Sophie Campbell and Erin Watson

title logo by
Amanda Lafrenais and Sophie Campbell

prepress by
Rhiannon Rasmussen-Silverstein and Matt Sheridan

proofreading by
Abby Lehrke

managing editor
C. Spike Trotman

special thanks to
Heather Nunnelly
Bo Bradshaw
Jennifer de Guzman

published by
Iron Circus Comics
ironcircus@gmail.com
www.ironcircus.com

first Iron Circus Comics printing: **January 2016**
softcover ISBN: **978-0-9890207-2-5**
hardcover ISBN: **978-0-9890207-3-2**
printed in China

SHADOW EYES

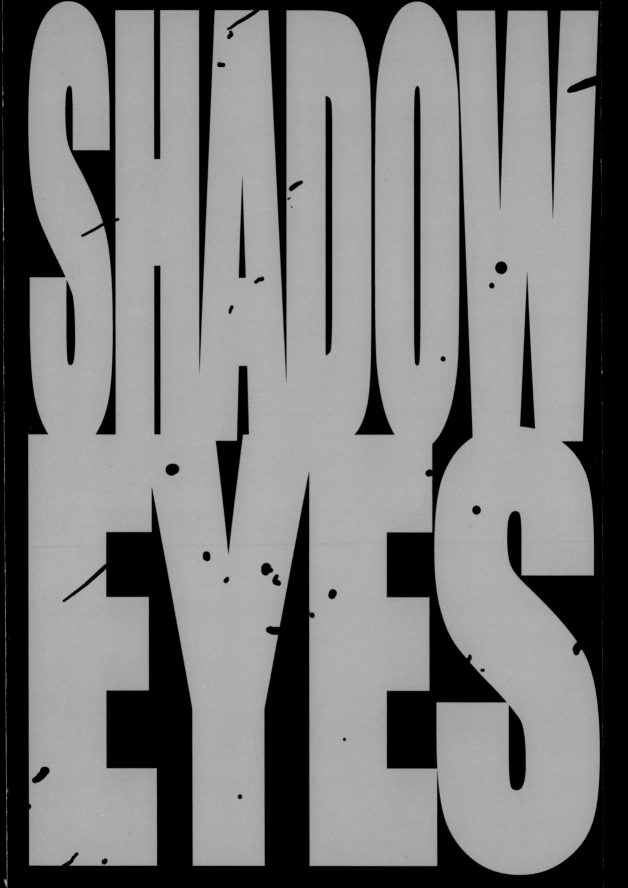

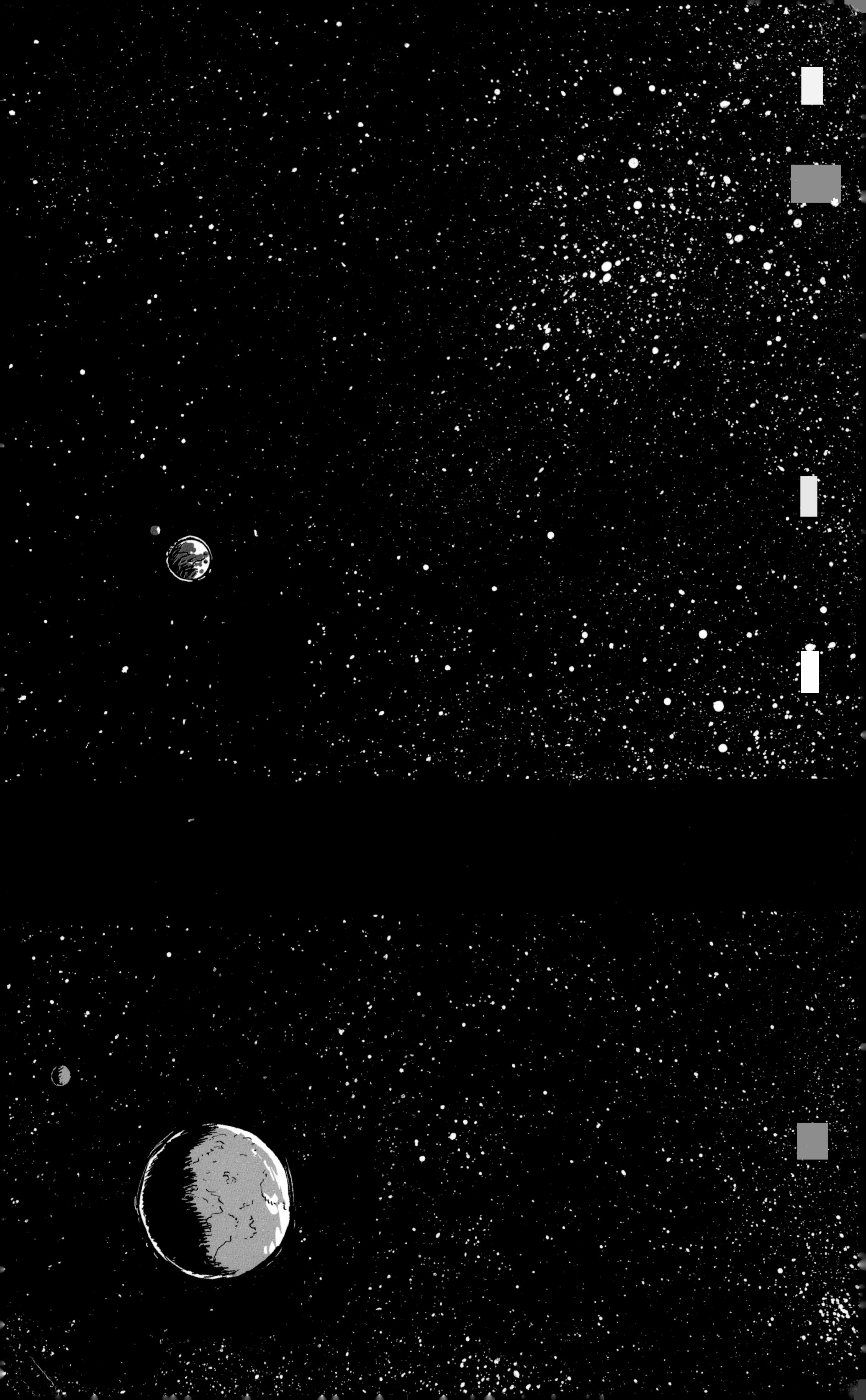

Earth.

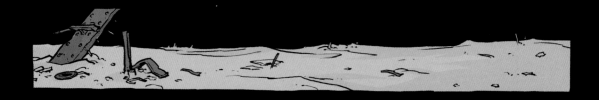

the year 200X.

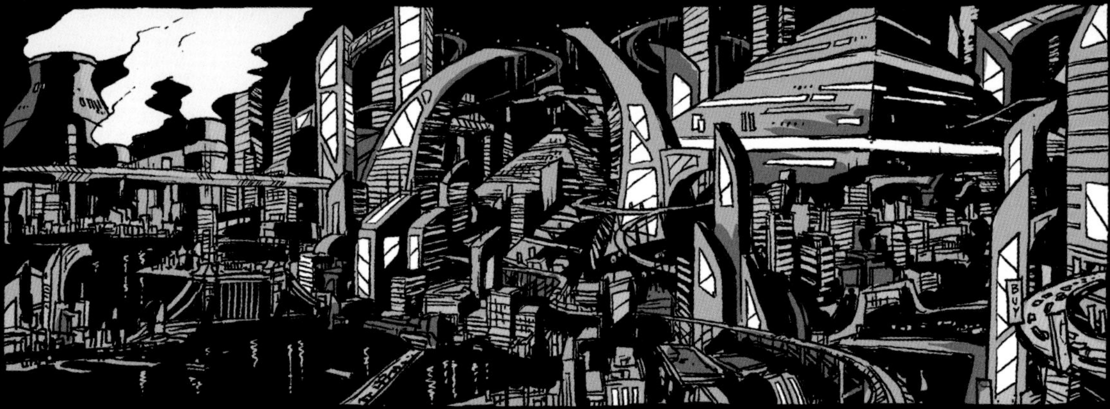

the city of Dranac.

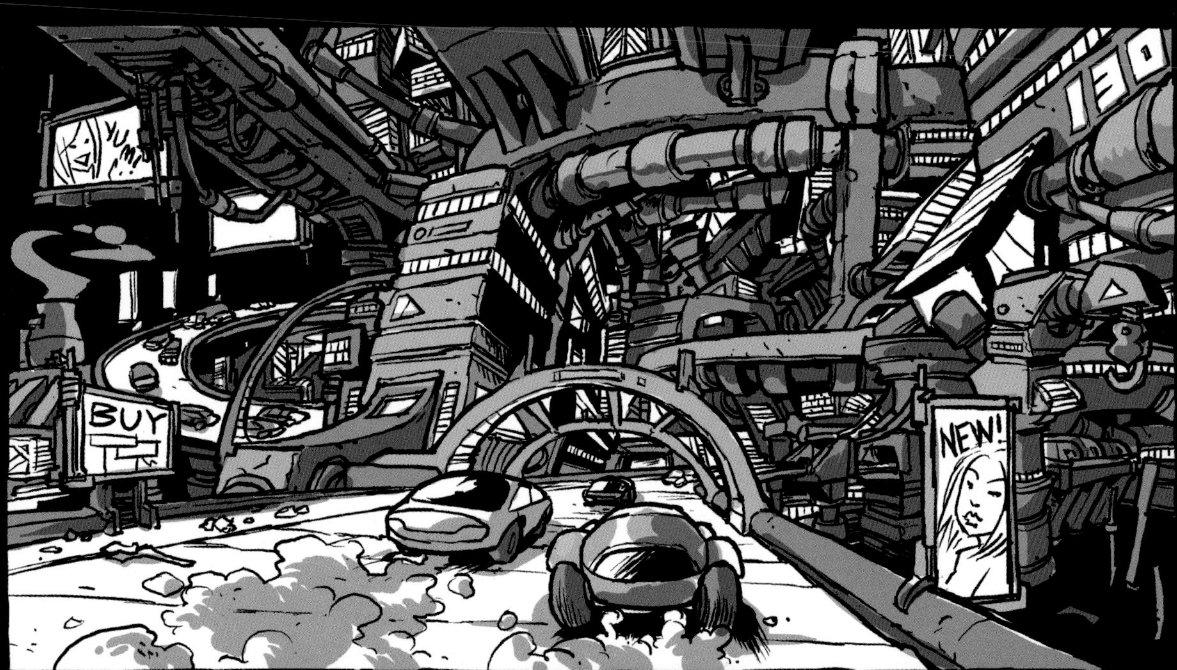
BUY
NEW!

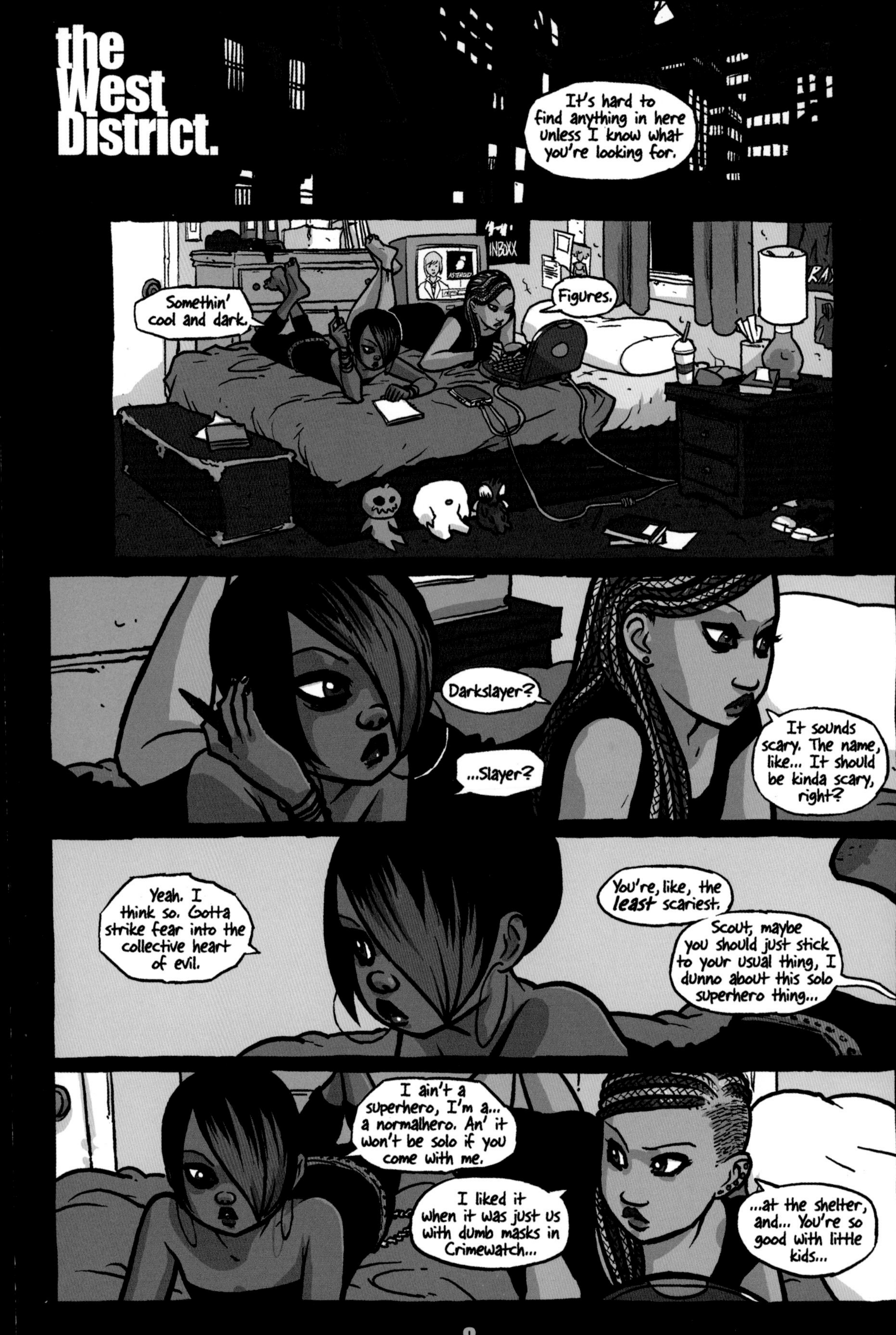

the West District.
It's hard to find anything in here unless I know what you're looking for.
Somethin' cool and dark.
Figures.
INBOXX
ASTEROID
Darkslayer?
...Slayer?
It sounds scary. The name, like... It should be kinda scary, right?
Yeah. I think so. Gotta strike fear into the collective heart of evil.
You're, like, the least scariest.
Scout, maybe you should just stick to your usual thing, I dunno about this solo superhero thing...
I ain't a superhero, I'm a... a normalhero. An' it won't be solo if you come with me.
I liked it when it was just us with dumb masks in Crimewatch...
...at the shelter, and... You're so good with little kids...

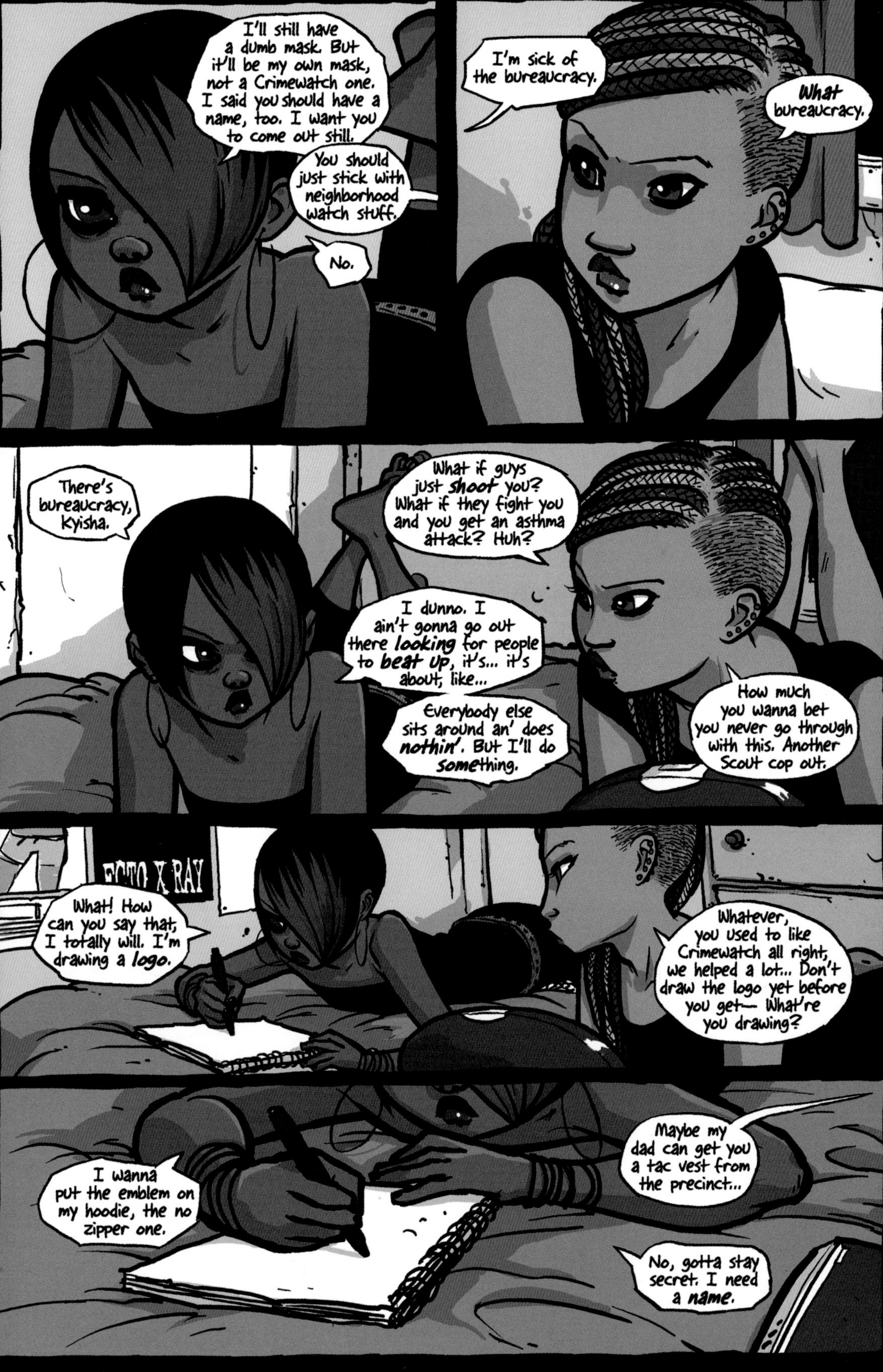
I'll still have a dumb mask. But it'll be my own mask, not a Crimewatch one. I said you should have a name, too. I want you to come out still.
You should just stick with neighborhood watch stuff.
No.
I'm sick of the bureaucracy.
What bureaucracy.
There's bureaucracy, Kyisha.
What if guys just shoot you? What if they fight you and you get an asthma attack? Huh?
I dunno. I ain't gonna go out there looking for people to beat up, it's... it's about, like...
Everybody else sits around an' does nothin'. But I'll do something.
How much you wanna bet you never go through with this. Another Scout cop out.
ECTO X RAY
What! How can you say that, I totally will. I'm drawing a logo.
Whatever, you used to like Crimewatch all right, we helped a lot... Don't draw the logo yet before you get— What're you drawing?
I wanna put the emblem on my hoodie, the no zipper one.
Maybe my dad can get you a tac vest from the precinct...
No, gotta stay secret. I need a name.

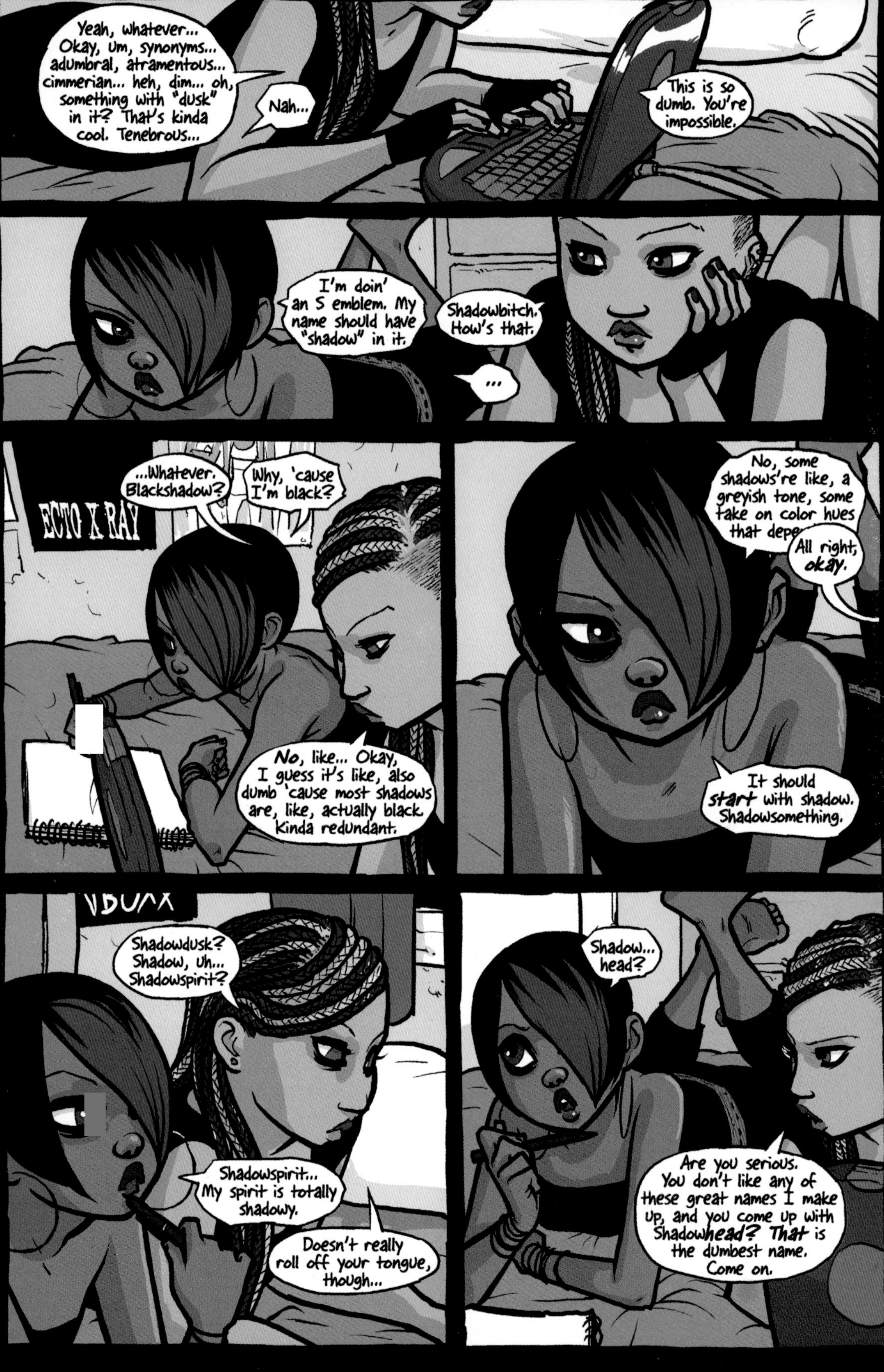
Yeah, whatever... Okay, um, synonyms... adumbral, atramentous... cimmerian... heh, dim... oh, something with "dusk" in it? That's kinda cool. Tenebrous...
Nah...
This is so dumb. You're impossible.
I'm doin' an S emblem. My name should have "shadow" in it.
Shadowbitch. How's that.
...
ECTO X RAY
...Whatever. Blackshadow?
Why, 'cause I'm black?
No, like... Okay, I guess it's like, also dumb 'cause most shadows are, like, actually black. Kinda redundant.
No, some shadows're like, a greyish tone, some take on color hues that depe
All right, okay.
It should start with shadow. Shadowsomething.
Shadowdusk? Shadow, uh... Shadowspirit?
Shadowspirit... My spirit is totally shadowy.
Doesn't really roll off your tongue, though...
Shadow... head?
Are you serious. You don't like any of these great names I make up, and you come up with Shadowhead? That is the dumbest name. Come on.

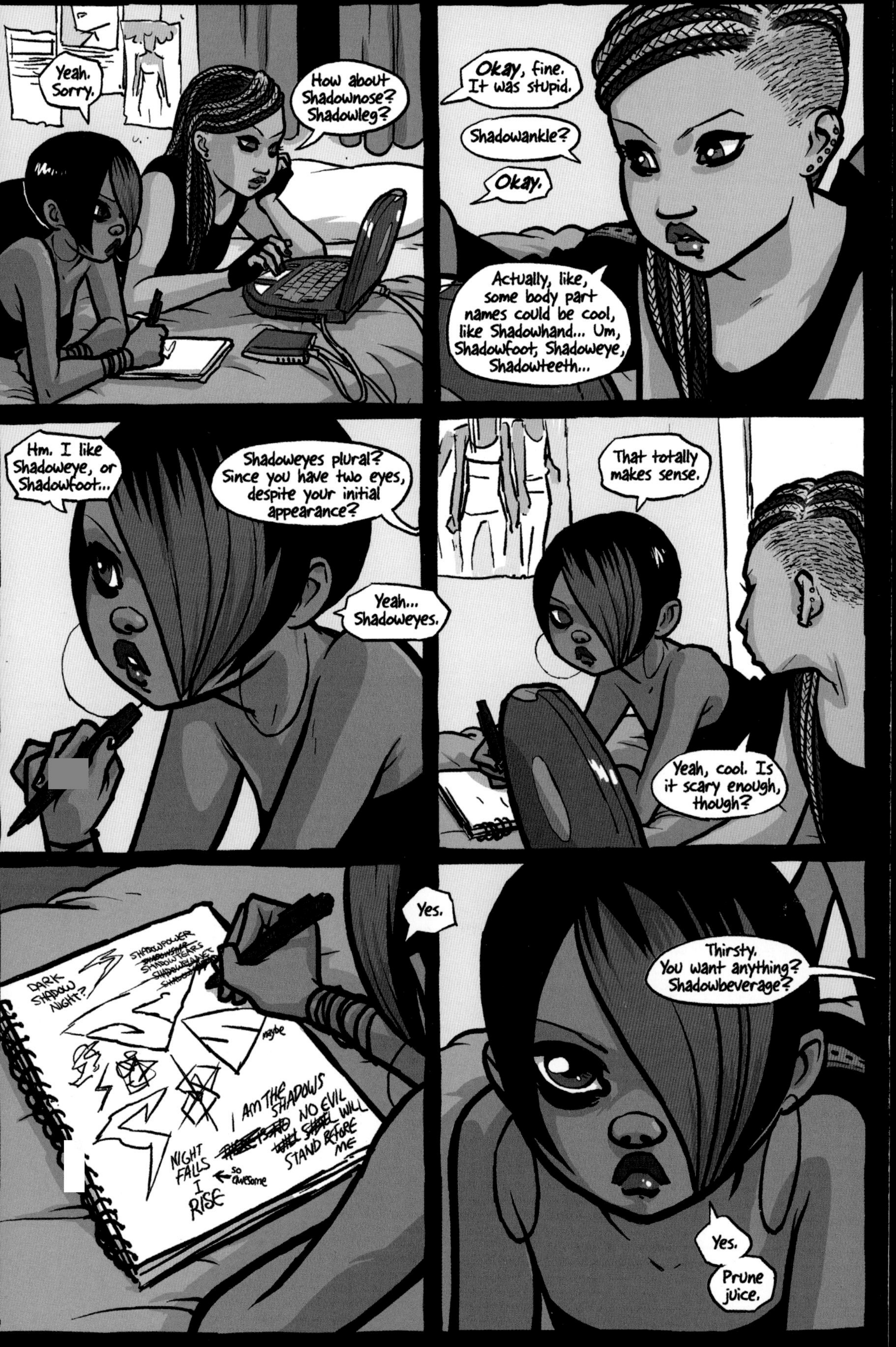
Yeah. Sorry.
How about Shadownose? Shadowleg?
Okay, fine. It was stupid.
Shadowankle?
Okay.
Actually, like, some body part names could be cool, like Shadowhand... Um, Shadowfoot, Shadoweye, Shadowteeth...
Hm. I like Shadoweye, or Shadowfoot...
Shadoweyes plural? Since you have two eyes, despite your initial appearance?
Yeah... Shadoweyes.
That totally makes sense.
Yeah, cool. Is it scary enough, though?
Yes.
DARK SHADOW NIGHT?
SHADOWPOWER
maybe
I AM THE SHADOWS
NO EVIL WILL STAND BEFORE ME
NIGHT FALLS I RISE
so awesome
Thirsty. You want anything? Shadowbeverage?
Yes.
Prune juice.

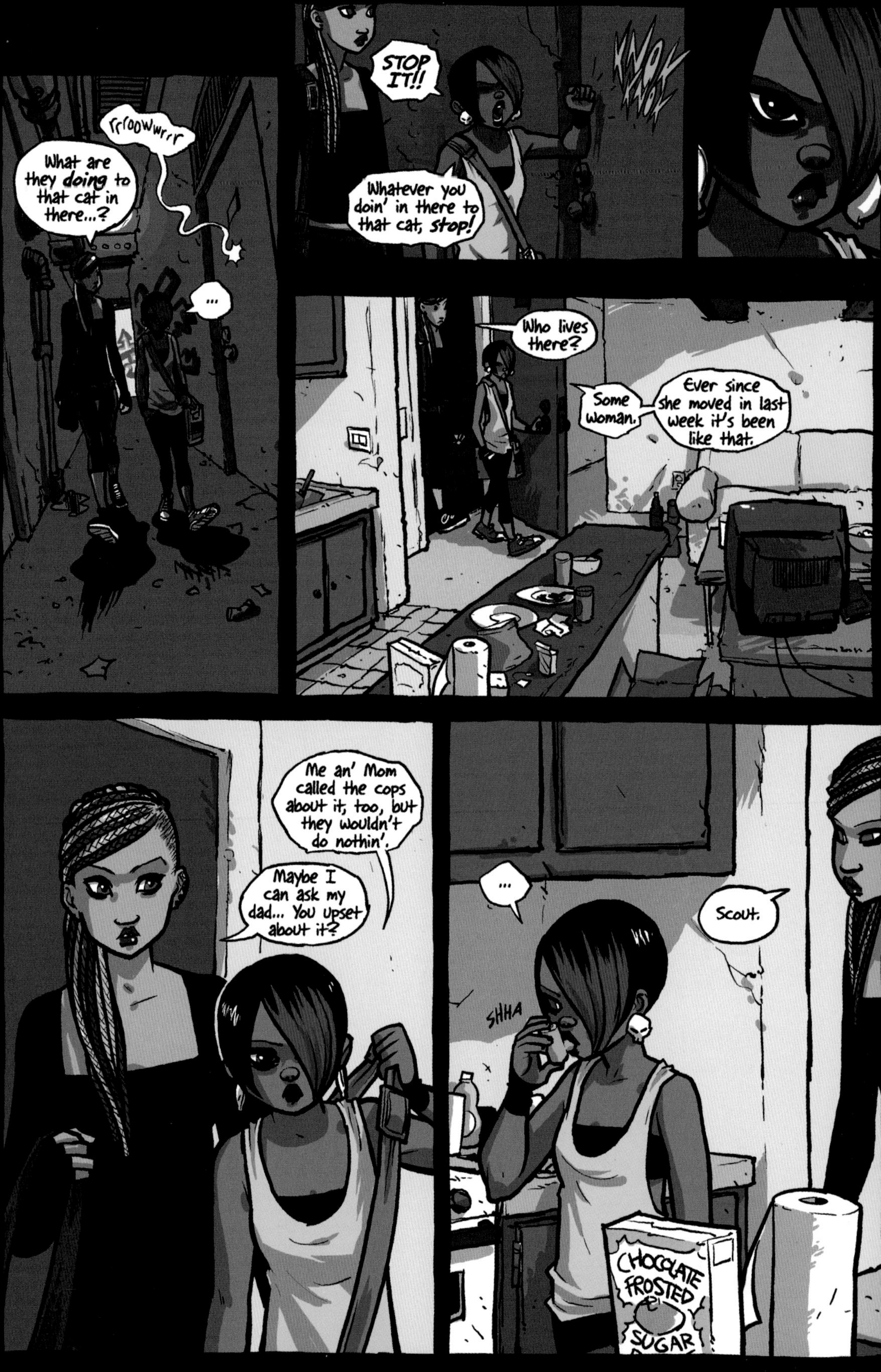
rrroowwrrr
What are they doing to that cat in there...?
...
STOP IT!!
Whatever you doin' in there to that cat, stop!
KNOK KNOK
Who lives there?
Some woman.
Ever since she moved in last week it's been like that.
Me an' Mom called the cops about it, too, but they wouldn't do nothin'.
Maybe I can ask my dad... You upset about it?
...
SHHA
Scout.
CHOCOLATE FROSTED SUGAR

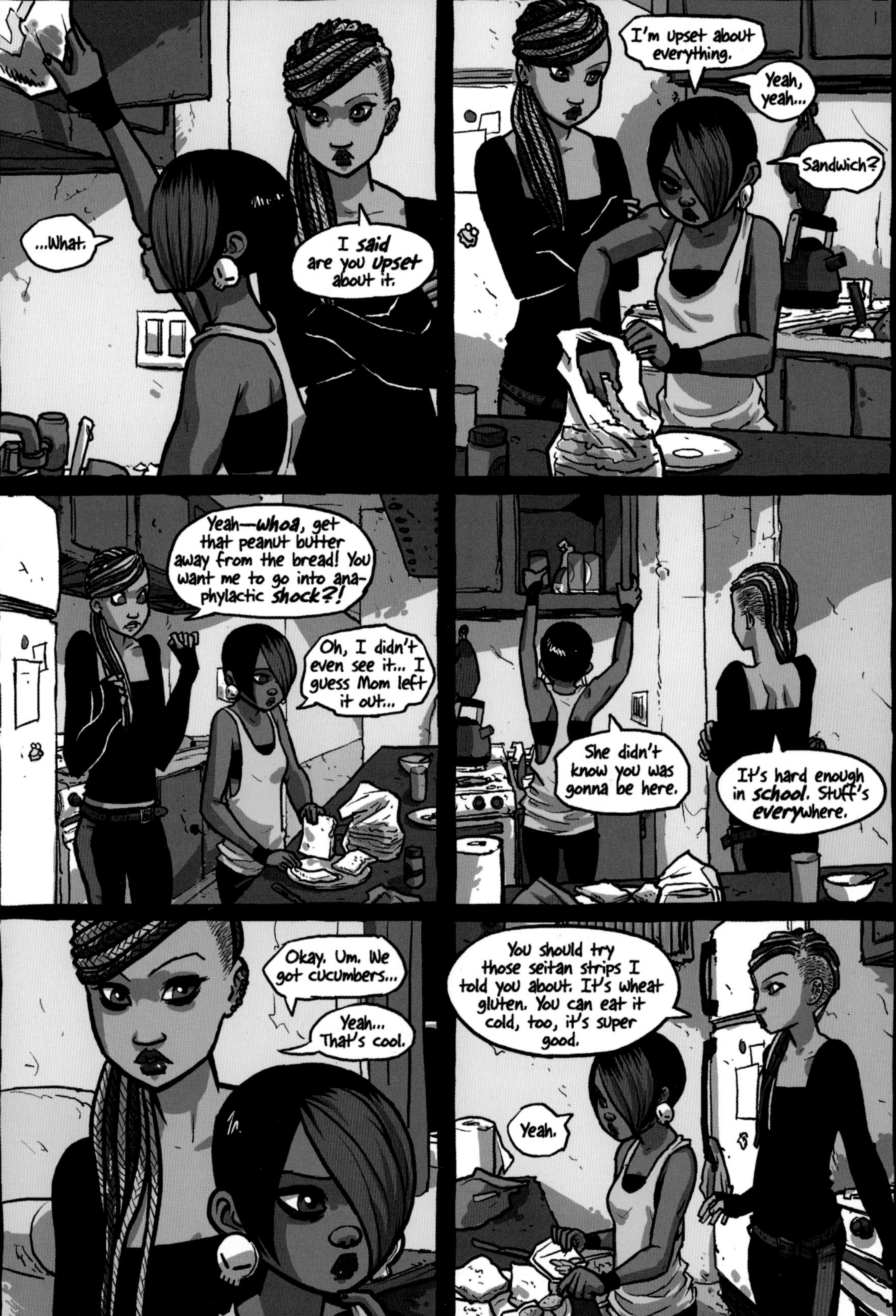

...What.
I said are you upset about it.
I'm upset about everything.
Yeah, yeah...
Sandwich?
Yeah—whoa, get that peanut butter away from the bread! You want me to go into anaphylactic shock?!
Oh, I didn't even see it... I guess Mom left it out...
She didn't know you was gonna be here.
It's hard enough in school. Stuff's everywhere.
Okay. Um. We got cucumbers...
Yeah... That's cool.
You should try those seitan strips I told you about. It's wheat gluten. You can eat it cold, too, it's super good.
Yeah.

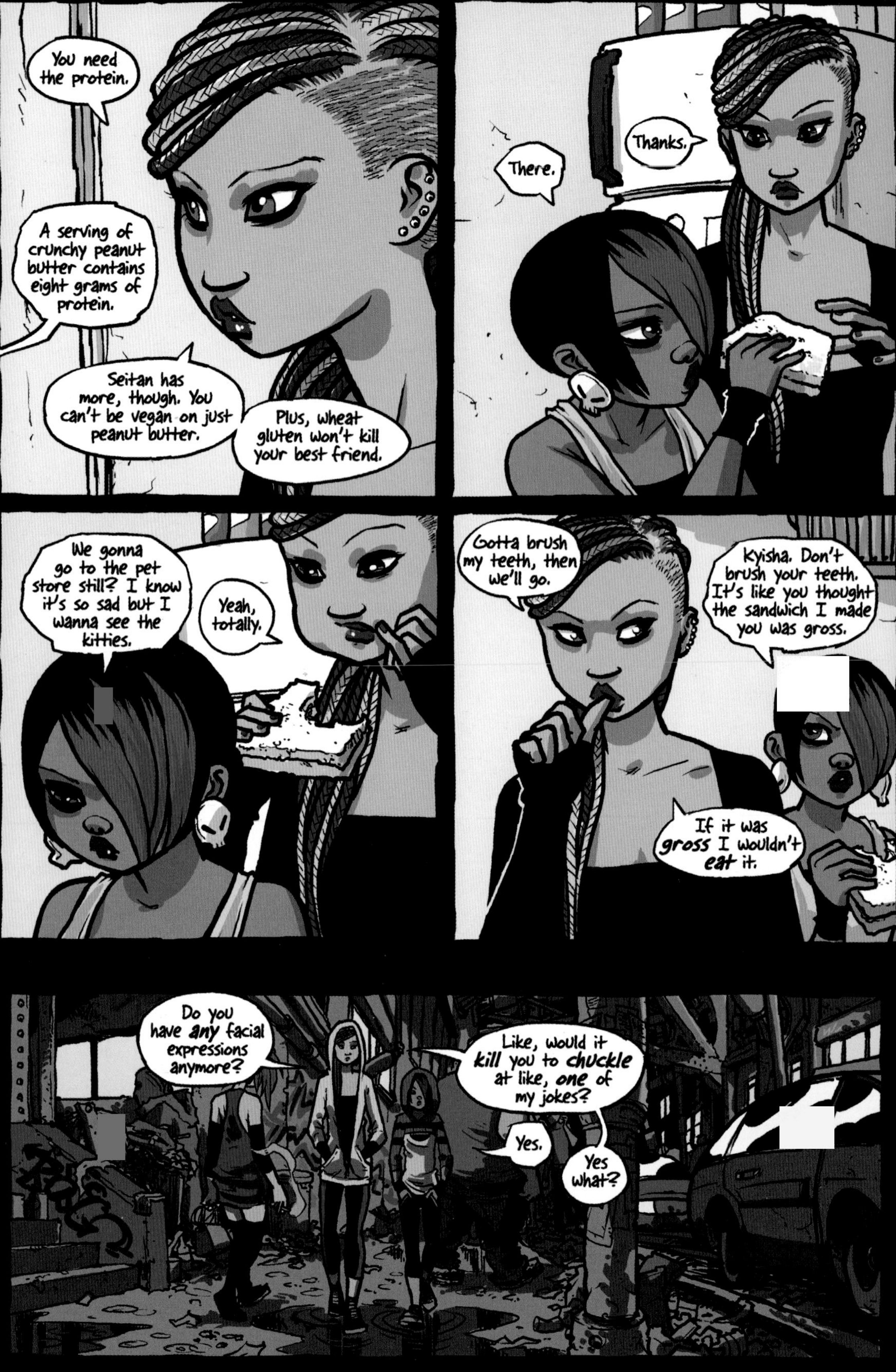
You need the protein.
A serving of crunchy peanut butter contains eight grams of protein.
Seitan has more, though. You can't be vegan on just peanut butter.
Plus, wheat gluten won't kill your best friend.
There.
Thanks.
We gonna go to the pet store still? I know it's so sad but I wanna see the kitties.
Yeah, totally.
Gotta brush my teeth, then we'll go.
Kyisha. Don't brush your teeth. It's like you thought the sandwich I made you was gross.
If it was gross I wouldn't eat it.
Do you have any facial expressions anymore?
Like, would it kill you to chuckle at like, one of my jokes?
Yes.
Yes what?

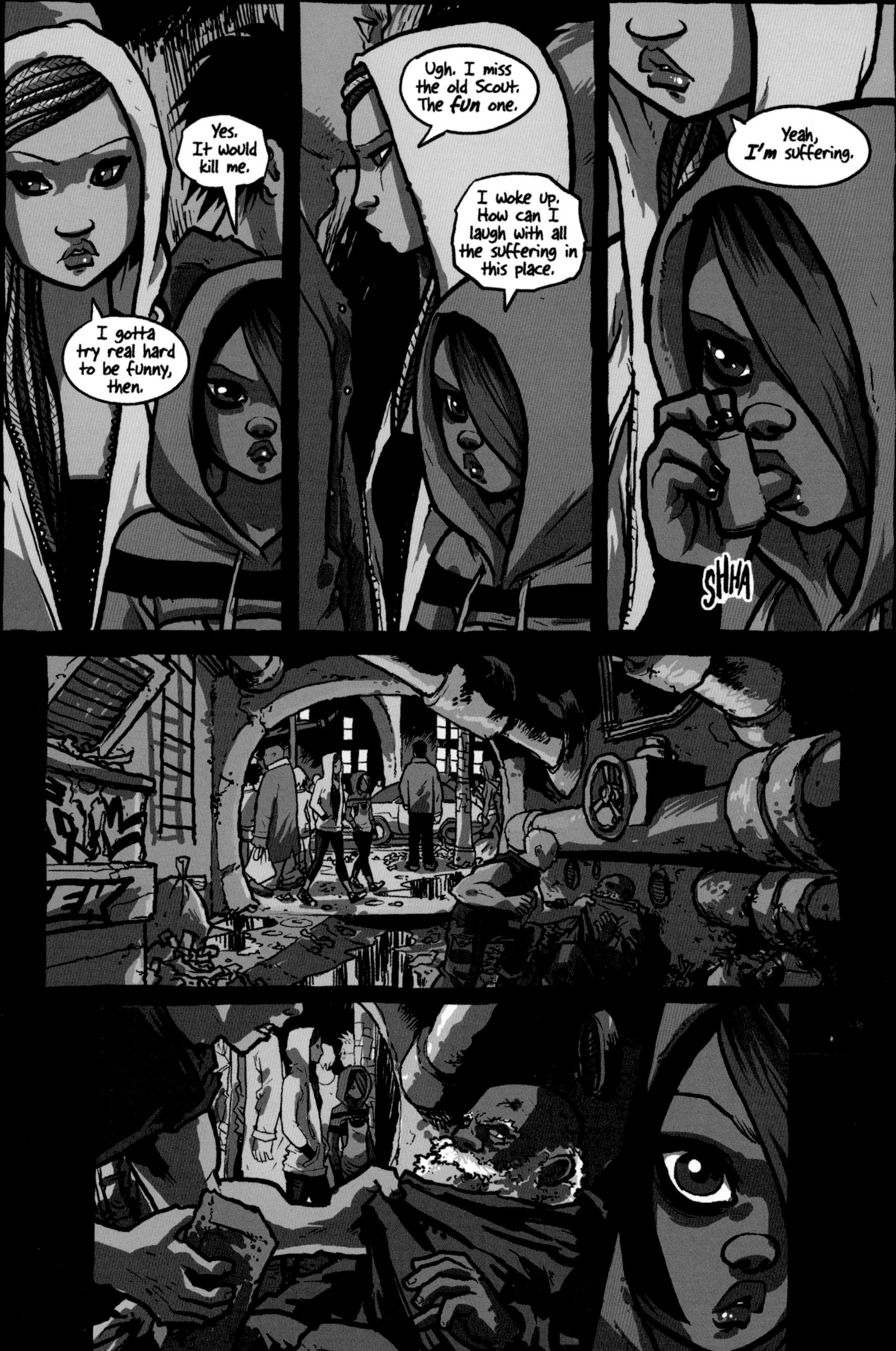
Yes. It would kill me.
I gotta try real hard to be funny, then.
Ugh. I miss the old Scout. The fun one.
I woke up. How can I laugh with all the suffering in this place.
Yeah, I'm suffering.
SHHA

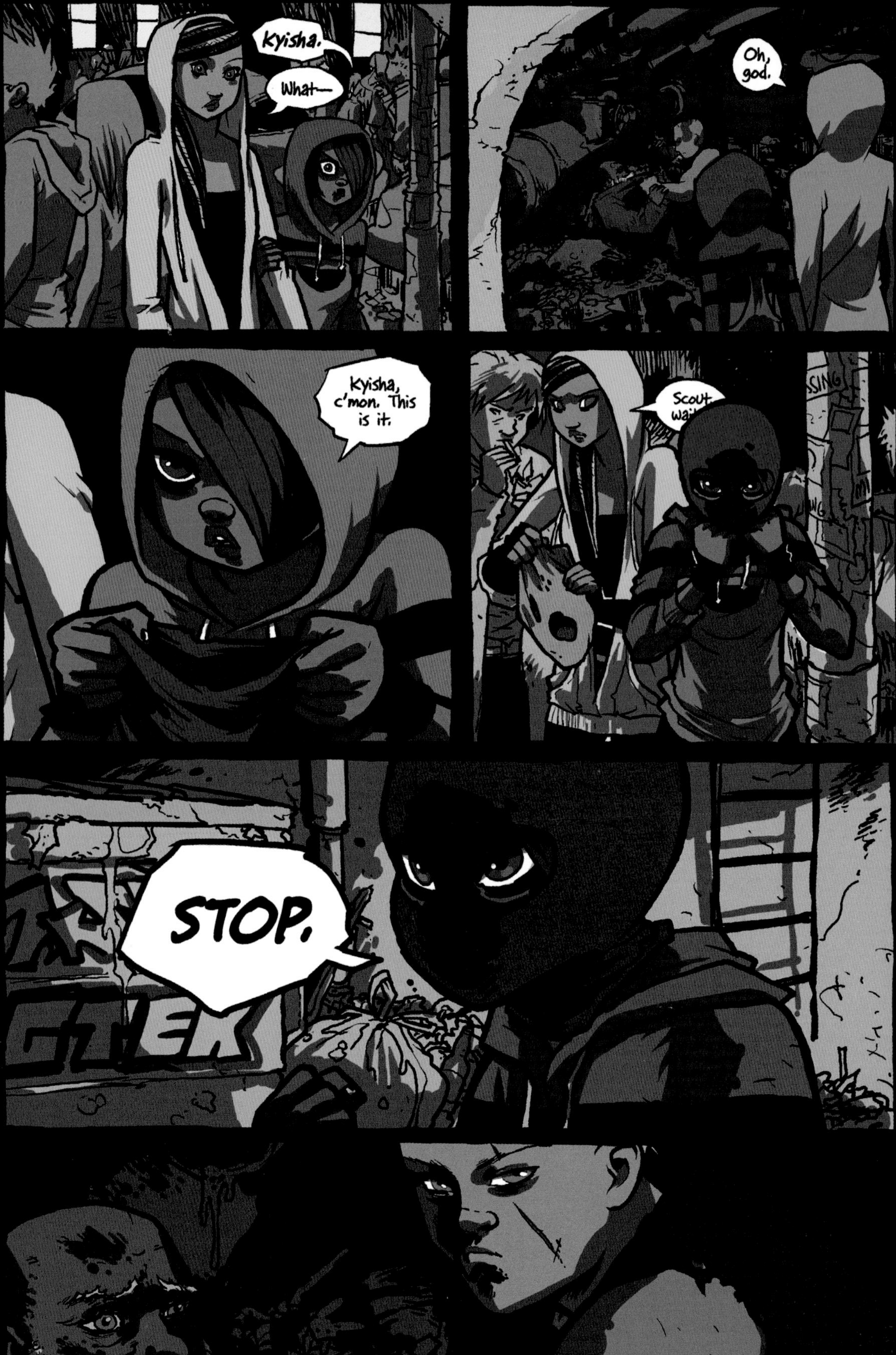
Kyisha.
What—
Oh, god.
Kyisha, c'mon. This is it.
Scout, wai
STOP.

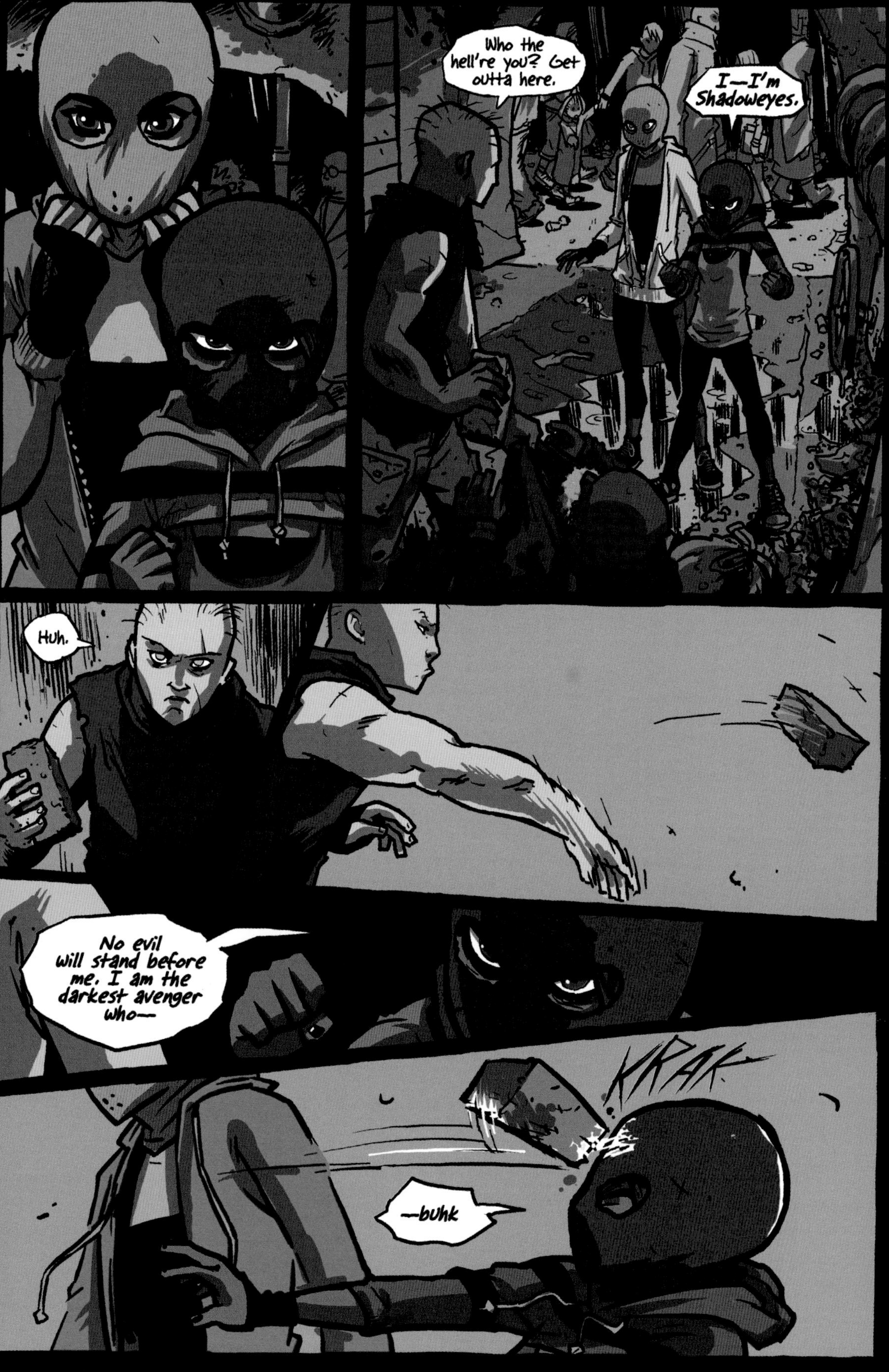
Who the hell're you? Get outta here.
I—I'm Shadoweyes.
Huh.
No evil will stand before me. I am the darkest avenger who—
KRAK
—buhk

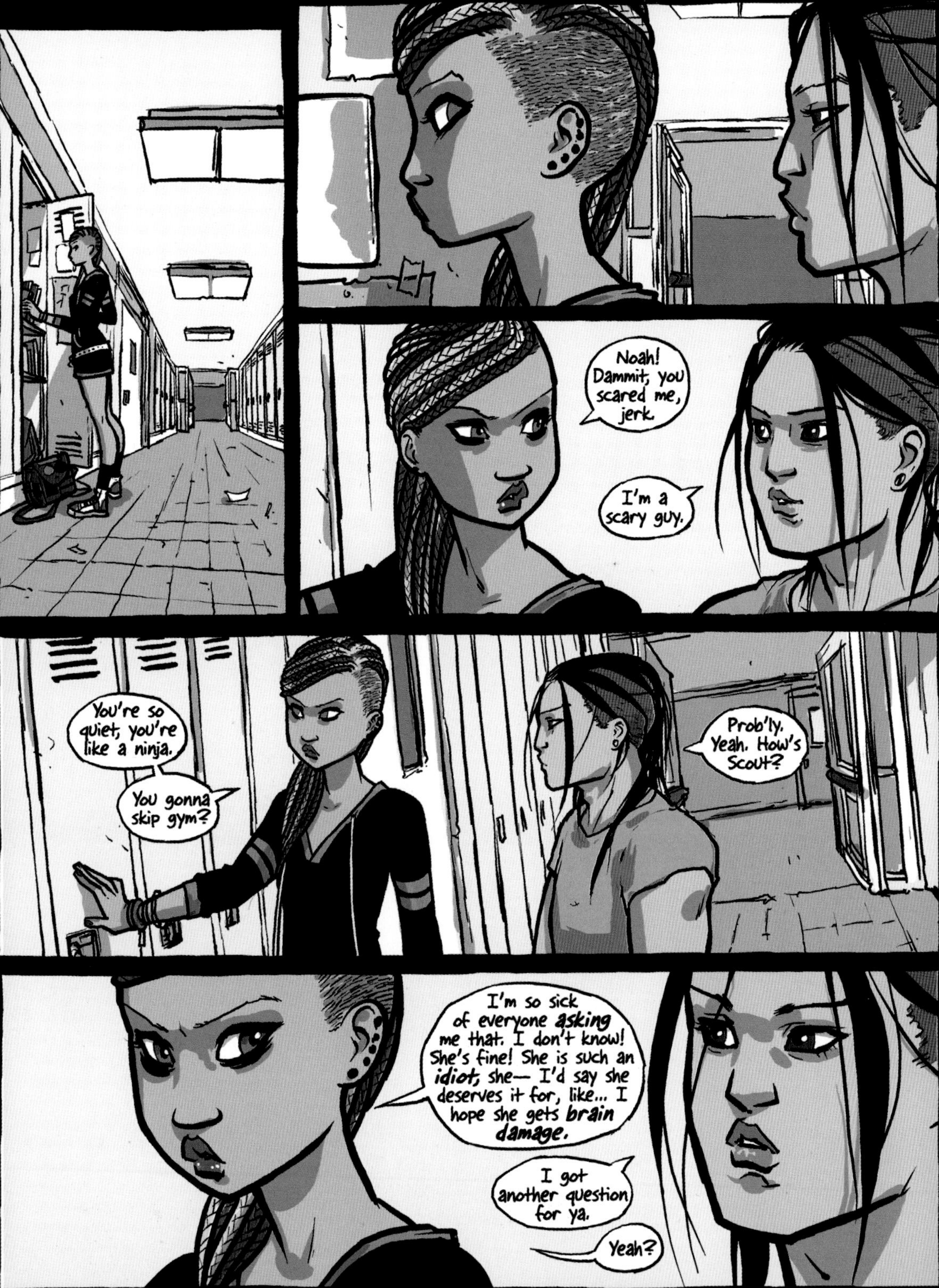
Noah! Dammit, you scared me, jerk.
I'm a scary guy.
You're so quiet, you're like a ninja.
You gonna skip gym?
Prob'ly. Yeah. How's Scout?
I'm so sick of everyone asking me that. I don't know! She's fine! She is such an idiot, she— I'd say she deserves it for, like... I hope she gets brain damage.
I got another question for ya.
Yeah?

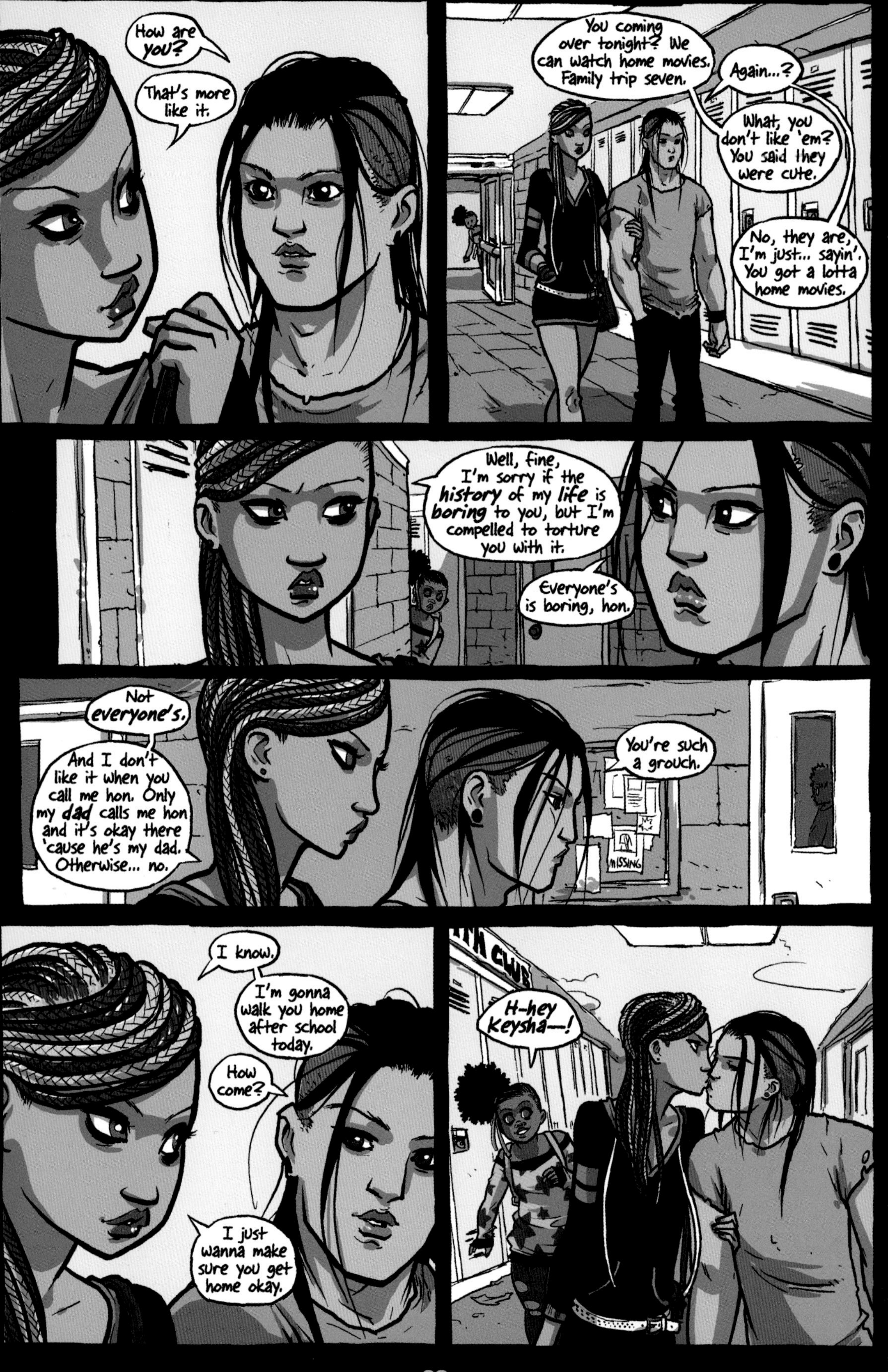
How are you?
That's more like it.
You coming over tonight? We can watch home movies. Family trip seven.
Again...?
What, you don't like 'em? You said they were cute.
No, they are, I'm just... sayin'. You got a lotta home movies.
Well, fine, I'm sorry if the history of my life is boring to you, but I'm compelled to torture you with it.
Everyone's is boring, hon.
Not everyone's.
And I don't like it when you call me hon. Only my dad calls me hon and it's okay there 'cause he's my dad. Otherwise... no.
You're such a grouch.
MISSING
I know.
I'm gonna walk you home after school today.
How come?
I just wanna make sure you get home okay.
H-hey Keysha—!

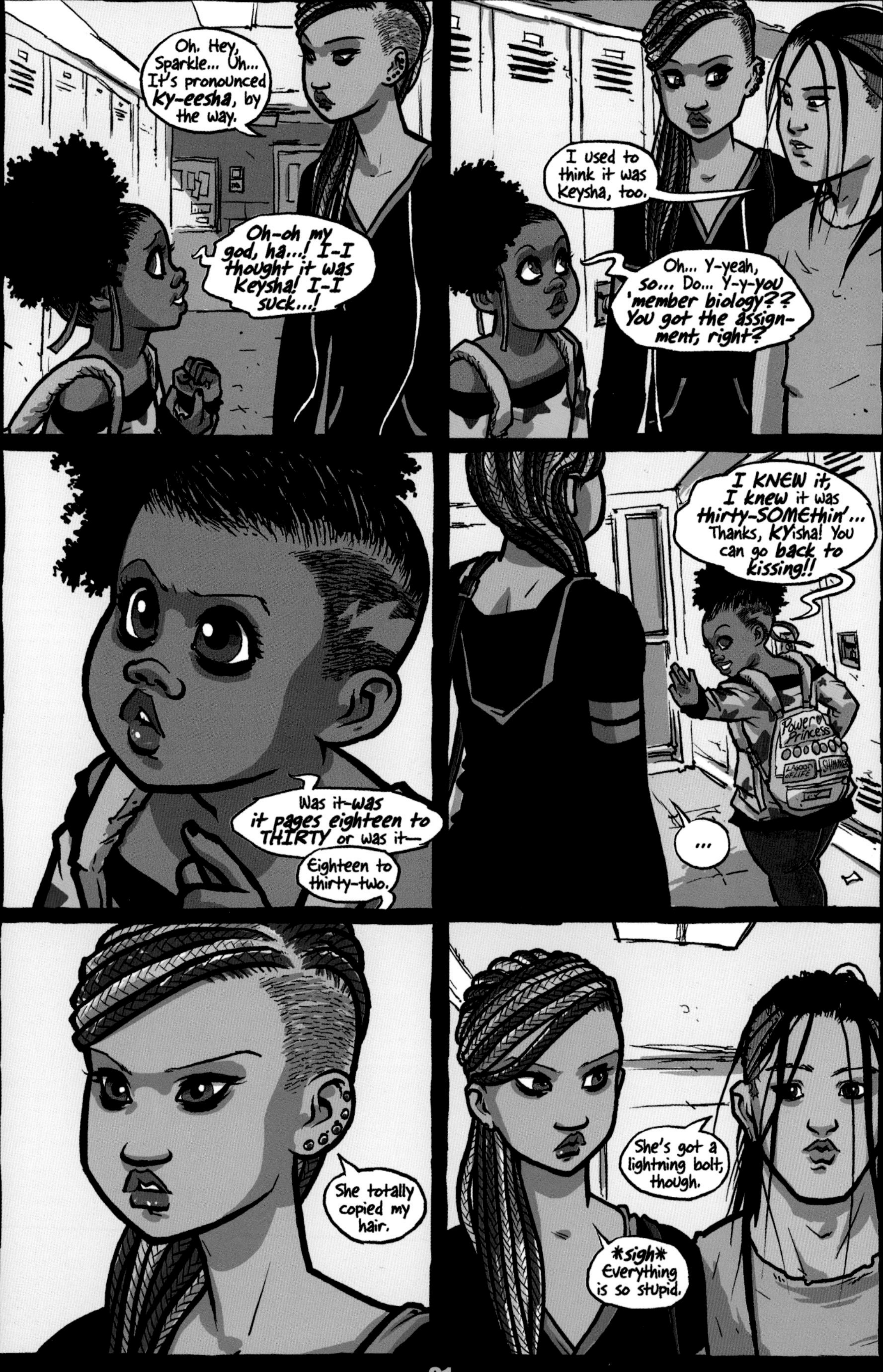
Oh. Hey, Sparkle... Uh... It's pronounced Ky-eesha, by the way.
Oh-oh my god, ha...! I-I thought it was Keysha! I-I suck...!
I used to think it was Keysha, too.
Oh... Y-yeah, so... Do... Y-y-you 'member biology?? You got the assignment, right?
Was it-was it pages eighteen to THIRTY or was it—
Eighteen to thirty-two.
I KNEW it, I knew it was thirty-SOMEthin'... Thanks, KYisha! You can go back to kissing!!
...
Power Princess
Lagoon of Life
She totally copied my hair.
She's got a lightning bolt, though.
sigh Everything is so stupid.

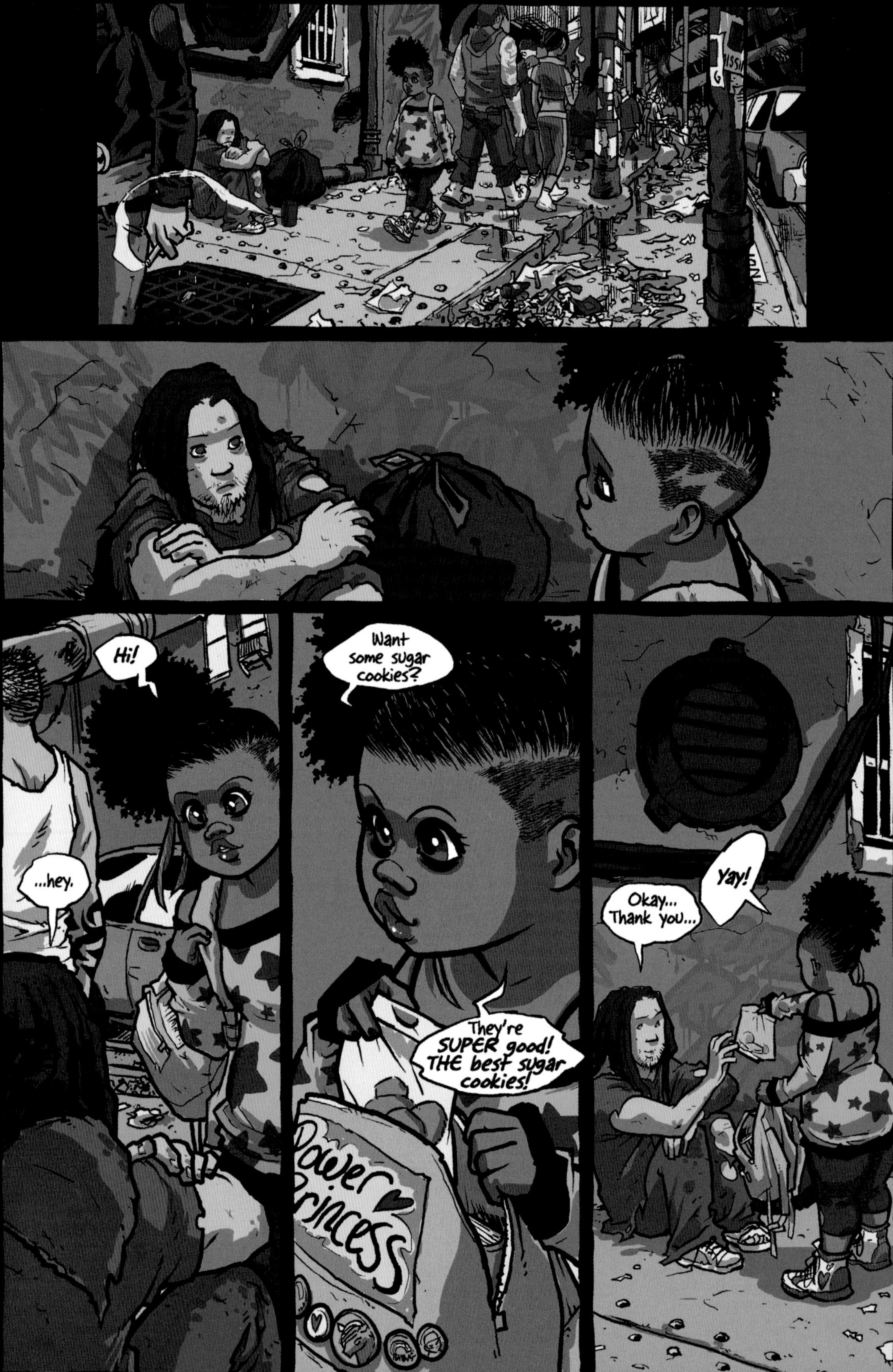
Hi!
...hey.
Want some sugar cookies?
They're SUPER good! THE best sugar cookies!
Power Princess
Okay... Thank you...
Yay!

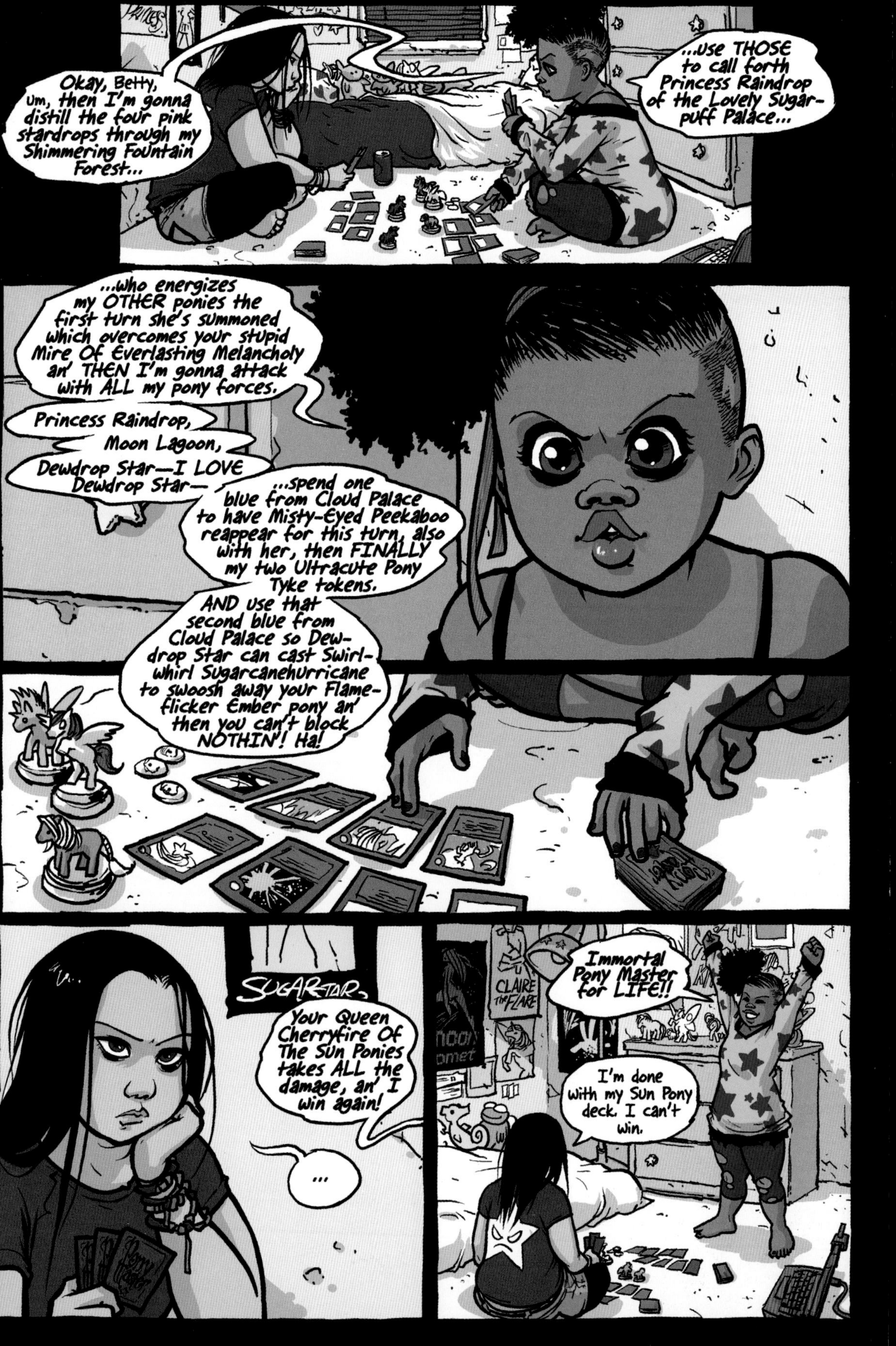
Okay, Betty, um, then I'm gonna distill the four pink stardrops through my Shimmering Fountain Forest...
...use THOSE to call forth Princess Raindrop of the Lovely Sugar-puff Palace...
...who energizes my OTHER ponies the first turn she's summoned which overcomes your stupid Mire Of Everlasting Melancholy an' THEN I'm gonna attack with ALL my pony forces.
Princess Raindrop,
Moon Lagoon,
Dewdrop Star—I LOVE Dewdrop Star—
...spend one blue from Cloud Palace to have Misty-Eyed Peekaboo reappear for this turn, also with her, then FINALLY my two Ultracute Pony Tyke tokens.
AND use that second blue from Cloud Palace so Dew-drop Star can cast Swirl-whirl Sugarcanehurricane to swoosh away your Flame-flicker Ember pony an' then you can't block NOTHIN'! Ha!
SUGARSTAR
Your Queen Cherryfire Of The Sun Ponies takes ALL the damage, an' I win again!
...
Immortal Pony Master for LIFE!!
CLAIRE the FLARE
I'm done with my Sun Pony deck. I can't win.

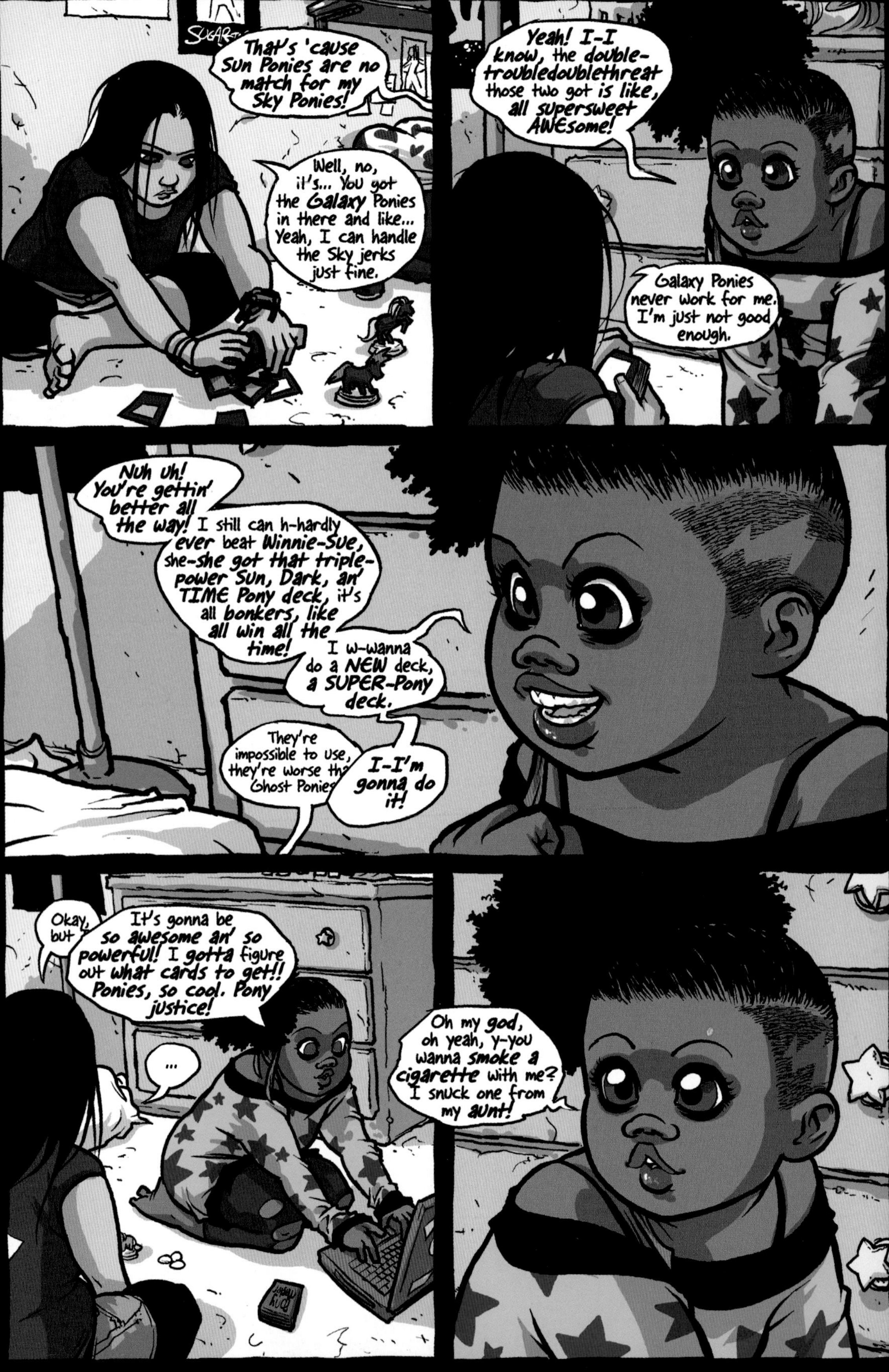

That's 'cause Sun Ponies are no match for my Sky Ponies!
Well, no, it's... You got the Galaxy Ponies in there and like... Yeah, I can handle the Sky jerks just fine.
Yeah! I-I know, the double-troubledoublethreat those two got is like, all supersweet AWEsome!
Galaxy Ponies never work for me. I'm just not good enough.
Nuh uh! You're gettin' better all the way! I still can h-hardly ever beat Winnie-Sue, she-she got that triple-power Sun, Dark, an' TIME Pony deck, it's all bonkers, like all win all the time!
I w-wanna do a NEW deck, a SUPER-Pony deck.
They're impossible to use, they're worse th Ghost Ponies
I-I'm gonna do it!
Okay, but
It's gonna be so awesome an' so powerful! I gotta figure out what cards to get!! Ponies, so cool. Pony justice!
...
Oh my god, oh yeah, y-you wanna smoke a cigarette with me? I snuck one from my aunt!

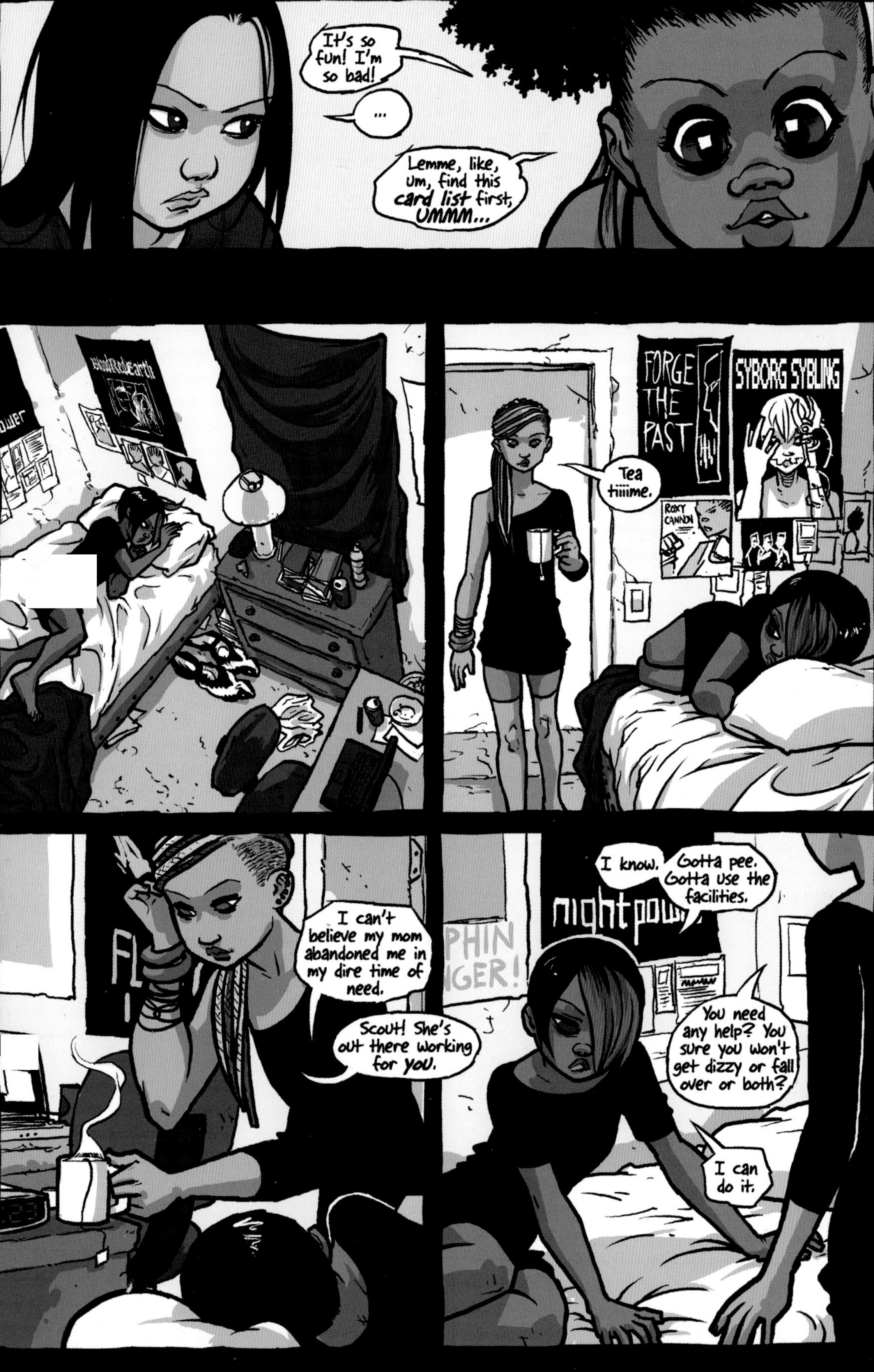
It's so fun! I'm so bad!
...
Lemme, like, um, find this card list first, UMMM...
FORGE THE PAST
SYBORG SYBLING
ROXY CANNON
Tea tiiiime.
I can't believe my mom abandoned me in my dire time of need.
Scout! She's out there working for you.
I know.
Gotta pee. Gotta use the facilities.
You need any help? You sure you won't get dizzy or fall over or both?
I can do it.

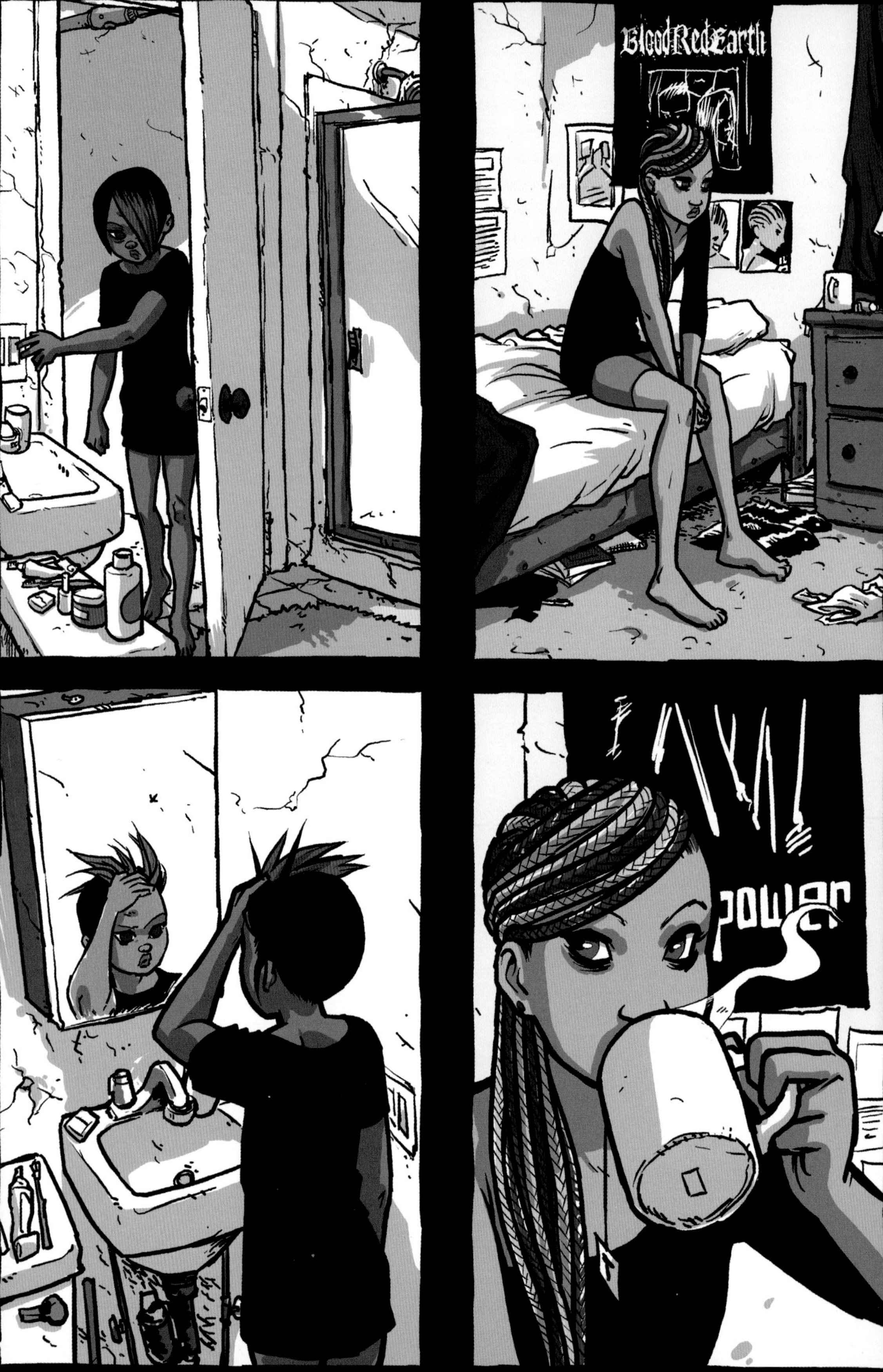
BloodRedEarth
power

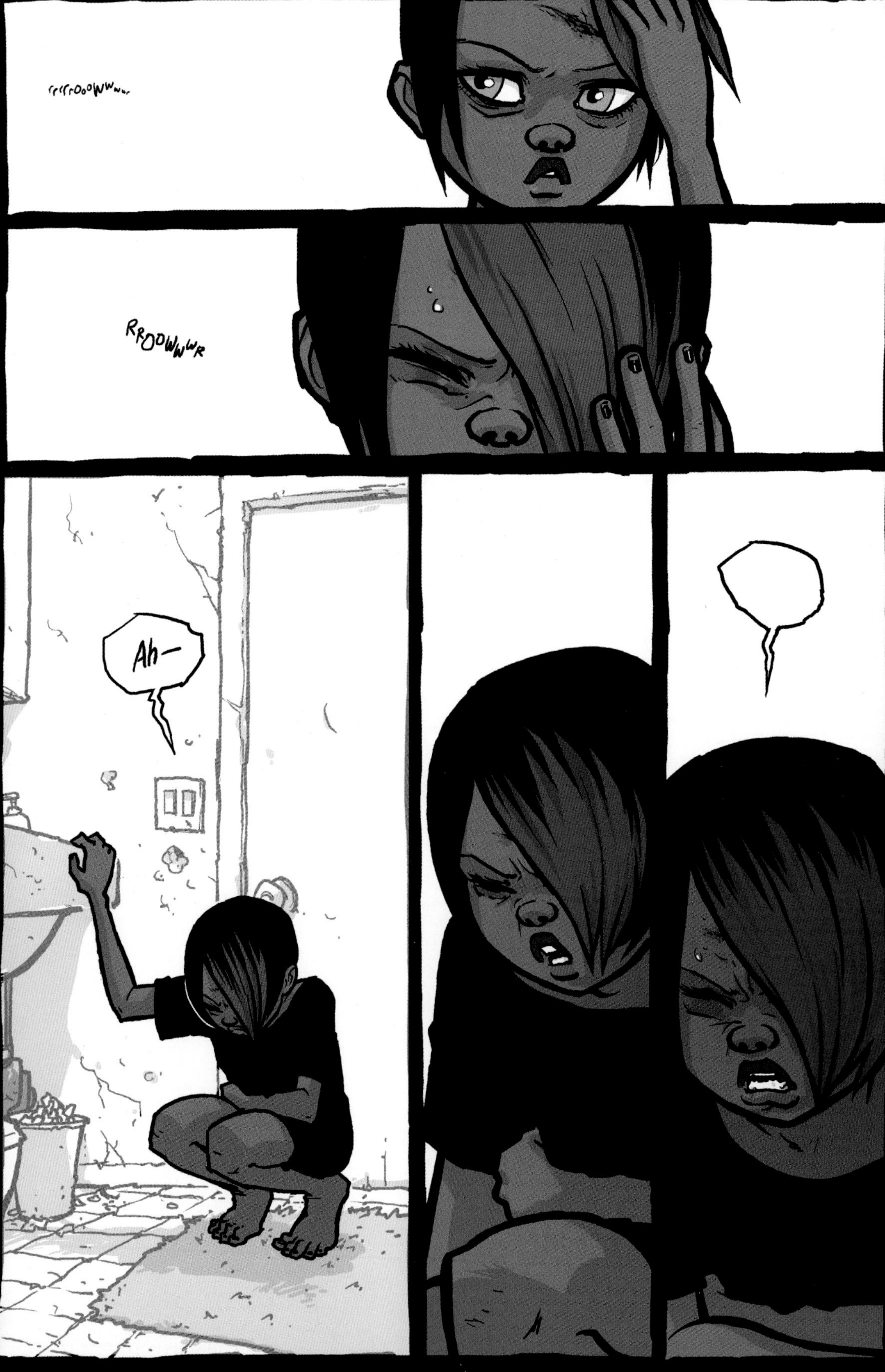
rrrrooowwwr
RRROOWWWR
Ah—

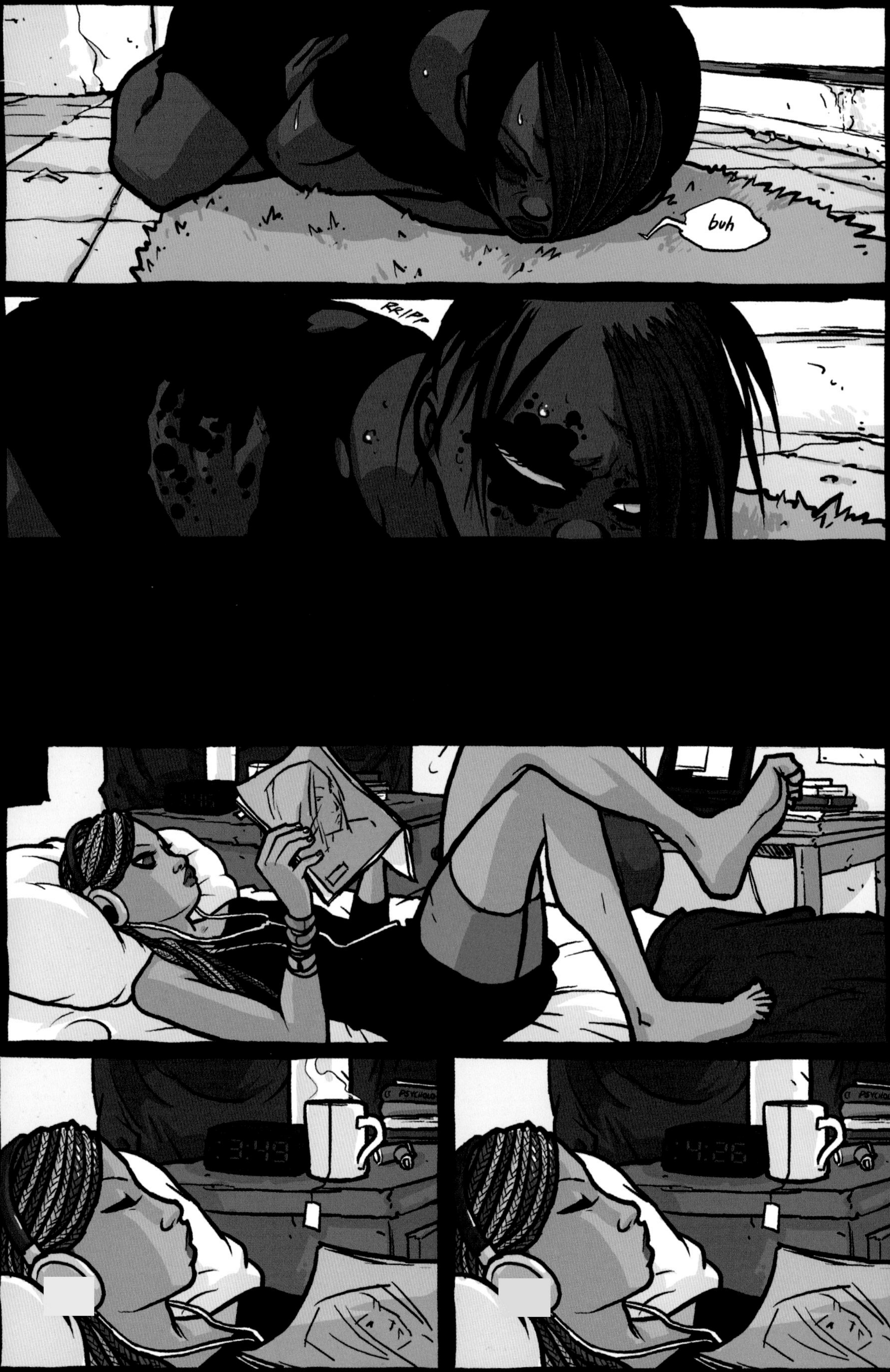
buh
RRIPP
3:49
4:26

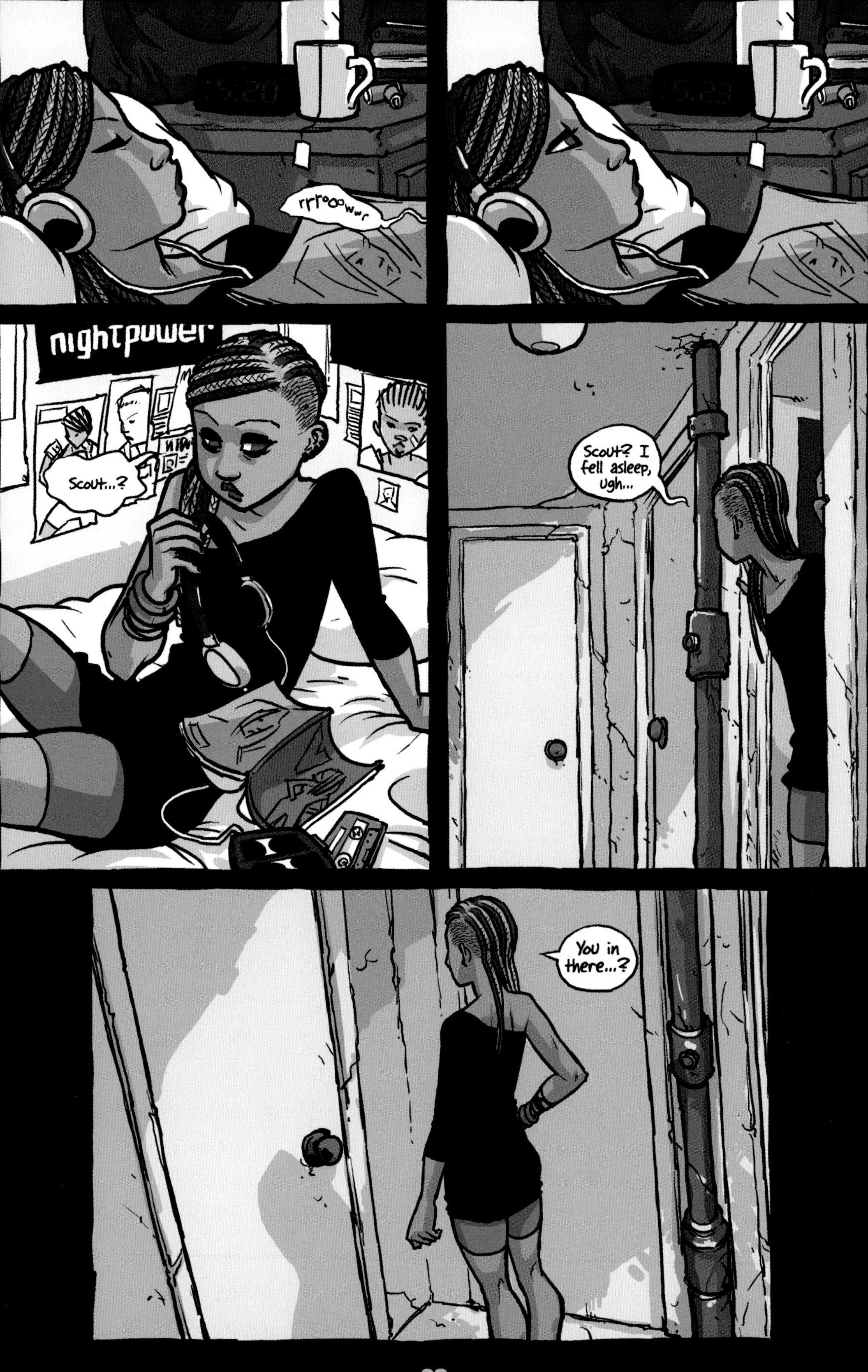
rrrooowwr
nightpower
Scout...?
Scout? I fell asleep, ugh...
You in there...?

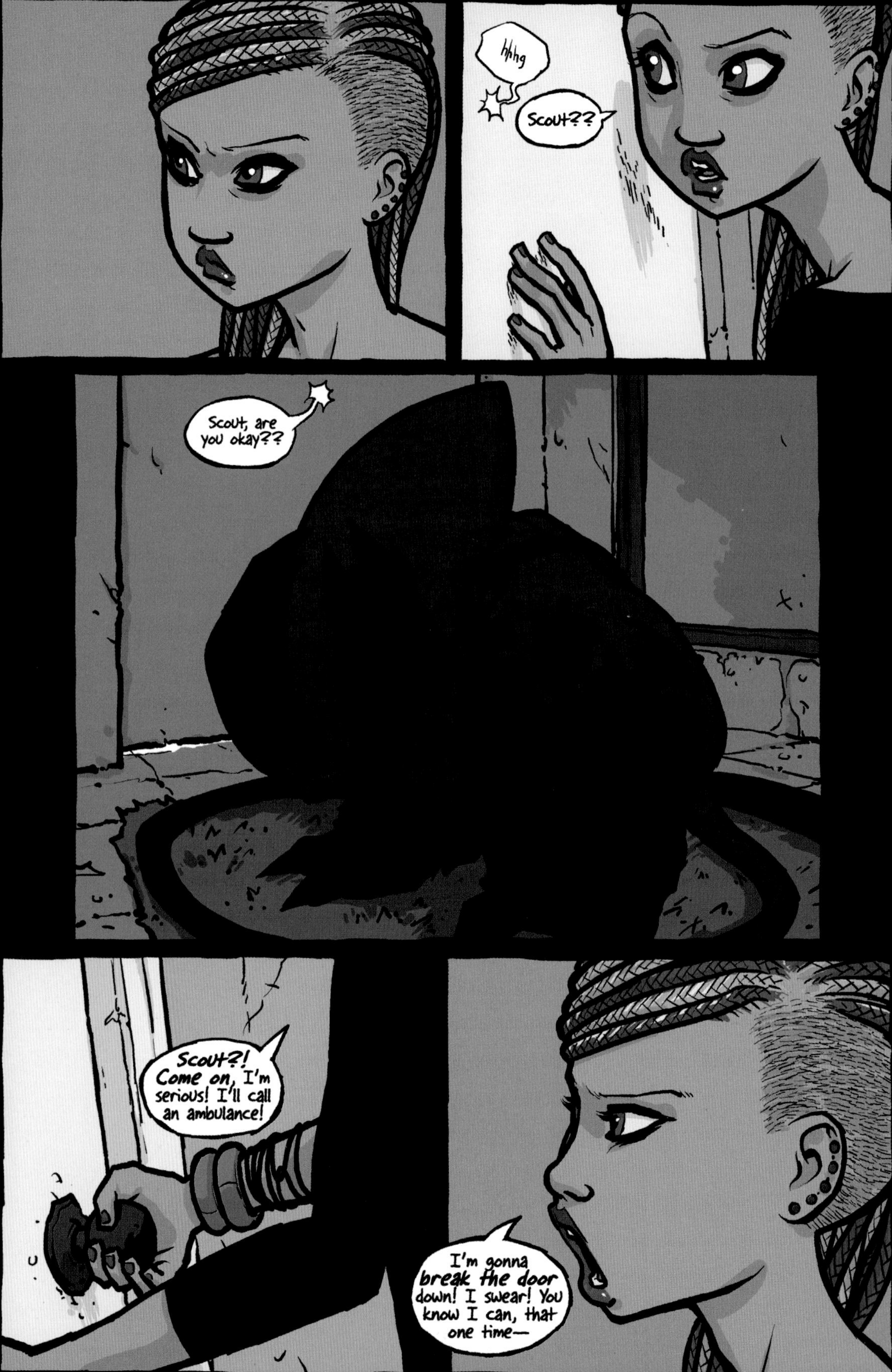

hhhg
Scout??
Scout, are you okay??
Scout?! Come on, I'm serious! I'll call an ambulance!
I'm gonna break the door down! I swear! You know I can, that one time—

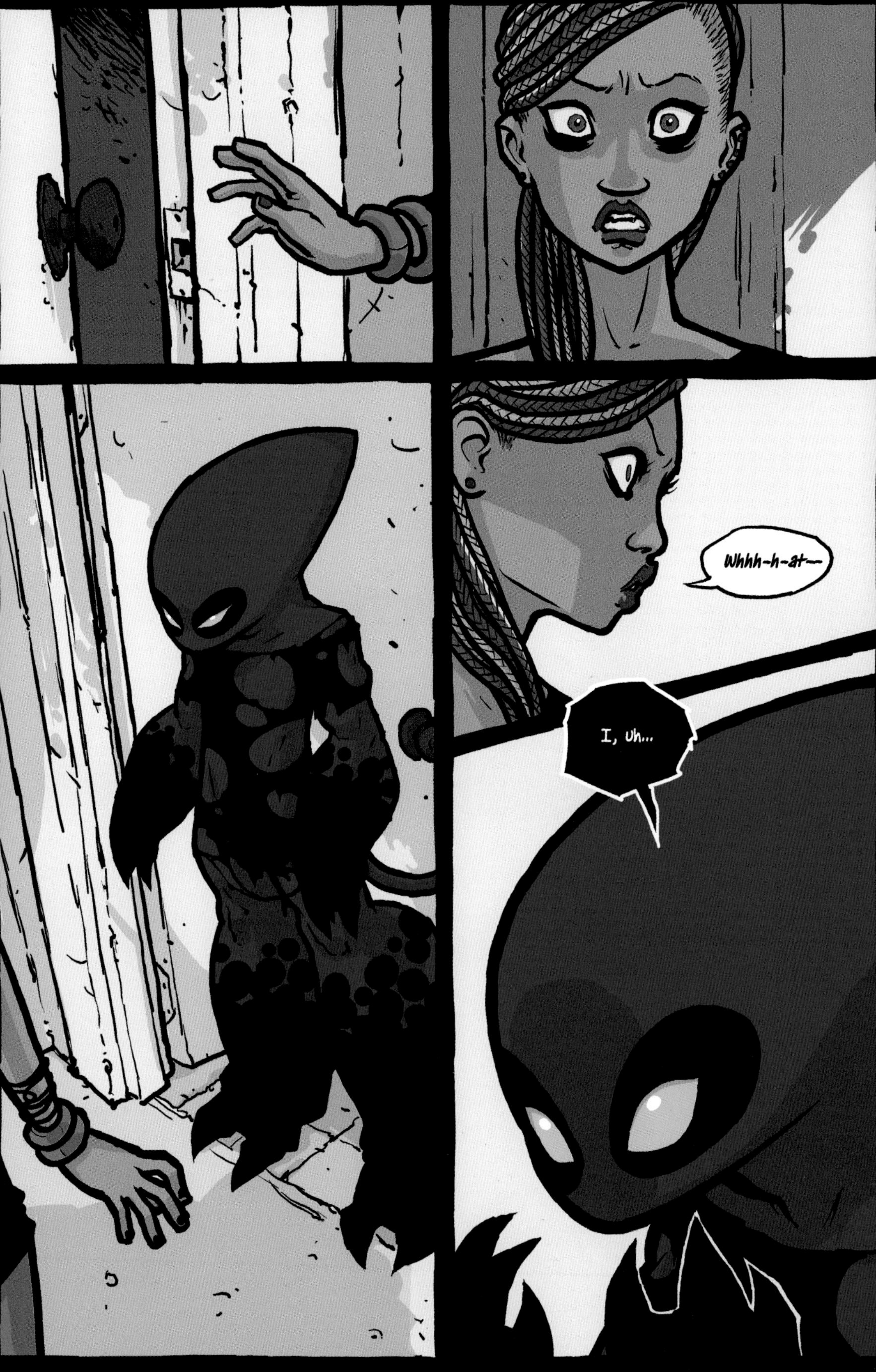
Whhh-h-at--
I, uh...

Oh my god... Scout?!?

Kyisha...

I... I changed... I had a... a thing, I'm a monster thing or somethin'... oh my god... don't be scared...

What...

don't be scared of me, okay...

I'm not! You're adorable, not scary...!

I'm just— What the hell is this...

I... The light hurts my eyes...

rrooooow

...Are you okay, at least...? Is it okay to touch you...?

...

rrooowwwr

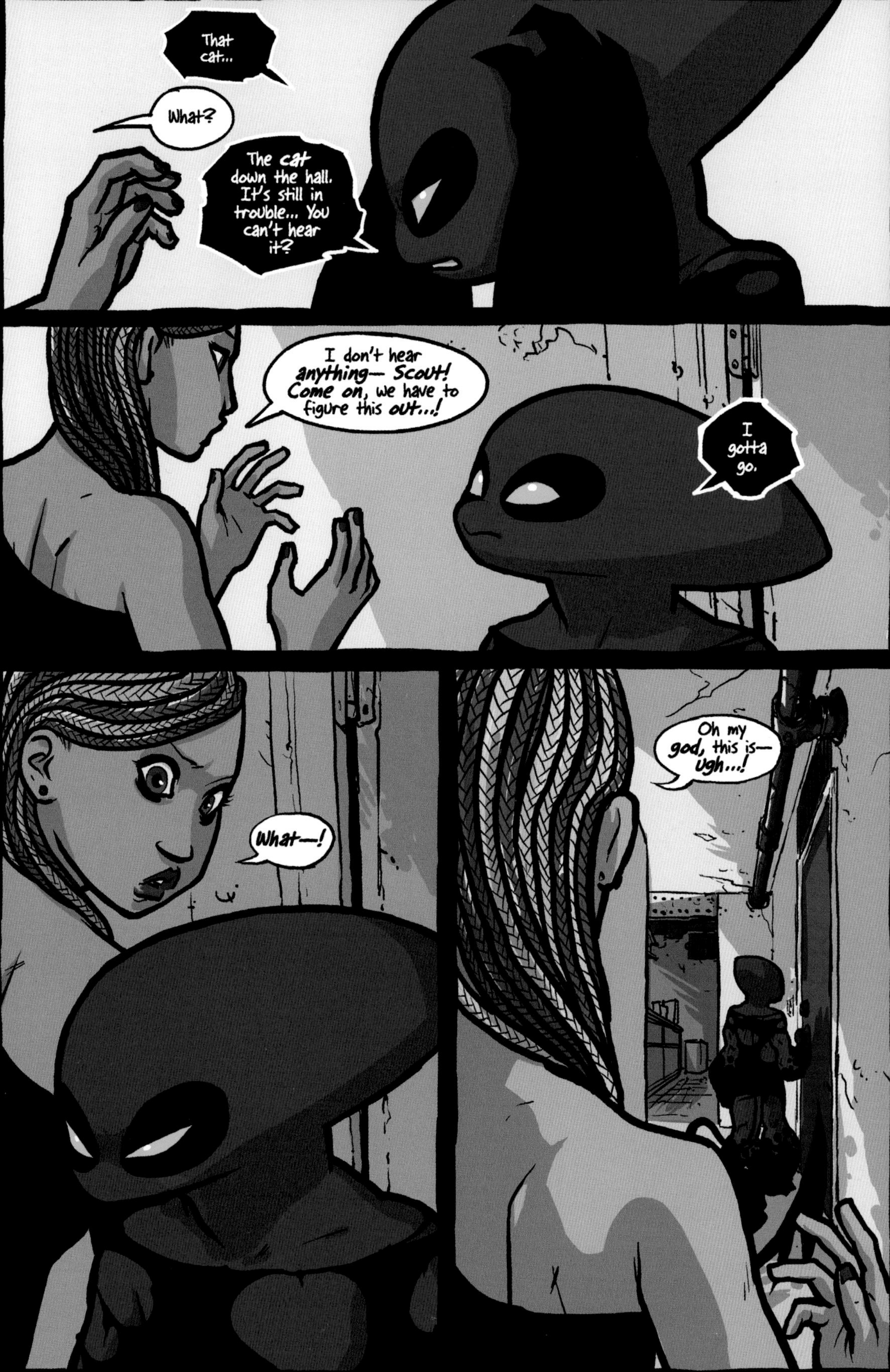
That cat...
What?
The cat down the hall. It's still in trouble... You can't hear it?
I don't hear anything— Scout! Come on, we have to figure this out...!
I gotta go.
What—!
Oh my god, this is— ugh...!

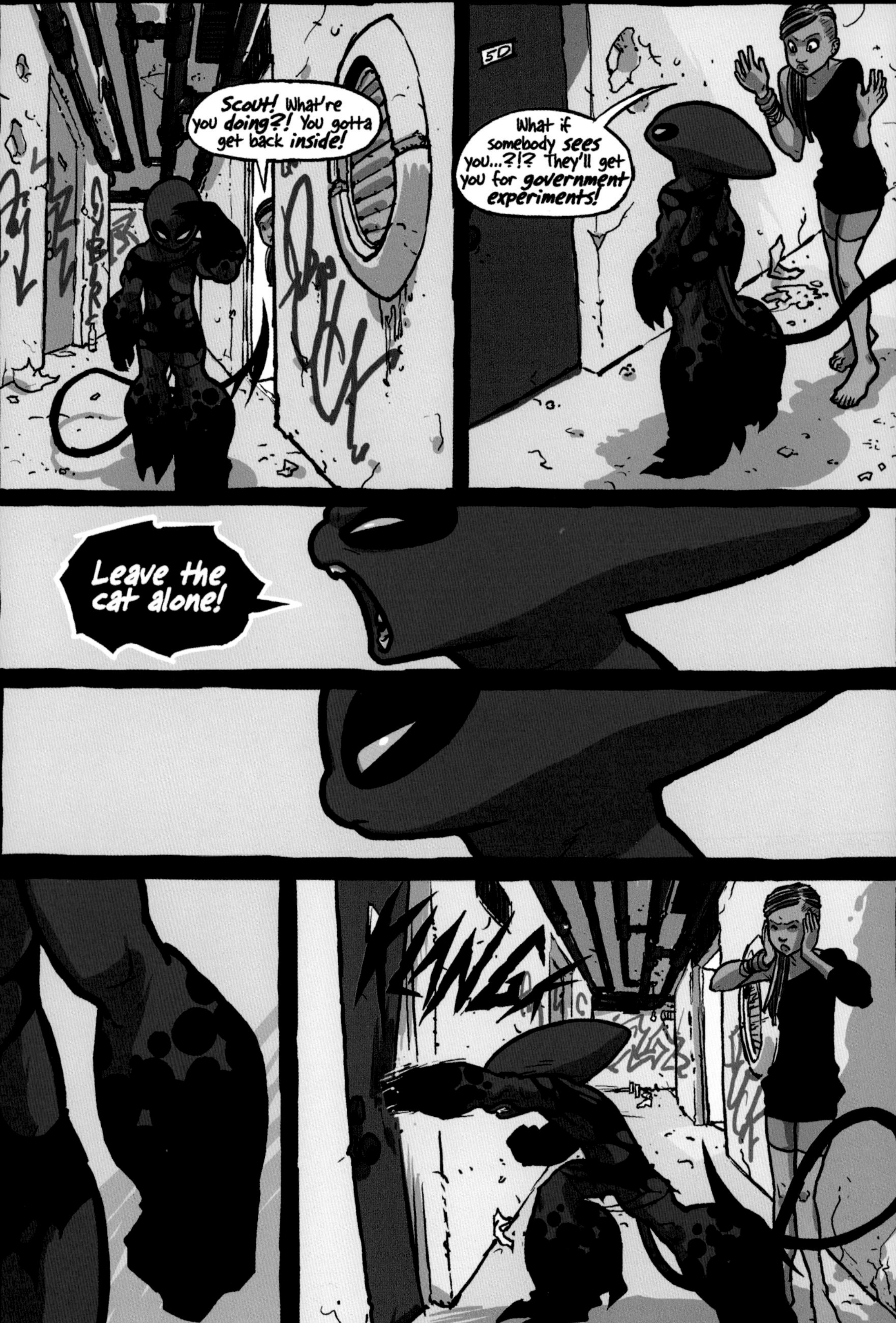
Scout! What're you doing?! You gotta get back inside!
5D
What if somebody sees you...?!? They'll get you for government experiments!
Leave the cat alone!

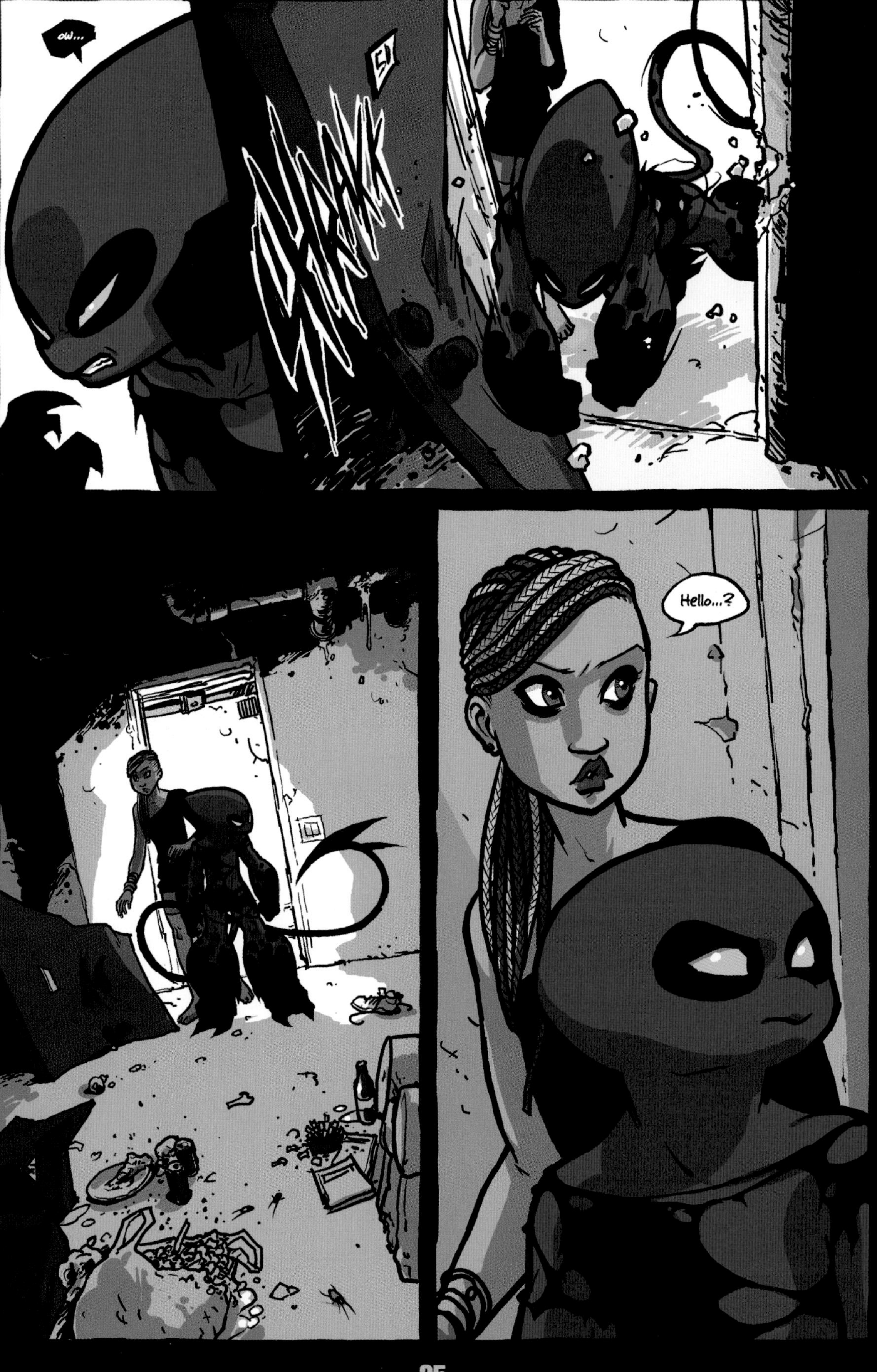
OW...
Hello...?

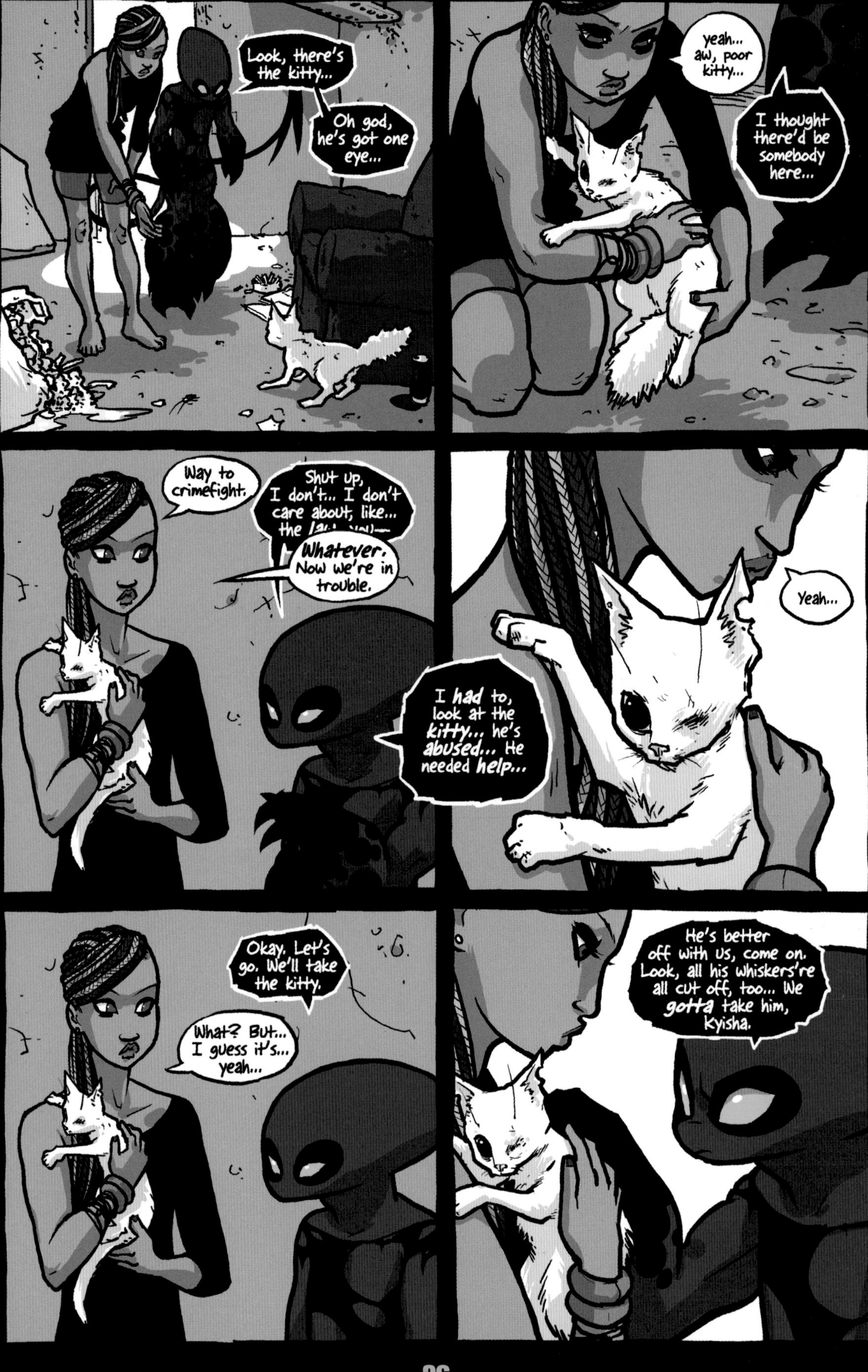
Look, there's the kitty...
Oh god, he's got one eye...
yeah... aw, poor kitty...
I thought there'd be somebody here...
Way to crimefight.
Shut up, I don't... I don't care about, like... the
Whatever. Now we're in trouble.
I had to, look at the kitty... he's abused... He needed help...
Yeah...
Okay. Let's go. We'll take the kitty.
What? But... I guess it's... yeah...
He's better off with us, come on. Look, all his whiskers're all cut off, too... We gotta take him, Kyisha.

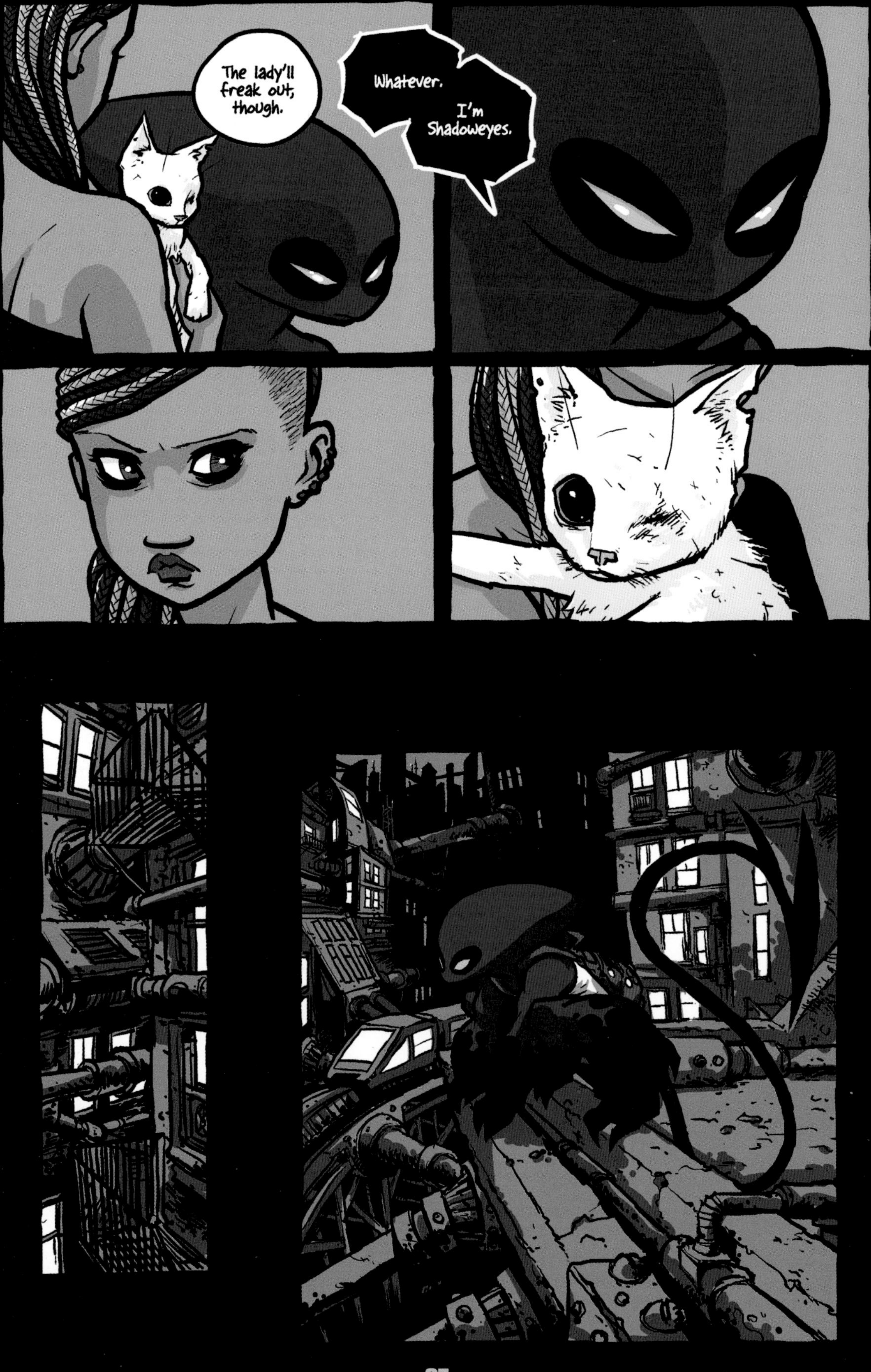
The lady'll freak out, though.
Whatever.
I'm Shadoweyes.

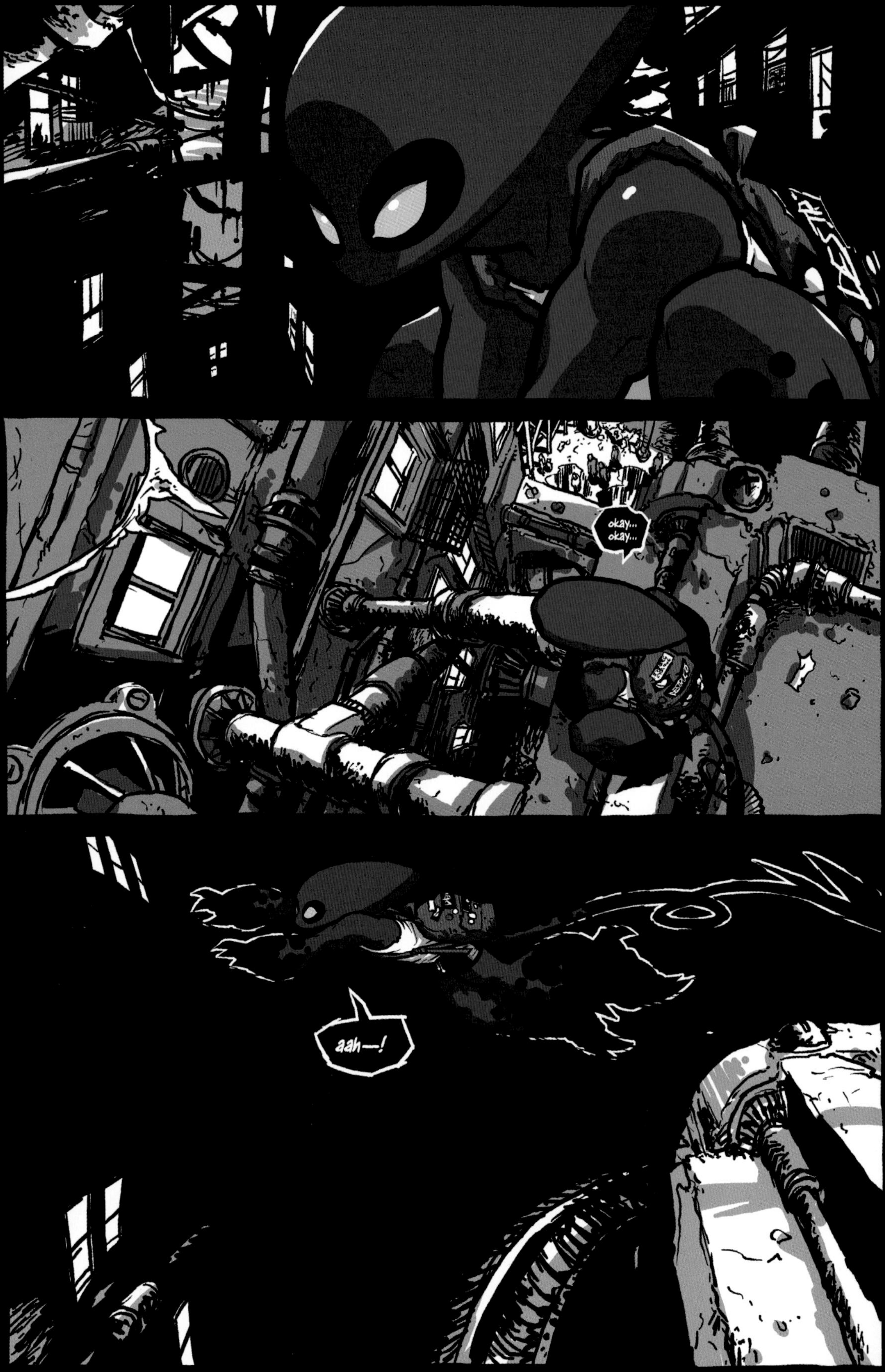
okay... okay...
aah—!

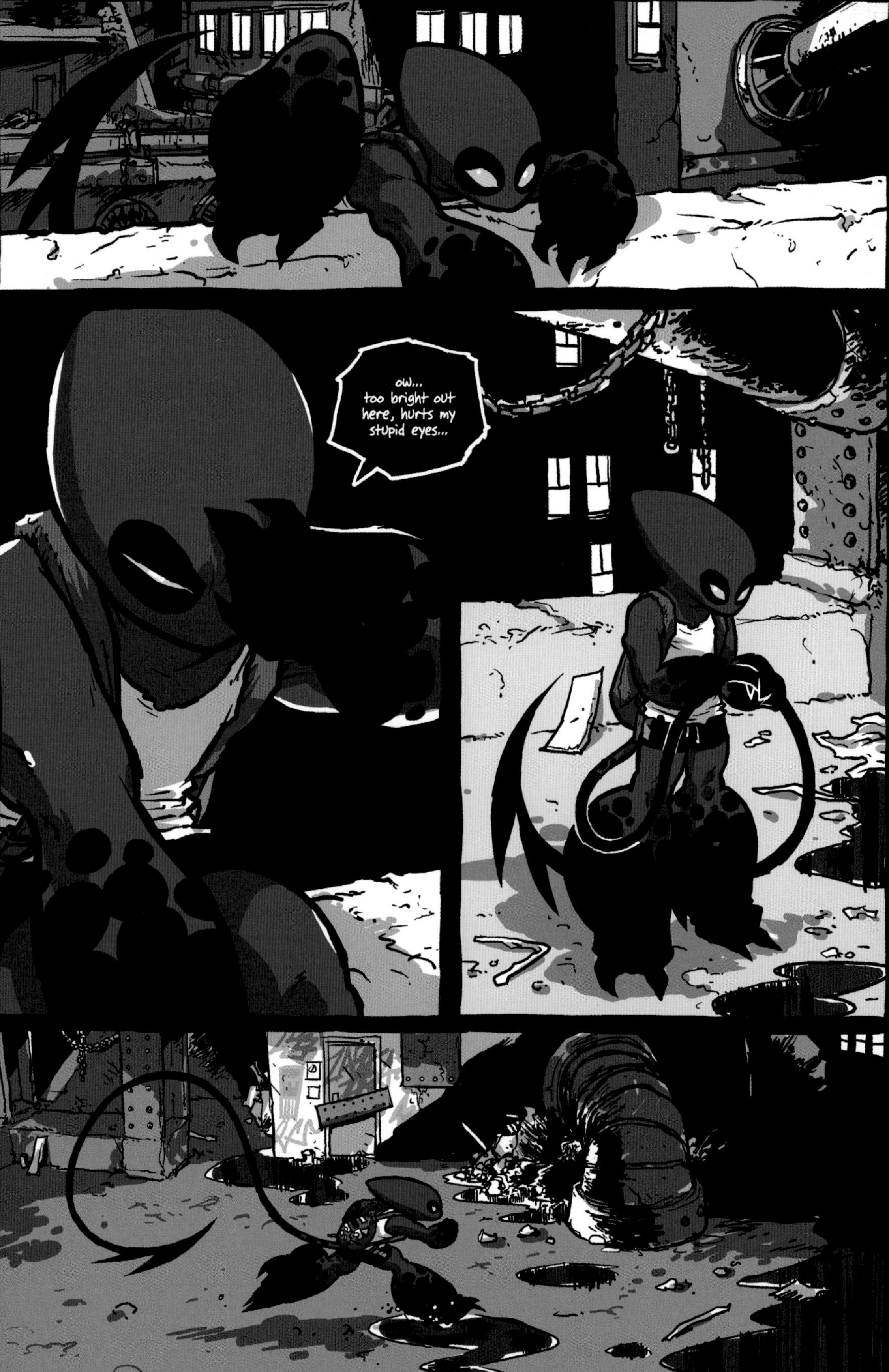
ow...
too bright out here, hurts my stupid eyes...

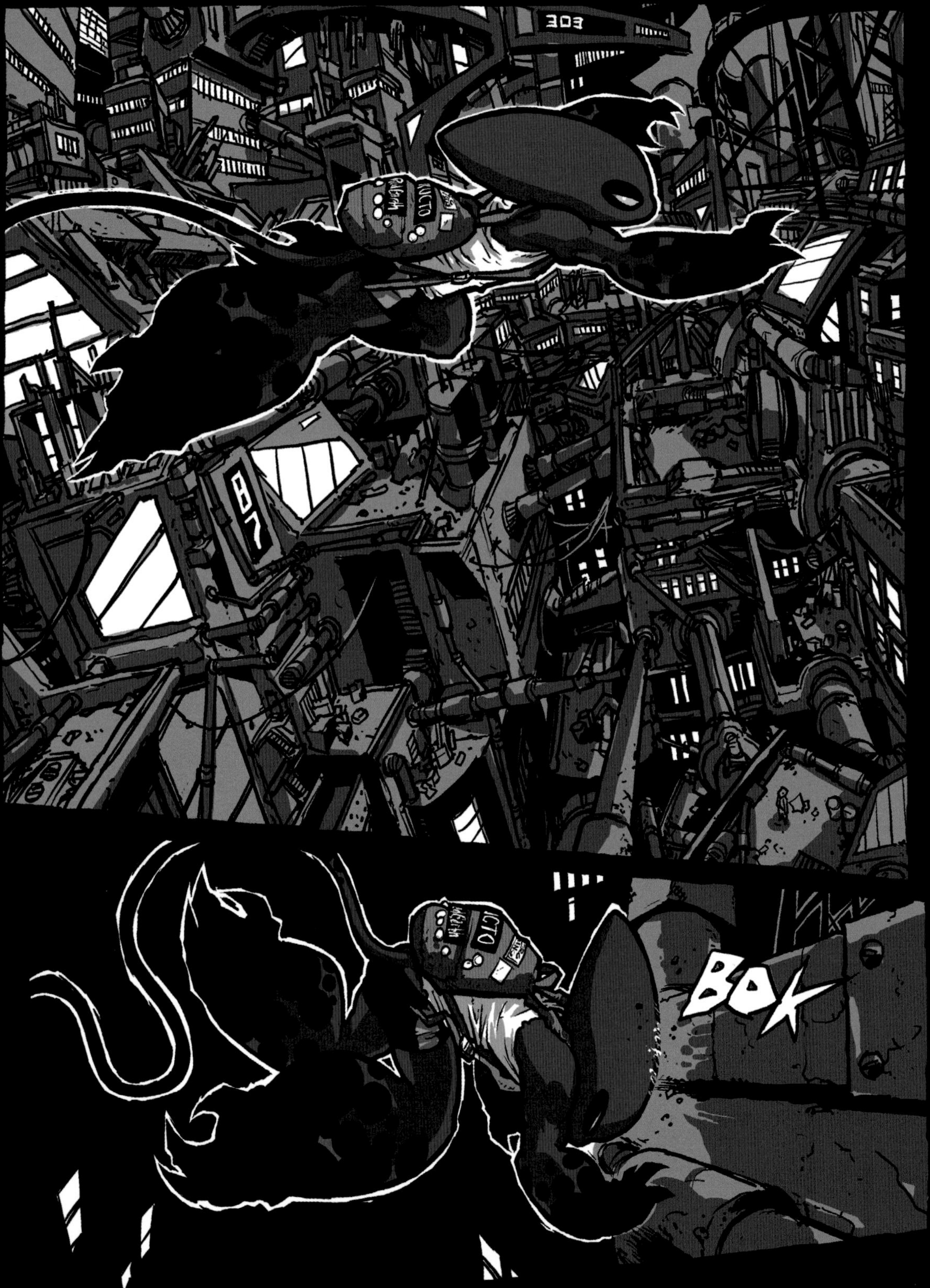
87
BOK

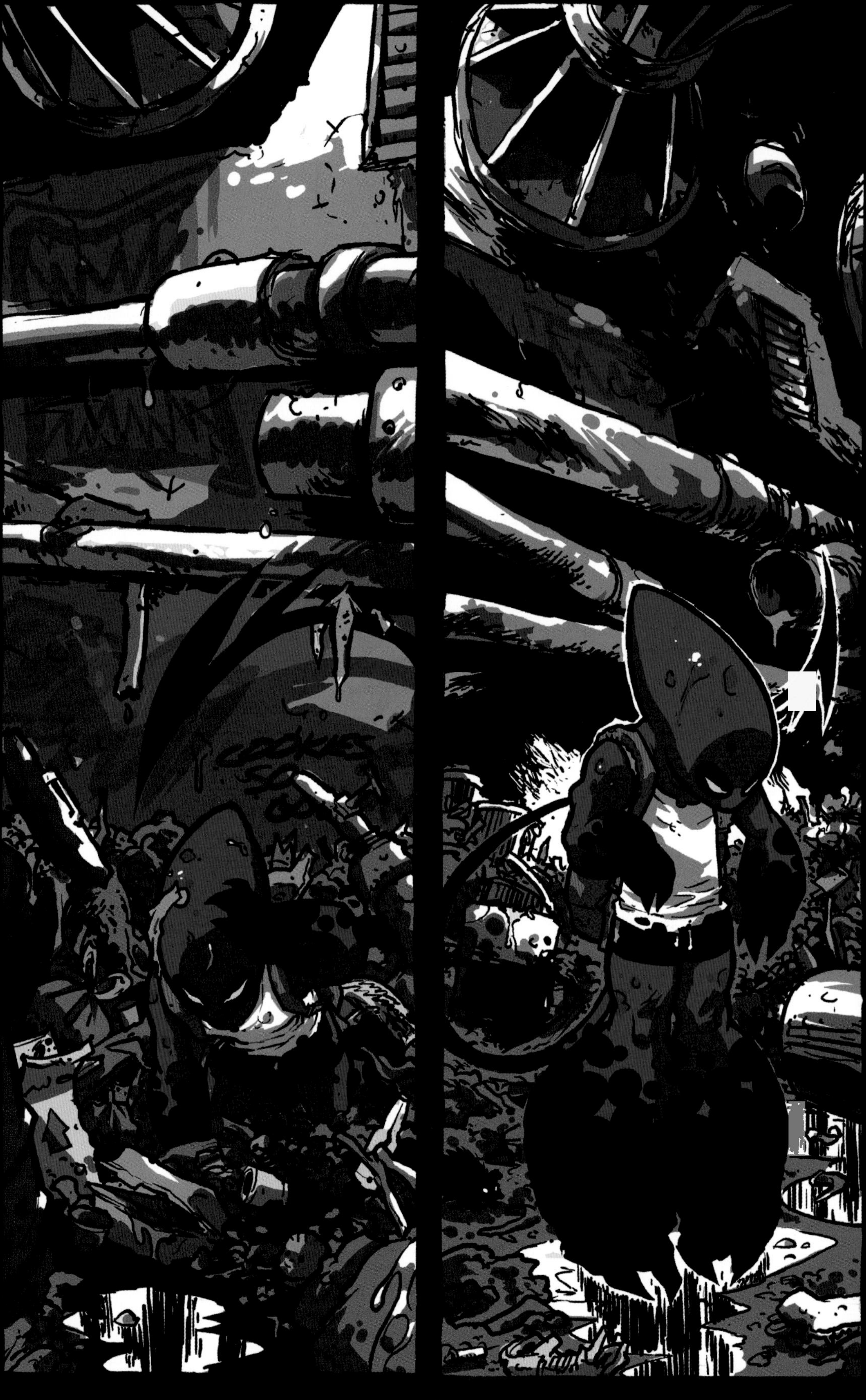

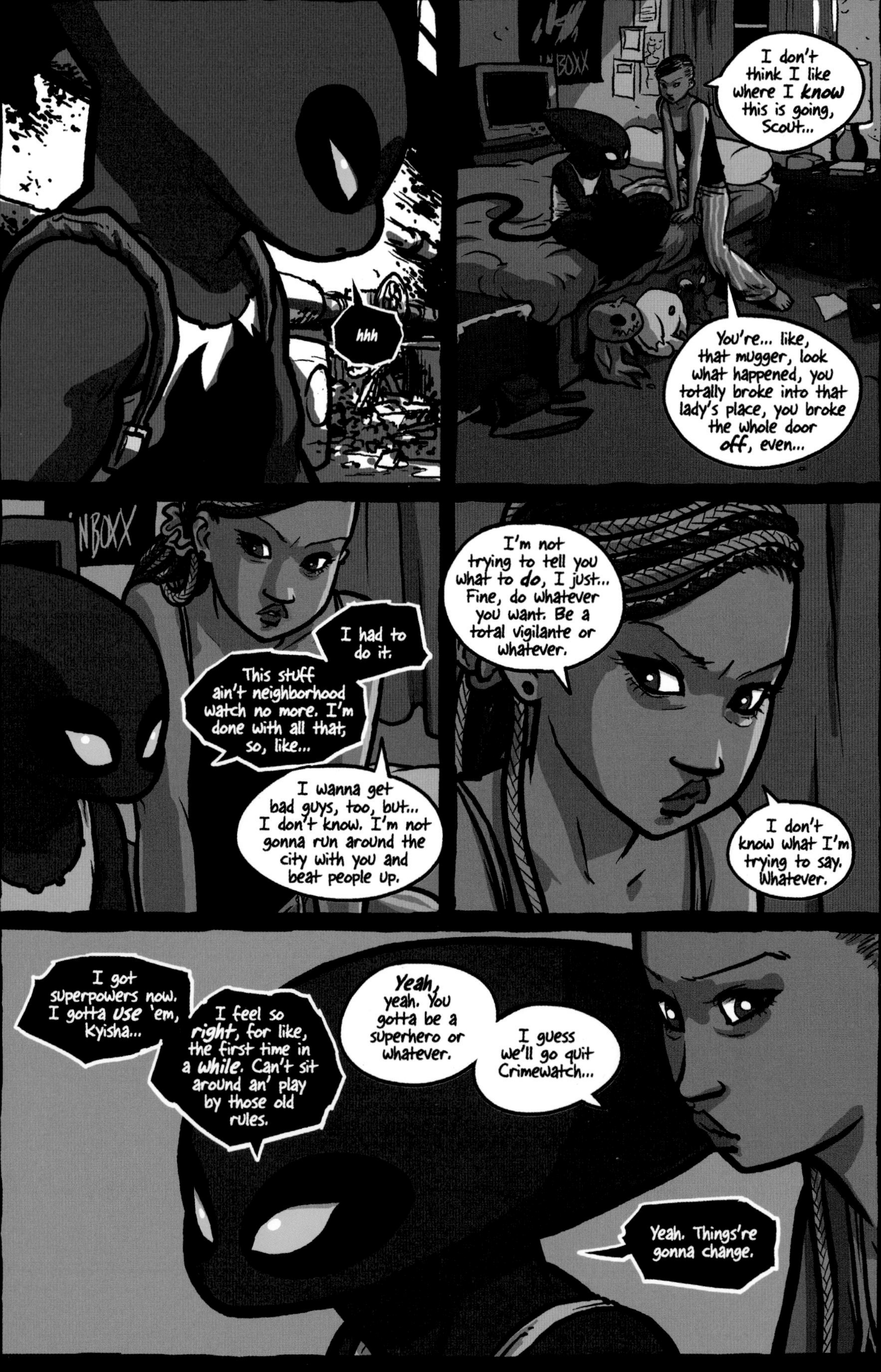
hhh
I don't think I like where I *know* this is going, Scout...
You're... like, that mugger, look what happened, you totally broke into that lady's place, you broke the whole door *off*, even...
I had to do it.
This stuff ain't neighborhood watch no more. I'm done with all that, so, like...
I wanna get bad guys, too, but... I don't know. I'm not gonna run around the city with you and beat people up.
I'm not trying to tell you what to *do*, I just... Fine, do whatever you want. Be a total vigilante or whatever.
I don't know what I'm trying to say. Whatever.
I got superpowers now. I gotta *use* 'em, Kyisha...
I feel so *right*, for like, the first time in a *while*. Can't sit around an' play by those old rules.
Yeah, yeah. You gotta be a superhero or whatever.
I guess we'll go quit Crimewatch...
Yeah. Things're gonna change.

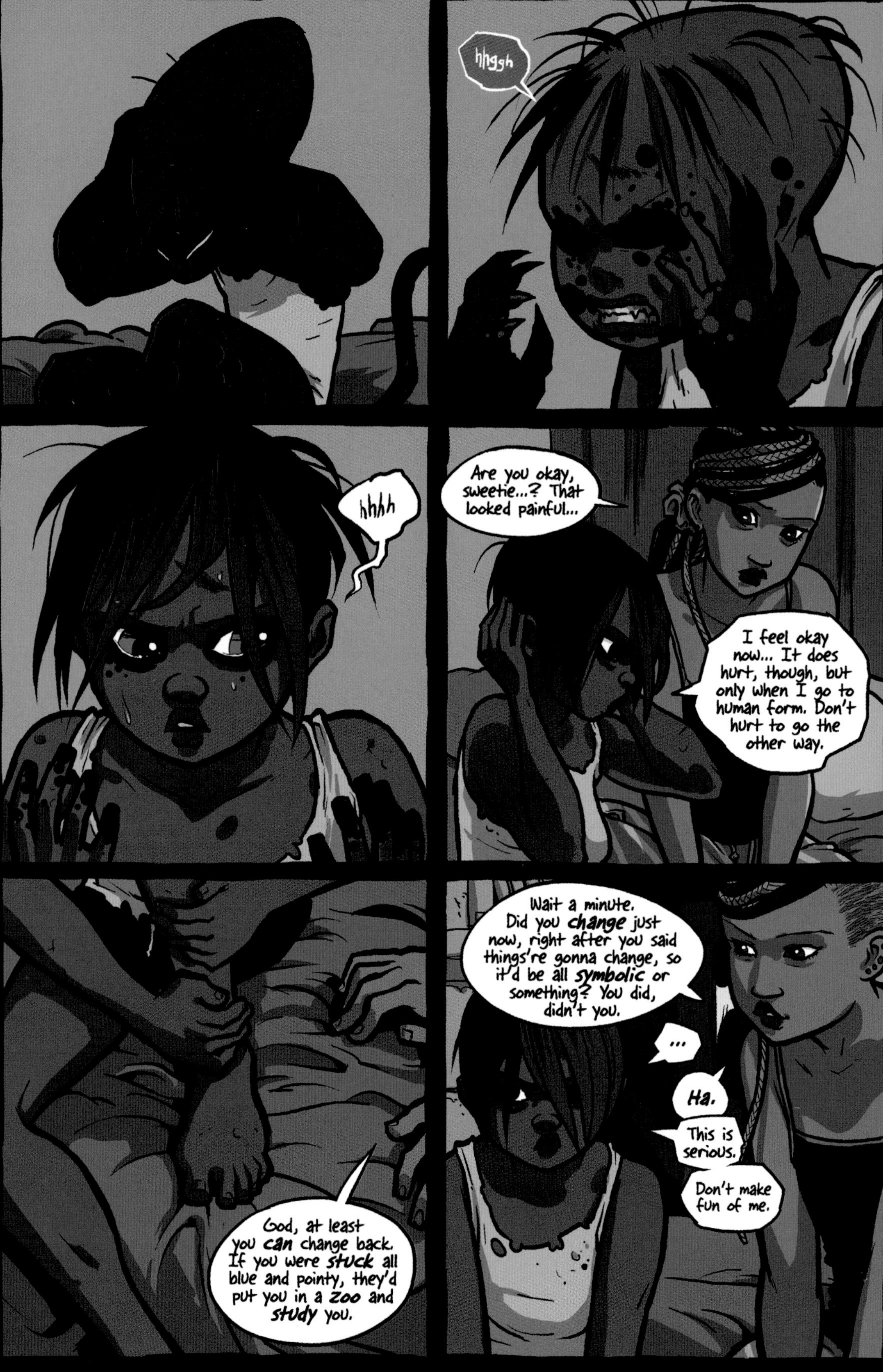
hhggh
hhhh
Are you okay, sweetie...? That looked painful...
I feel okay now... It does hurt, though, but only when I go to human form. Don't hurt to go the other way.
God, at least you can change back. If you were stuck all blue and pointy, they'd put you in a zoo and study you.
Wait a minute. Did you change just now, right after you said things're gonna change, so it'd be all symbolic or something? You did, didn't you.
...
Ha.
This is serious.
Don't make fun of me.

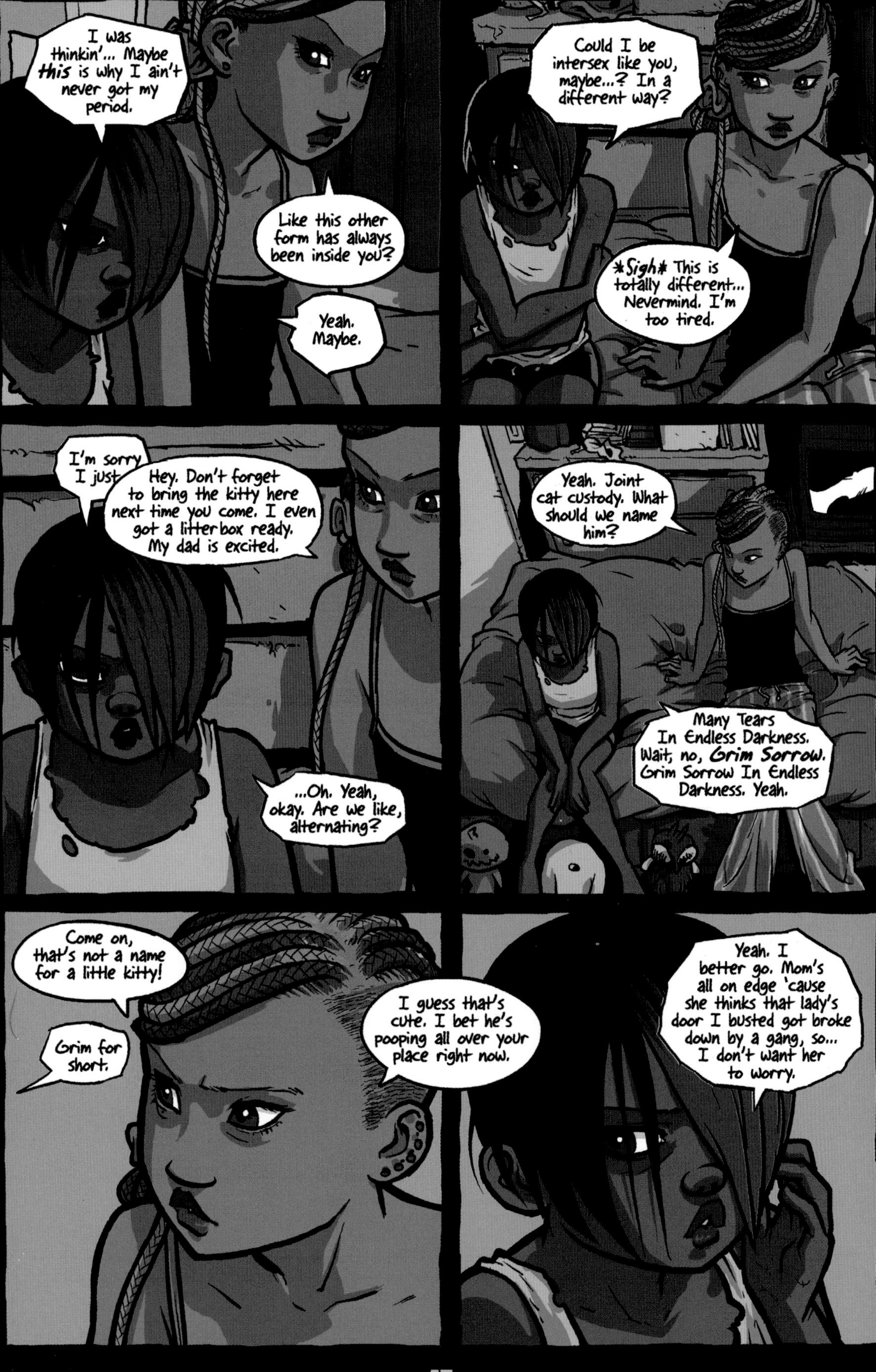
I was thinkin'... Maybe *this* is why I ain't never got my period.
Like this other form has always been inside you?
Yeah. Maybe.
Could I be intersex like you, maybe...? In a different way?
Sigh This is totally different... Nevermind. I'm too tired.
I'm sorry I just
Hey. Don't forget to bring the kitty here next time you come. I even got a litterbox ready. My dad is excited.
...Oh. Yeah, okay. Are we like, alternating?
Yeah. Joint cat custody. What should we name him?
Many Tears In Endless Darkness. Wait, no, *Grim Sorrow*. Grim Sorrow In Endless Darkness. Yeah.
Come on, that's not a name for a little kitty!
Grim for short.
I guess that's cute. I bet he's pooping all over your place right now.
Yeah. I better go. Mom's all on edge 'cause she thinks that lady's door I busted got broke down by a gang, so... I don't want her to worry.

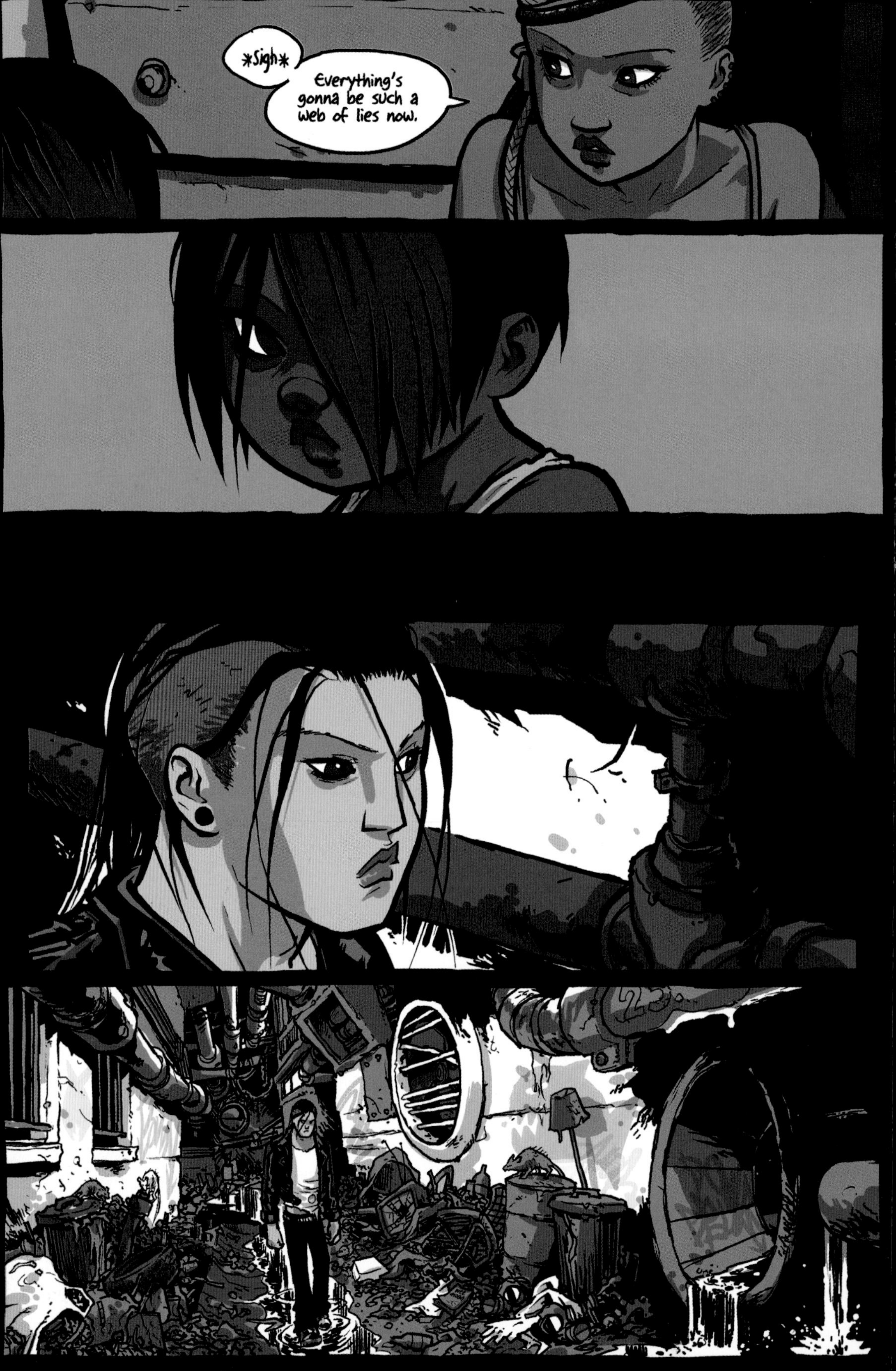
Sigh
Everything's gonna be such a web of lies now.

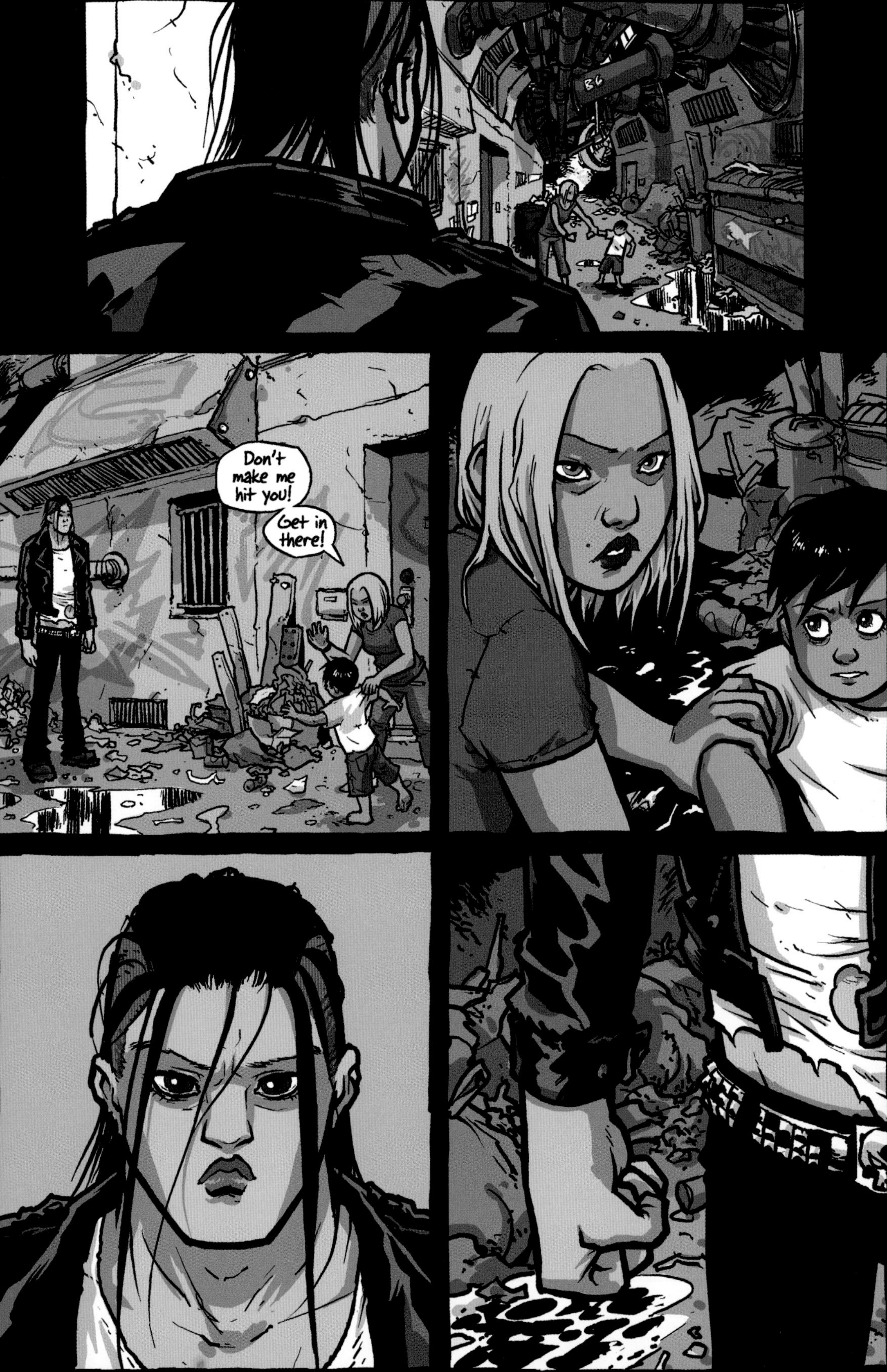

Don't make me hit you!
Get in there!

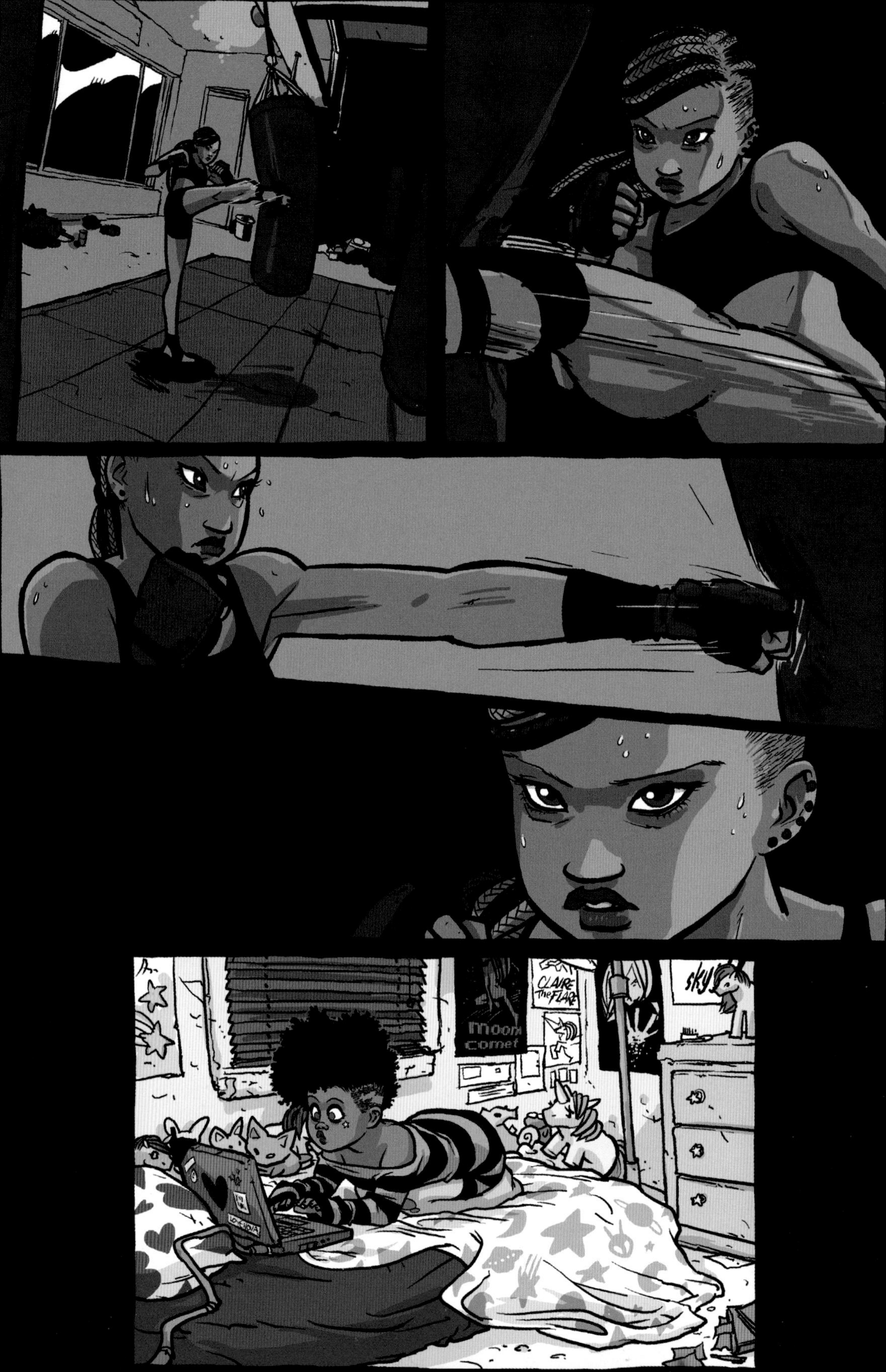
moon
comet
CLAIRE
The FLARE
sky
LOVE NOVA

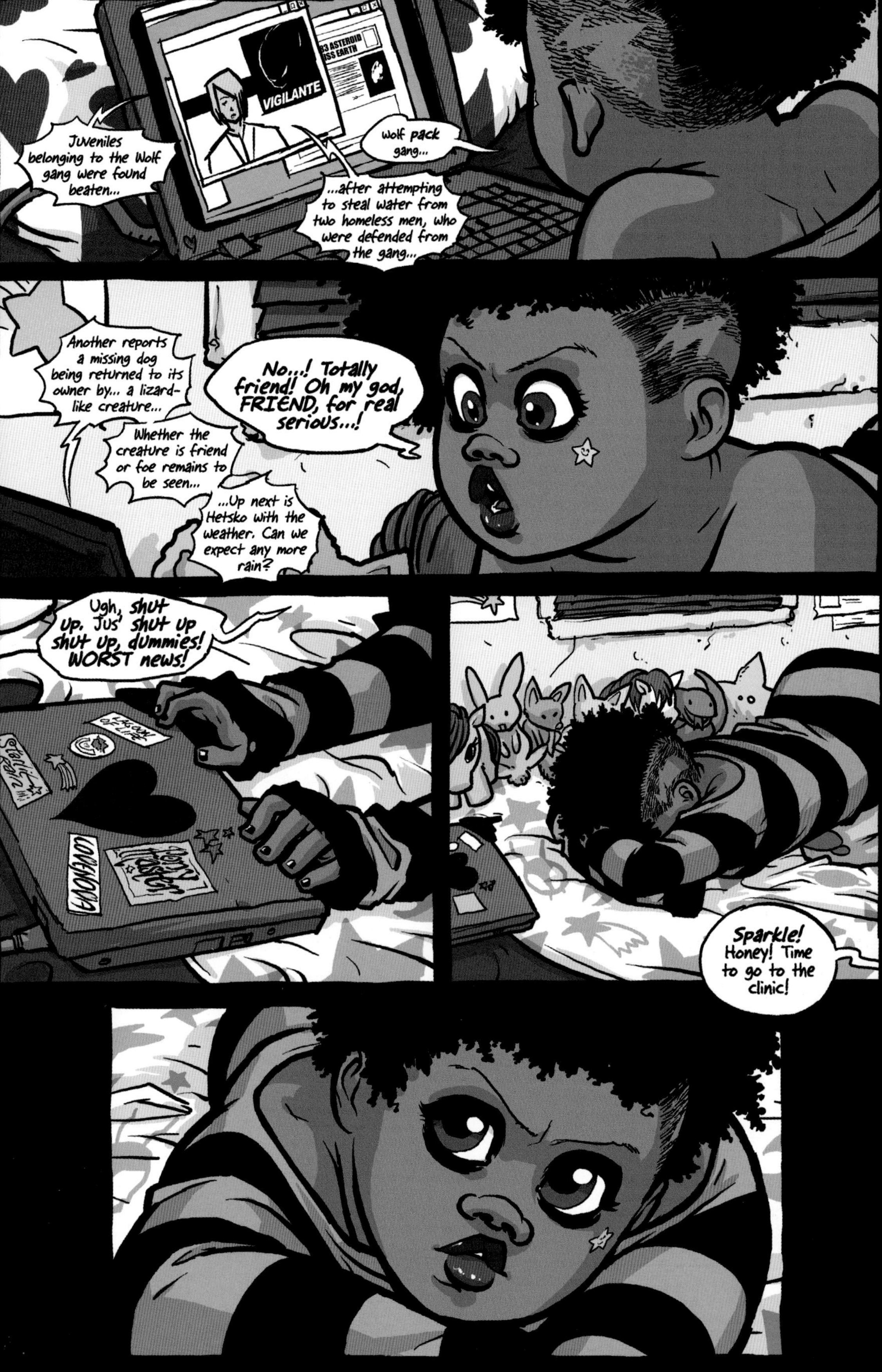
VIGILANTE
Juveniles belonging to the Wolf gang were found beaten...
Wolf pack gang...
...after attempting to steal water from two homeless men, who were defended from the gang...
Another reports a missing dog being returned to its owner by... a lizard-like creature...
No...! Totally friend! Oh my god, FRIEND, for real serious...!
Whether the creature is friend or foe remains to be seen...
...Up next is Hetsko with the weather. Can we expect any more rain?
Ugh, shut up. Jus' shut up shut up, dummies! WORST news!
Sparkle! Honey! Time to go to the clinic!

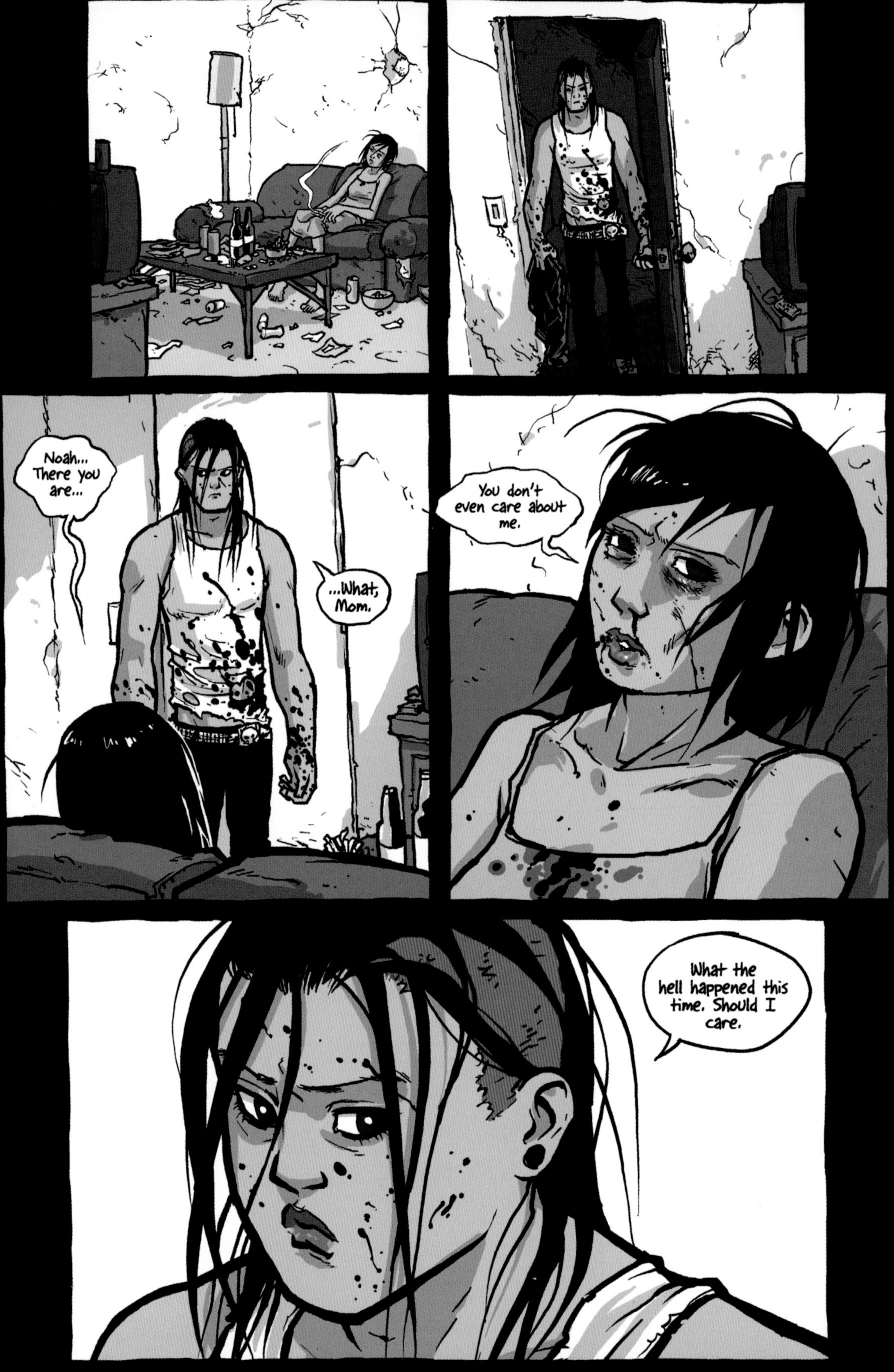
Noah... There you are...
...What, Mom.
You don't even care about me.
What the hell happened this time. Should I care.

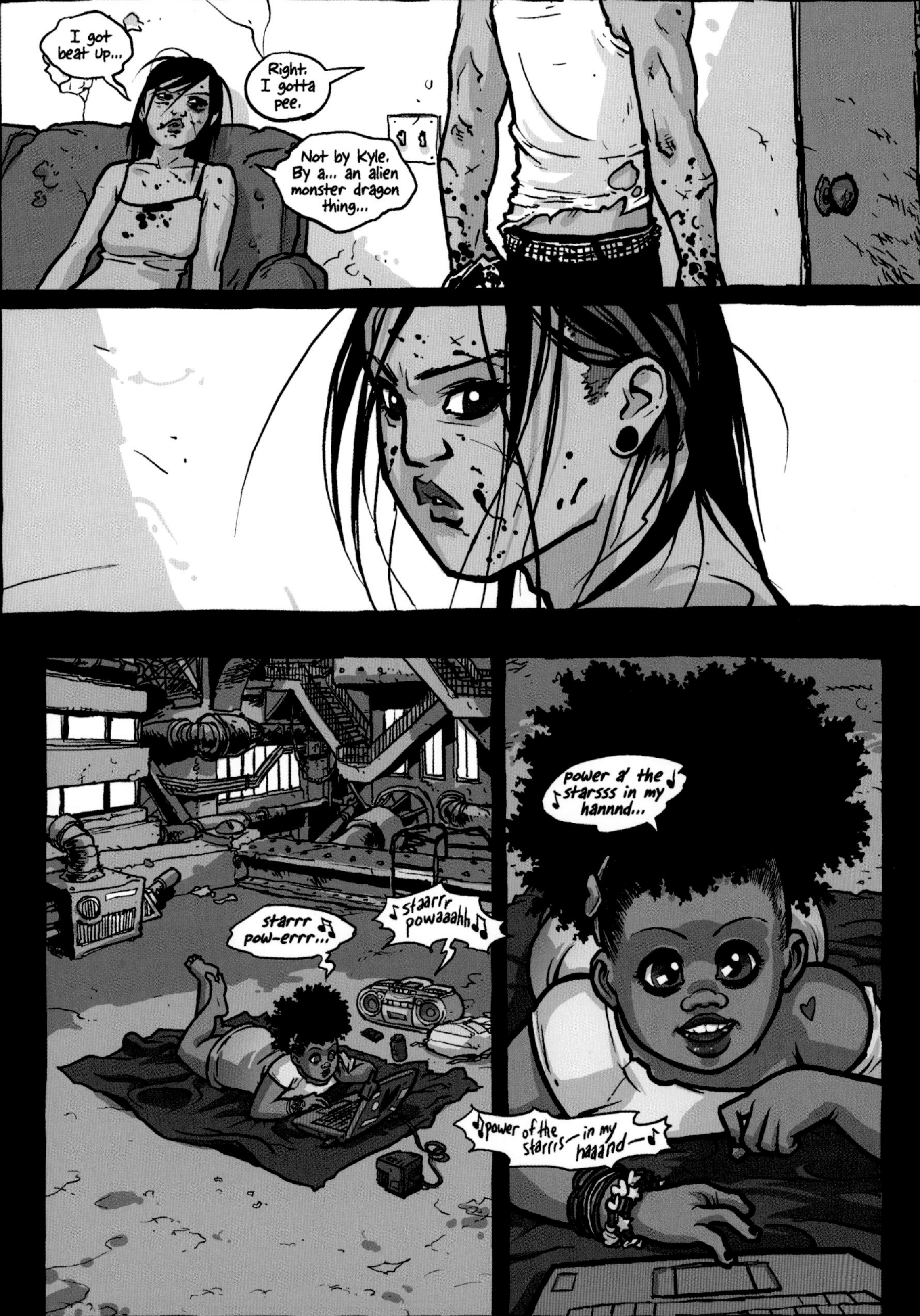
I got beat up...
Right. I gotta pee.
Not by Kyle. By a... an alien monster dragon thing...
starrr pow-errr...
staarrr powaaaahh
power a' the starsss in my hannnd...
power of the starrrs— in my haaand—

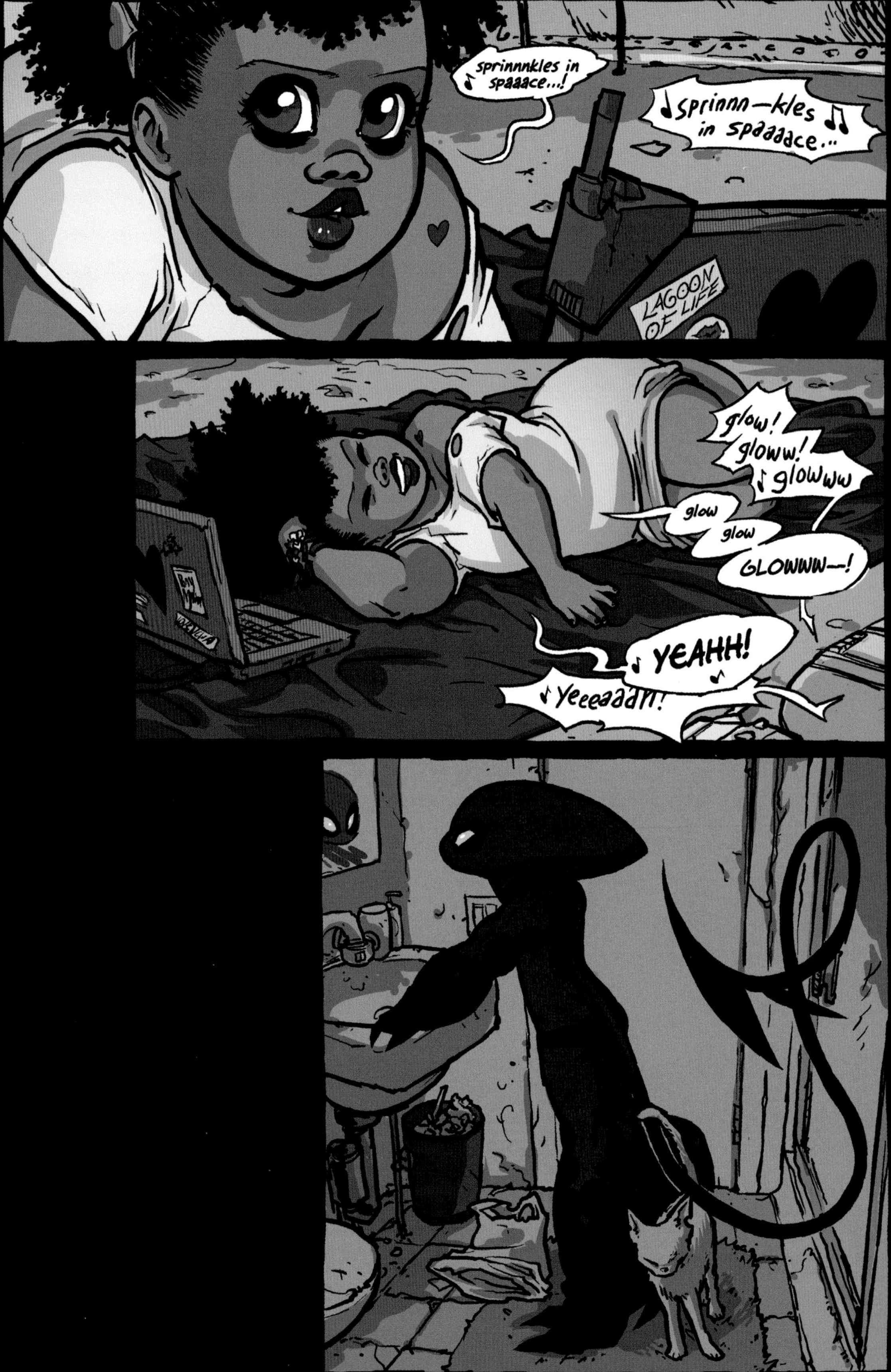
sprinnnkles in spaaace...!
sprinnn—kles in spaaaace...
LAGOON OF LIFE
glow! gloww! glowww
glow glow GLOWWW—!
YEAHH!
Yeeeaaah!

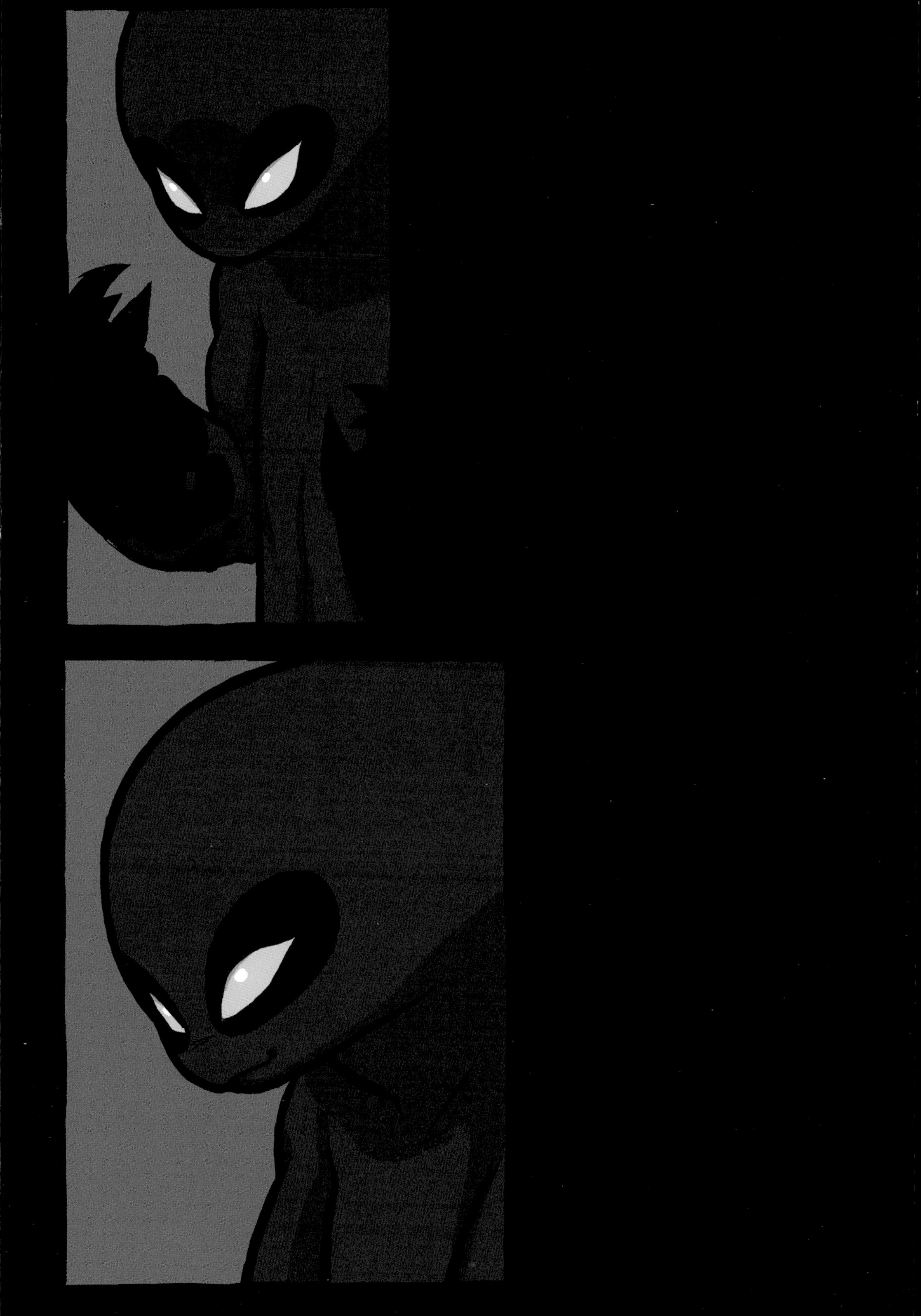

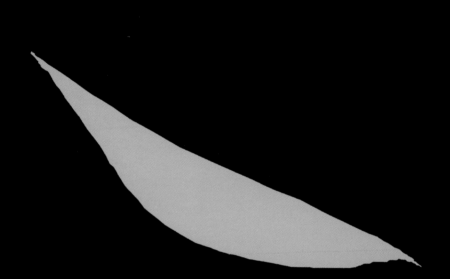

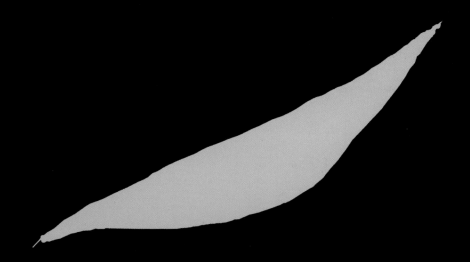

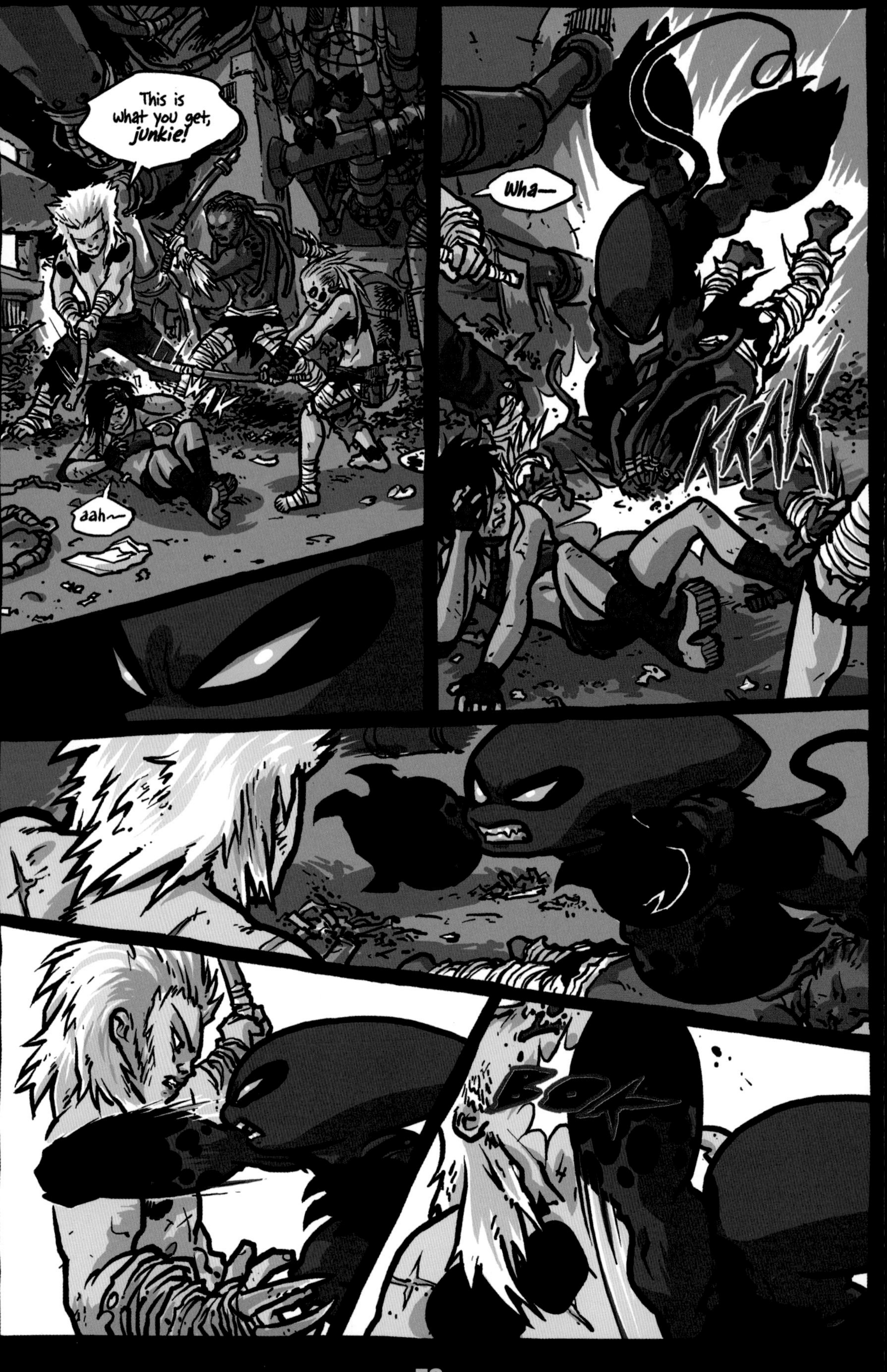
This is what you get, junkie!
aah~
Wha—
KRAK
BOK

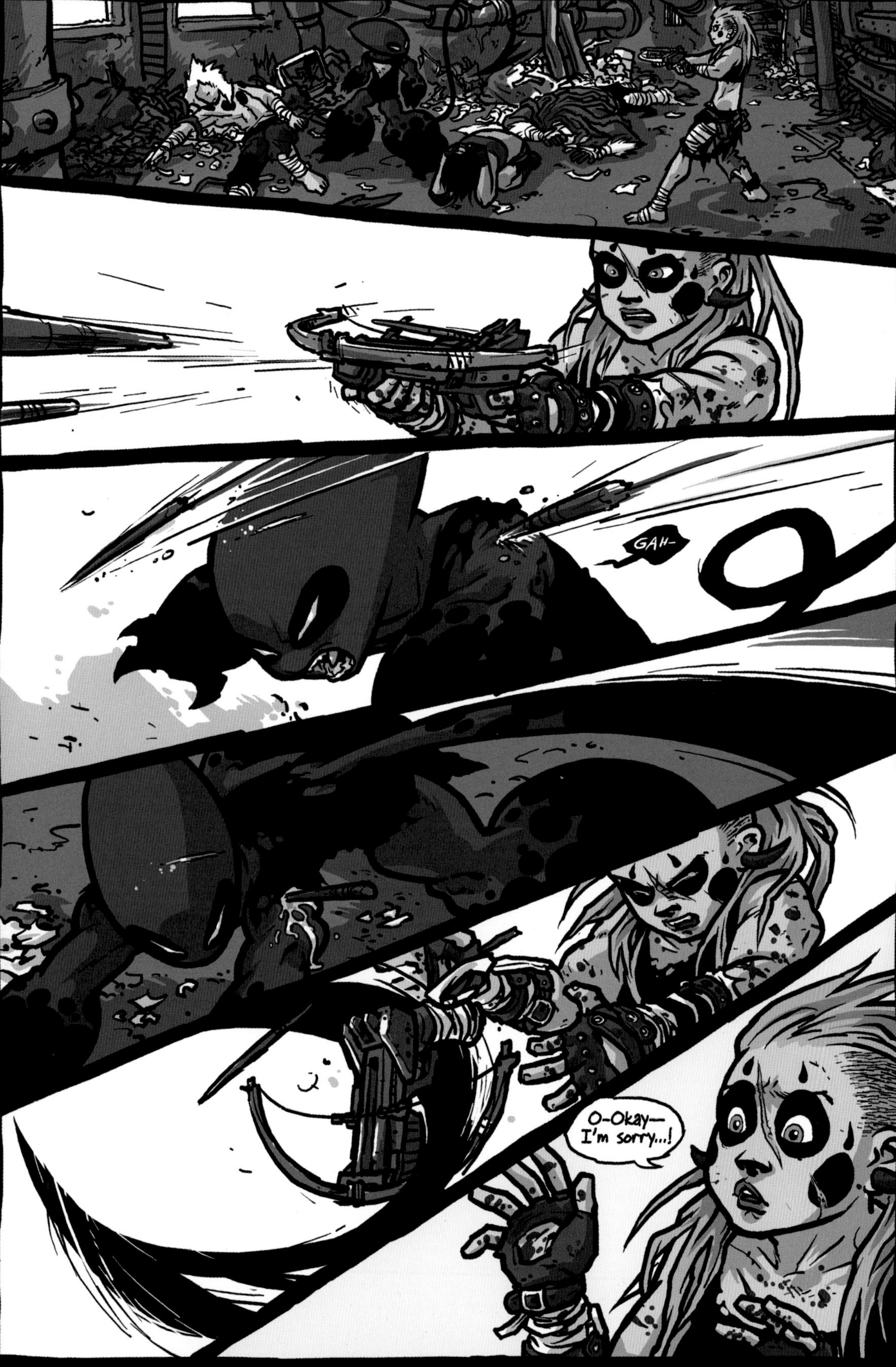
GAH–
O-Okay—
I'm sorry...!

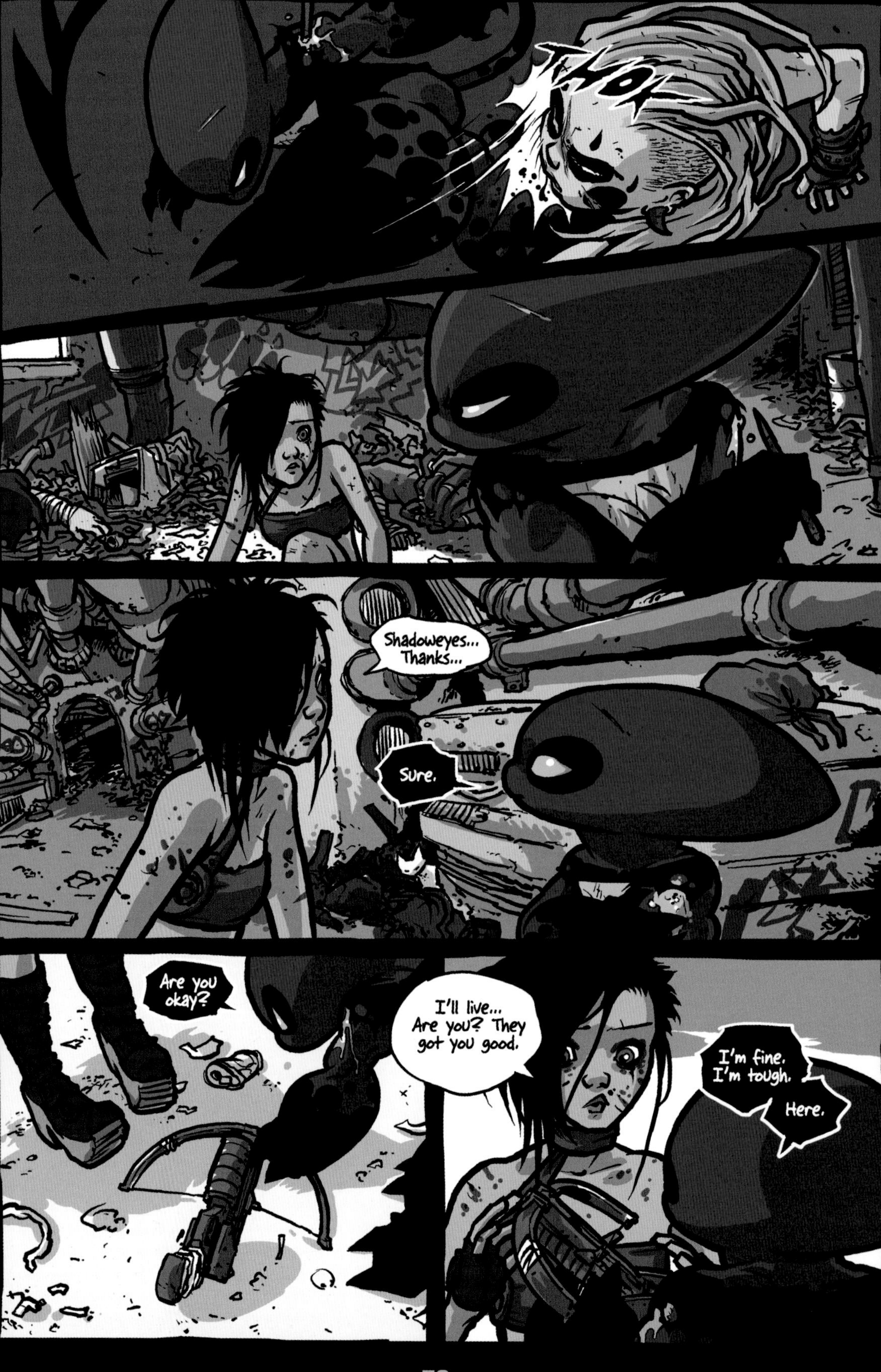
Shadoweyes...
Thanks...
Sure.
Are you okay?
I'll live... Are you? They got you good.
I'm fine. I'm tough.
Here.

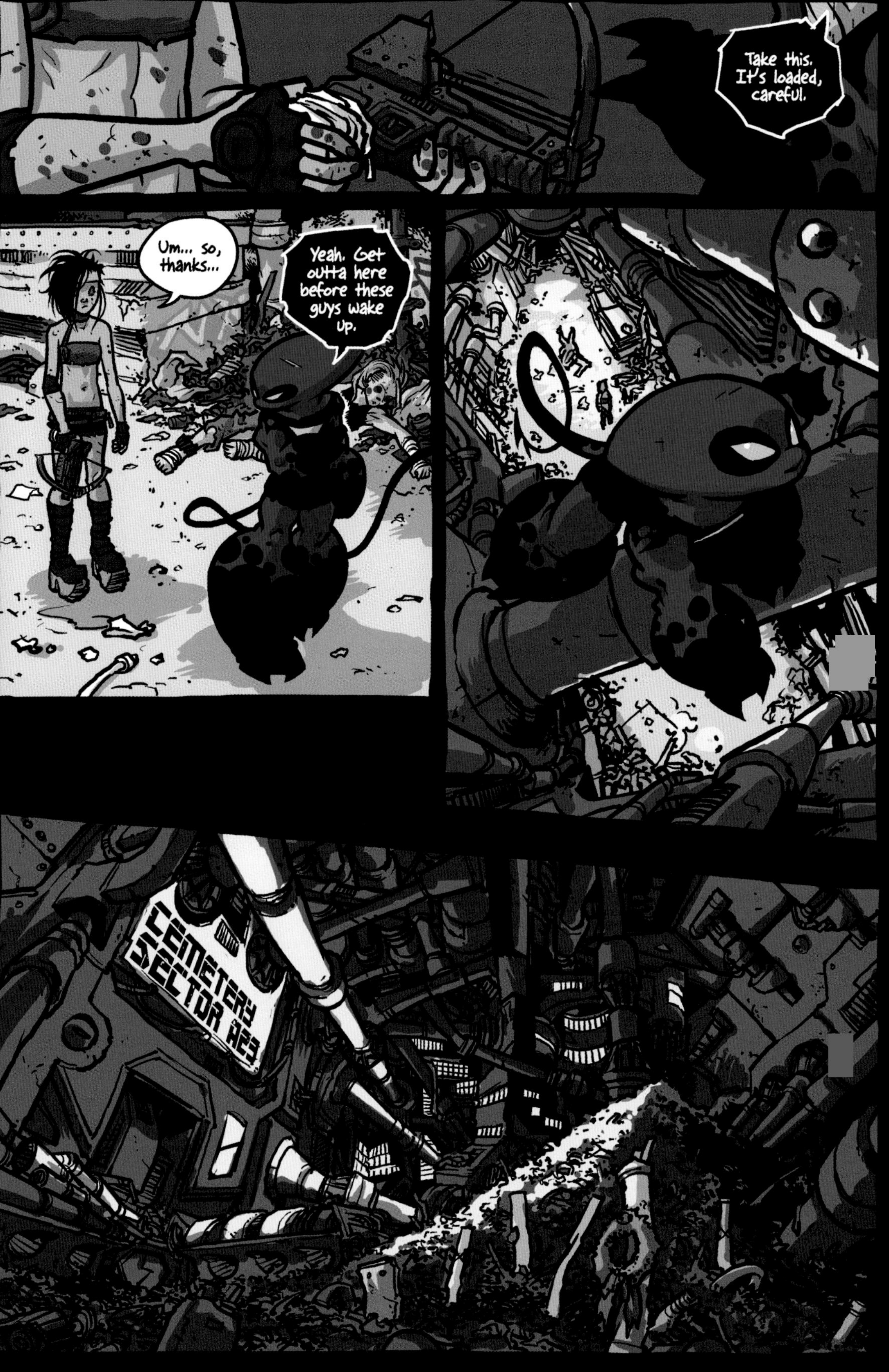
Take this. It's loaded, careful.
Um... so, thanks...
Yeah. Get outta here before these guys wake up.
CEMETERY SECTOR A23

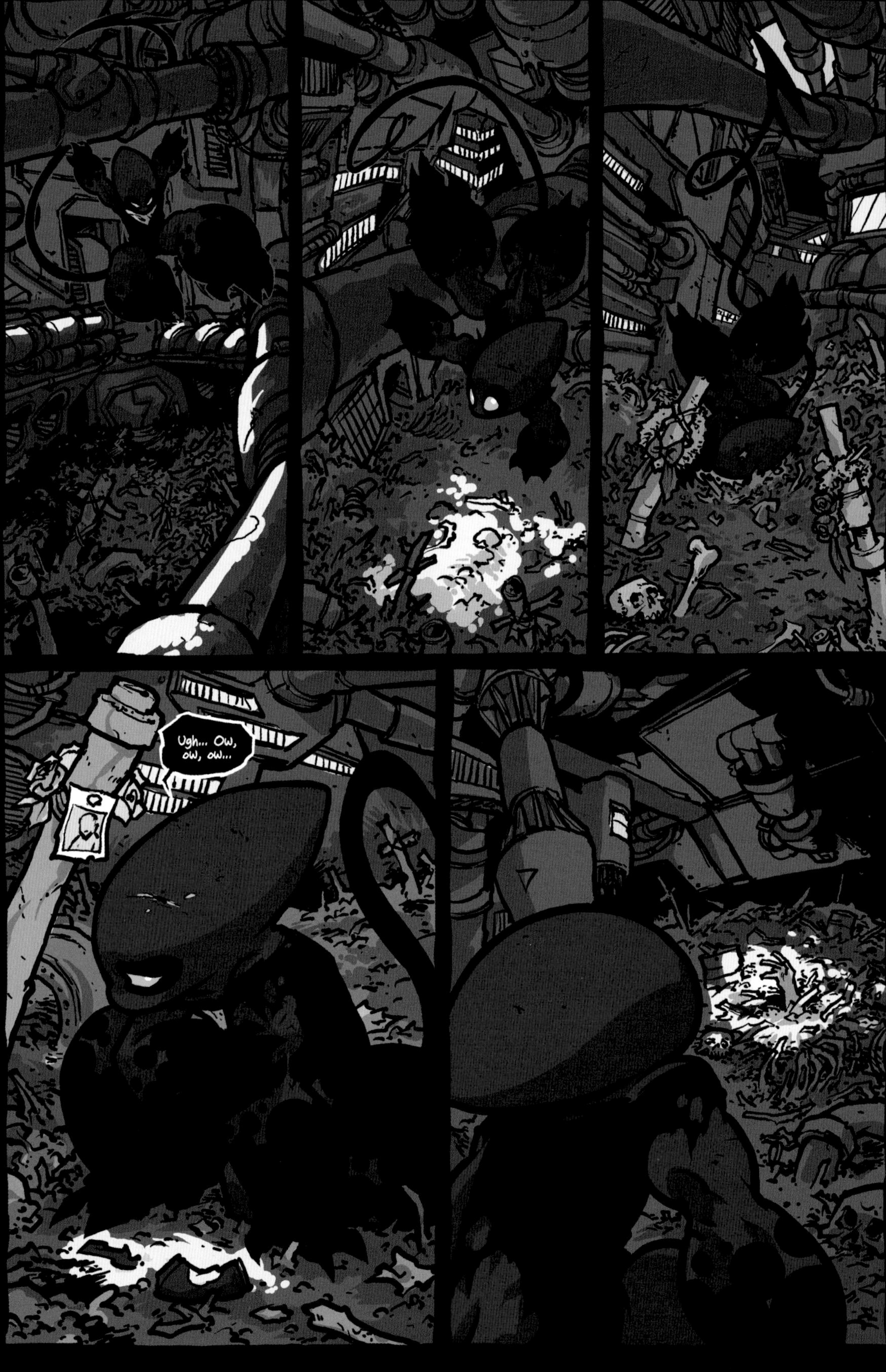
Ugh... Ow, ow, ow...

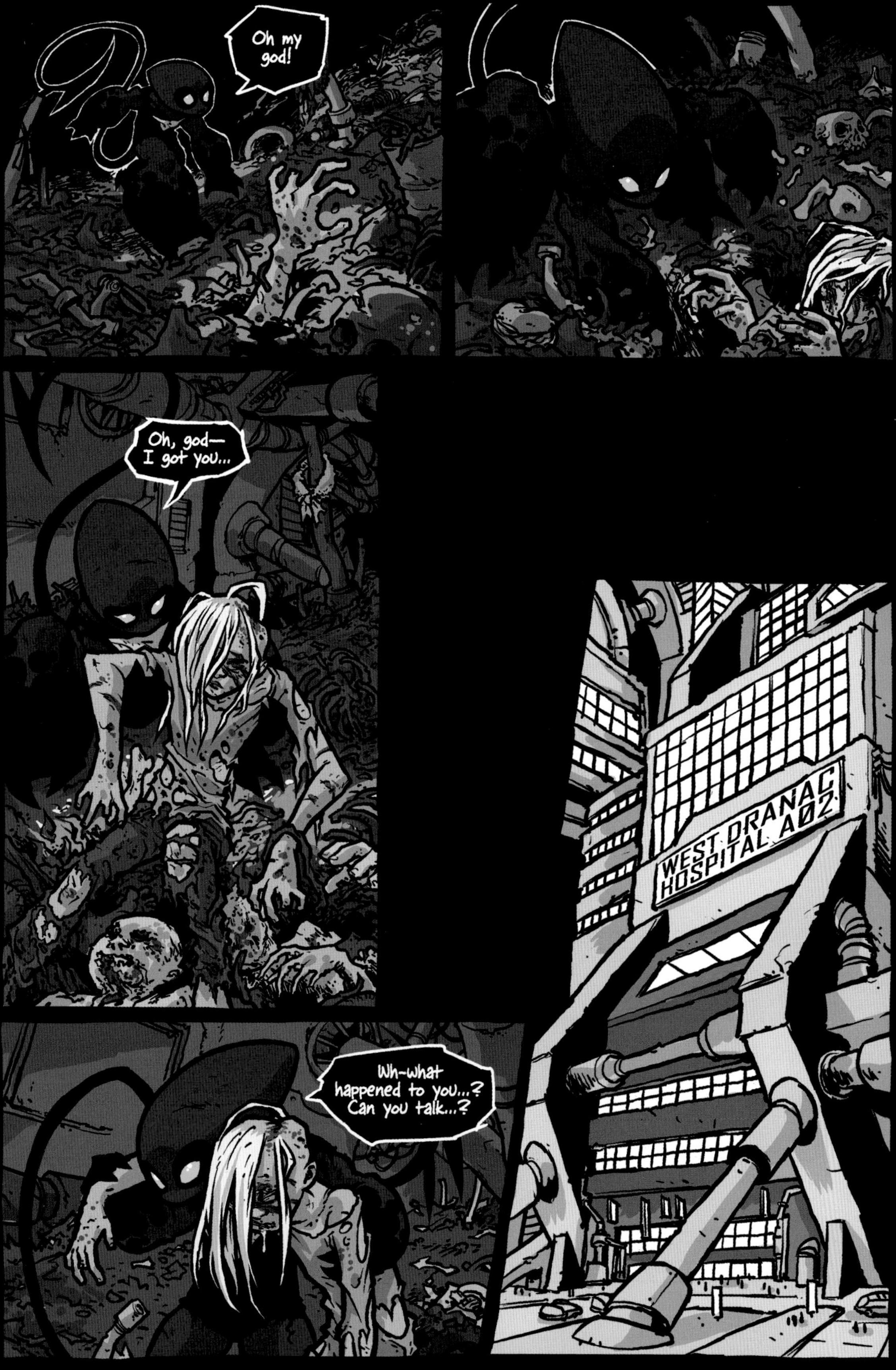
Oh my god!
Oh, god— I got you...
Wh-what happened to you...? Can you talk...?
WEST DRANAC HOSPITAL A02

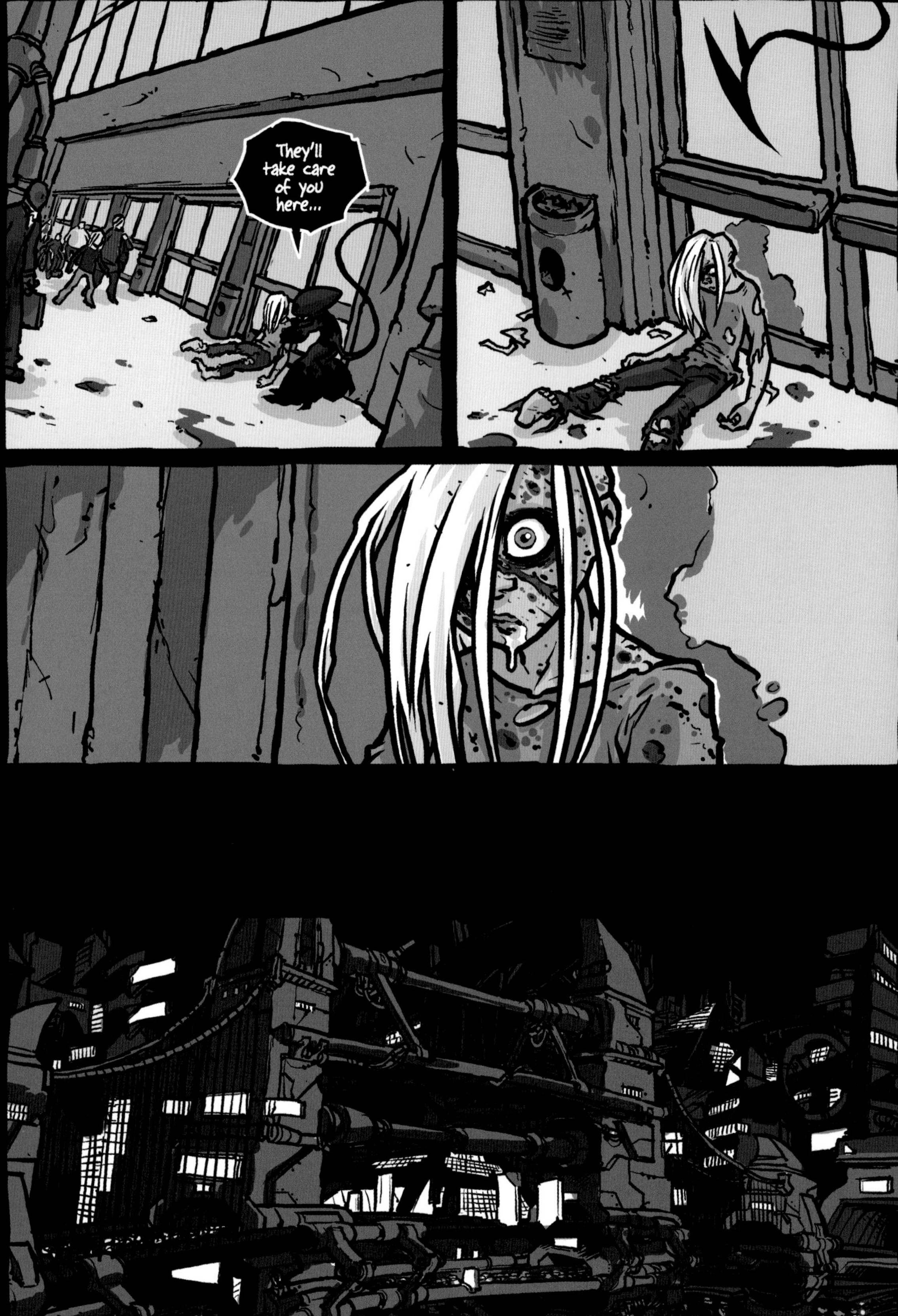
They'll take care of you here...

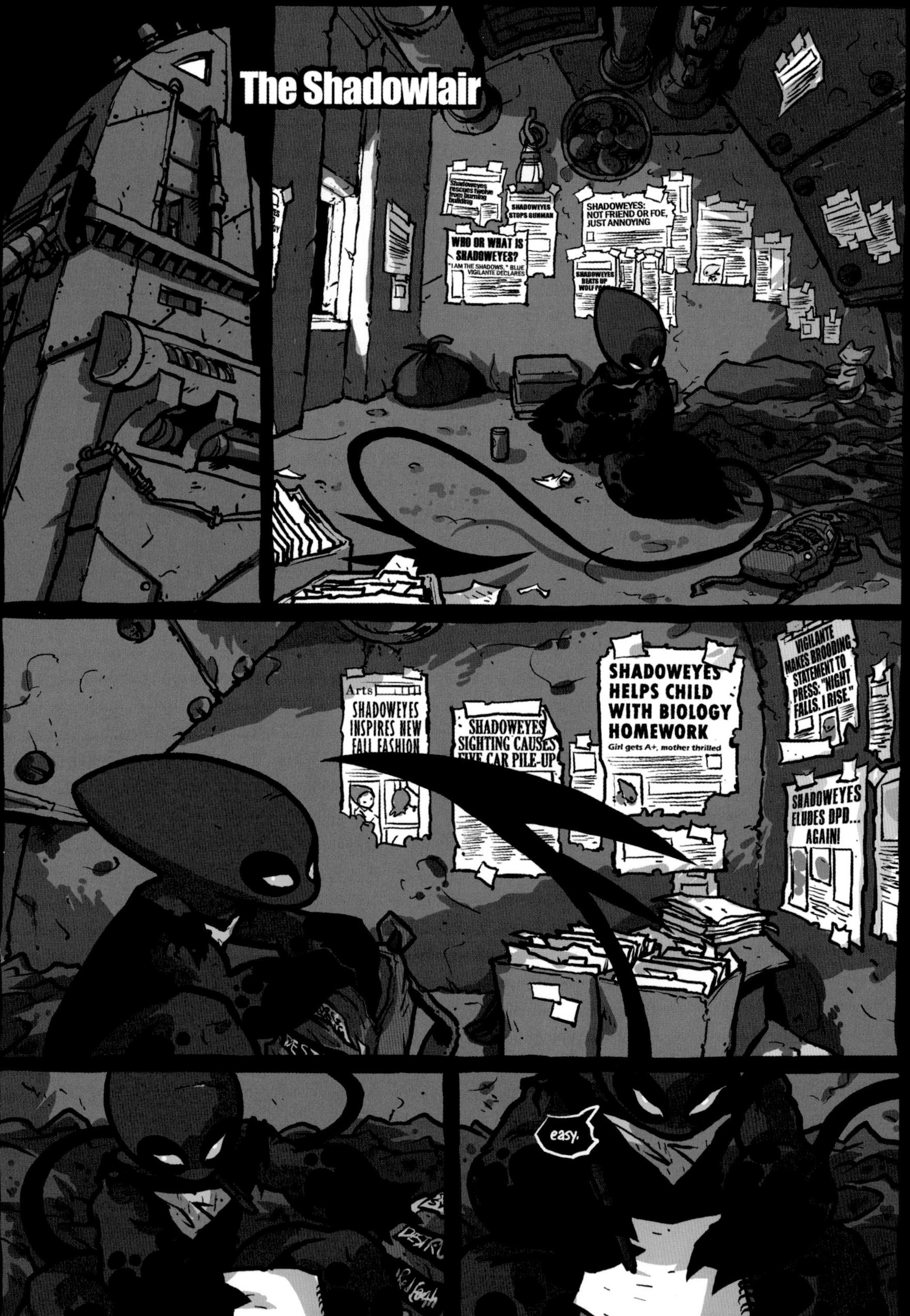
The Shadowlair
Shadoweyes rescues twelve from burning building
SHADOWEYES STOPS GUNMAN
SHADOWEYES: NOT FRIEND OR FOE, JUST ANNOYING
WHO OR WHAT IS SHADOWEYES?
"I AM THE SHADOWS," BLUE VIGILANTE DECLARES
Arts
SHADOWEYES INSPIRES NEW FALL FASHION
SHADOWEYES SIGHTING CAUSES FIVE CAR PILE-UP
SHADOWEYES HELPS CHILD WITH BIOLOGY HOMEWORK
Girl gets A+, mother thrilled
VIGILANTE MAKES BROODING STATEMENT TO PRESS: "NIGHT FALLS. I RISE."
SHADOWEYES ELUDES DPD... AGAIN!
easy.

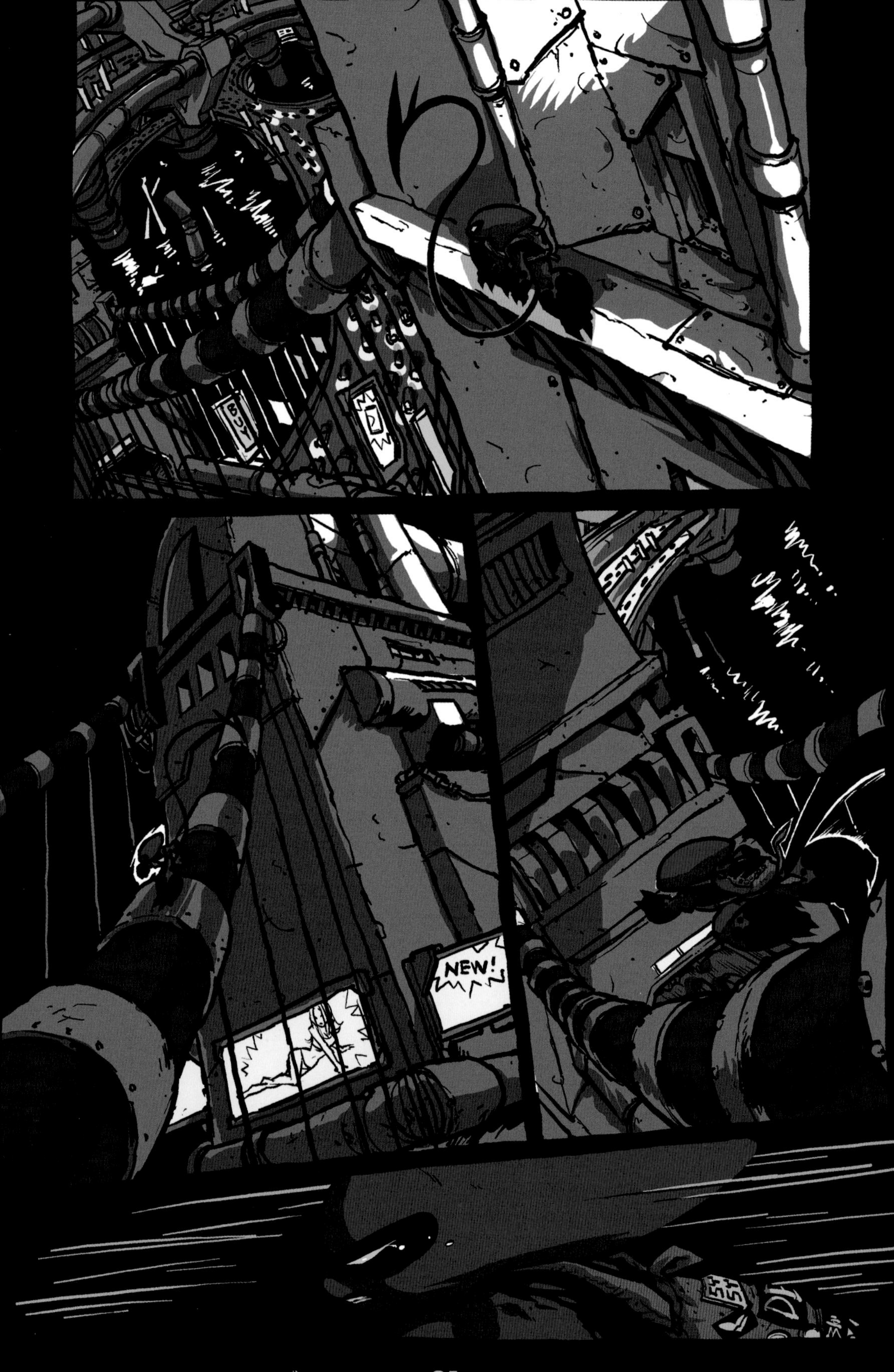
BUY
NEW!

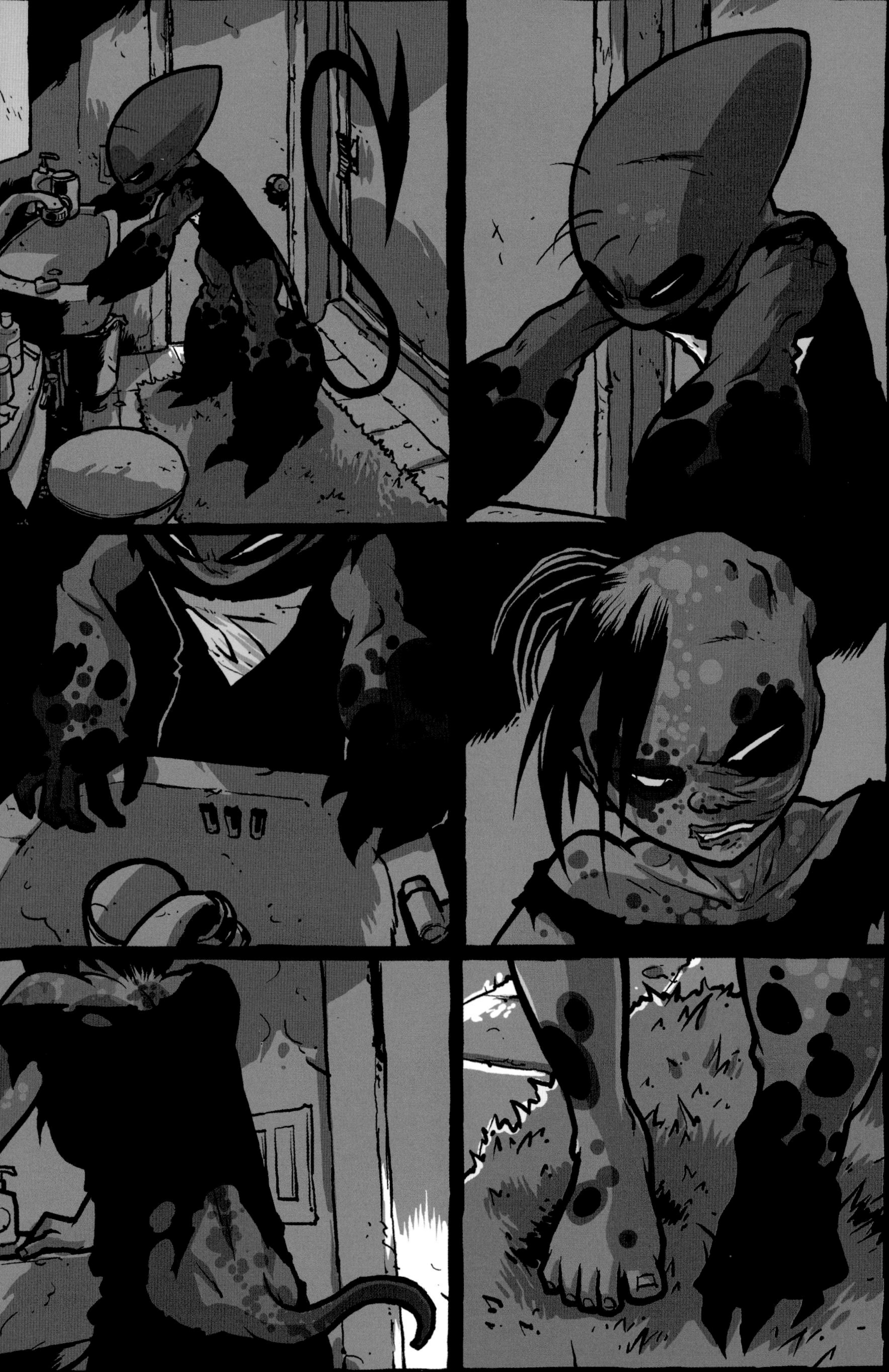

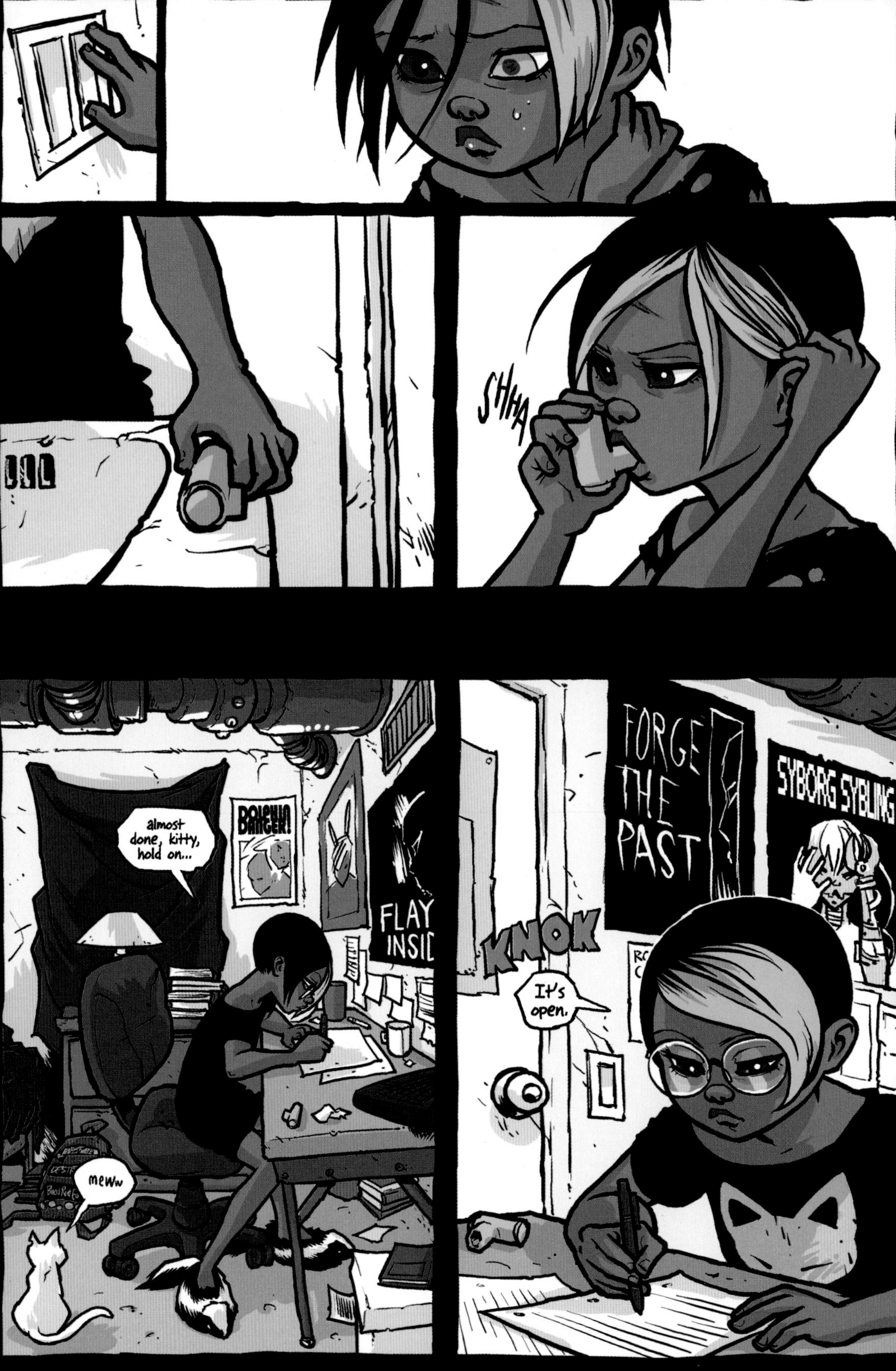
SHHA
almost done, kitty, hold on...
DOLPHIN DANGER!
FLAY INSID
mewww
FORGE THE PAST
SYBORG SYBLING
KNOK
It's open.

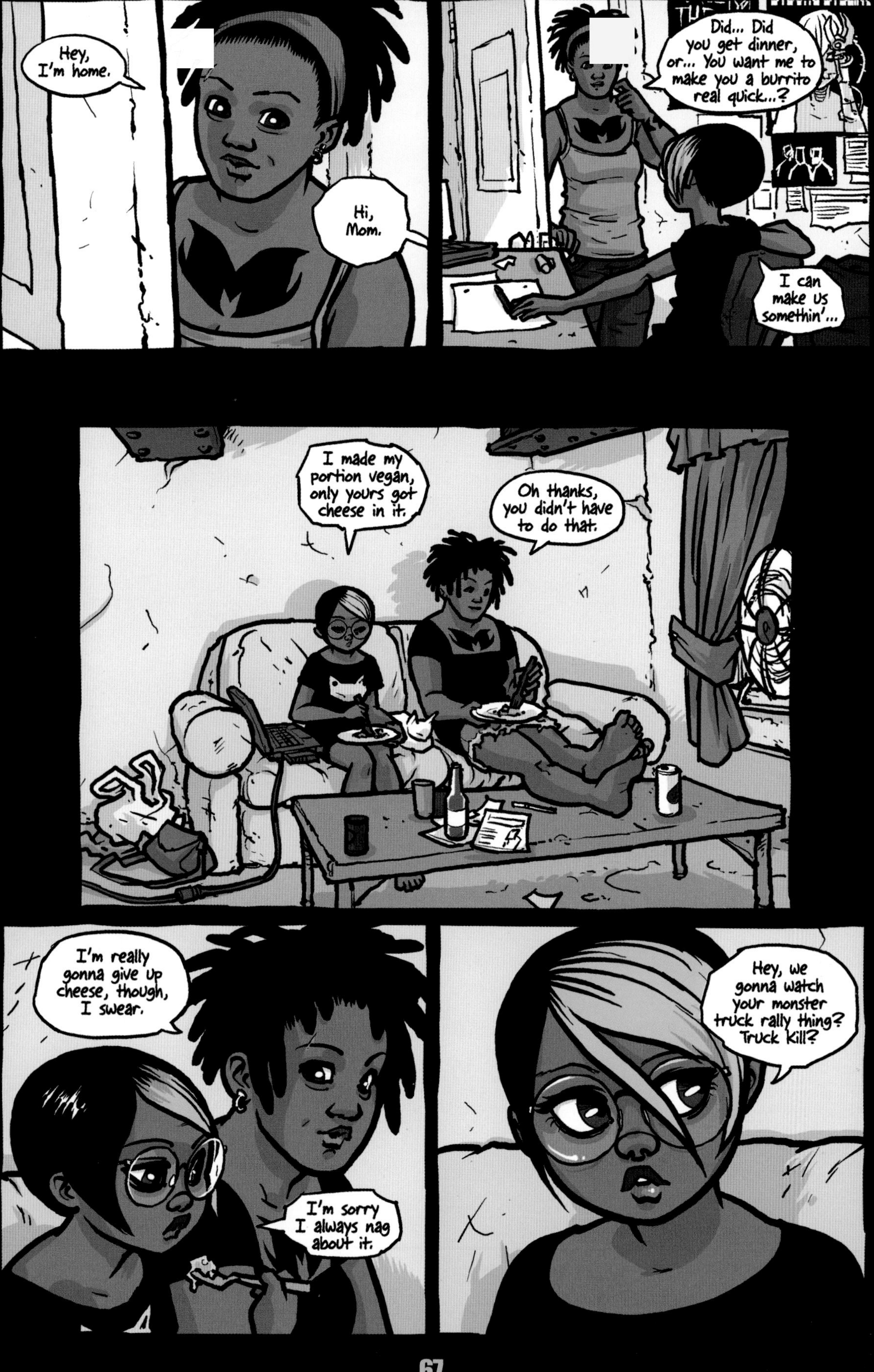

Hey, I'm home.
Hi, Mom.
Did... Did you get dinner, or... You want me to make you a burrito real quick...?
I can make us somethin'...
I made my portion vegan, only yours got cheese in it.
Oh thanks, you didn't have to do that.
I'm really gonna give up cheese, though, I swear.
I'm sorry I always nag about it.
Hey, we gonna watch your monster truck rally thing? Truck Kill?

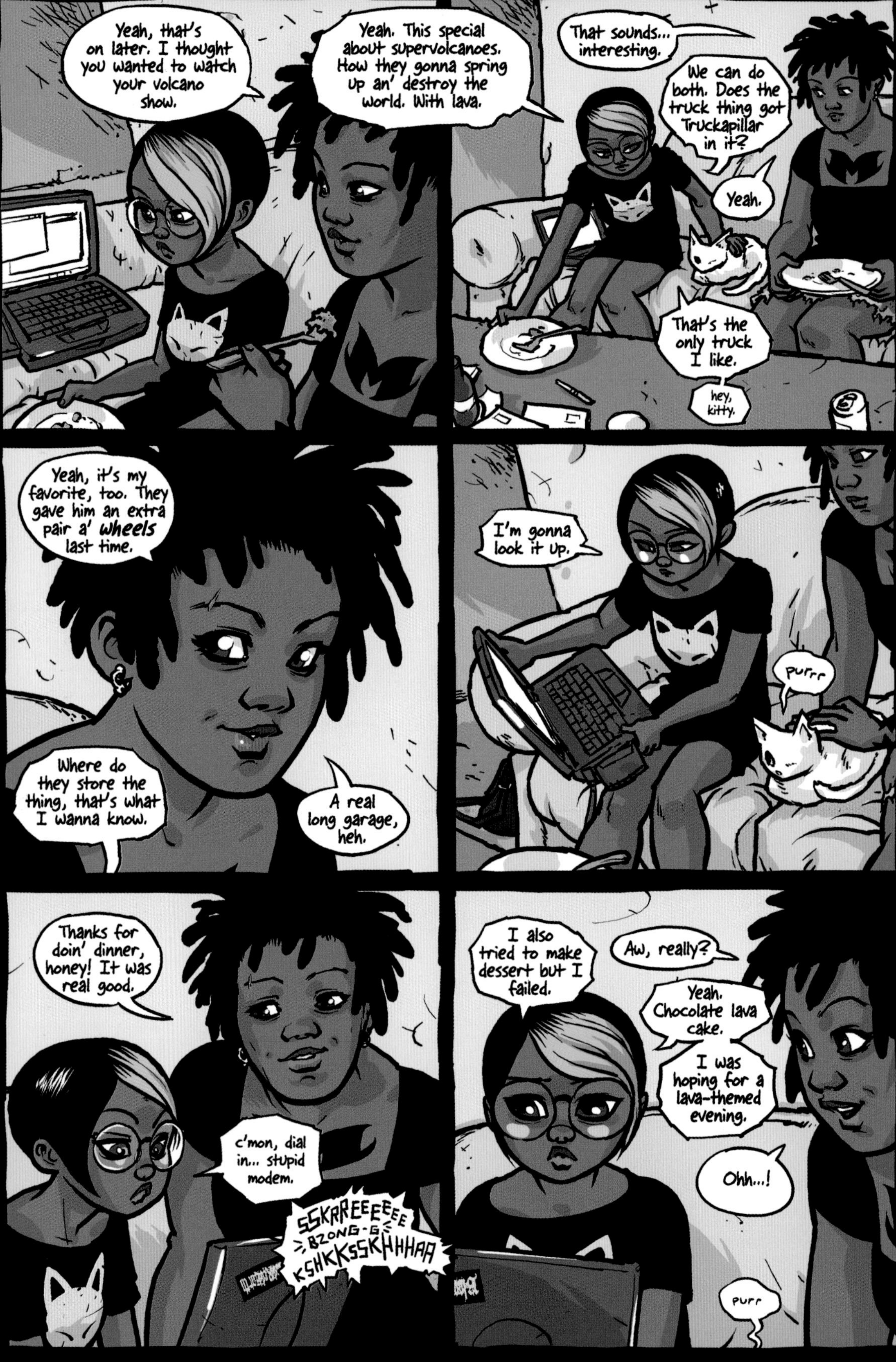
Yeah, that's on later. I thought you wanted to watch your volcano show.
Yeah. This special about supervolcanoes. How they gonna spring up an' destroy the world. With lava.
That sounds... interesting.
We can do both. Does the truck thing got Truckapillar in it?
Yeah.
That's the only truck I like.
hey, kitty.
Yeah, it's my favorite, too. They gave him an extra pair a' *wheels* last time.
Where do they store the thing, that's what I wanna know.
A real long garage, heh.
I'm gonna look it up.
purrr
Thanks for doin' dinner, honey! It was real good.
c'mon, dial in... stupid modem.
SSKRREEEEEEE BZONG-G KSHKKSSKHHHAA
I also tried to make dessert but I failed.
Aw, really?
Yeah. Chocolate lava cake.
I was hoping for a lava-themed evening.
Ohh...!
purr

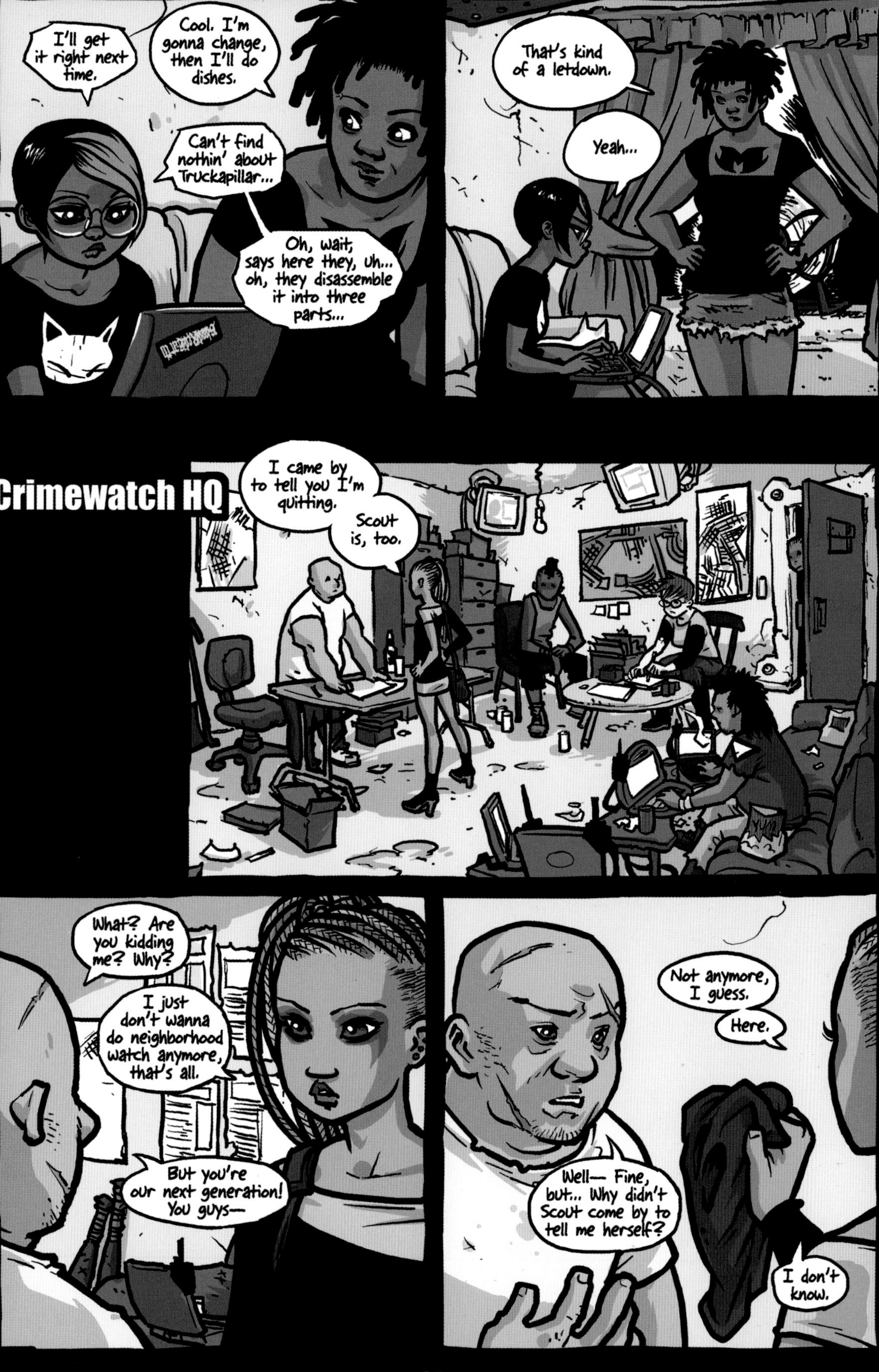
I'll get it right next time.
Cool. I'm gonna change, then I'll do dishes.
Can't find nothin' about Truckapillar...
Oh, wait, says here they, uh... oh, they disassemble it into three parts...
That's kind of a letdown.
Yeah...
Crimewatch HQ
I came by to tell you I'm quitting.
Scout is, too.
What? Are you kidding me? Why?
I just don't wanna do neighborhood watch anymore, that's all.
But you're our next generation! You guys—
Not anymore, I guess.
Here.
Well— Fine, but... Why didn't Scout come by to tell me herself?
I don't know.

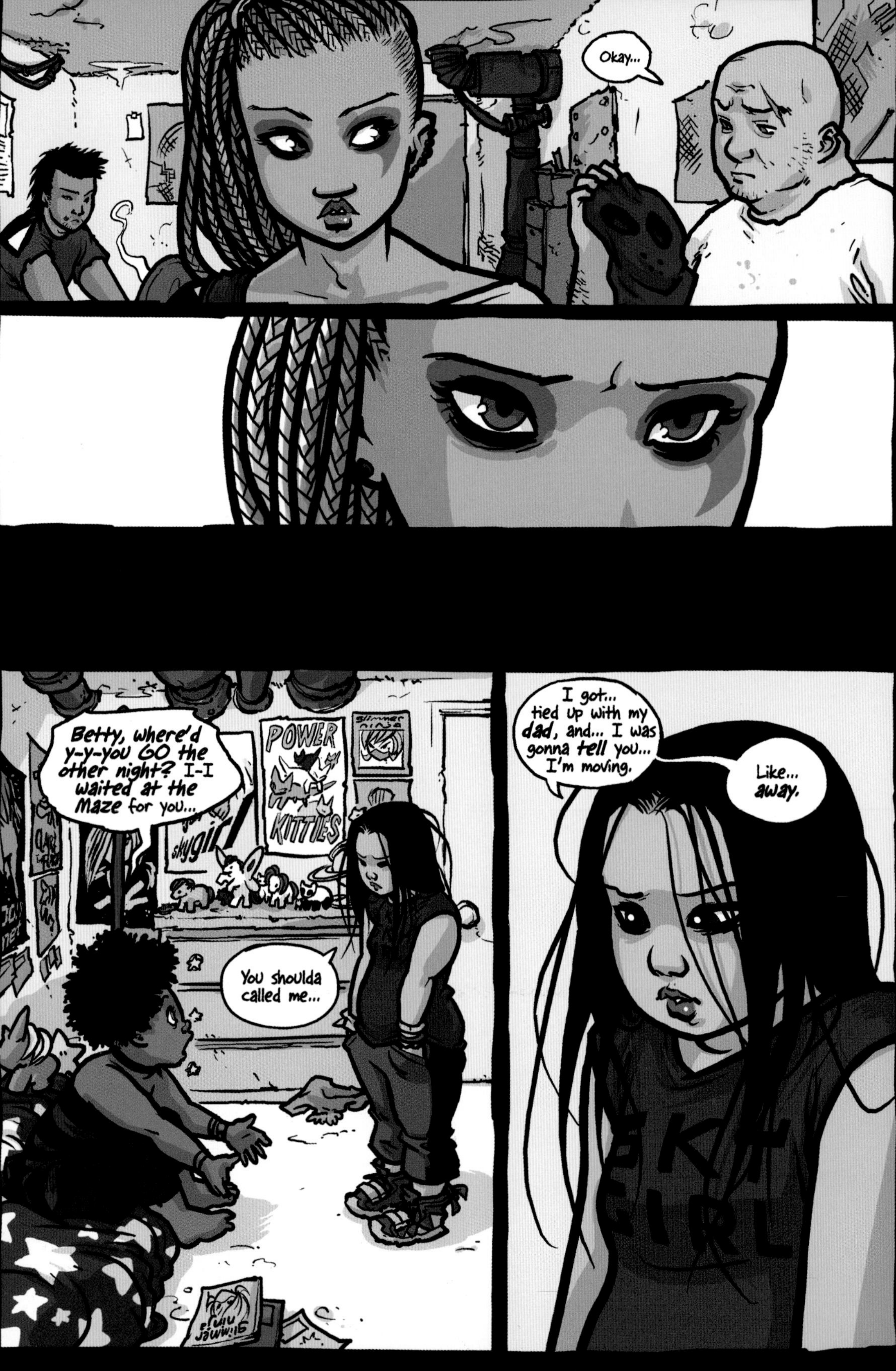
Okay...
POWER
KITTIES
Betty, where'd y-y-you GO the other night? I-I waited at the Maze for you...
You shoulda called me...
I got... tied up with my dad, and... I was gonna tell you... I'm moving.
Like... away.

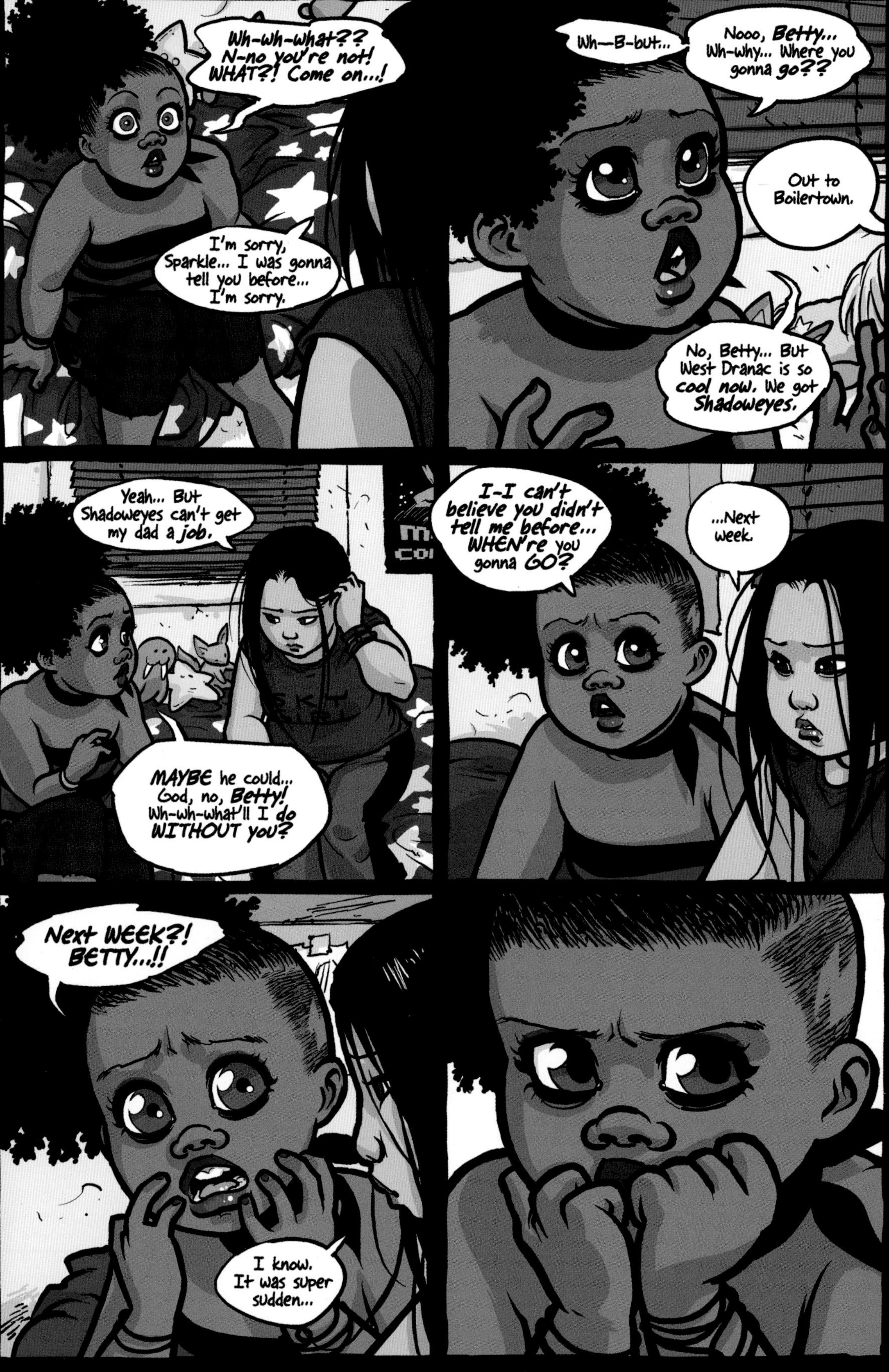

Wh-wh-what?? N-no you're not! WHAT?! Come on...!
I'm sorry, Sparkle... I was gonna tell you before... I'm sorry.
Wh—B-but...
Nooo, Betty... Wh-why... Where you gonna go??
Out to Boilertown.
No, Betty... But West Dranac is so cool now. We got Shadoweyes.
Yeah... But Shadoweyes can't get my dad a job.
MAYBE he could... God, no, Betty! Wh-wh-what'll I do WITHOUT you?
I-I can't believe you didn't tell me before... WHEN're you gonna GO?
...Next week.
Next WEEK?! BETTY...!!
I know. It was super sudden...

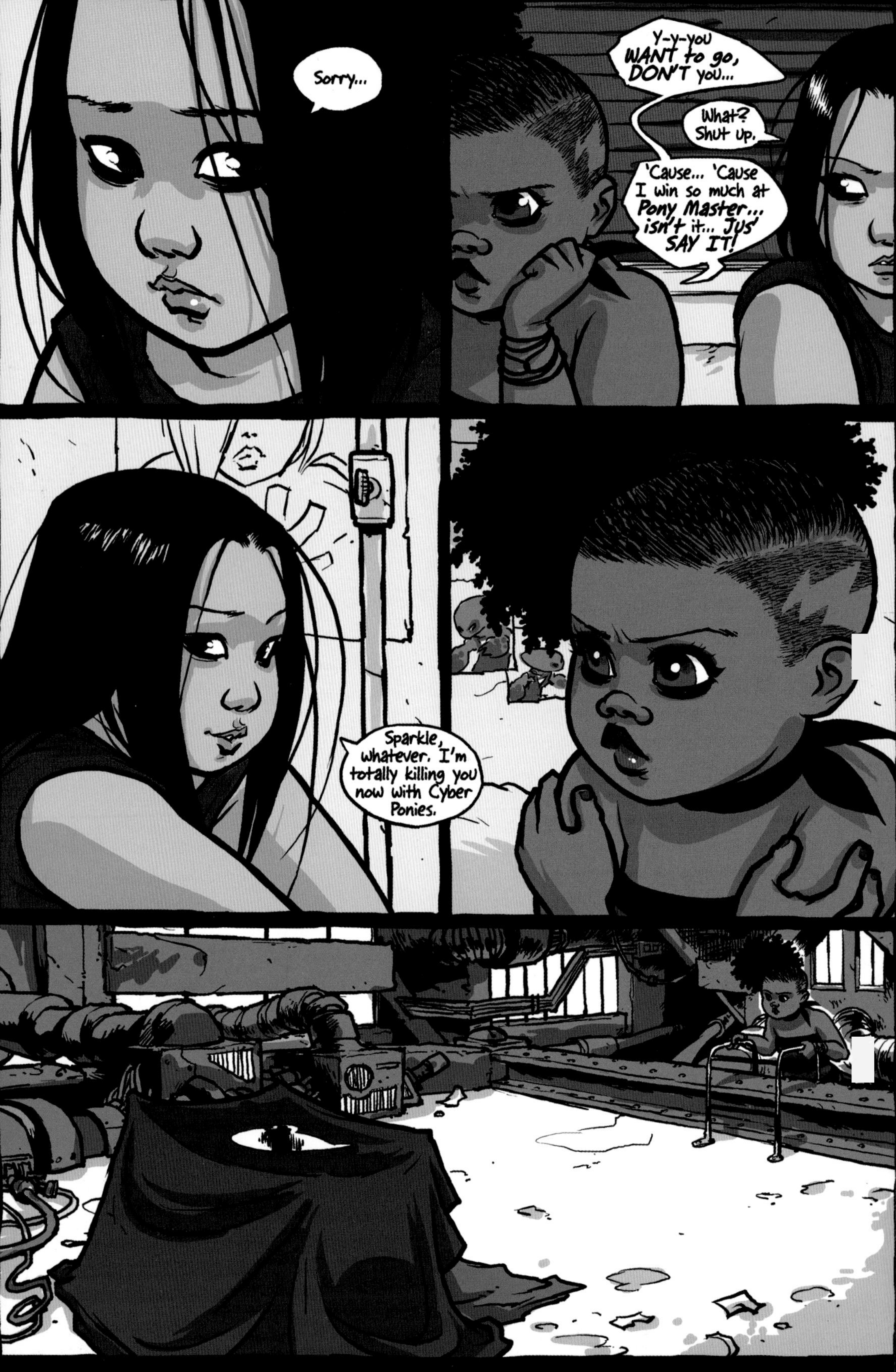
Sorry...
Y-y-you WANT to go, DON'T you...
What? Shut up.
'Cause... 'Cause I win so much at Pony Master... isn't it... Jus' SAY IT!
Sparkle, whatever. I'm totally killing you now with Cyber Ponies.

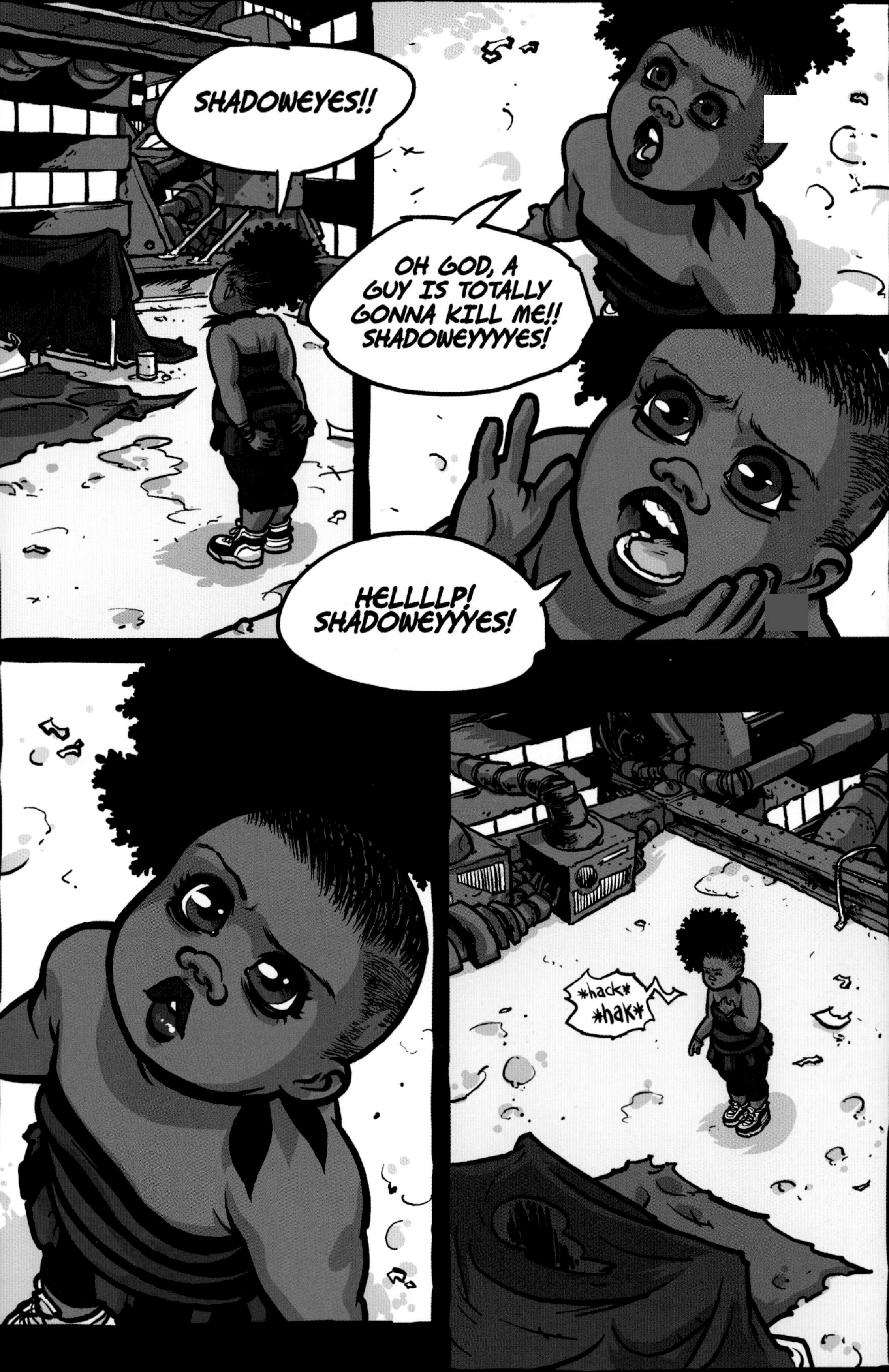
SHADOWEYES!!
OH GOD, A GUY IS TOTALLY GONNA KILL ME!! SHADOWEYYYYES!
HELLLLP! SHADOWEYYYES!
hack *hak*

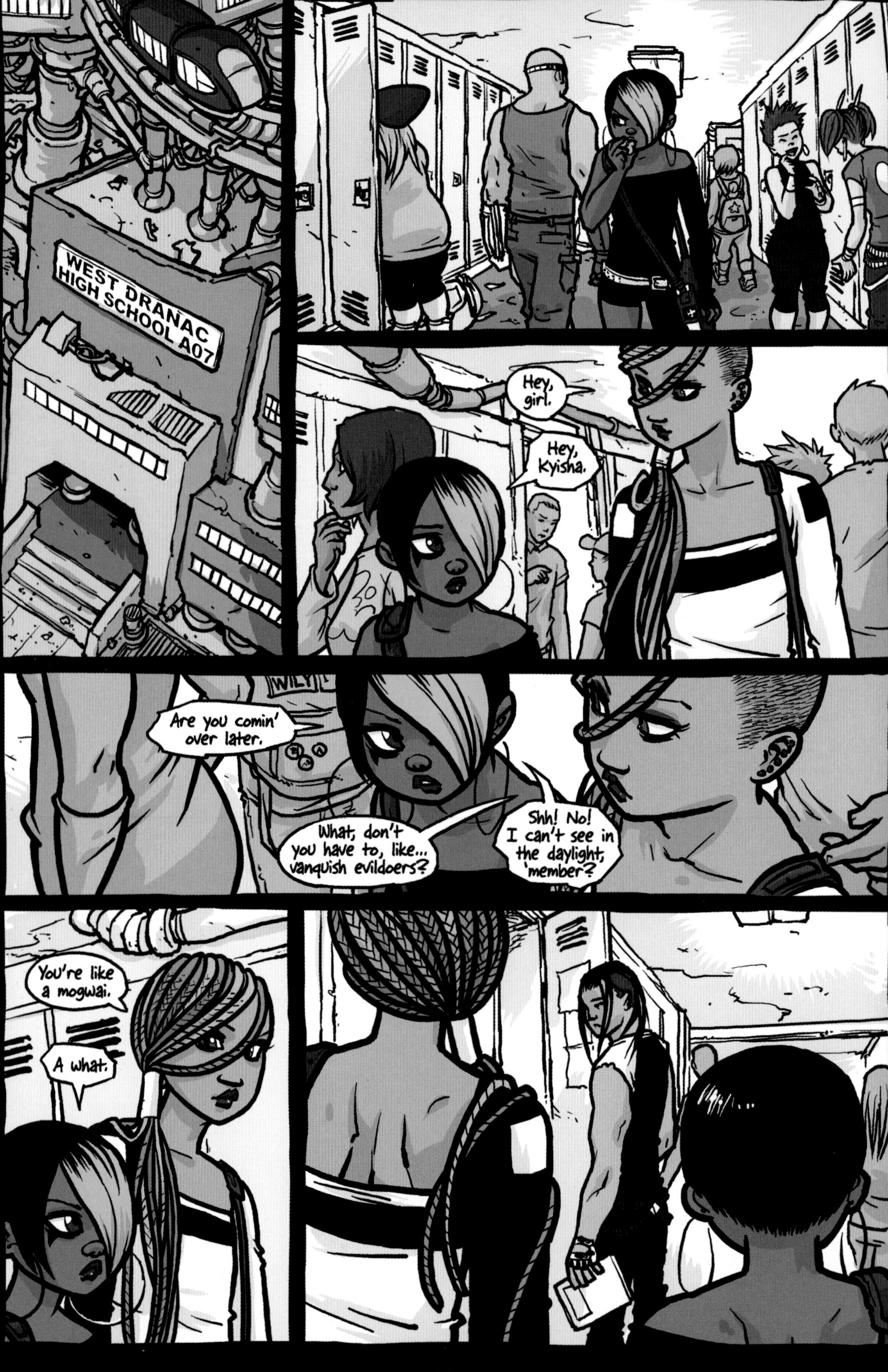
WEST DRANAC HIGH SCHOOL A07
Hey, girl.
Hey, Kyisha.
Are you comin' over later.
What, don't you have to, like... vanquish evildoers?
Shh! No! I can't see in the daylight, 'member?
You're like a mogwai.
A what.

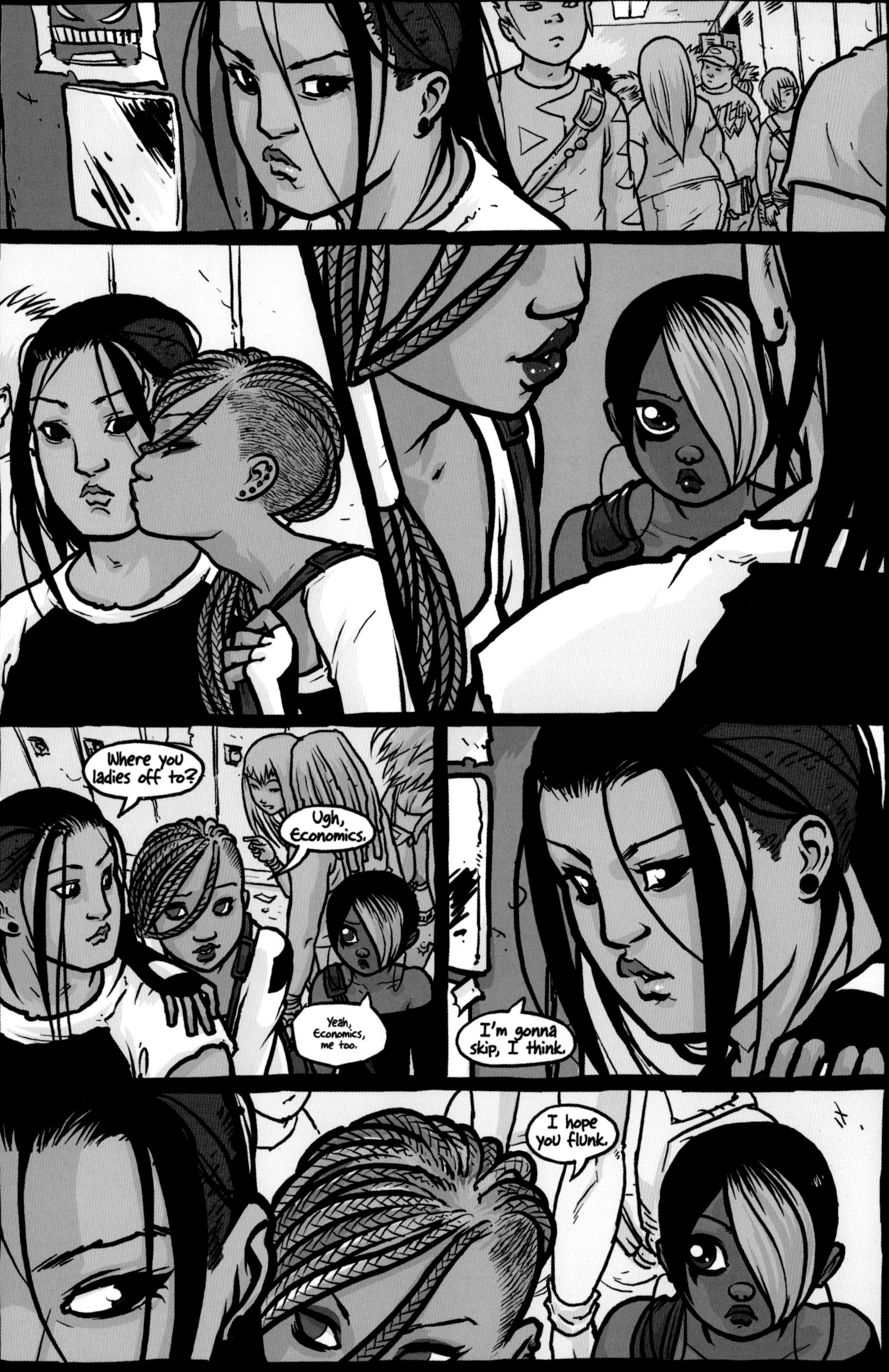
Where you ladies off to?
Ugh, Economics.
Yeah, Economics, me too.
I'm gonna skip, I think.
I hope you flunk.

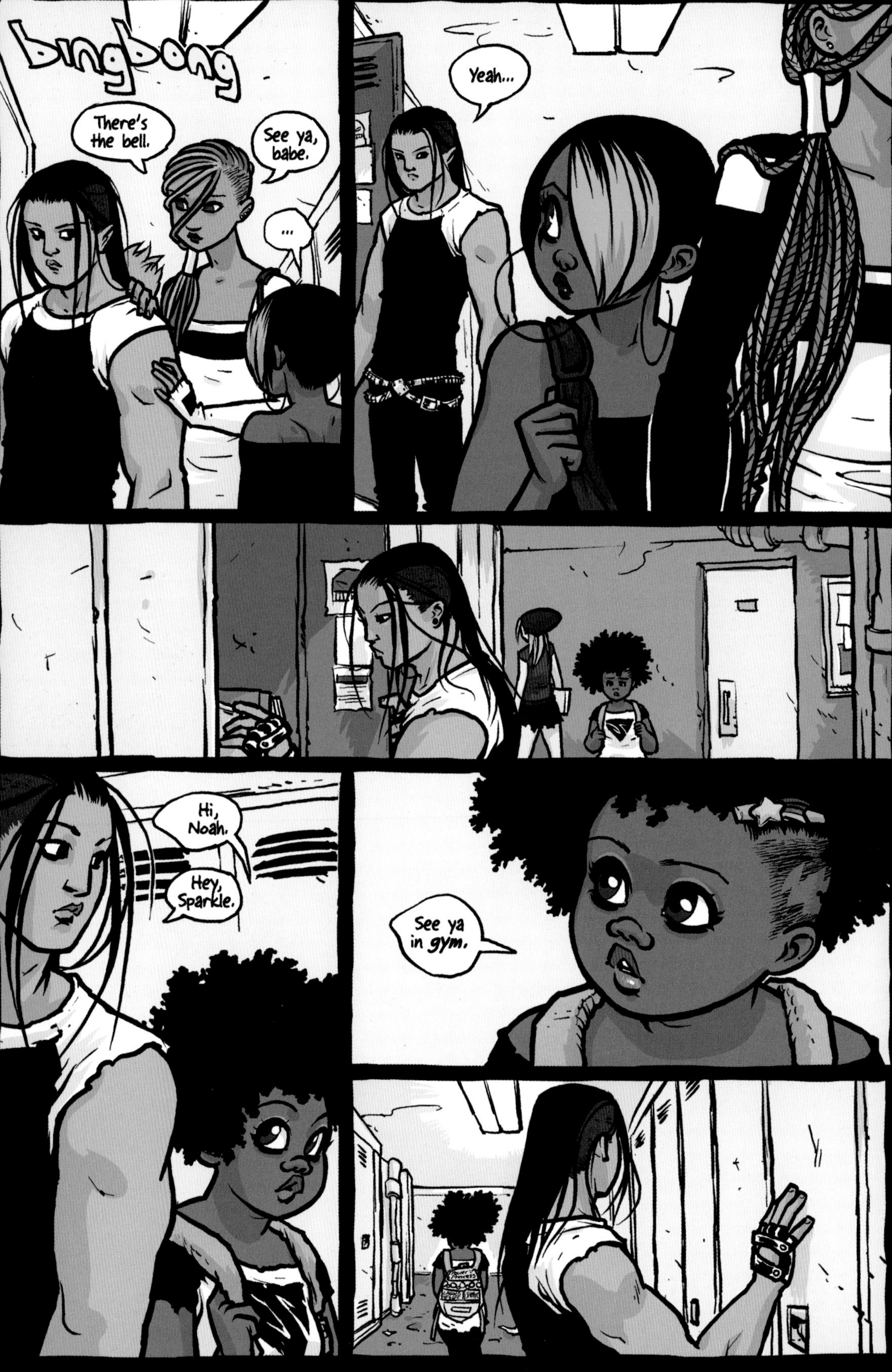
bingbong
There's the bell.
See ya, babe.
...
Yeah...
Hi, Noah.
Hey, Sparkle.
See ya in gym.

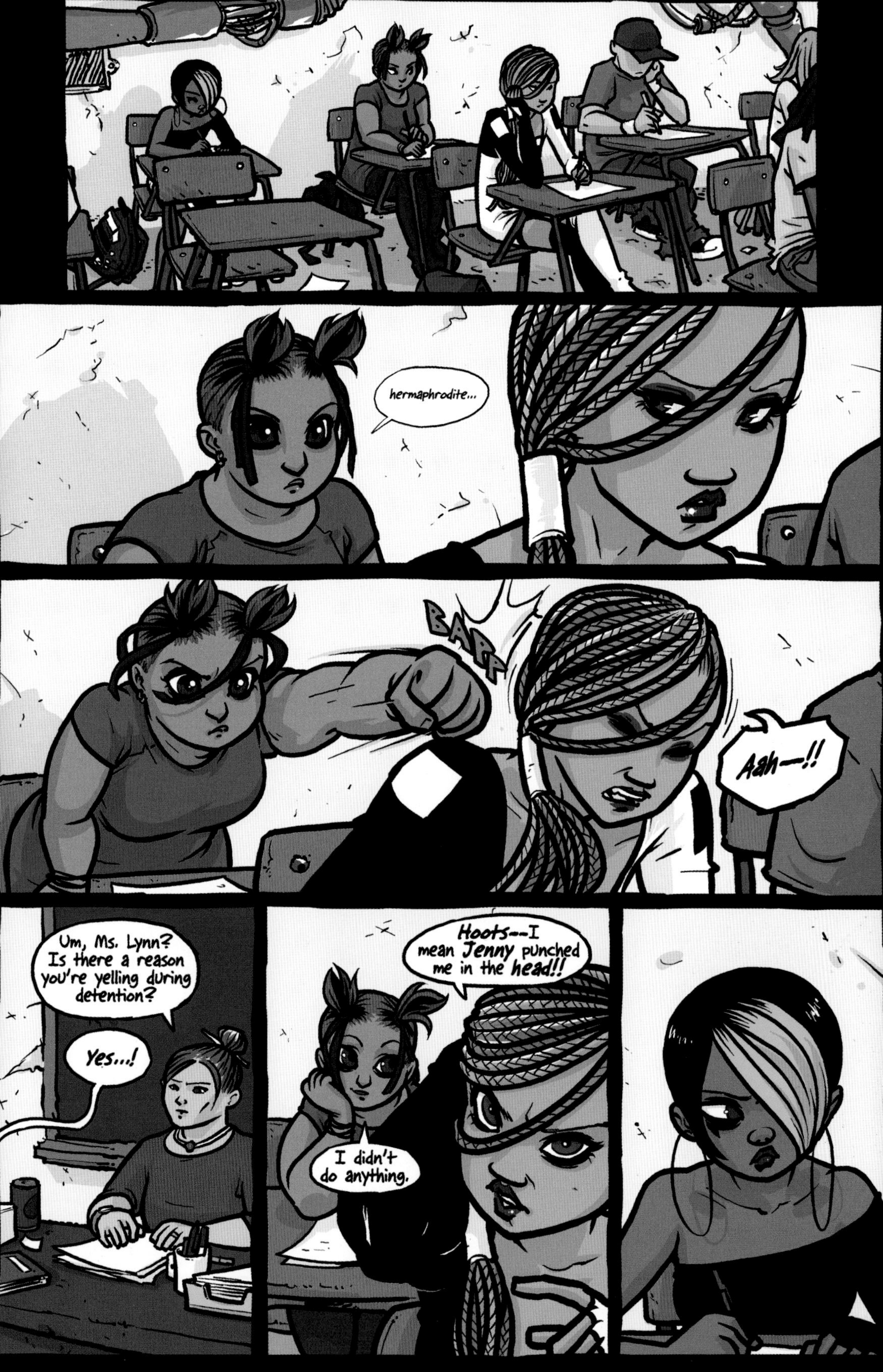
hermaphrodite...
BAPP
Aah—!!
Um, Ms. Lynn? Is there a reason you're yelling during detention?
Yes...!
Hoots--I mean Jenny punched me in the head!!
I didn't do anything.

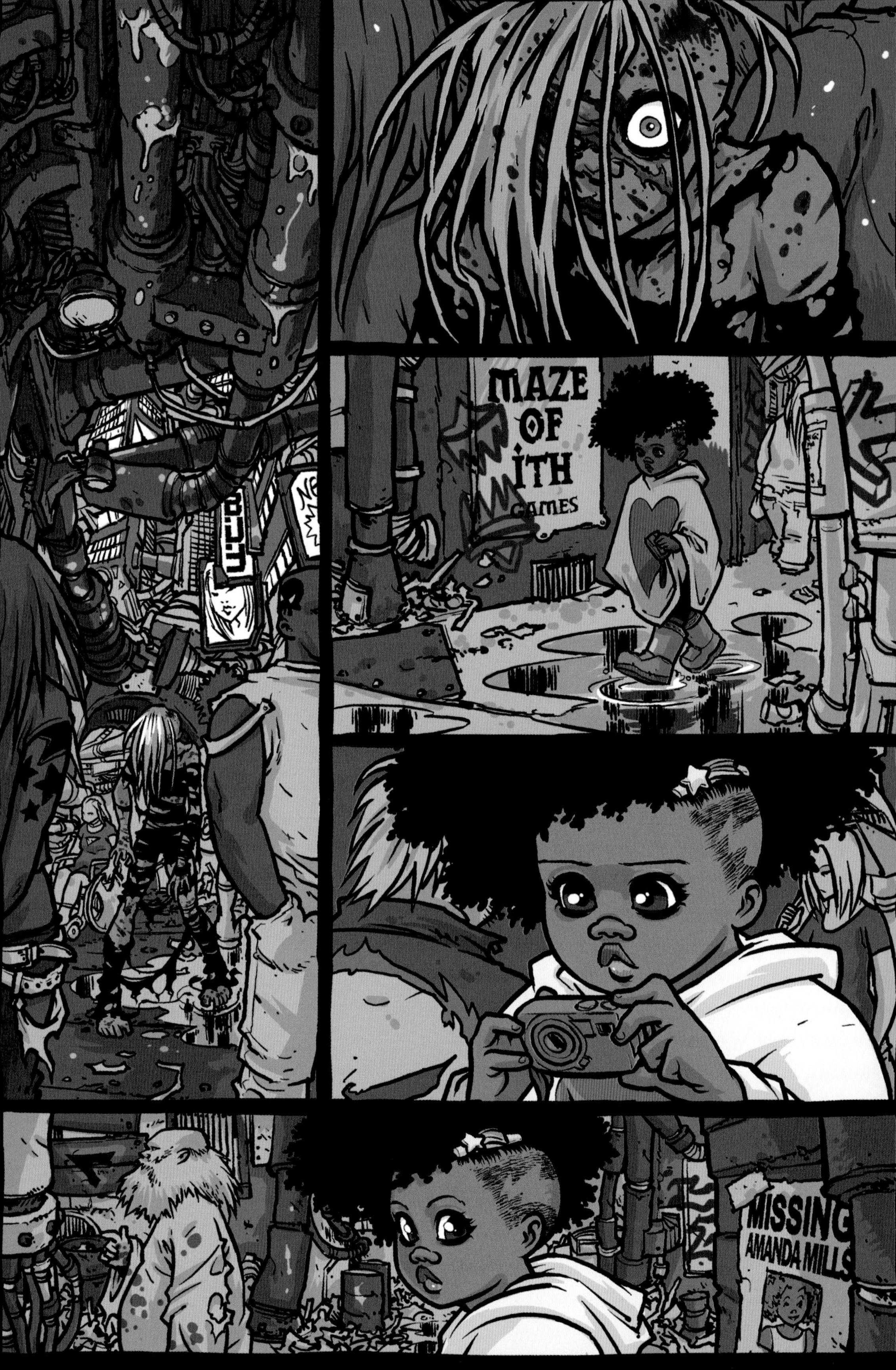
BUY
MAZE OF ITH GAMES
MISSING
AMANDA MILLS

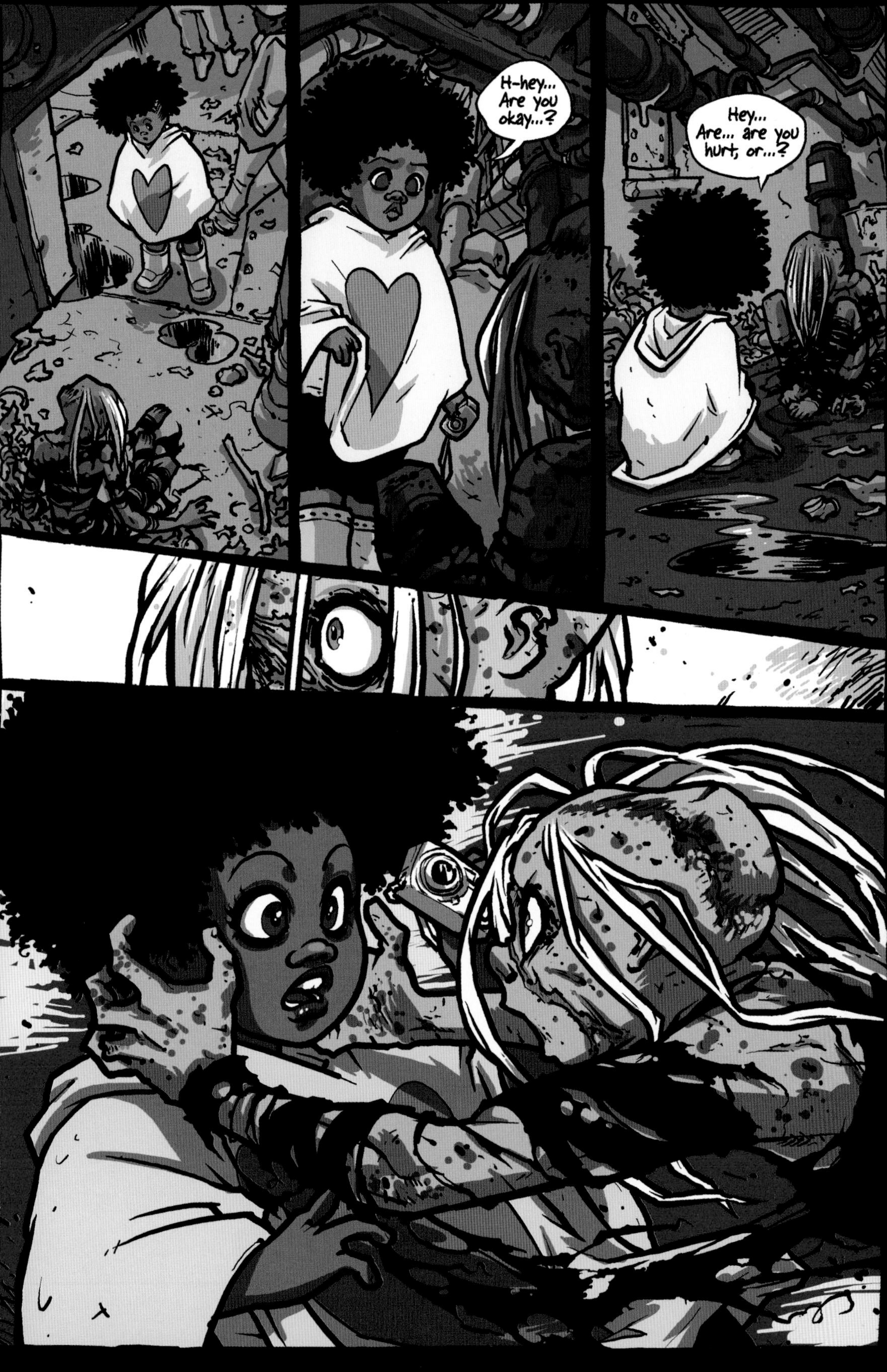
H-hey... Are you okay...?
Hey... Are... are you hurt, or...?

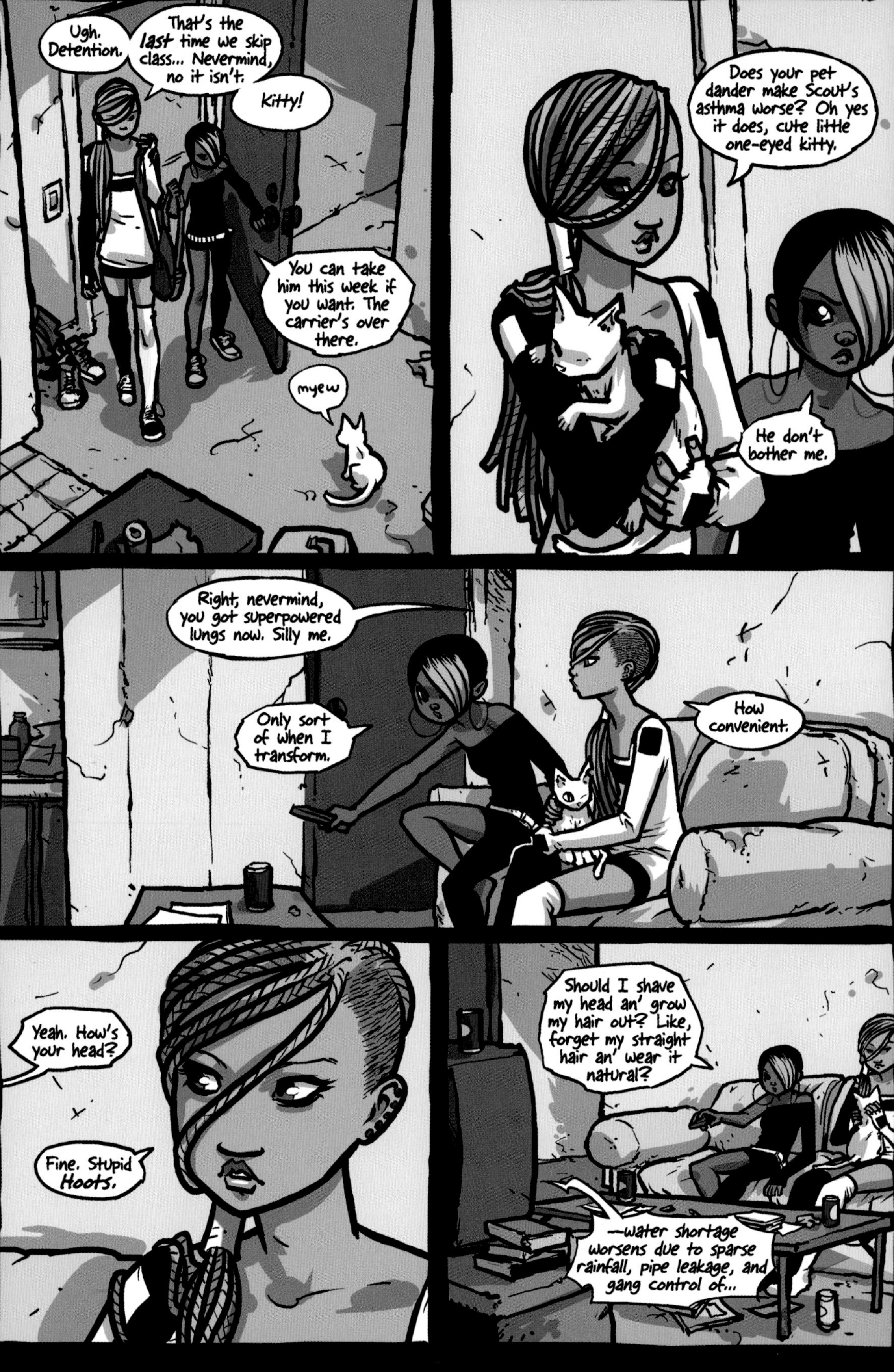
Ugh. Detention.
That's the last time we skip class... Nevermind, no it isn't.
Kitty!
You can take him this week if you want. The carrier's over there.
myew
Does your pet dander make Scout's asthma worse? Oh yes it does, cute little one-eyed kitty.
He don't bother me.
Right, nevermind, you got superpowered lungs now. Silly me.
Only sort of when I transform.
How convenient.
Yeah. How's your head?
Fine. Stupid Hoots.
Should I shave my head an' grow my hair out? Like, forget my straight hair an' wear it natural?
—water shortage worsens due to sparse rainfall, pipe leakage, and gang control of...

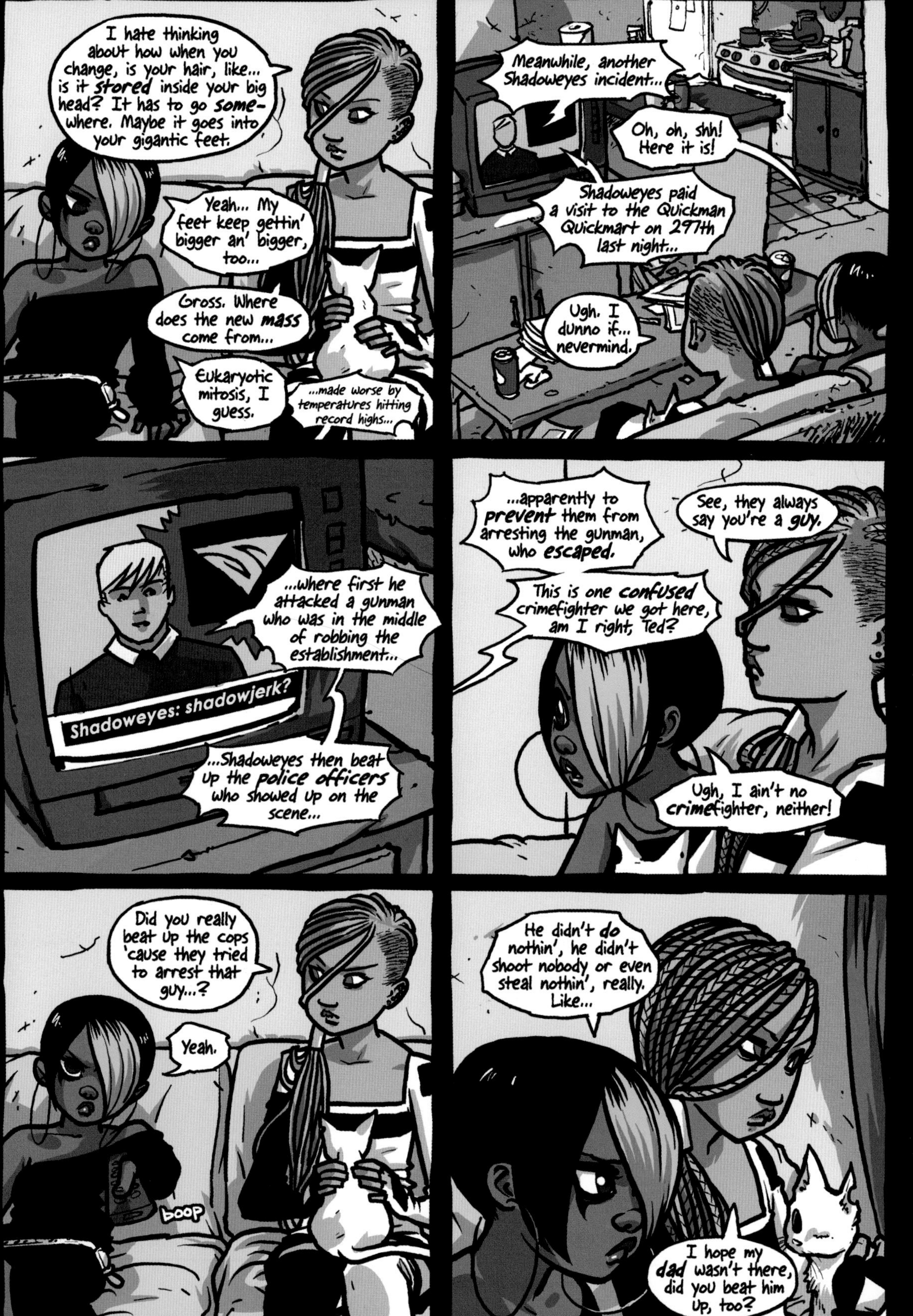
I hate thinking about how when you change, is your hair, like... is it stored inside your big head? It has to go some-where. Maybe it goes into your gigantic feet.
Yeah... My feet keep gettin' bigger an' bigger, too...
Gross. Where does the new mass come from...
Eukaryotic mitosis, I guess.
...made worse by temperatures hitting record highs...
Meanwhile, another Shadoweyes incident...
Oh, oh, shh! Here it is!
Shadoweyes paid a visit to the Quickman Quickmart on 297th last night...
Ugh. I dunno if... nevermind.
...where first he attacked a gunman who was in the middle of robbing the establishment...
Shadoweyes: shadowjerk?
...Shadoweyes then beat up the police officers who showed up on the scene...
...apparently to prevent them from arresting the gunman, who escaped.
See, they always say you're a guy.
This is one confused crimefighter we got here, am I right, Ted?
Ugh, I ain't no crimefighter, neither!
Did you really beat up the cops 'cause they tried to arrest that guy...?
Yeah.
boop
He didn't do nothin', he didn't shoot nobody or even steal nothin', really. Like...
I hope my dad wasn't there, did you beat him up, too?

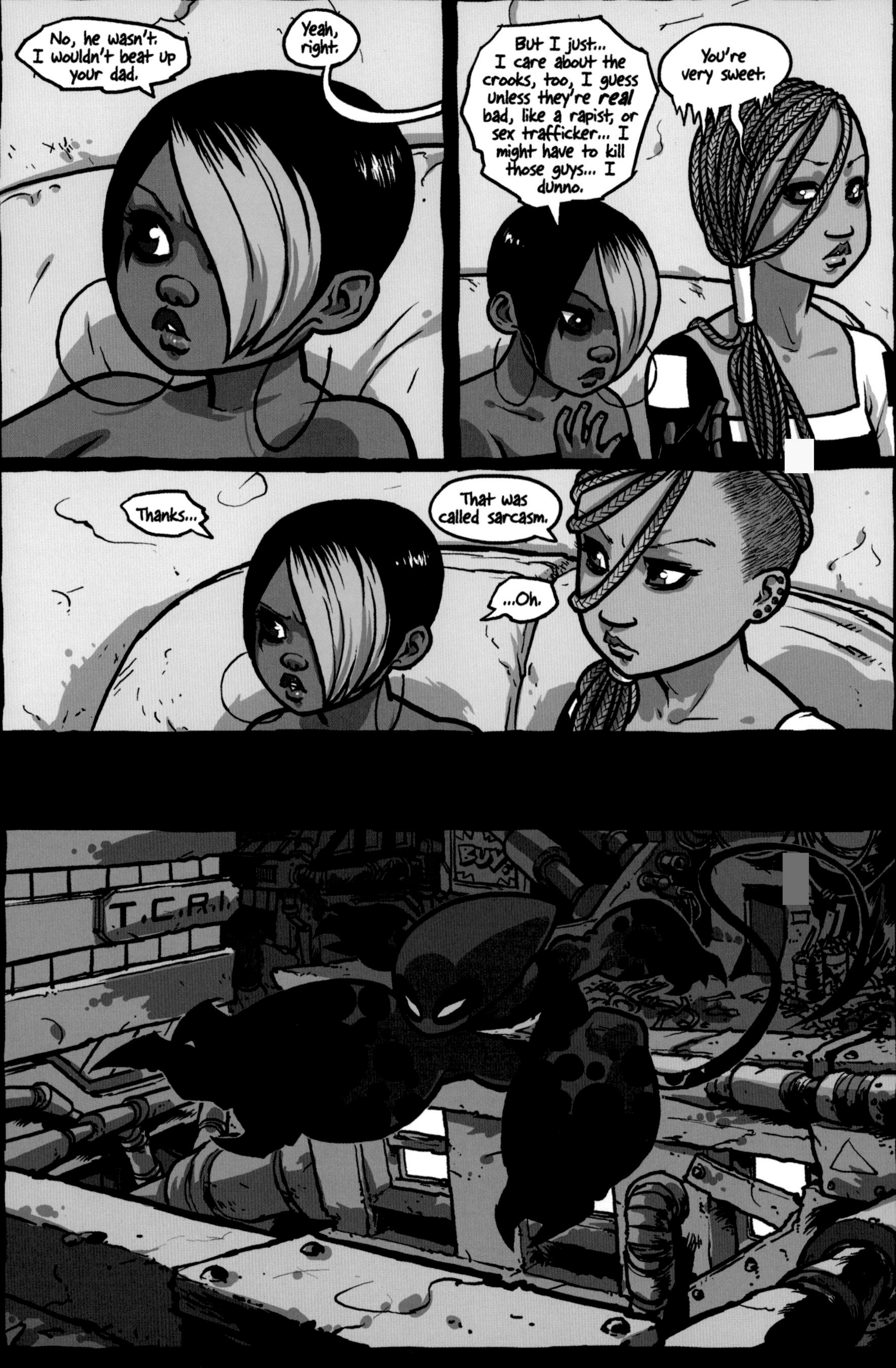
No, he wasn't. I wouldn't beat up your dad.
Yeah, right.
But I just... I care about the crooks, too, I guess unless they're *real* bad, like a rapist, or sex trafficker... I might have to kill those guys... I dunno.
You're very sweet.
Thanks...
That was called sarcasm.
...Oh.
BUY
T.C.R.I.

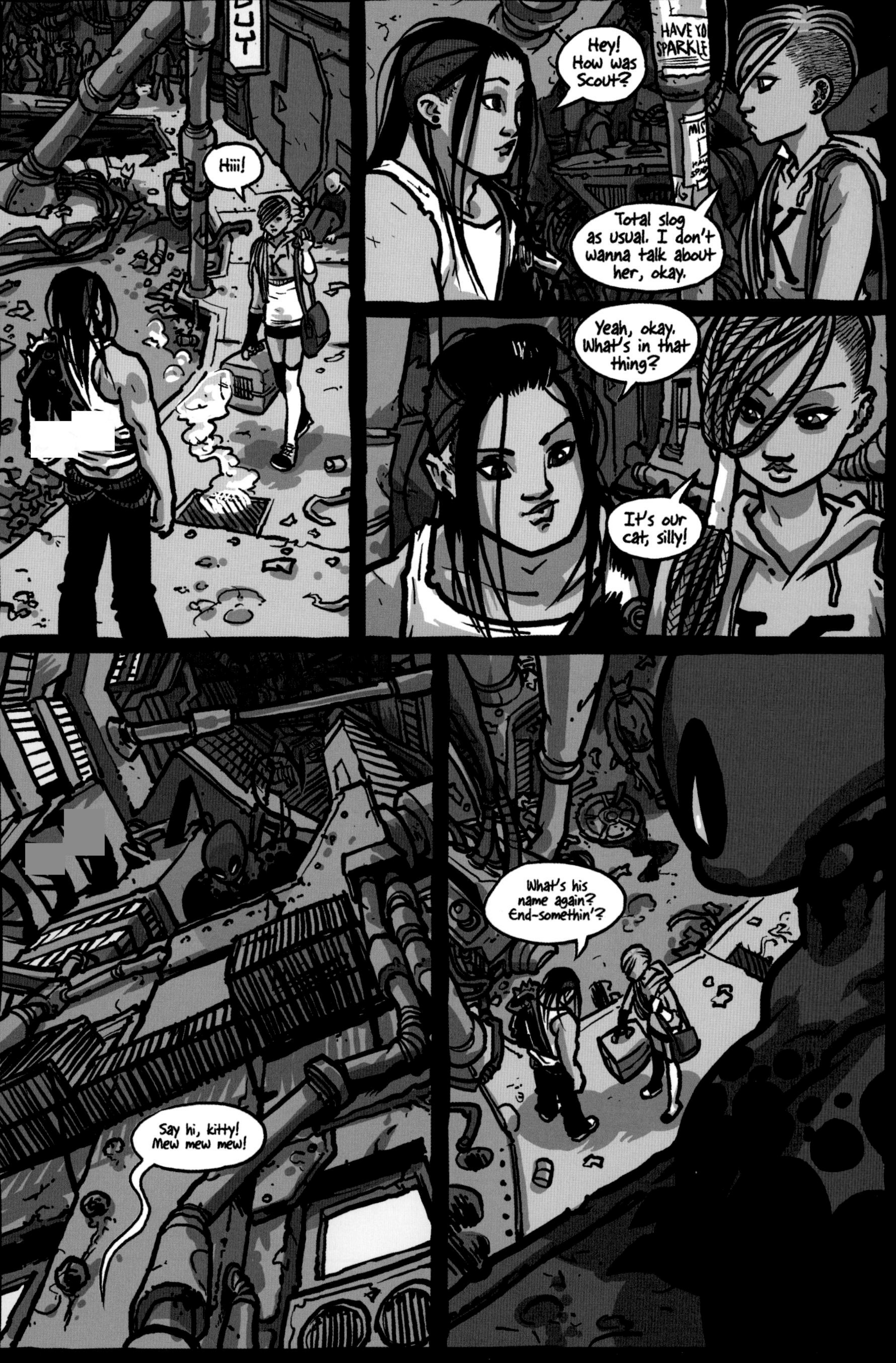
Hiii!
Hey! How was Scout?
Total slog as usual. I don't wanna talk about her, okay.
Yeah, okay. What's in that thing?
It's our cat, silly!
Say hi, kitty! Mew mew mew!
What's his name again? End-somethin'?

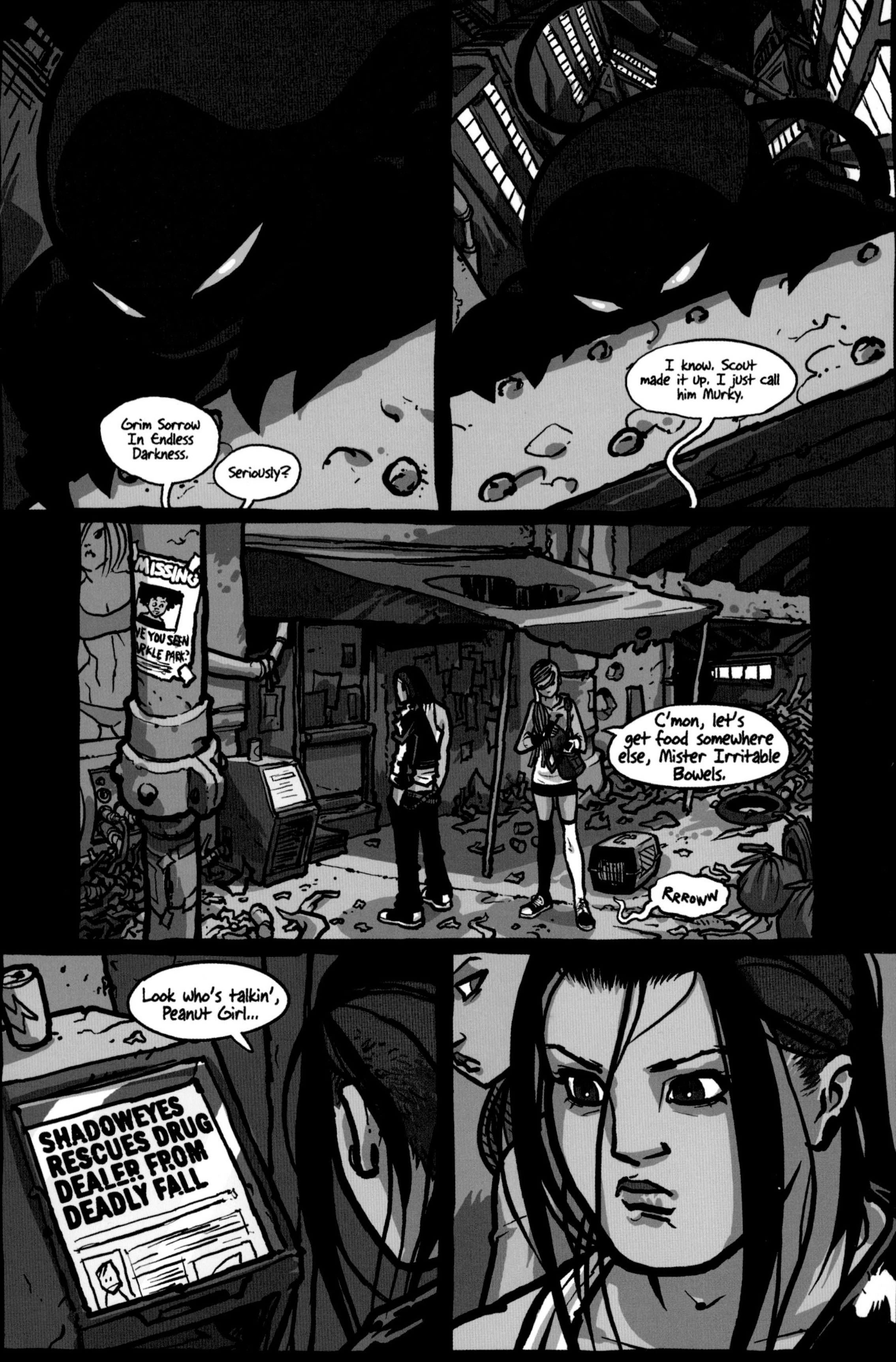
Grim Sorrow In Endless Darkness.
Seriously?
I know. Scout made it up. I just call him Murky.
MISSING
C'mon, let's get food somewhere else, Mister Irritable Bowels.
RRROWW
Look who's talkin', Peanut Girl...
SHADOWEYES RESCUES DRUG DEALER FROM DEADLY FALL

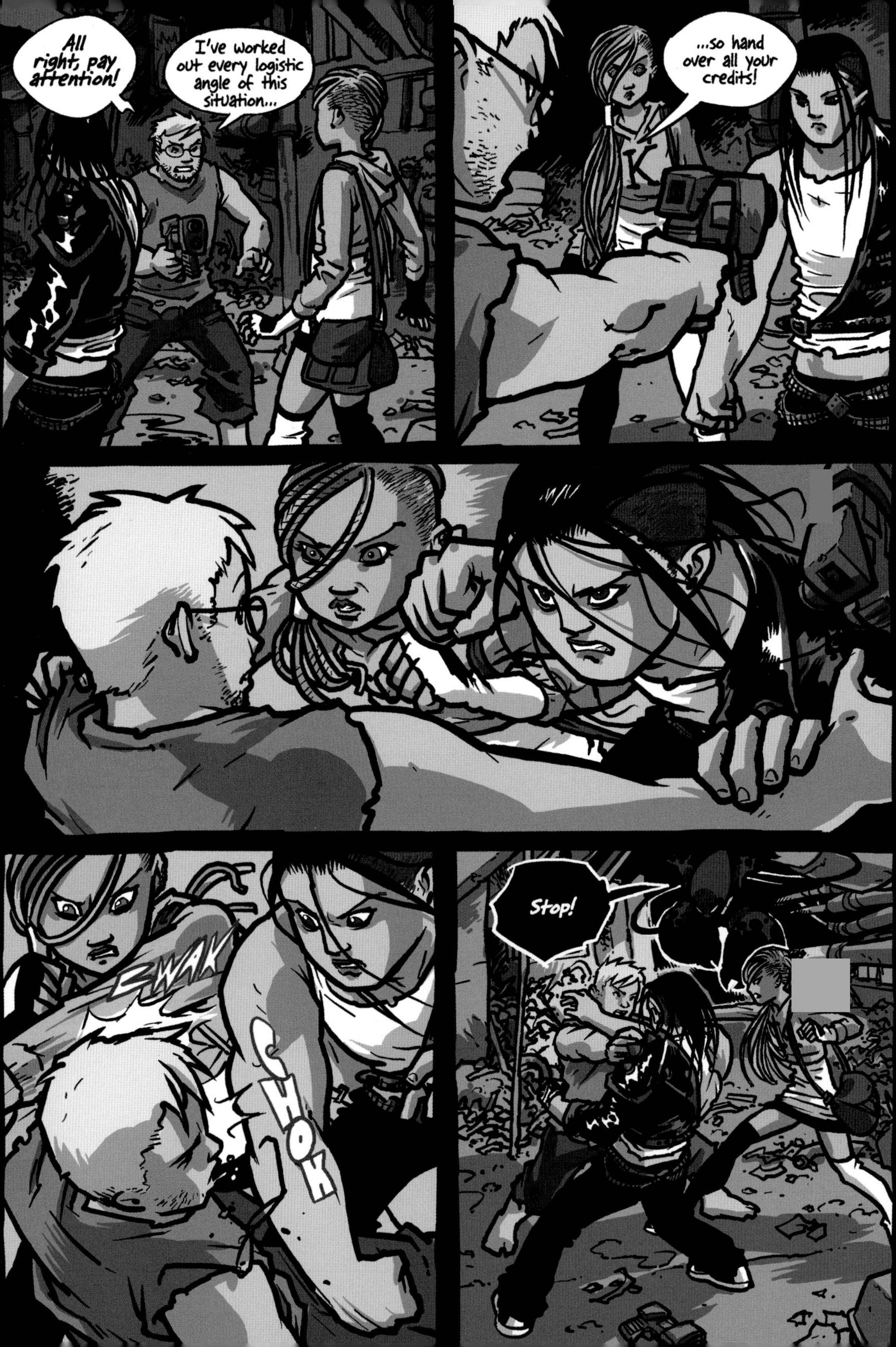
All right, pay attention!
I've worked out every logistic angle of this situation...
...so hand over all your credits!
SWAK
CHOK
Stop!

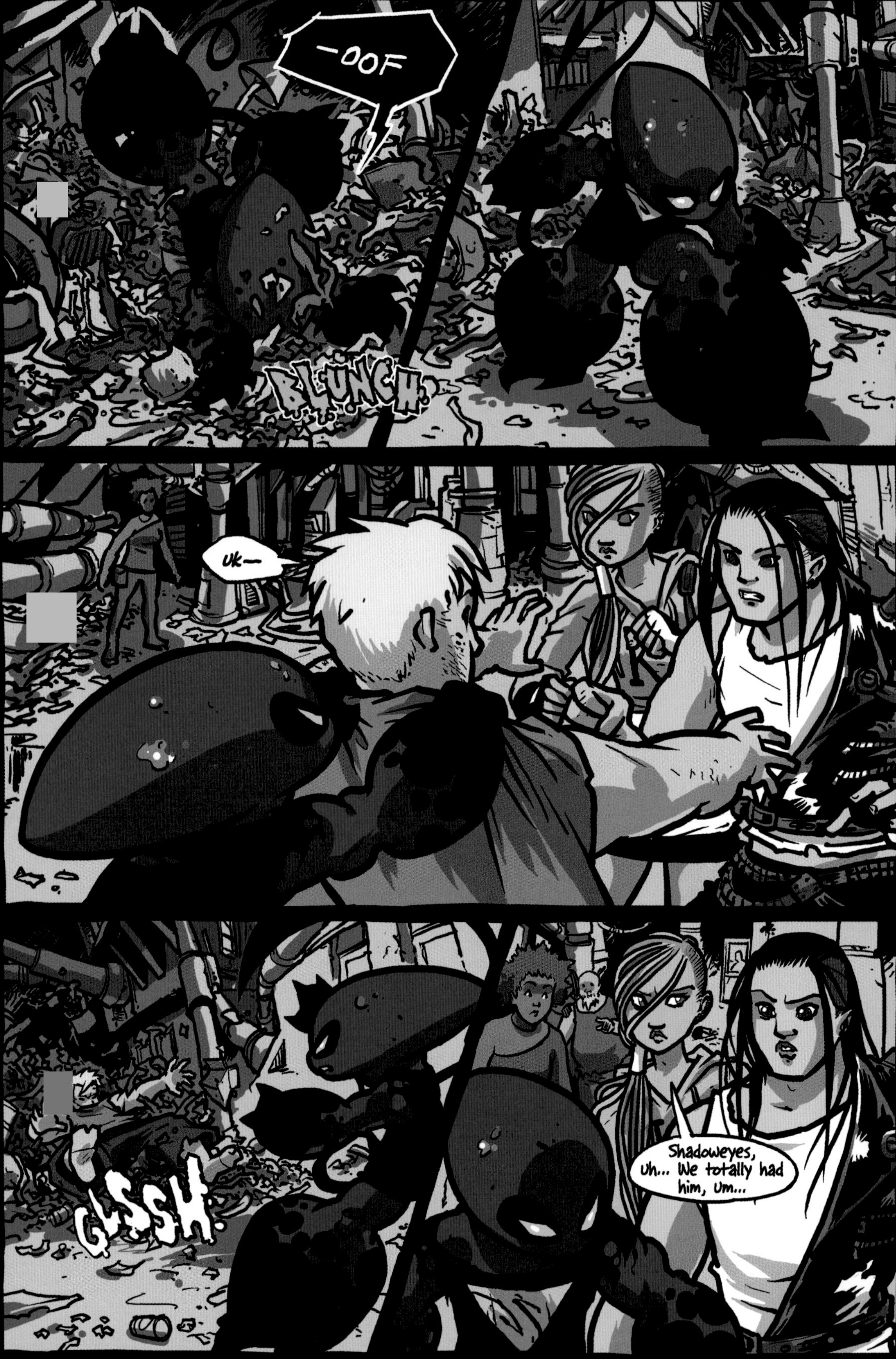
-OOF
BLUNCH
UK—
GSSH
Shadoweyes, Uh... We totally had him, Um...

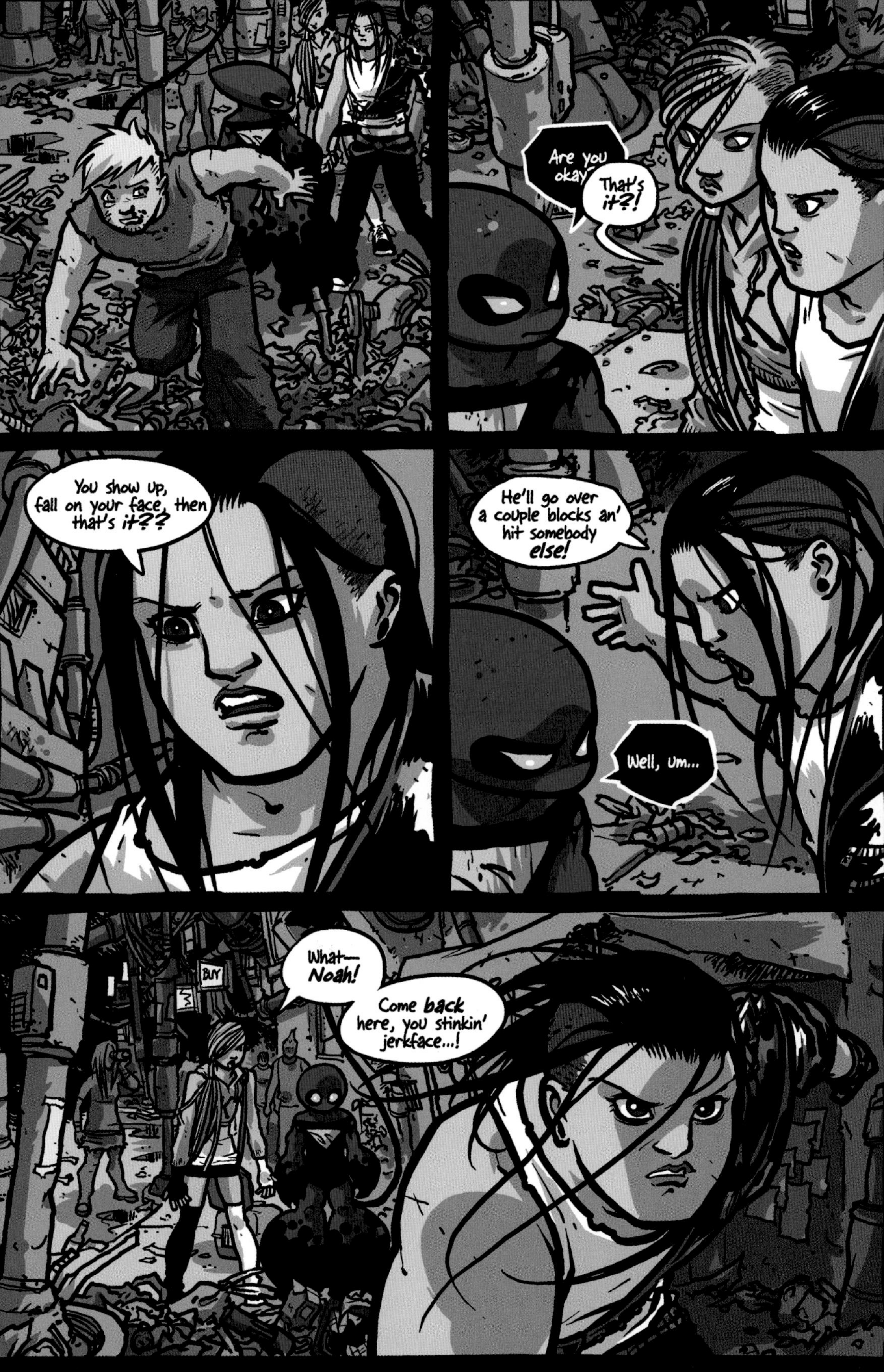
Are you okay?
That's it?!
You show up, fall on your face, then that's it??
He'll go over a couple blocks an' hit somebody else!
Well, um...
What— Noah!
Come back here, you stinkin' jerkface...!
BUY

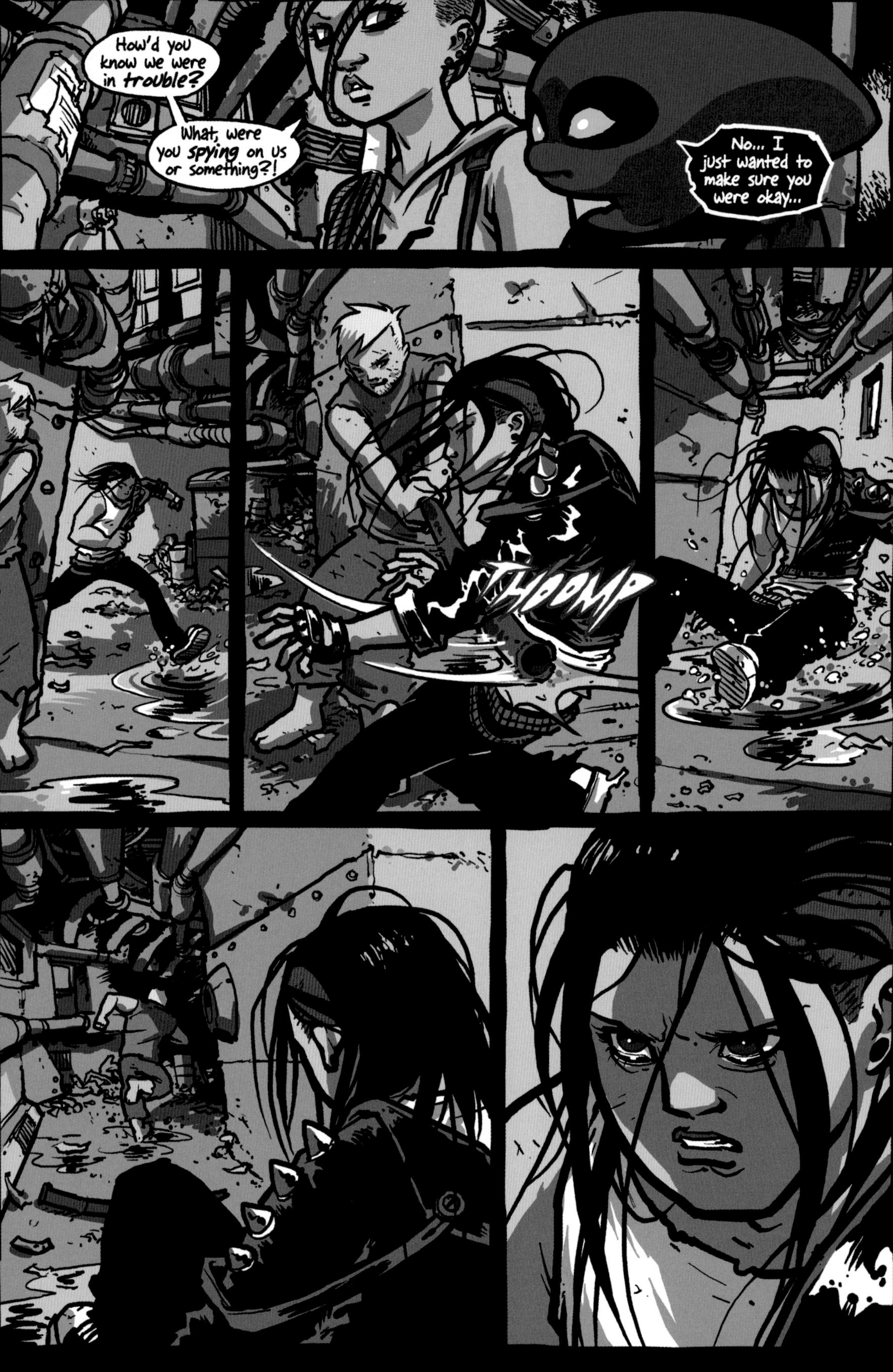
How'd you know we were in trouble?
What, were you spying on us or something?!
No... I just wanted to make sure you were okay...
THOOMP

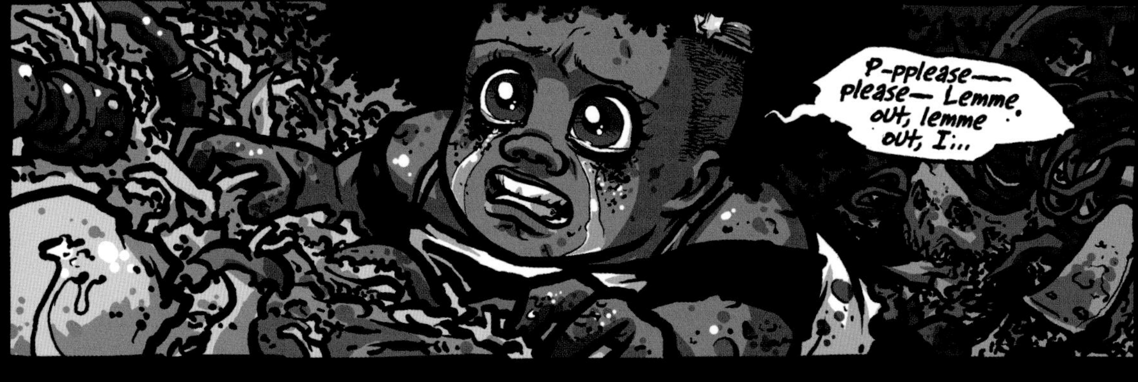
P-pplease— please— Lemme out, lemme out, I...

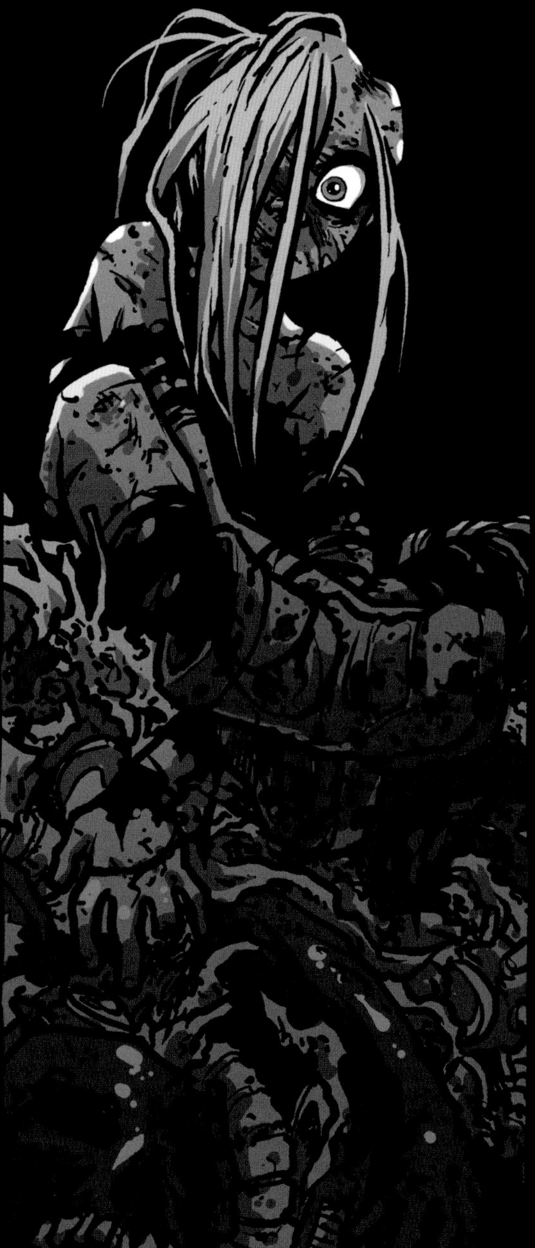

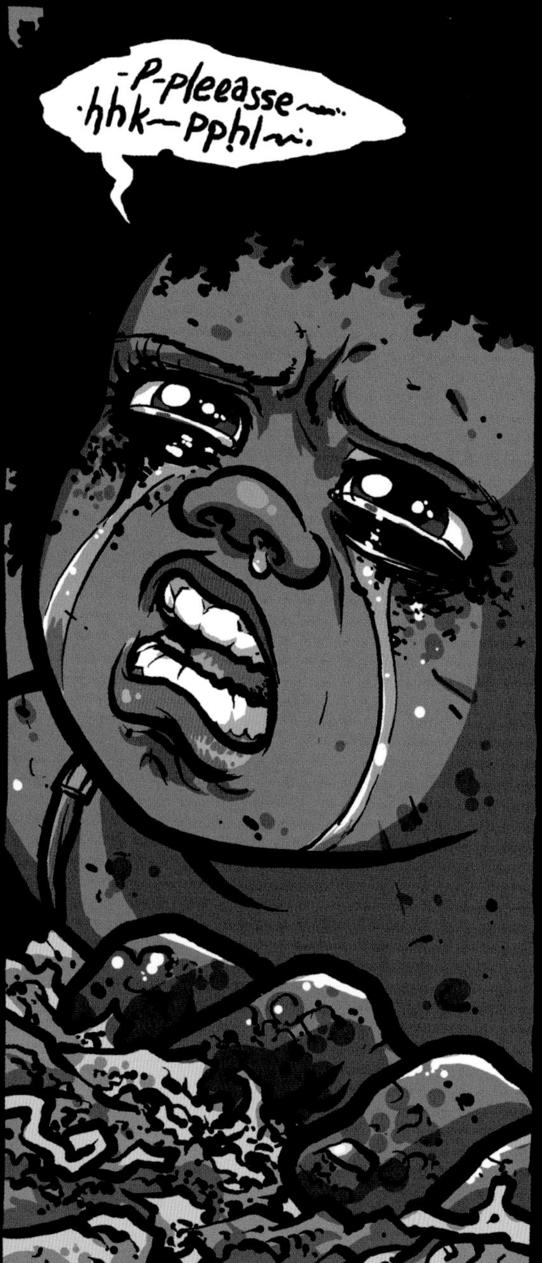
-P-pleeasse— ·hhk—pphl—.

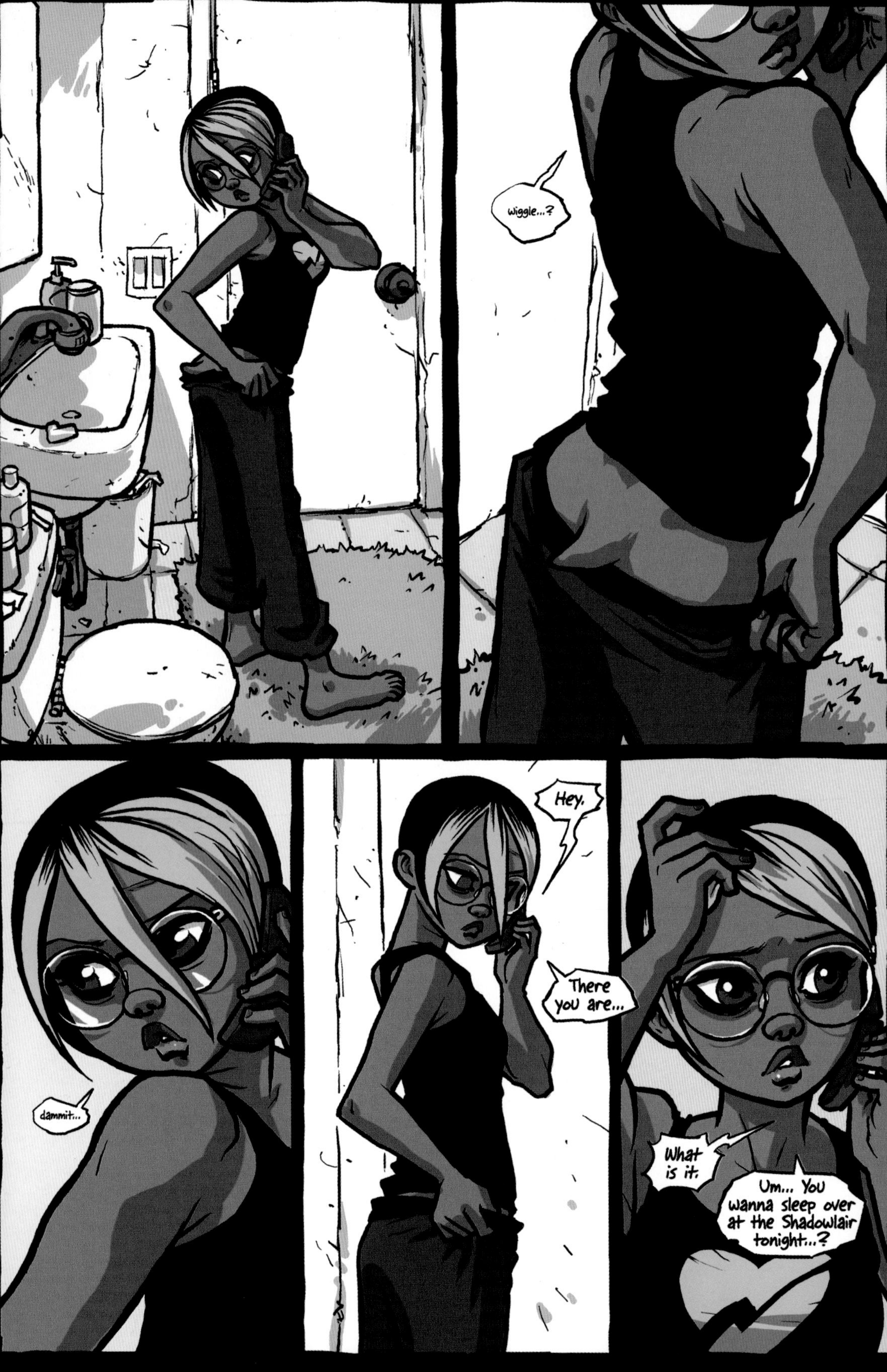
wiggle...?
dammit...
Hey.
There you are...
What is it.
Um... You wanna sleep over at the Shadowlair tonight...?

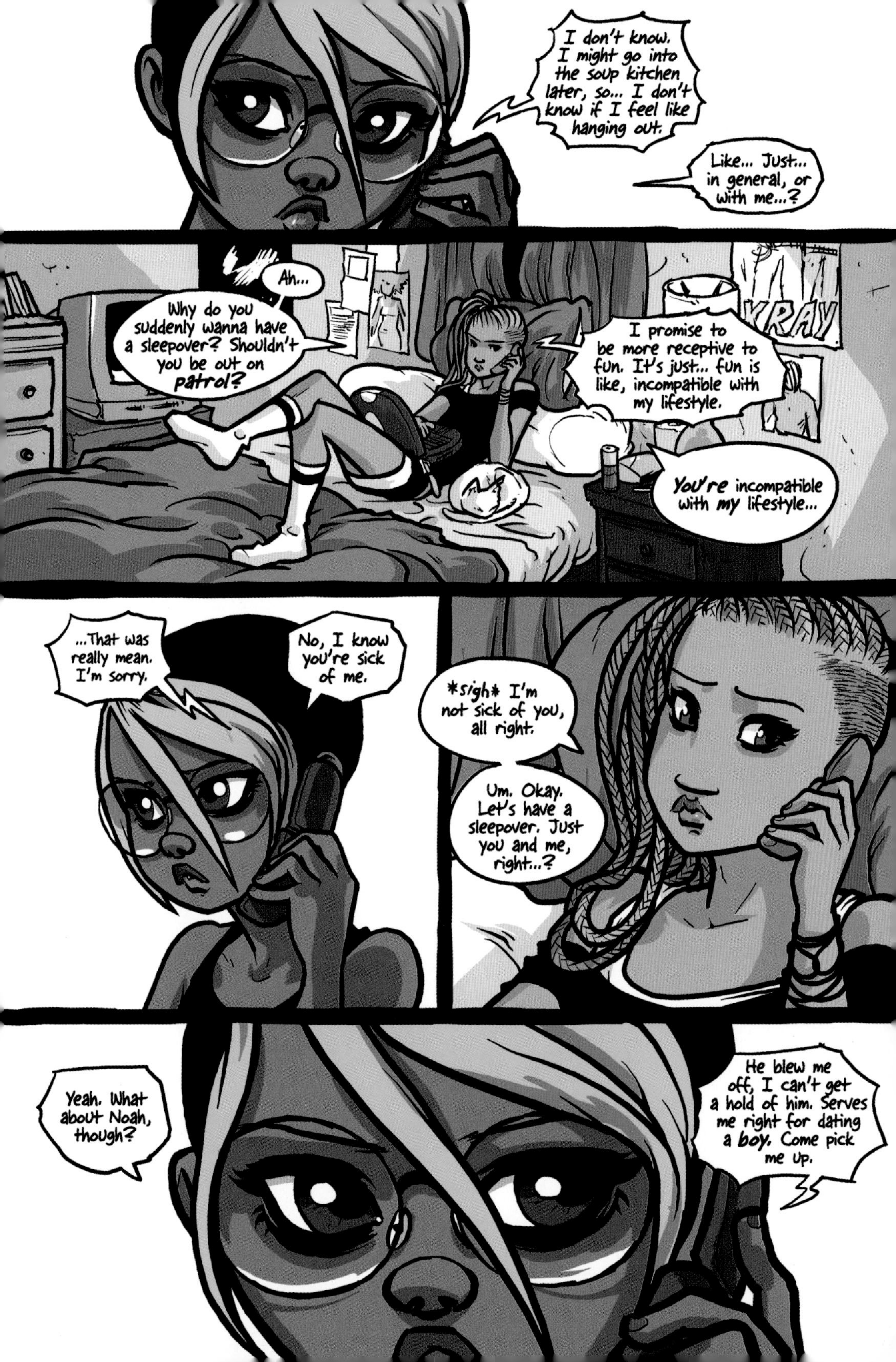

I don't know. I might go into the soup kitchen later, so... I don't know if I feel like hanging out.
Like... Just... in general, or with me...?
Ah...
Why do you suddenly wanna have a sleepover? Shouldn't you be out on **patrol**?
I promise to be more receptive to fun. It's just... fun is like, incompatible with my lifestyle.
You're incompatible with ***my*** lifestyle...
...That was really mean. I'm sorry.
No, I know you're sick of me.
sigh I'm not sick of you, all right.
Um. Okay. Let's have a sleepover. Just you and me, right...?
Yeah. What about Noah, though?
He blew me off, I can't get a hold of him. Serves me right for dating a ***boy***. Come pick me up.

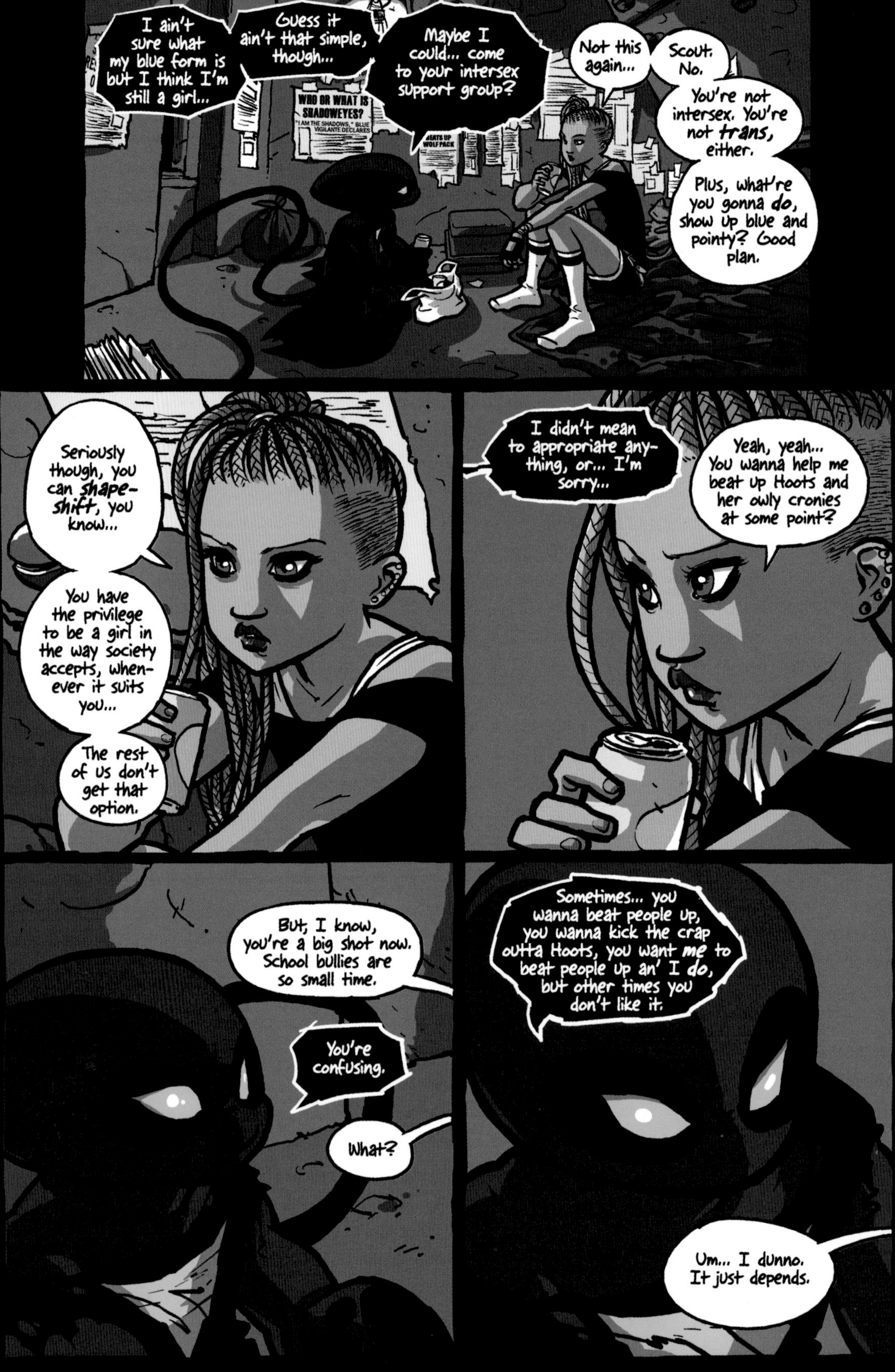
I ain't sure what my blue form is but I think I'm still a girl...
Guess it ain't that simple, though...
WHO OR WHAT IS SHADOWEYES?
"I AM THE SHADOWS," BLUE VIGILANTE DECLARES
Maybe I could... come to your intersex support group?
BEATS UP WOLF PACK
Not this again...
Scout. No.
You're not intersex. You're not *trans,* either.
Plus, what're you gonna *do,* show up blue and pointy? Good plan.
Seriously though, you can *shape-shift,* you know...
You have the privilege to be a girl in the way society accepts, whenever it suits you...
The rest of us don't get that option.
I didn't mean to appropriate anything, or... I'm sorry...
Yeah, yeah... You wanna help me beat up Hoots and her owly cronies at some point?
But, I know, you're a big shot now. School bullies are so small time.
You're confusing.
What?
Sometimes... you wanna beat people up, you wanna kick the crap outta Hoots, you want *me* to beat people up an' I *do,* but other times you don't like it.
Um... I dunno. It just depends.

Some people sure deserve it, right? Like people who make someone's life *hell*.

I dunno, it makes sense in my head.

You're the confusing one, though, you go around not only letting the bad guys get away but then you beat up the *good* guys when they try to *get* the bad guys.

SHADOWEYES BEATS UP WOLF PACK

No wonder everybody hates you.

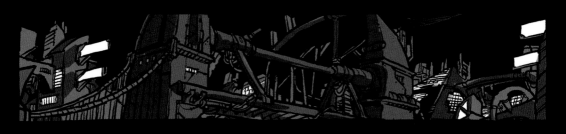

SHADOWEYES BEATS UP WOLF PACK

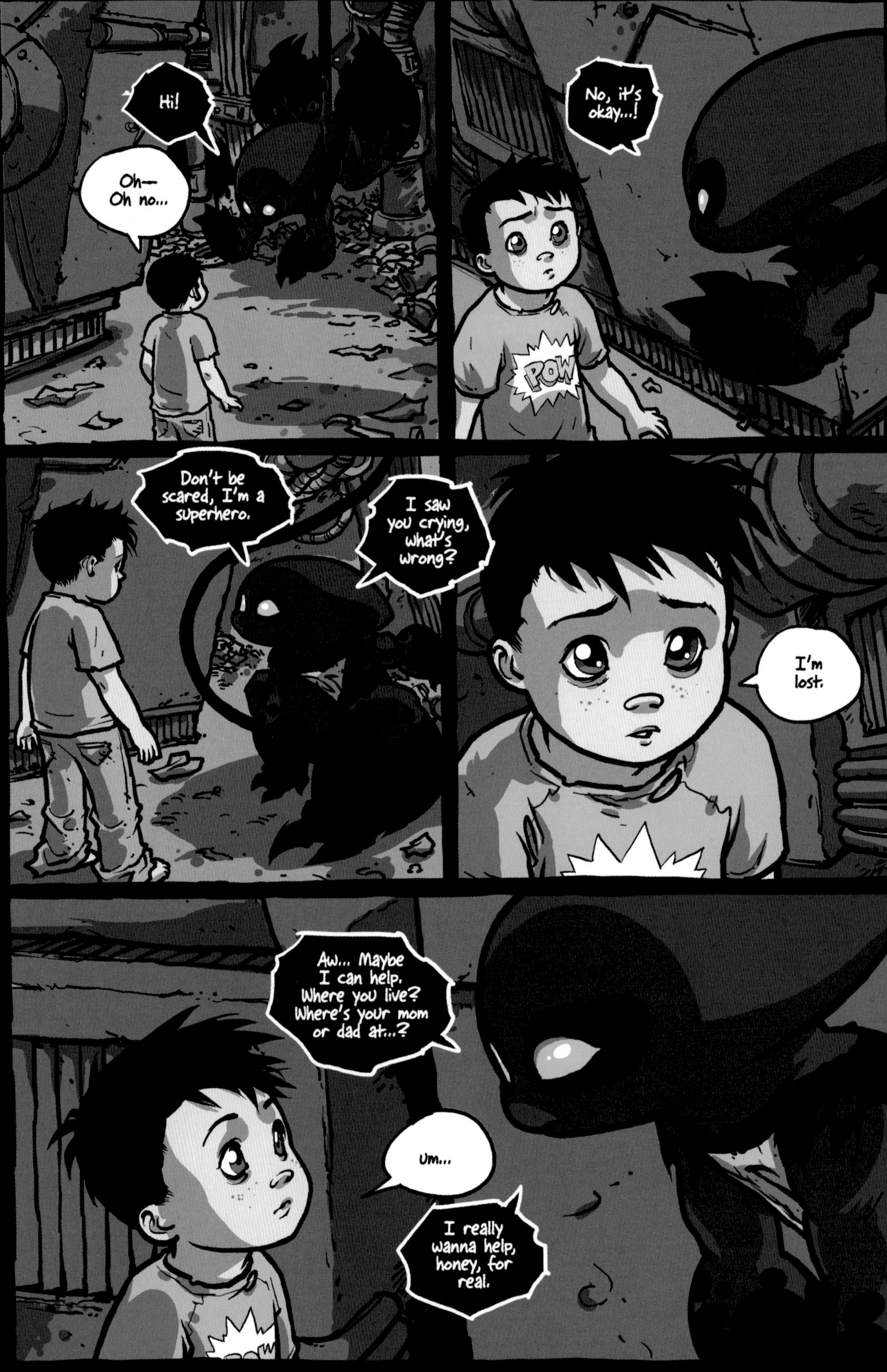
Hi!
Oh— Oh no...
No, it's okay...!
Don't be scared, I'm a superhero.
I saw you crying, what's wrong?
I'm lost.
Aw... Maybe I can help. Where you live? Where's your mom or dad at...?
Um...
I really wanna help, honey, for real.

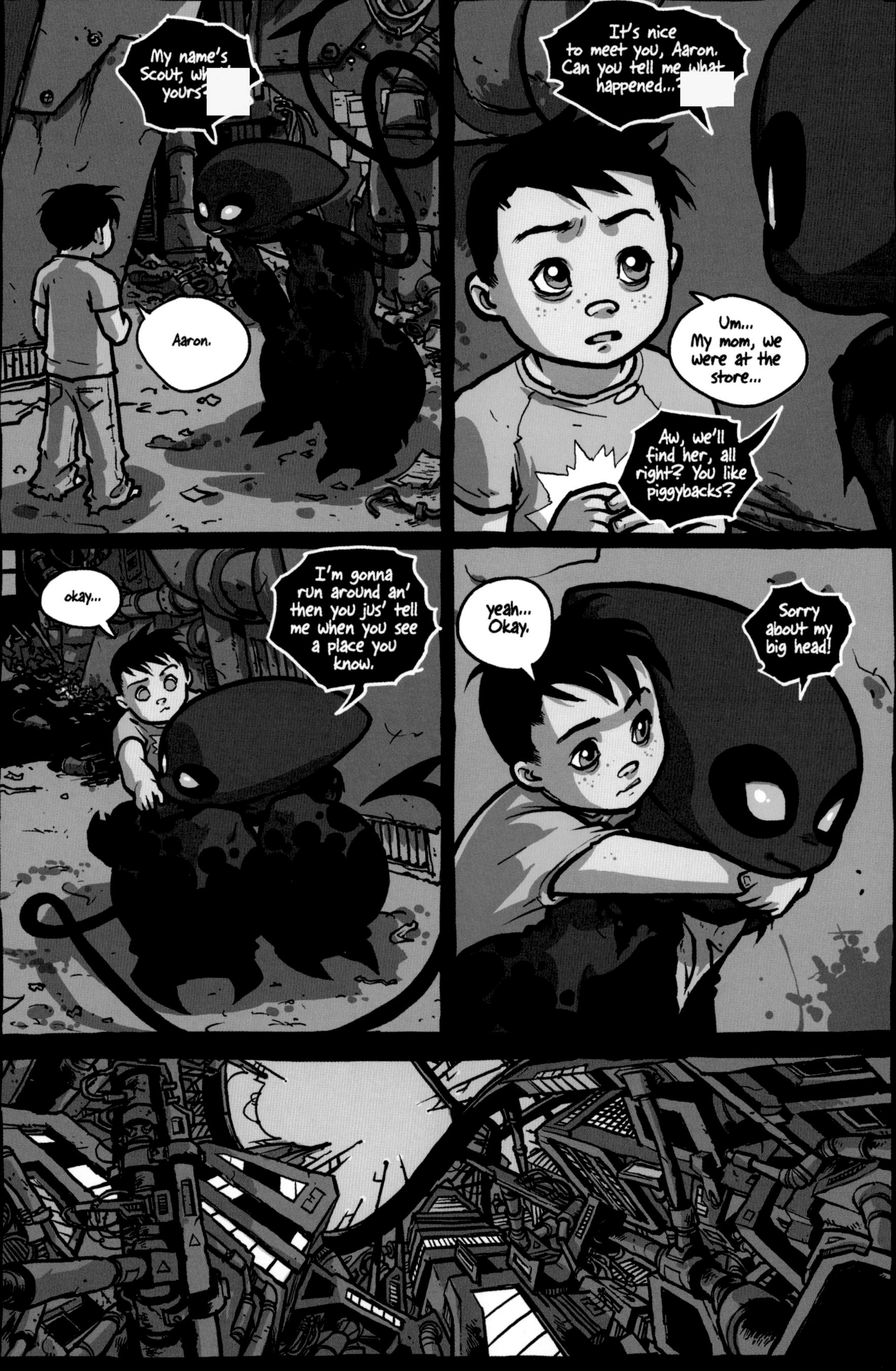

My name's Scout, wh yours?
Aaron.
It's nice to meet you, Aaron. Can you tell me what happened...?
Um... My mom, we were at the store...
Aw, we'll find her, all right? You like piggybacks?
okay...
I'm gonna run around an' then you jus' tell me when you see a place you know.
yeah... Okay.
Sorry about my big head!

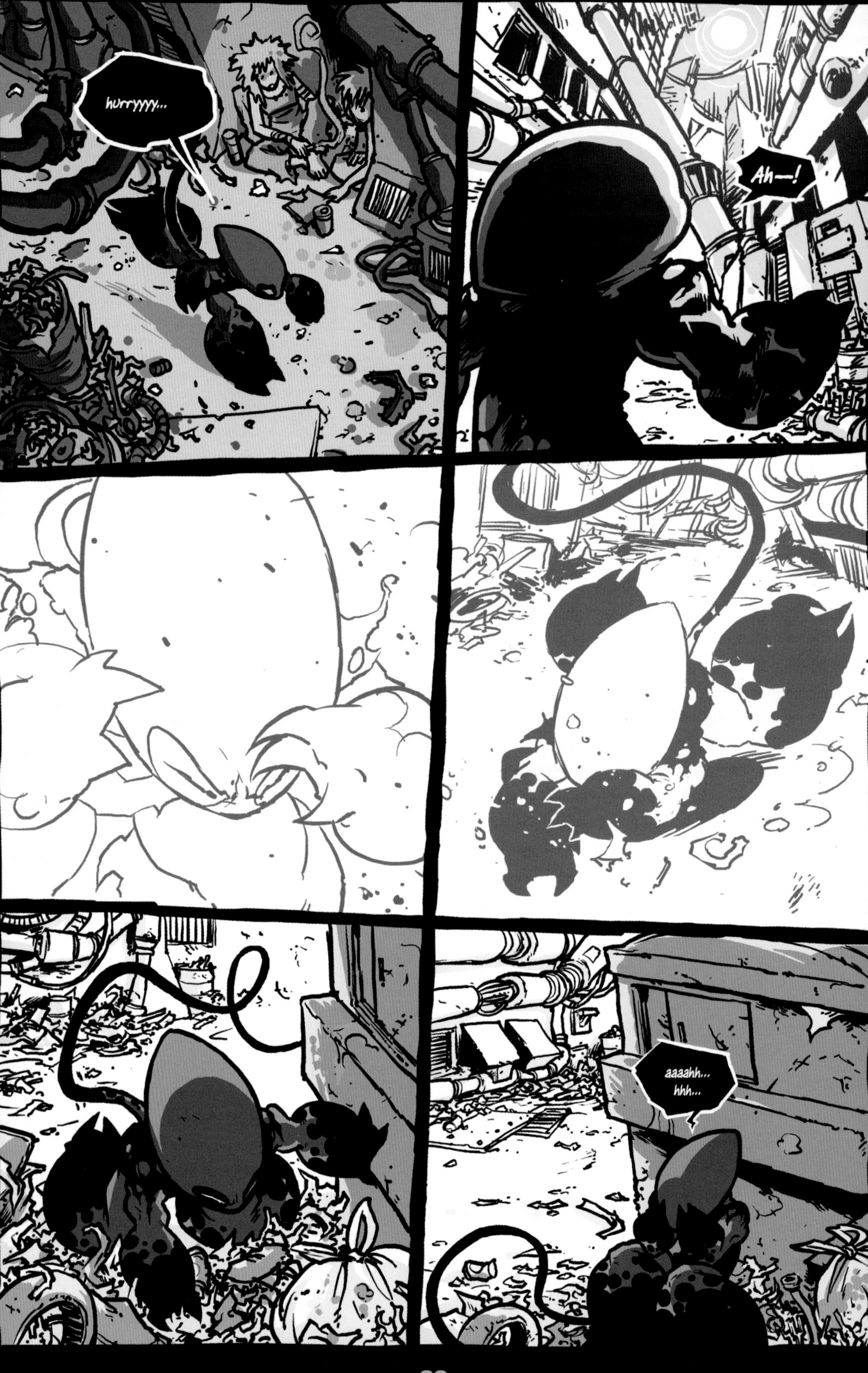
hurryyyy...
Ah—!
aaaahh...
hhh...

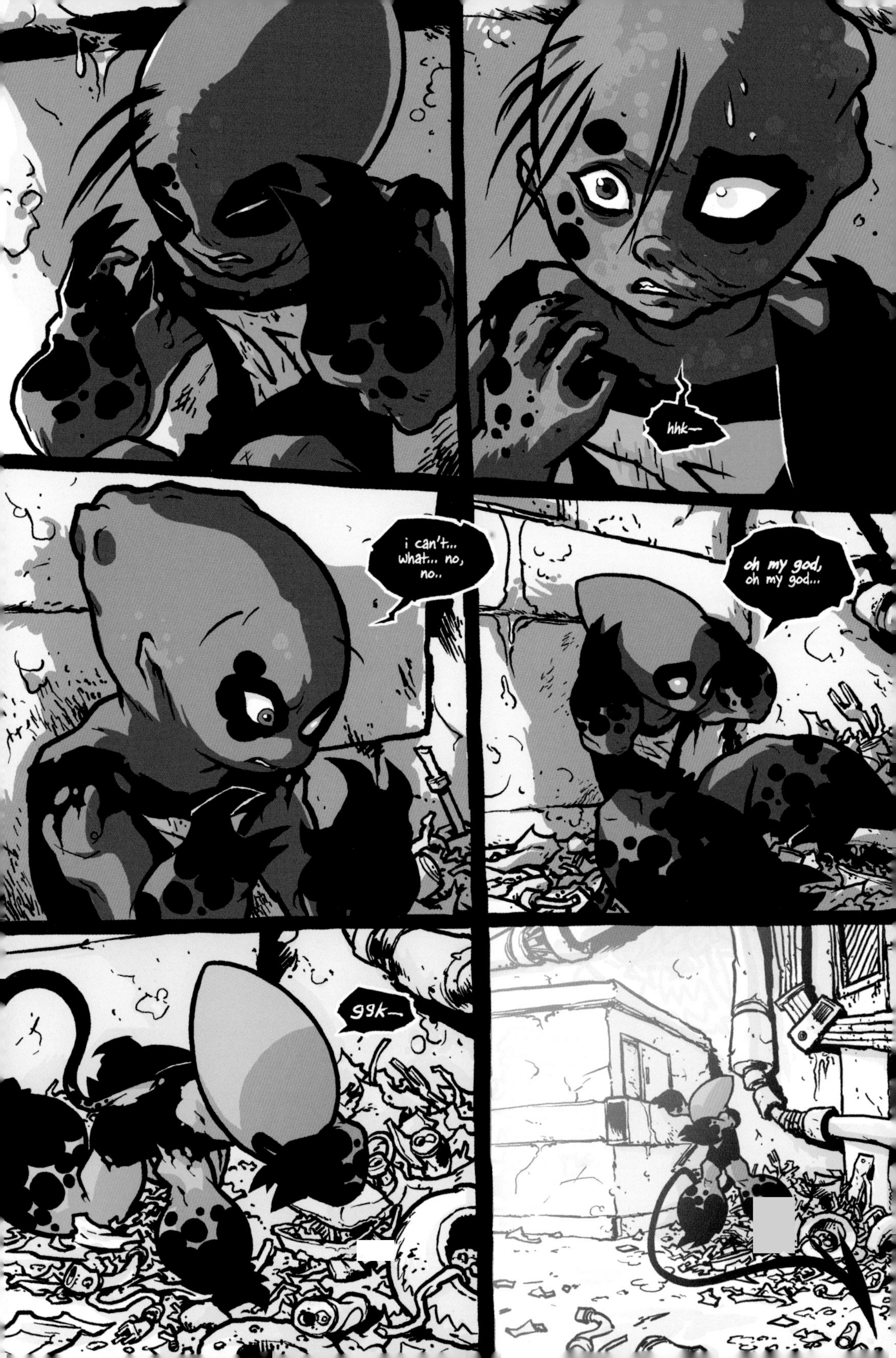
hhk–
i can't...
what... no,
no..
oh my god,
oh my god...
ggk–

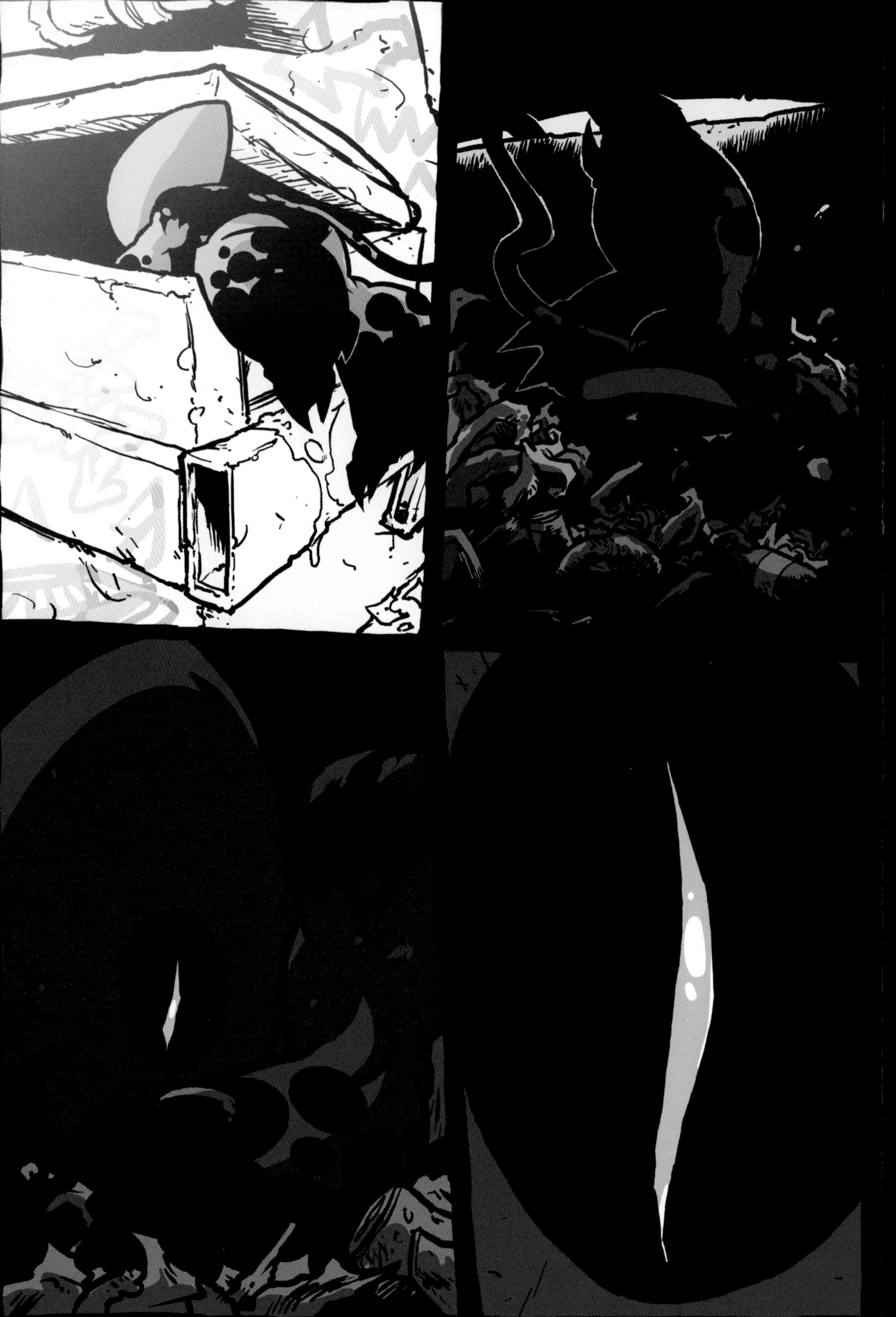

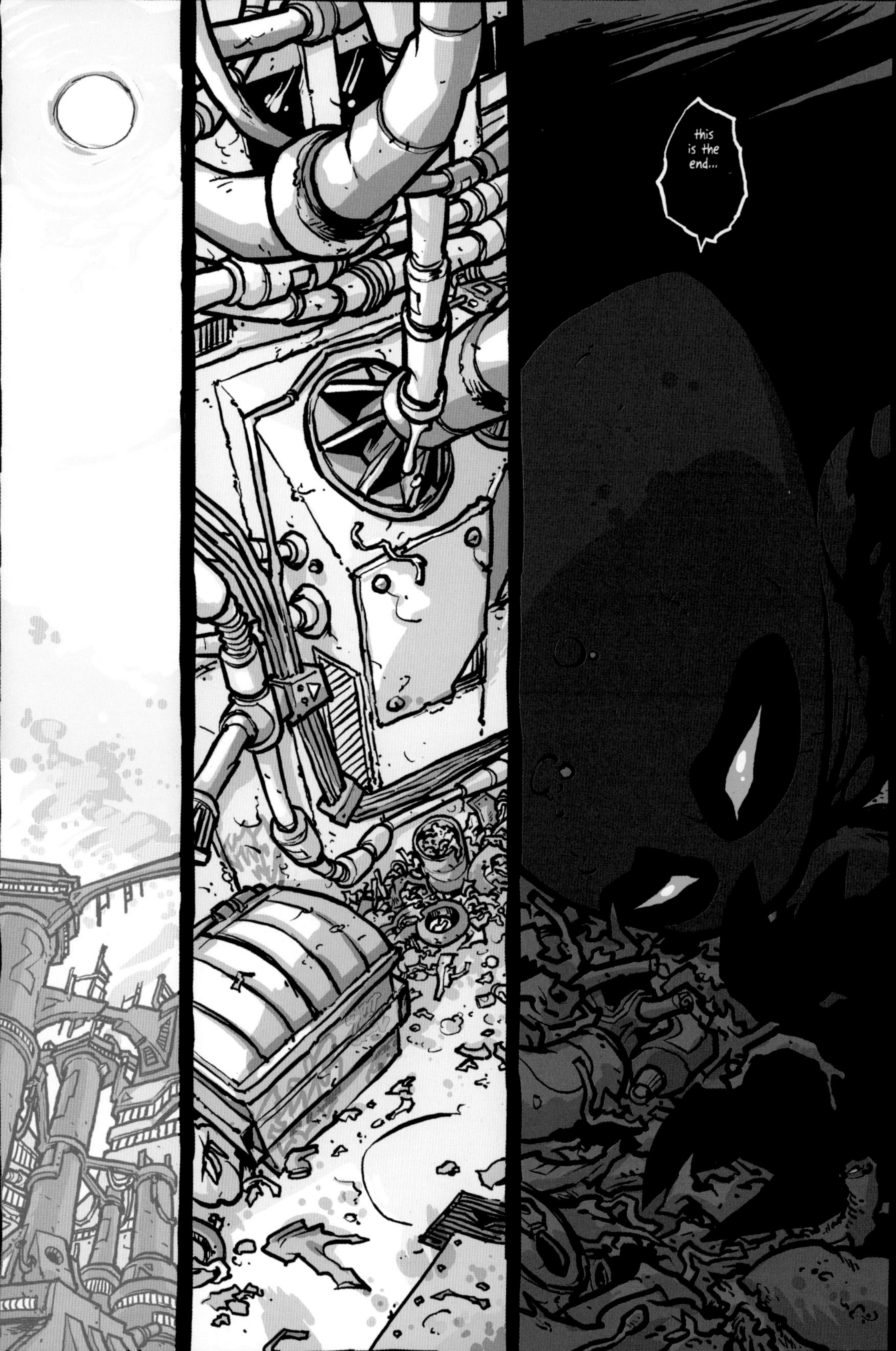
this is the end...

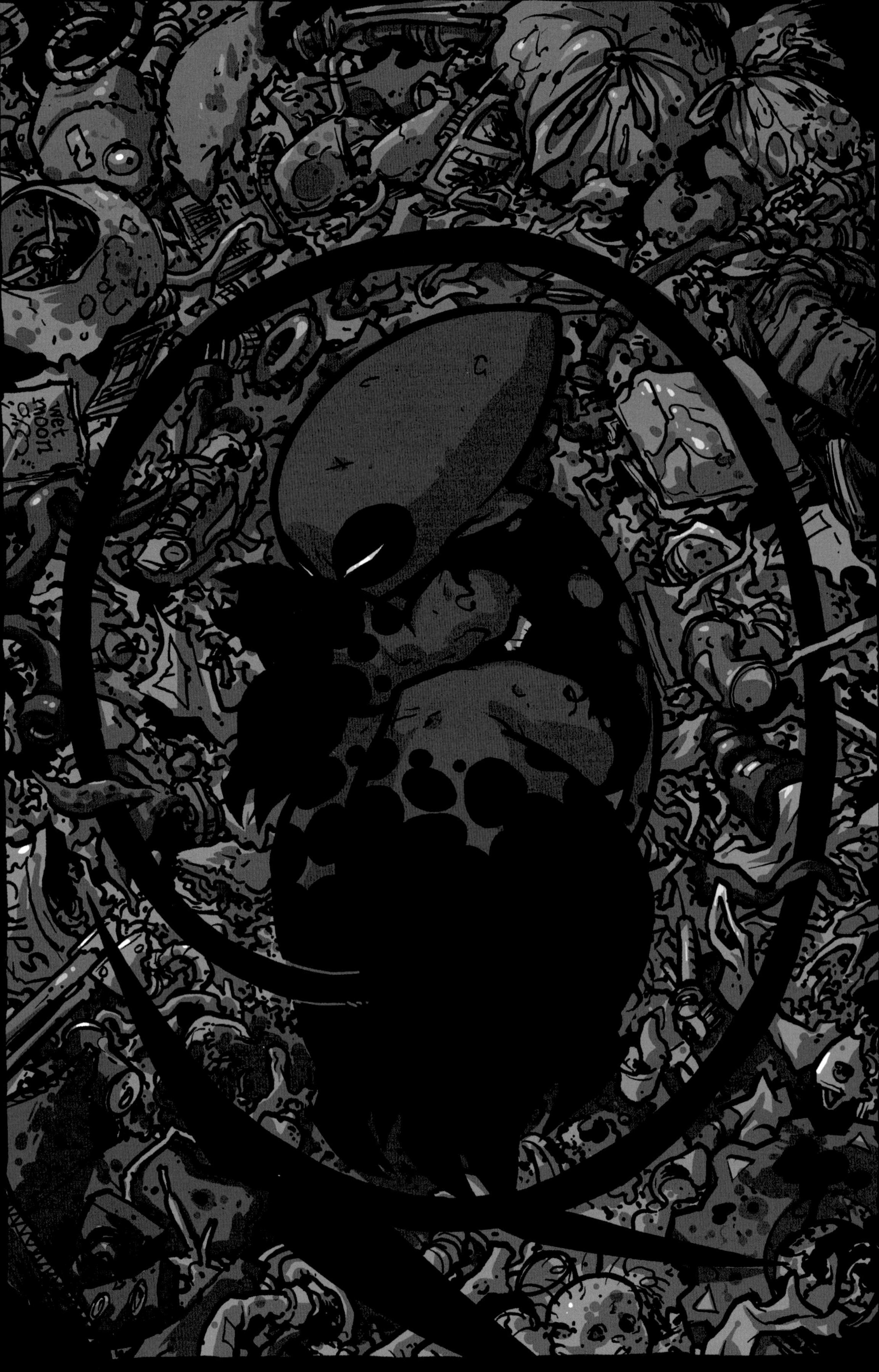
wet moon
CHIPS

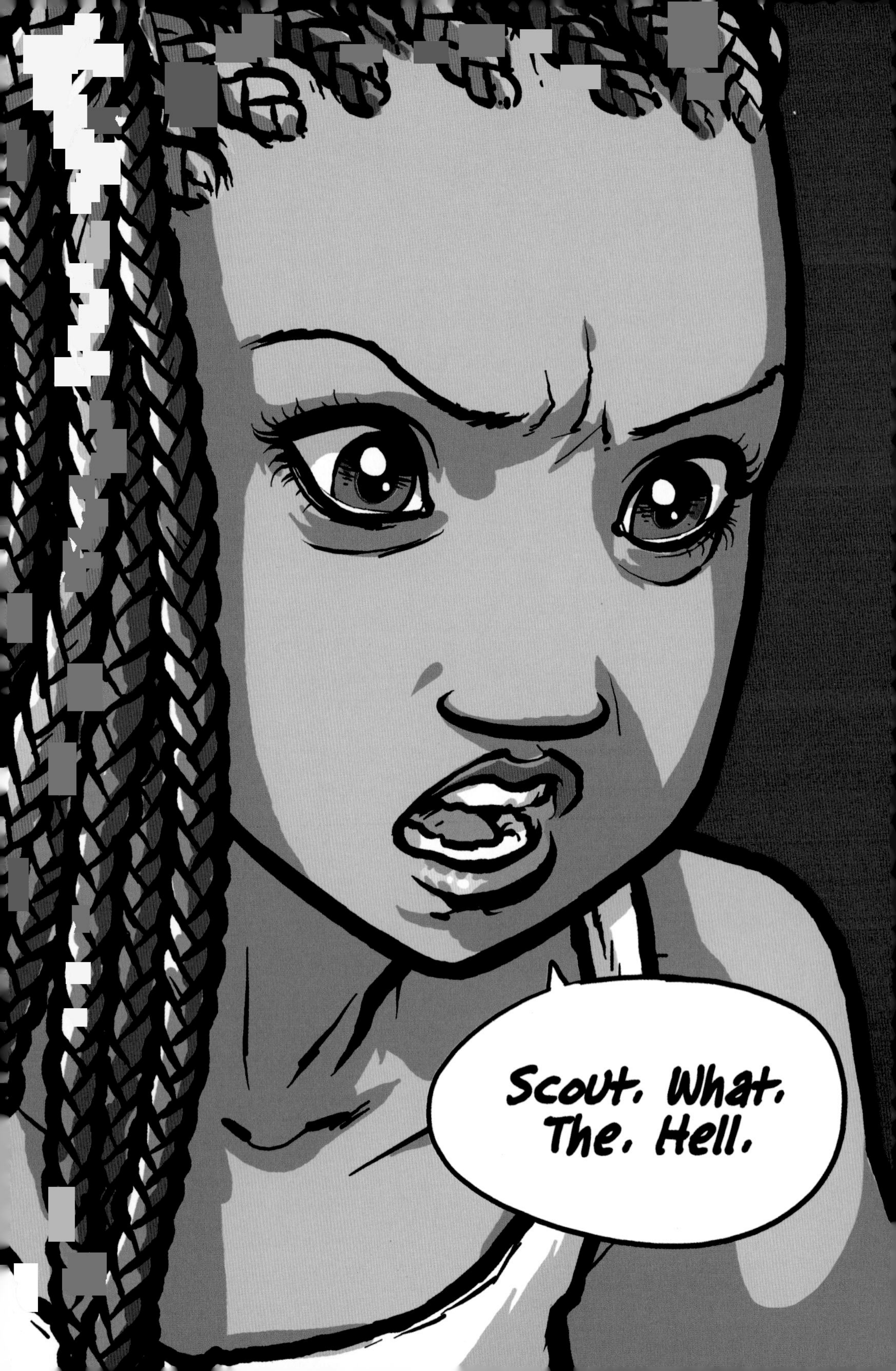
Scout. What. The. Hell.

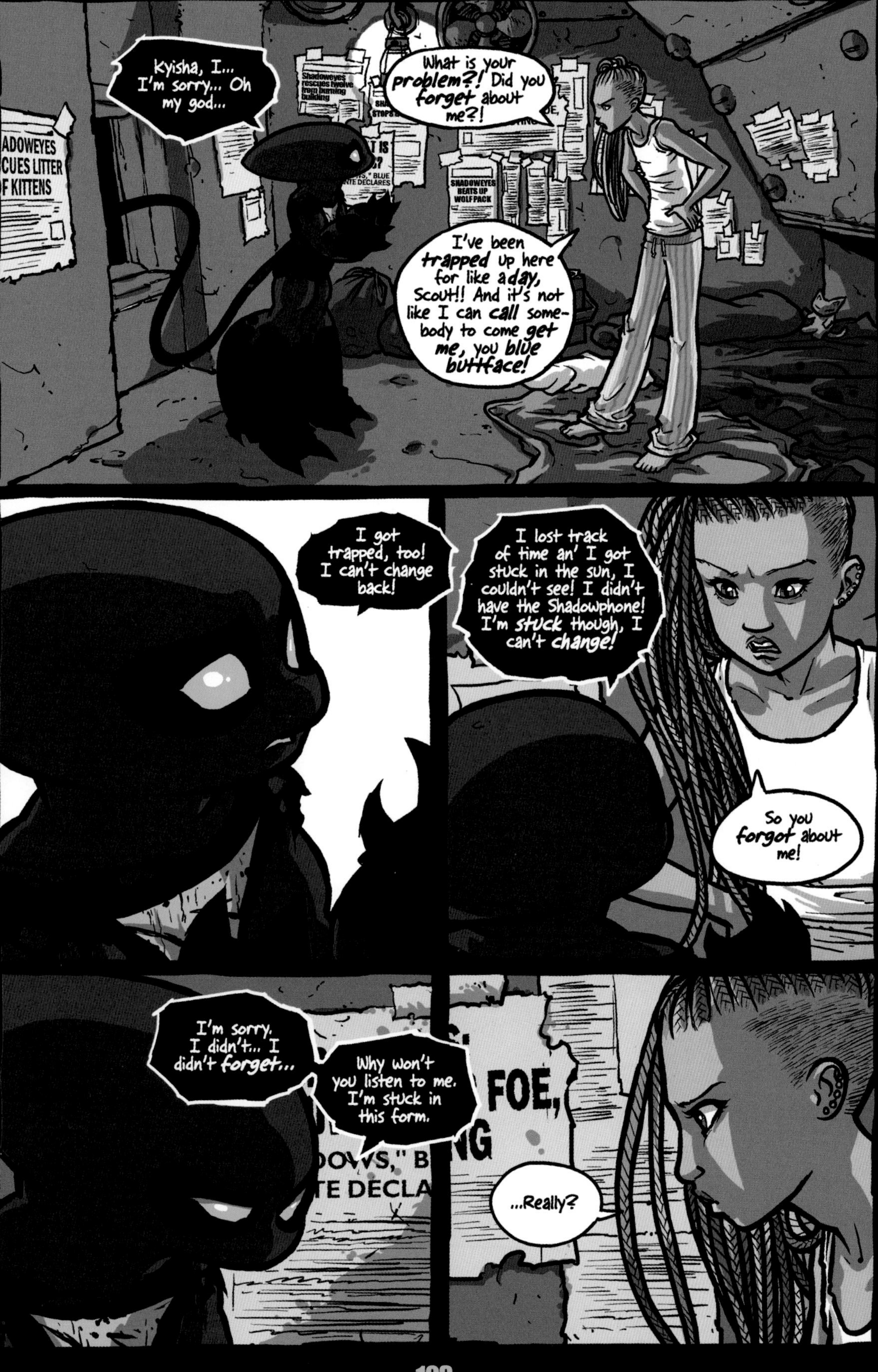
ADOWEYES
CUES LITTER
F KITTENS
Shadoweyes rescues twelve from burning building
SHADOWEYES BEATS UP WOLF PACK
Kyisha, I... I'm sorry... Oh my god...
What is your problem?! Did you forget about me?!
I've been trapped up here for like a day, Scout!! And it's not like I can call somebody to come get me, you blue buttface!
I got trapped, too! I can't change back!
I lost track of time an' I got stuck in the sun, I couldn't see! I didn't have the Shadowphone! I'm stuck though, I can't change!
So you forgot about me!
I'm sorry. I didn't... I didn't forget...
Why won't you listen to me. I'm stuck in this form.
...Really?

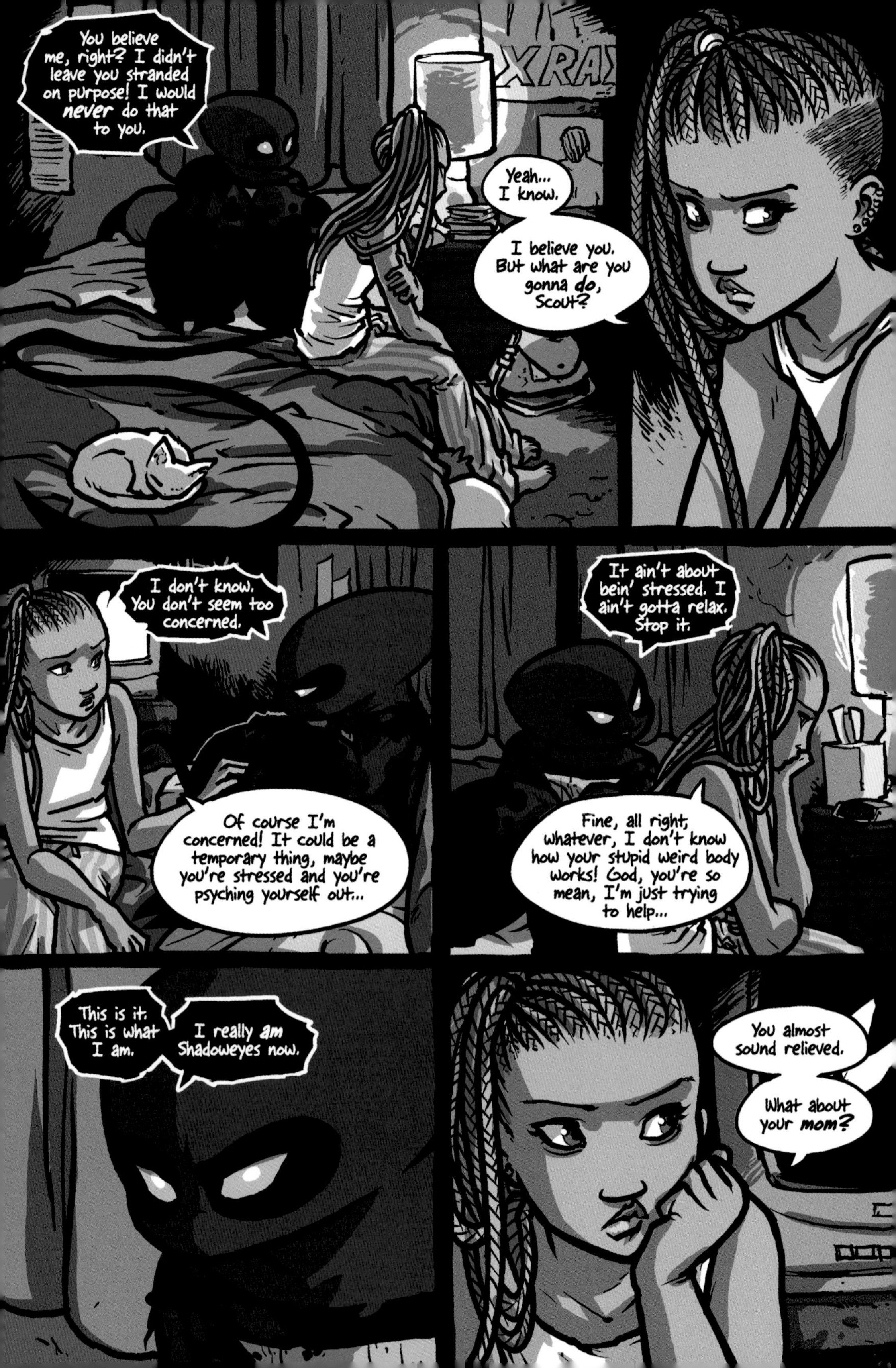
You believe me, right? I didn't leave you stranded on purpose! I would never do that to you.
XRAY
Yeah... I know.
I believe you. But what are you gonna do, Scout?
I don't know. You don't seem too concerned.
Of course I'm concerned! It could be a temporary thing, maybe you're stressed and you're psyching yourself out...
It ain't about bein' stressed. I ain't gotta relax. Stop it.
Fine, all right, whatever, I don't know how your stupid weird body works! God, you're so mean, I'm just trying to help...
This is it. This is what I am.
I really am Shadoweyes now.
You almost sound relieved.
What about your mom?

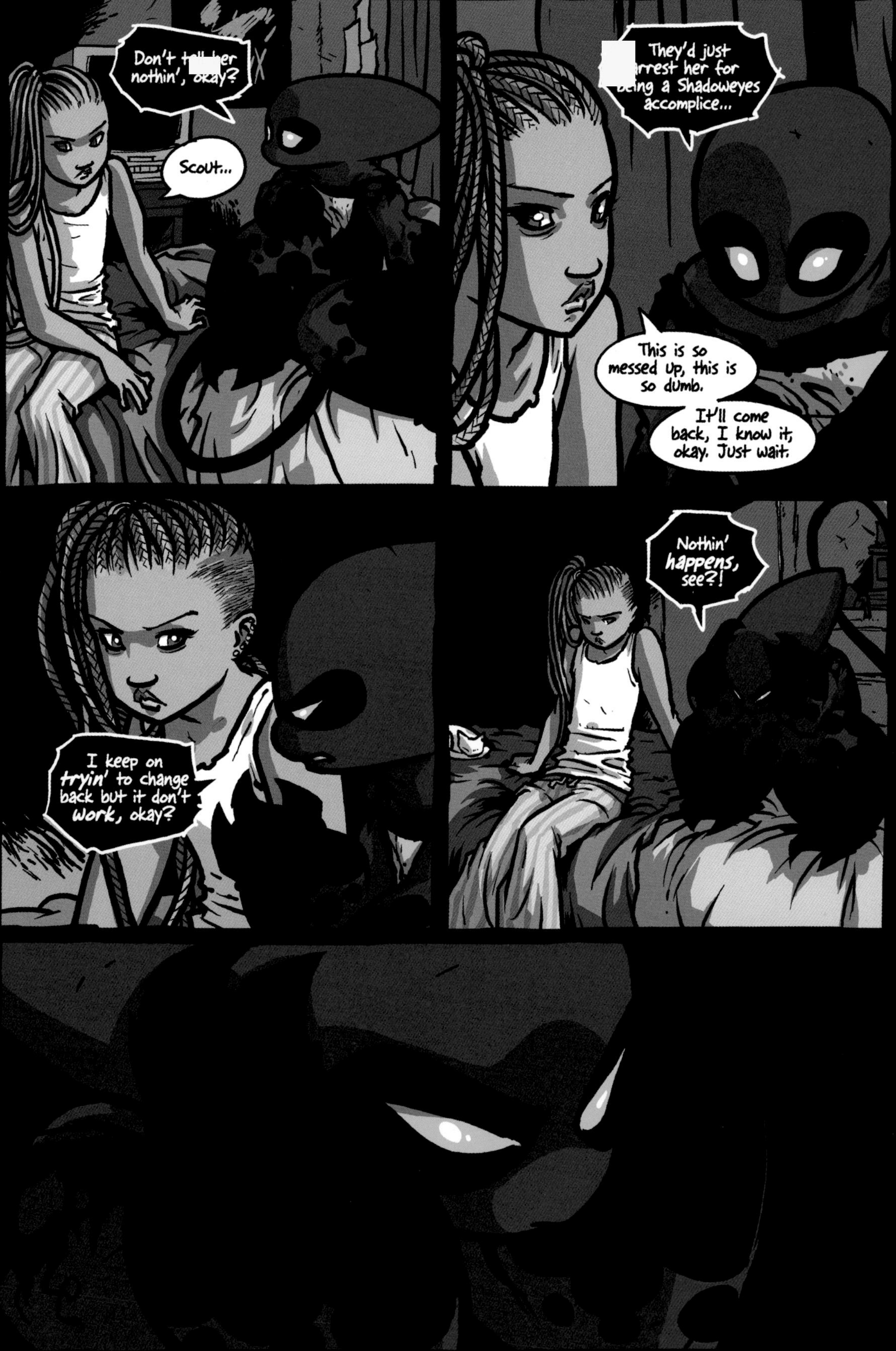
Don't tell her nothin', okay?
Scout...
They'd just arrest her for being a Shadoweyes accomplice...
This is so messed up, this is so dumb.
It'll come back, I know it, okay. Just wait.
I keep on tryin' to change back but it don't work, okay?
Nothin' happens, see?!

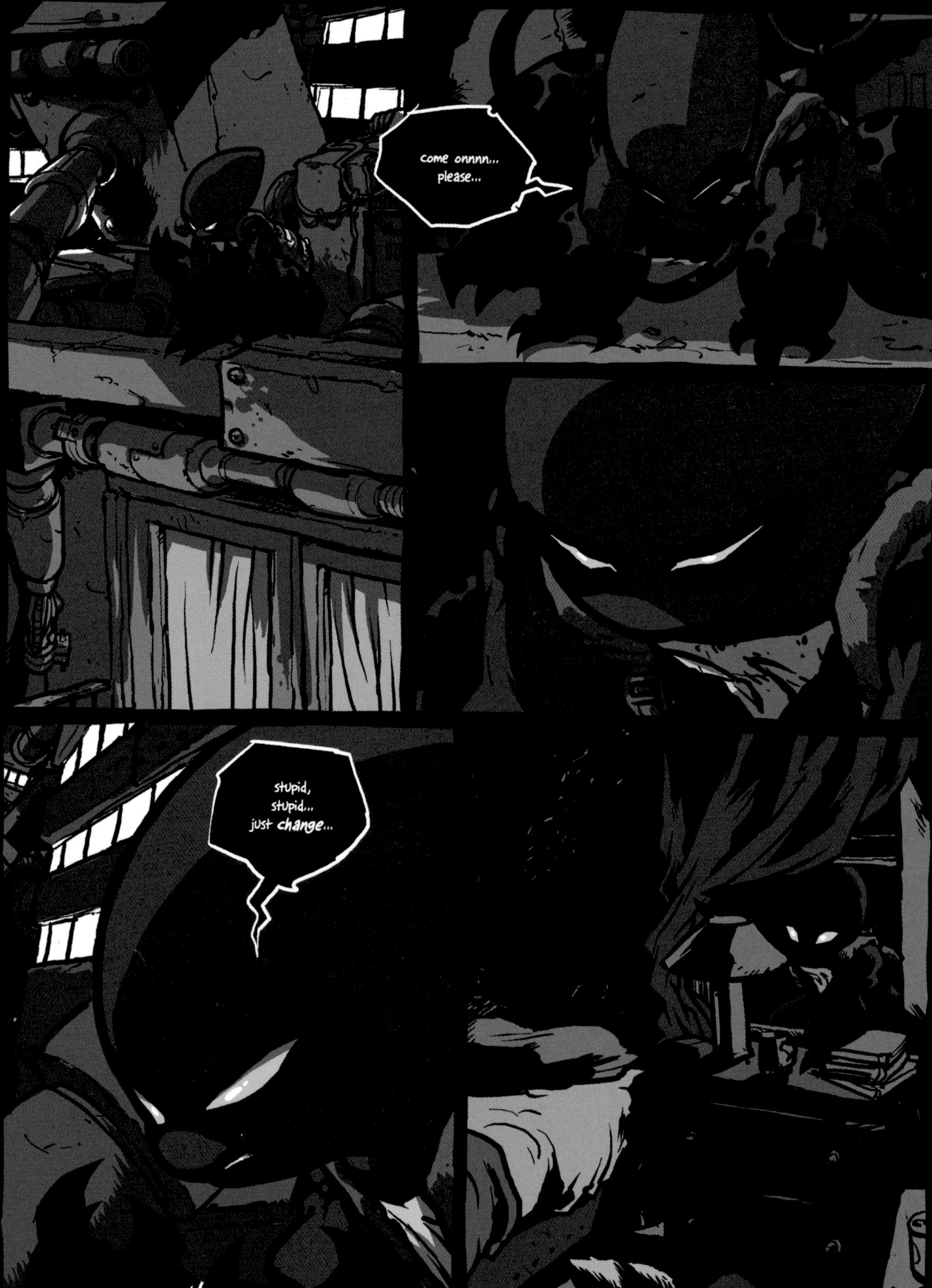
come onnnn...
please...
stupid,
stupid...
just change...

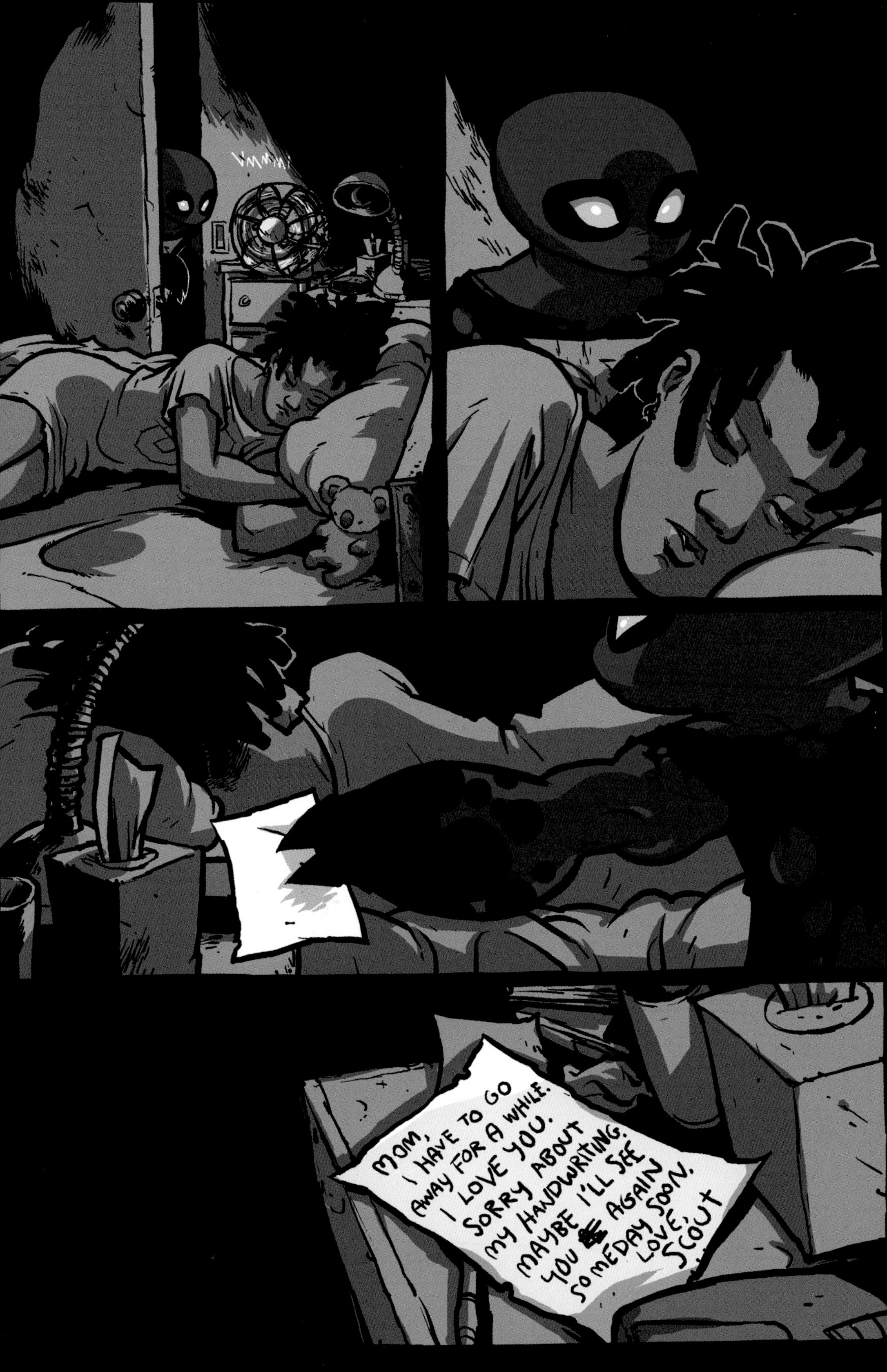
VMMM
MOM,
I HAVE TO GO
AWAY FOR A WHILE.
I LOVE YOU.
SORRY ABOUT
MY HANDWRITING.
MAYBE I'LL SEE
YOU AGAIN
SOMEDAY SOON.
LOVE,
SCOUT

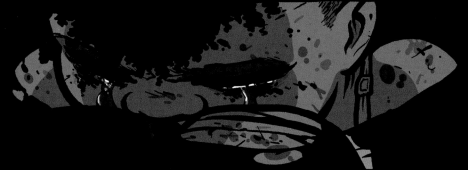

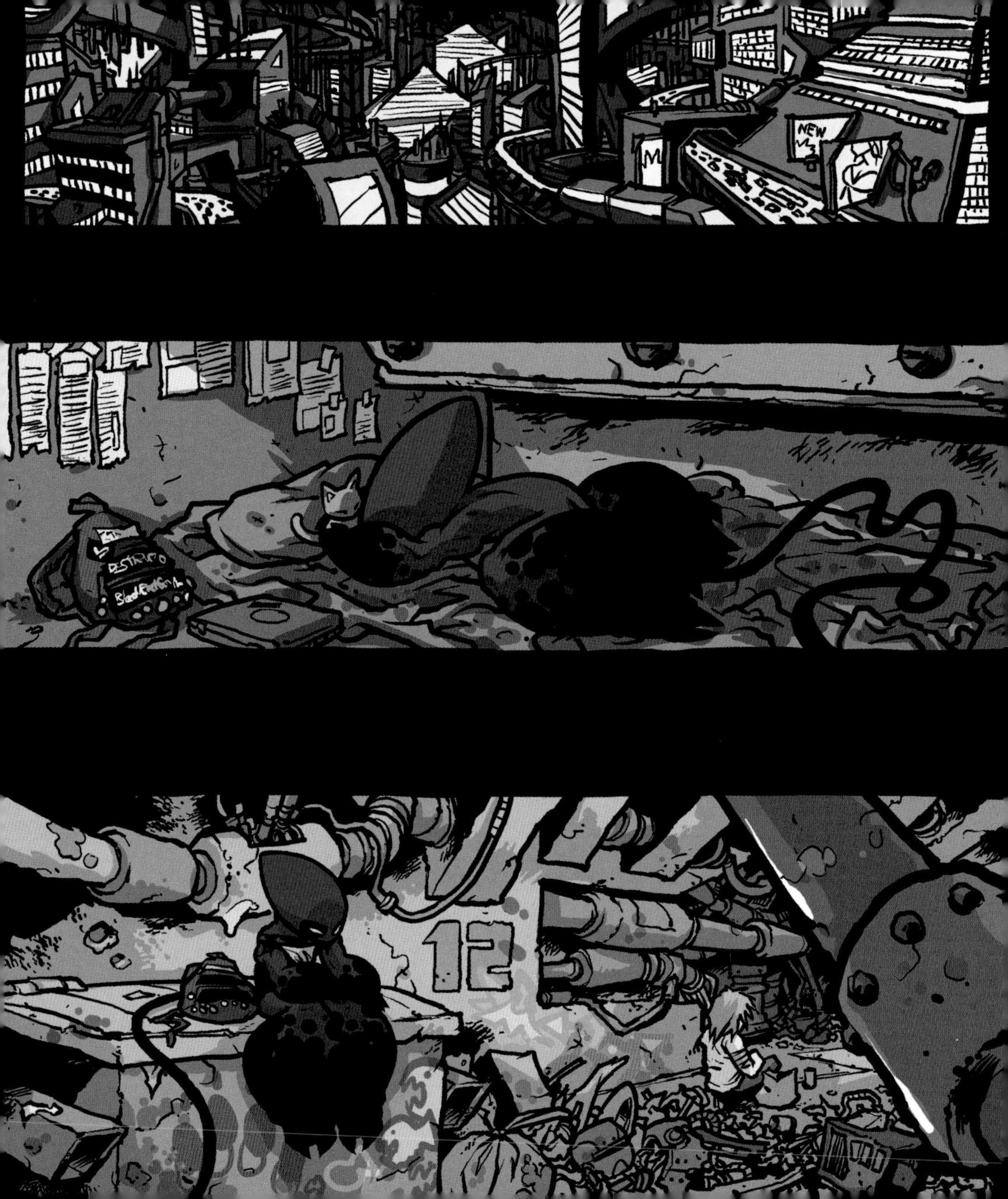

NEW
12

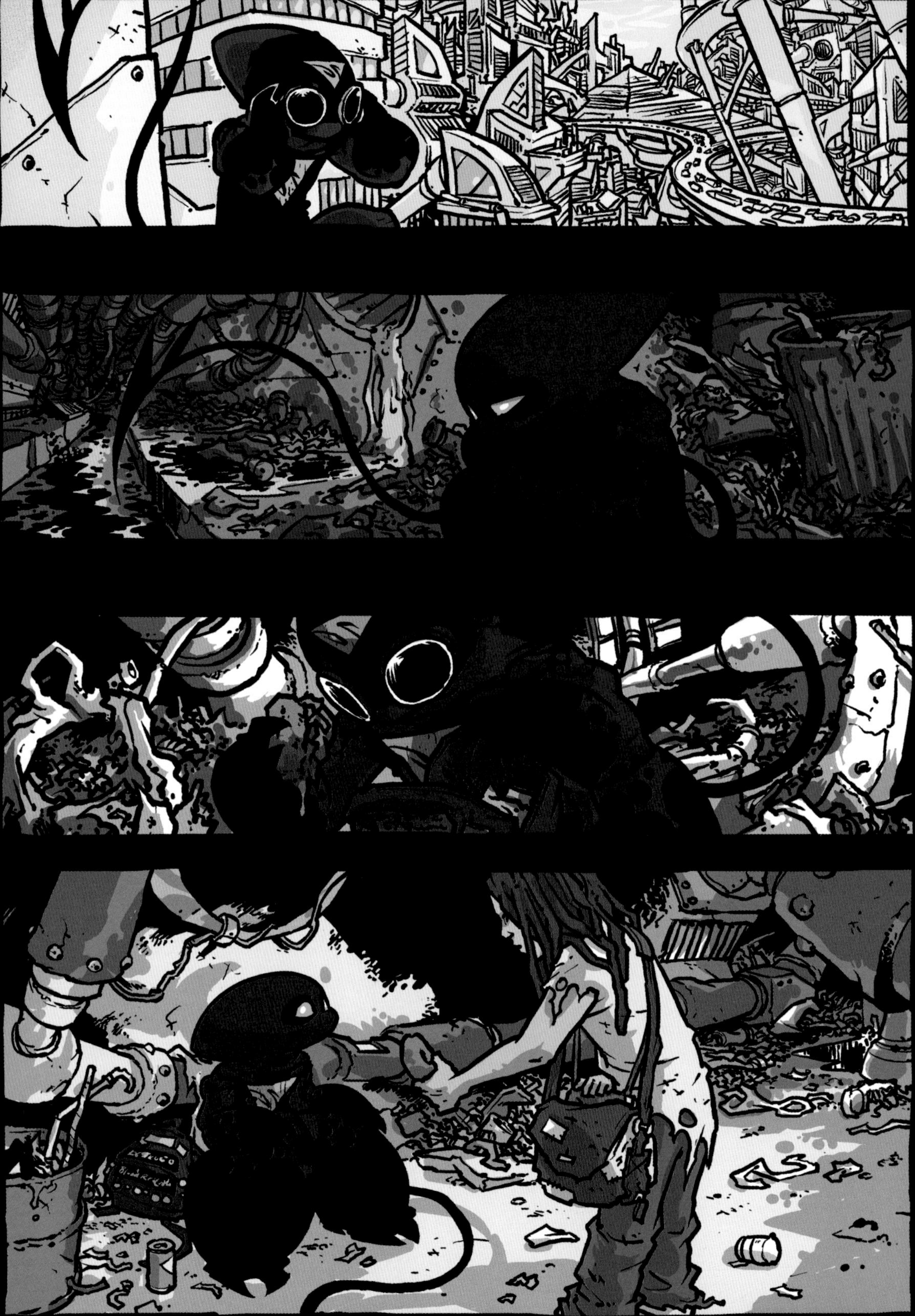

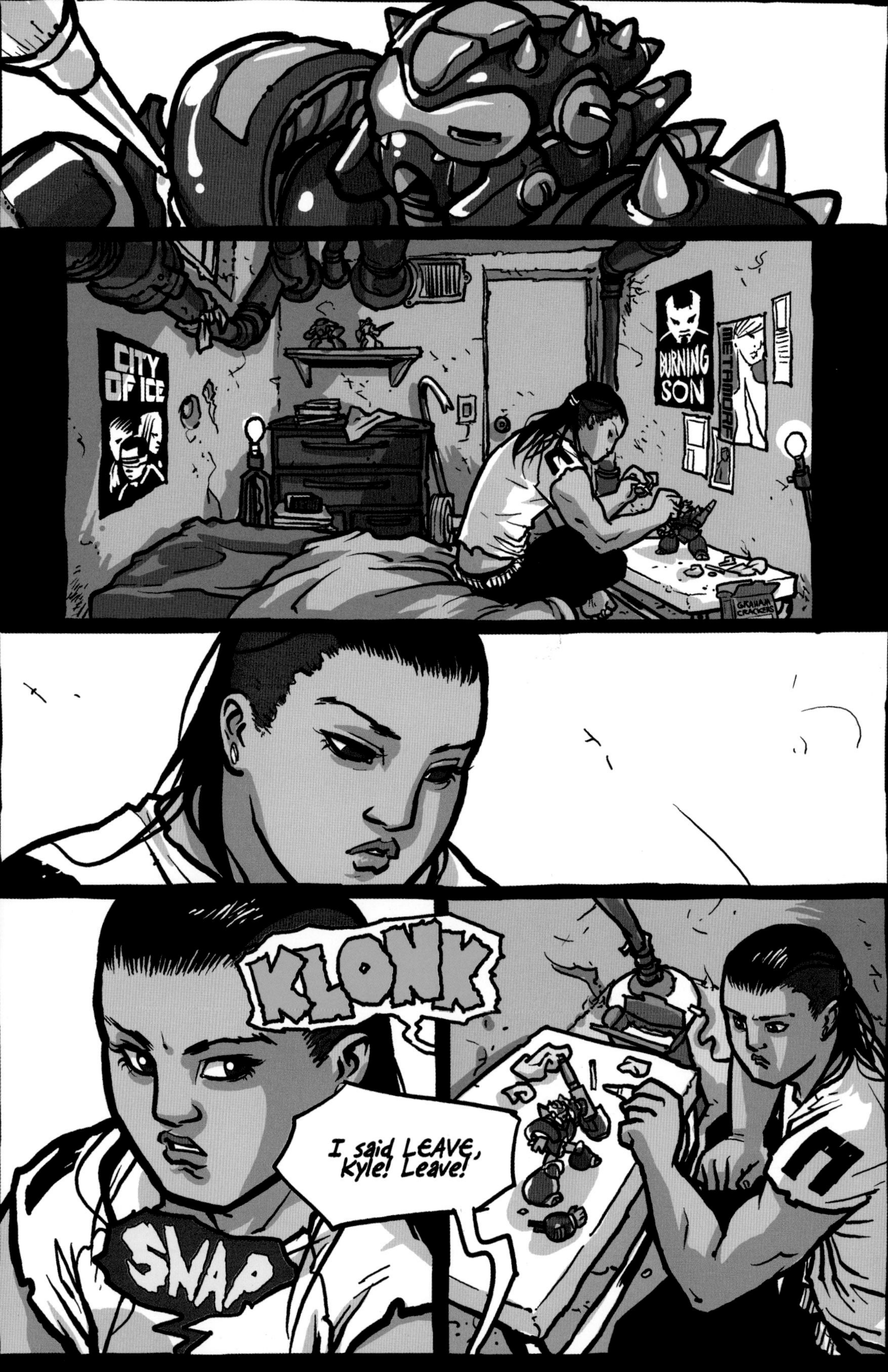
CITY OF ICE
BURNING SON
METAMORF
GRAHAM CRACKERS
KLONK
I said LEAVE, Kyle! Leave!
SNAP

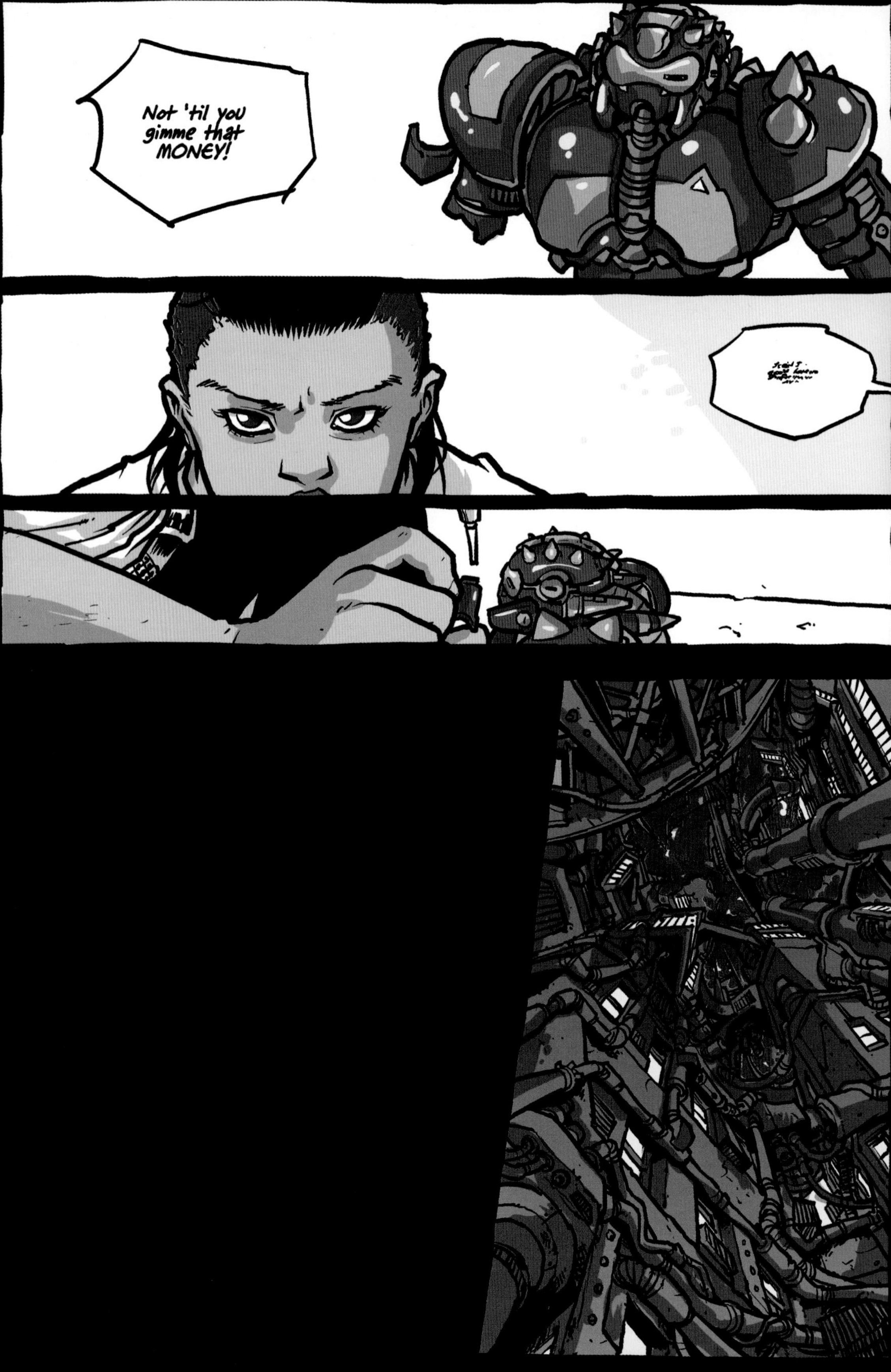
Not 'til you gimme that MONEY!

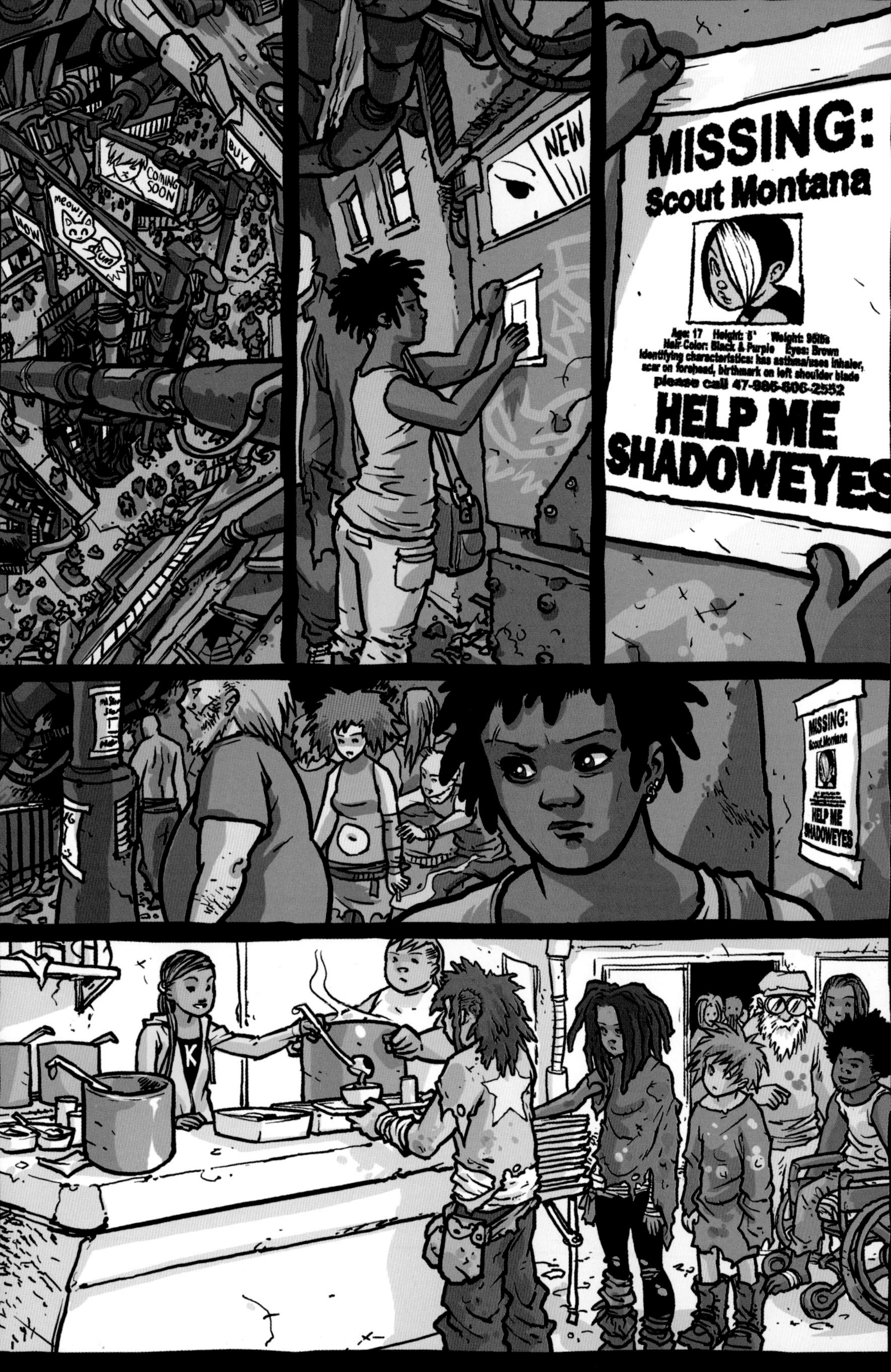
BUY
COMING SOON
MEOW!
NOW
YUM
NEW
MISSING:
Scout Montana
Age: 17 Height: 5' Weight: 95lbs
Hair Color: Black & Purple Eyes: Brown
Identifying characteristics: has asthma/uses inhaler, scar on forehead, birthmark on left shoulder blade
please call 47-986-606-2552
HELP ME
SHADOWEYES
MISSING:
Scout Montana
HELP ME
SHADOWEYES
K

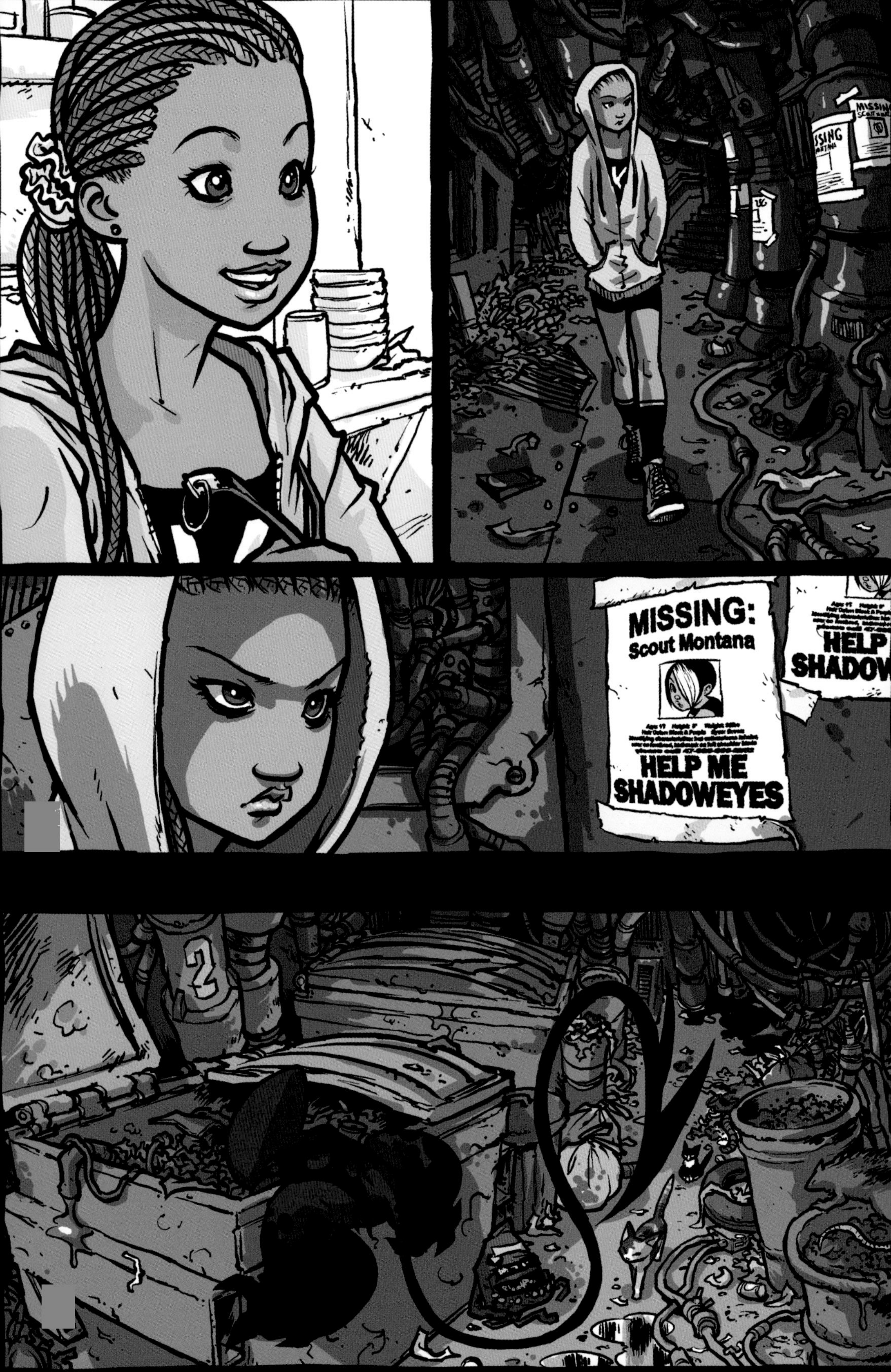
MISSING:
Scout Montana
HELP ME
SHADOWEYES

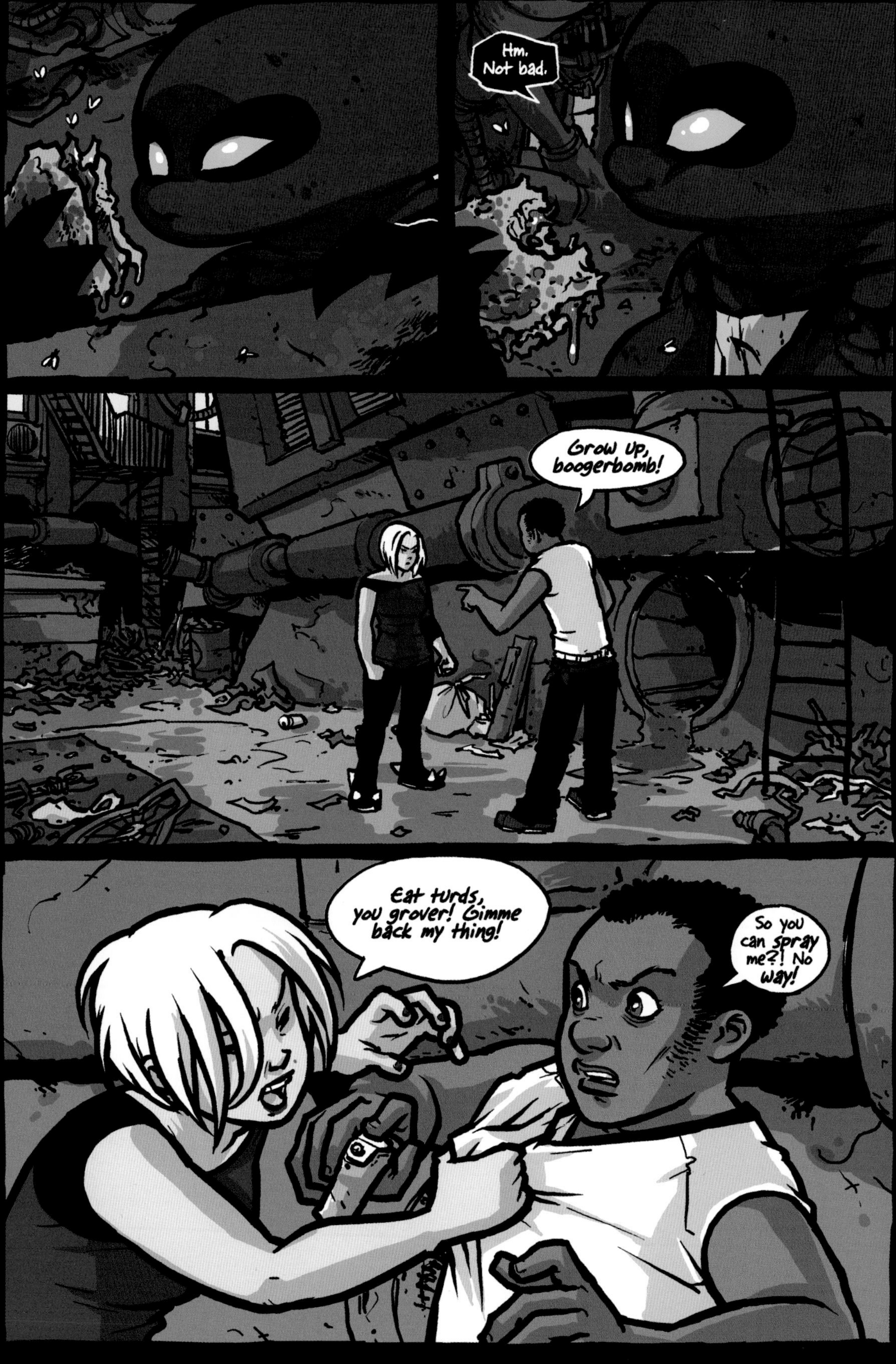
Hm. Not bad.
Grow up, boogerbomb!
Eat turds, you grover! Gimme back my thing!
So you can spray me?! No way!

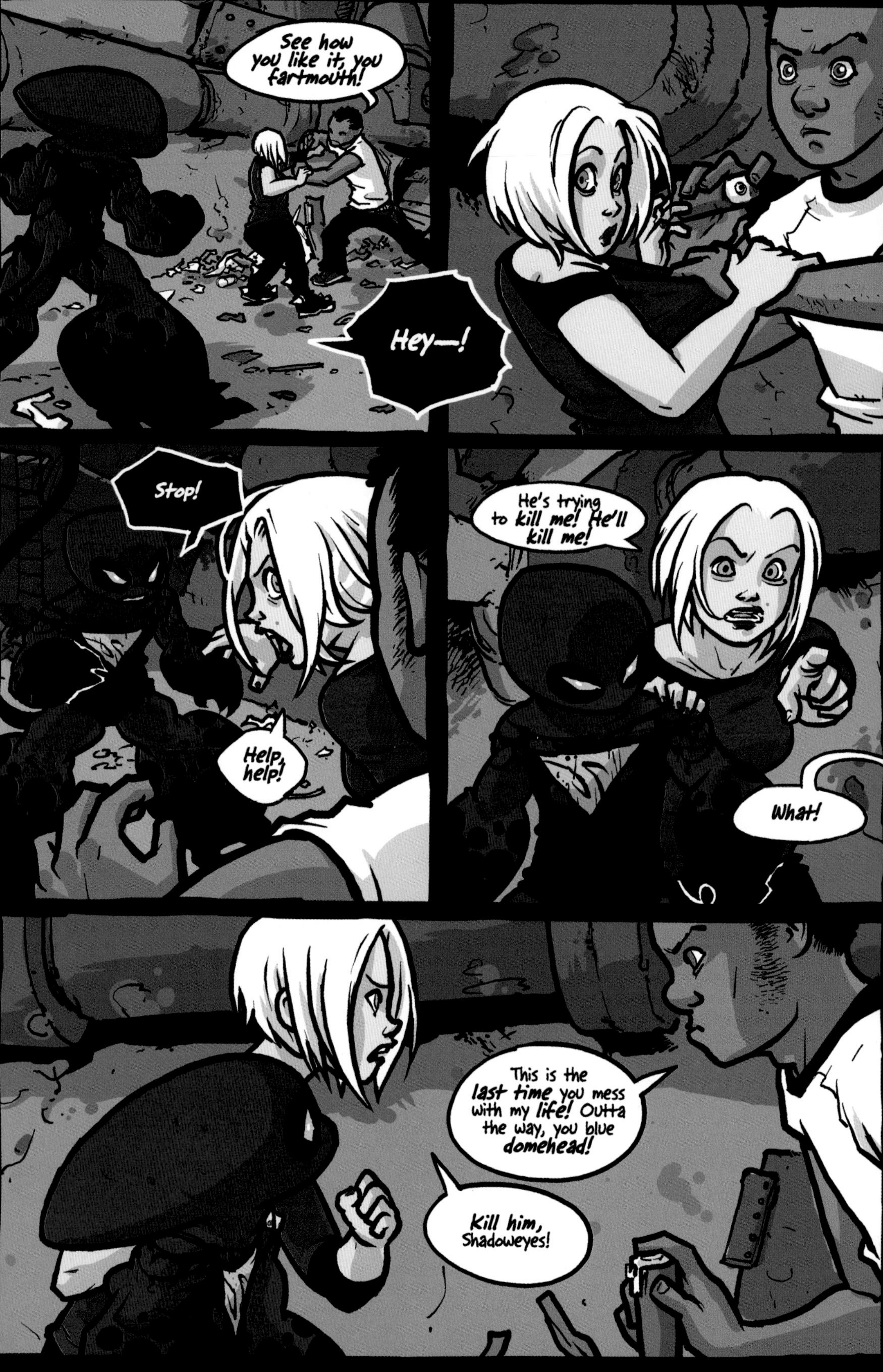
See how you like it, you fartmouth!
Hey—!
Stop!
Help, help!
He's trying to kill me! He'll kill me!
What!
This is the last time you mess with my life! Outta the way, you blue domehead!
Kill him, Shadoweyes!

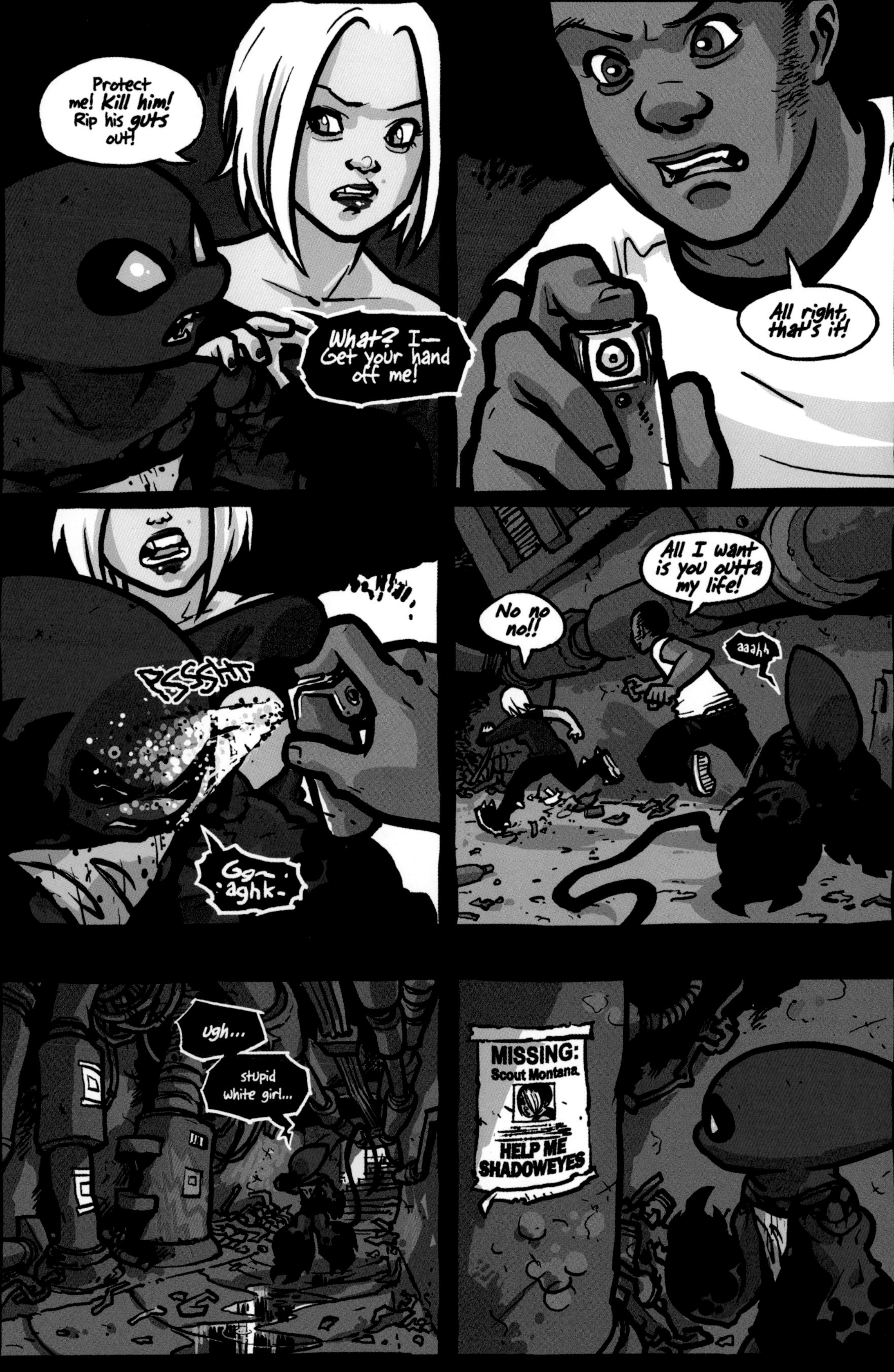
Protect me! Kill him! Rip his guts out!
What? I— Get your hand off me!
All right, that's it!
PSSSHT
Gg-aghk-
All I want is you outta my life!
No no no!!
aaahh
ugh...
stupid white girl...
MISSING:
Scout Montana
HELP ME SHADOWEYES

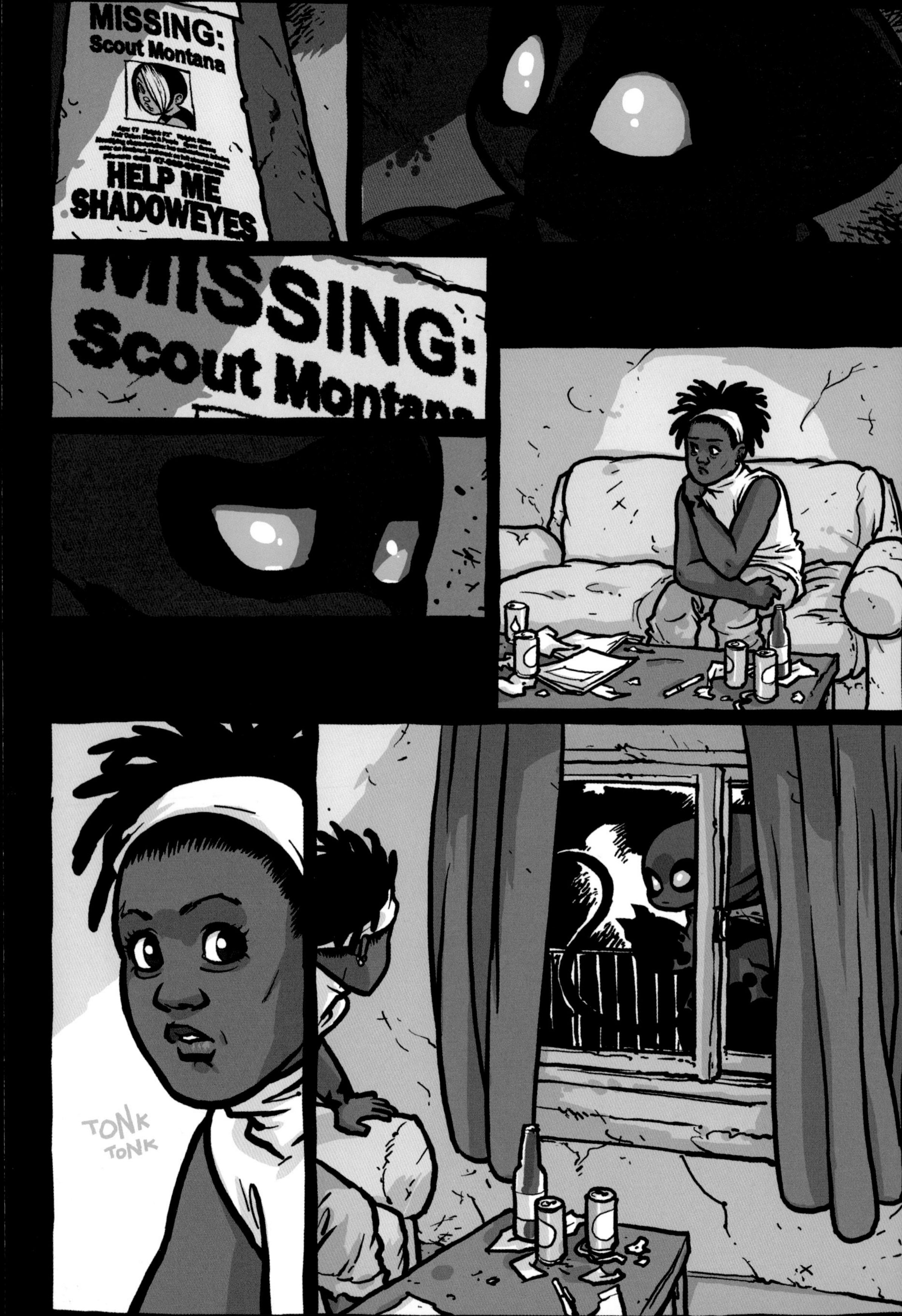
MISSING:
Scout Montana
HELP ME
SHADOWEYES
MISSING:
Scout Montana
TONK
TONK

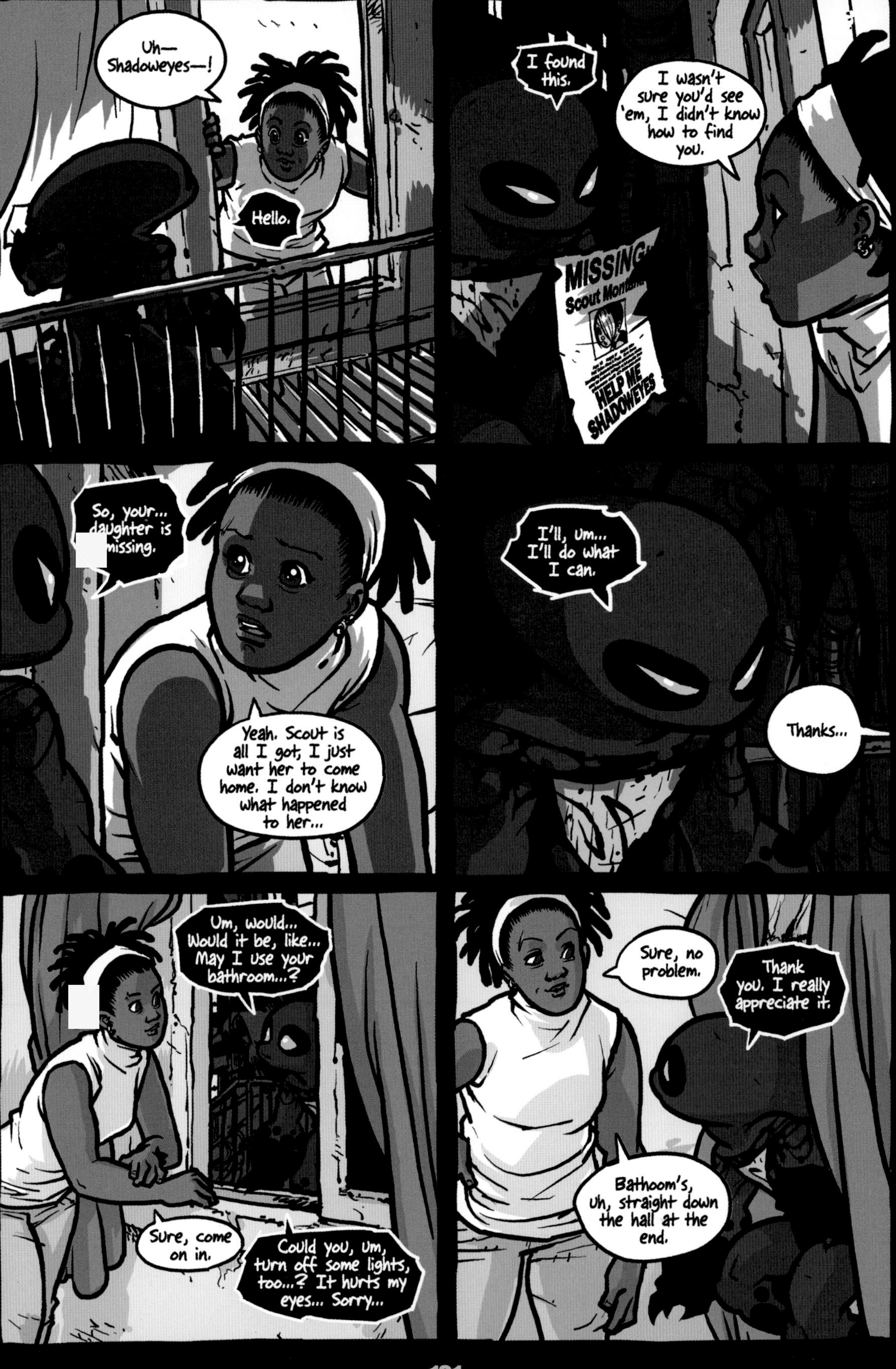
Uh— Shadoweyes—!
Hello.
I found this.
I wasn't sure you'd see 'em, I didn't know how to find you.
MISSING
HELP ME SHADOWEYES
So, your... daughter is missing.
Yeah. Scout is all I got, I just want her to come home. I don't know what happened to her...
I'll, um... I'll do what I can.
Thanks...
Um, would... Would it be, like... May I use your bathroom...?
Sure, come on in.
Could you, um, turn off some lights, too...? It hurts my eyes... Sorry...
Sure, no problem.
Thank you. I really appreciate it.
Bathoom's, uh, straight down the hall at the end.

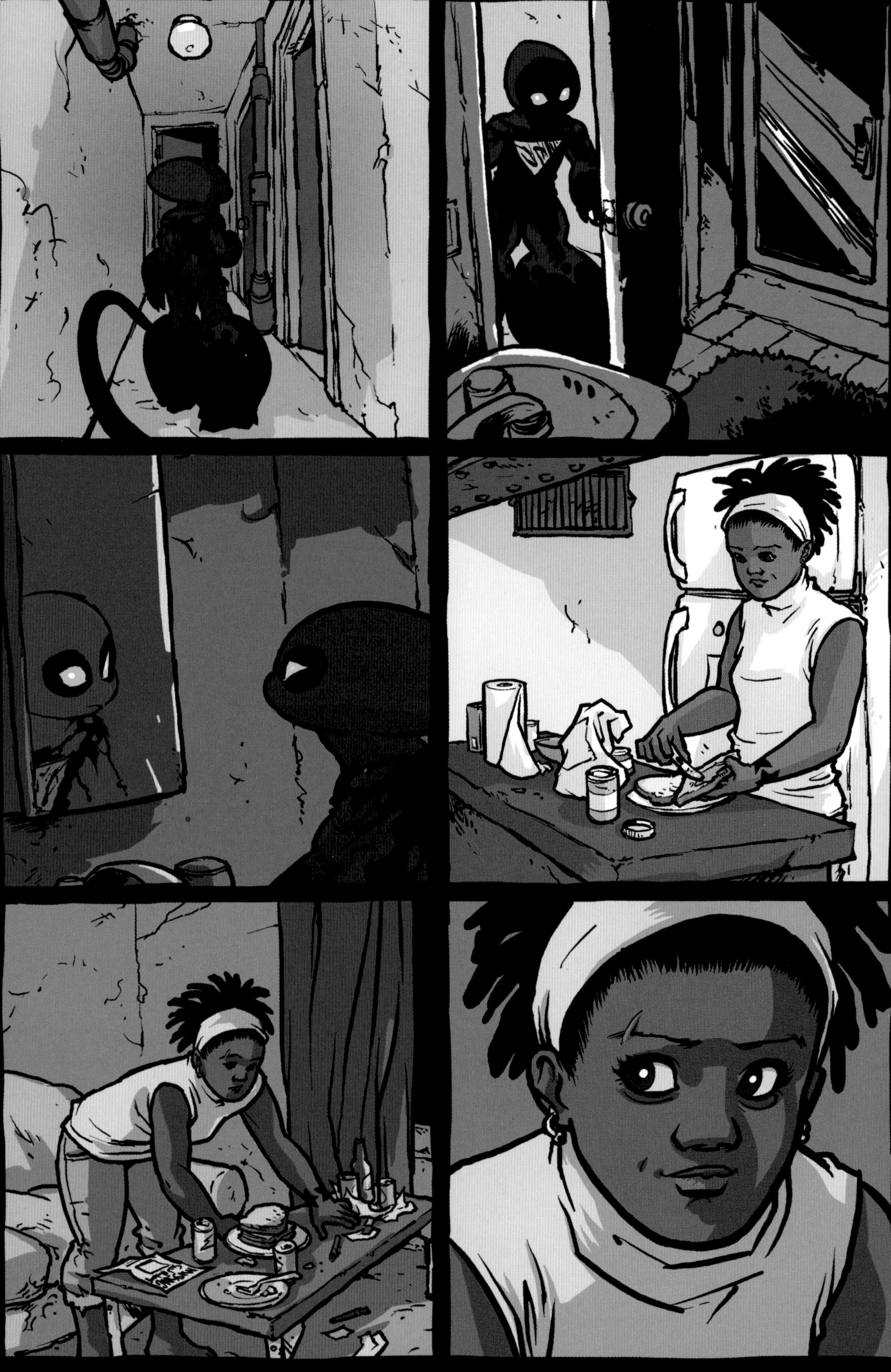

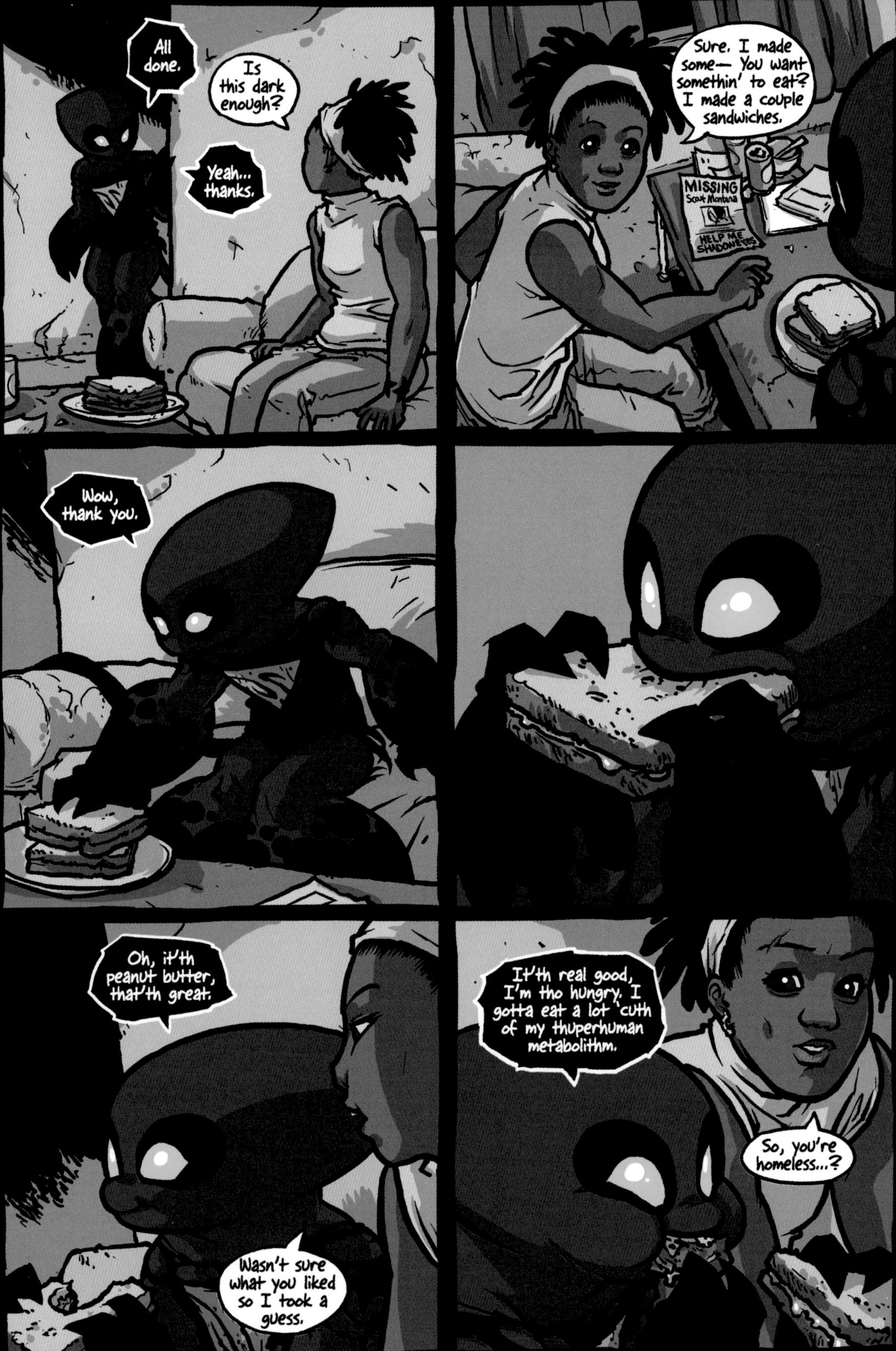
All done.
Is this dark enough?
Yeah... thanks.
Sure. I made some— You want somethin' to eat? I made a couple sandwiches.
MISSING Scout Montana
HELP ME SHADOWEYES
Wow, thank you.
Oh, it'th peanut butter, that'th great.
Wasn't sure what you liked so I took a guess.
It'th real good, I'm tho hungry. I gotta eat a lot 'cuth of my thuperhuman metabolithm.
So, you're homeless...?

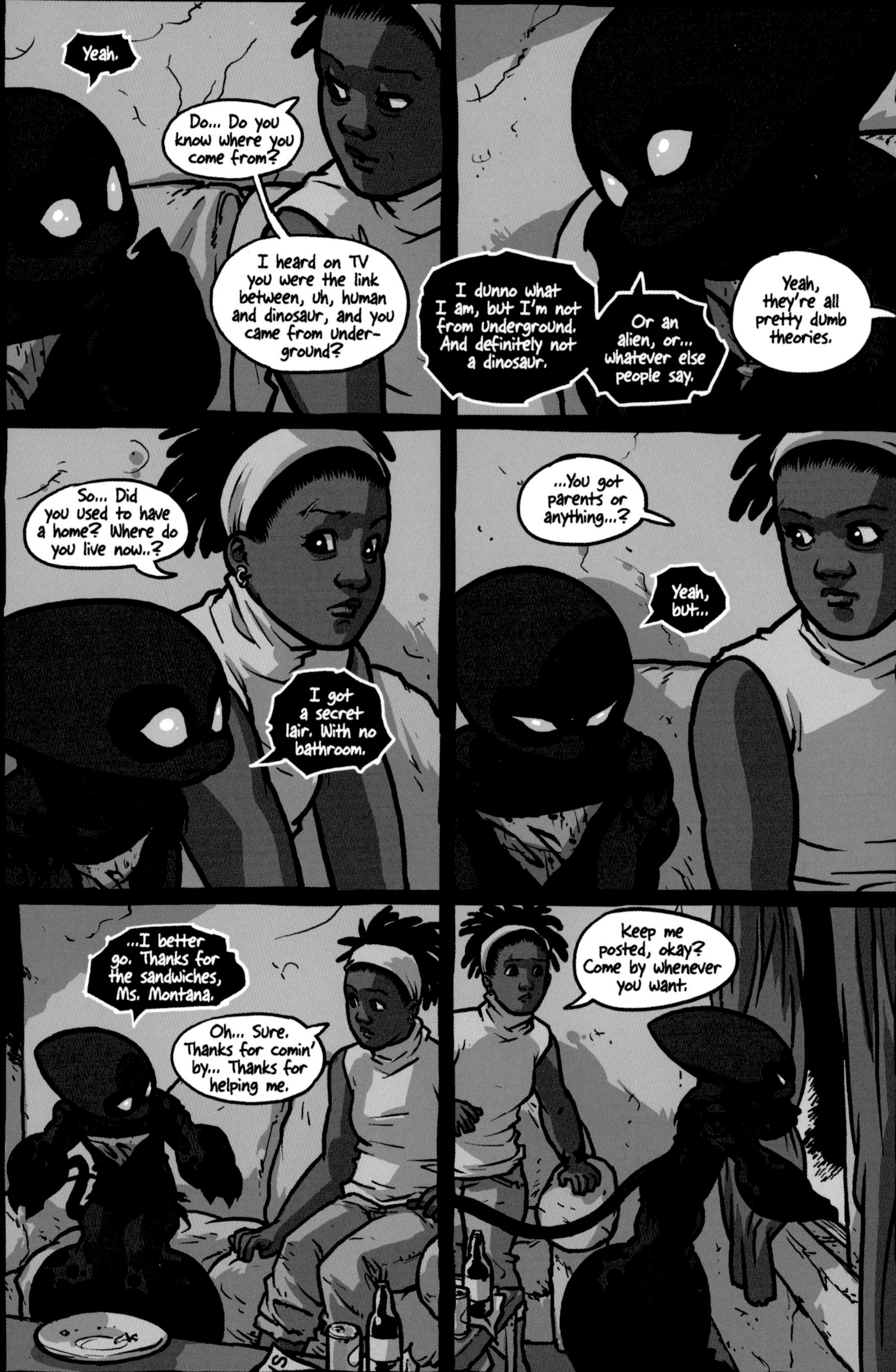
Yeah.
Do... Do you know where you come from?
I heard on TV you were the link between, uh, human and dinosaur, and you came from under-ground?
I dunno what I am, but I'm not from underground. And definitely not a dinosaur.
Or an alien, or... whatever else people say.
Yeah, they're all pretty dumb theories.
So... Did you used to have a home? Where do you live now..?
I got a secret lair. With no bathroom.
...You got parents or anything...?
Yeah, but...
...I better go. Thanks for the sandwiches, Ms. Montana.
Oh... Sure. Thanks for comin' by... Thanks for helping me.
Keep me posted, okay? Come by whenever you want.

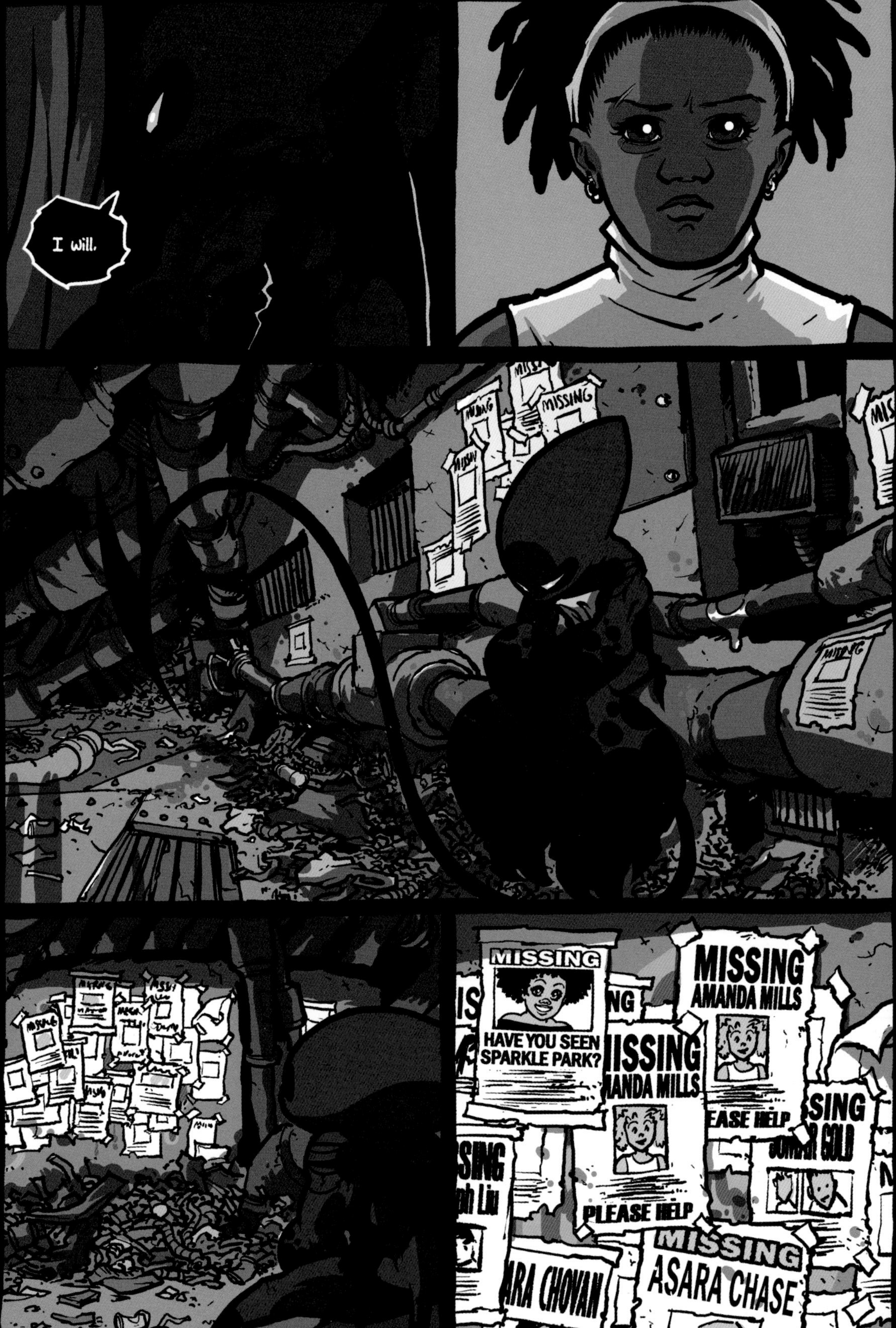
I will.
MISSING
MISSING
MISSING
HAVE YOU SEEN SPARKLE PARK?
MISSING
AMANDA MILLS
MISSING
ANDA MILLS
PLEASE HELP
PLEASE HELP
MISSING
ASARA CHASE
ARA CHOVAN

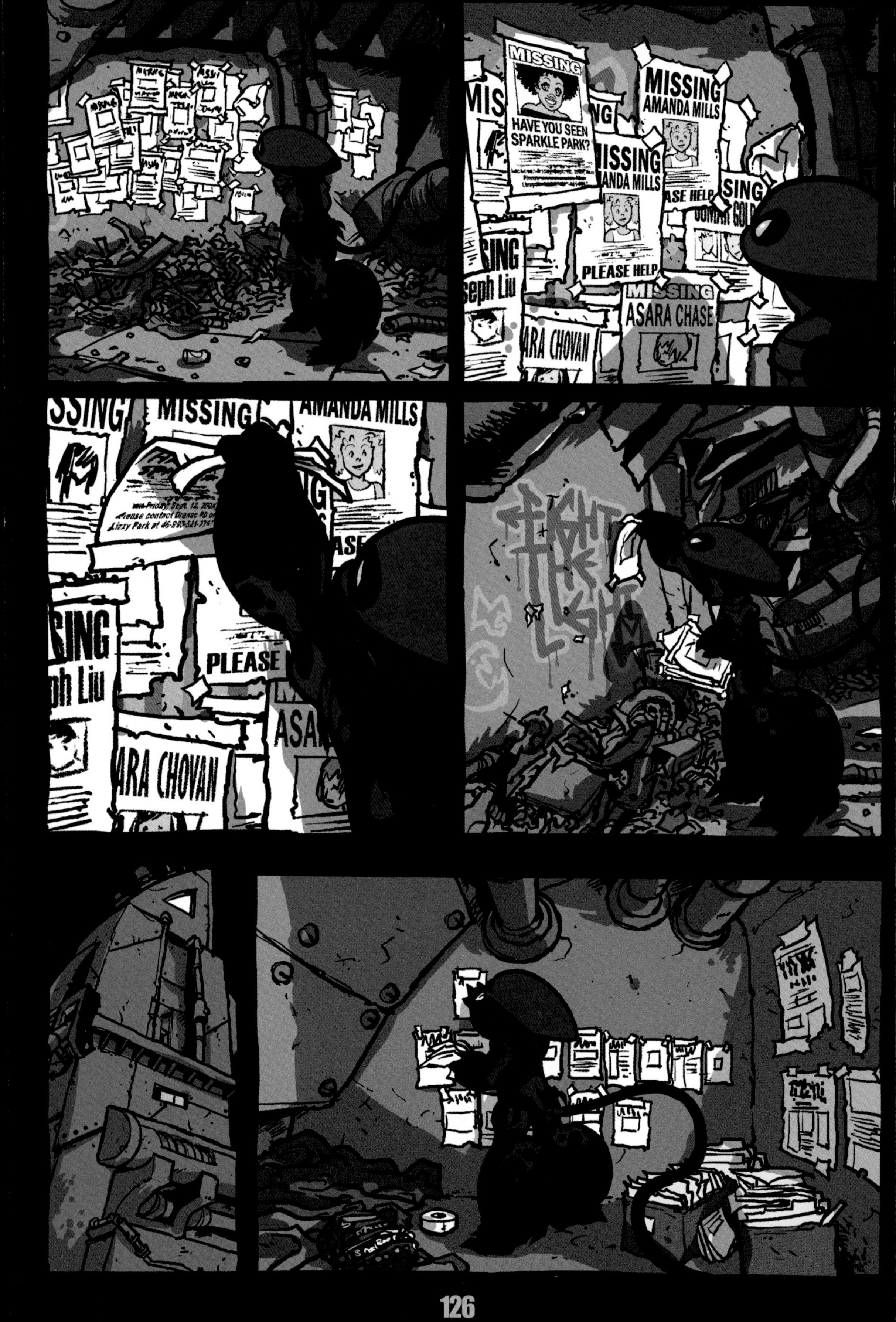
MISSING
HAVE YOU SEEN SPARKLE PARK?
MISSING
AMANDA MILLS
MISSING
PLEASE HELP
MISSING
ASARA CHASE
ARA CHOVAN
eph Liu
MISSING
AMANDA MILLS
Friday, Sept. 12, 20XX
Please contact Orange PD or
Lizzy Park at
PLEASE
ASA
ARA CHOVAN
ph Liu

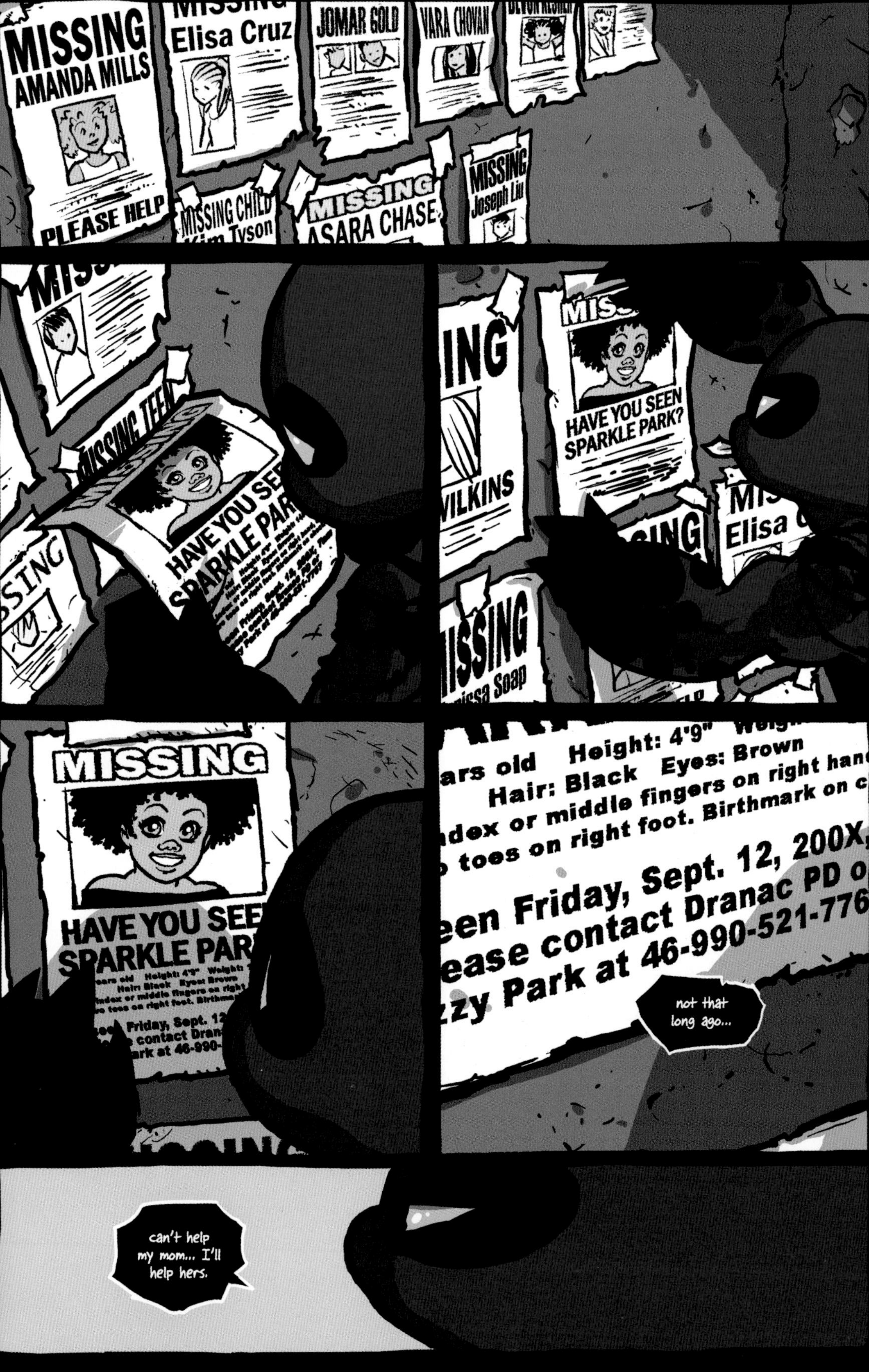
MISSING
AMANDA MILLS
PLEASE HELP
MISSING
Elisa Cruz
JOMAR GOLD
VARA CHOVAN
MISSING CHILD
MISSING
ASARA CHASE
MISSING
Joseph Liu
HAVE YOU SEEN
SPARKLE PARK?
WILKINS
MISSING
HAVE YOU SEE
SPARKLE PAR
Height: 4'9"
Hair: Black Eyes: Brown
Friday, Sept. 12, 200X,
Please contact Dranac PD o
Park at 46-990-521-776
not that long ago...
can't help my mom... I'll help hers.

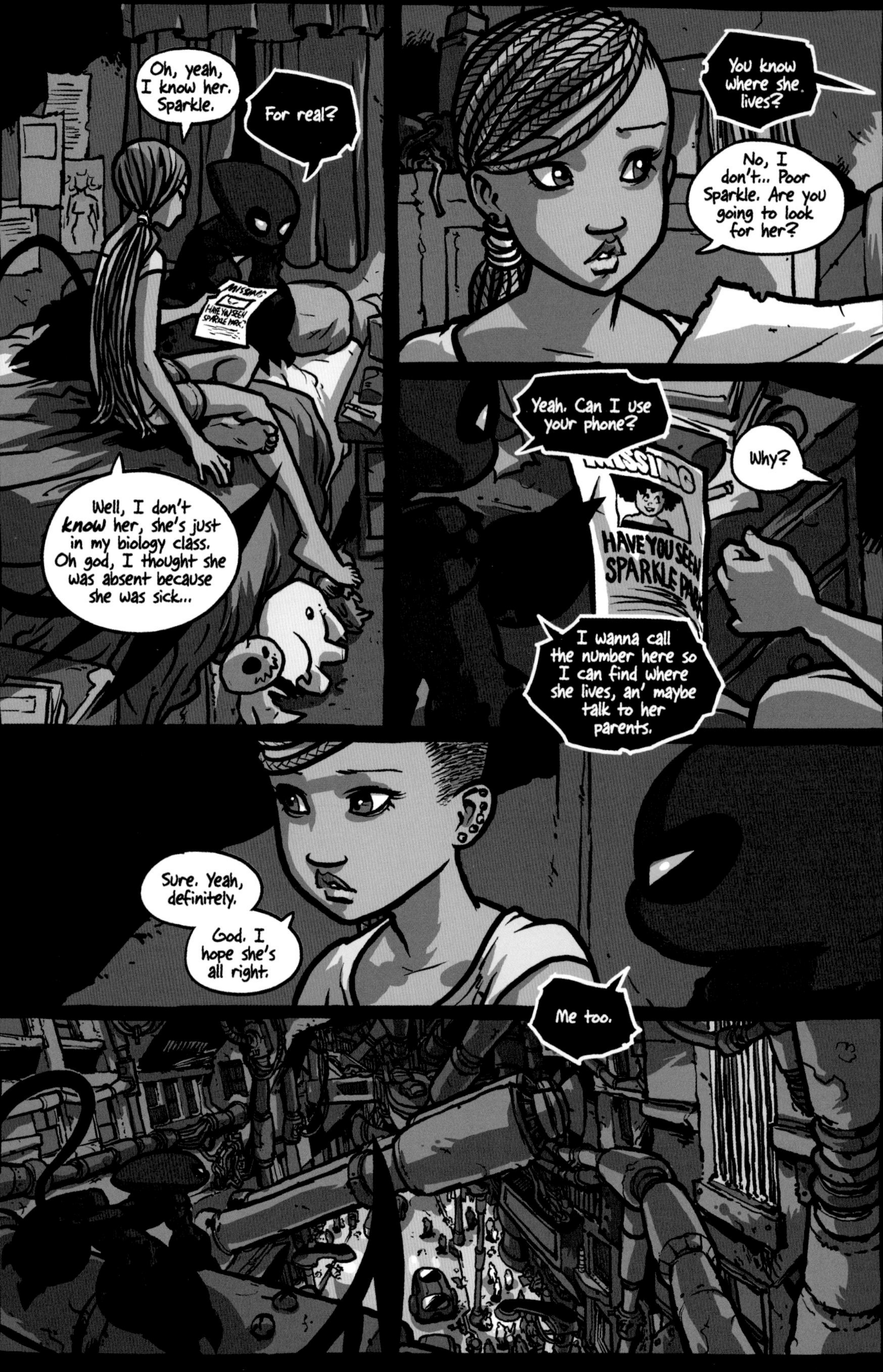
Oh, yeah, I know her. Sparkle.
For real?
Well, I don't **know** her, she's just in my biology class. Oh god, I thought she was absent because she was sick...
You know where she lives?
No, I don't... Poor Sparkle. Are you going to look for her?
Yeah. Can I use your phone?
Why?
I wanna call the number here so I can find where she lives, an' maybe talk to her parents.
Sure. Yeah, definitely.
God. I hope she's all right.
Me too.

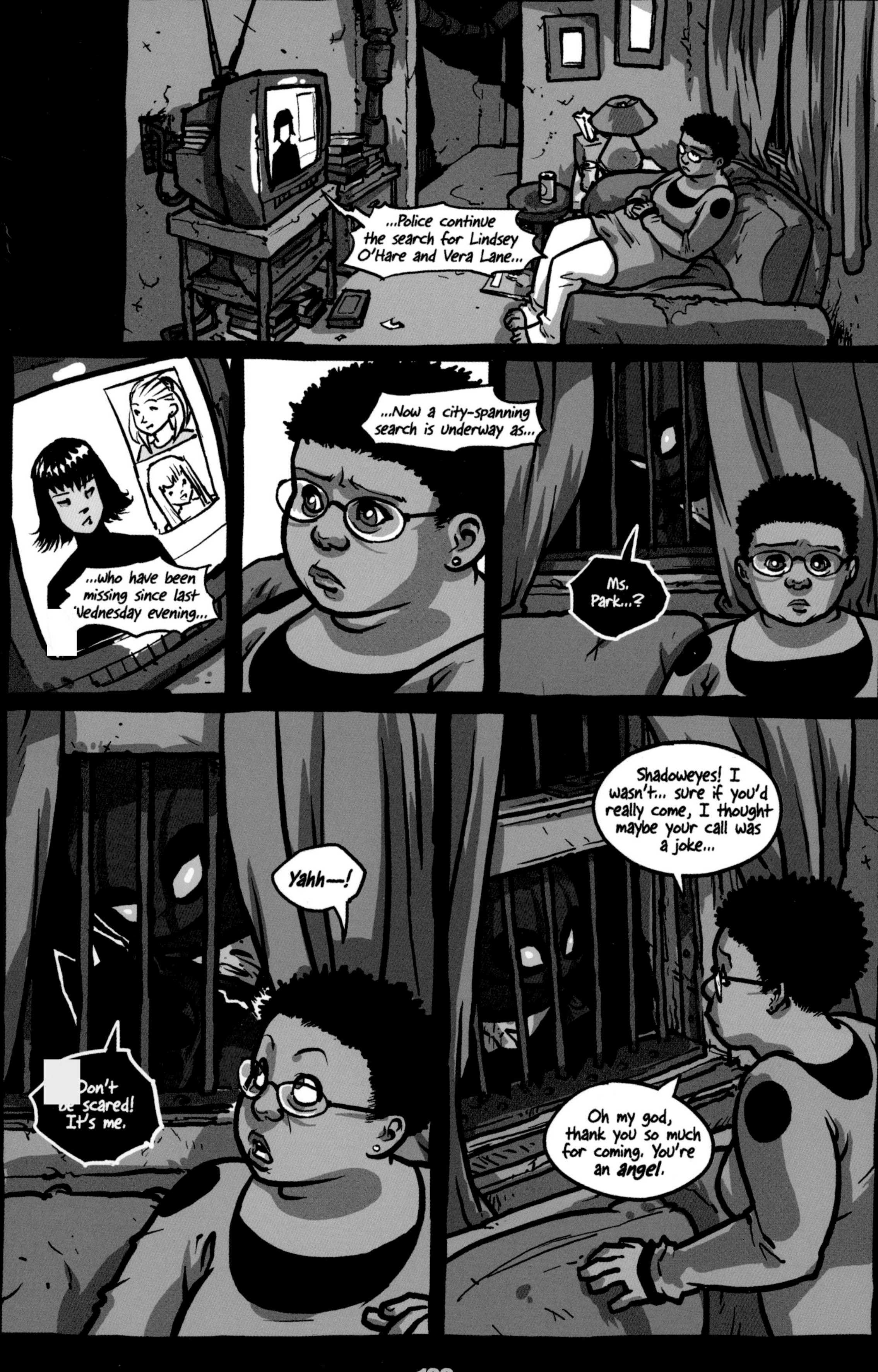
...Police continue the search for Lindsey O'Hare and Vera Lane...
...who have been missing since last Wednesday evening...
...Now a city-spanning search is underway as...
Ms. Park...?
Don't be scared! It's me.
Yahh—!
Shadoweyes! I wasn't... sure if you'd really come, I thought maybe your call was a joke...
Oh my god, thank you so much for coming. You're an *angel*.

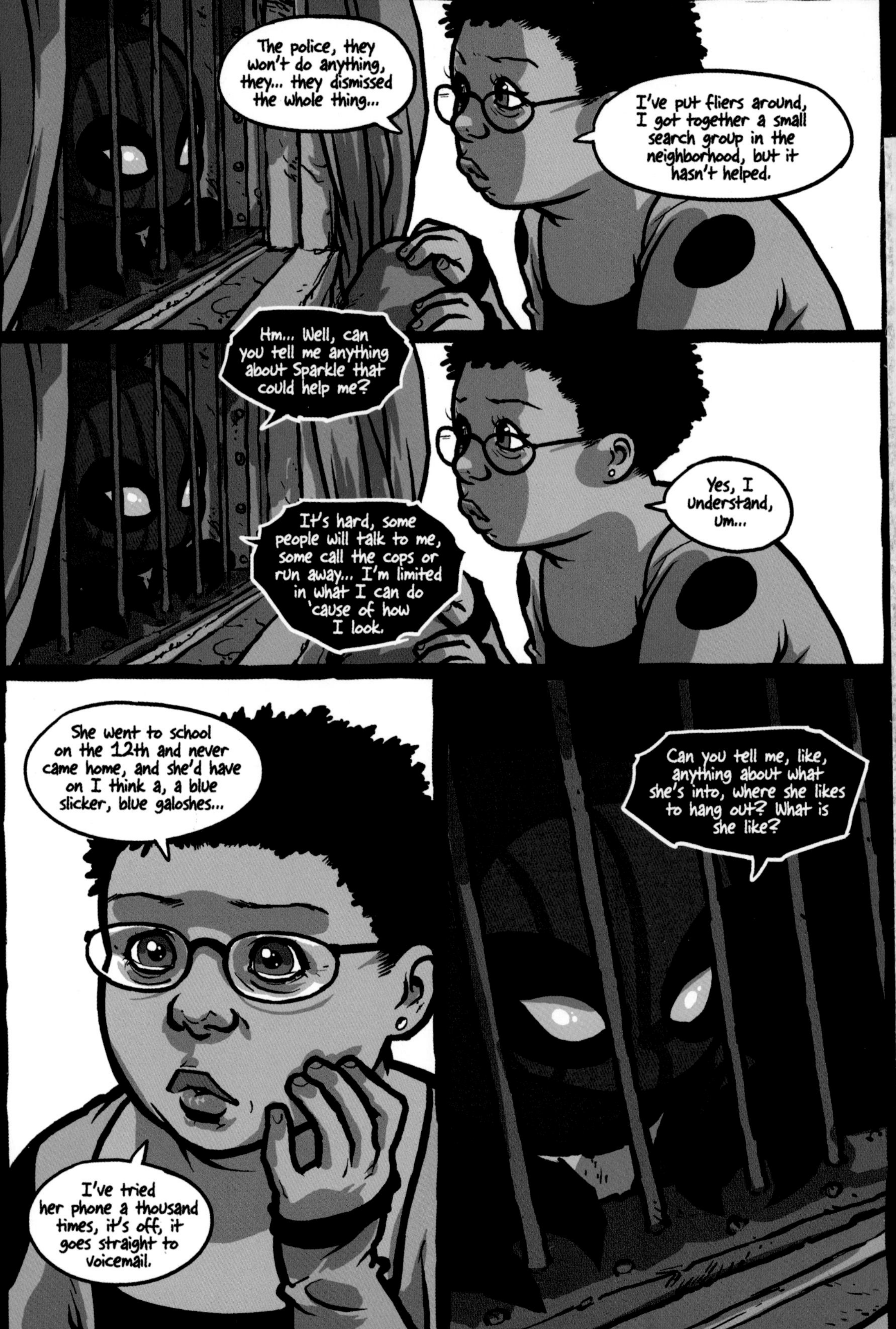
The police, they won't do anything, they... they dismissed the whole thing...
I've put fliers around, I got together a small search group in the neighborhood, but it hasn't helped.
Hm... Well, can you tell me anything about Sparkle that could help me?
Yes, I understand, um...
It's hard, some people will talk to me, some call the cops or run away... I'm limited in what I can do 'cause of how I look.
She went to school on the 12th and never came home, and she'd have on I think a, a blue slicker, blue galoshes...
Can you tell me, like, anything about what she's into, where she likes to hang out? What is she like?
I've tried her phone a thousand times, it's off, it goes straight to voicemail.

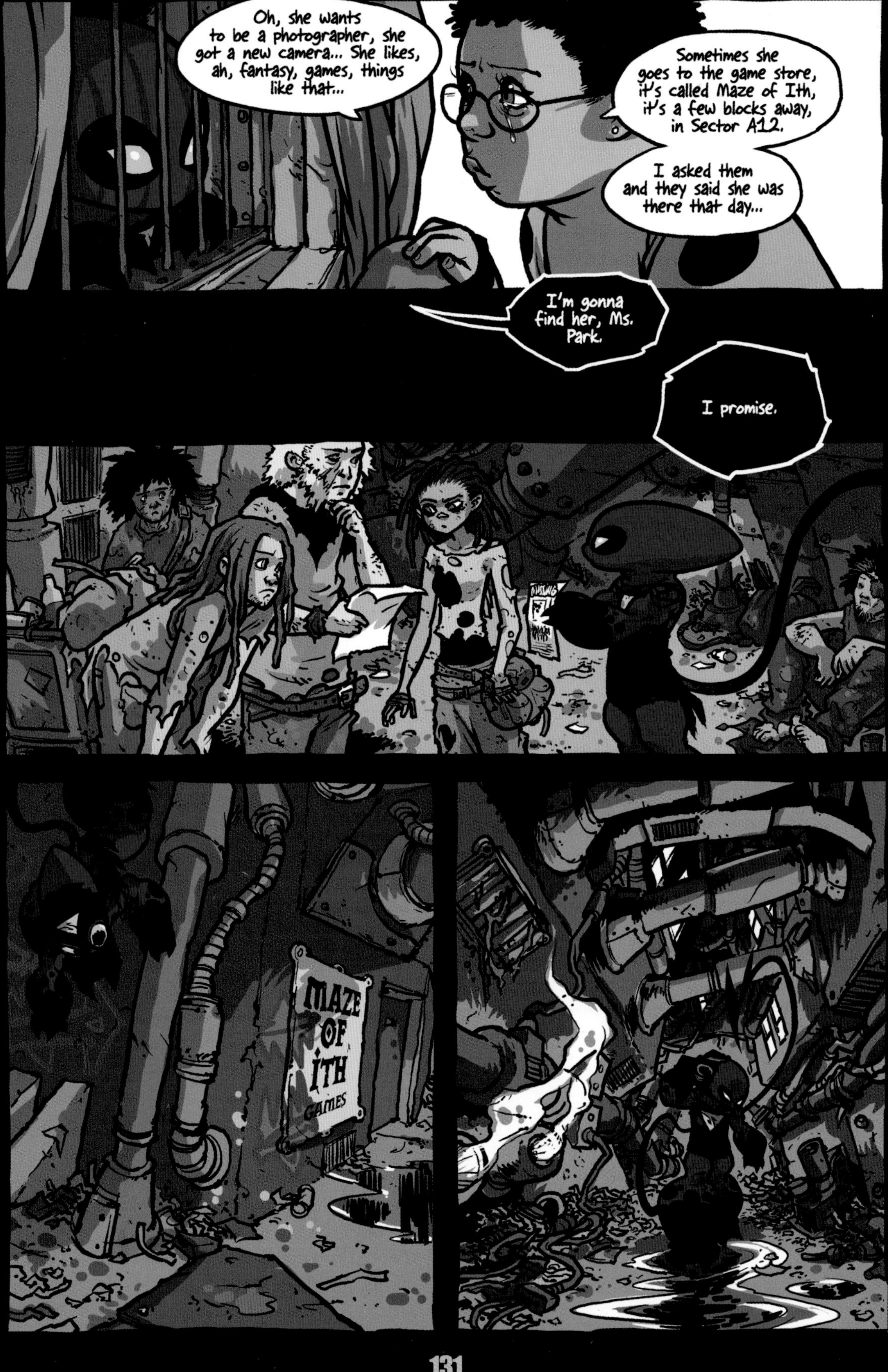
Oh, she wants to be a photographer, she got a new camera... She likes, ah, fantasy, games, things like that...
Sometimes she goes to the game store, it's called Maze of Ith, it's a few blocks away, in Sector A12.
I asked them and they said she was there that day...
I'm gonna find her, Ms. Park.
I promise.
MAZE OF ITH GAMES

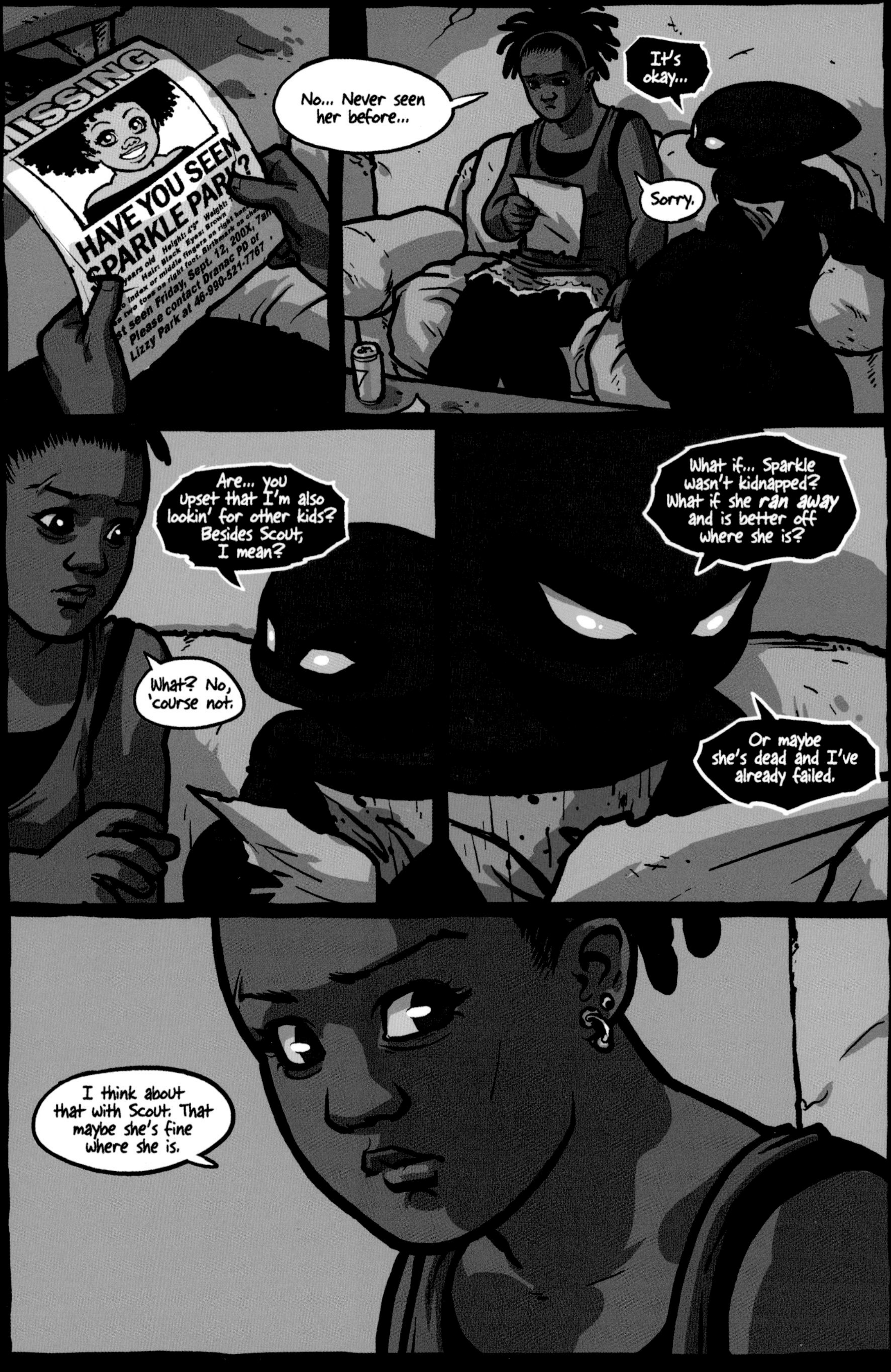
MISSING
HAVE YOU SEEN SPARKLE PARK?
No... Never seen her before...
It's okay...
Sorry.
Are... you upset that I'm also lookin' for other kids? Besides Scout, I mean?
What? No, 'course not.
What if... Sparkle wasn't kidnapped? What if she ran away and is better off where she is?
Or maybe she's dead and I've already failed.
I think about that with Scout. That maybe she's fine where she is.

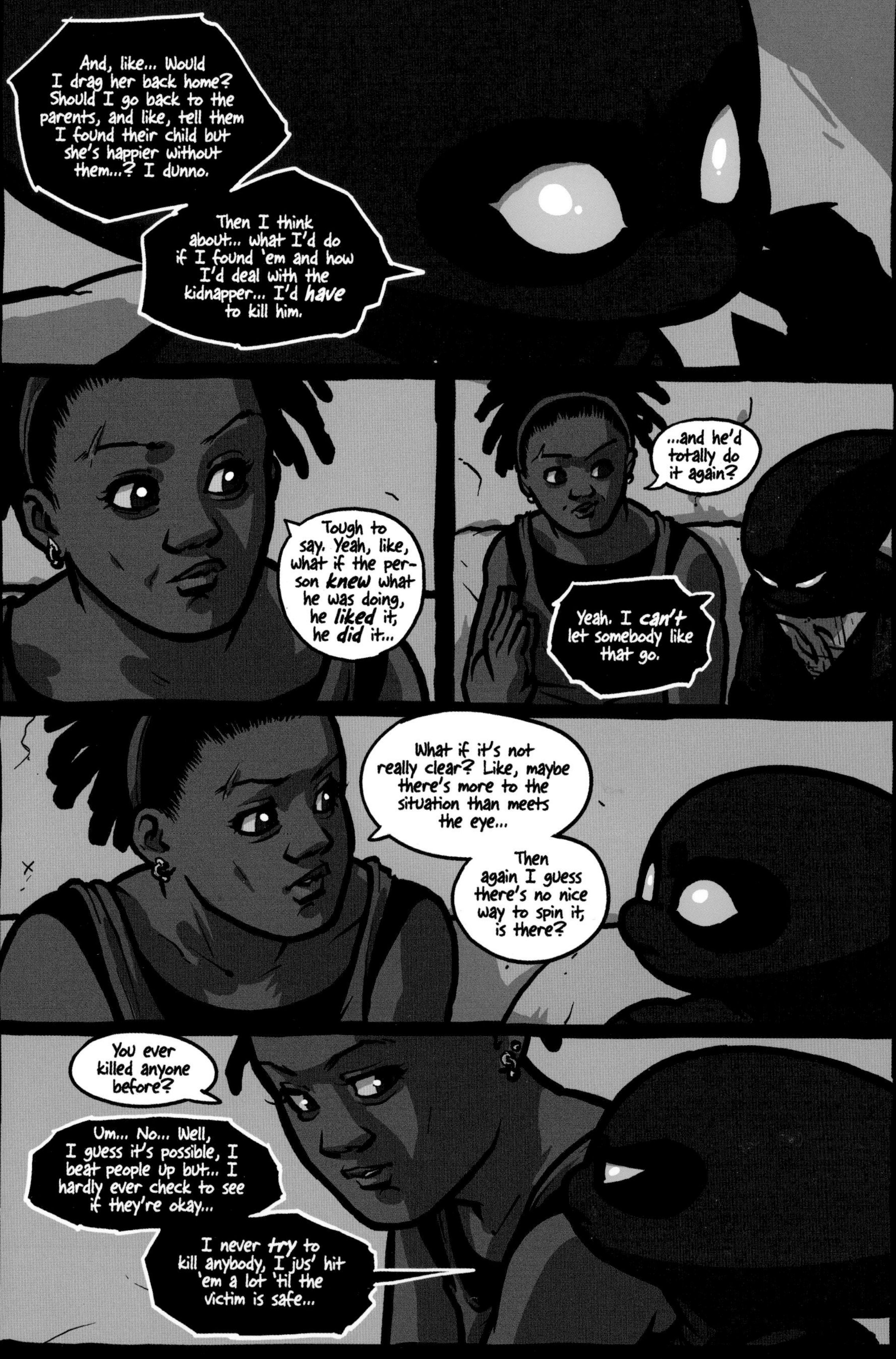

And, like... Would I drag her back home? Should I go back to the parents, and like, tell them I found their child but she's happier without them...? I dunno.
Then I think about... what I'd do if I found 'em and how I'd deal with the kidnapper... I'd *have* to kill him.
Tough to say. Yeah, like, what if the person *knew* what he was doing, he *liked* it, he *did* it...
...and he'd totally do it again?
Yeah. I *can't* let somebody like that go.
What if it's not really clear? Like, maybe there's more to the situation than meets the eye...
Then again I guess there's no nice way to spin it, is there?
You ever killed anyone before?
Um... No... Well, I guess it's possible, I beat people up but... I hardly ever check to see if they're okay...
I never *try* to kill anybody, I jus' hit 'em a lot 'til the victim is safe...

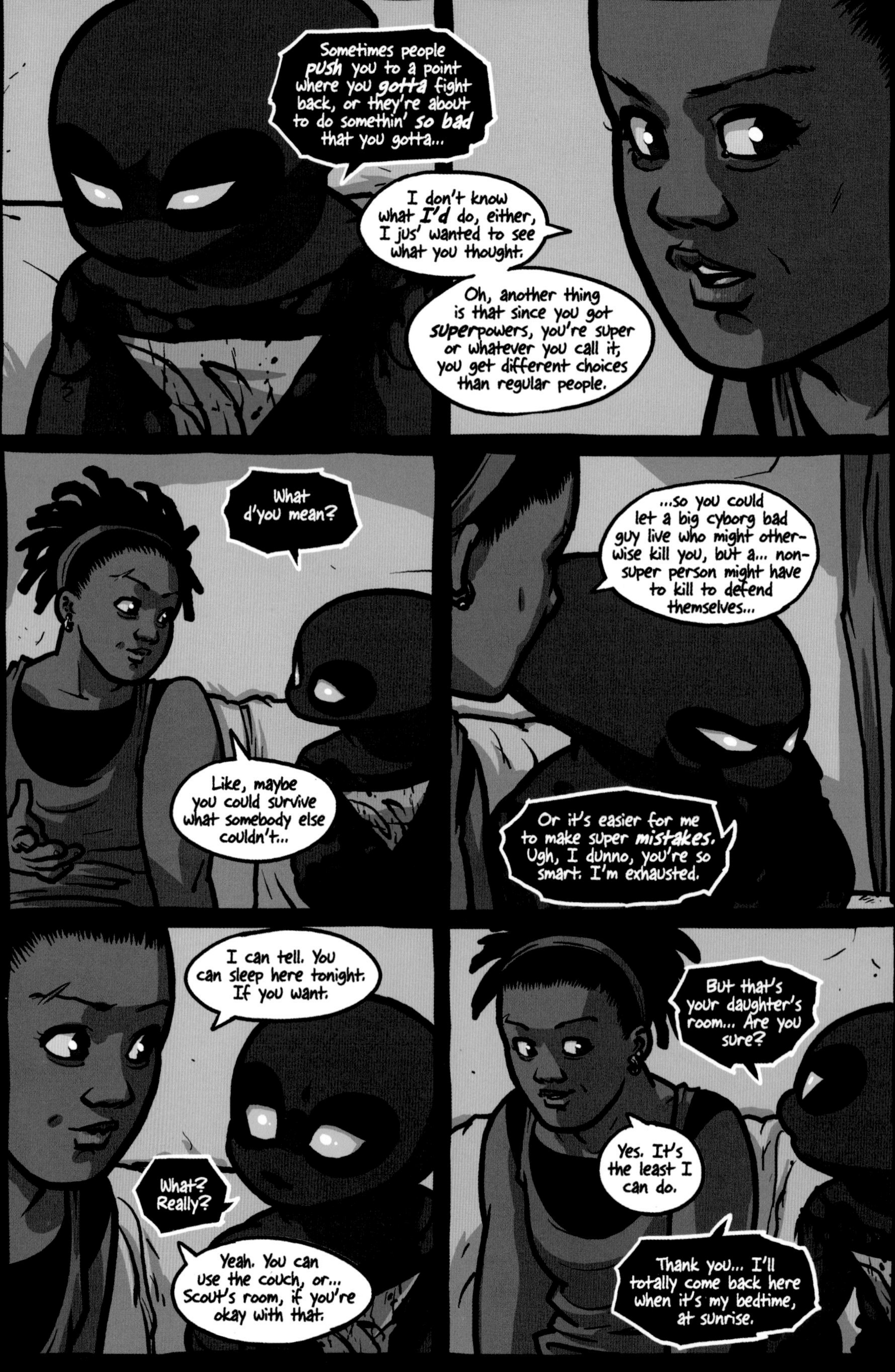

Sometimes people push you to a point where you gotta fight back, or they're about to do somethin' so bad that you gotta...
I don't know what I'd do, either, I jus' wanted to see what you thought.
Oh, another thing is that since you got superpowers, you're super or whatever you call it, you get different choices than regular people.
What d'you mean?
Like, maybe you could survive what somebody else couldn't...
...so you could let a big cyborg bad guy live who might otherwise kill you, but a... non-super person might have to kill to defend themselves...
Or it's easier for me to make super mistakes. Ugh, I dunno, you're so smart. I'm exhausted.
I can tell. You can sleep here tonight. If you want.
What? Really?
Yeah. You can use the couch, or... Scout's room, if you're okay with that.
But that's your daughter's room... Are you sure?
Yes. It's the least I can do.
Thank you... I'll totally come back here when it's my bedtime, at sunrise.

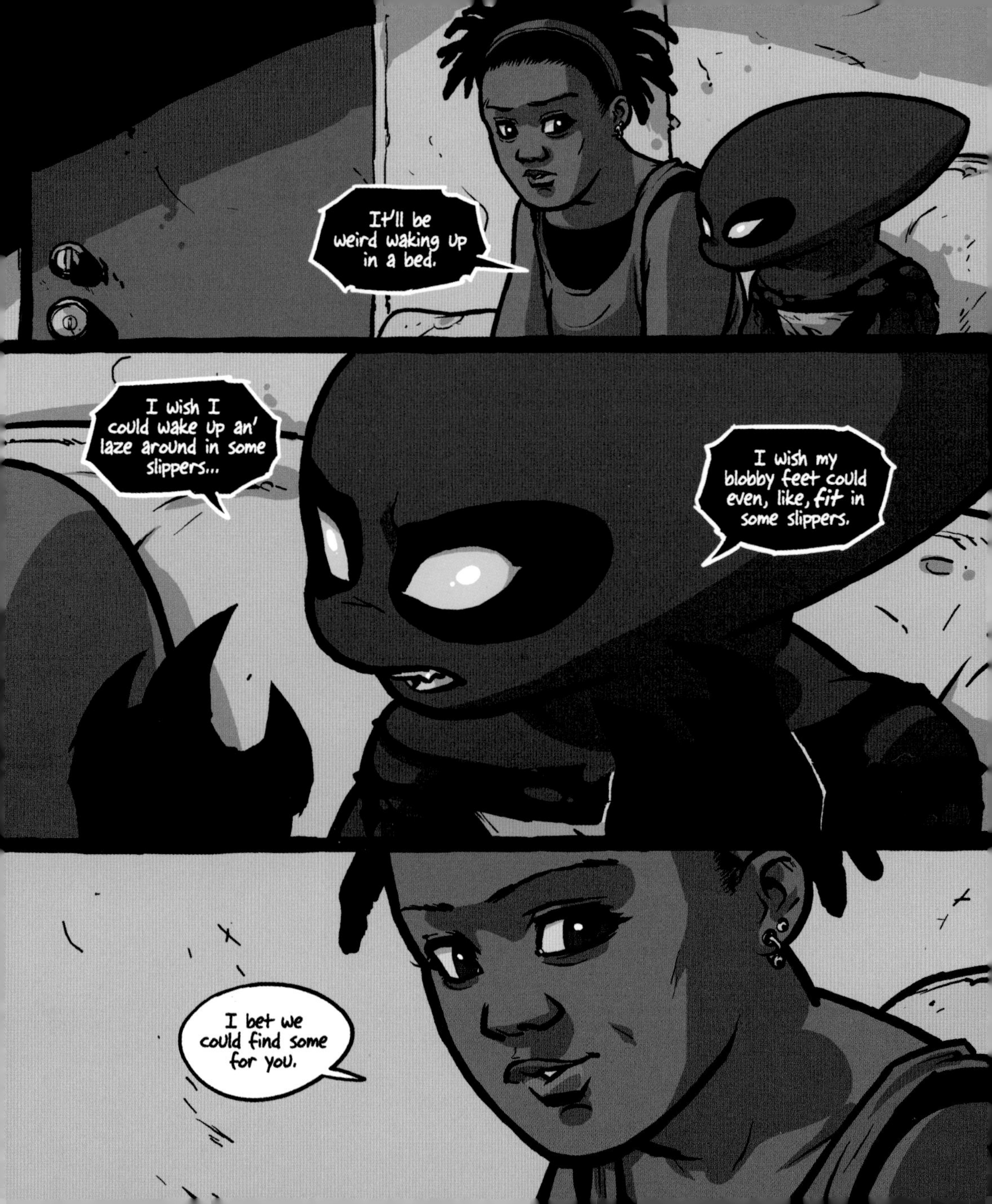
It'll be weird waking up in a bed.
I wish I could wake up an' laze around in some slippers...
I wish my blobby feet could even, like, fit in some slippers.
I bet we could find some for you.

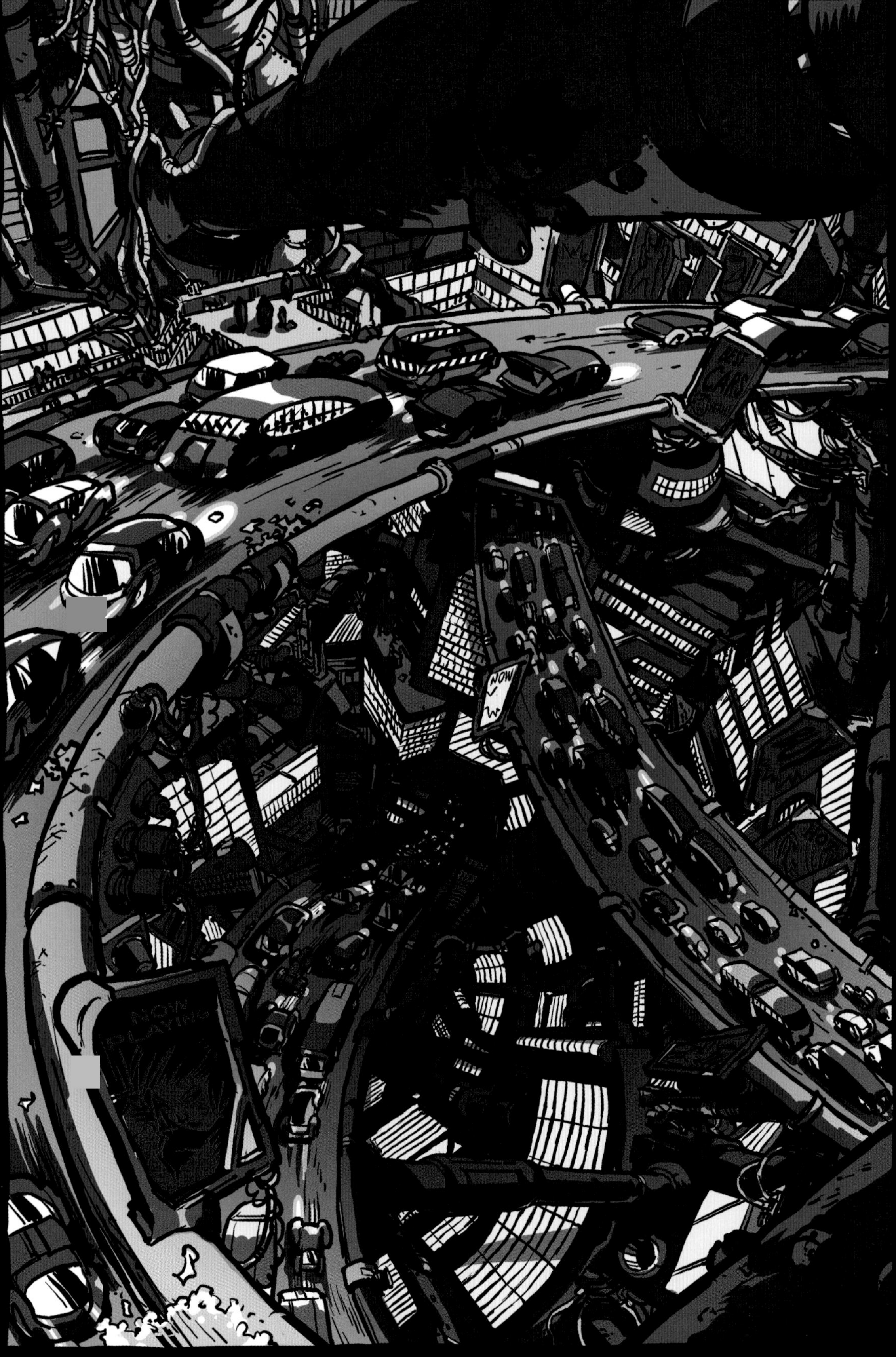
NOW
NOW PLAYING

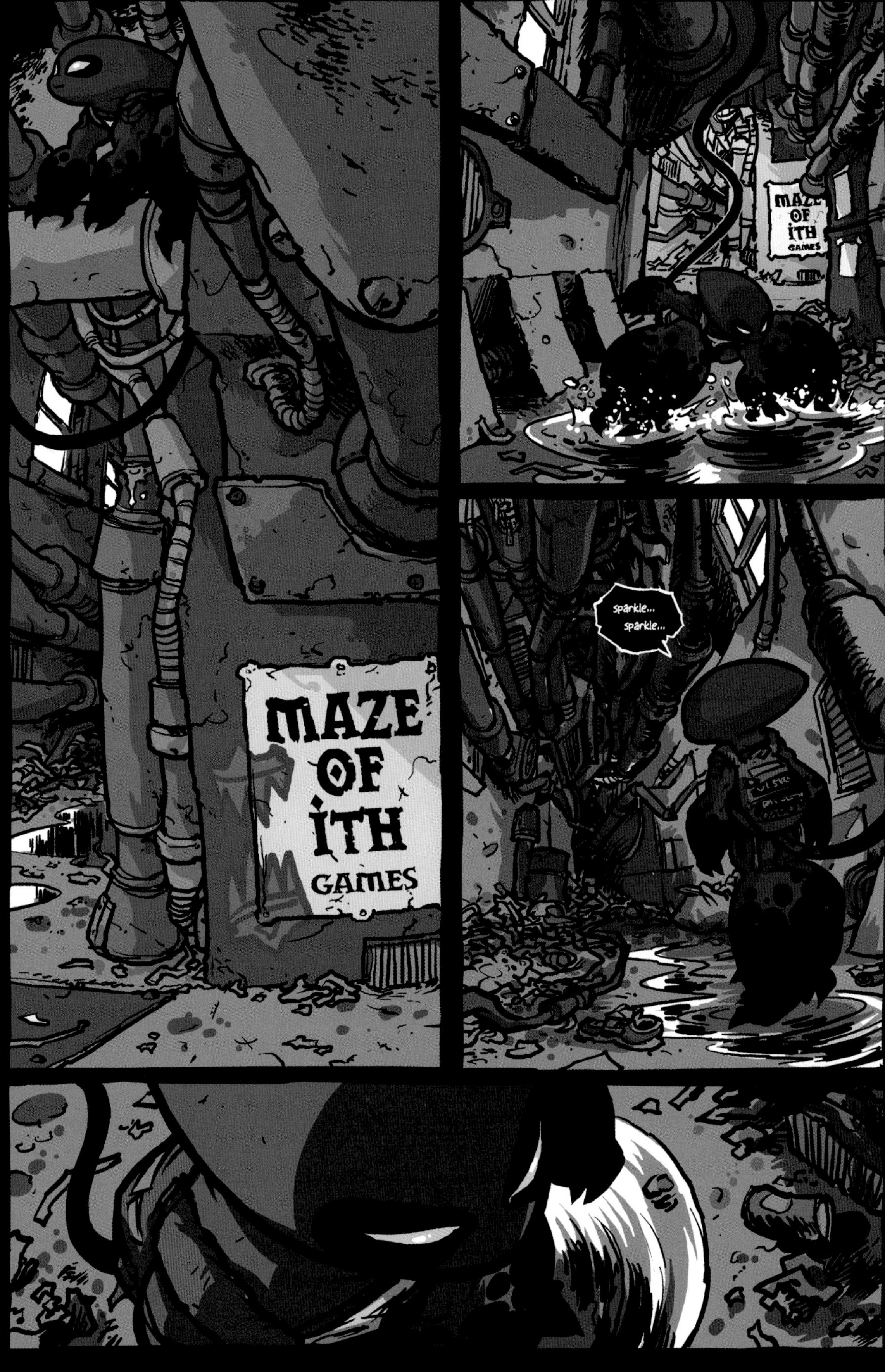
MAZE OF ITH GAMES
MAZE OF ITH GAMES
sparkle... sparkle...

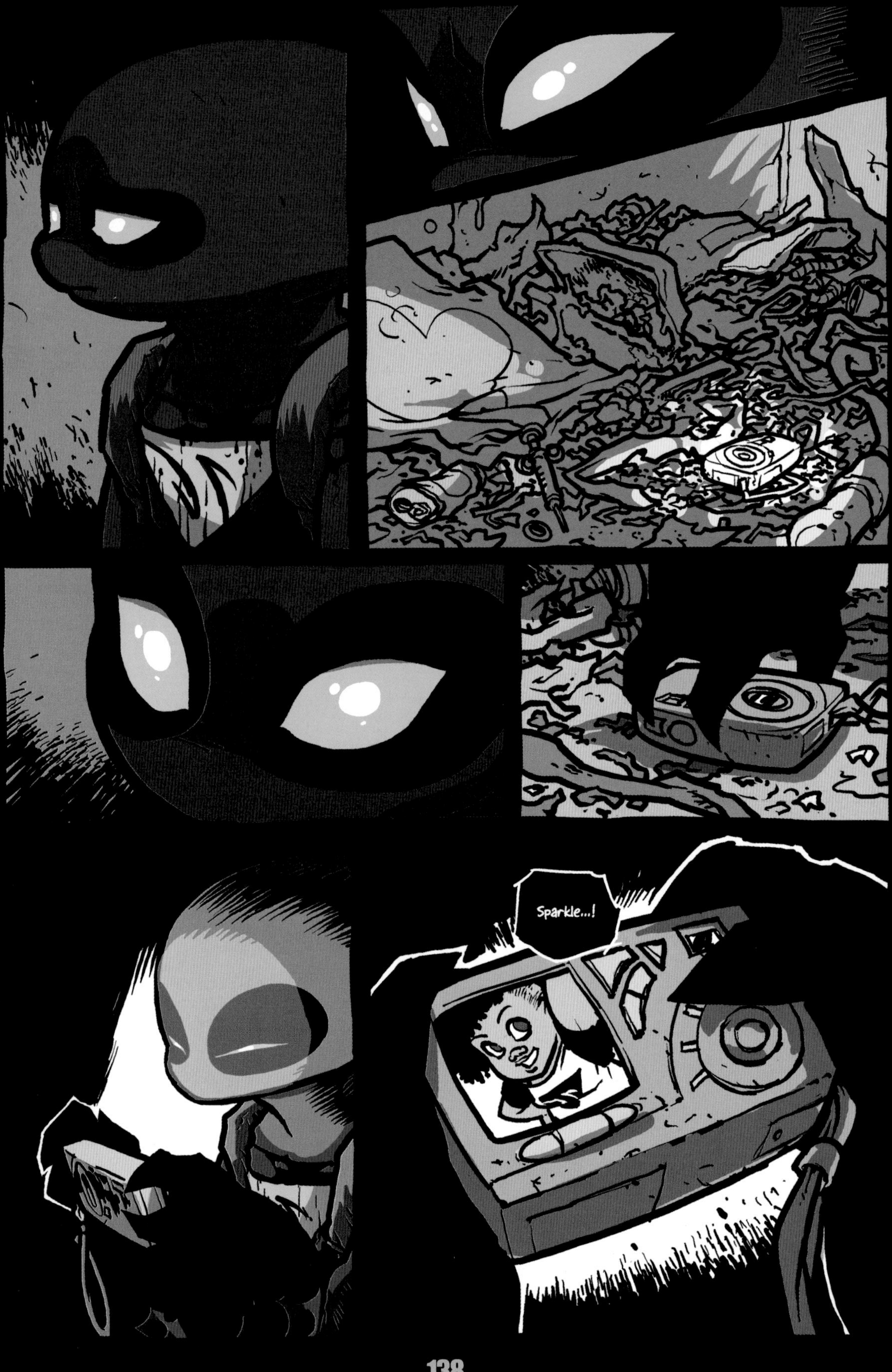
Sparkle...!

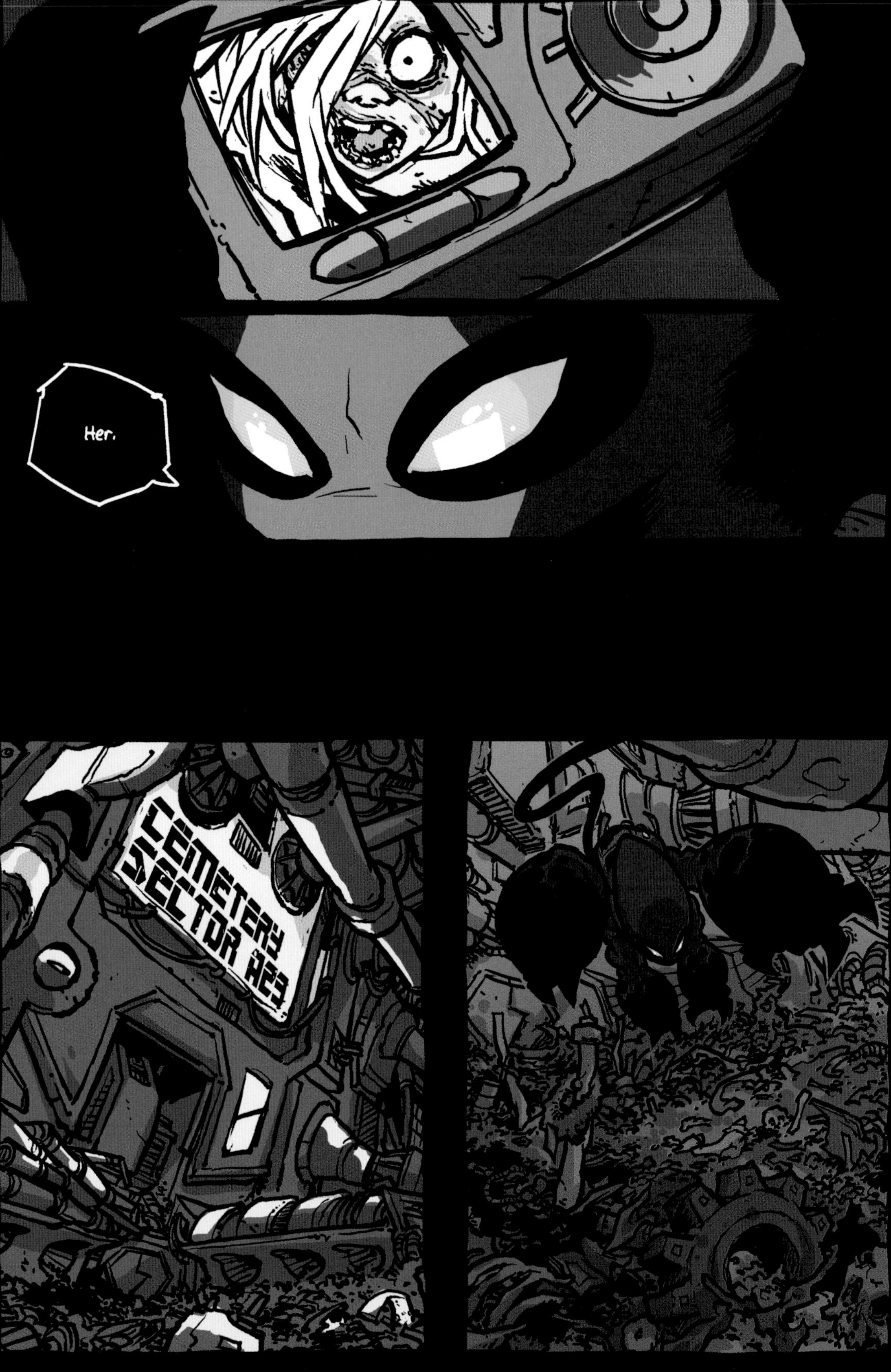
Her.
CEMETERY SECTOR A23

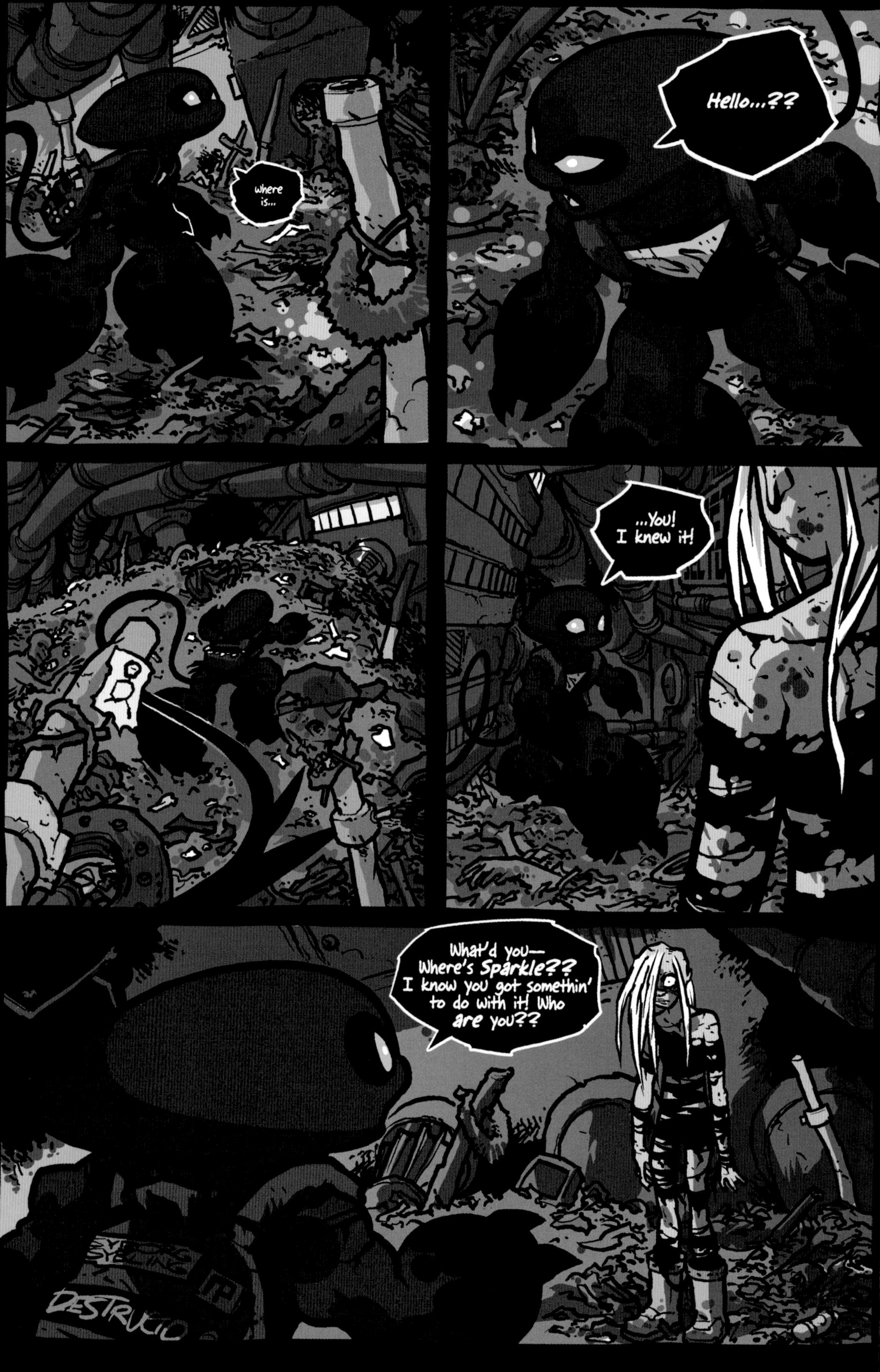
where is...
Hello...??
...You! I knew it!
What'd you— Where's Sparkle?? I know you got somethin' to do with it! Who are you??

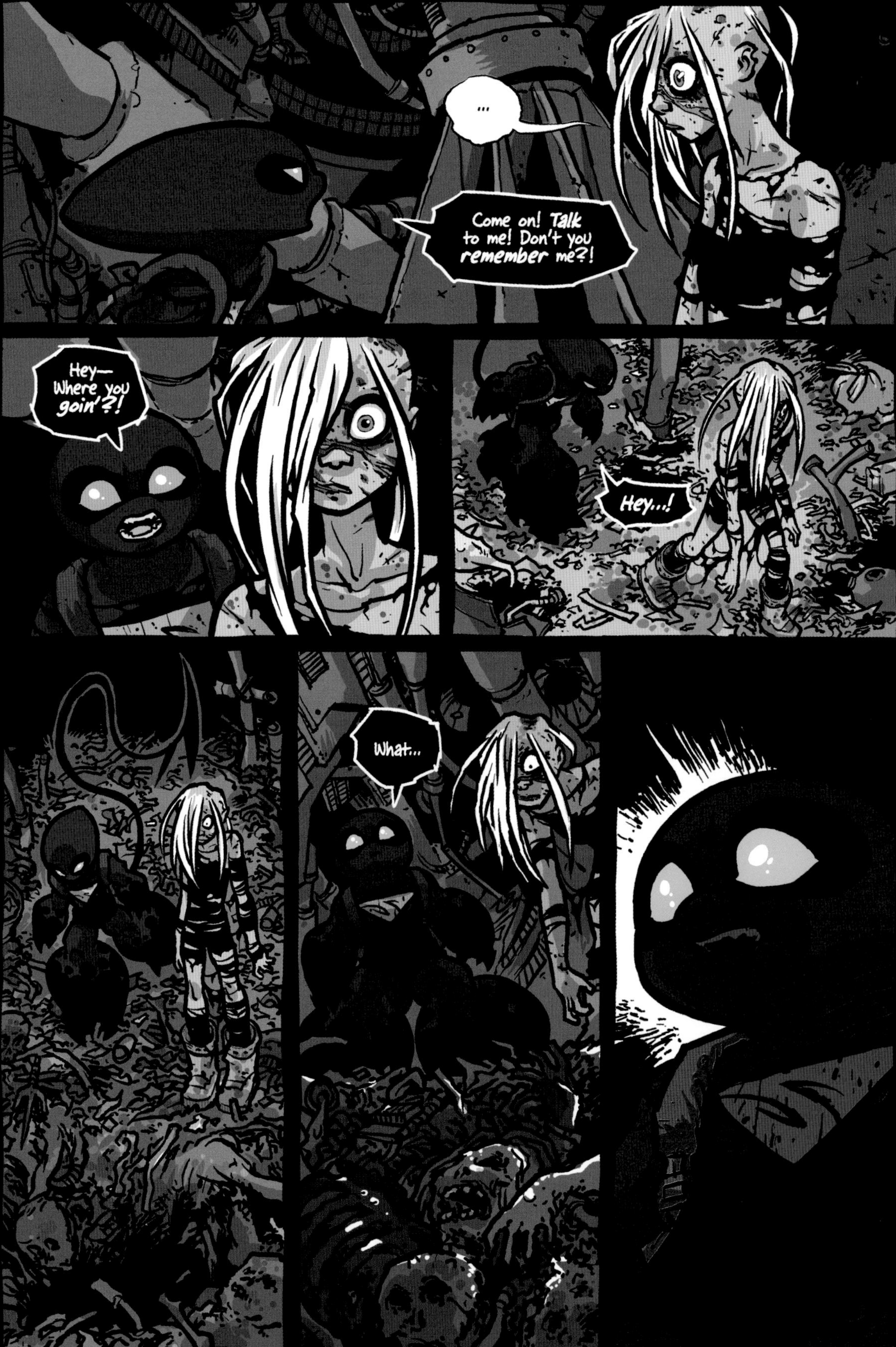
...
Come on! Talk to me! Don't you remember me?!
Hey— Where you goin'?!
Hey...!
What...

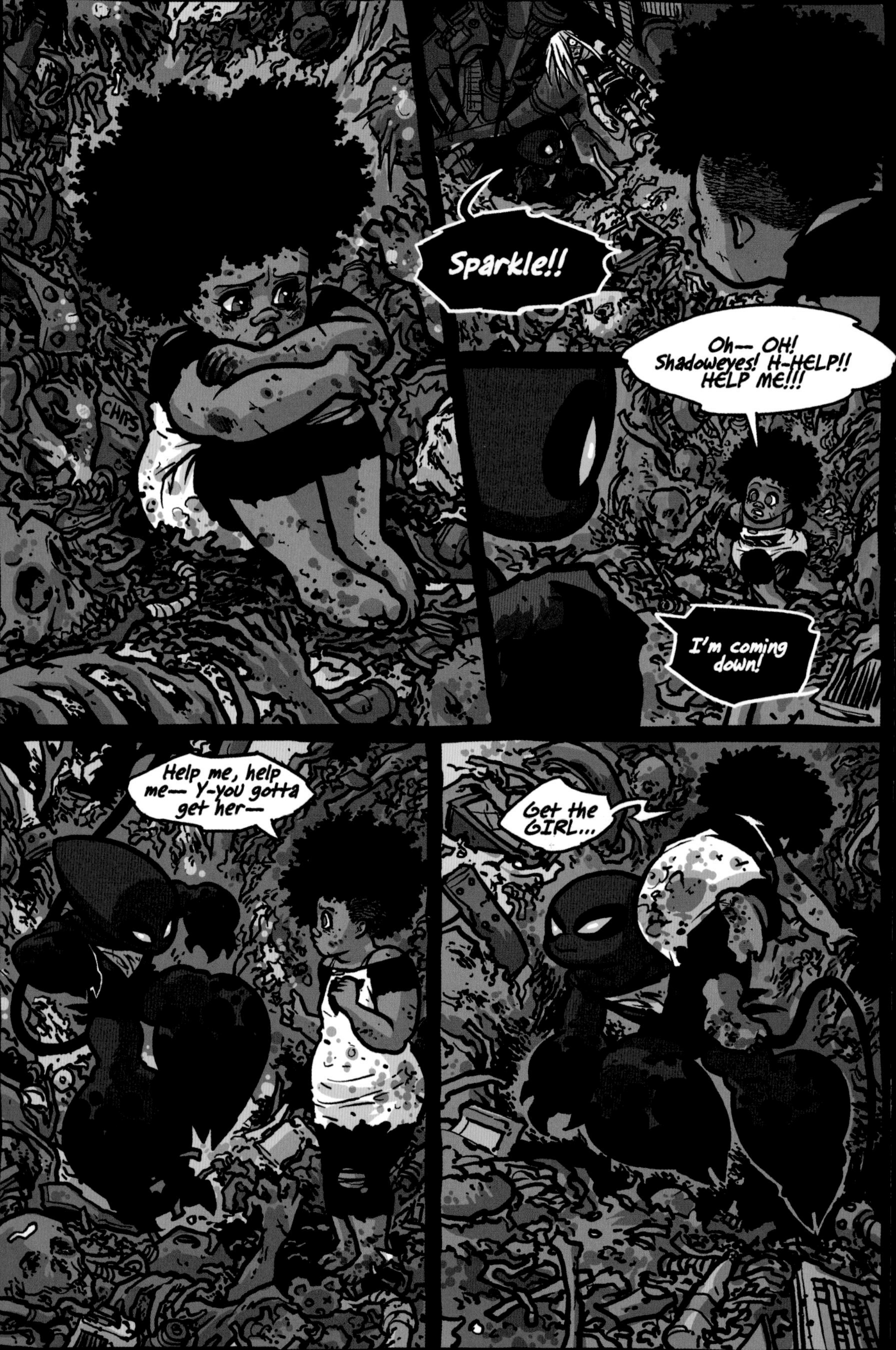
Sparkle!!
Oh-- OH! Shadoweyes! H-HELP!! HELP ME!!!
I'm coming down!
Help me, help me-- Y-you gotta get her--
Get the GIRL...

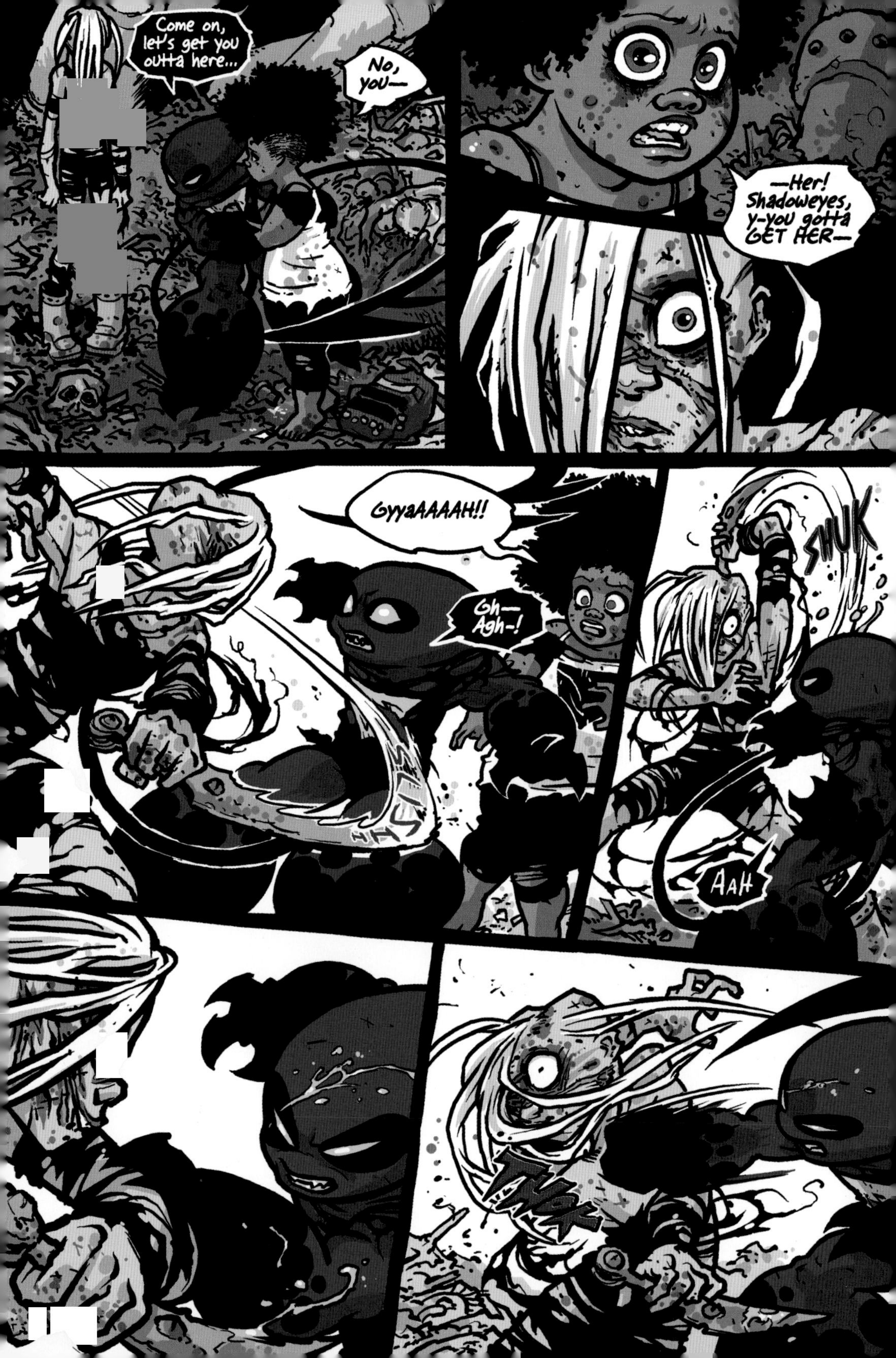

Come on, let's get you outta here...
No, you—
—Her! Shadoweyes, y-you gotta GET HER—
GyyaAAAAH!!
Gh— Agh-!
SHUK
AAH

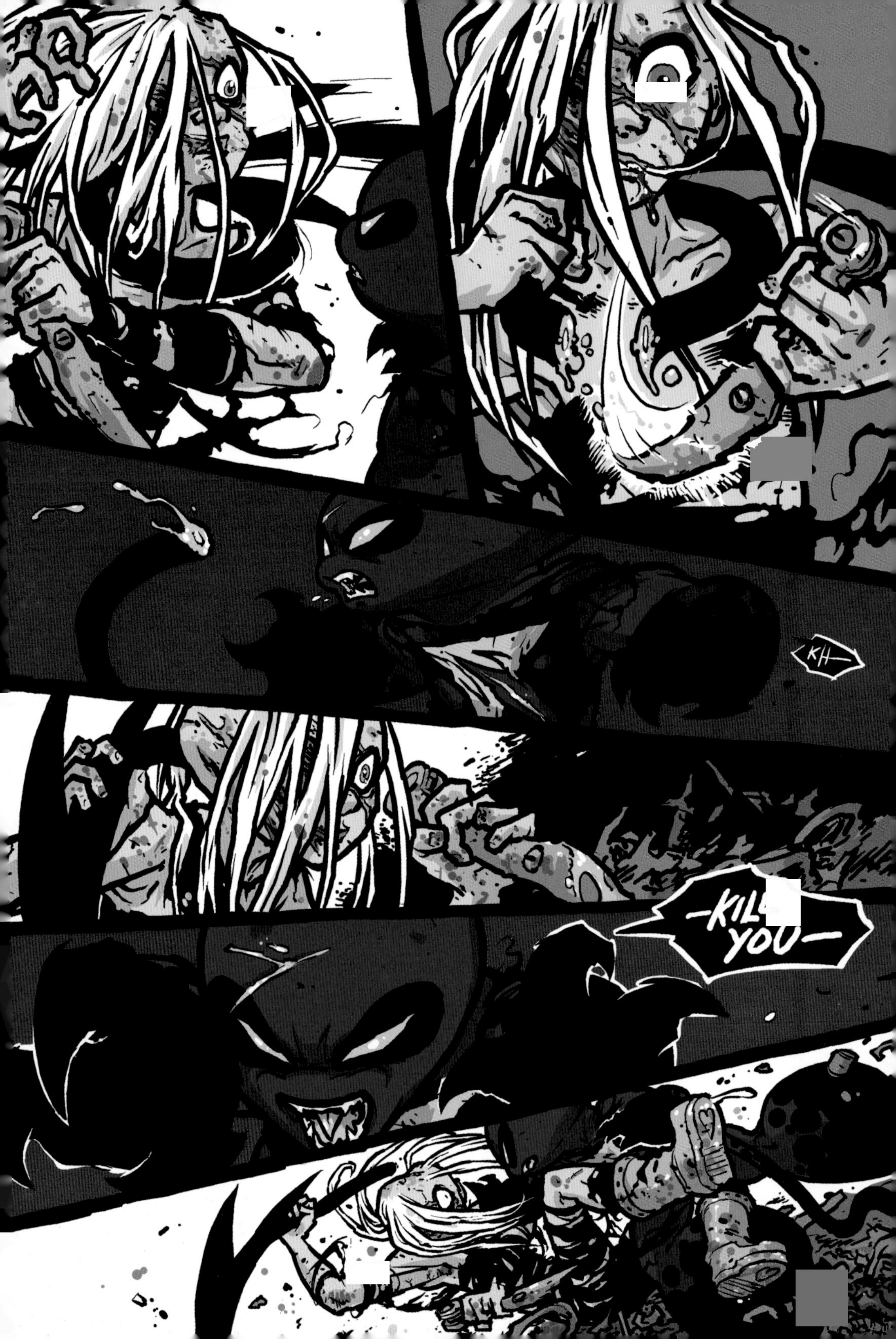
-KIL
YOU-

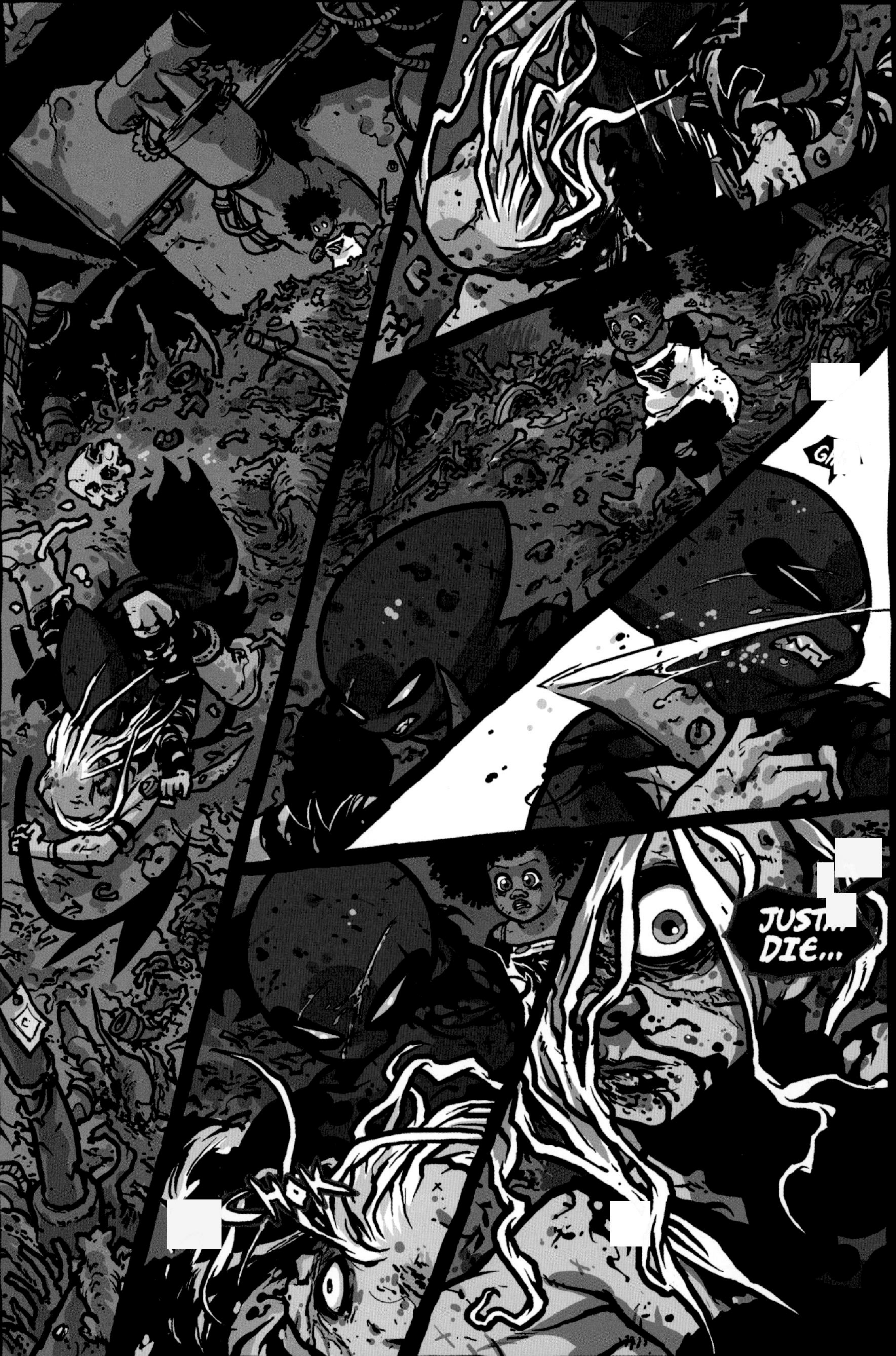
JUST
DIE...

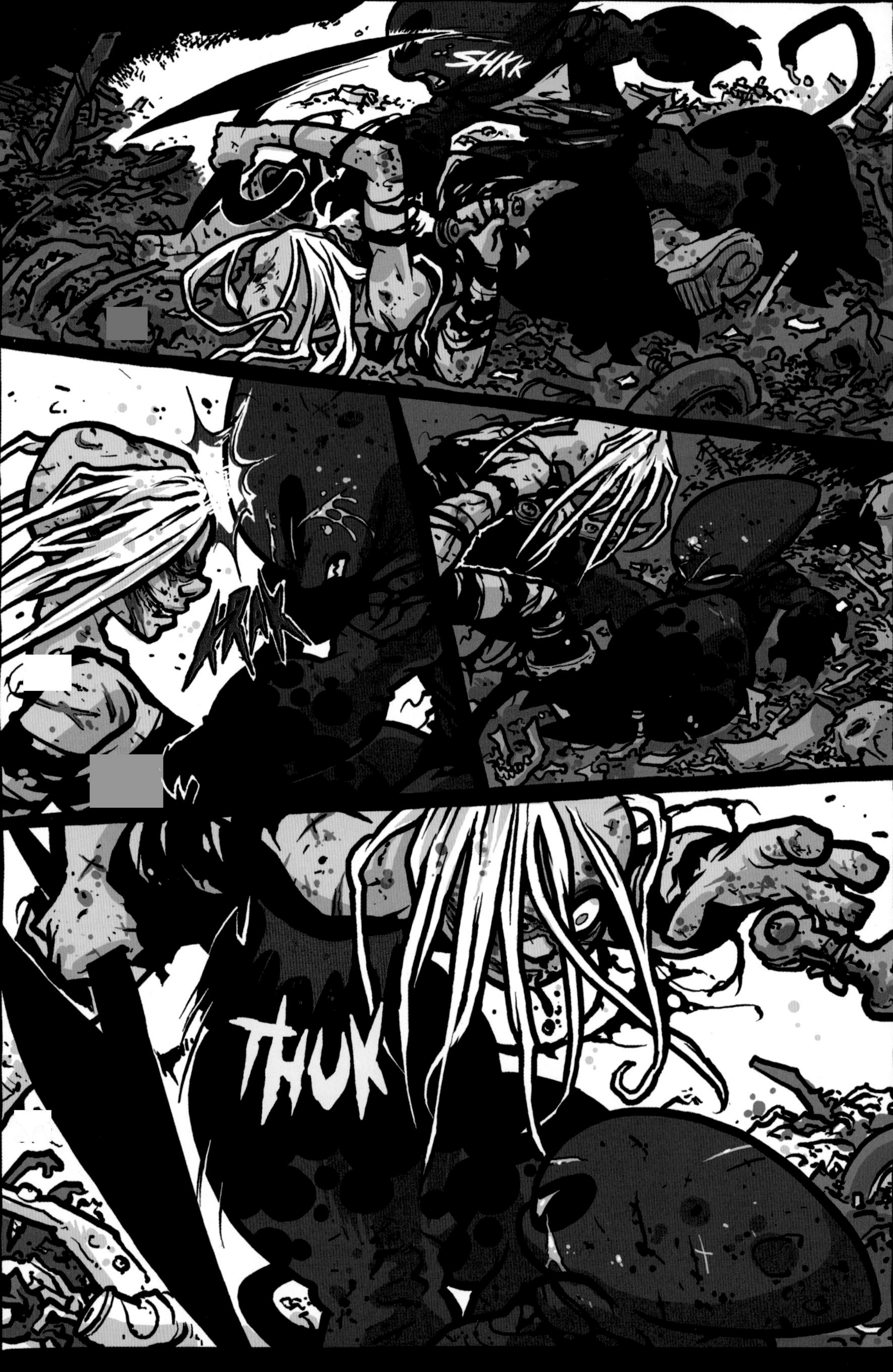
SHKK
THUK

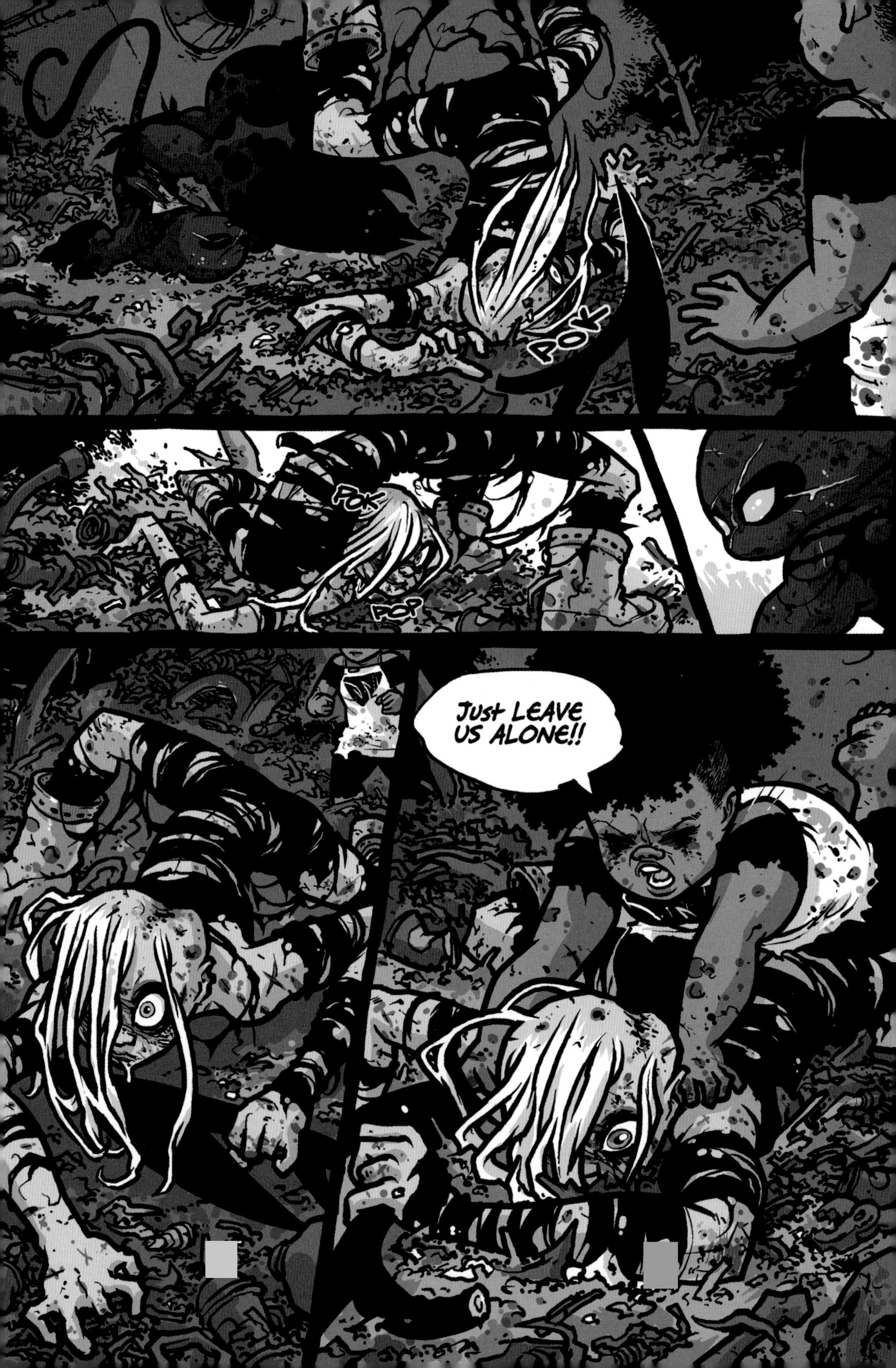
POK
POK
POP
JUST LEAVE US ALONE!!

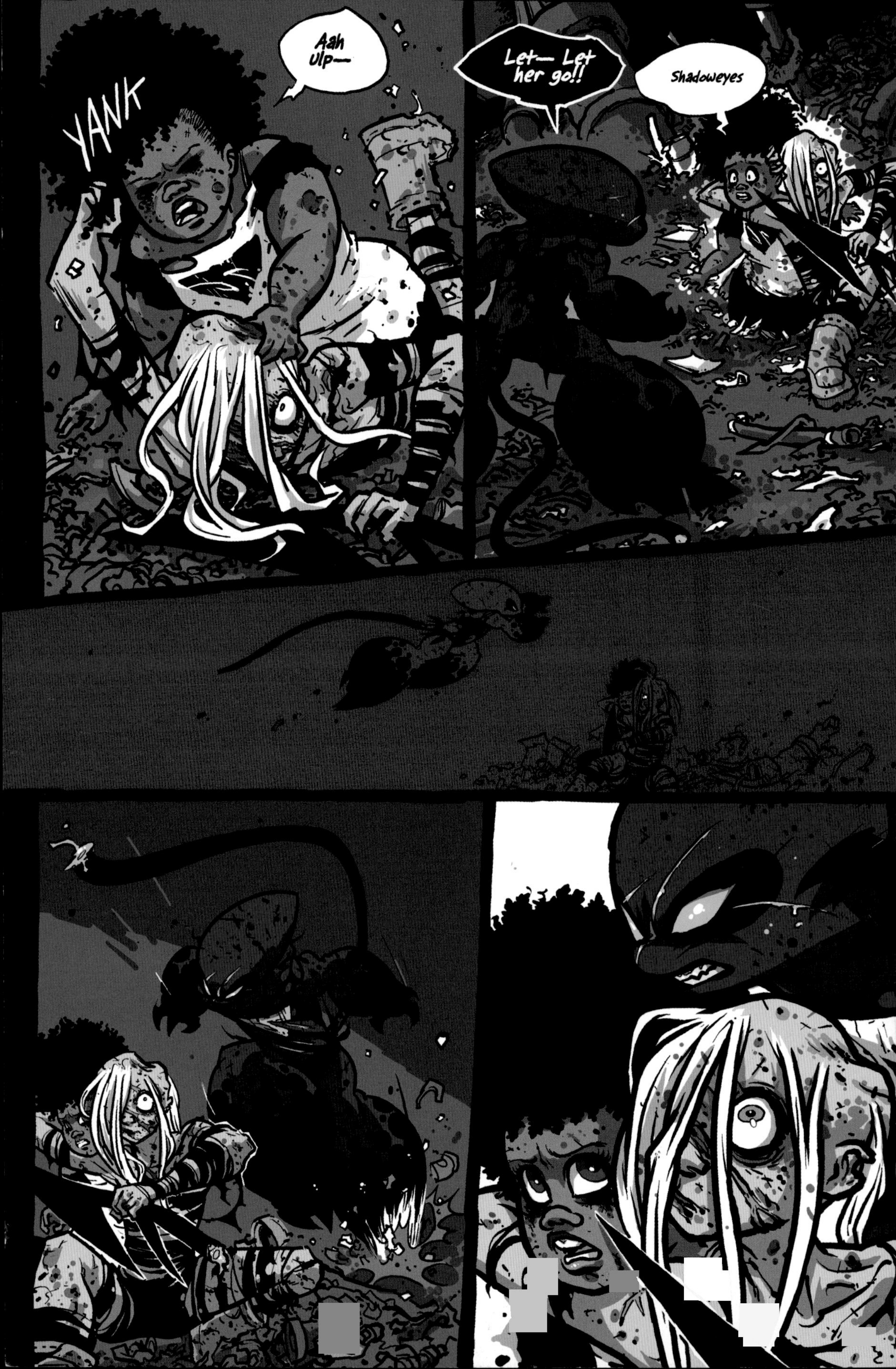
YANK
Aah Ulp—
Let— Let her go!!
Shadoweyes

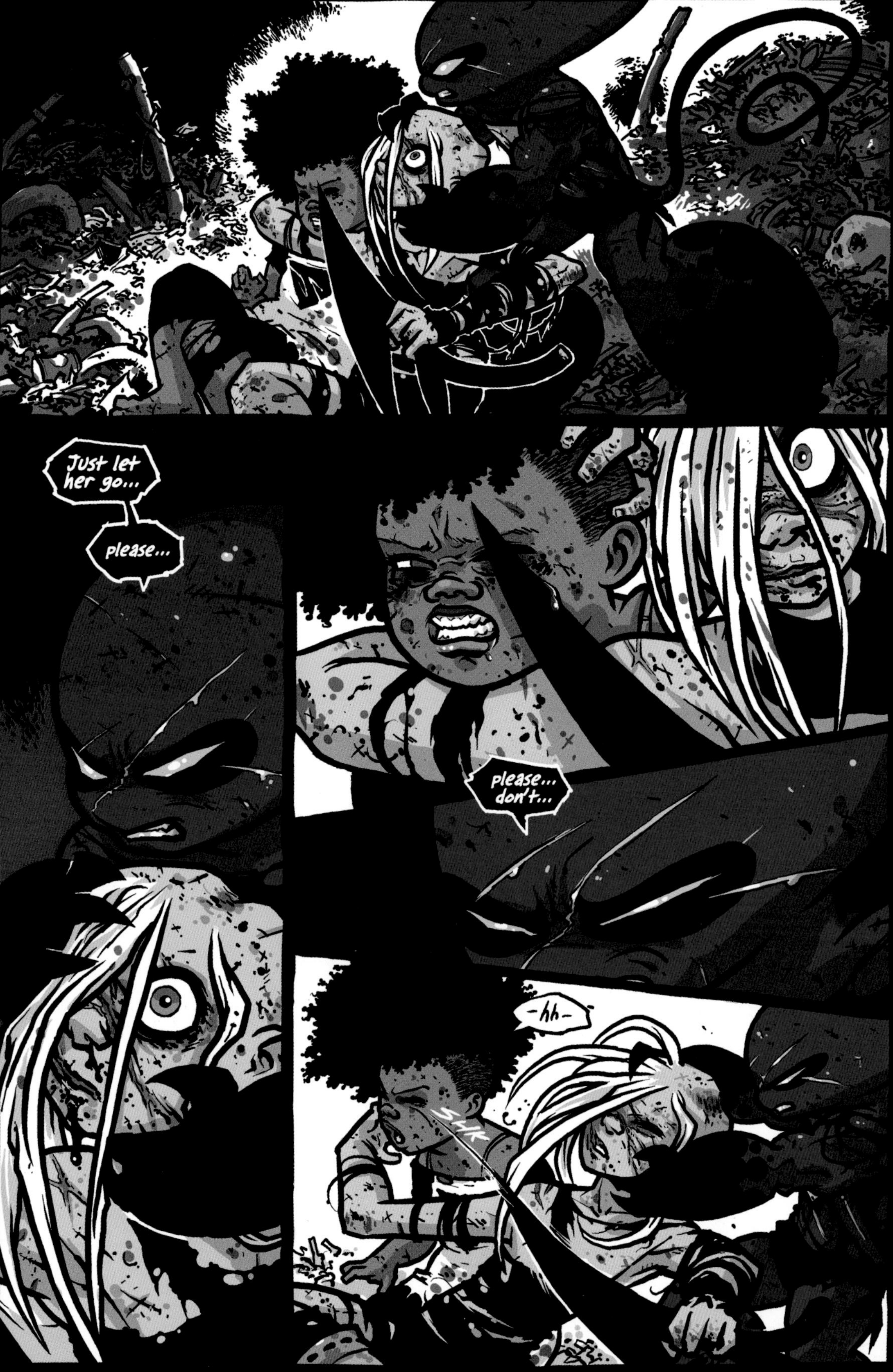
Just let her go...
please...
please... don't...
-hh-
SHK

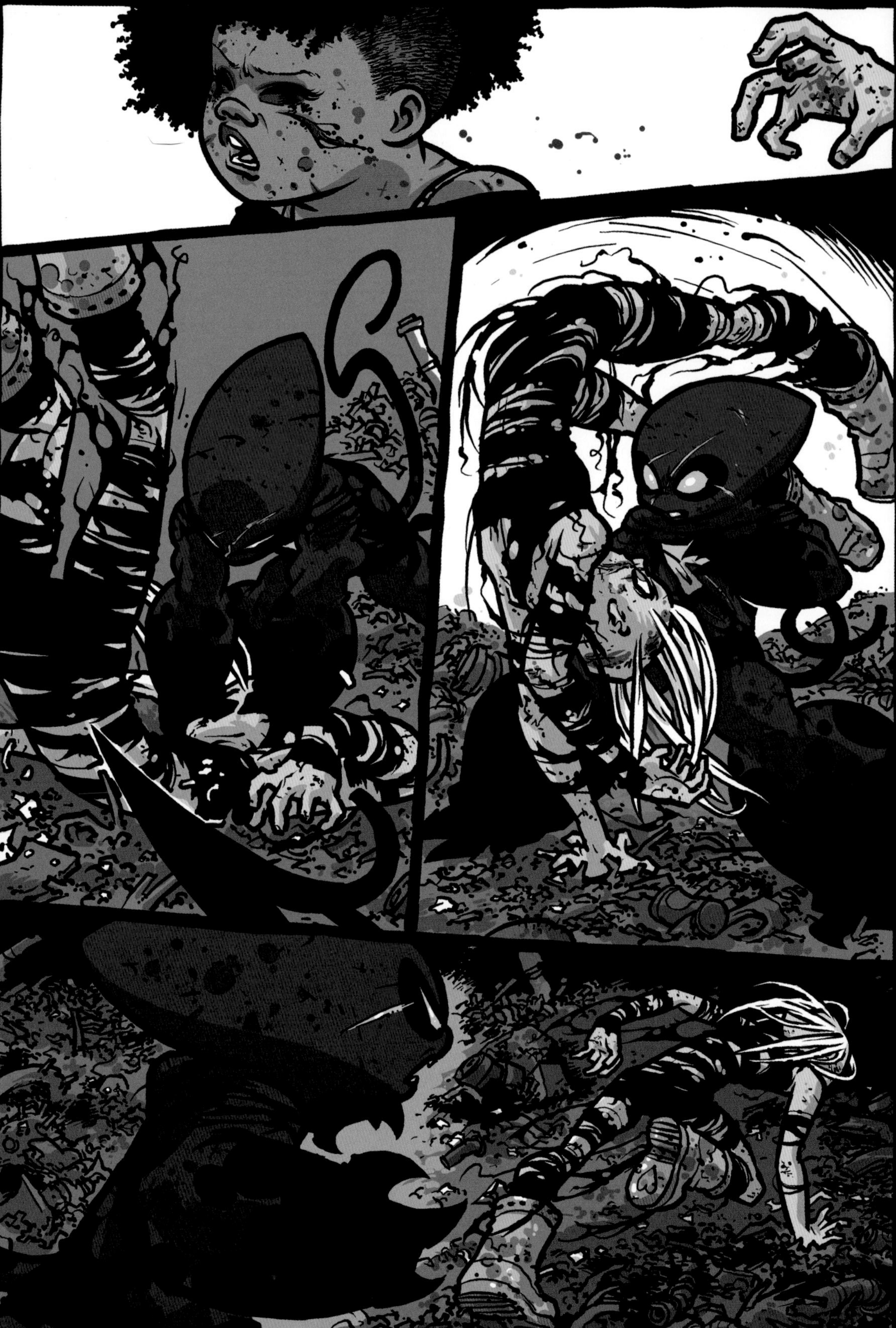

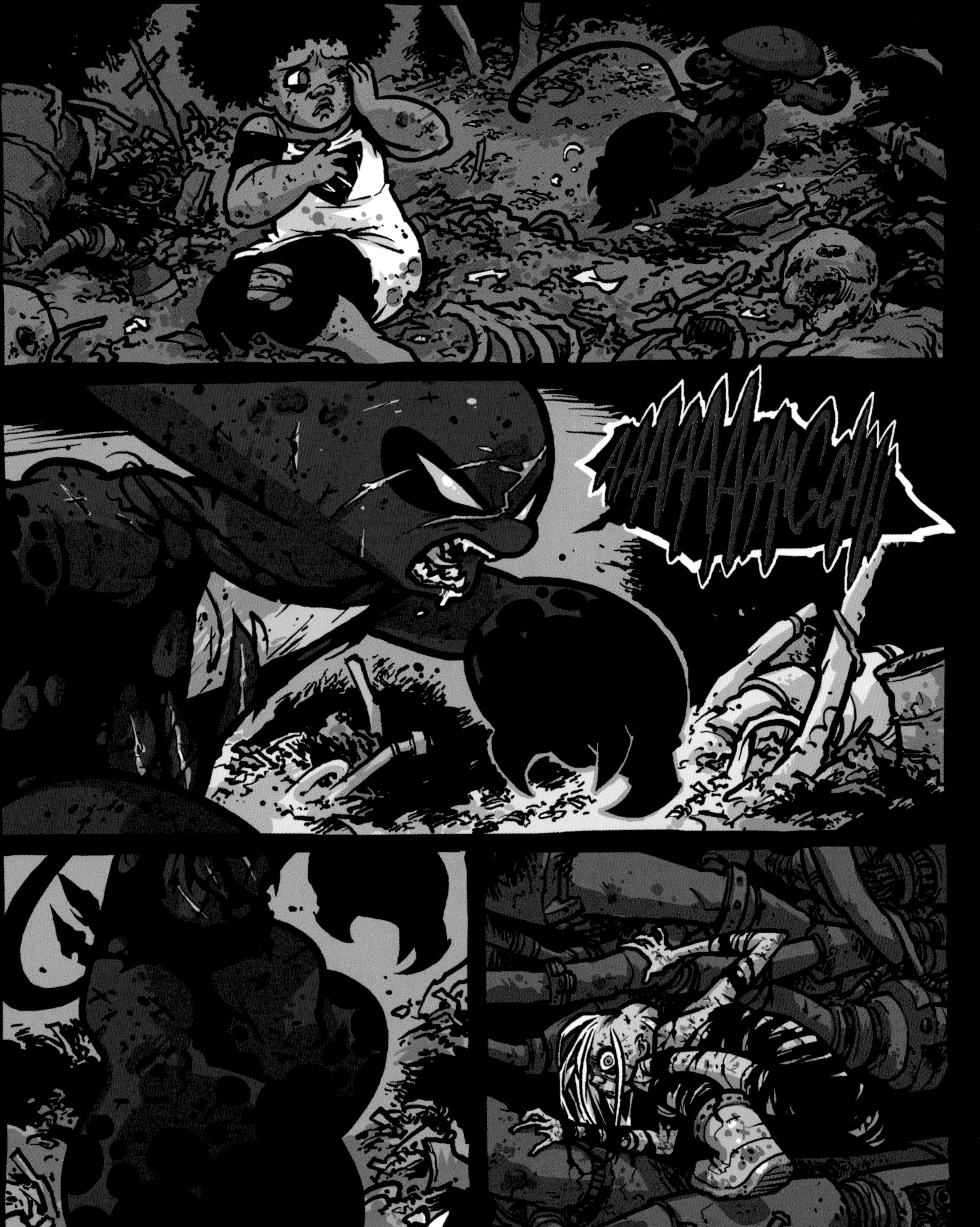
AAAAAAAAACGHH

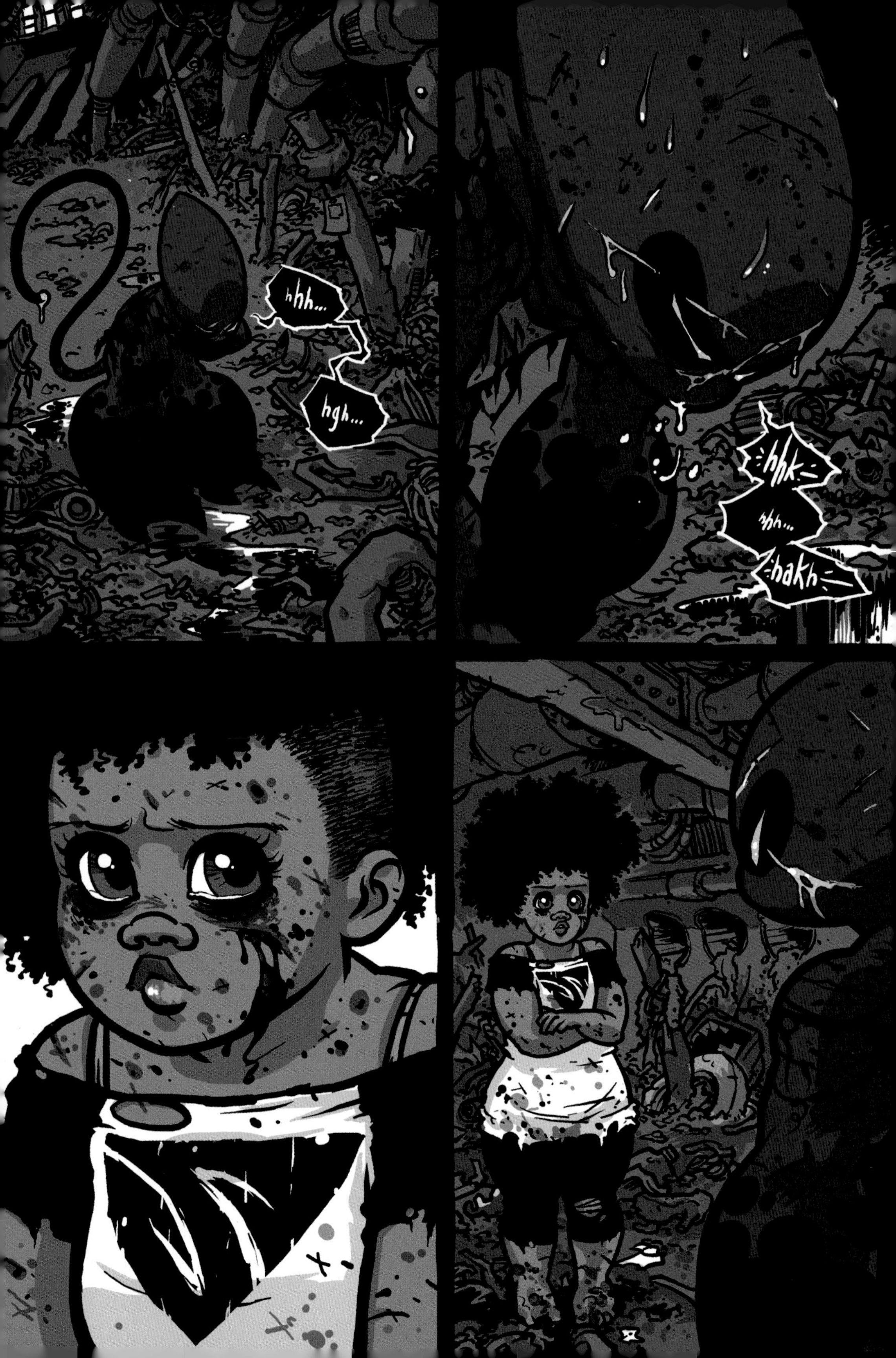
hhh...
hgh...
hhk
hhh...
hakh

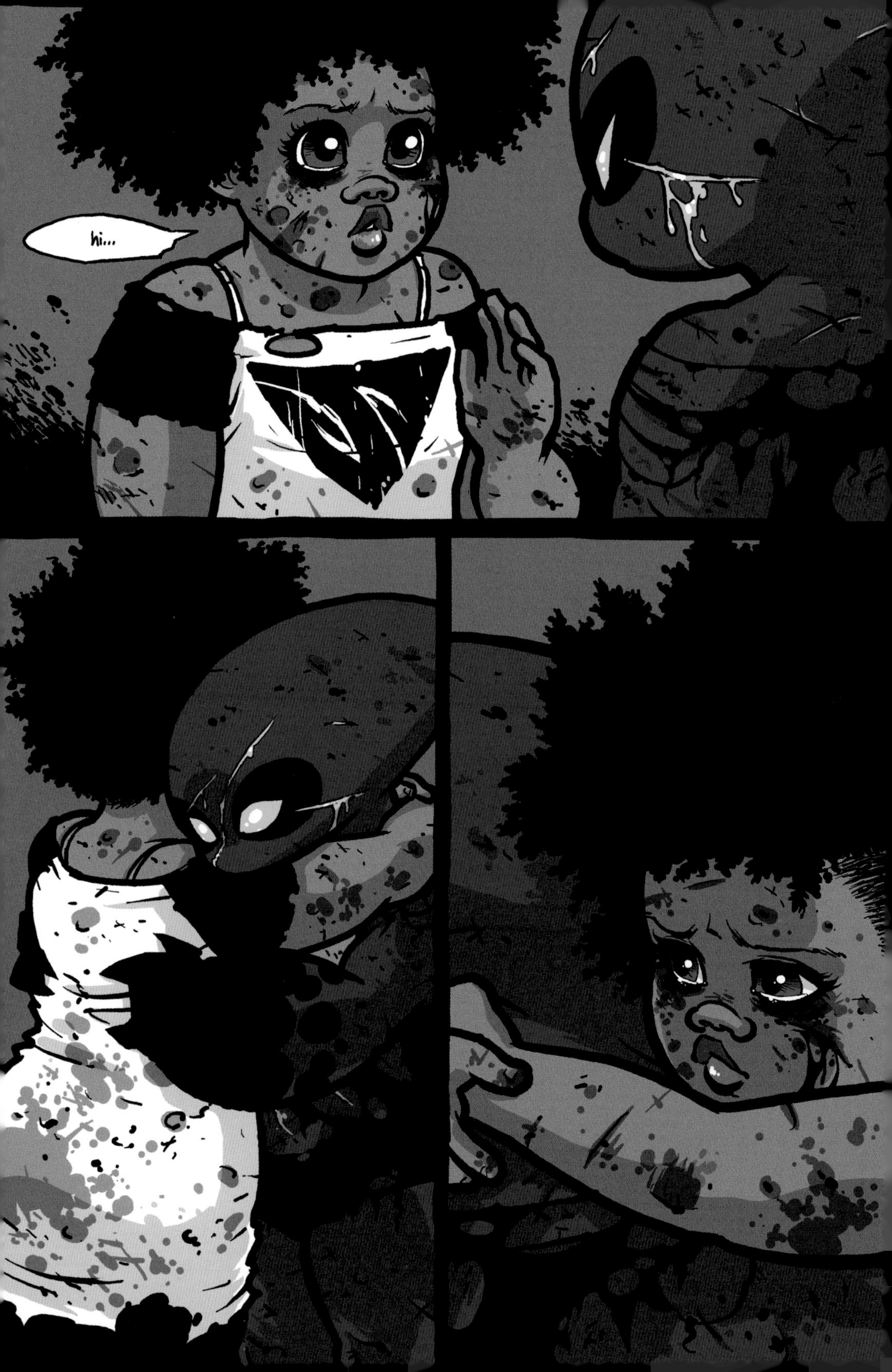
hi...

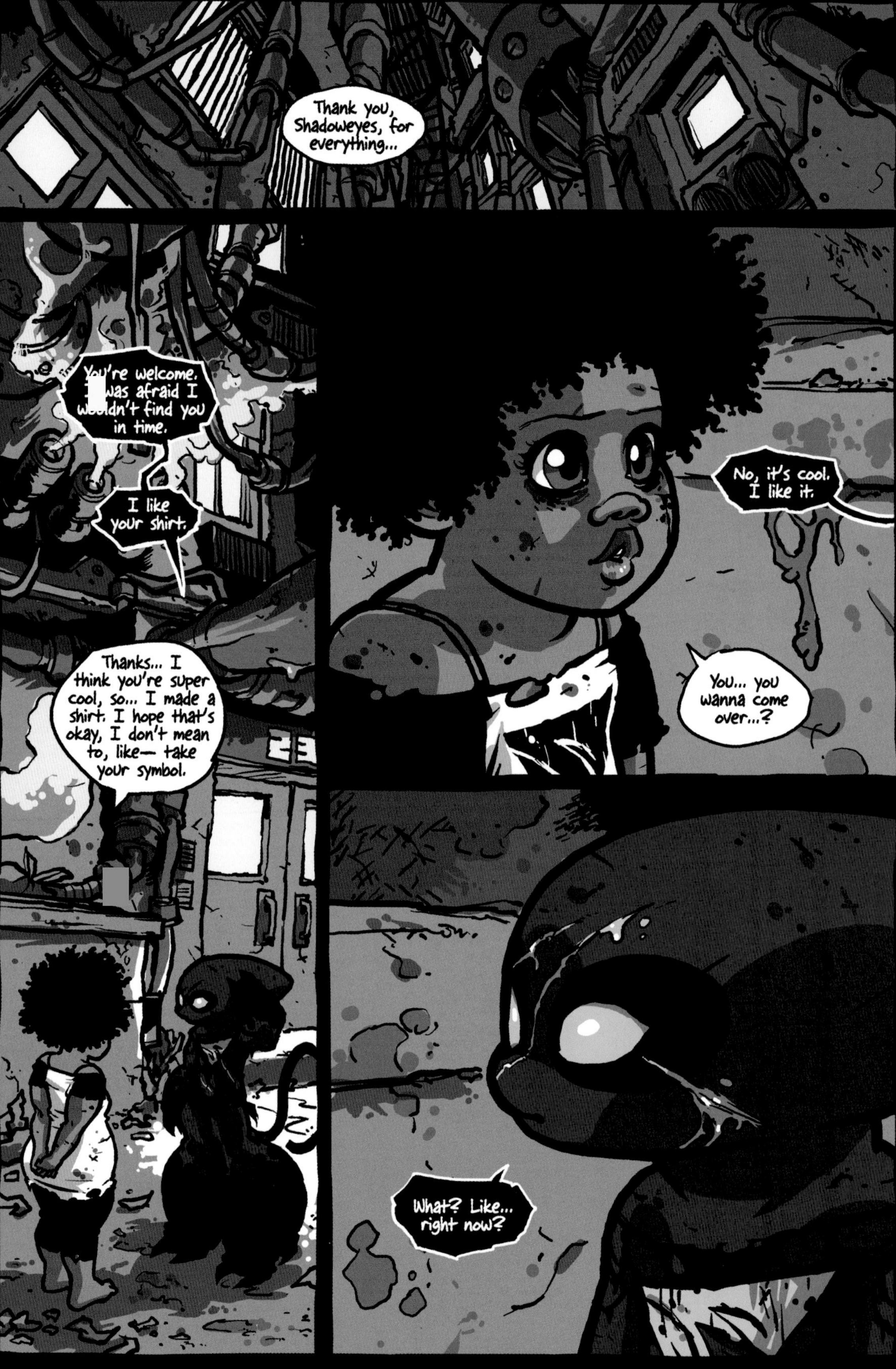

Thank you, Shadoweyes, for everything...
You're welcome. I was afraid I wouldn't find you in time.
I like your shirt.
Thanks... I think you're super cool, so... I made a shirt. I hope that's okay, I don't mean to, like— take your symbol.
No, it's cool. I like it.
You... you wanna come over...?
What? Like... right now?

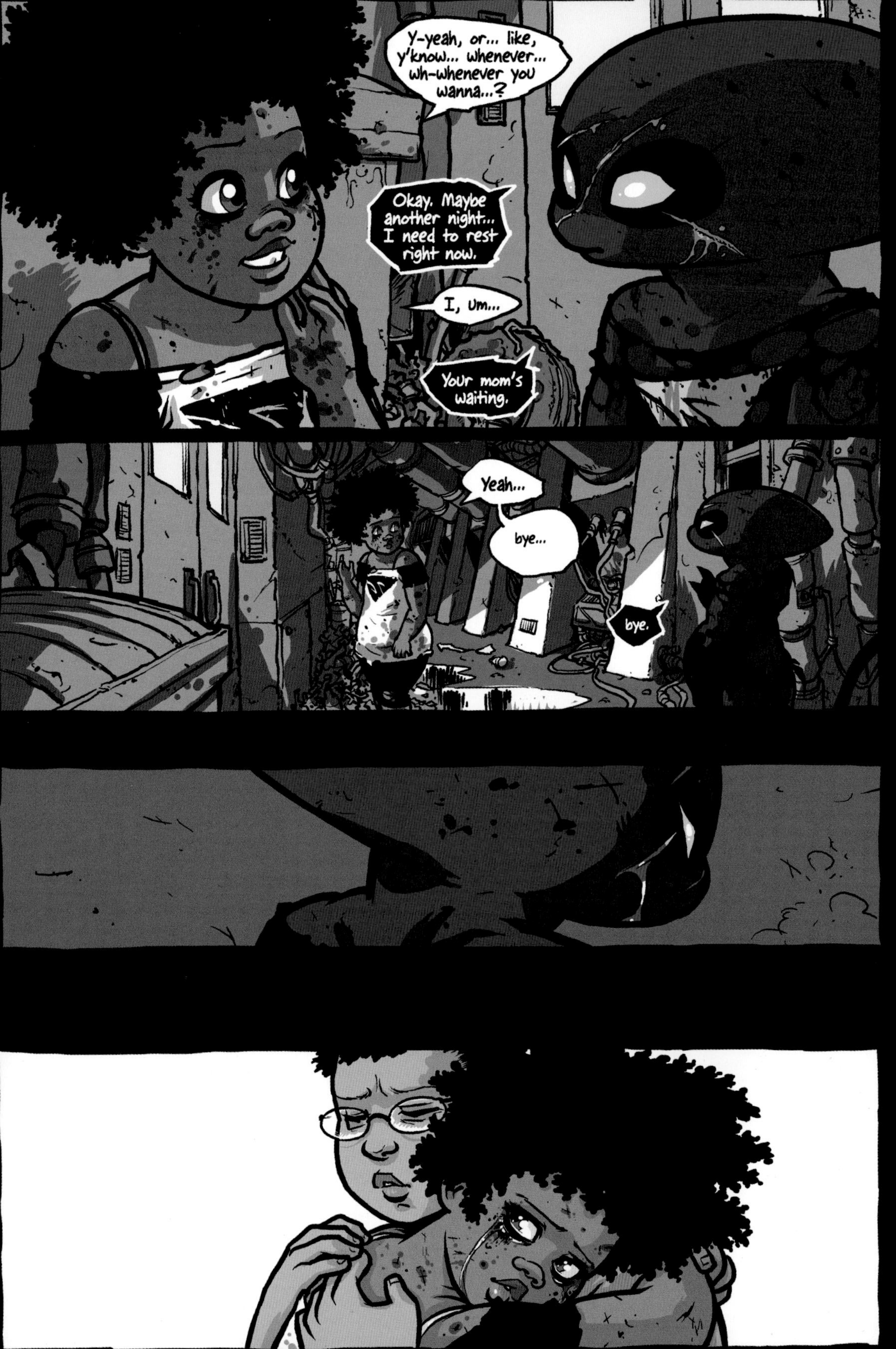
Y-yeah, or... like, y'know... whenever... wh-whenever you wanna...?
Okay. Maybe another night... I need to rest right now.
I, um...
Your mom's waiting.
Yeah...
bye...
bye.

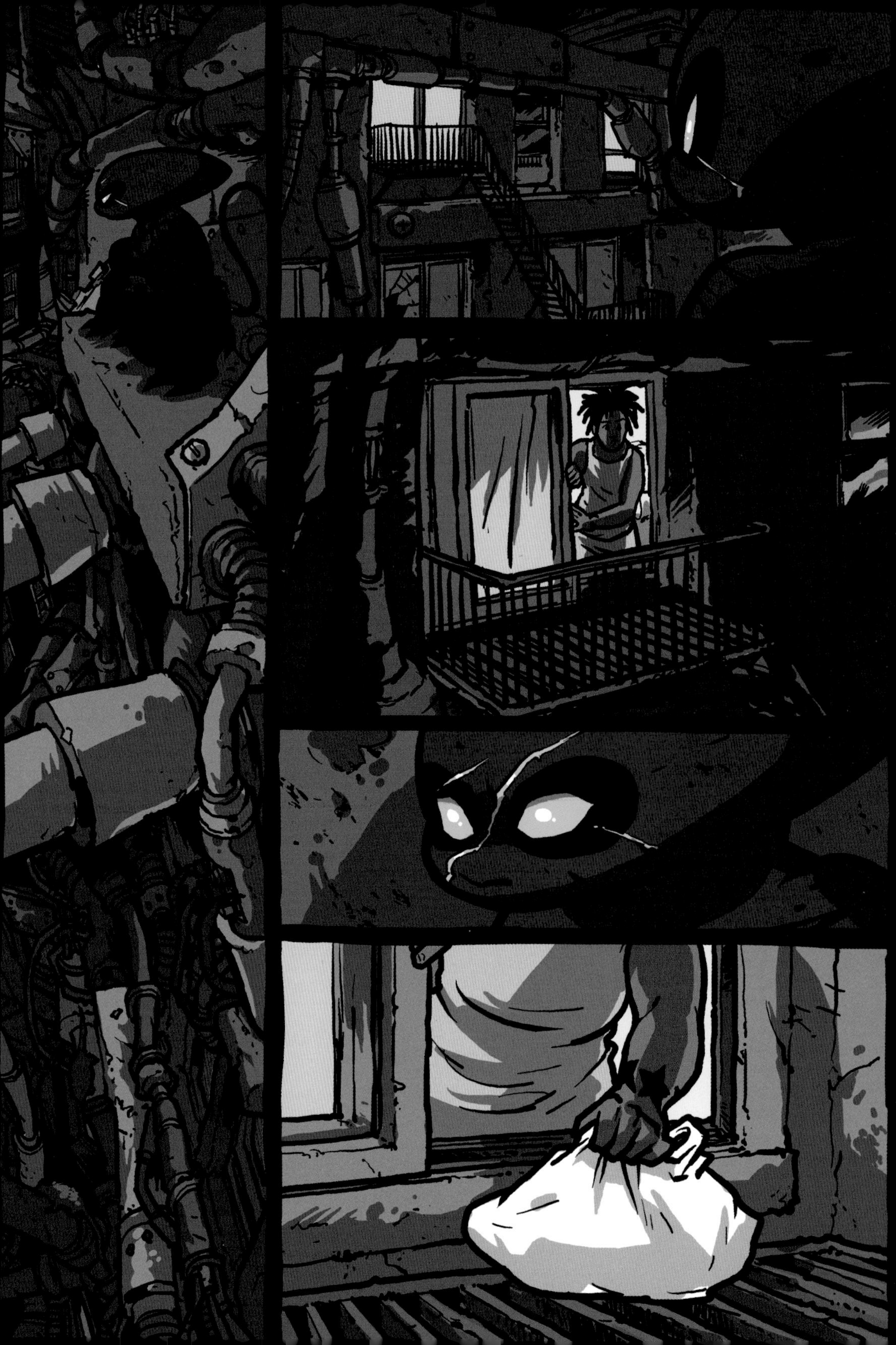

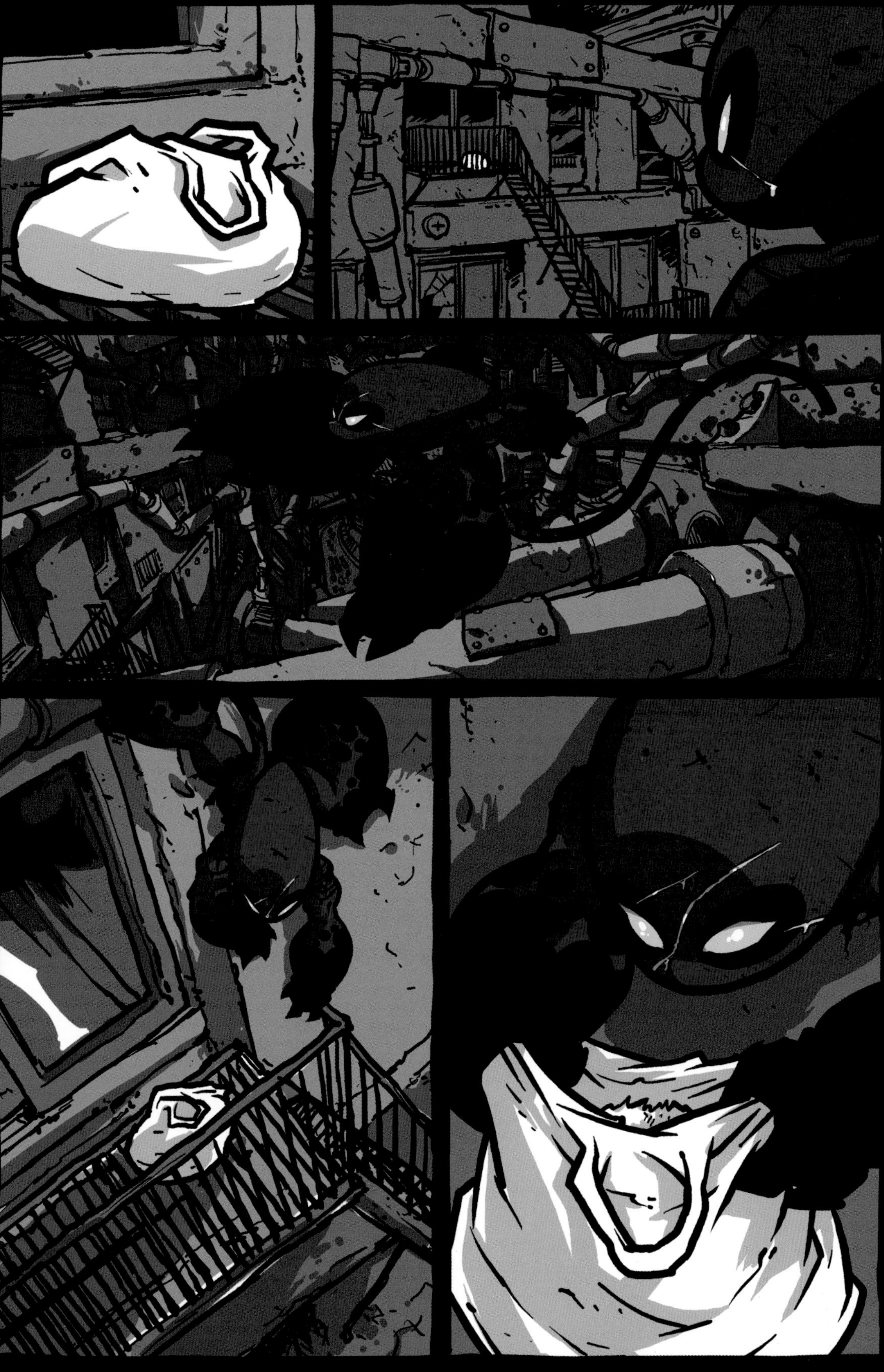

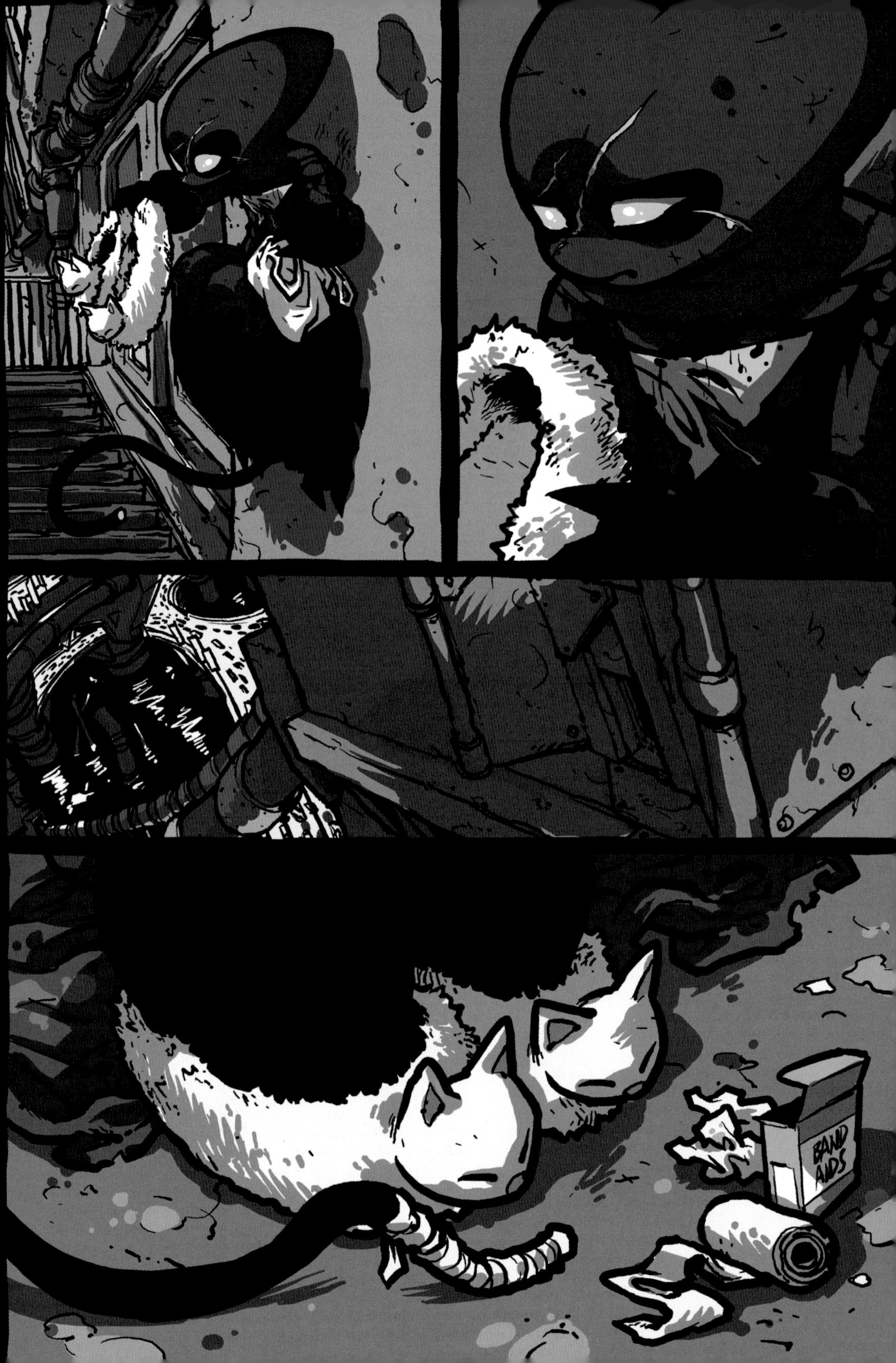
BAND AIDS

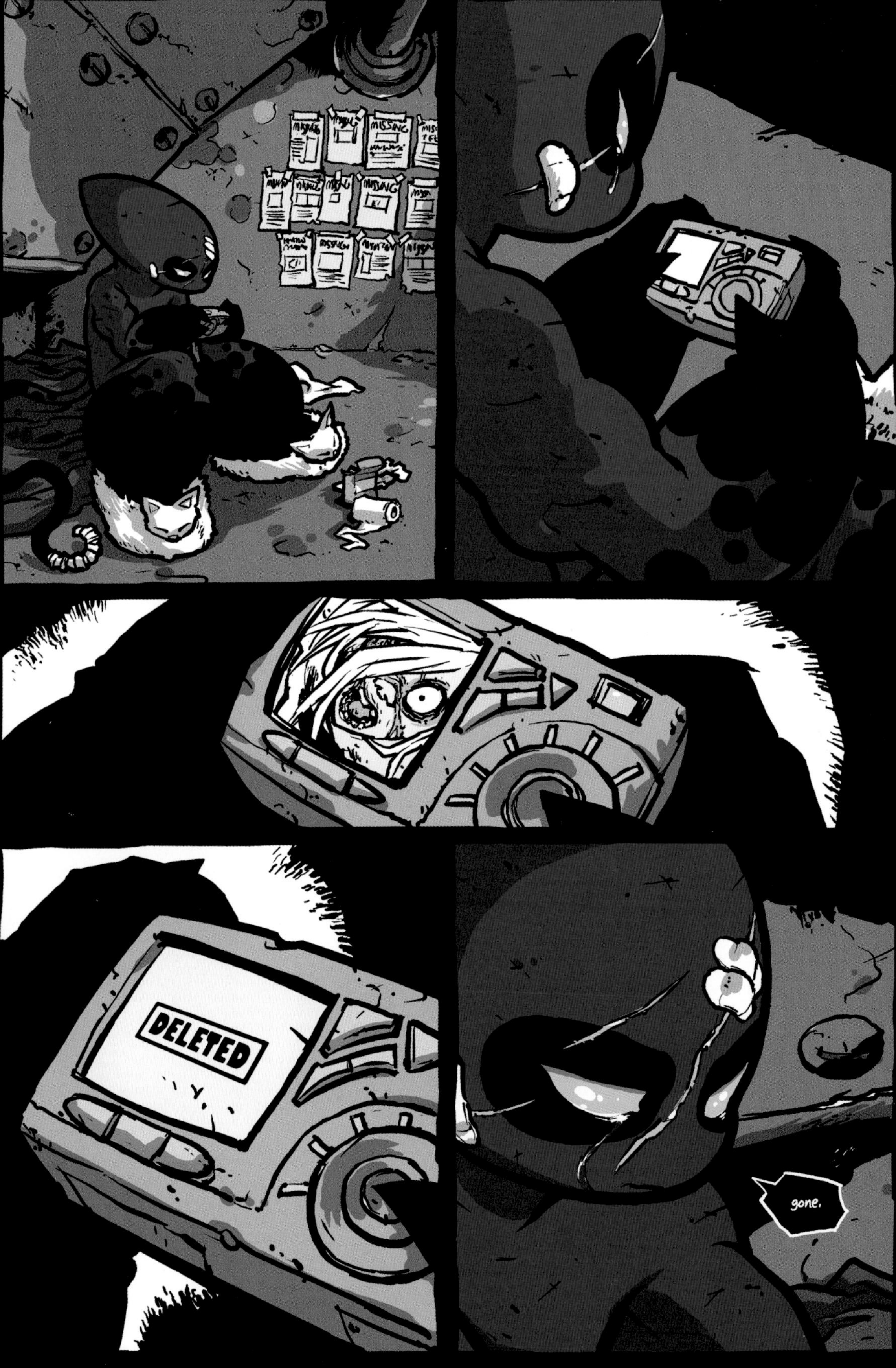
DELETED
gone.

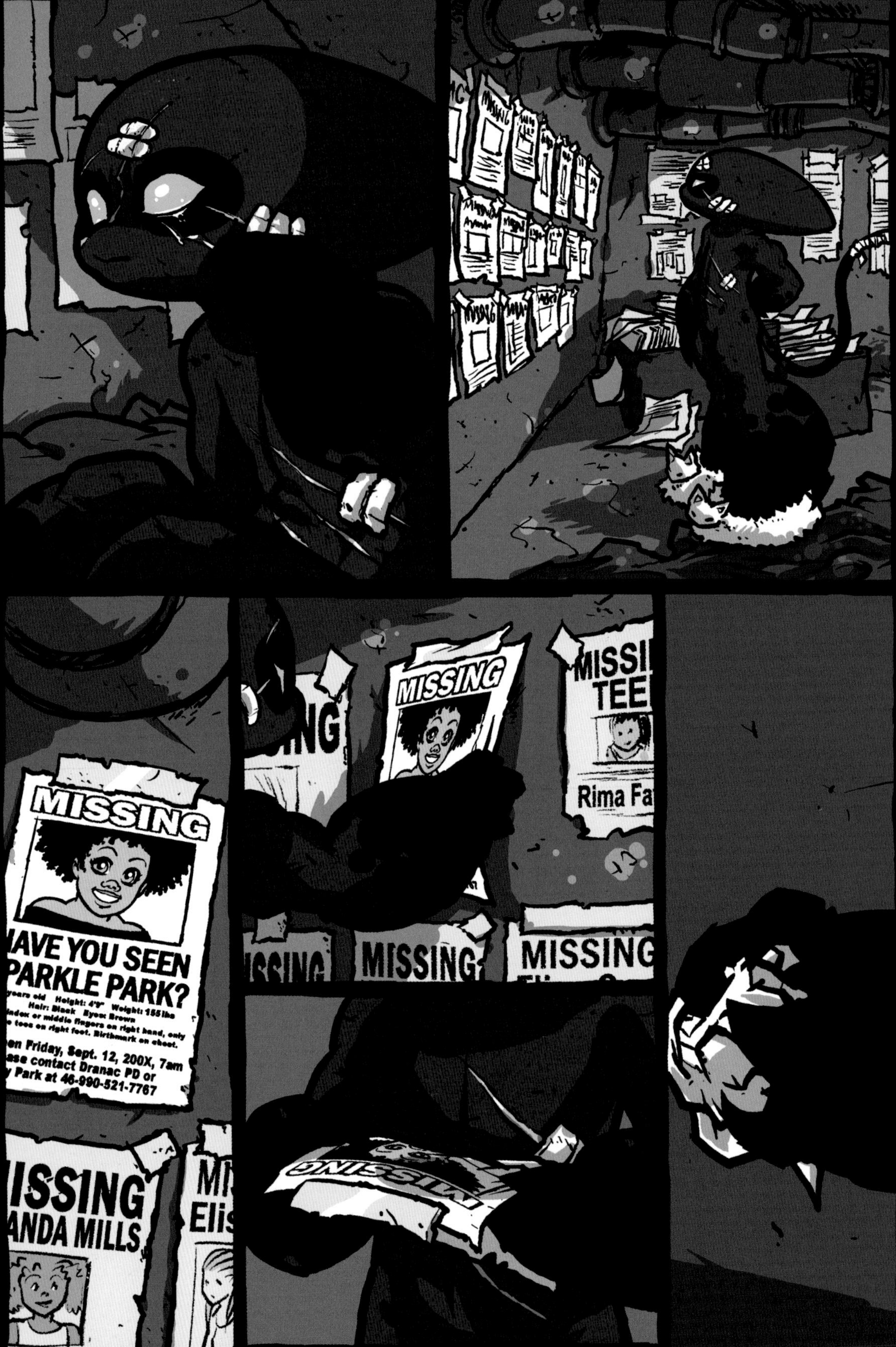
MISSING
MISSING
MISSI
TEE
Rima Fa
MISSING
HAVE YOU SEEN
PARKLE PARK?
years old Height: 4'9" Weight: 155lbs
Hair: Black Eyes: Brown
index or middle fingers on right hand, only
toes on right foot. Birthmark on chest.
en Friday, Sept. 12, 200X, 7am
ase contact Dranac PD or
y Park at 46-990-521-7767
MISSING
MISSING
MISSING
ISSING
ANDA MILLS
Mi
Elis
MISSING

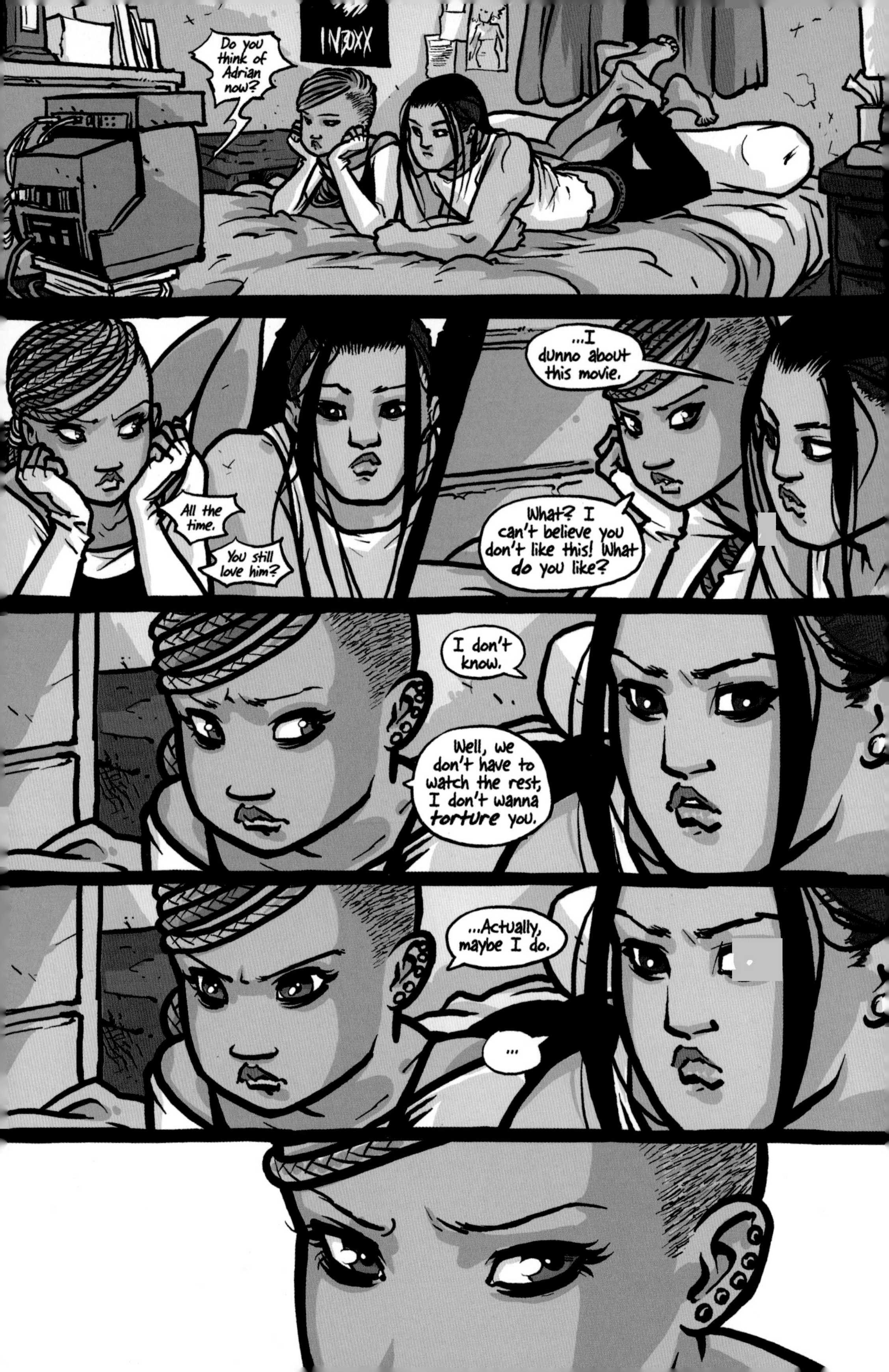

IN3OXX
Do you think of Adrian now?
All the time.
You still love him?
...I dunno about this movie.
What? I can't believe you don't like this! What do you like?
I don't know.
Well, we don't have to watch the rest, I don't wanna torture you.
...Actually, maybe I do.
...

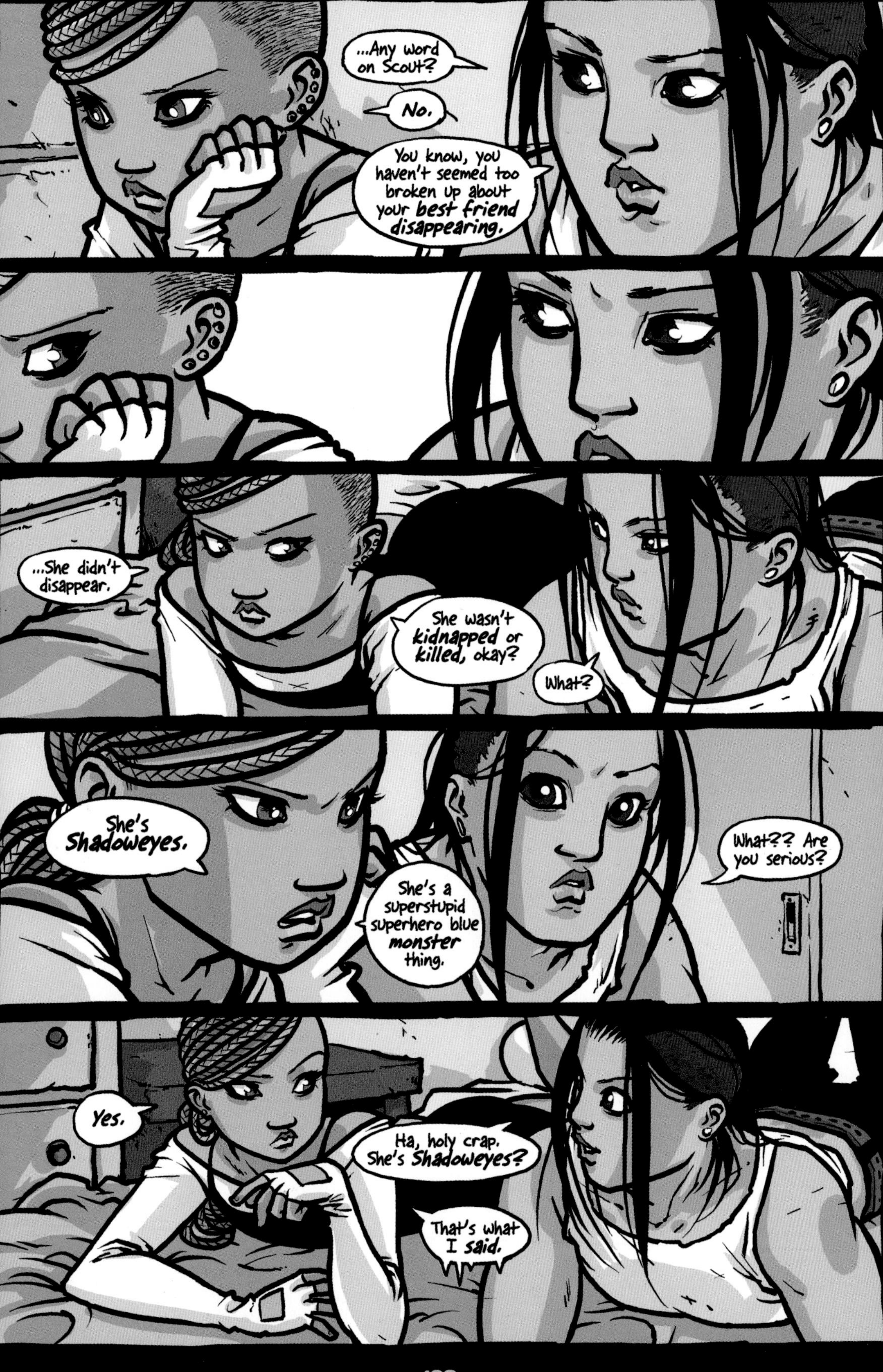
...Any word on Scout?
No.
You know, you haven't seemed too broken up about your **best friend disappearing.**
...She didn't disappear.
She wasn't **kidnapped** or **killed**, okay?
What?
She's **Shadoweyes.**
She's a superstupid superhero blue **monster** thing.
What?? Are you serious?
Yes.
Ha, holy crap. She's **Shadoweyes?**
That's what I **said.**

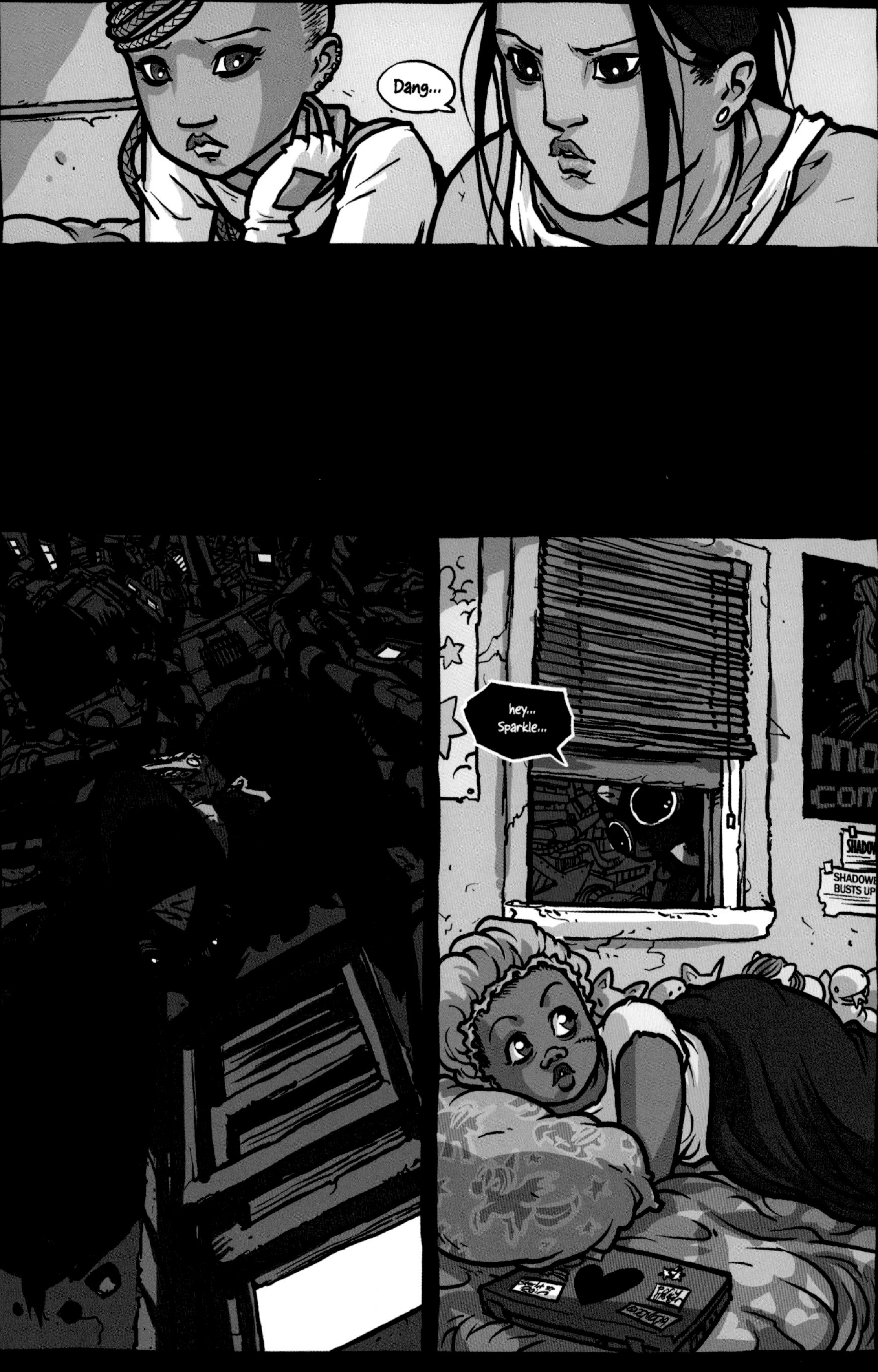
Dang...
hey...
Sparkle...

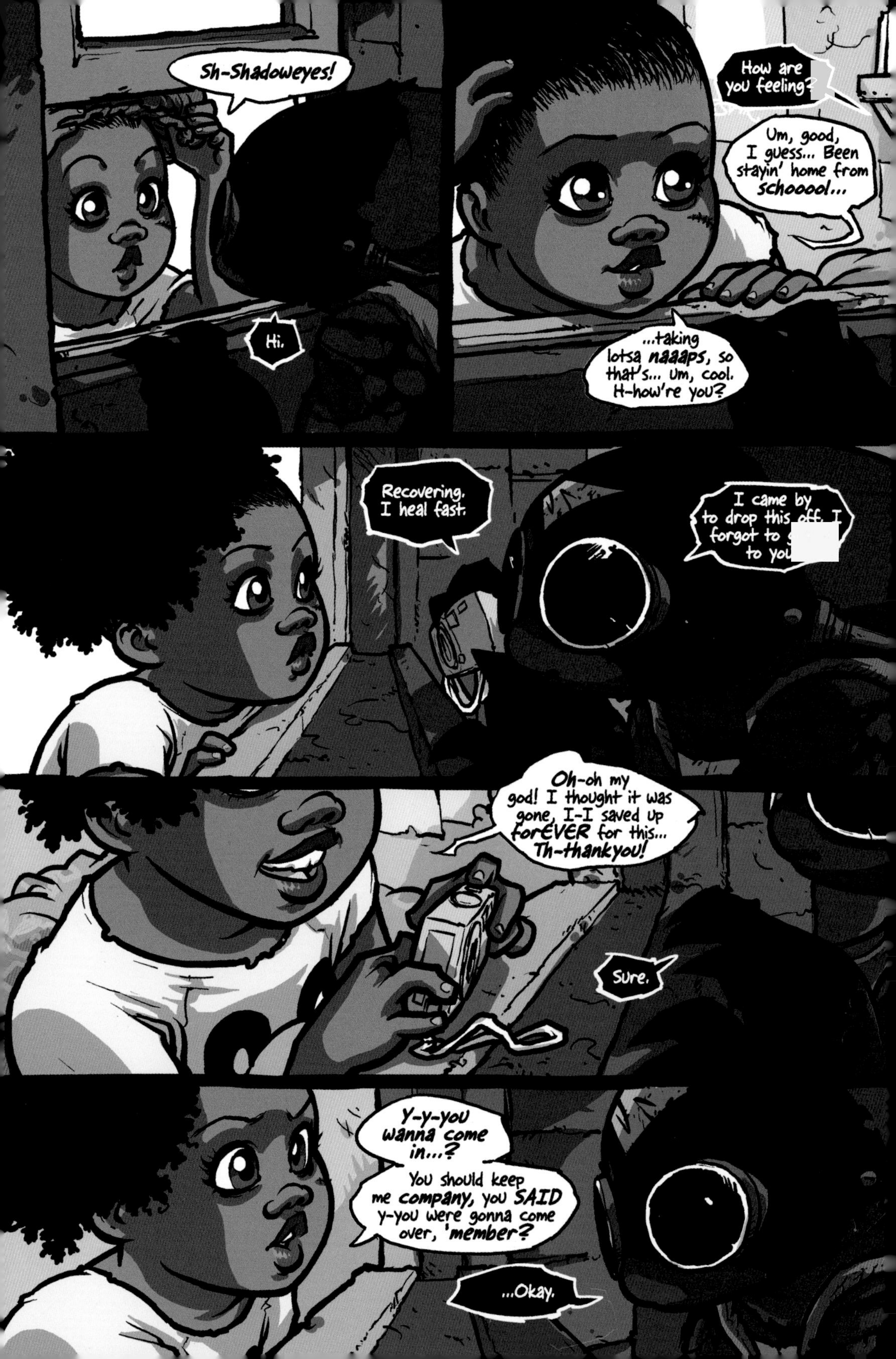
Sh-Shadoweyes!
Hi.
How are you feeling?
Um, good, I guess... Been stayin' home from schoooool...
...taking lotsa naaaps, so that's... um, cool. H-how're you?
Recovering. I heal fast.
I came by to drop this off. I forgot to g
to you
Oh-oh my god! I thought it was gone, I-I saved up forEVER for this... Th-thankyou!
Sure.
Y-y-you wanna come in...?
You should keep me company, you SAID y-you were gonna come over, 'member?
...Okay.

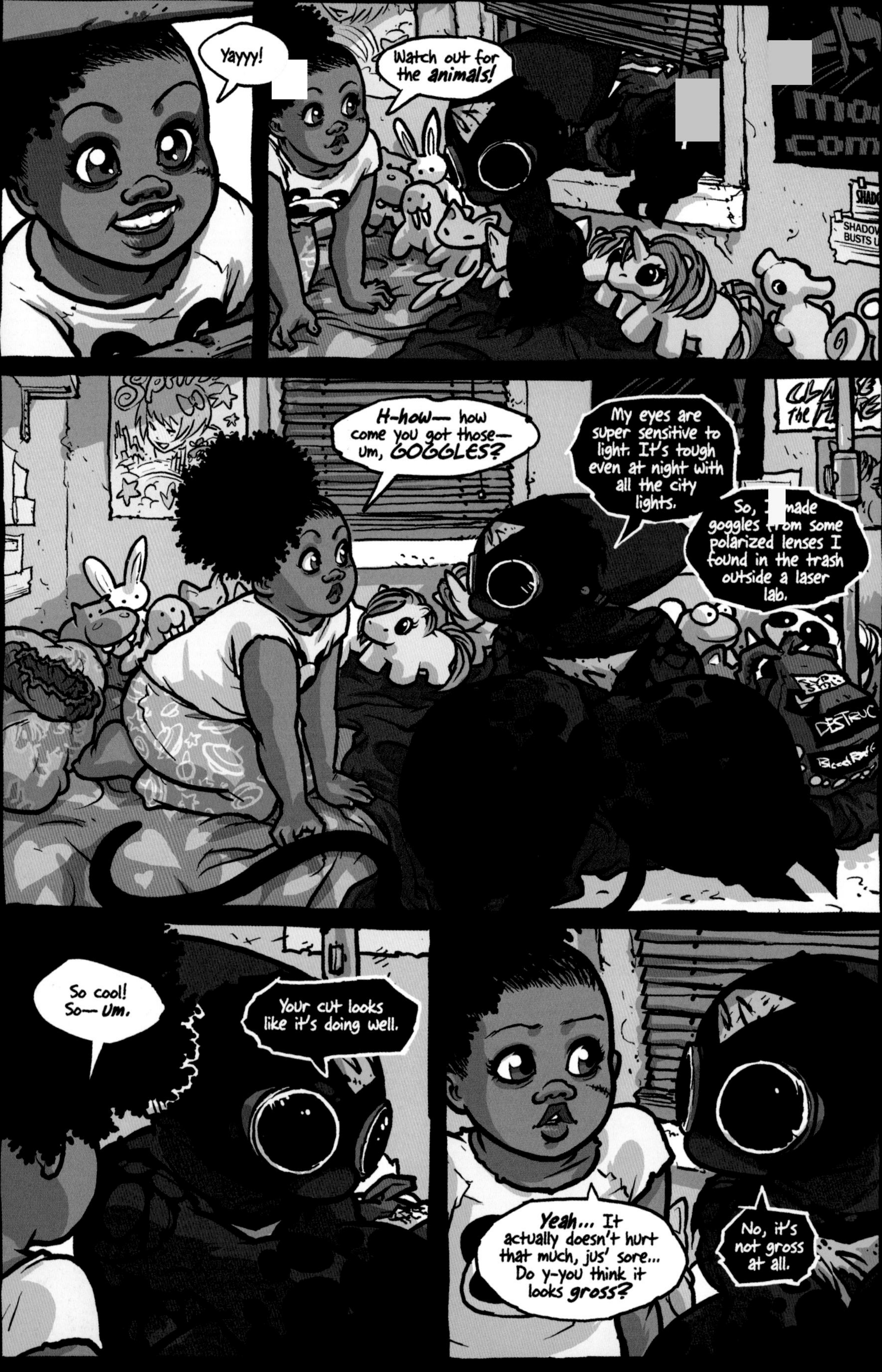

Yayyy!
Watch out for the animals!
H-how— how come you got those— um, GOGGLES?
My eyes are super sensitive to light. It's tough even at night with all the city lights.
So, I made goggles from some polarized lenses I found in the trash outside a laser lab.
So cool! So— Um.
Your cut looks like it's doing well.
Yeah... It actually doesn't hurt that much, jus' sore... Do y-you think it looks gross?
No, it's not gross at all.

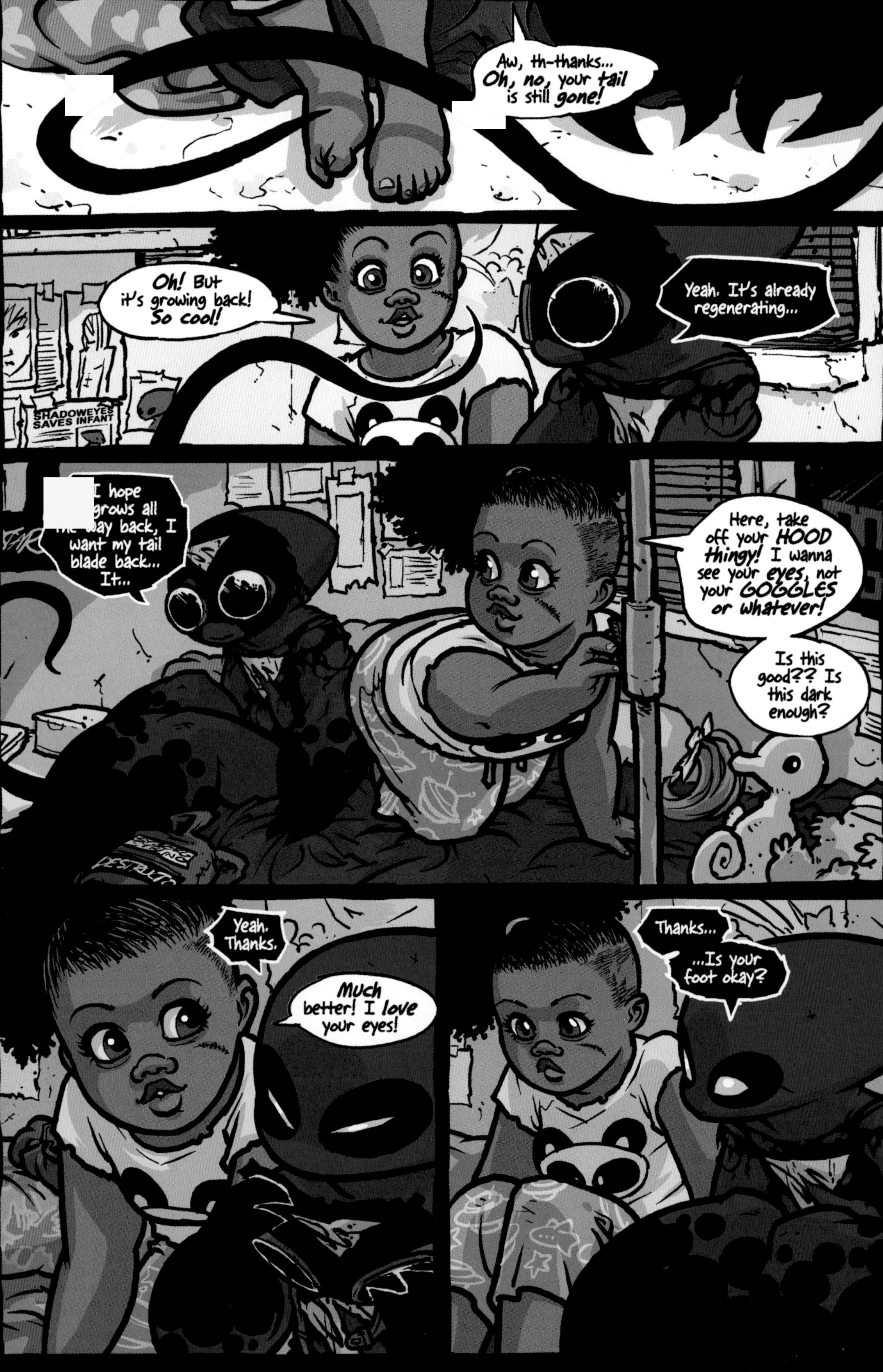
Aw, th-thanks... Oh, no, your tail is still gone!
Oh! But it's growing back! So cool!
Yeah. It's already regenerating...
SHADOWEYES SAVES INFANT
I hope grows all way back, I want my tail blade back... It...
Here, take off your HOOD thingy! I wanna see your eyes, not your GOGGLES or whatever!
Is this good?? Is this dark enough?
Yeah. Thanks.
Much better! I love your eyes!
Thanks...
...Is your foot okay?

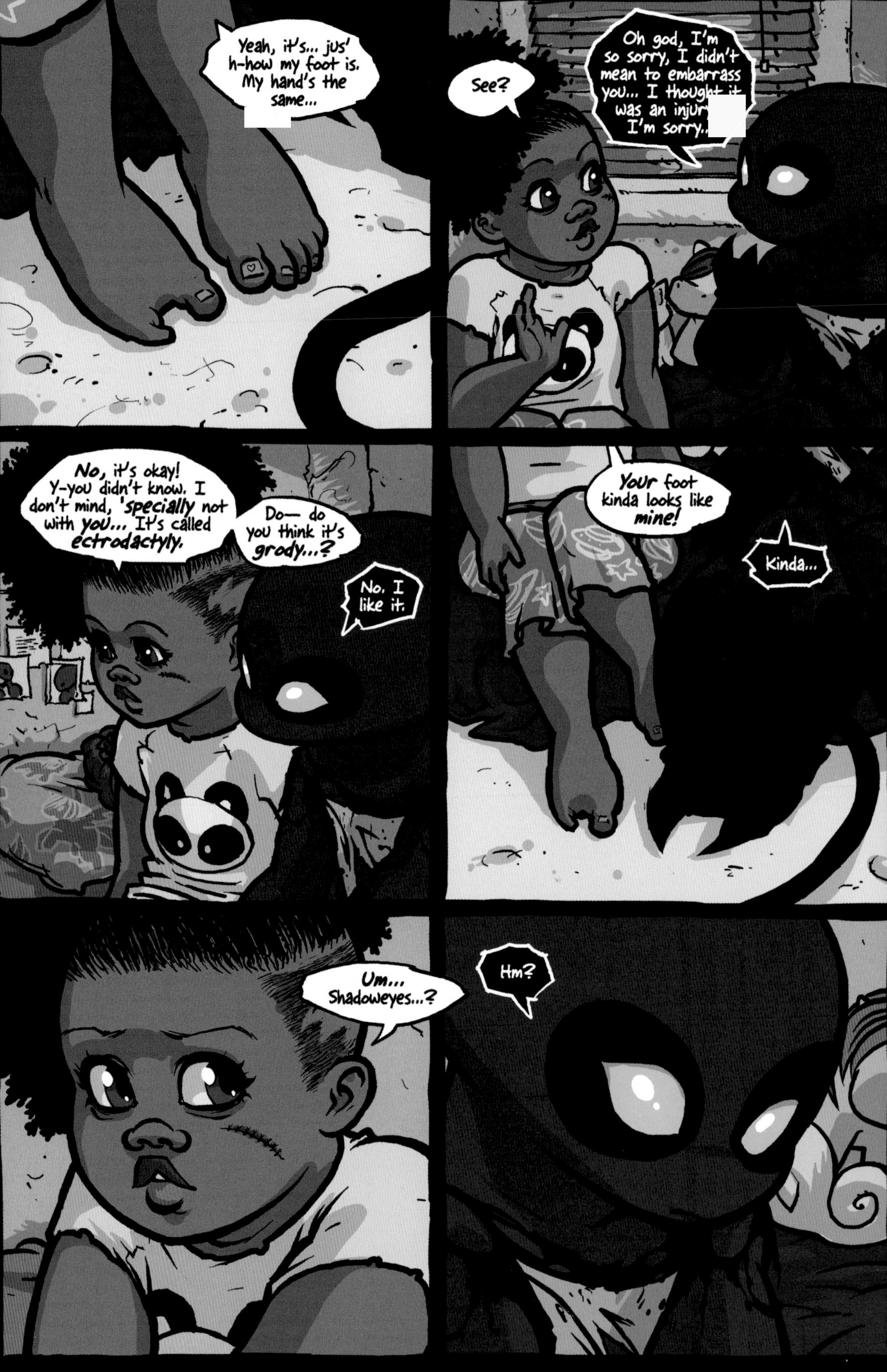
Yeah, it's... jus' h-how my foot is. My hand's the same...
See?
Oh god, I'm so sorry, I didn't mean to embarrass you... I thought it was an injury I'm sorry...
No, it's okay! Y-you didn't know. I don't mind, 'specially not with you... It's called ectrodactyly.
Do— do you think it's grody...?
No. I like it.
Your foot kinda looks like mine!
Kinda...
Um... Shadoweyes...?
Hm?

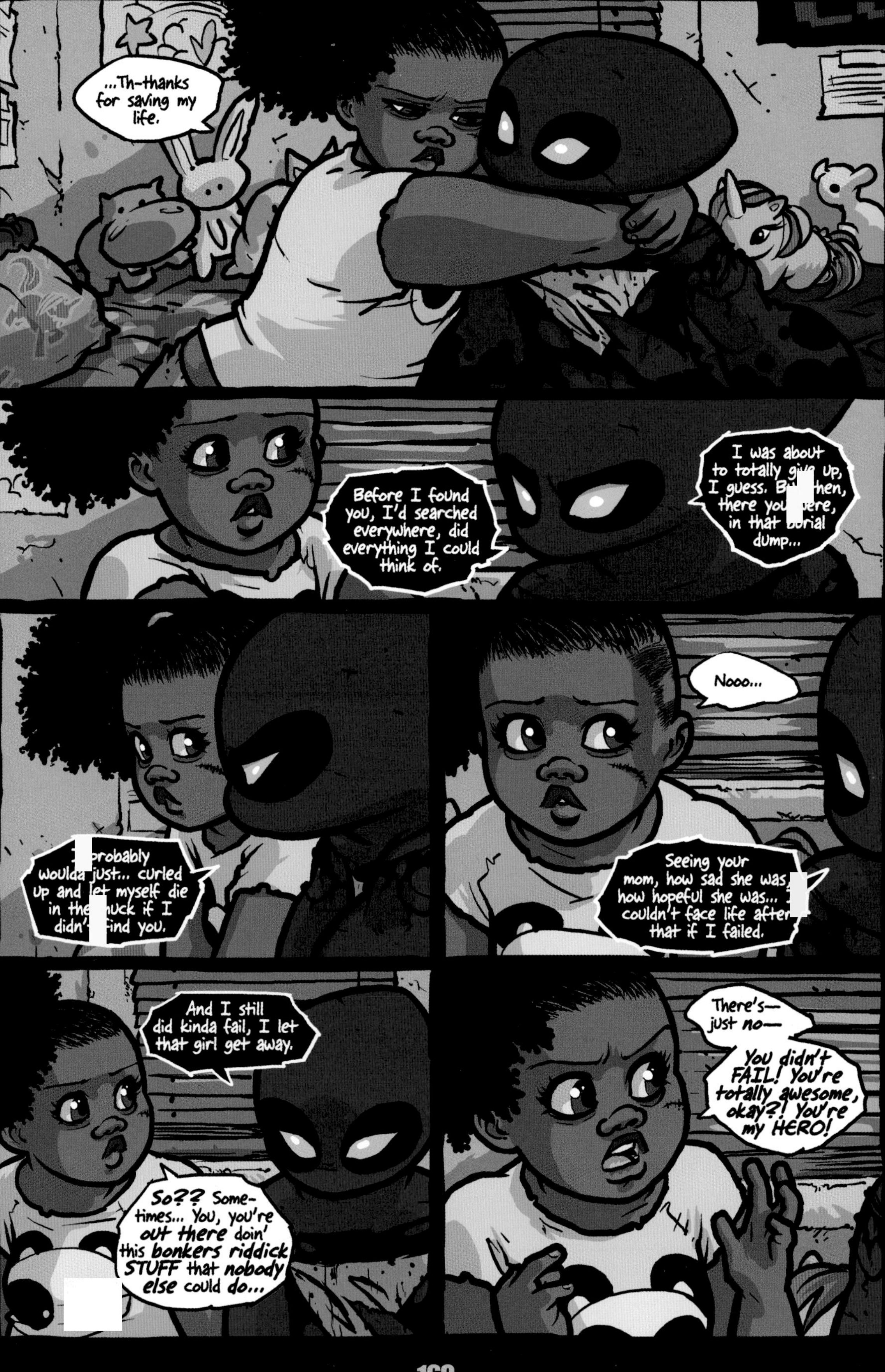
...Th-thanks for saving my life.
Before I found you, I'd searched everywhere, did everything I could think of.
I was about to totally gi up, I guess. B hen, there you ere, in that urial dump...
Nooo...
robably woulda just... curled up and let myself die in the uck if I didn' find you.
Seeing your mom, how sad she was, how hopeful she was... couldn't face life after that if I failed.
And I still did kinda fail, I let that girl get away.
So?? Sometimes... You, you're out there doin' this bonkers riddick STUFF that nobody else could do...
There's— just no—
You didn't FAIL! You're totally awesome, okay?! You're my HERO!

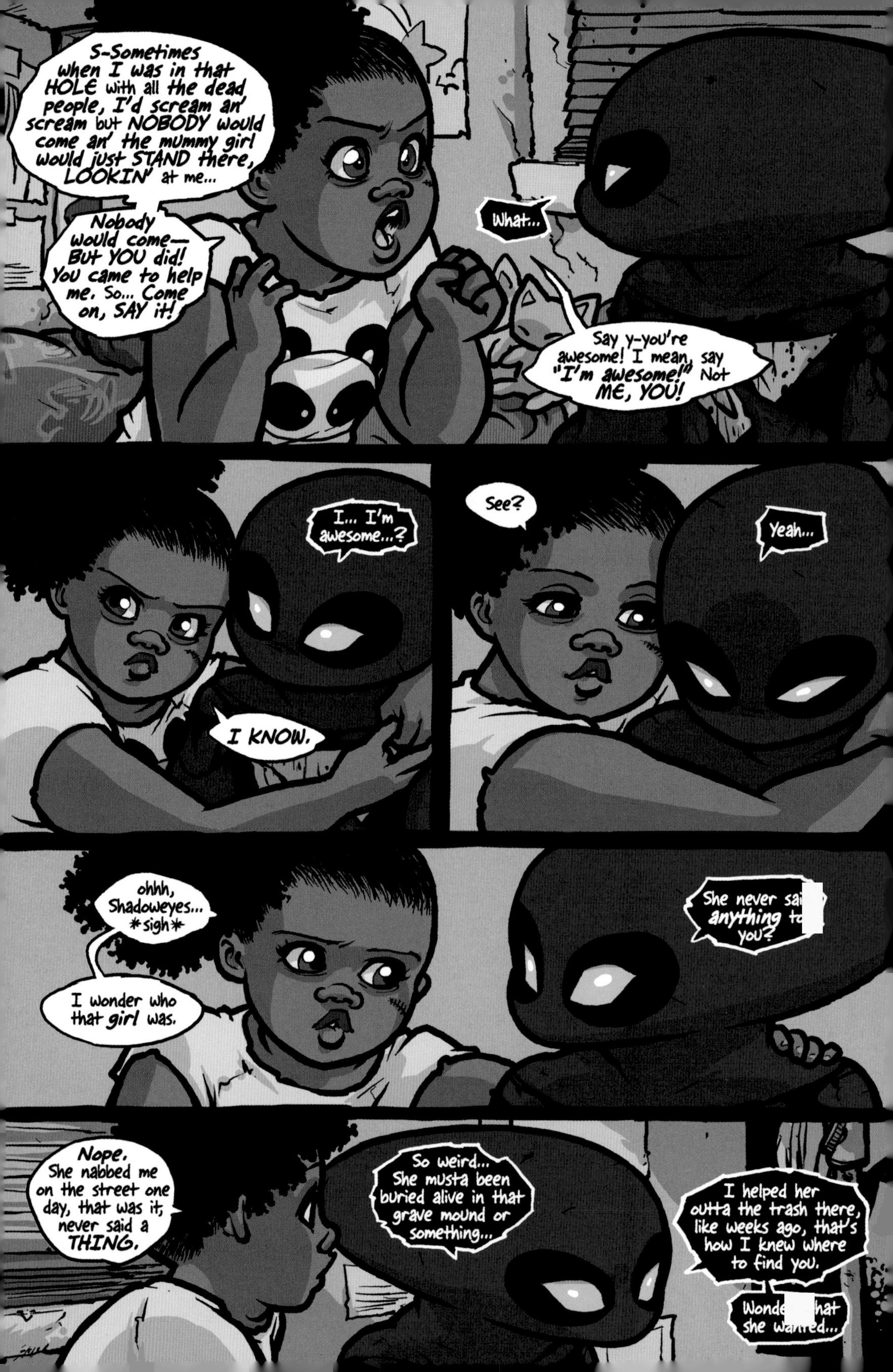
S-Sometimes when I was in that HOLE with all the dead people, I'd scream an' scream but NOBODY would come an' the mummy girl would just STAND there, LOOKIN' at me...
Nobody would come— But YOU did! You came to help me. So... Come on, SAY it!
What...
Say y-you're awesome! I mean, say "I'm awesome!" Not ME, YOU!
I... I'm awesome...?
I KNOW.
See?
Yeah...
ohhh, Shadoweyes... *sigh*
I wonder who that girl was.
She never sai anything t you?
Nope. She nabbed me on the street one day, that was it, never said a THING.
So weird... She musta been buried alive in that grave mound or something...
I helped her outta the trash there, like weeks ago, that's how I knew where to find you.
Wonde hat she wanted...

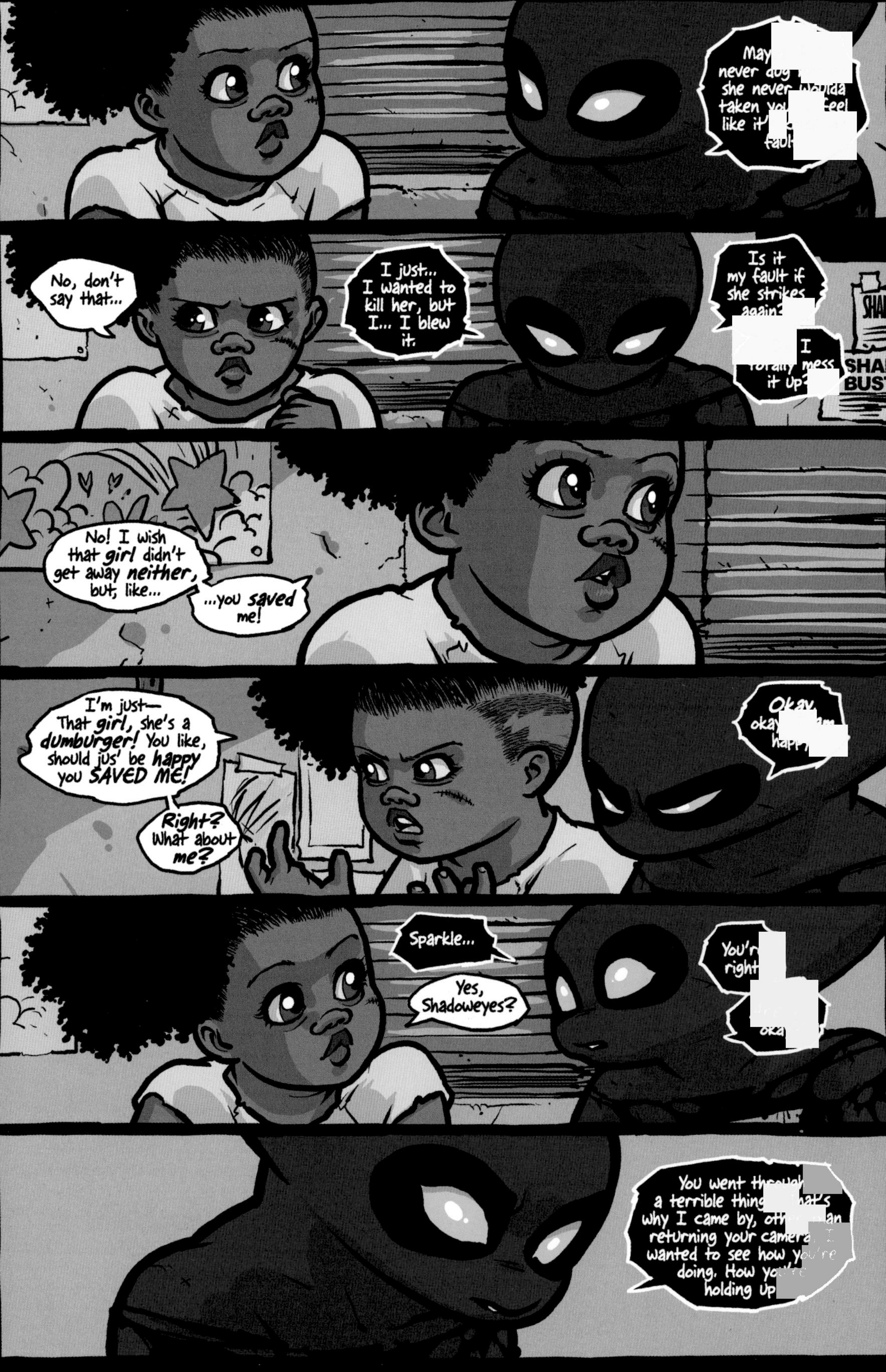
No, don't say that...
I just... I wanted to kill her, but I... I blew it.
Is it my fault if she strikes
No! I wish that girl didn't get away neither, but, like...
...you saved me!
I'm just— That girl, she's a dumburger! You like, should jus' be happy you SAVED ME!
Right? What about me?
Sparkle...
Yes, Shadoweyes?

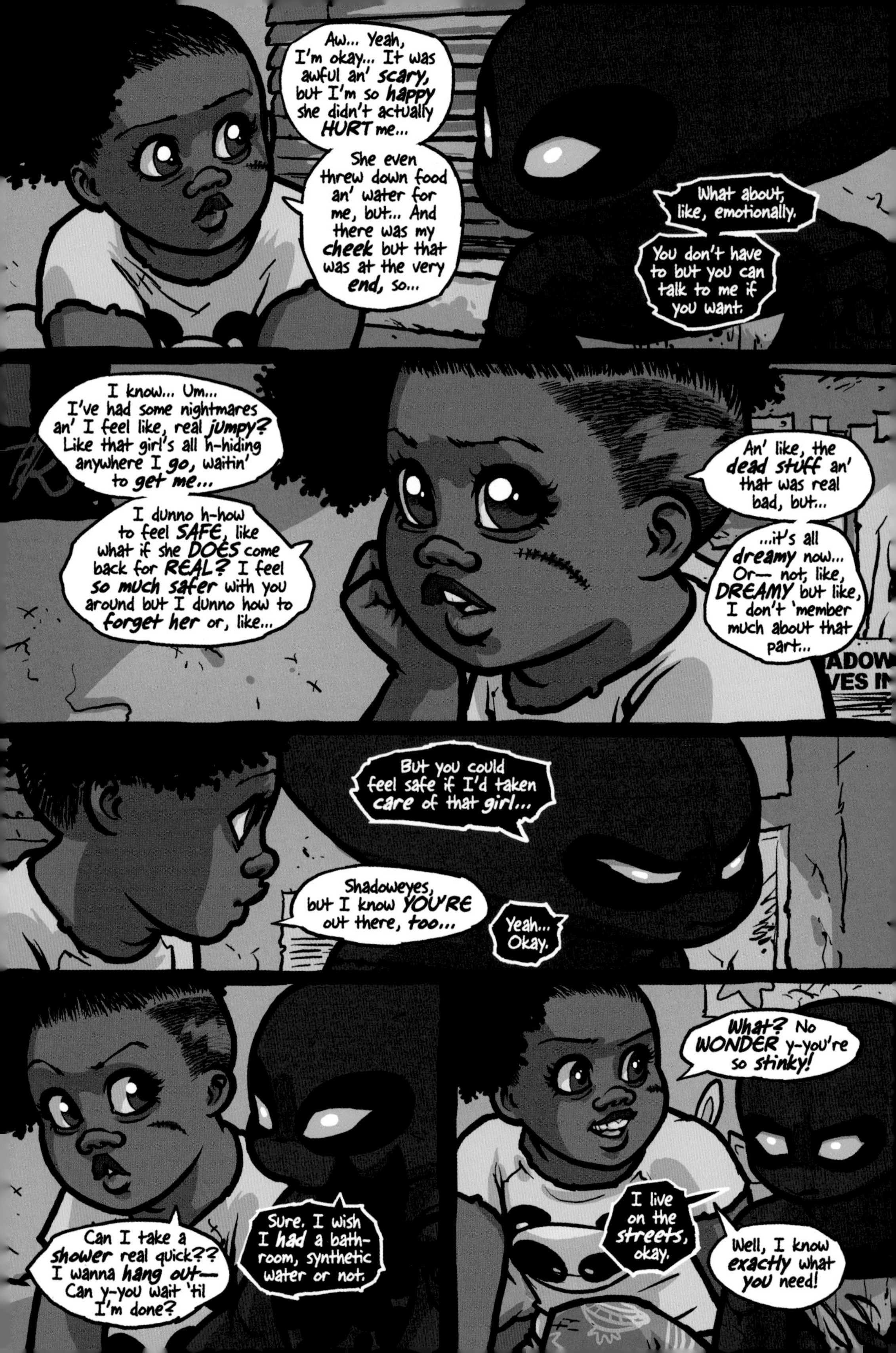
Aw... Yeah, I'm okay... It was awful an' scary, but I'm so happy she didn't actually HURT me...
She even threw down food an' water for me, but... And there was my cheek but that was at the very end, so...
What about, like, emotionally.
You don't have to but you can talk to me if you want.
I know... Um... I've had some nightmares an' I feel like, real jumpy? Like that girl's all h-hiding anywhere I go, waitin' to get me...
I dunno h-how to feel SAFE, like what if she DOES come back for REAL? I feel so much safer with you around but I dunno how to forget her or, like...
An' like, the dead stuff an' that was real bad, but...
...it's all dreamy now... Or— not, like, DREAMY but like, I don't 'member much about that part...
ADOW
VES IN
But you could feel safe if I'd taken care of that girl...
Shadoweyes, but I know YOU'RE out there, too...
Yeah... Okay.
Can I take a shower real quick?? I wanna hang out— Can y-you wait 'til I'm done?
Sure. I wish I had a bath-room, synthetic water or not.
What? No WONDER y-you're so stinky!
I live on the streets, okay.
Well, I know exactly what you need!

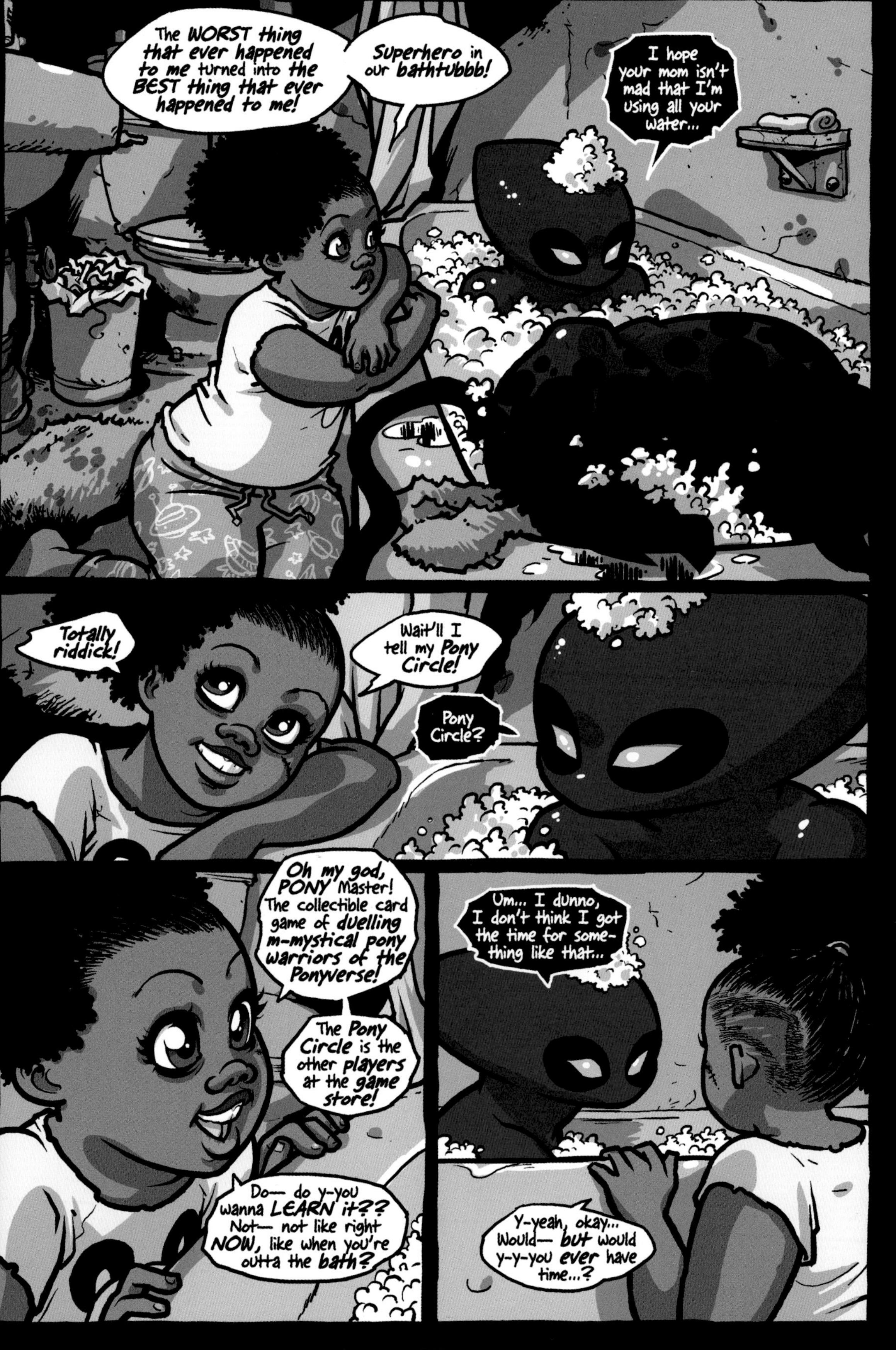
The WORST thing that ever happened to me turned into the BEST thing that ever happened to me!
Superhero in our bathtubbb!
I hope your mom isn't mad that I'm using all your water...
Totally riddick!
Wait'll I tell my Pony Circle!
Pony Circle?
Oh my god, PONY Master! The collectible card game of duelling m-mystical pony warriors of the Ponyverse!
The Pony Circle is the other players at the game store!
Do— do y-you wanna LEARN it?? Not— not like right NOW, like when you're outta the bath?
Um... I dunno, I don't think I got the time for some-thing like that...
Y-yeah, okay... Would— but would y-y-you ever have time...?

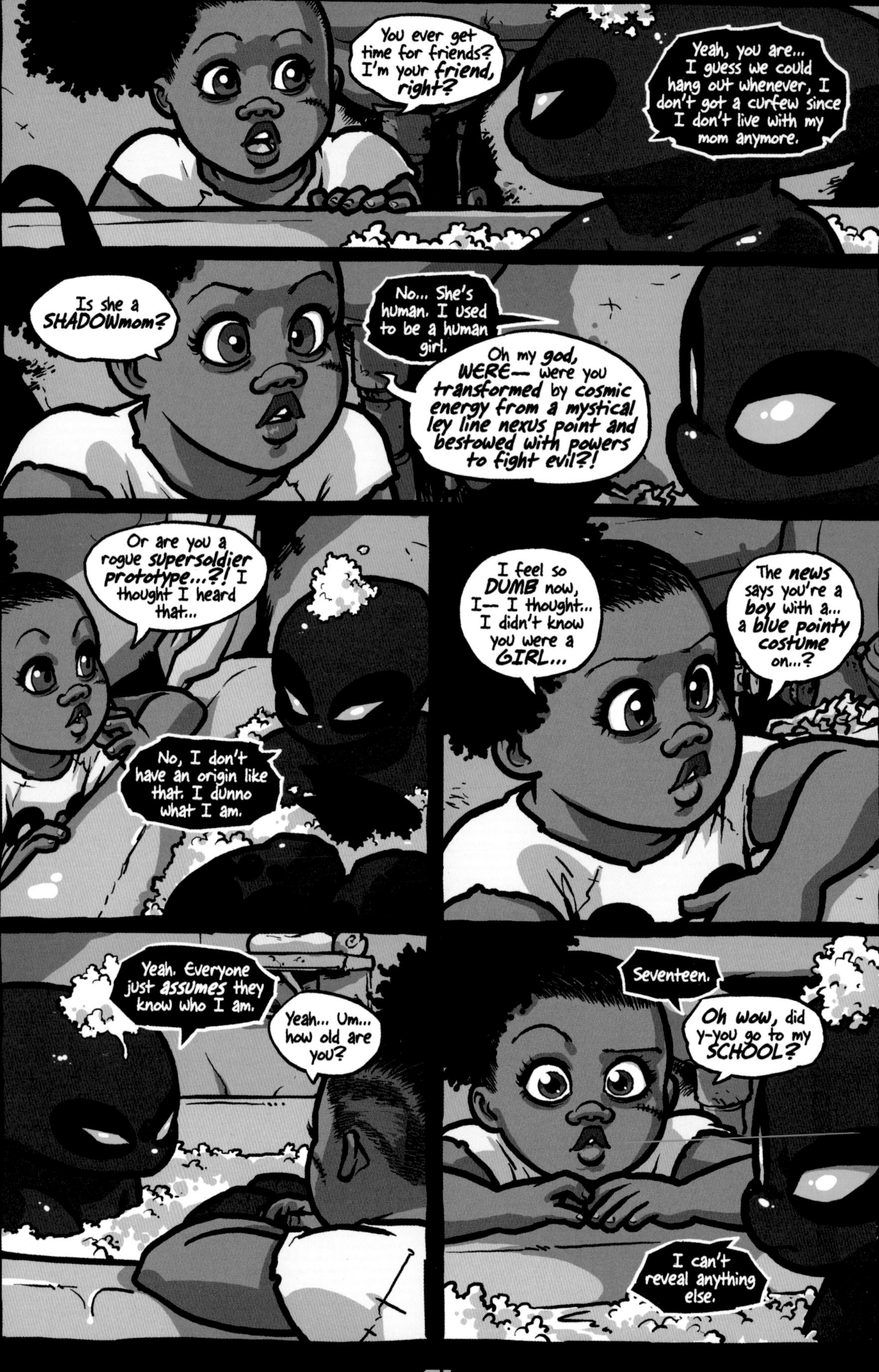
You ever get time for friends? I'm your friend, right?
Yeah, you are... I guess we could hang out whenever, I don't got a curfew since I don't live with my mom anymore.
Is she a SHADOWmom?
No... She's human. I used to be a human girl.
Oh my god, WERE— were you transformed by cosmic energy from a mystical ley line nexus point and bestowed with powers to fight evil?!
Or are you a rogue supersoldier prototype...?! I thought I heard that...
No, I don't have an origin like that. I dunno what I am.
I feel so DUMB now, I— I thought... I didn't know you were a GIRL...
The news says you're a boy with a... a blue pointy costume on...?
Yeah. Everyone just assumes they know who I am.
Yeah... Um... how old are you?
Seventeen.
Oh wow, did y-you go to my SCHOOL?
I can't reveal anything else.

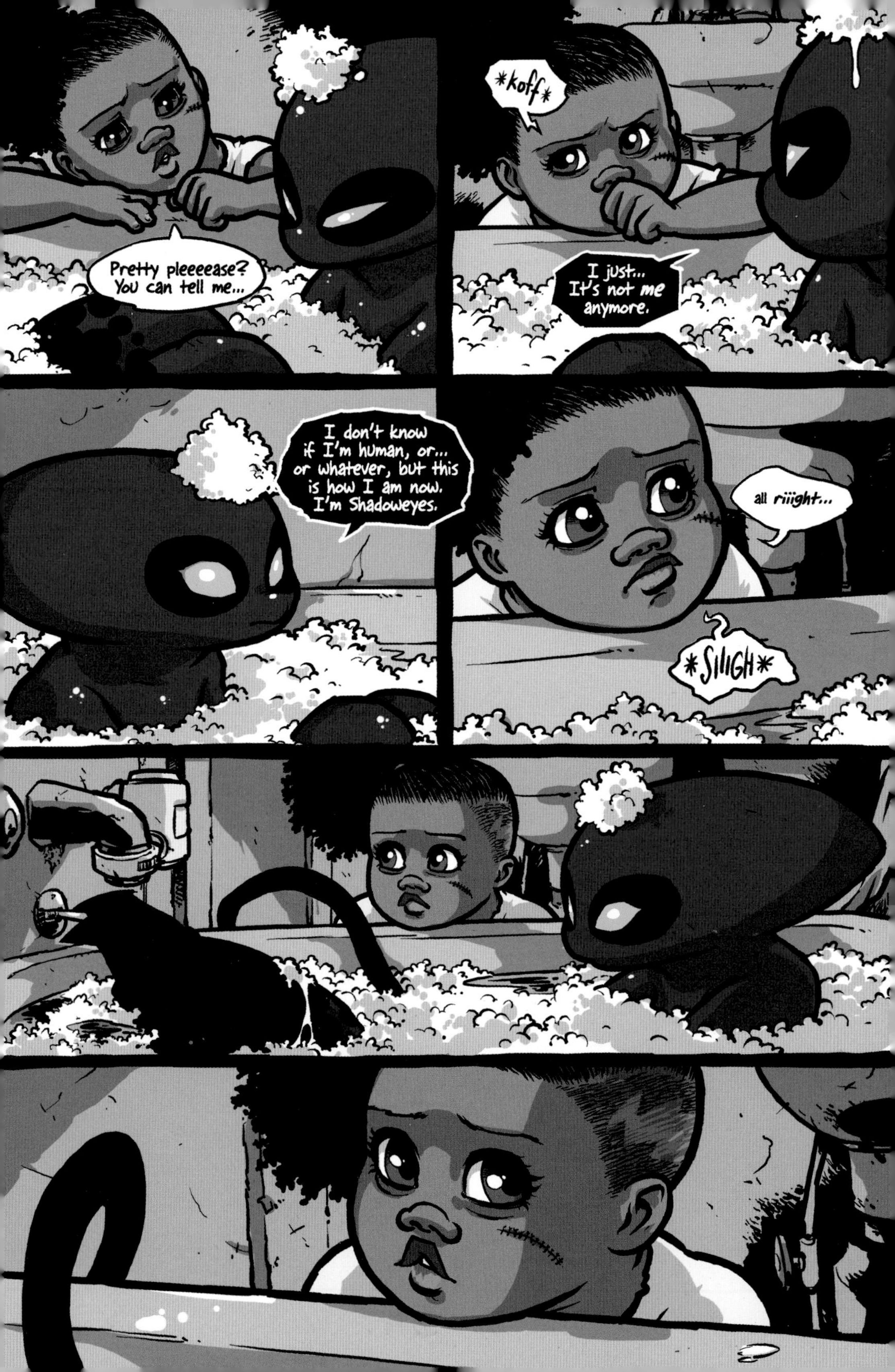
Pretty pleeeease? You can tell me...
koff
I just... It's not me anymore.
I don't know if I'm human, or... or whatever, but this is how I am now. I'm Shadoweyes.
all riiight...
SIIIGH

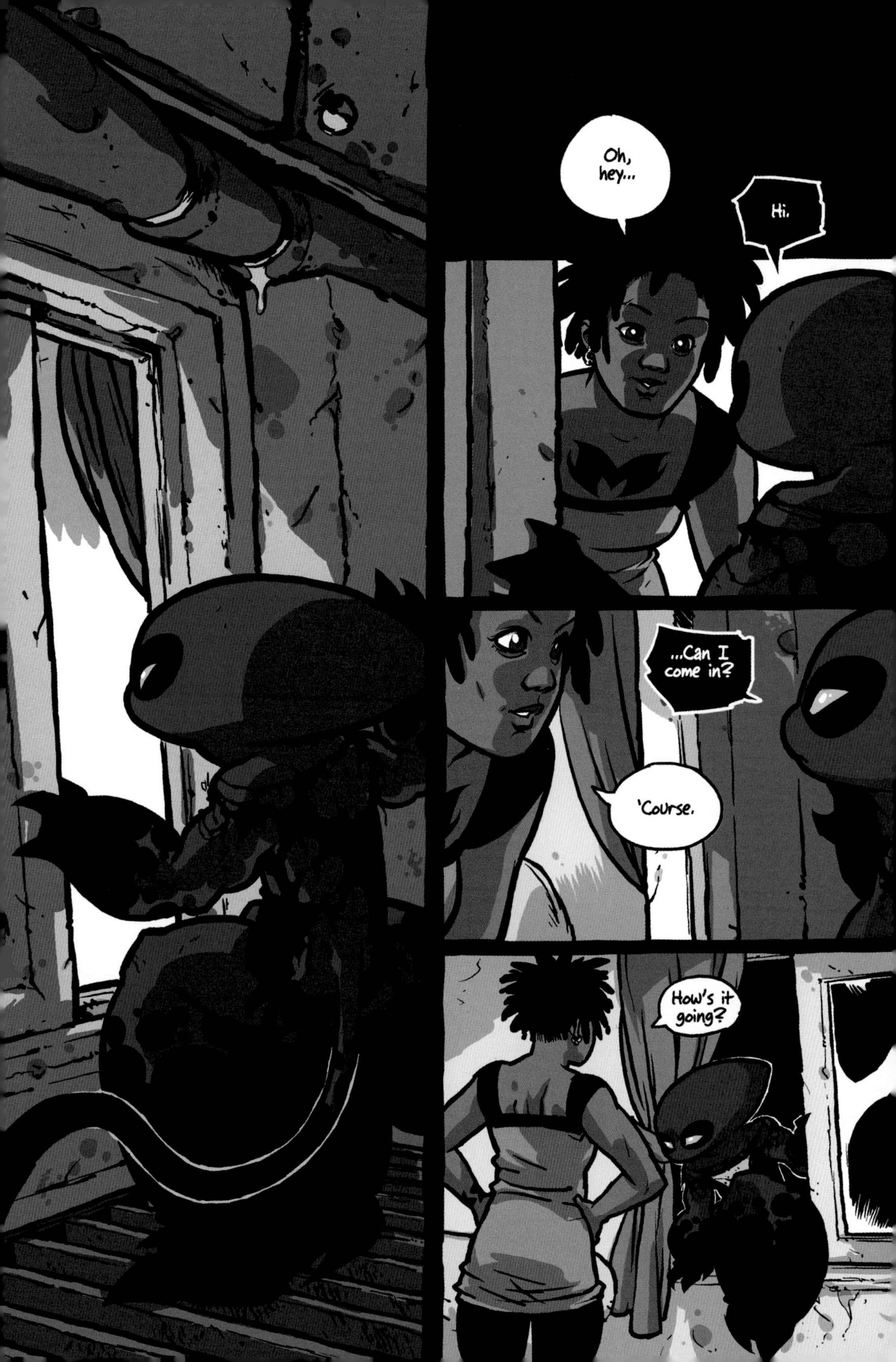
Oh, hey...
Hi.
...Can I come in?
'Course.
How's it going?

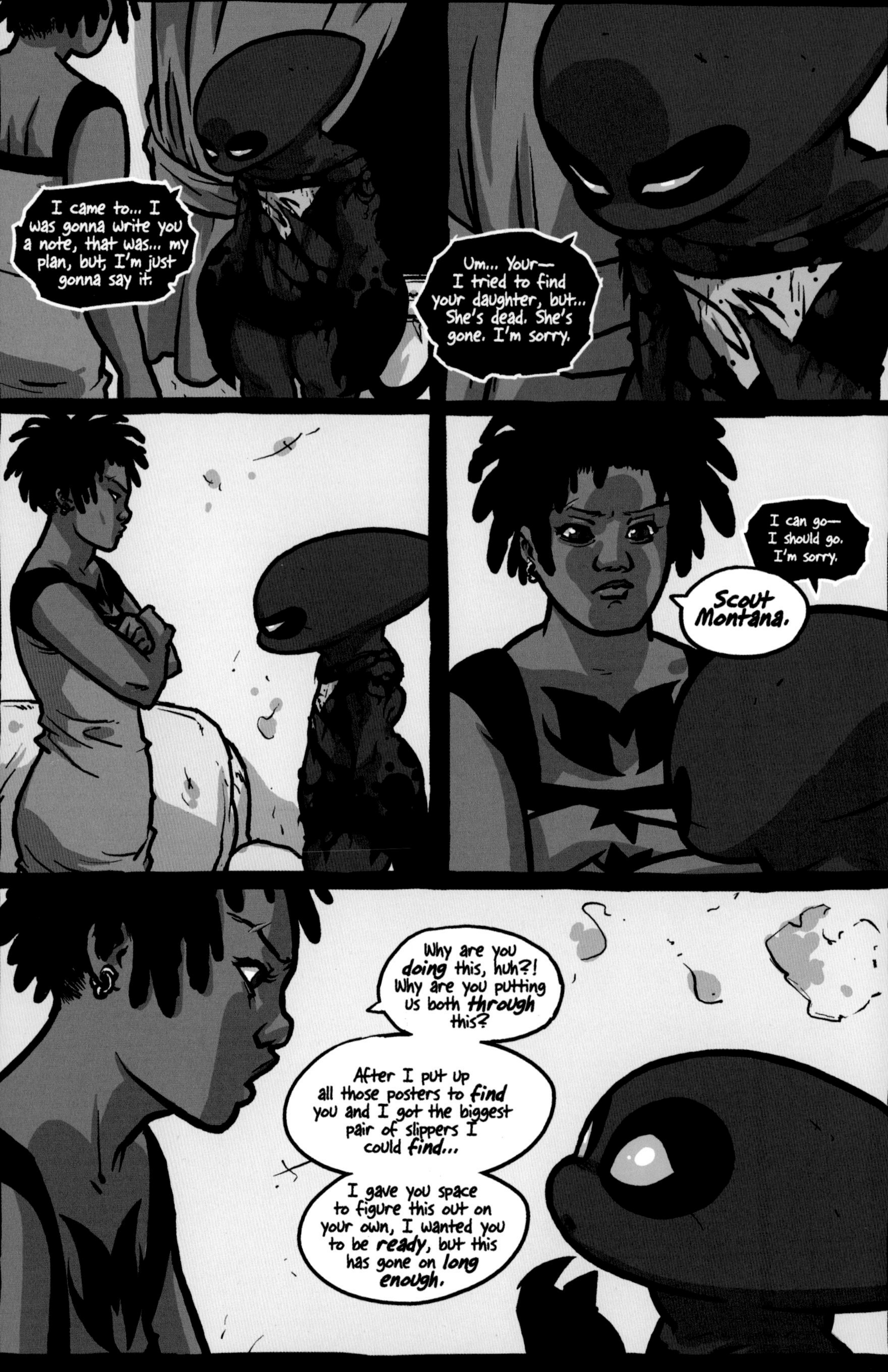

I came to... I was gonna write you a note, that was... my plan, but, I'm just gonna say it.
Um... Your— I tried to find your daughter, but... She's dead. She's gone. I'm sorry.
I can go— I should go. I'm sorry.
Scout Montana.
Why are you doing this, huh?! Why are you putting us both through this?
After I put up all those posters to find you and I got the biggest pair of slippers I could find...
I gave you space to figure this out on your own, I wanted you to be ready, but this has gone on long enough.

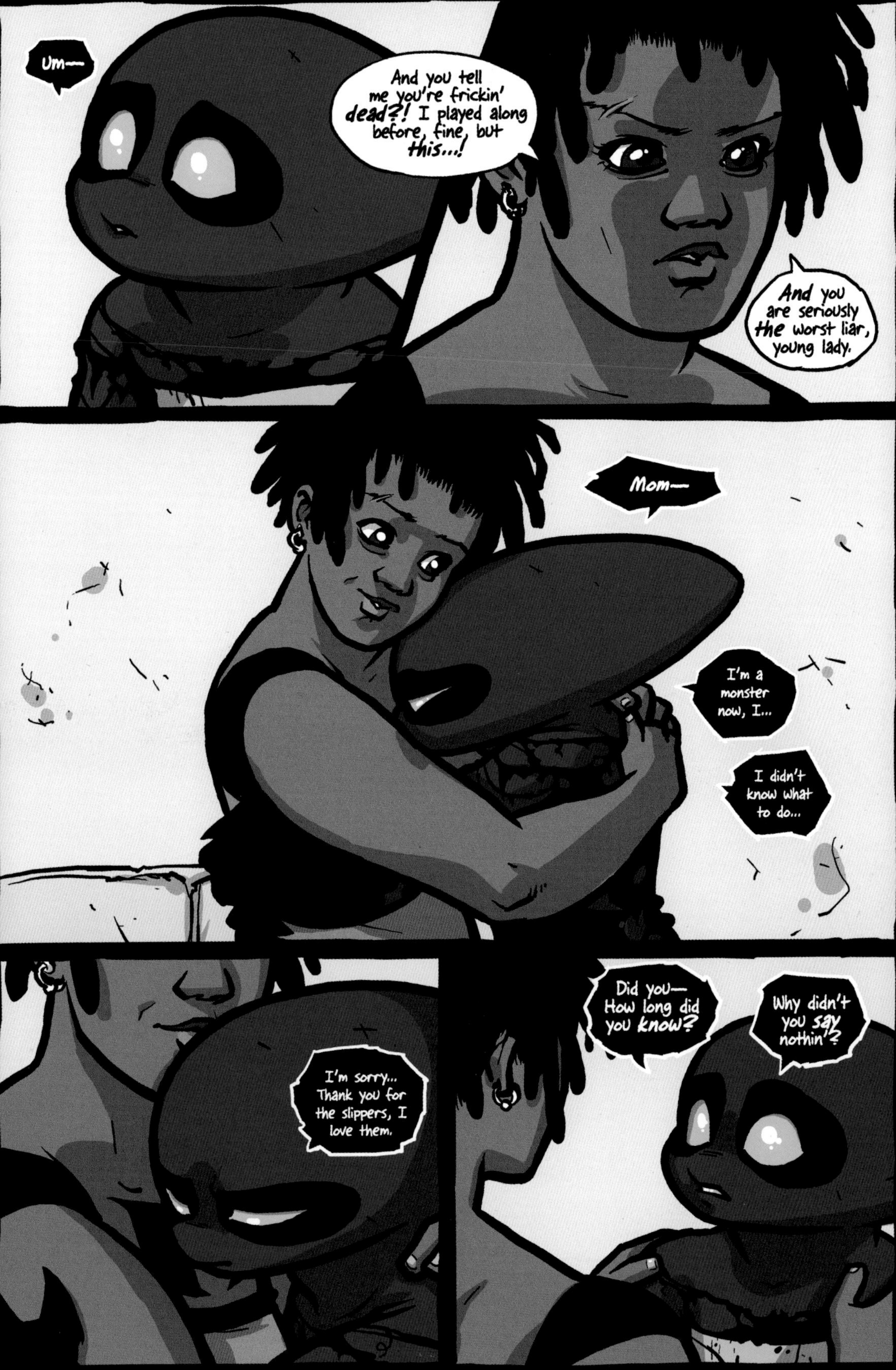
Um—
And you tell me you're frickin' dead?! I played along before, fine, but this...!
And you are seriously the worst liar, young lady.
Mom—
I'm a monster now, I...
I didn't know what to do...
I'm sorry... Thank you for the slippers, I love them.
Did you— How long did you know?
Why didn't you say nothin'?

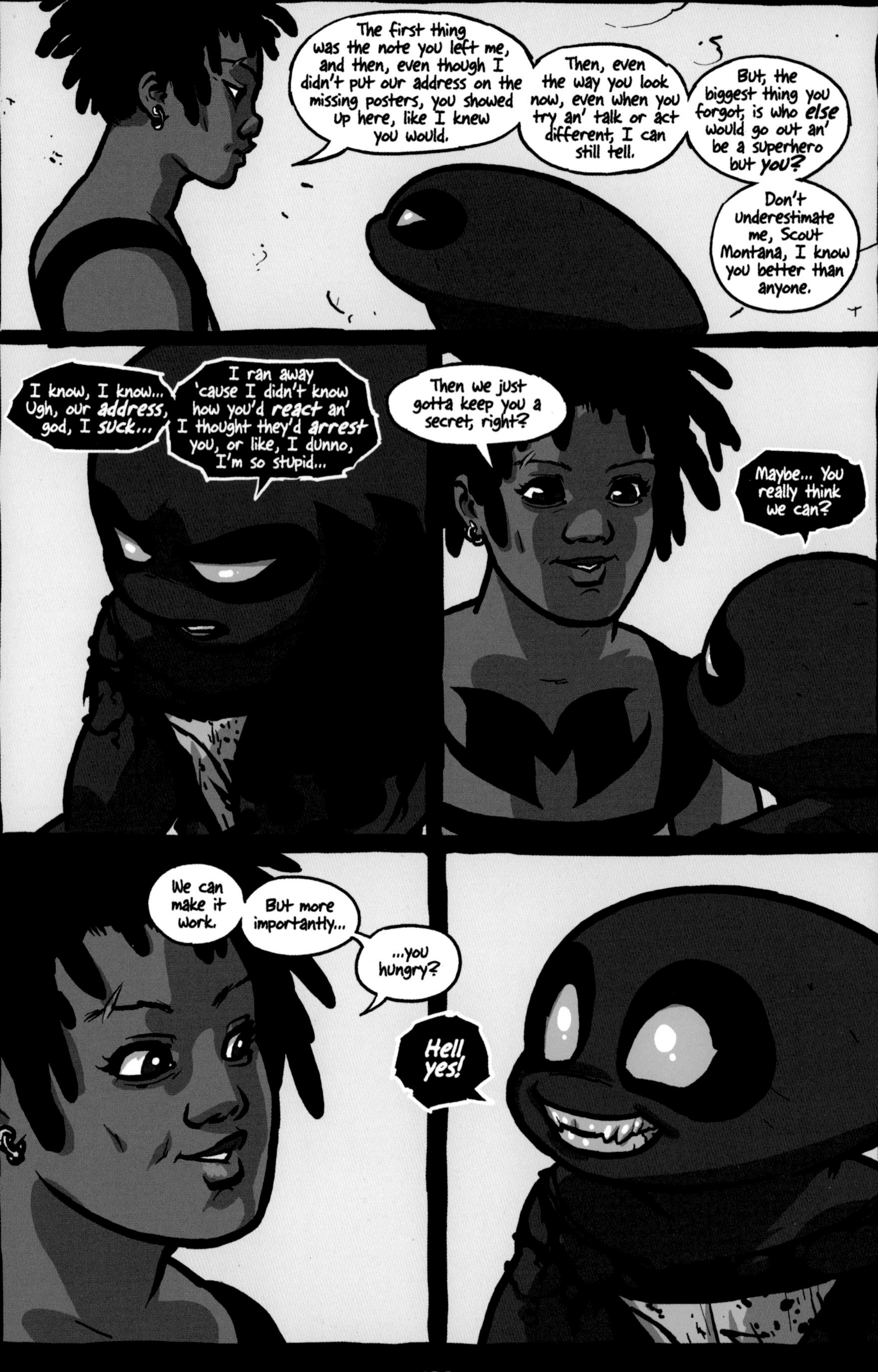
The first thing was the note you left me, and then, even though I didn't put our address on the missing posters, you showed up here, like I knew you would.
Then, even the way you look now, even when you try an' talk or act different, I can still tell.
But, the biggest thing you forgot, is who else would go out an' be a superhero but you?
Don't underestimate me, Scout Montana, I know you better than anyone.
I know, I know... Ugh, our address, god, I suck...
I ran away 'cause I didn't know how you'd react an' I thought they'd arrest you, or like, I dunno, I'm so stupid...
Then we just gotta keep you a secret, right?
Maybe... You really think we can?
We can make it work.
But more importantly...
...you hungry?
Hell yes!

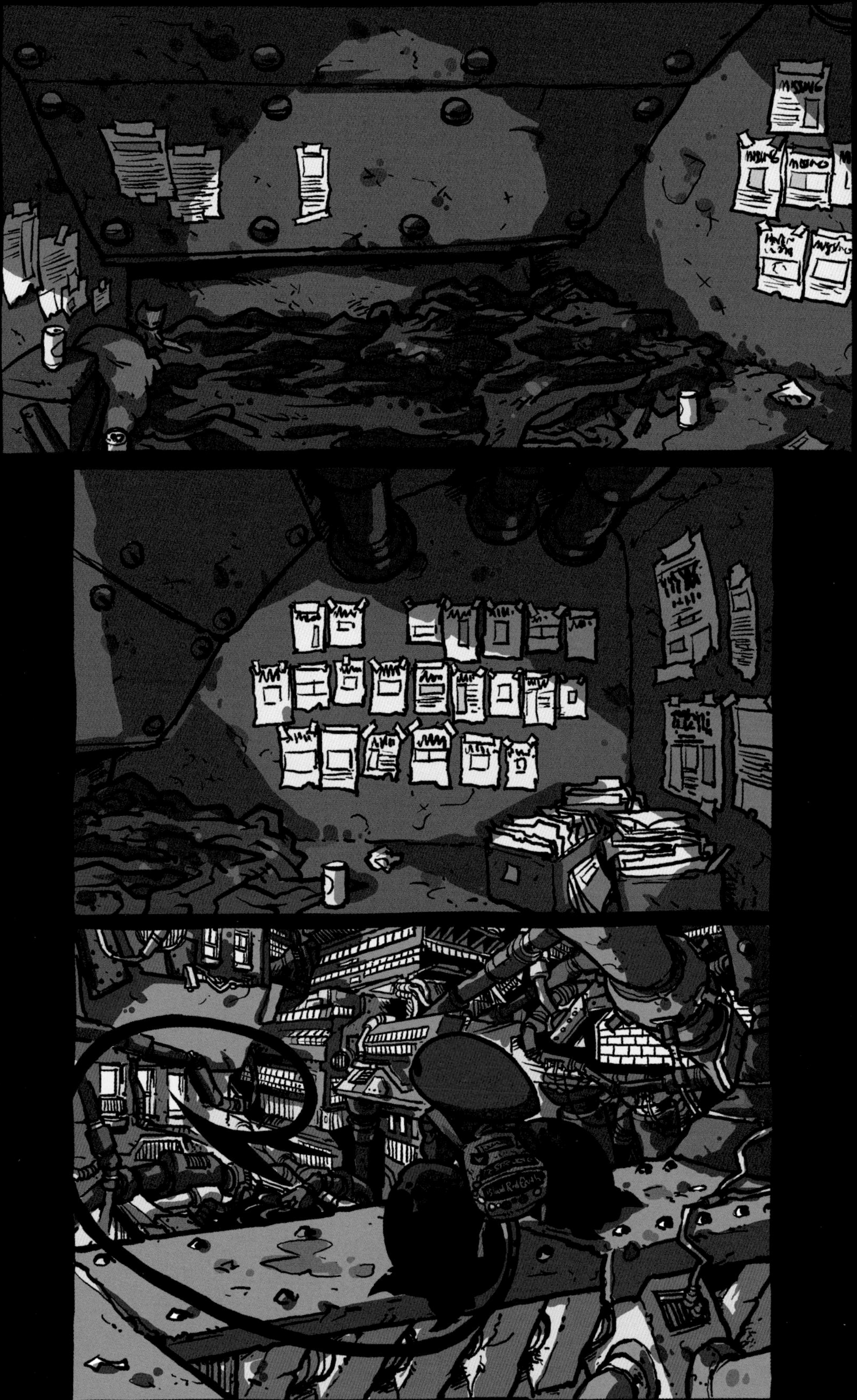
MISSING

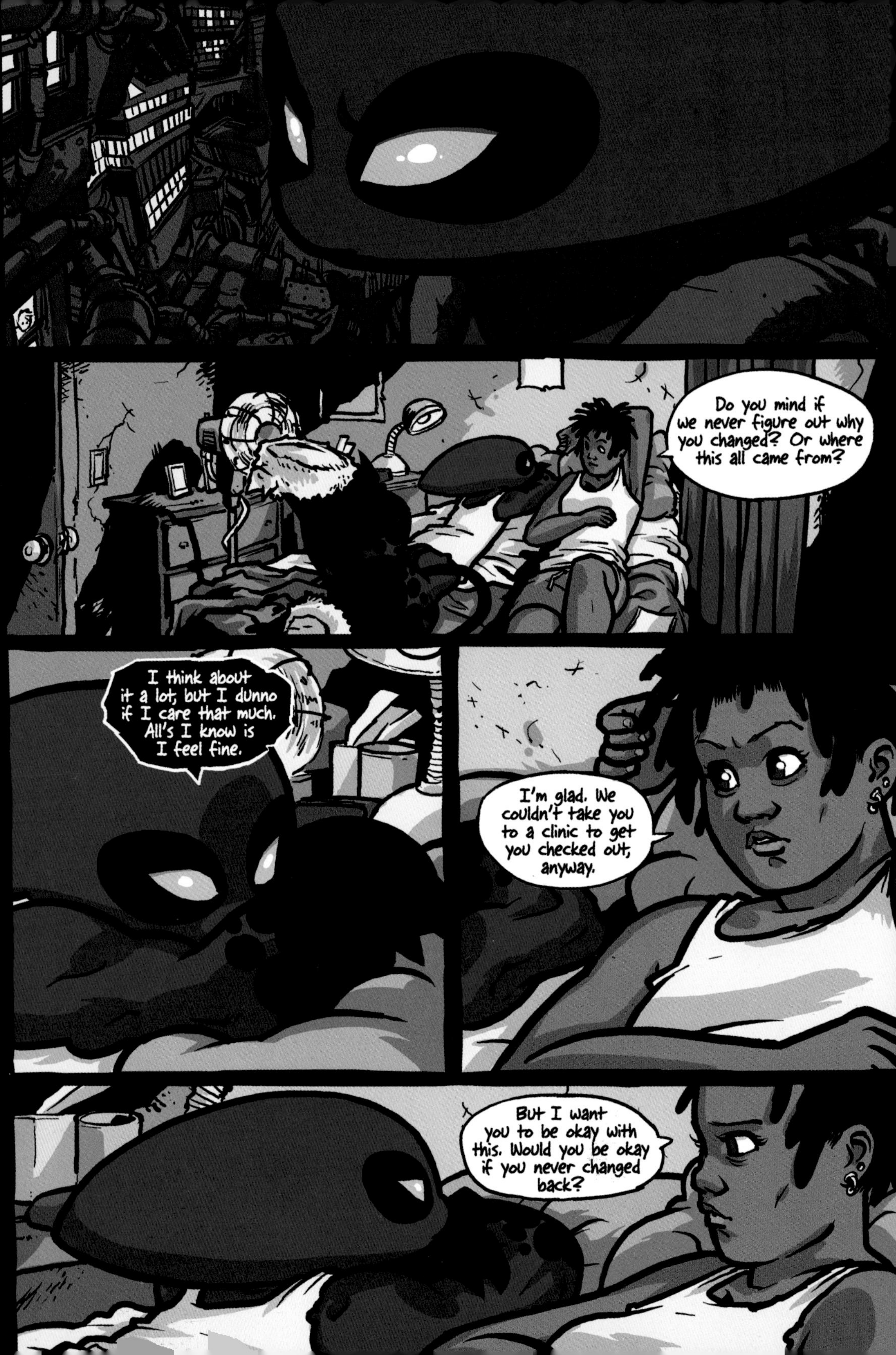
Do you mind if we never figure out why you changed? Or where this all came from?
I think about it a lot, but I dunno if I care that much. All's I know is I feel fine.
I'm glad. We couldn't take you to a clinic to get you checked out, anyway.
But I want you to be okay with this. Would you be okay if you never changed back?

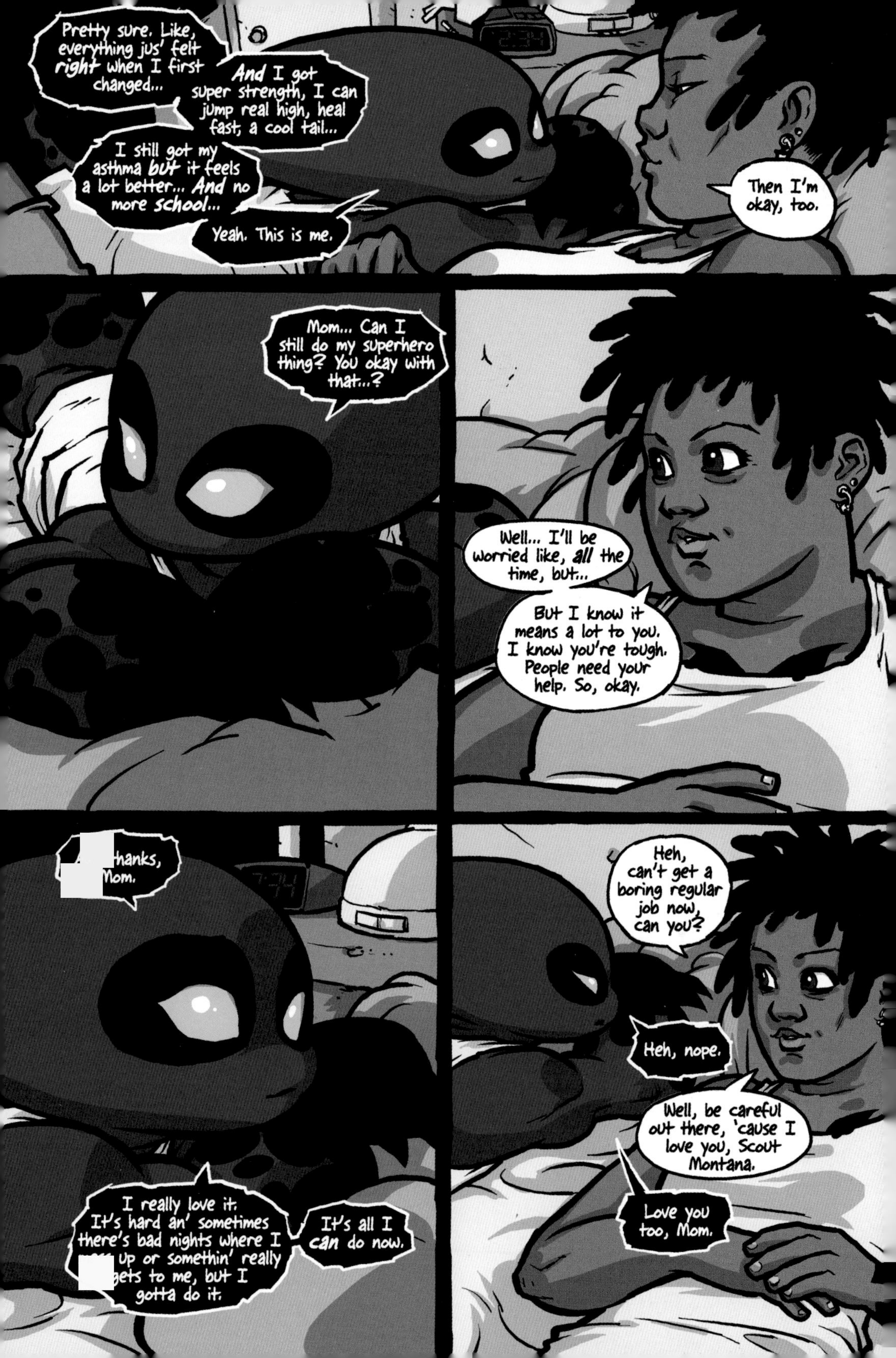
Pretty sure. Like, everything jus' felt right when I first changed...
And I got super strength, I can jump real high, heal fast, a cool tail...
I still got my asthma but it feels a lot better... And no more school...
Yeah. This is me.
Then I'm okay, too.
Mom... Can I still do my superhero thing? You okay with that...?
Well... I'll be worried like, all the time, but...
But I know it means a lot to you. I know you're tough. People need your help. So, okay.
hanks, Mom.
I really love it. It's hard an' sometimes there's bad nights where I up or somethin' really gets to me, but I gotta do it.
It's all I can do now.
Heh, can't get a boring regular job now, can you?
Heh, nope.
Well, be careful out there, 'cause I love you, Scout Montana.
Love you too, Mom.

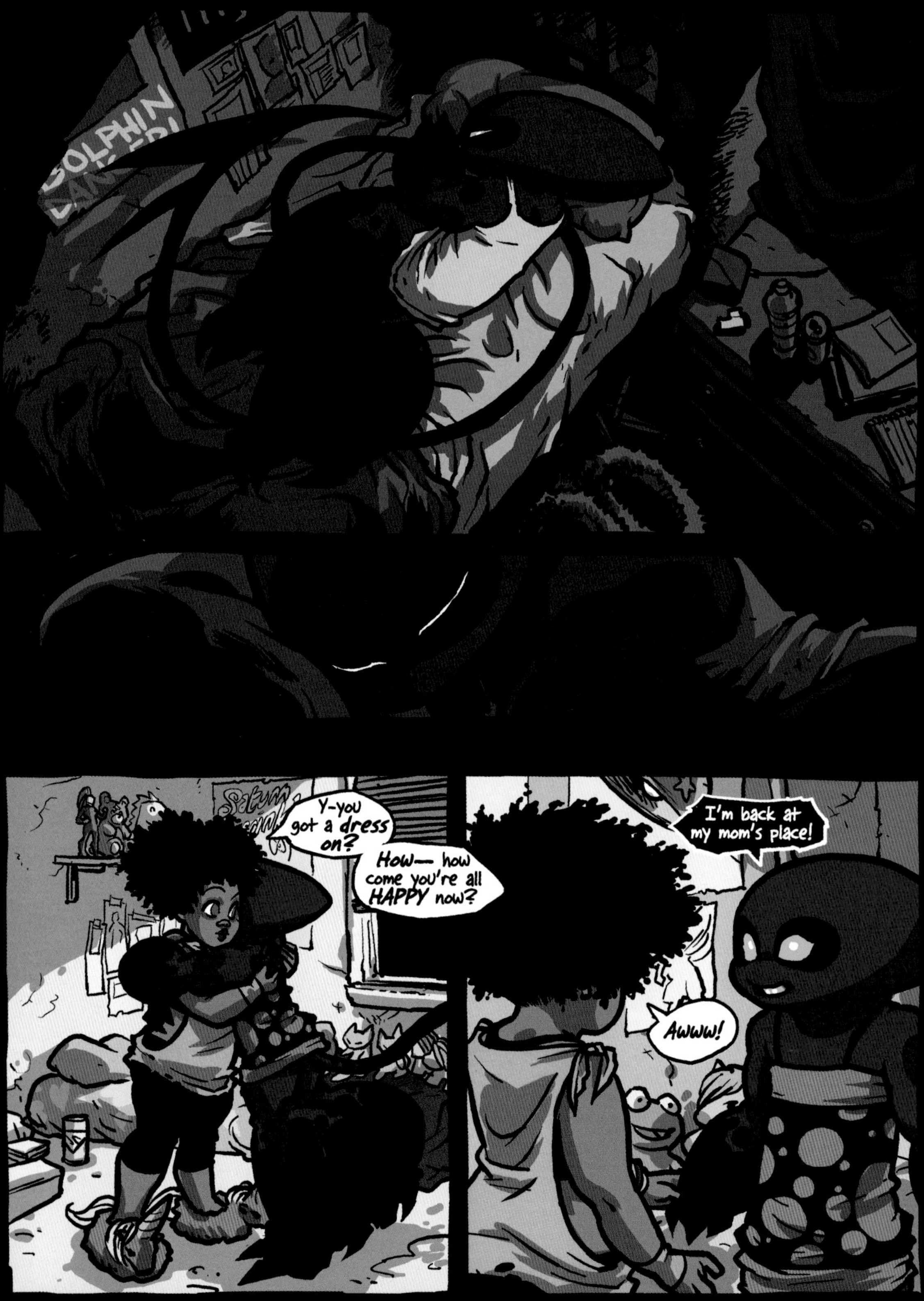

DOLPHIN
Y-you got a dress on?
How— how come you're all HAPPY now?
I'm back at my mom's place!
AWWW!

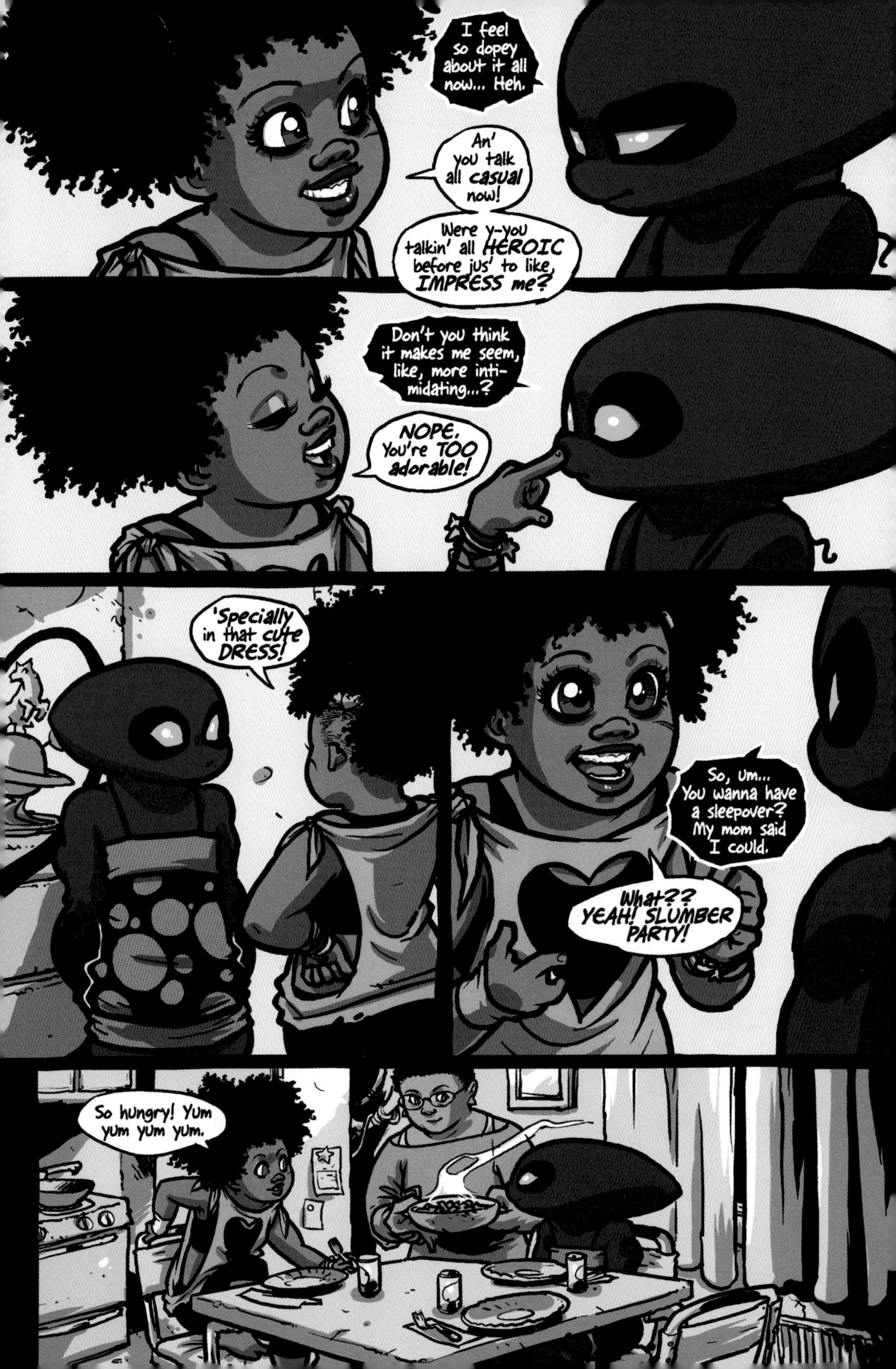

I feel so dopey about it all now... Heh.
An' you talk all casual now!
Were y-you talkin' all HEROIC before jus' to like, IMPRESS me?
Don't you think it makes me seem, like, more intimidating...?
NOPE. You're TOO adorable!
'Specially in that cute DRESS!
So, um... You wanna have a sleepover? My mom said I could.
What?? YEAH! SLUMBER PARTY!
So hungry! Yum yum yum yum.

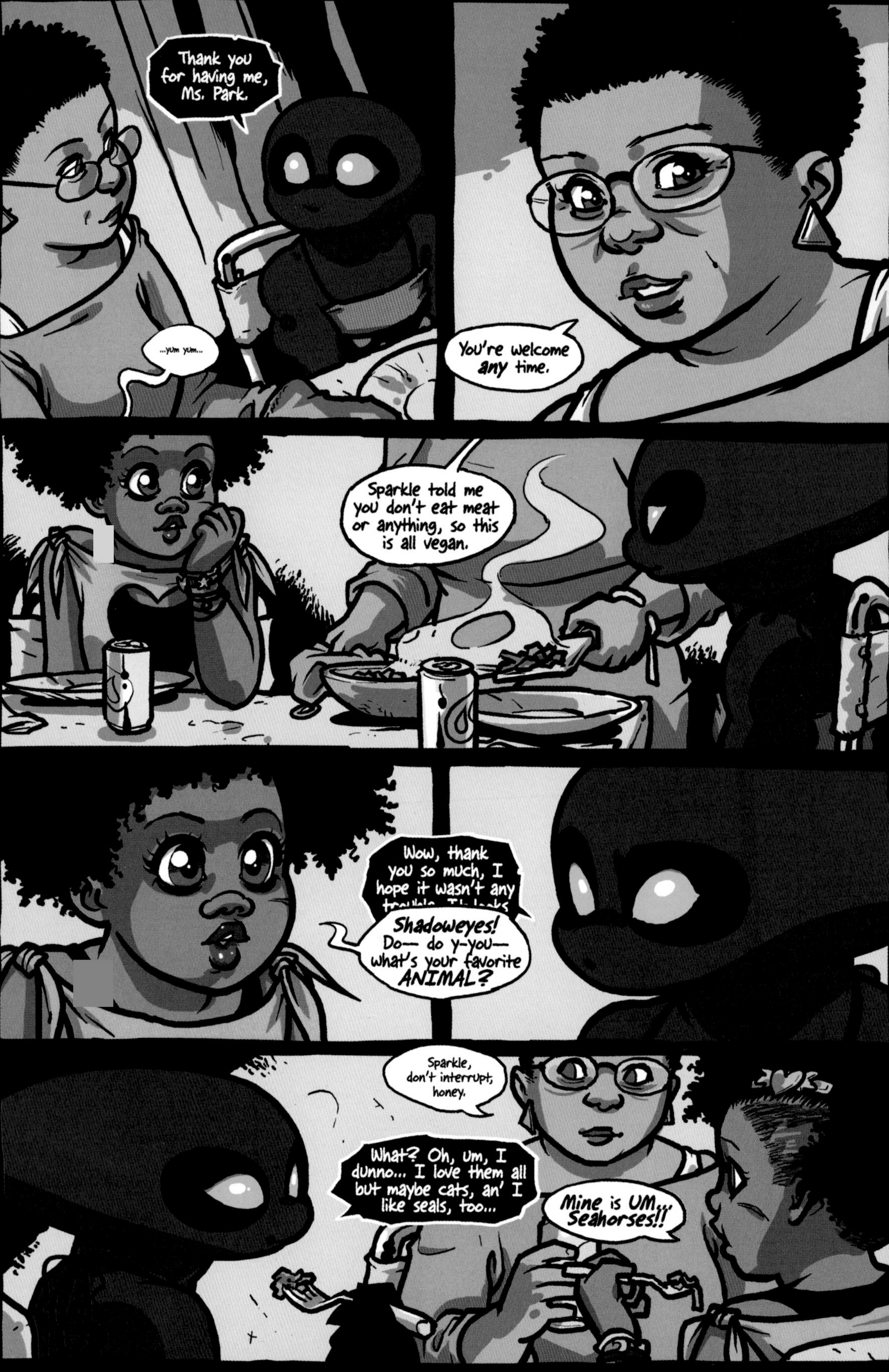
Thank you for having me, Ms. Park.
...yum yum...
You're welcome any time.
Sparkle told me you don't eat meat or anything, so this is all vegan.
Wow, thank you so much, I hope it wasn't any
Shadoweyes! Do— do y-you— what's your favorite ANIMAL?
Sparkle, don't interrupt, honey.
What? Oh, um, I dunno... I love them all but maybe cats, an' I like seals, too...
Mine is UM... Seahorses!!

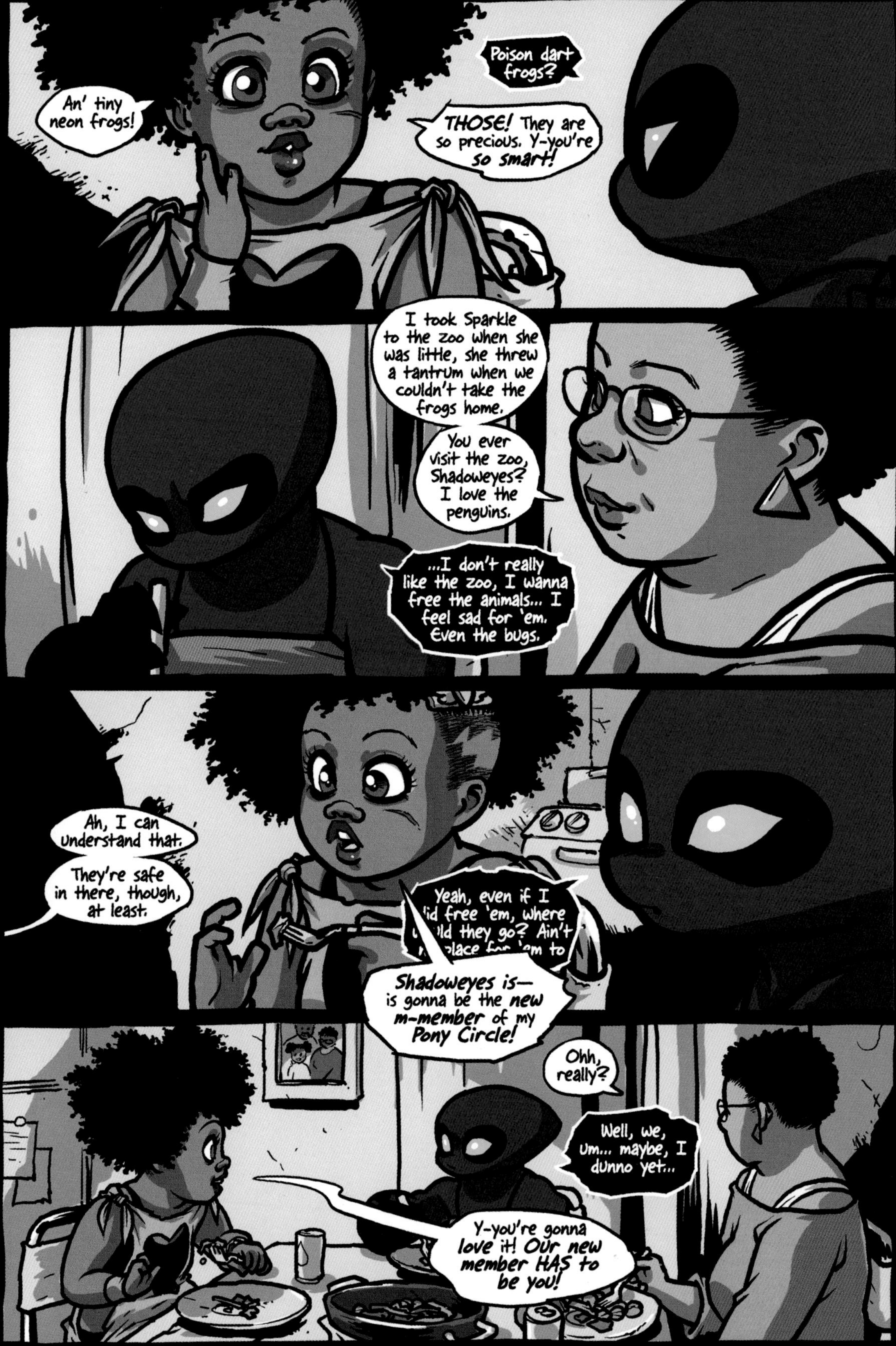
An' tiny neon frogs!
Poison dart frogs?
THOSE! They are so precious. Y-you're so smart!
I took Sparkle to the zoo when she was little, she threw a tantrum when we couldn't take the frogs home.
You ever visit the zoo, Shadoweyes? I love the penguins.
...I don't really like the zoo, I wanna free the animals... I feel sad for 'em. Even the bugs.
Ah, I can understand that.
They're safe in there, though, at least.
Yeah, even if I
free 'em, where
they go? Ain't
place for 'em to
Shadoweyes is— is gonna be the new m-member of my Pony Circle!
Ohh, really?
Well, we, um... maybe, I dunno yet...
Y-you're gonna love it! Our new member HAS to be you!

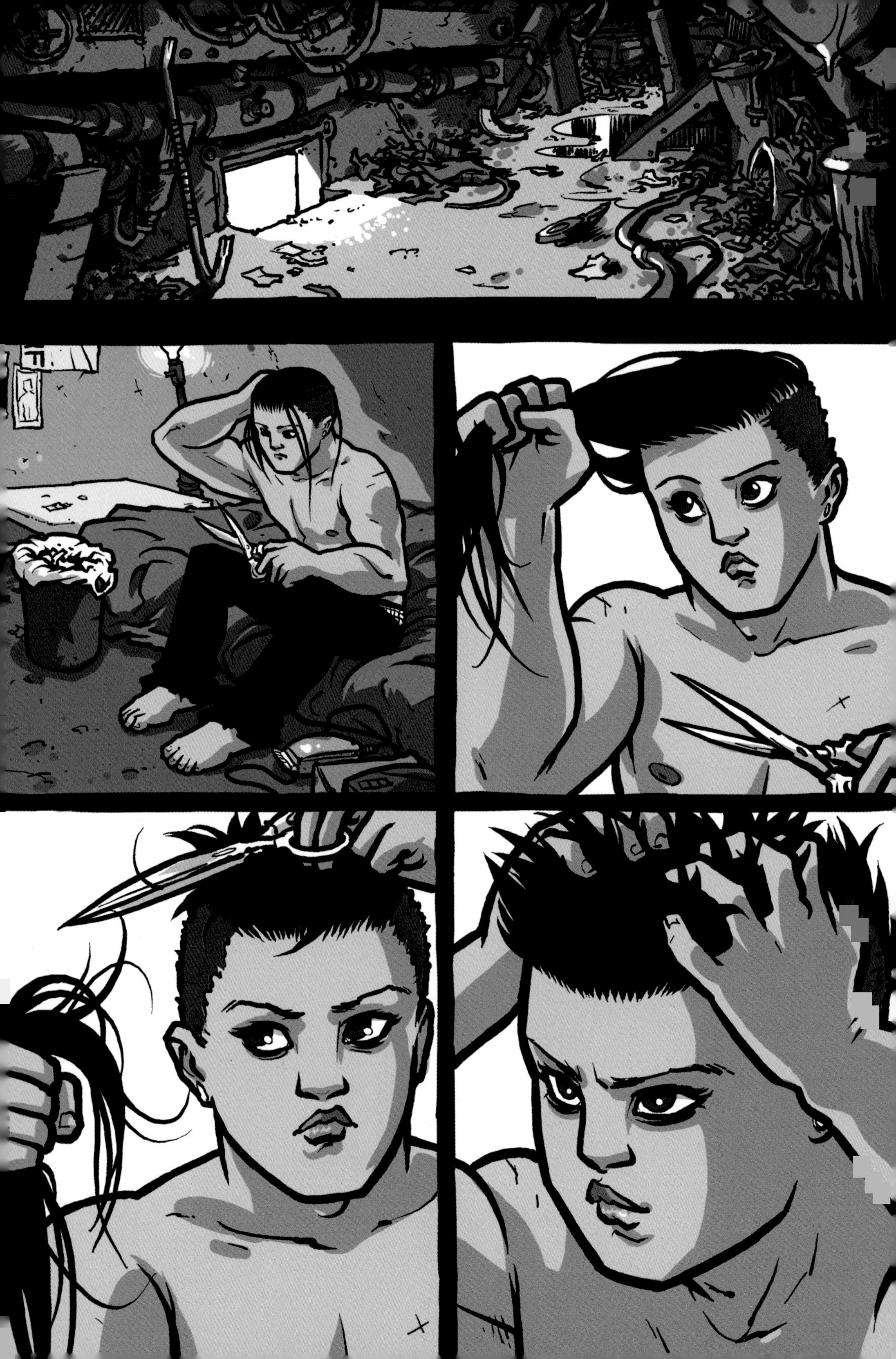

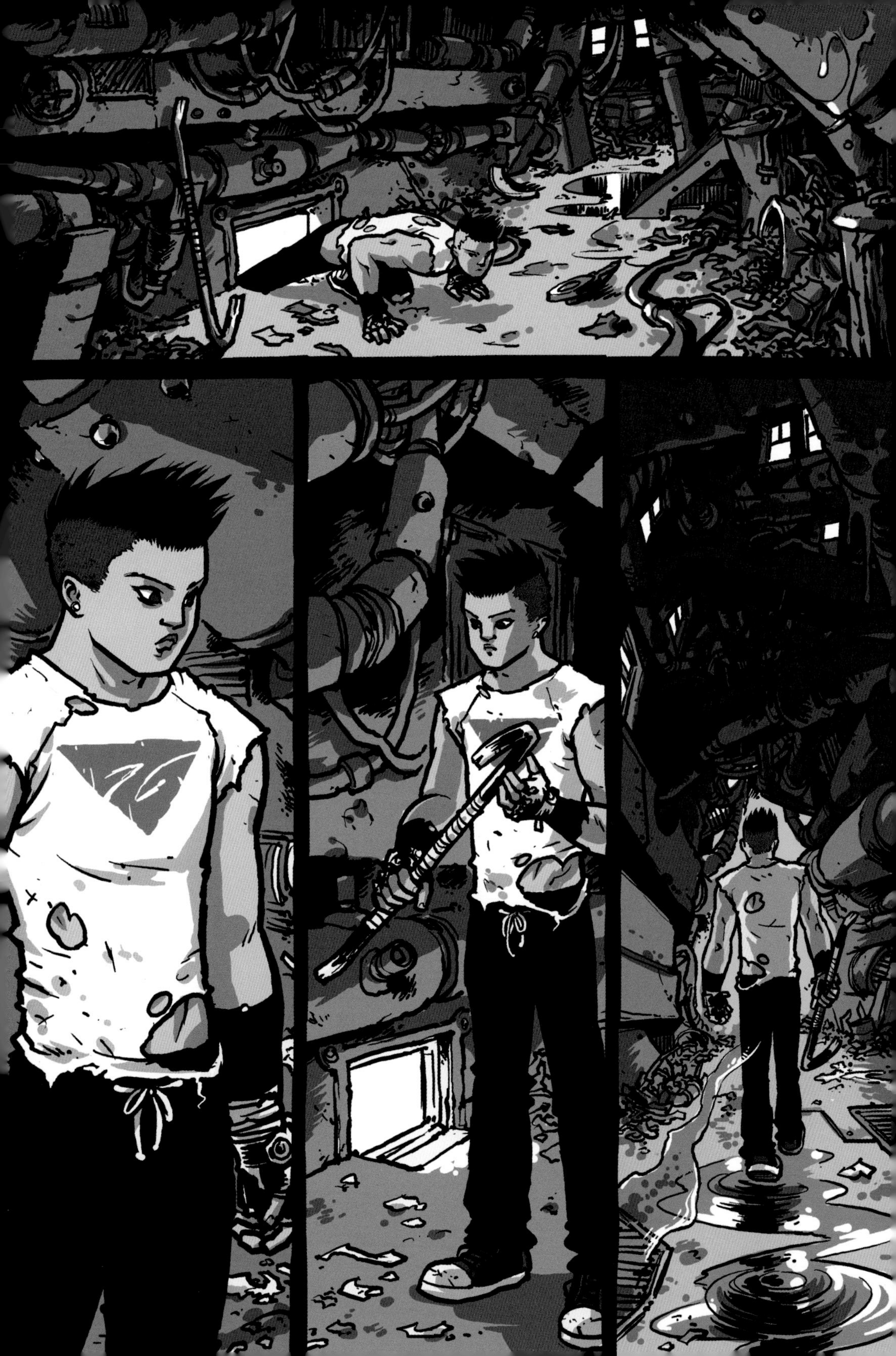

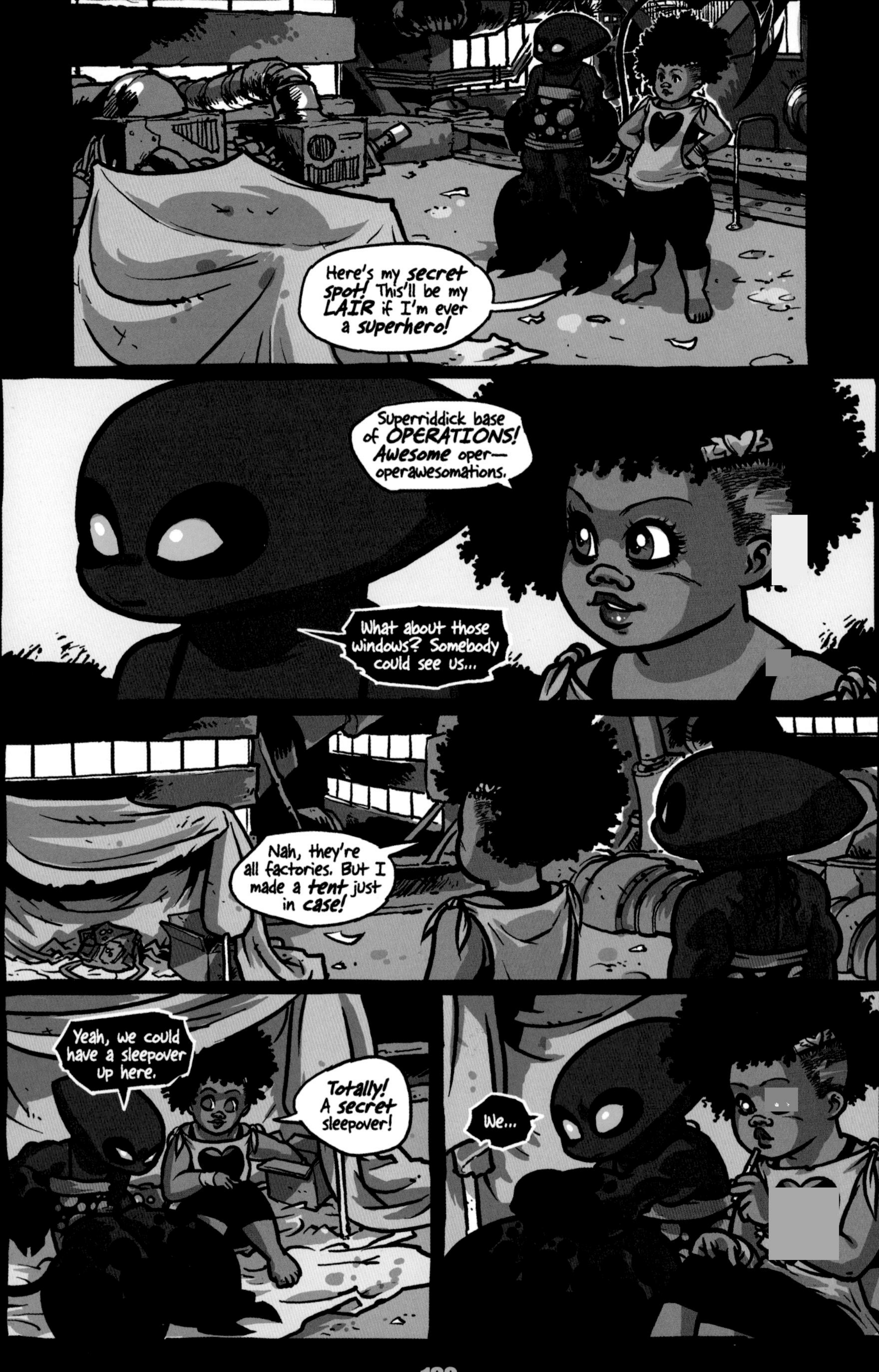
Here's my secret spot! This'll be my LAIR if I'm ever a superhero!
Superriddick base of OPERATIONS! Awesome oper— operawesomations.
What about those windows? Somebody could see us...
Nah, they're all factories. But I made a tent just in case!
Yeah, we could have a sleepover up here.
Totally! A secret sleepover!
We...

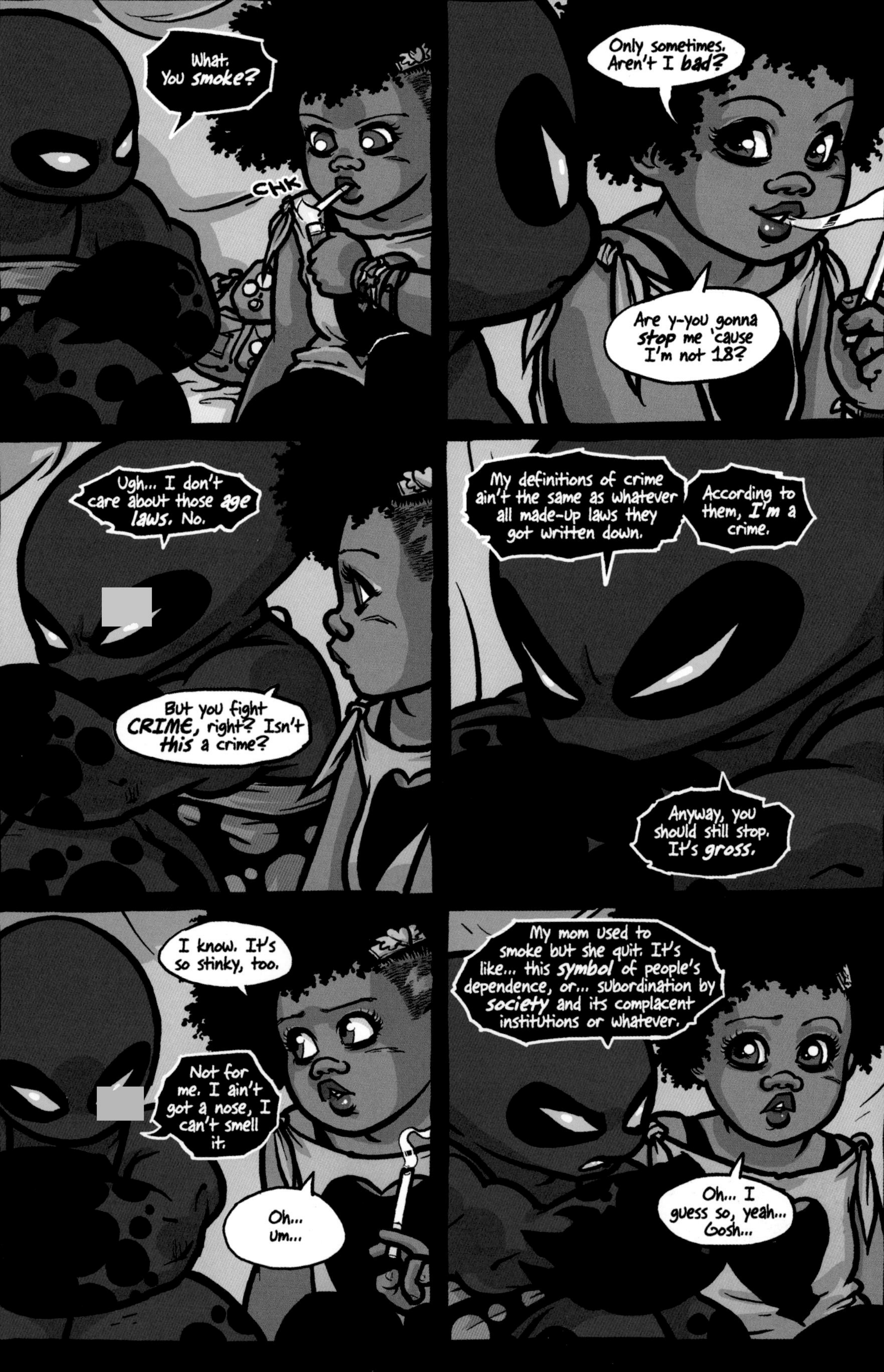

What. You smoke?
CHK
Only sometimes. Aren't I bad?
Are y-you gonna stop me 'cause I'm not 18?
Ugh... I don't care about those age laws. No.
But you fight CRIME, right? Isn't this a crime?
My definitions of crime ain't the same as whatever all made-up laws they got written down.
According to them, I'm a crime.
Anyway, you should still stop. It's gross.
I know. It's so stinky, too.
Not for me. I ain't got a nose, I can't smell it.
Oh... um...
My mom used to smoke but she quit. It's like... this symbol of people's dependence, or... subordination by society and its complacent institutions or whatever.
Oh... I guess so, yeah... Gosh...

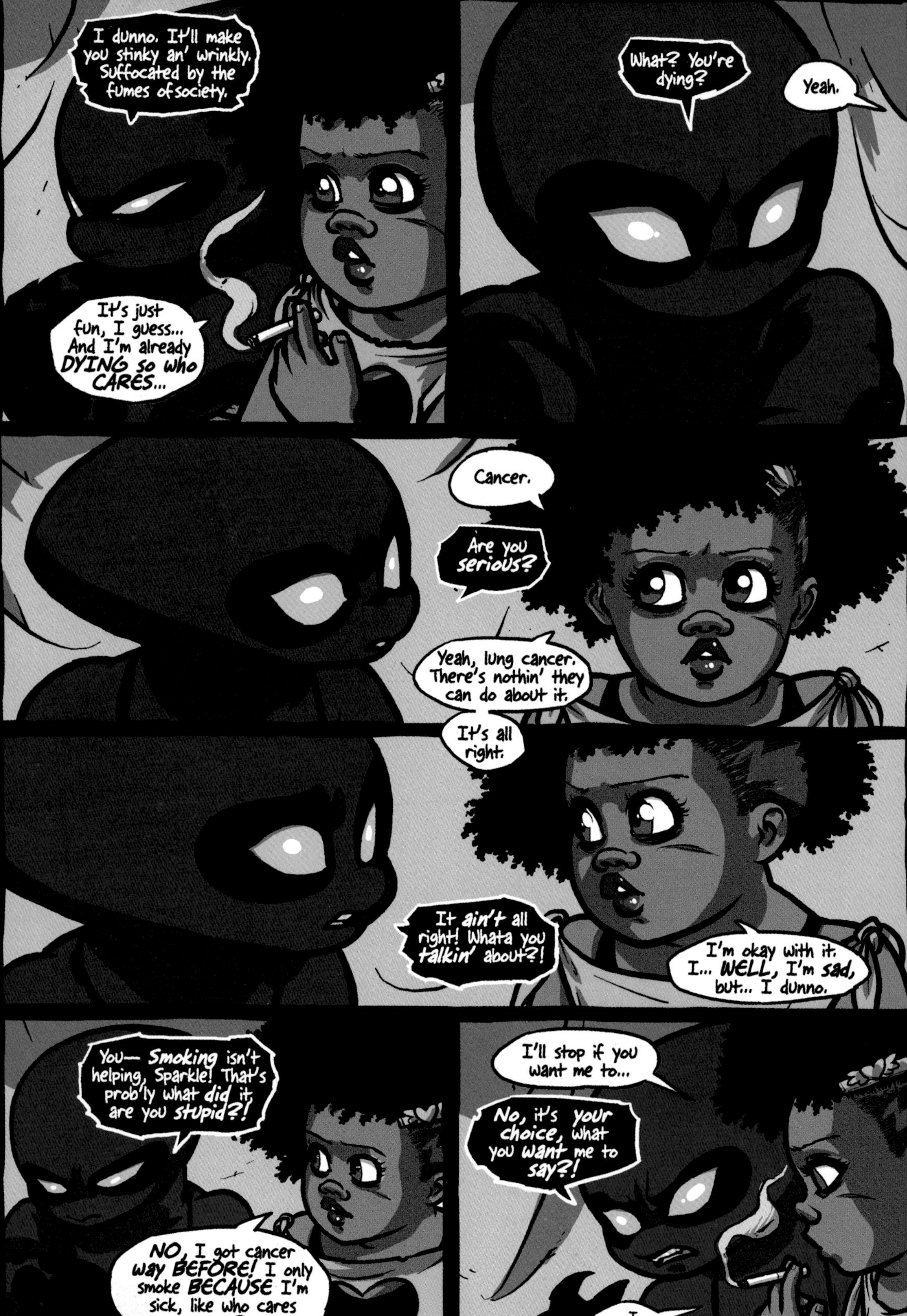
I dunno. It'll make you stinky an' wrinkly. Suffocated by the fumes of society.
It's just fun, I guess... And I'm already DYING so who CARES...
What? You're dying?
Yeah.
Cancer.
Are you serious?
Yeah, lung cancer. There's nothin' they can do about it.
It's all right.
It ain't all right! Whata you talkin' about?!
I'm okay with it. I... WELL, I'm sad, but... I dunno.
You— Smoking isn't helping, Sparkle! That's prob'ly what did it, are you stupid?!
NO, I got cancer way BEFORE! I only smoke BECAUSE I'm sick, like who cares now...?
I'll stop if you want me to...
No, it's your choice, what you want me to say?!
I dunno...

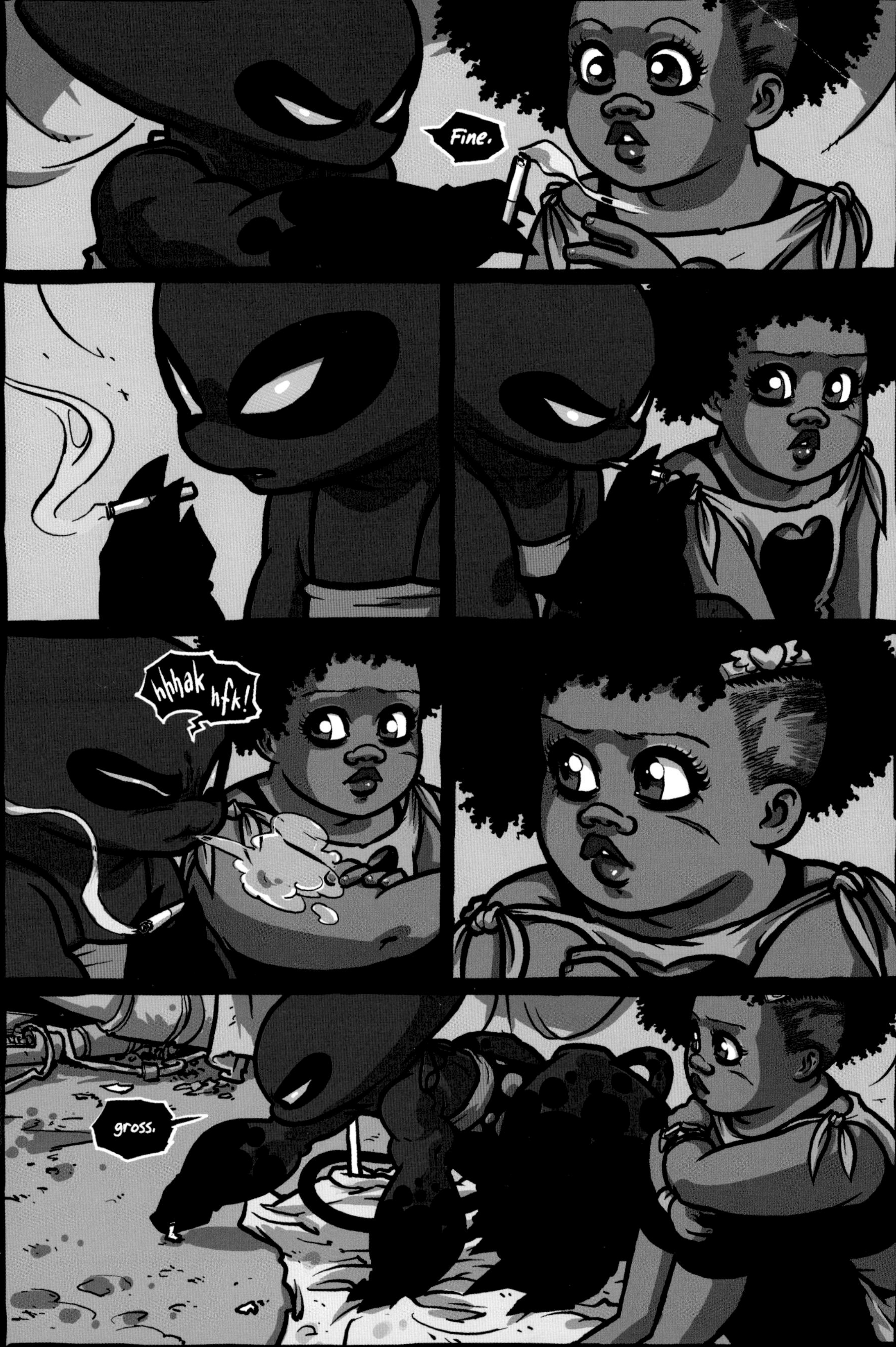
Fine.
hhhak
hfk!
gross.

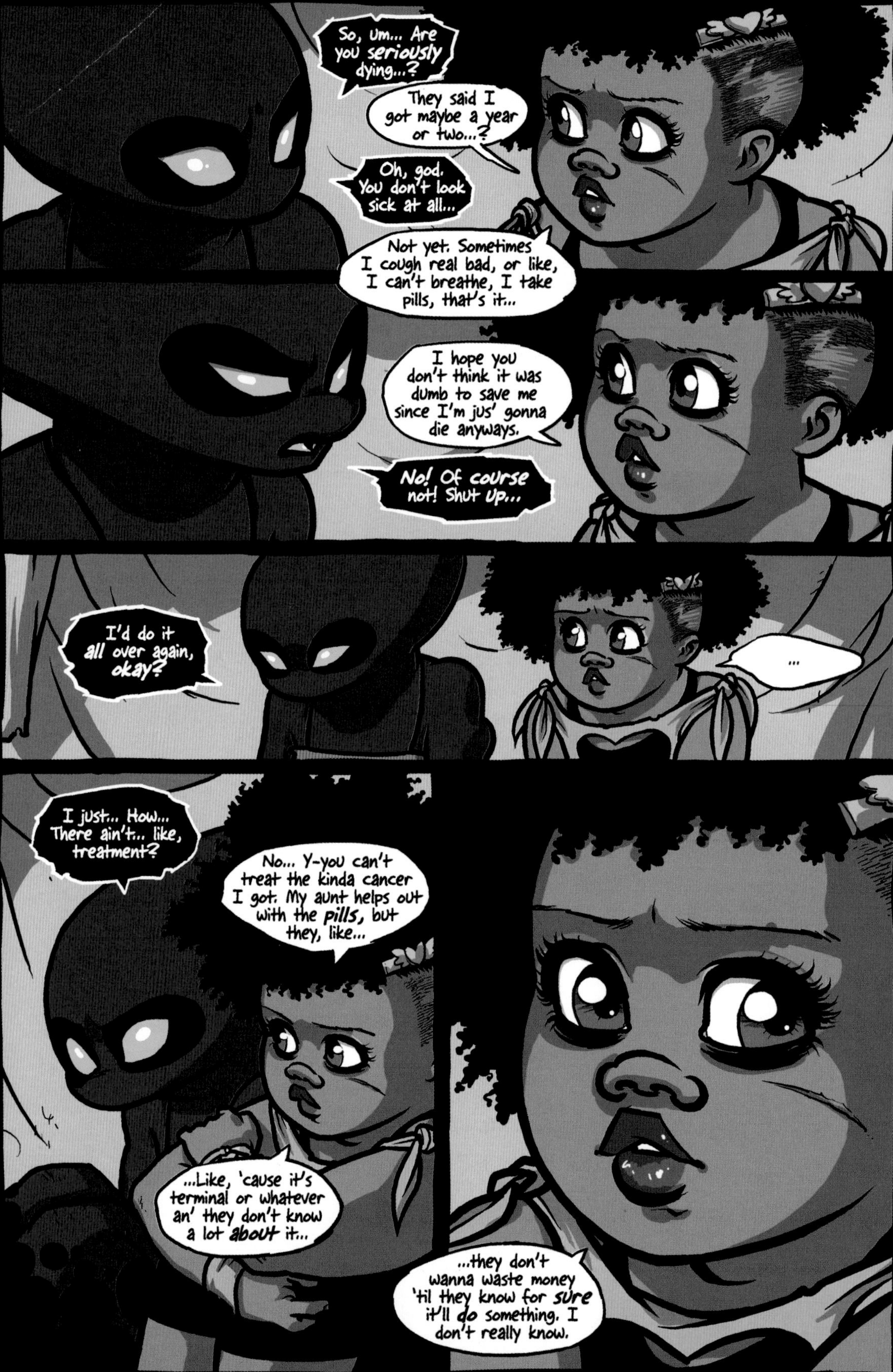
So, um... Are you seriously dying...?
They said I got maybe a year or two...?
Oh, god. You don't look sick at all...
Not yet. Sometimes I cough real bad, or like, I can't breathe, I take pills, that's it...
I hope you don't think it was dumb to save me since I'm jus' gonna die anyways.
No! Of course not! Shut up...
I'd do it all over again, okay?
...
I just... How... There ain't... like, treatment?
No... Y-you can't treat the kinda cancer I got. My aunt helps out with the pills, but they, like...
...Like, 'cause it's terminal or whatever an' they don't know a lot about it...
...they don't wanna waste money 'til they know for sure it'll do something. I don't really know.

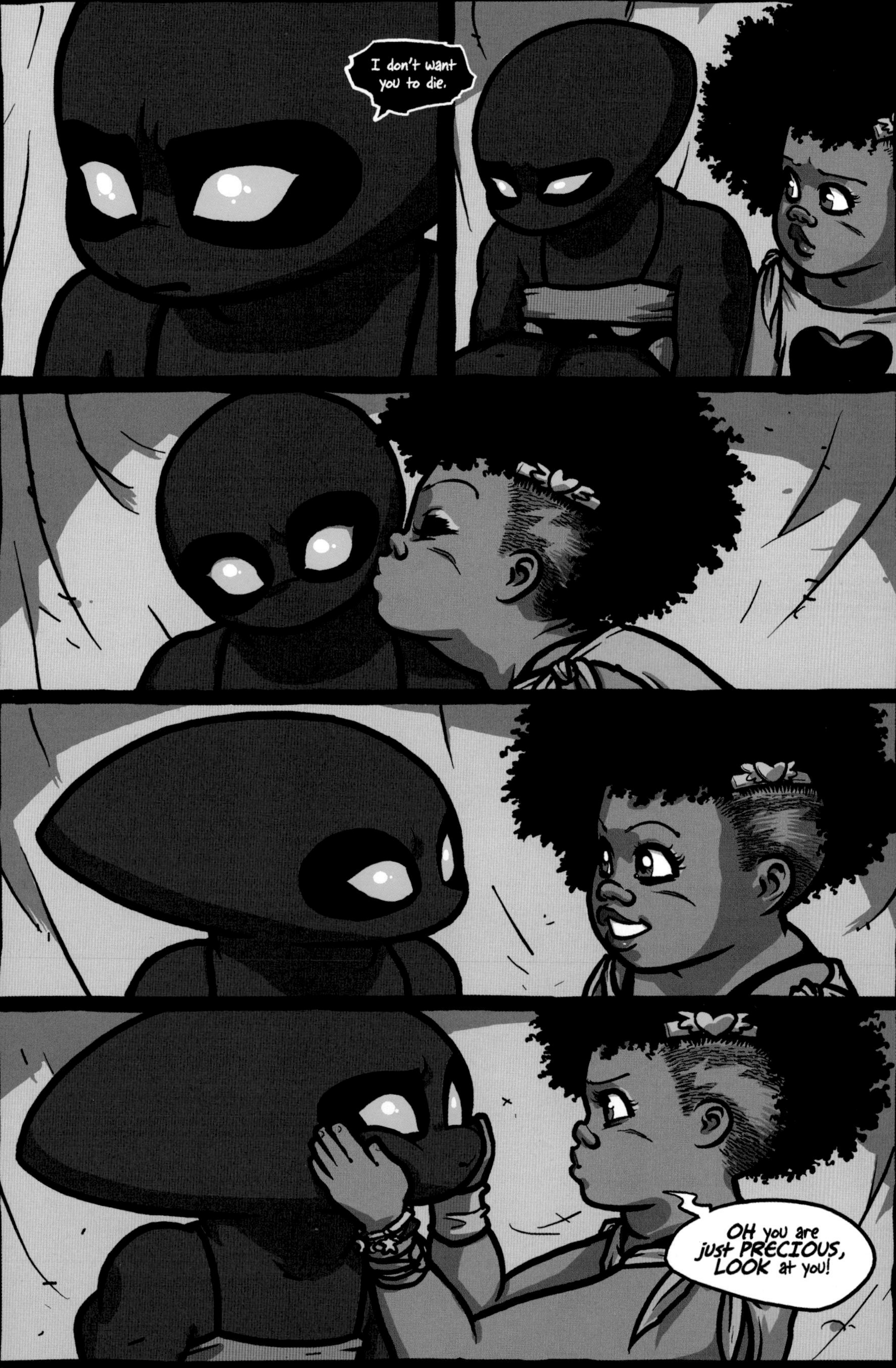
I don't want you to die.
OH you are just PRECIOUS, LOOK at you!

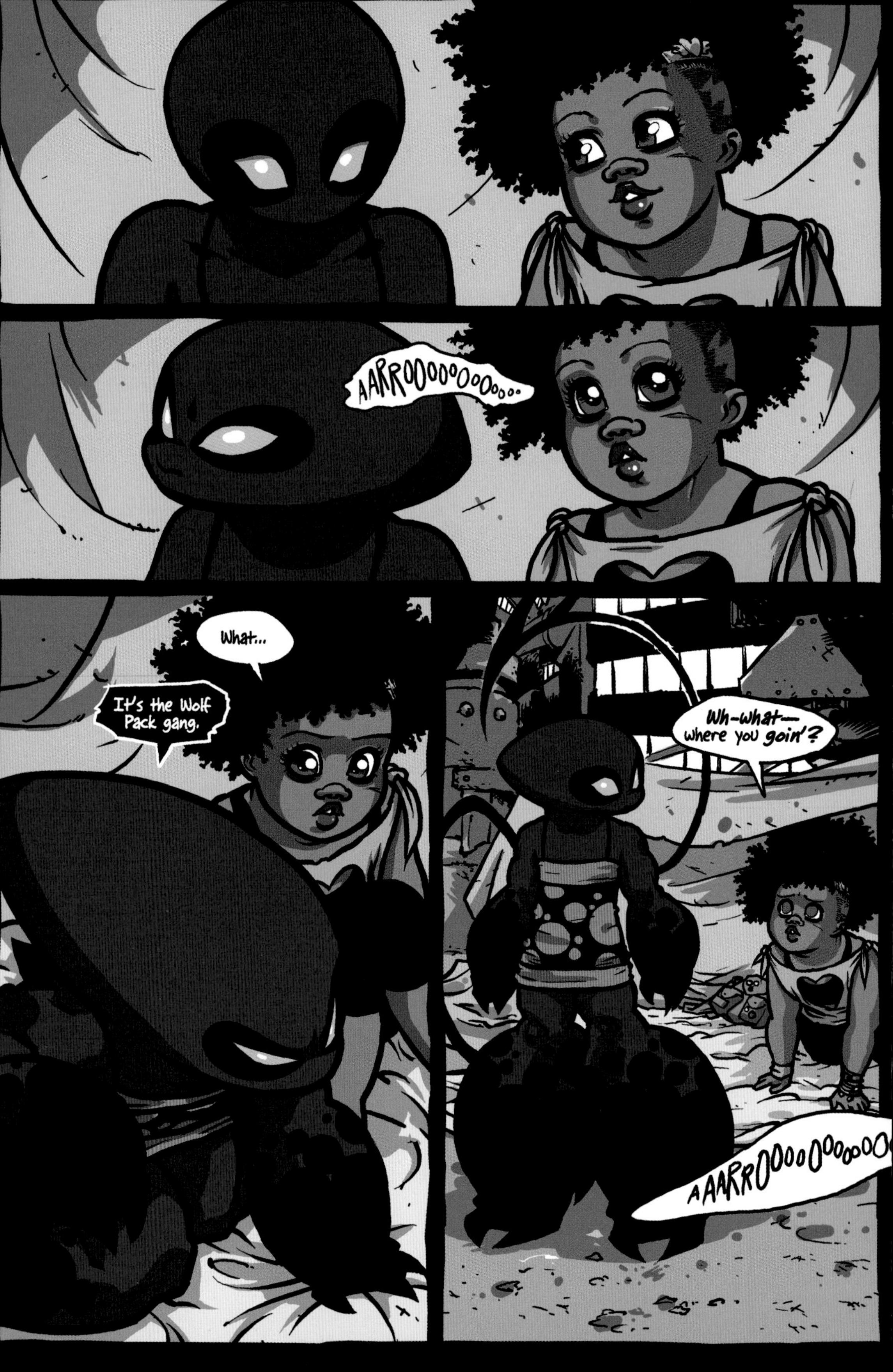
AARROOOOOOOOooo
What...
It's the Wolf Pack gang.
Wh-what— where you goin'?
AAARROOOOOOOOOOO

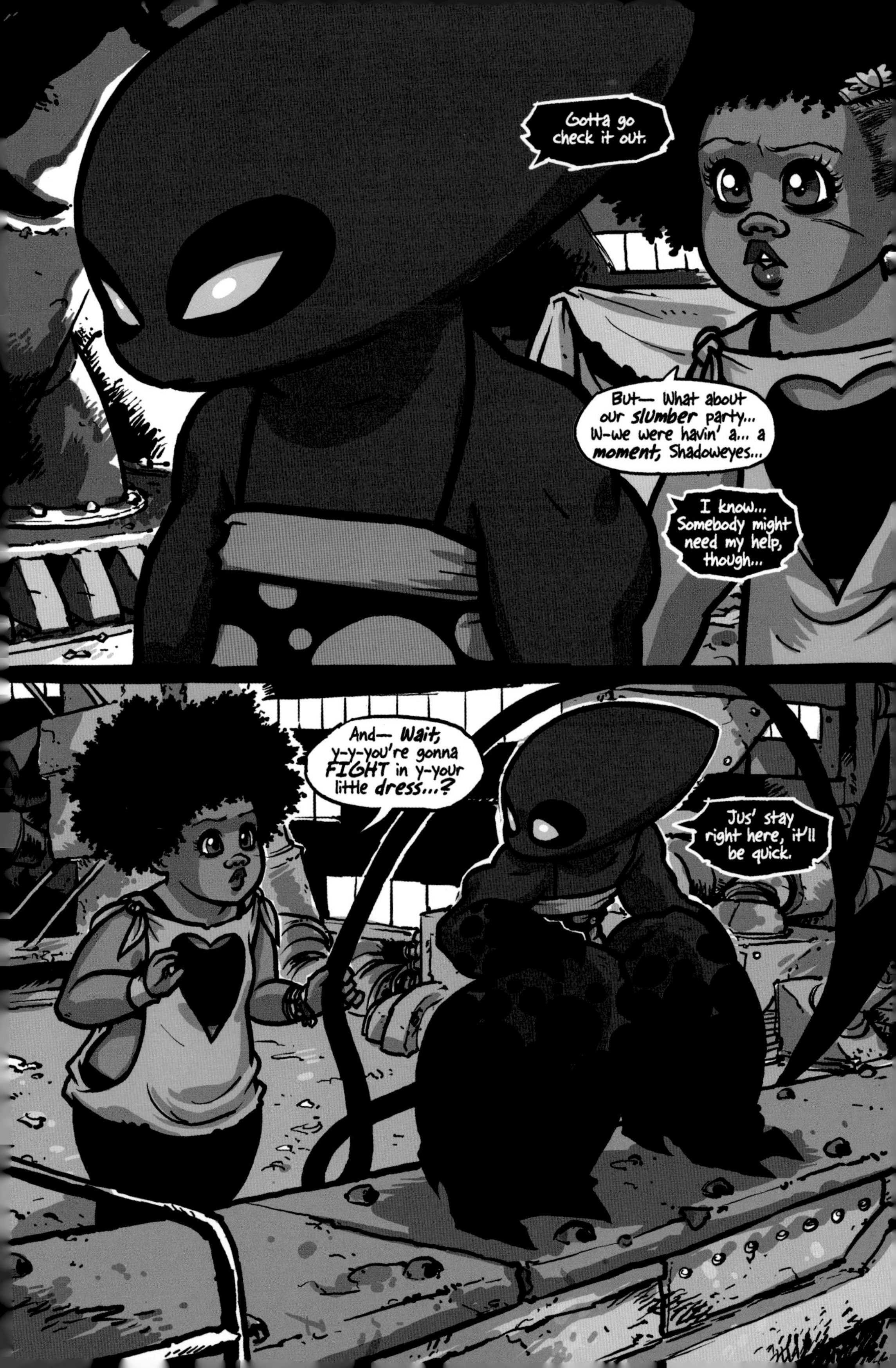
Gotta go check it out.
But— What about our slumber party... W-we were havin' a... a moment, Shadoweyes...
I know... Somebody might need my help, though...
And— Wait, y-y-you're gonna FIGHT in y-your little dress...?
Jus' stay right here, it'll be quick.

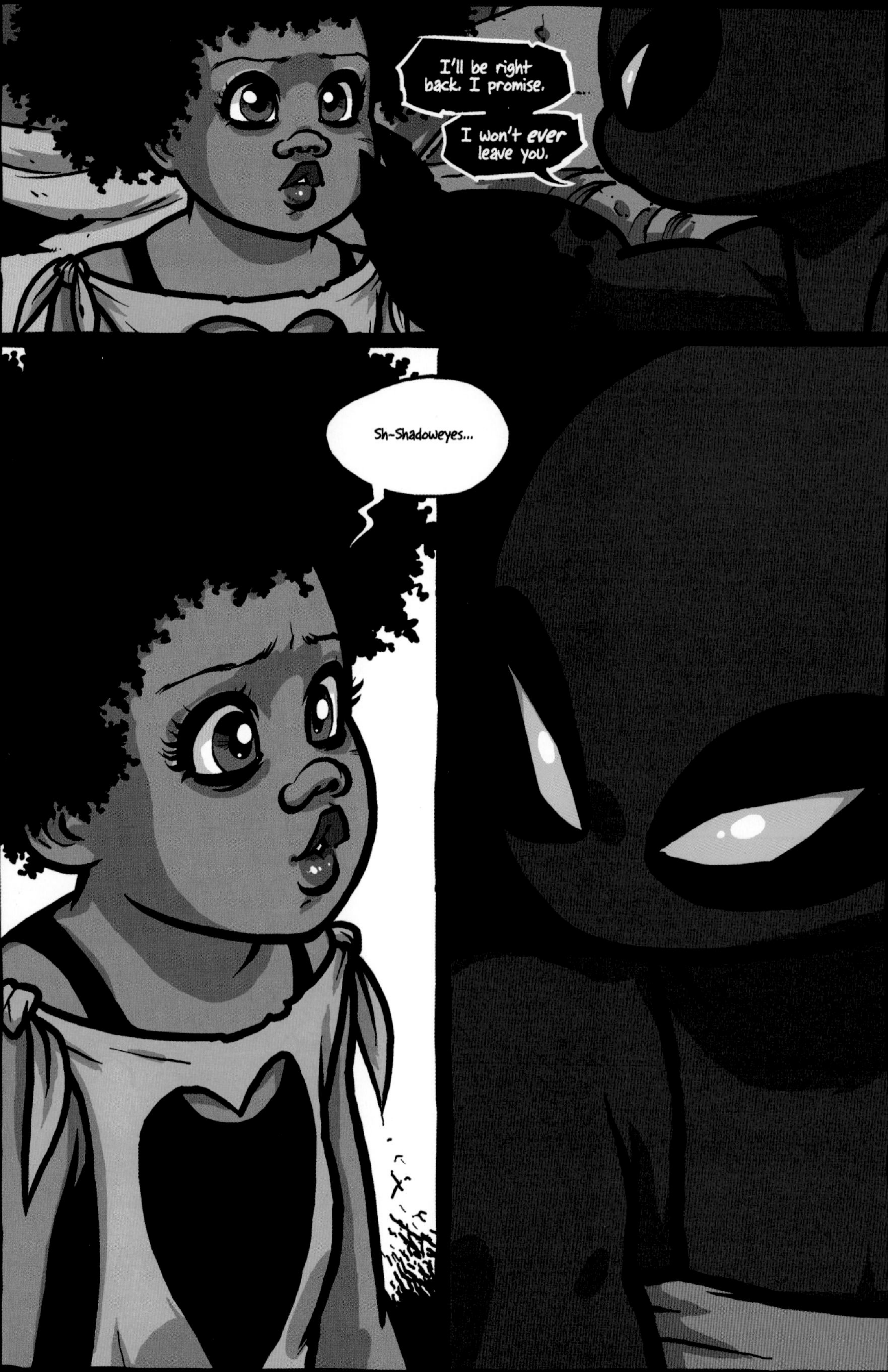
I'll be right back. I promise.
I won't ever leave you.
Sh-Shadoweyes...

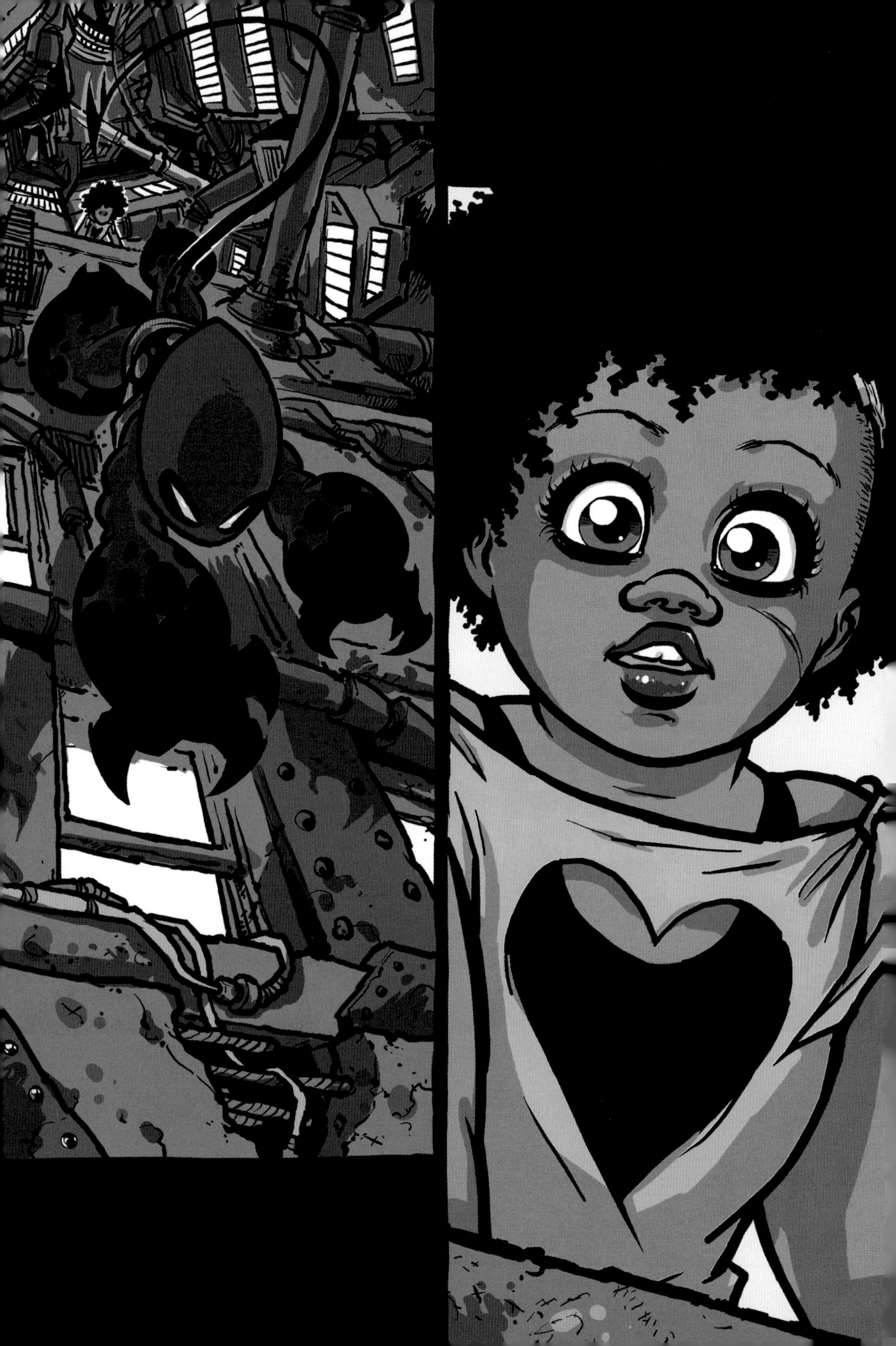

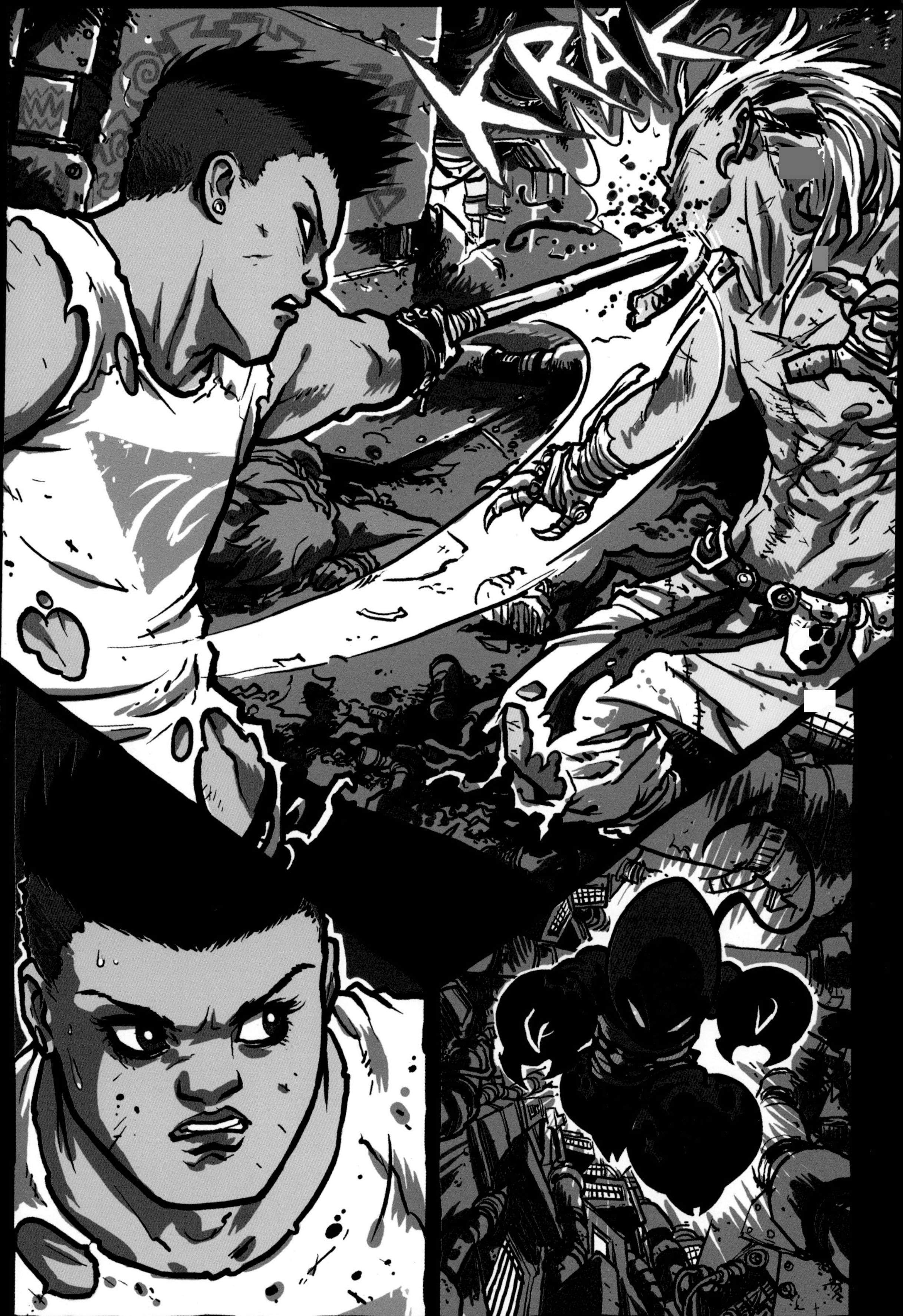
KRAK

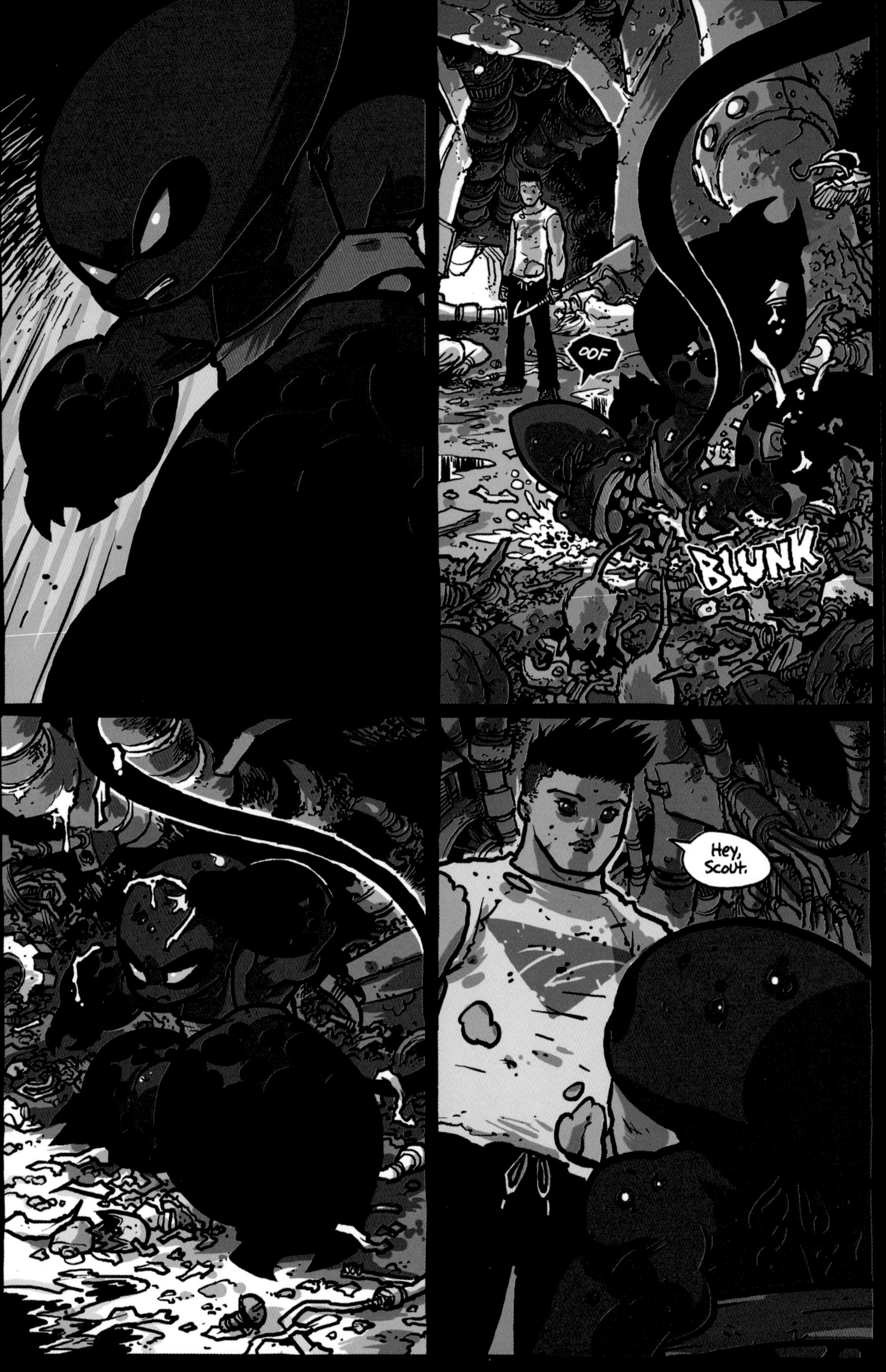
OOF
BLUNK
Hey, Scout.

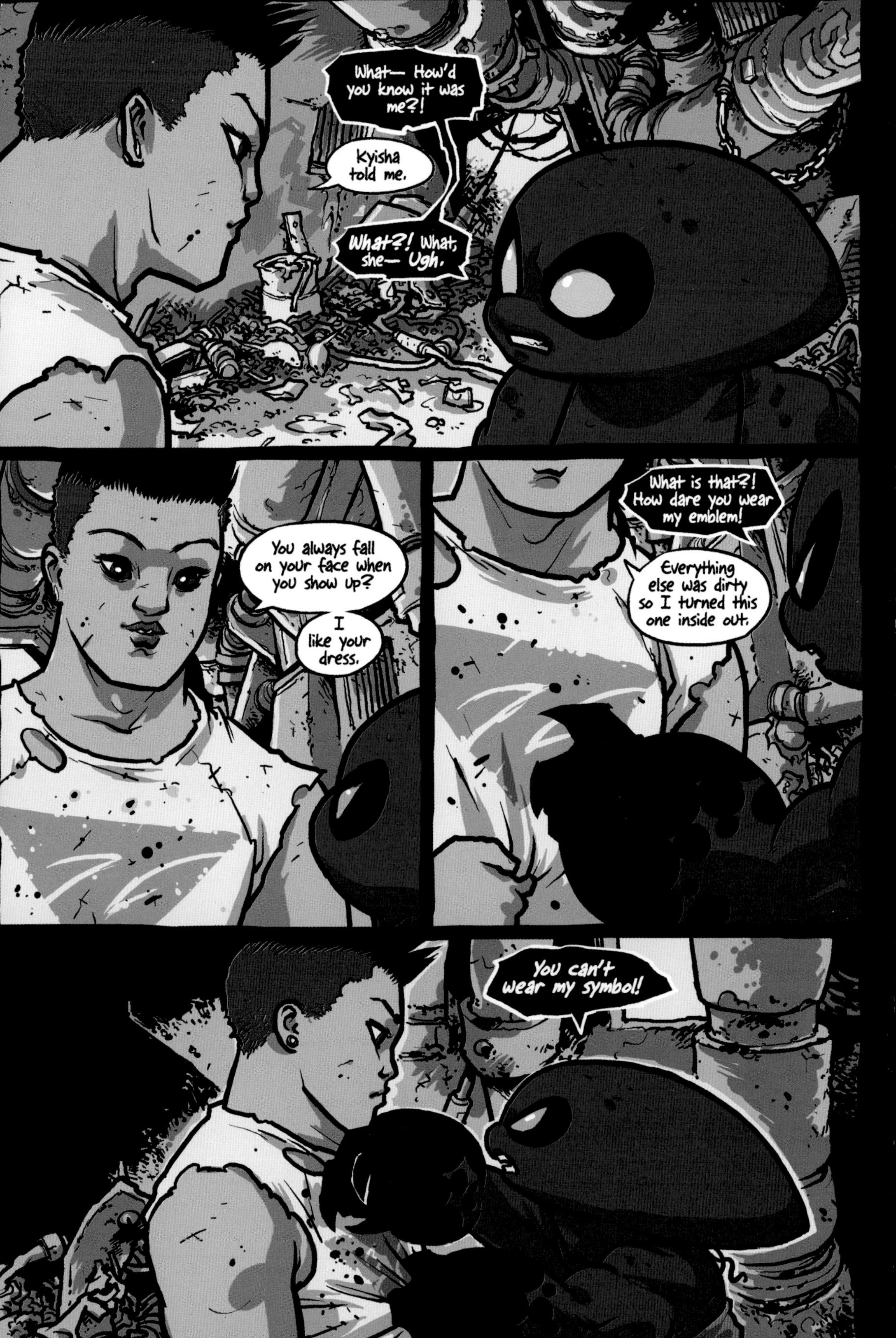
What— How'd you know it was me?!
Kyisha told me.
What?! What, she— Ugh.
You always fall on your face when you show up?
I like your dress.
What is that?! How dare you wear my emblem!
Everything else was dirty so I turned this one inside out.
You can't wear my symbol!

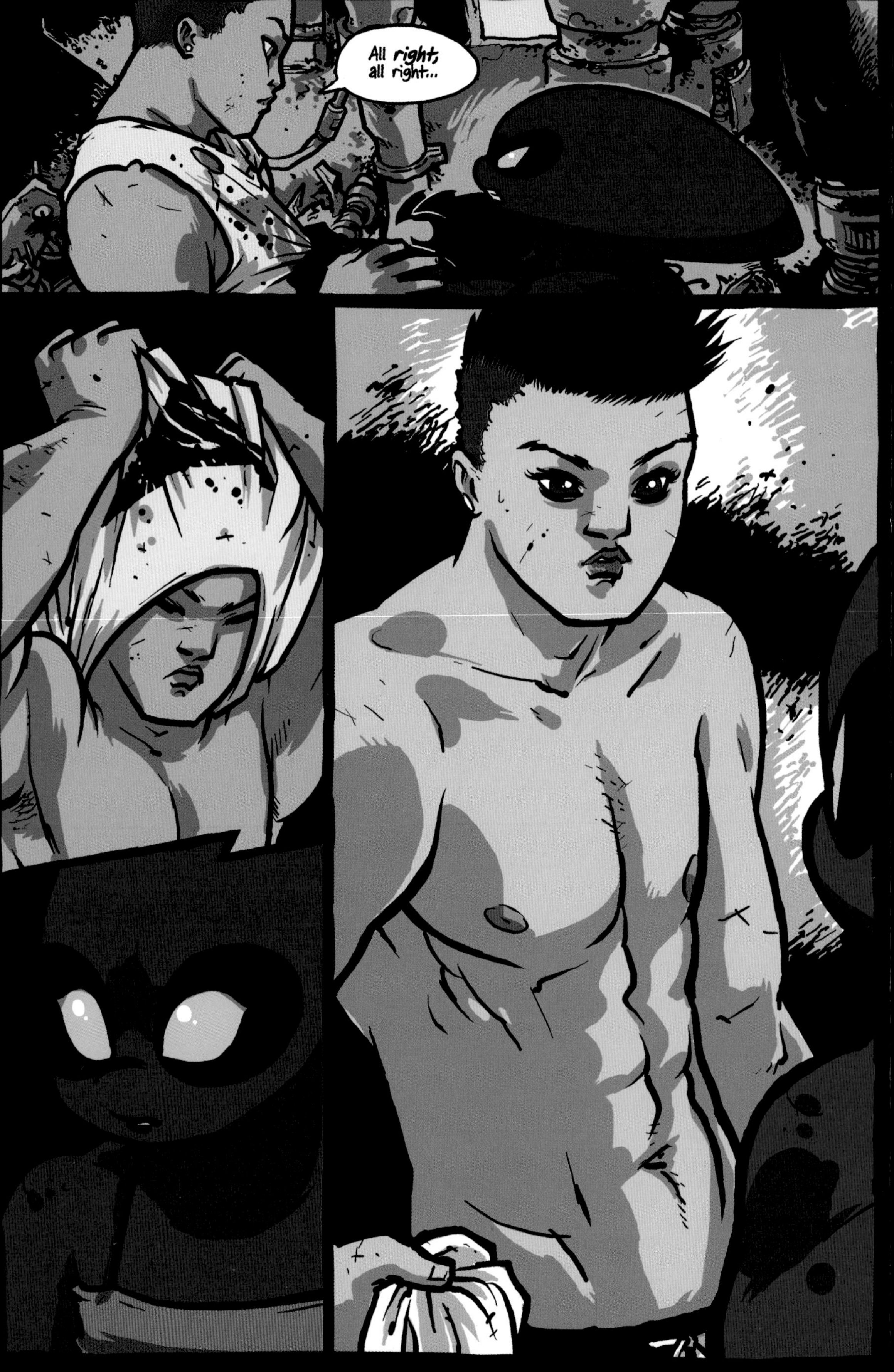
All right,
all right...

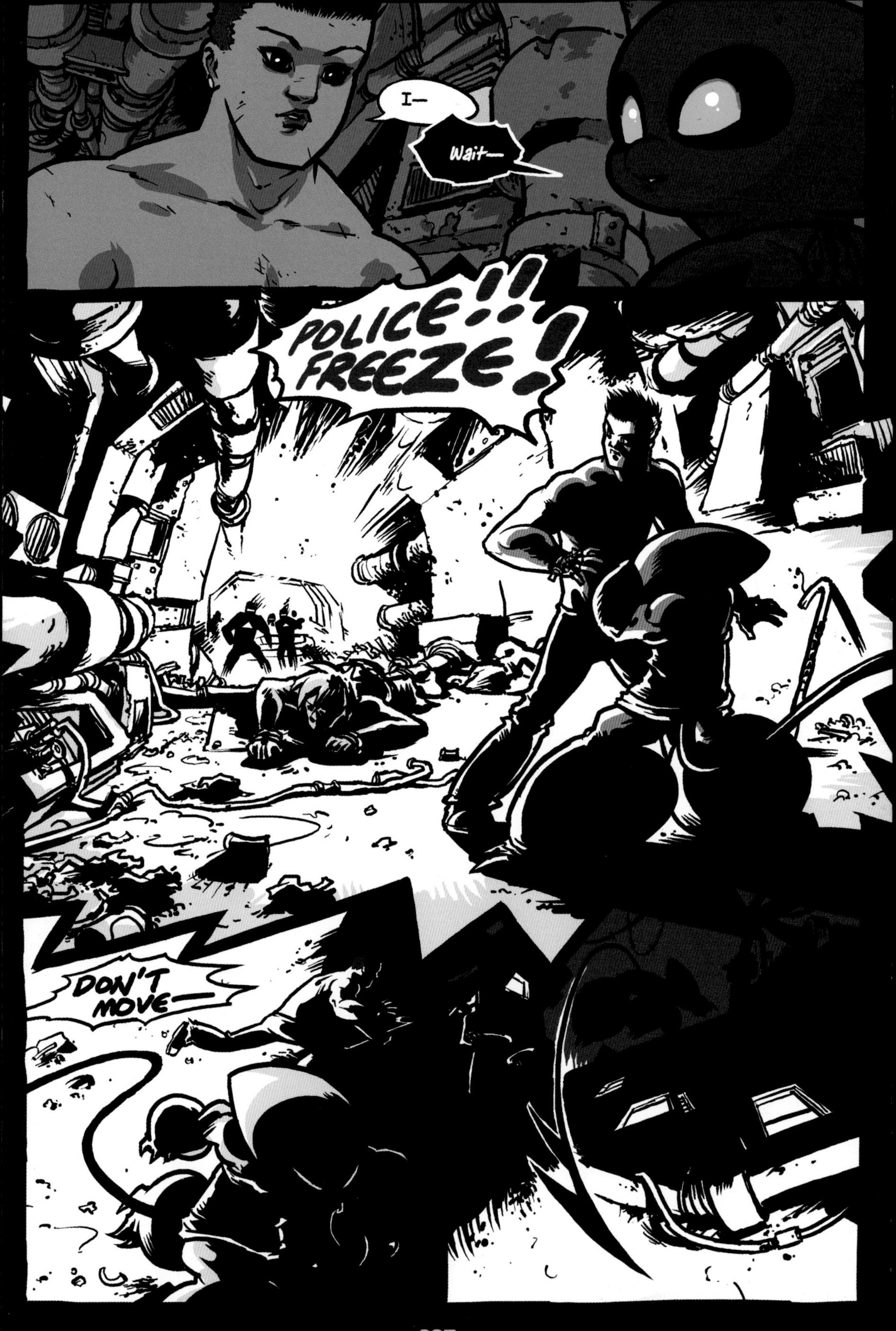
I—
Wait—
POLICE!! FREEZE!
DON'T MOVE—

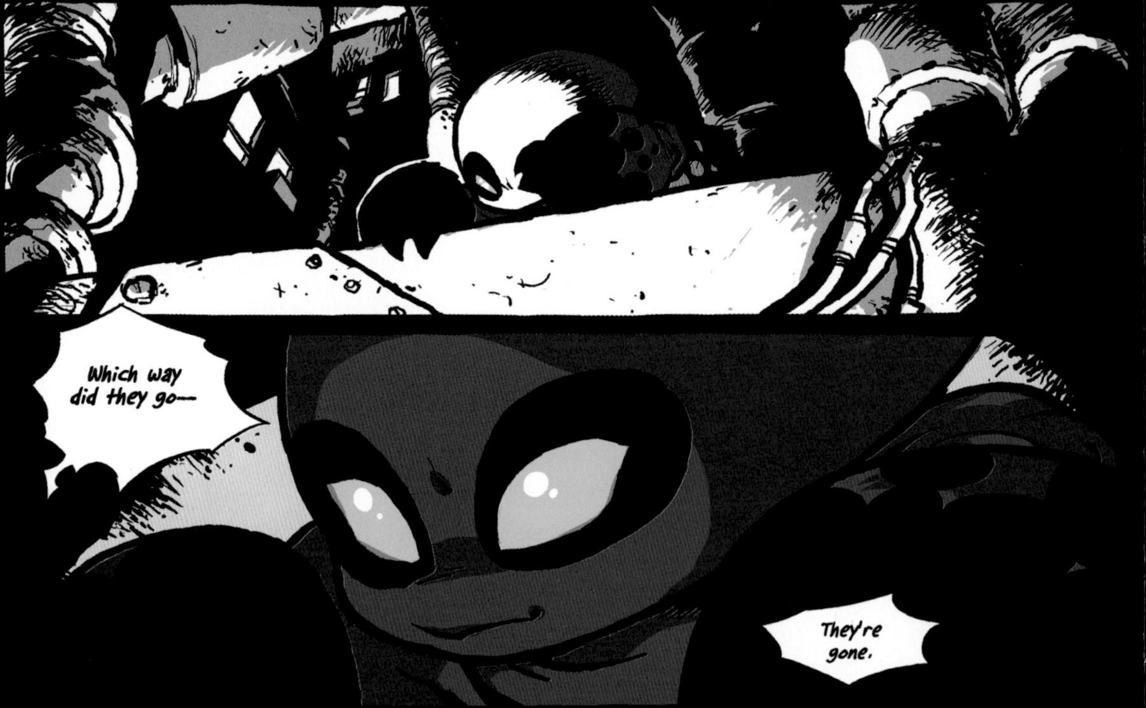
Which way did they go—
They're gone.

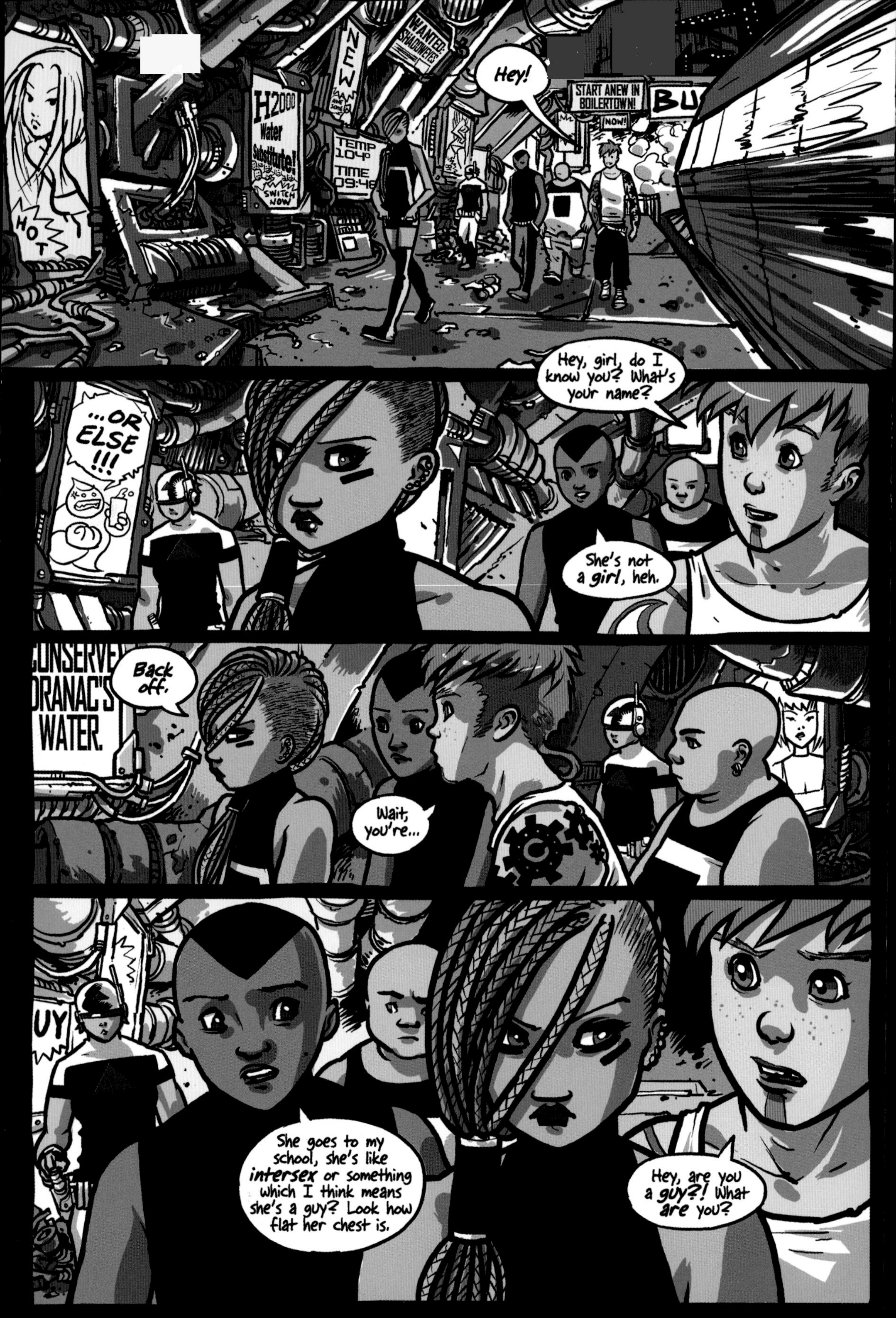
HOT
H2000 Water Substitute!
SWITCH NOW
NEW
WANTED: SHADOWEYES
TEMP 104°
TIME 09:48
[redacted]
Hey!
START ANEW IN BOILERTOWN!
NOW!
...OR ELSE!!!
Hey, girl, do I know you? What's your name?
She's not a *girl*, heh.
CONSERVE ORANAC'S WATER.
Back off.
Wait, you're...
She goes to my school, she's like ***intersex*** or something which I think means she's a guy? Look how flat her chest is.
Hey, are you a ***guy?!*** What ***are*** you?

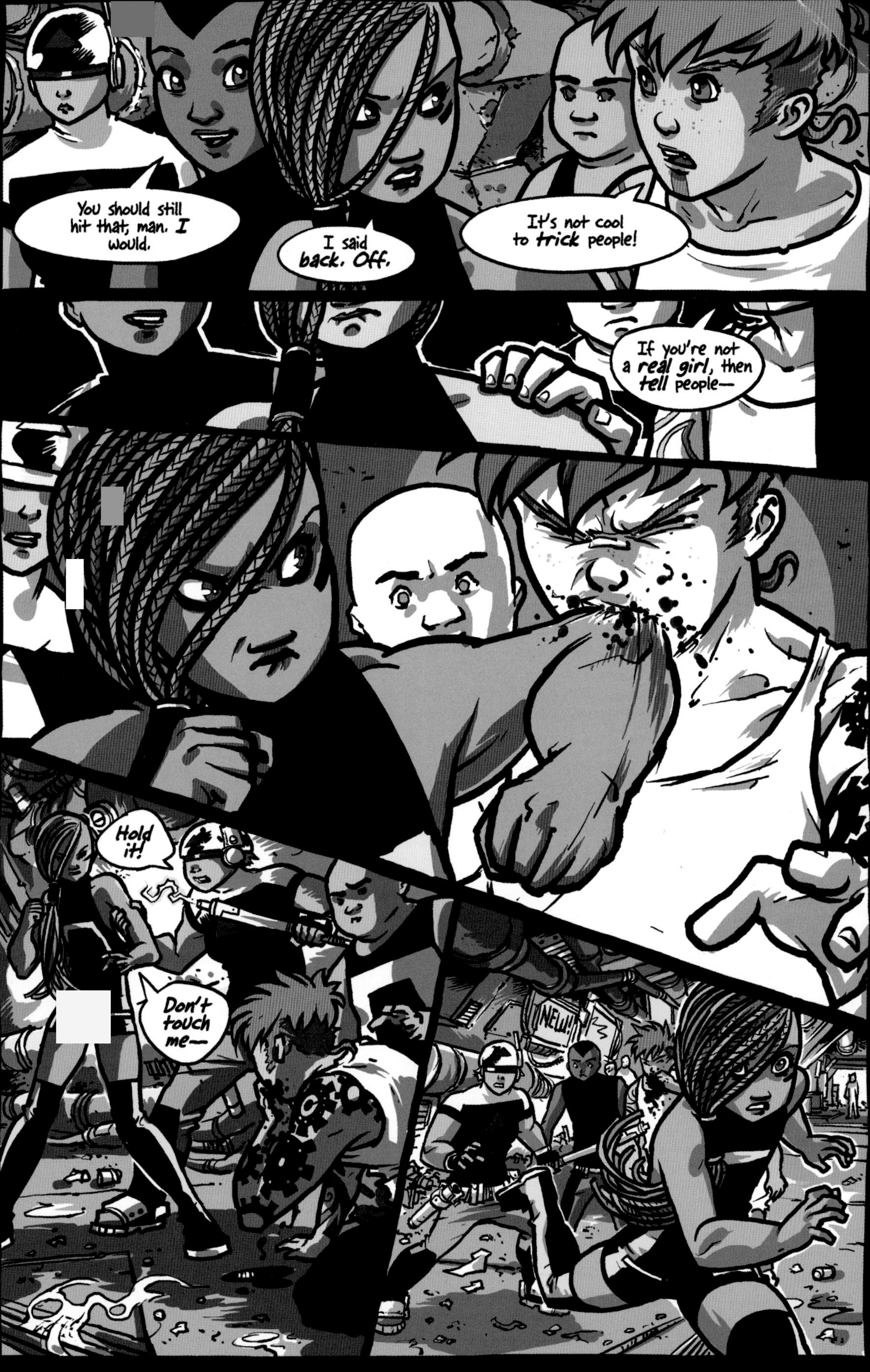
You should still hit that, man. I would.
I said back. Off.
It's not cool to trick people!
If you're not a real girl, then tell people—
Hold it!
Don't touch me—

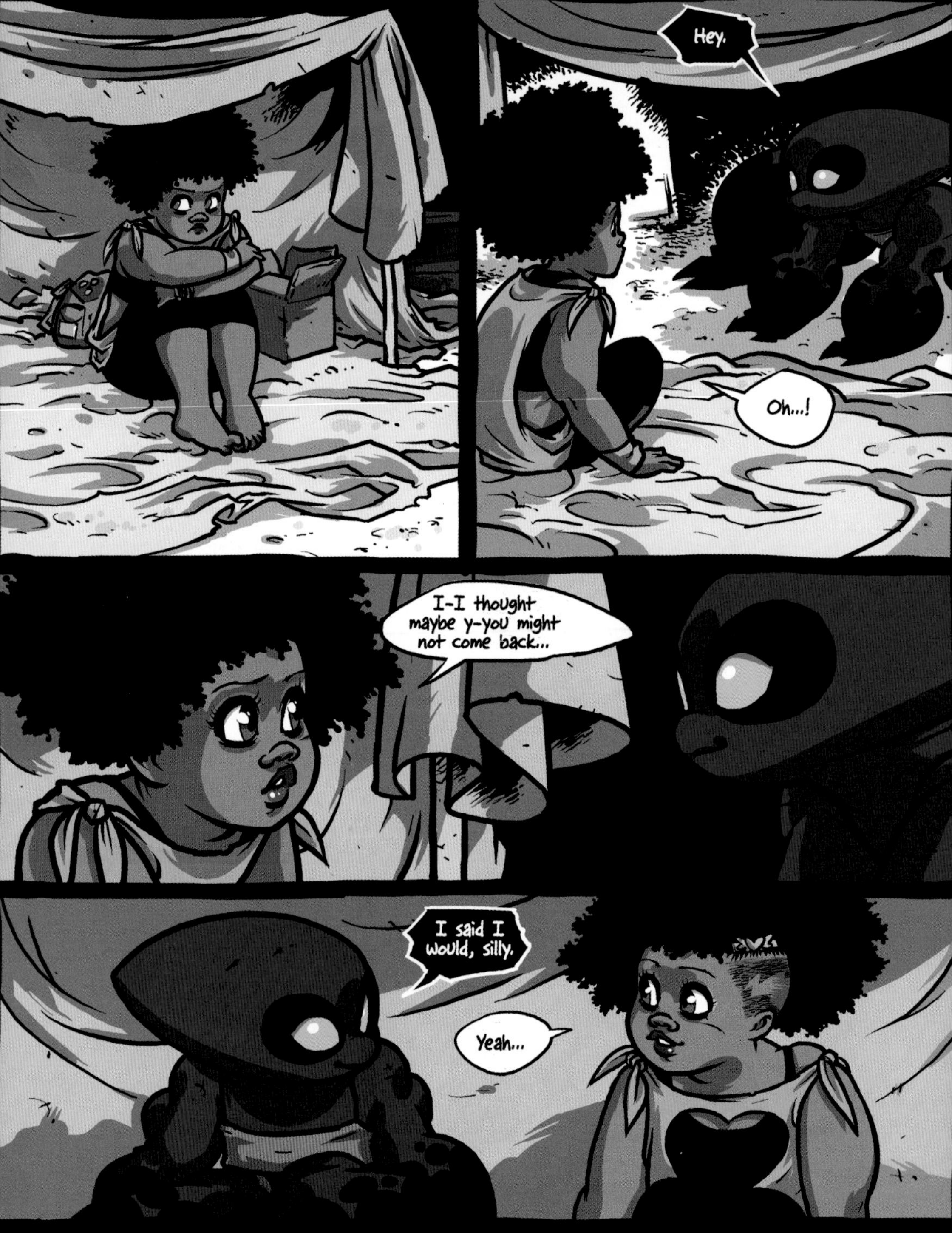
Hey.
Oh...!
I-I thought maybe y-you might not come back...
I said I would, silly.
Yeah...

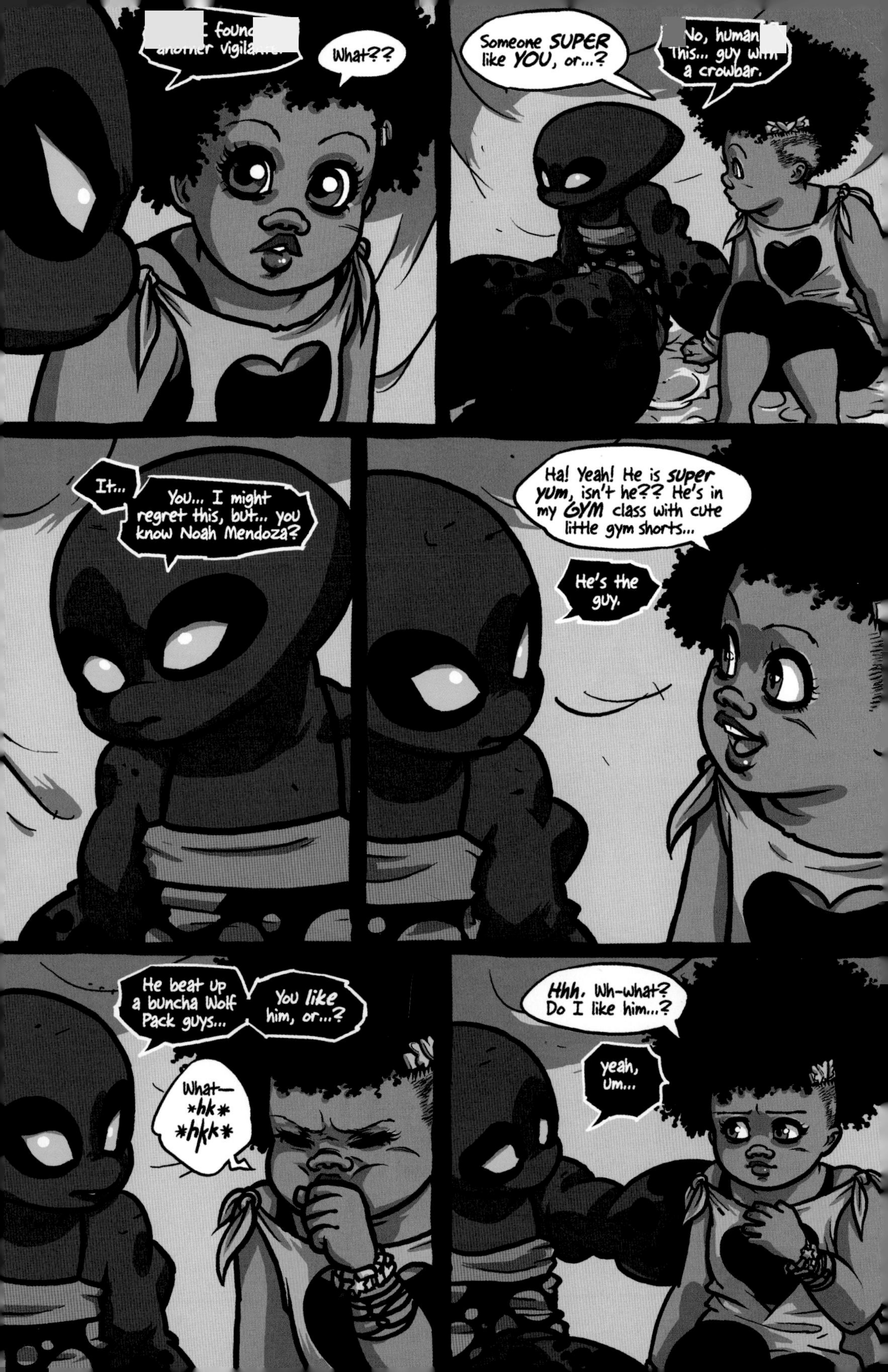
I found another vigil
What??
Someone SUPER like YOU, or...?
No, human This... guy with a crowbar.
It...
You... I might regret this, but... you know Noah Mendoza?
Ha! Yeah! He is super yum, isn't he?? He's in my GYM class with cute little gym shorts...
He's the guy.
He beat up a buncha Wolf Pack guys...
You like him, or...?
What— *hk* *hkk*
Hhh. Wh-what? Do I like him...?
yeah, um...

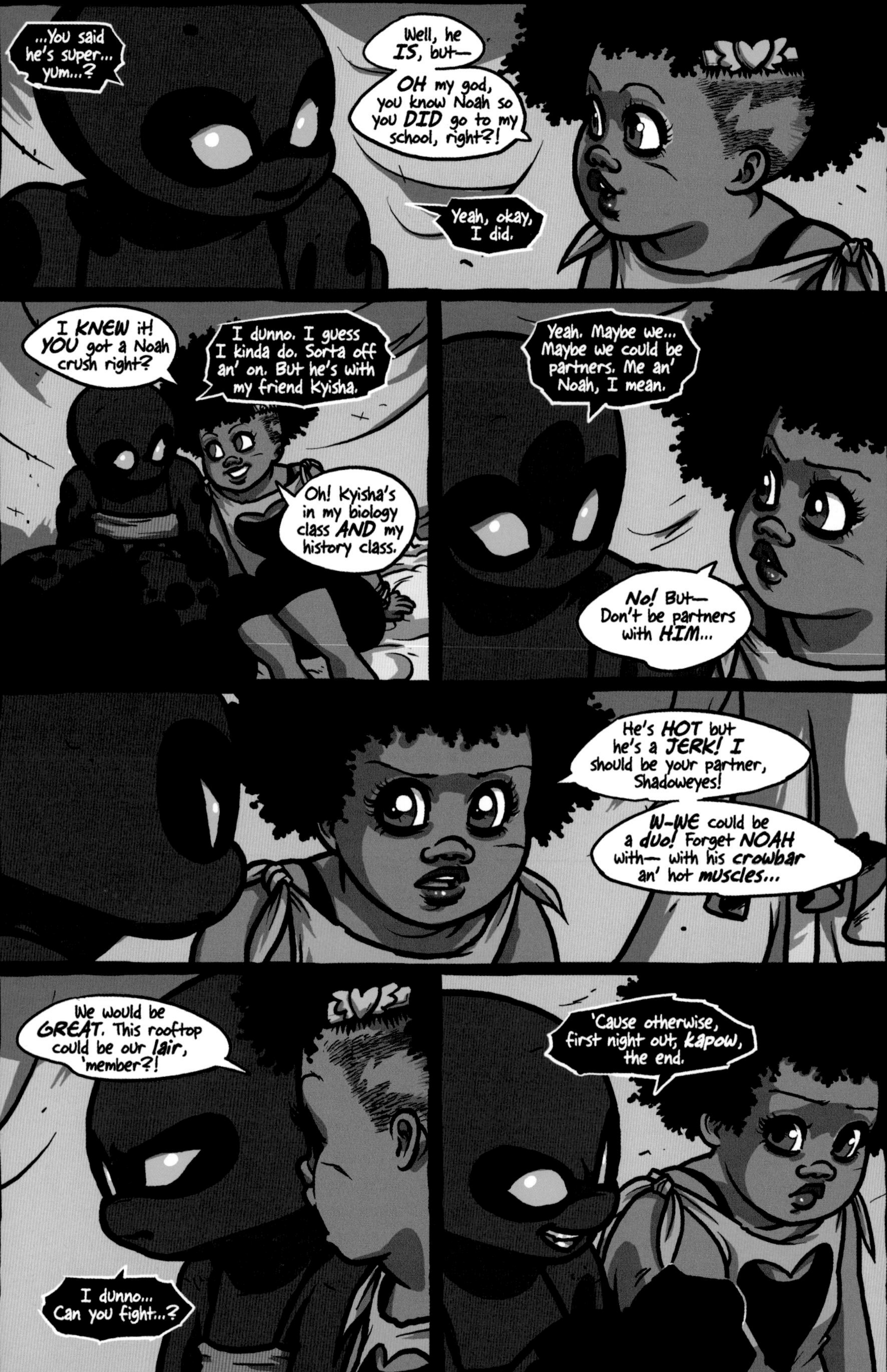
...You said he's super... yum...?
Well, he IS, but—
OH my god, you know Noah so you DID go to my school, right?!
Yeah, okay, I did.
I KNEW it! YOU got a Noah crush right?
I dunno. I guess I kinda do. Sorta off an' on. But he's with my friend Kyisha.
Oh! Kyisha's in my biology class AND my history class.
Yeah. Maybe we... Maybe we could be partners. Me an' Noah, I mean.
No! But— Don't be partners with HIM...
He's HOT but he's a JERK! I should be your partner, Shadoweyes!
W-WE could be a duo! Forget NOAH with— with his crowbar an' hot muscles...
We would be GREAT. This rooftop could be our lair, 'member?!
I dunno... Can you fight...?
'Cause otherwise, first night out, kapow, the end.

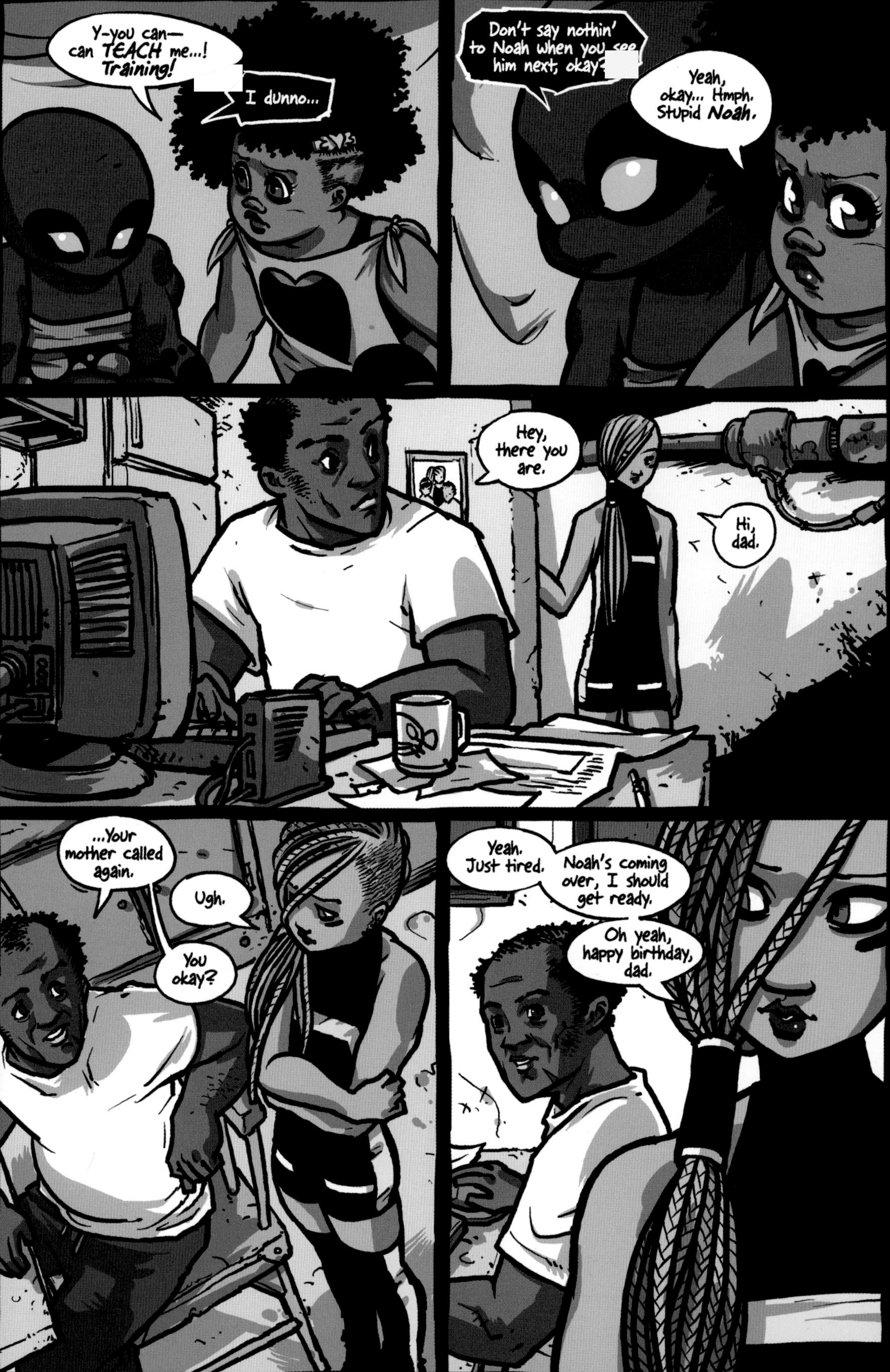
Y-you can—
can TEACH me...!
Training!
I dunno...
Don't say nothin' to Noah when you see him next, okay?
Yeah, okay... Hmph. Stupid Noah.
Hey, there you are.
Hi, dad.
...Your mother called again.
Ugh.
You okay?
Yeah. Just tired.
Noah's coming over, I should get ready.
Oh yeah, happy birthday, dad.

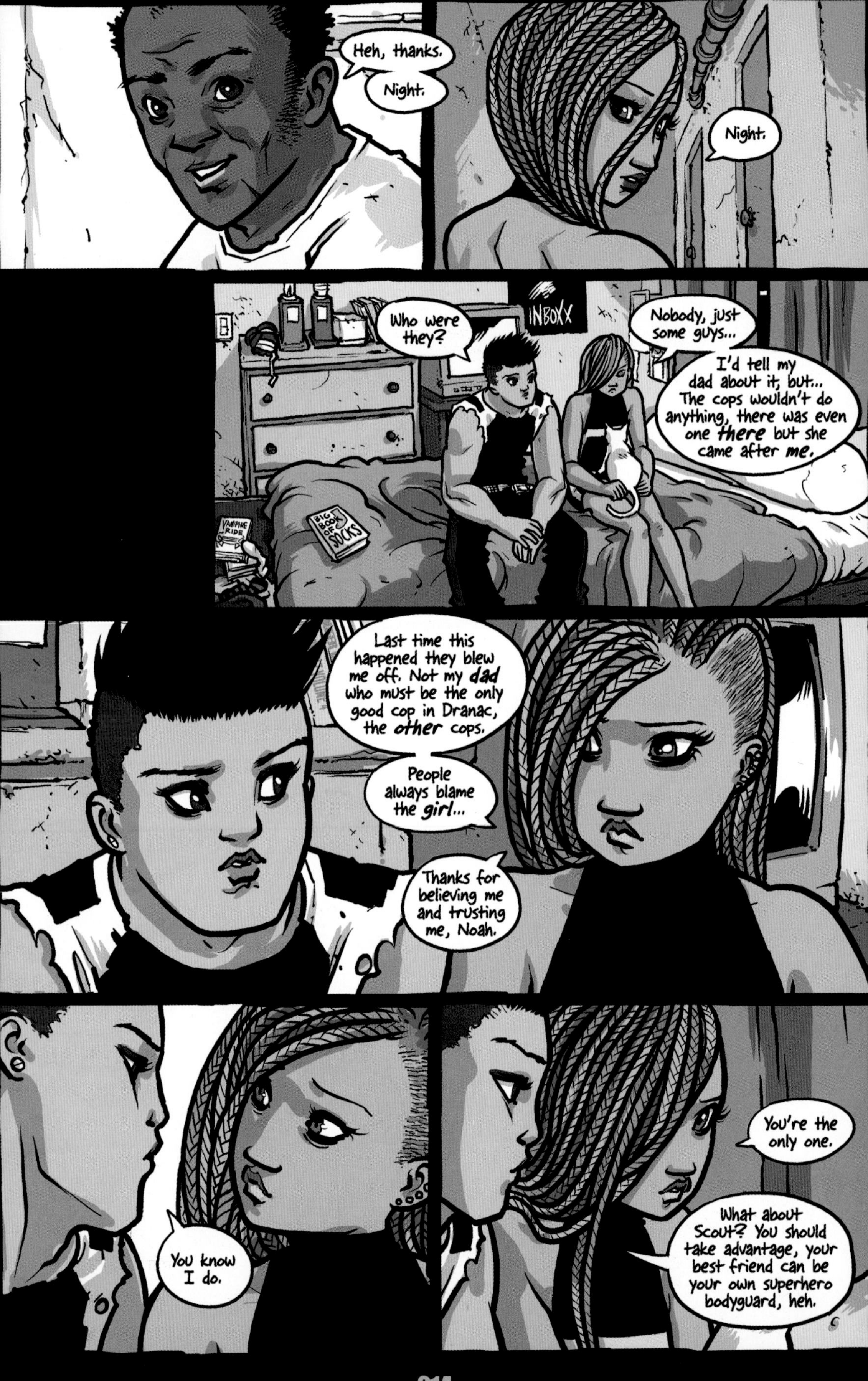
Heh, thanks.
Night.
Night.
Who were they?
INBOXX
Nobody, just some guys...
I'd tell my dad about it, but... The cops wouldn't do anything, there was even one *there* but she came after *me*.
VAMPIRE RIDE
BIG BOOK OF SOCKS
Last time this happened they blew me off. Not my *dad* who must be the only good cop in Dranac, the *other* cops.
People always blame the *girl*...
Thanks for believing me and trusting me, Noah.
You know I do.
You're the only one.
What about Scout? You should take advantage, your best friend can be your own superhero bodyguard, heh.

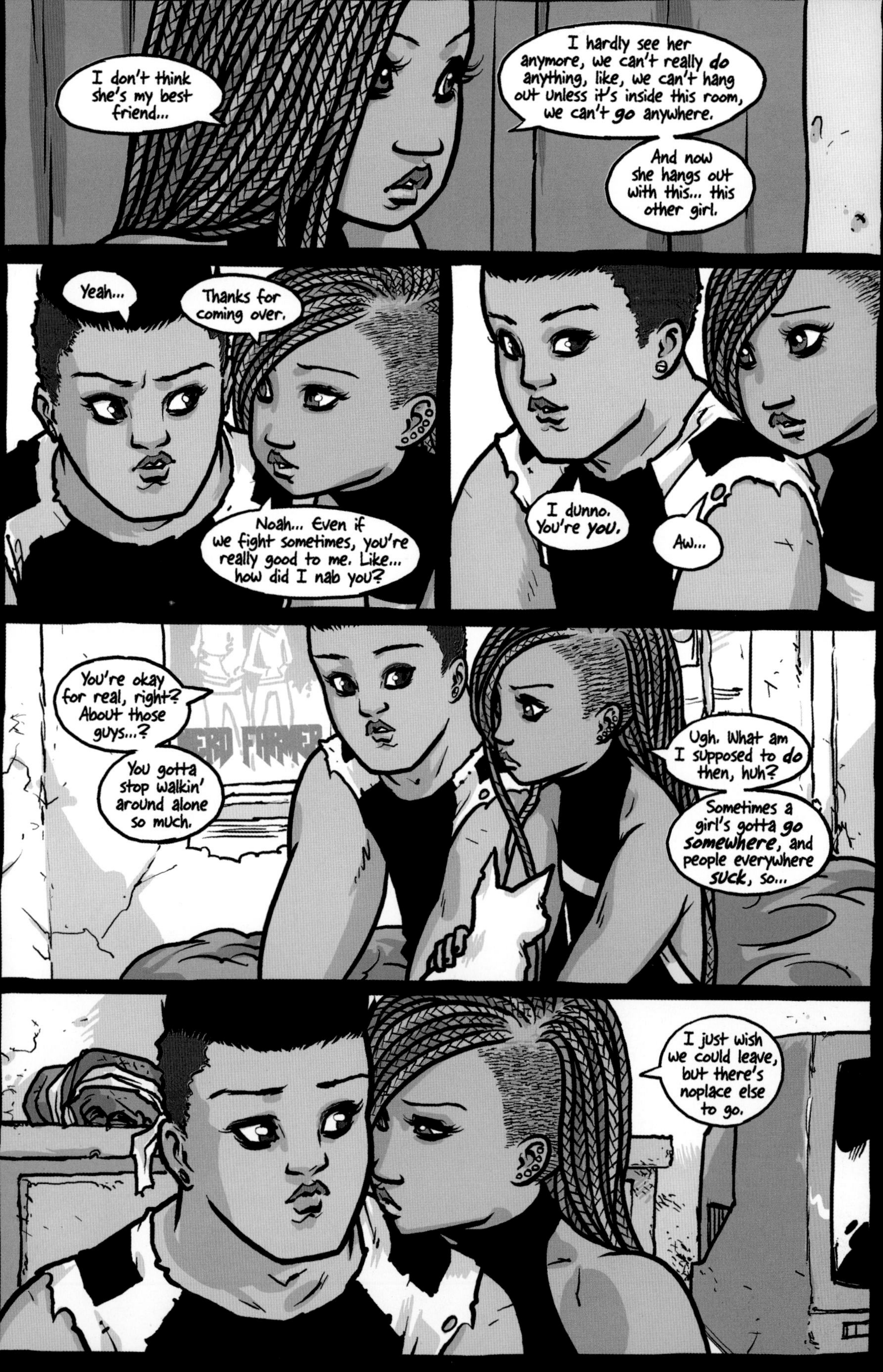

I don't think she's my best friend...
I hardly see her anymore, we can't really do anything, like, we can't hang out unless it's inside this room, we can't go anywhere.
And now she hangs out with this... this other girl.
Yeah...
Thanks for coming over.
Noah... Even if we fight sometimes, you're really good to me. Like... how did I nab you?
I dunno. You're you.
Aw...
You're okay for real, right? About those guys...?
You gotta stop walkin' around alone so much.
Ugh. What am I supposed to do then, huh?
Sometimes a girl's gotta go somewhere, and people everywhere suck, so...
I just wish we could leave, but there's noplace else to go.

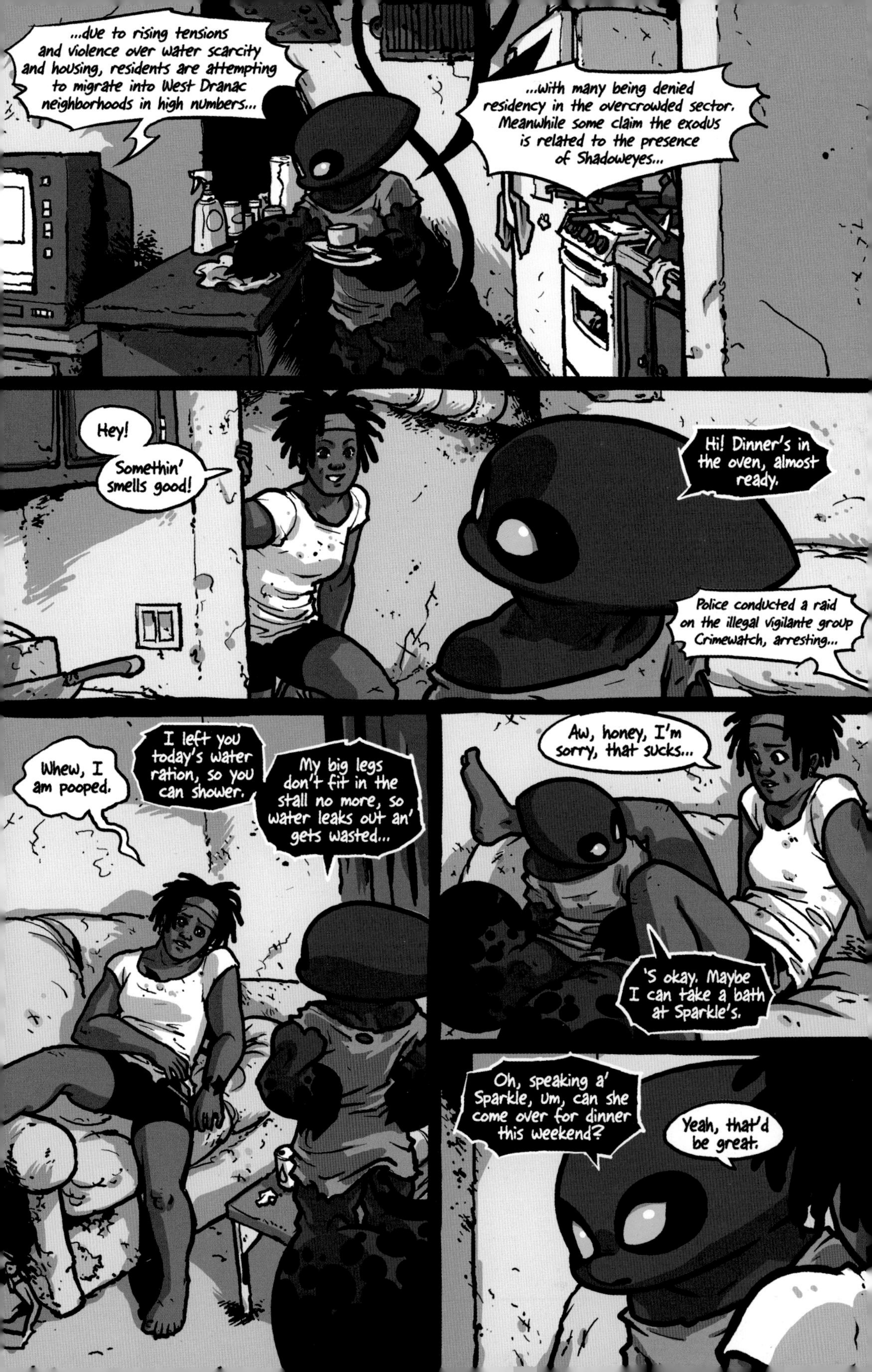
...due to rising tensions and violence over water scarcity and housing, residents are attempting to migrate into West Dranac neighborhoods in high numbers...
...with many being denied residency in the overcrowded sector. Meanwhile some claim the exodus is related to the presence of Shadoweyes...
Hey!
Somethin' smells good!
Hi! Dinner's in the oven, almost ready.
Police conducted a raid on the illegal vigilante group Crimewatch, arresting...
Whew, I am pooped.
I left you today's water ration, so you can shower.
My big legs don't fit in the stall no more, so water leaks out an' gets wasted...
Aw, honey, I'm sorry, that sucks...
'S okay. Maybe I can take a bath at Sparkle's.
Oh, speaking a' Sparkle, um, can she come over for dinner this weekend?
Yeah, that'd be great.

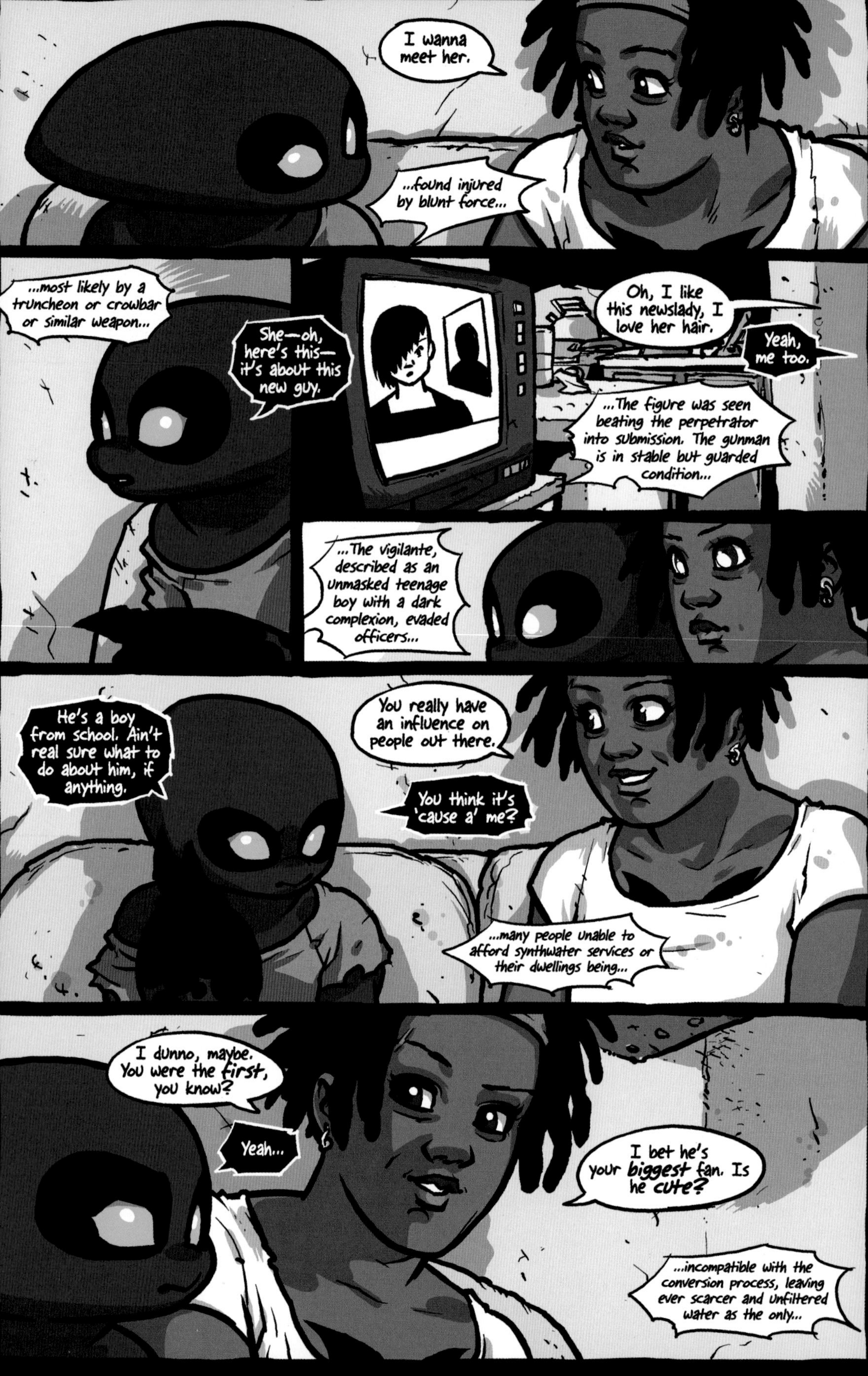
I wanna meet her.
...found injured by blunt force...
...most likely by a truncheon or crowbar or similar weapon...
She—oh, here's this—it's about this new guy.
Oh, I like this newslady, I love her hair.
Yeah, me too.
...The figure was seen beating the perpetrator into submission. The gunman is in stable but guarded condition...
...The vigilante, described as an unmasked teenage boy with a dark complexion, evaded officers...
He's a boy from school. Ain't real sure what to do about him, if anything.
You really have an influence on people out there.
You think it's 'cause a' me?
...many people unable to afford synthwater services or their dwellings being...
I dunno, maybe. You were the *first*, you know?
Yeah...
I bet he's your *biggest* fan. Is he *cute?*
...incompatible with the conversion process, leaving ever scarcer and unfiltered water as the only...

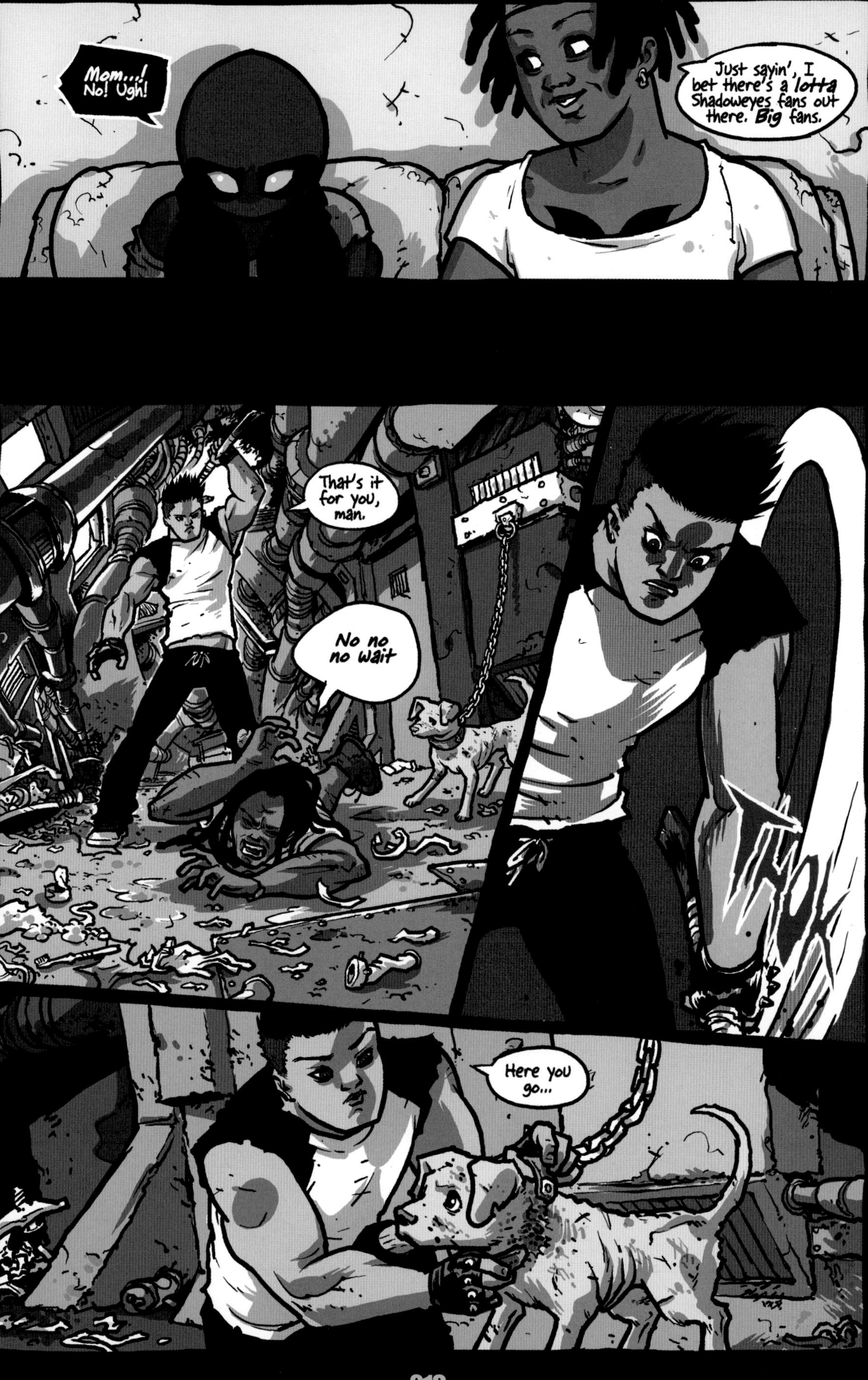

Mom...! No! Ugh!
Just sayin', I bet there's a lotta Shadoweyes fans out there. Big fans.
That's it for you, man.
No no no wait
Here you go...

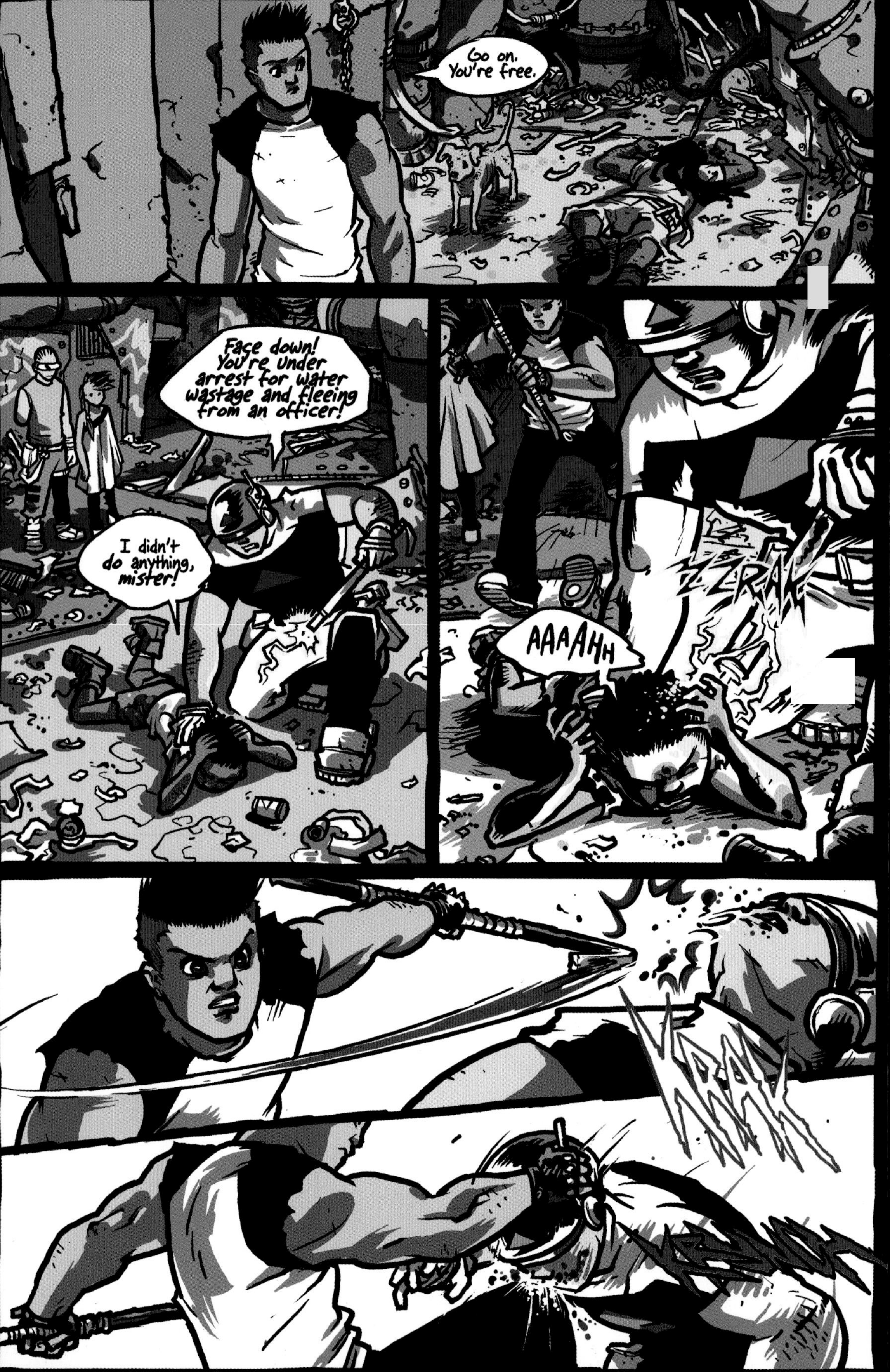
Go on. You're free.
Face down! You're under arrest for water wastage and fleeing from an officer!
I didn't do anything, mister!
AAAAHH

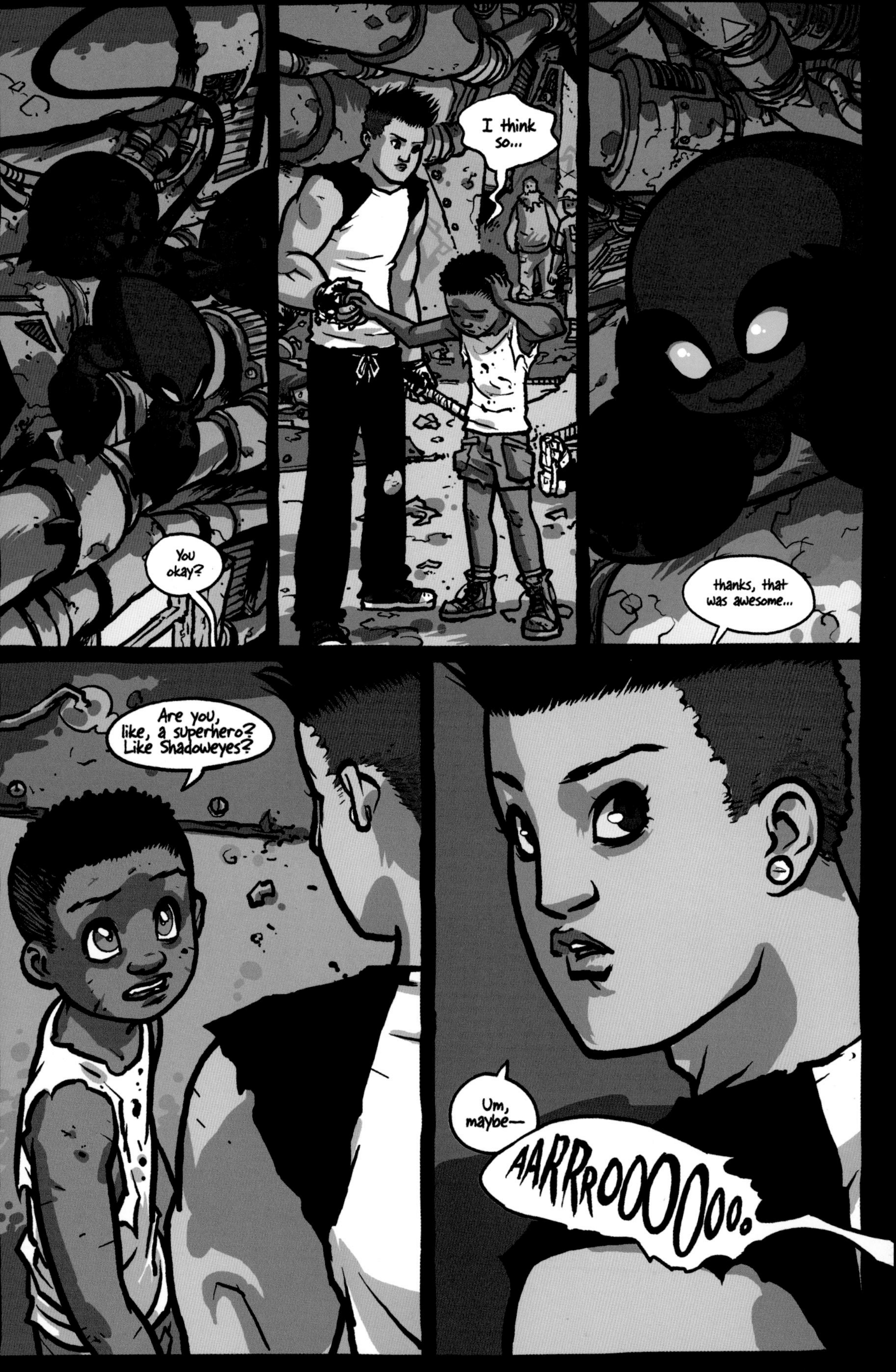
You okay?
I think so...
thanks, that was awesome...
Are you, like, a superhero? Like Shadoweyes?
Um, maybe—
AARRROOOOOoo.

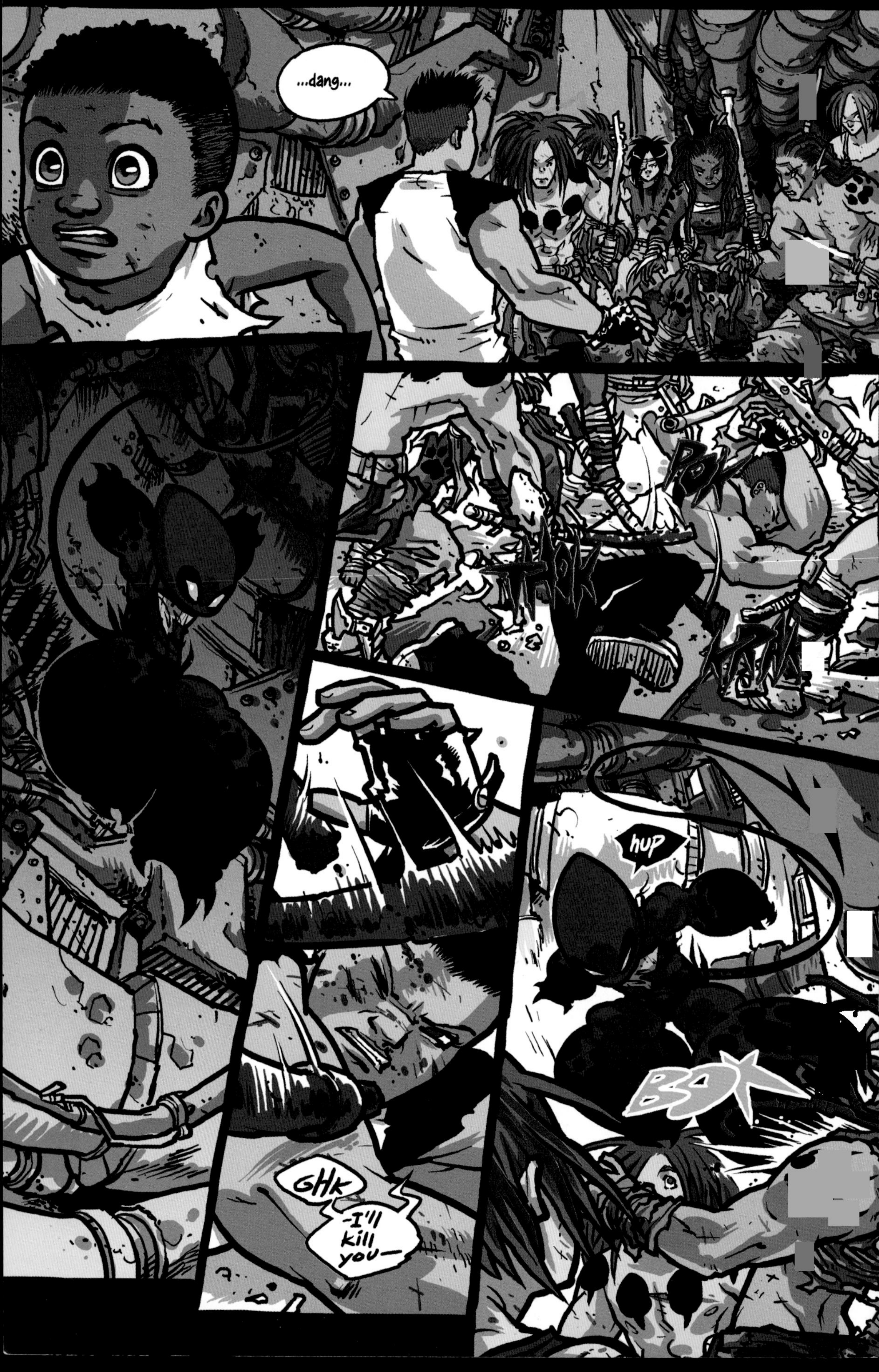

...dang...
POK
THOK
WHAK
hup
BOK
GHK
-I'll kill you—

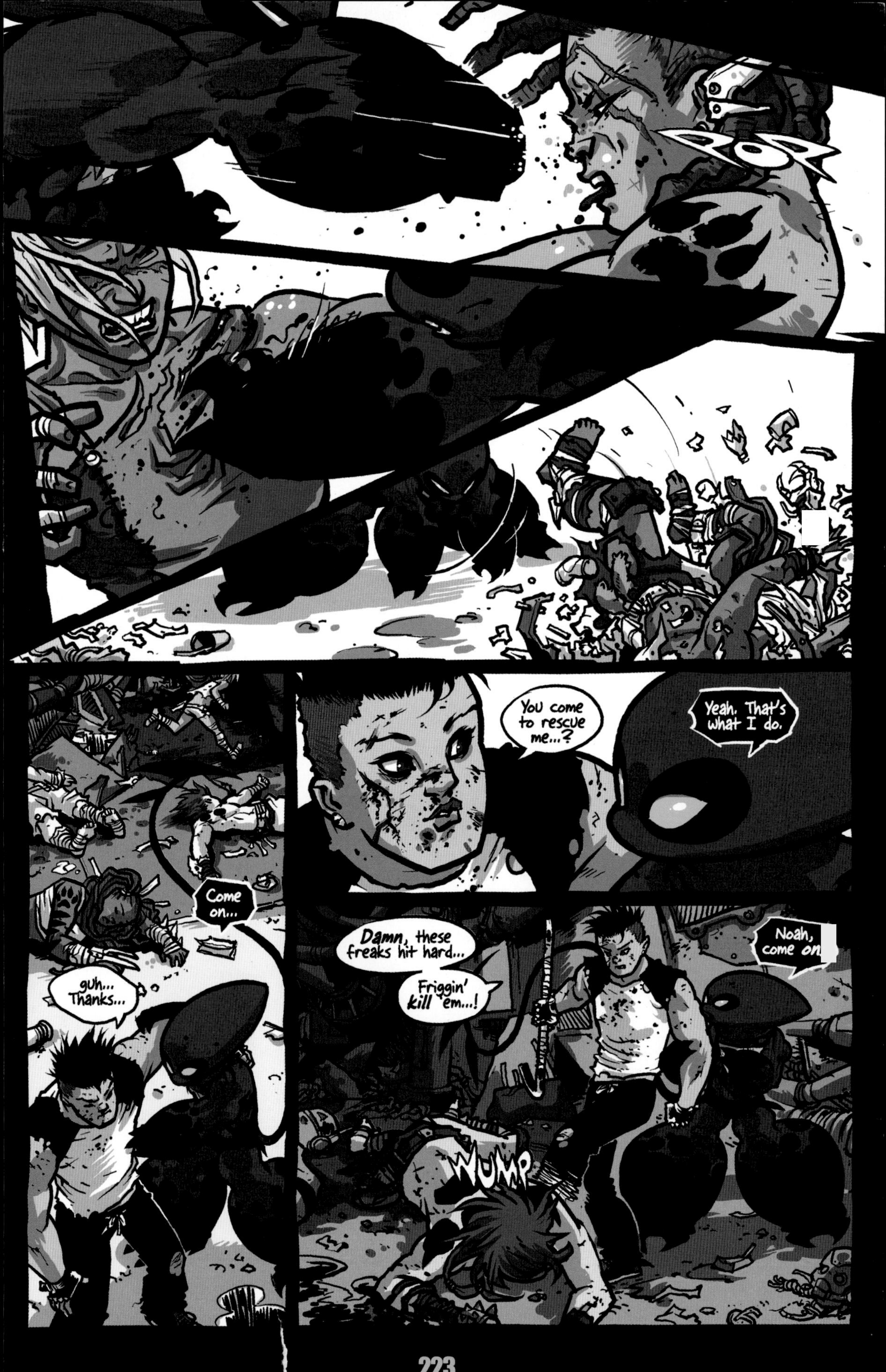
You come to rescue me...?
Yeah. That's what I do.
Come on...
guh... Thanks...
Damn, these freaks hit hard...
Friggin' kill 'em...!
Noah, come on
WUMP

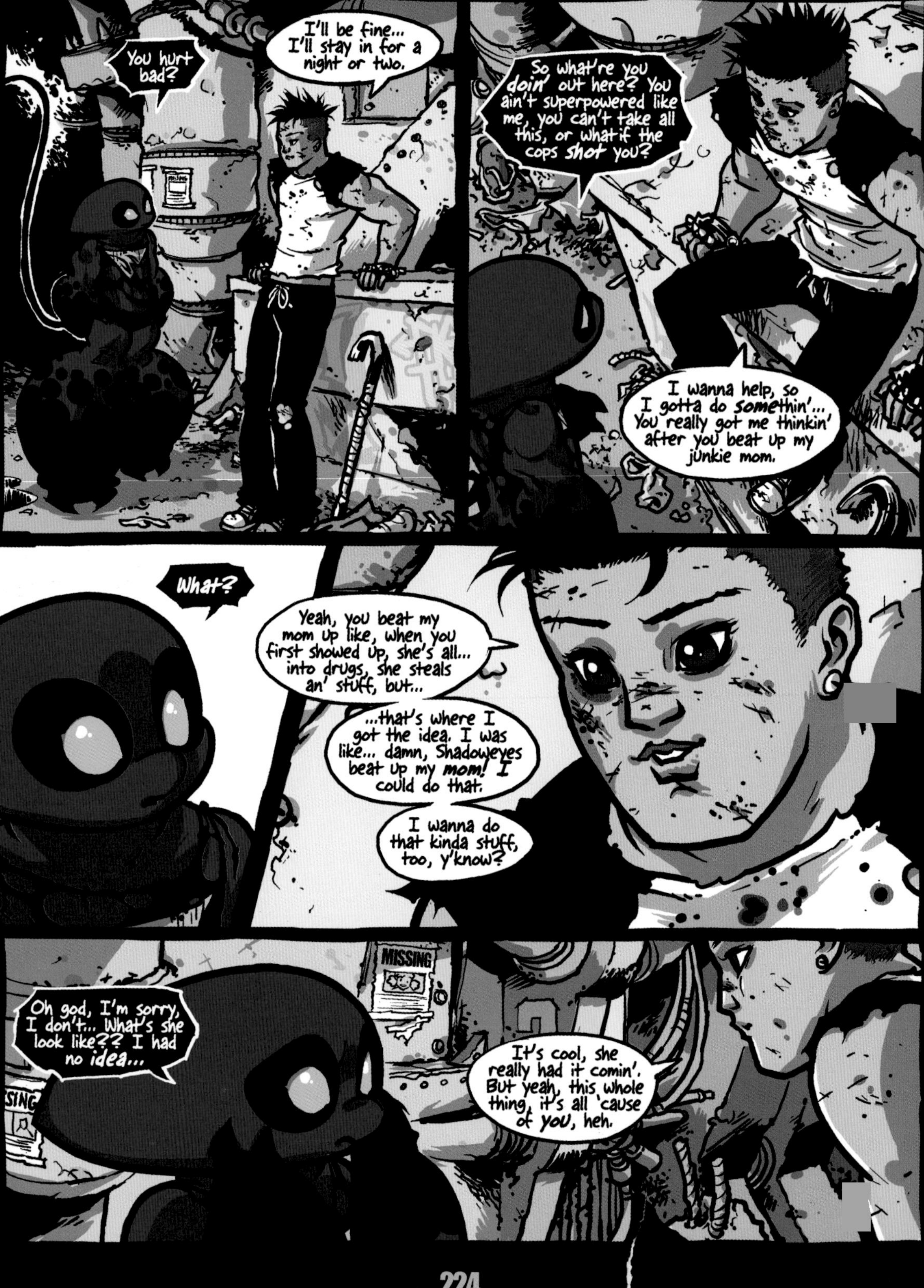
You hurt bad?
I'll be fine... I'll stay in for a night or two.
MISSING
So what're you doin' out here? You ain't superpowered like me, you can't take all this, or what if the cops shot you?
I wanna help, so I gotta do somethin'... You really got me thinkin' after you beat up my junkie mom.
What?
Yeah, you beat my mom up like, when you first showed up, she's all... into drugs, she steals an' stuff, but...
...that's where I got the idea. I was like... damn, Shadoweyes beat up my mom! I could do that.
I wanna do that kinda stuff, too, y'know?
MISSING
Oh god, I'm sorry, I don't... What's she look like?? I had no idea...
It's cool, she really had it comin'. But yeah, this whole thing, it's all 'cause of you, heh.

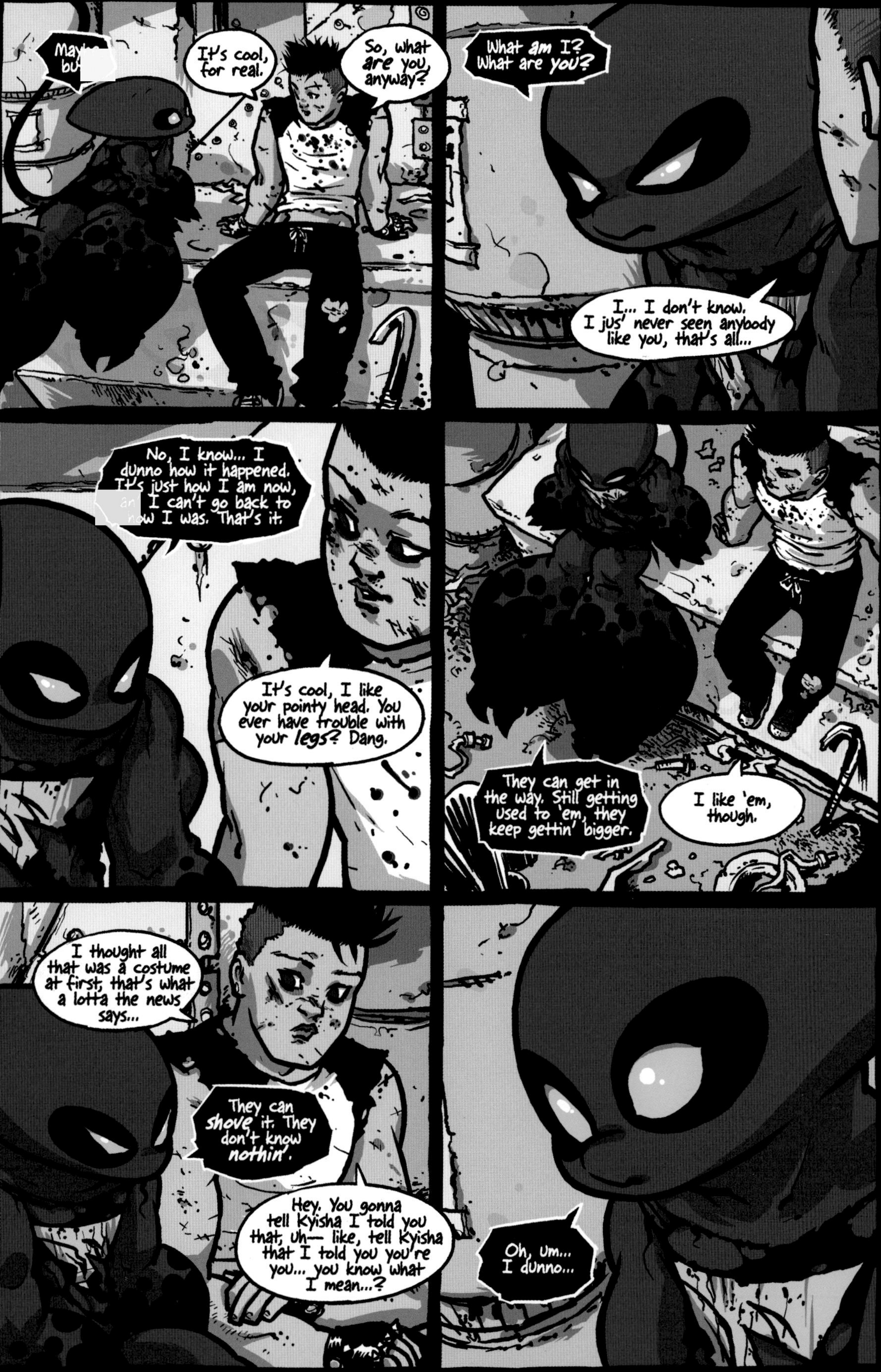
May bu
It's cool, for real.
So, what are you, anyway?
What am I? What are you?
I... I don't know. I jus' never seen anybody like you, that's all...
No, I know... I dunno how it happened. It's just how I am now, an I can't go back to ow I was. That's it.
It's cool, I like your pointy head. You ever have trouble with your legs? Dang.
They can get in the way. Still getting used to 'em, they keep gettin' bigger.
I like 'em, though.
I thought all that was a costume at first; that's what a lotta the news says...
They can shove it. They don't know nothin'.
Hey. You gonna tell Kyisha I told you that, uh— like, tell Kyisha that I told you you're you... you know what I mean...?
Oh, um... I dunno...

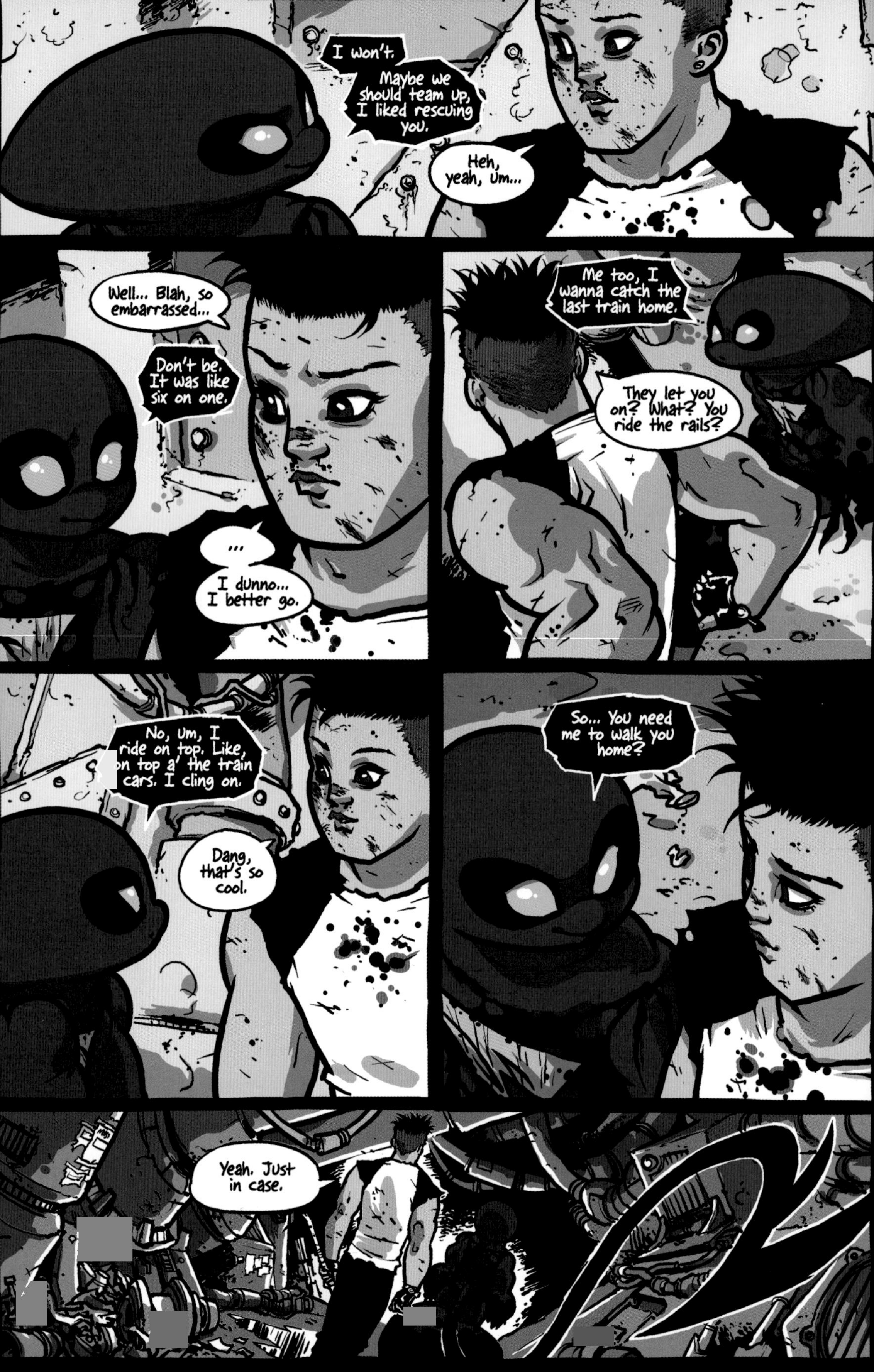
I won't.
Maybe we should team up, I liked rescuing you.
Heh, yeah, um...
Well... Blah, so embarrassed...
Don't be. It was like six on one.
...
I dunno... I better go.
Me too, I wanna catch the last train home.
They let you on? What? You ride the rails?
No, um, I ride on top. Like, on top a' the train cars. I cling on.
Dang, that's so cool.
So... You need me to walk you home?
Yeah. Just in case.

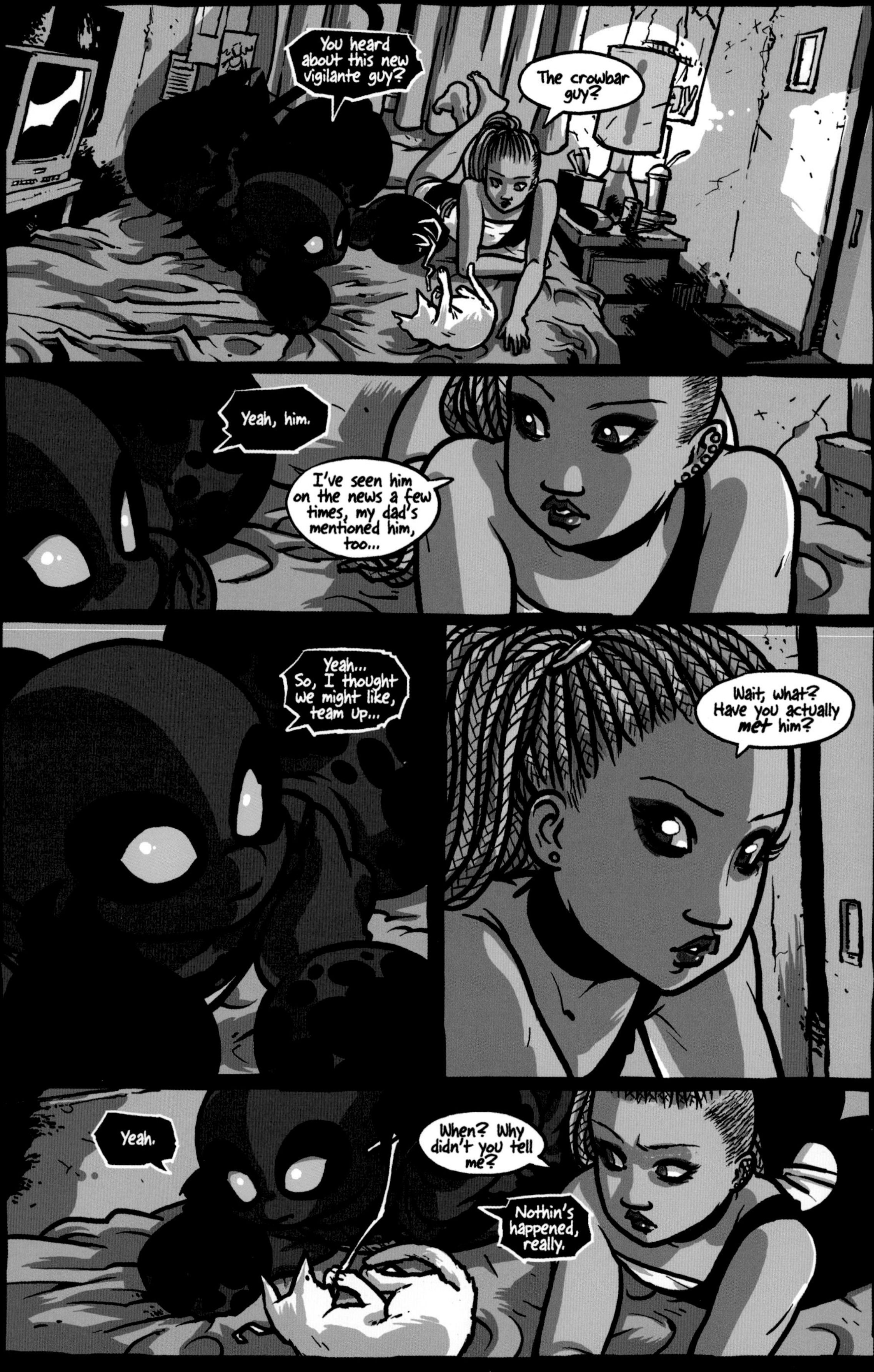
You heard about this new vigilante guy?
The crowbar guy?
Yeah, him.
I've seen him on the news a few times, my dad's mentioned him, too...
Yeah... So, I thought we might like, team up...
Wait, what? Have you actually *met* him?
Yeah.
When? Why didn't you tell me?
Nothin's happened, really.

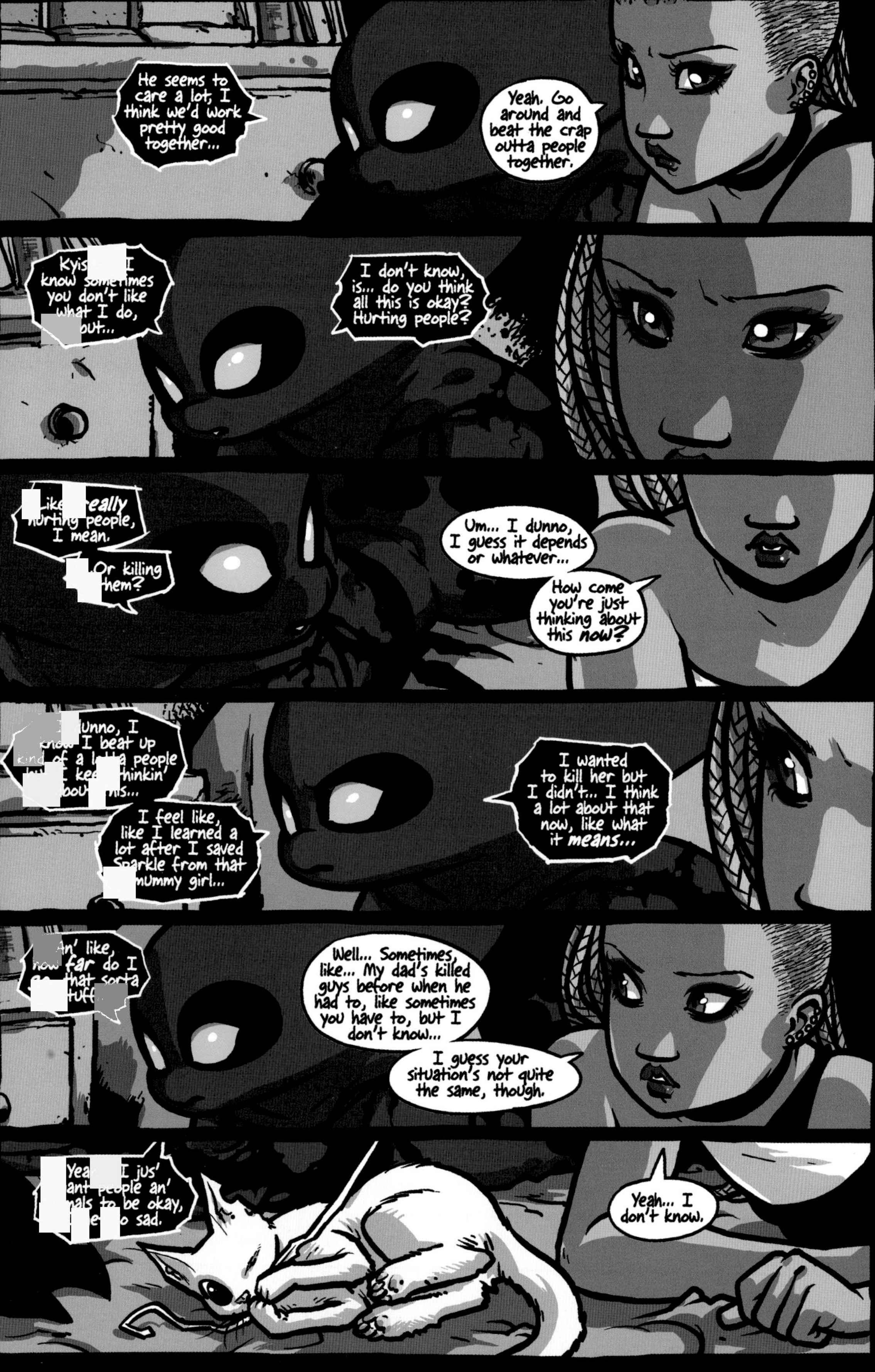
He seems to care a lot, I think we'd work pretty good together...
Yeah. Go around and beat the crap outta people together.
Kyis[redacted] I know sometimes you don't like what I do, [redacted]ut...
I don't know, is... do you think all this is okay? Hurting people?
[redacted]Like[redacted]eally hurting people, I mean.
[redacted]Or killing [redacted]hem?
Um... I dunno, I guess it depends or whatever...
How come you're just thinking about this *now?*
[redacted]unno, I know I beat up kind of a lo[redacted]a people [redacted] kee[redacted]hinkin' [redacted]bou[redacted]his...
I feel like, like I learned a lot after I saved Sparkle from that [redacted]ummy girl...
I wanted to kill her but I didn't... I think a lot about that now, like what it *means...*
[redacted]An' like, how *far* do I [redacted]that sorta [redacted]tuff[redacted]
Well... Sometimes, like... My dad's killed guys before when he had to, like sometimes you have to, but I don't know...
I guess your situation's not quite the same, though.
[redacted]Yea[redacted]I jus' [redacted]ant people an' [redacted]mals to be okay, [redacted]e[redacted]o sad.
Yeah... I don't know.

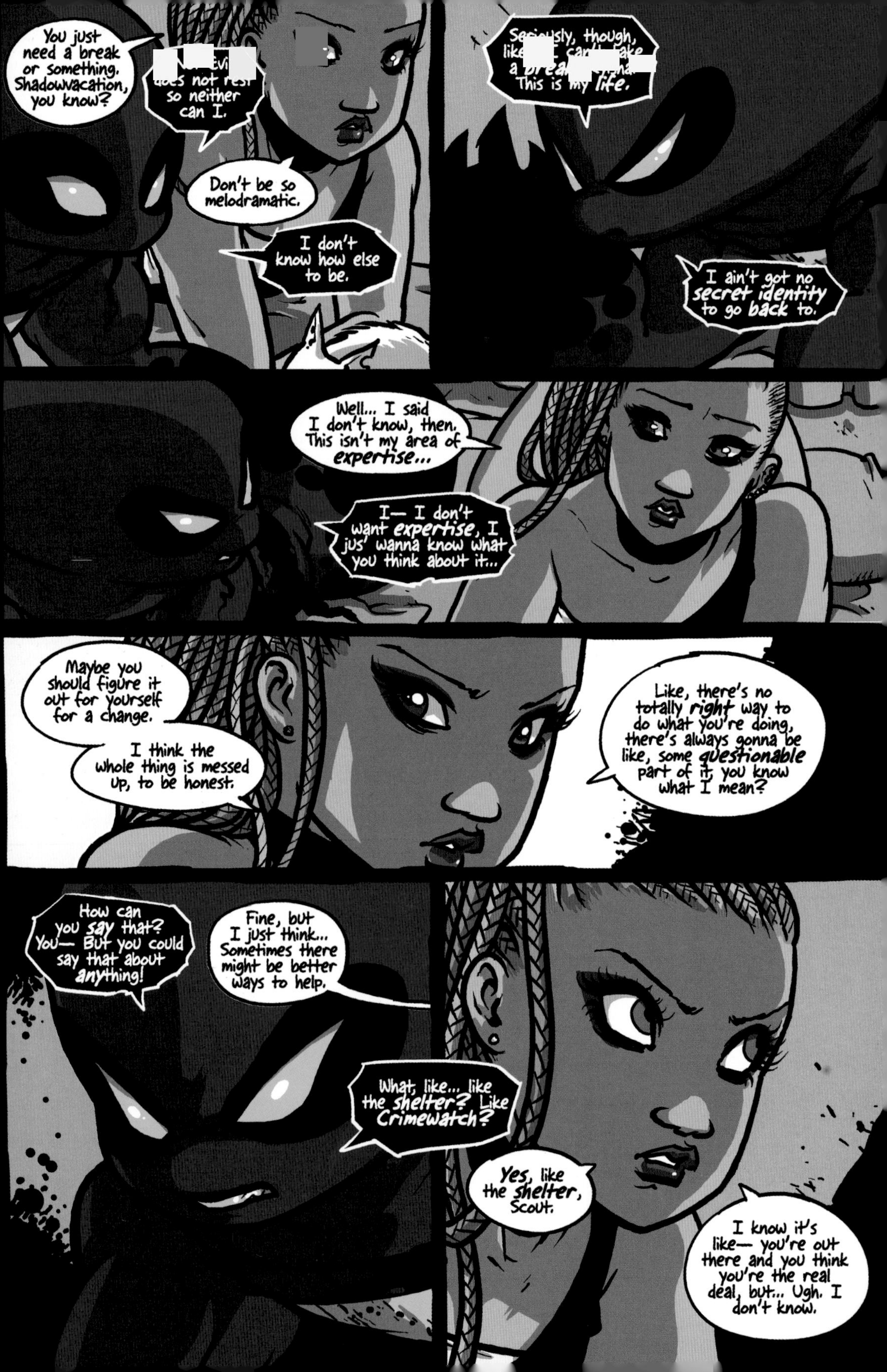

You just need a break or something. Shadowvacation, you know?
[redacted] does not rest so neither can I.
Don't be so melodramatic.
I don't know how else to be.
Seriously, though, like [redacted] can't take a break [redacted] This is my life.
I ain't got no secret identity to go back to.
Well... I said I don't know, then. This isn't my area of expertise...
I— I don't want expertise, I jus' wanna know what you think about it...
Maybe you should figure it out for yourself for a change.
I think the whole thing is messed up, to be honest.
Like, there's no totally right way to do what you're doing, there's always gonna be like, some questionable part of it, you know what I mean?
How can you say that? You— But you could say that about anything!
Fine, but I just think... Sometimes there might be better ways to help.
What, like... like the shelter? Like Crimewatch?
Yes, like the shelter, Scout.
I know it's like— you're out there and you think you're the real deal, but... Ugh. I don't know.

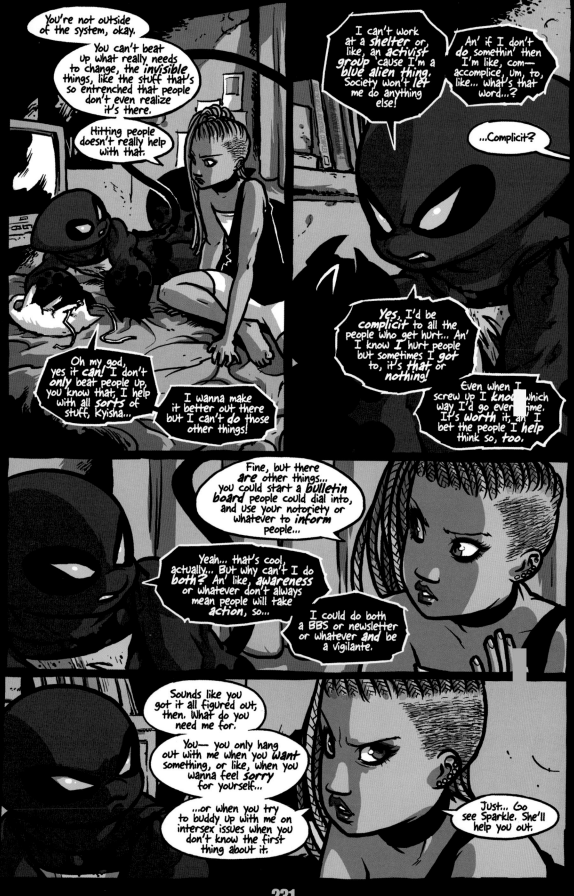

You're not outside of the system, okay.

You can't beat up what really needs to change, the *invisible* things, like the stuff that's so entrenched that people don't even realize it's there.

Hitting people doesn't really help with that.

Oh my god, yes it *can!* I don't *only* beat people up, you know that, I help with all *sorts* of stuff, Kyisha...

I wanna make it better out there but I can't do those other things!

I can't work at a *shelter* or, like, an *activist group* 'cause I'm a *blue alien thing.* Society won't *let* me do anything else!

An' if I don't *do somethin'* then I'm like, com— accomplice, um, to, like... what's that word...?

...Complicit?

Yes, I'd be *complicit* to all the people who get hurt... An' I know I hurt people but sometimes I *got* to, it's *that* or *nothing!*

Even when I screw up I *know* which way I'd go every time. It's *worth* it, an' I bet the people I *help* think so, *too.*

Fine, but there *are* other things... you could start a *bulletin board* people could dial into, and use your notoriety or whatever to *inform* people...

Yeah... that's cool, actually... But why can't I do *both?* An' like, *awareness* or whatever don't always mean people will take *action,* so...

I could do both a BBS or newsletter or whatever and be a vigilante.

Sounds like you got it all figured out, then. What do you need me for.

You— you only hang out with me when you *want* something, or like, when you wanna feel *sorry* for yourself...

...or when you try to buddy up with me on intersex issues when you don't know the first thing about it.

Just... Go see Sparkle. She'll help you out.

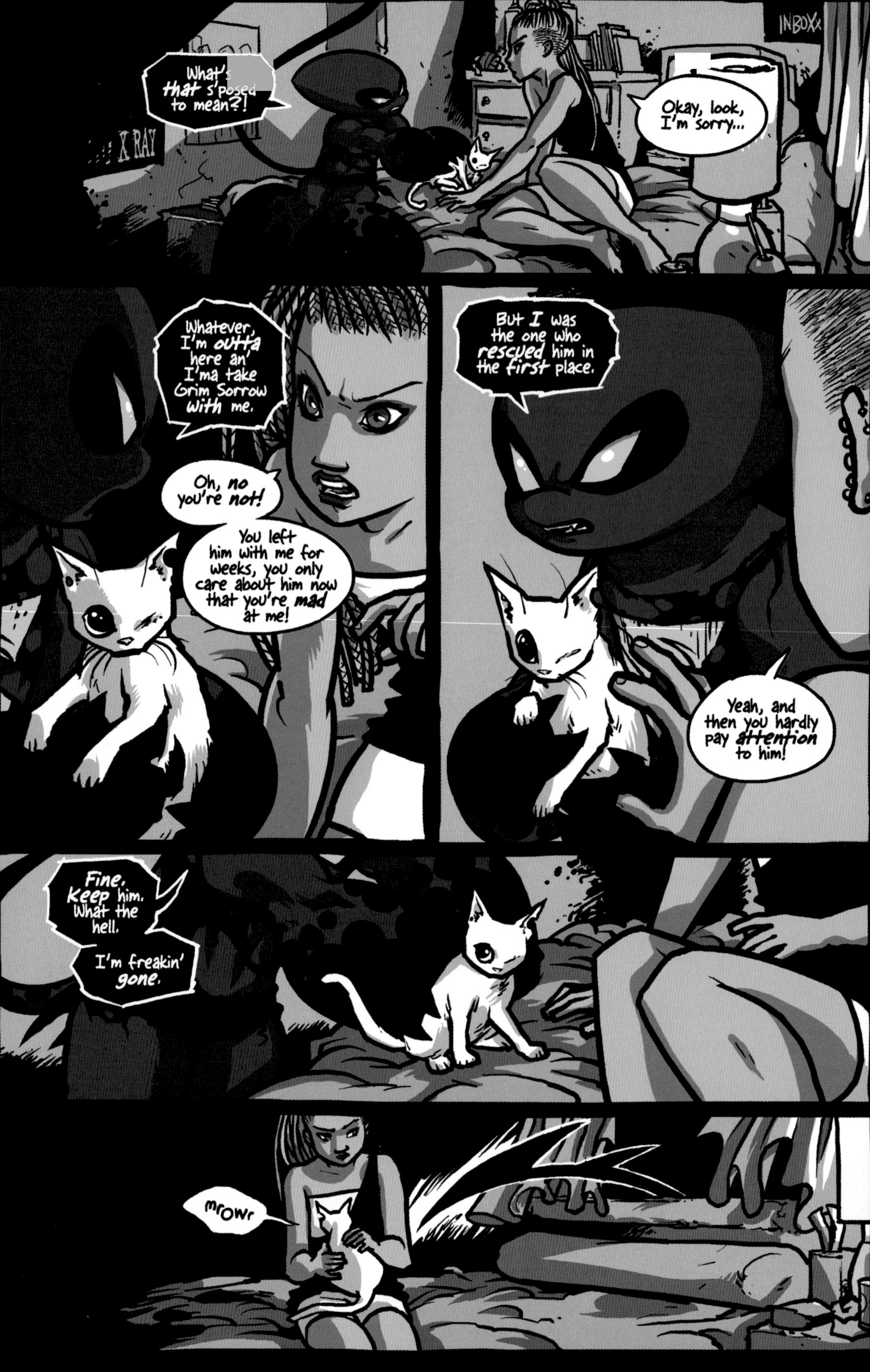
What's that s'posed to mean?!
Okay, look, I'm sorry...
Whatever, I'm outta here an' I'ma take Grim Sorrow with me.
Oh, no you're not!
You left him with me for weeks, you only care about him now that you're mad at me!
But I was the one who rescued him in the first place.
Yeah, and then you hardly pay attention to him!
Fine. Keep him. What the hell.
I'm freakin' gone.
mrowr

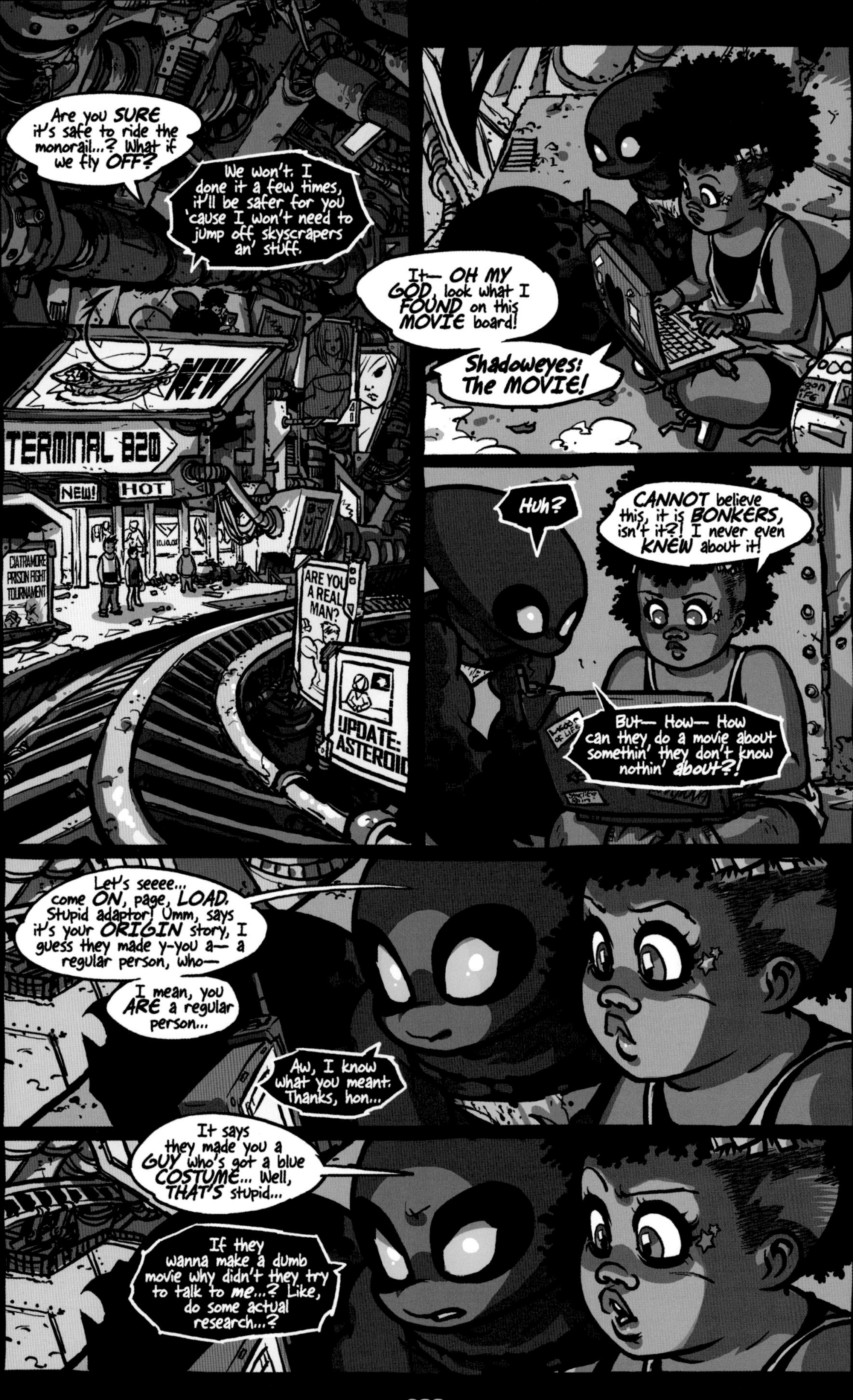
Are you SURE it's safe to ride the monorail...? What if we fly OFF?
We won't. I done it a few times, it'll be safer for you 'cause I won't need to jump off skyscrapers an' stuff.
NEW
TERMINAL B20
NEW!
HOT
CIATRAMORE PRISON FIGHT TOURNAMENT
ARE YOU A REAL MAN?
UPDATE: ASTEROID
It— OH MY GOD, look what I FOUND on this MOVIE board!
Shadoweyes: The MOVIE!
Huh?
CANNOT believe this, it is BONKERS, isn't it?! I never even KNEW about it!
But— How— How can they do a movie about somethin' they don't know nothin' about?!
Let's seeee... come ON, page, LOAD. Stupid adaptor! Umm, says it's your ORIGIN story, I guess they made y-you a— a regular person, who—
I mean, you ARE a regular person...
Aw, I know what you meant. Thanks, hon...
It says they made you a GUY who's got a blue COSTUME... Well, THAT'S stupid...
If they wanna make a dumb movie why didn't they try to talk to me...? Like, do some actual research...?

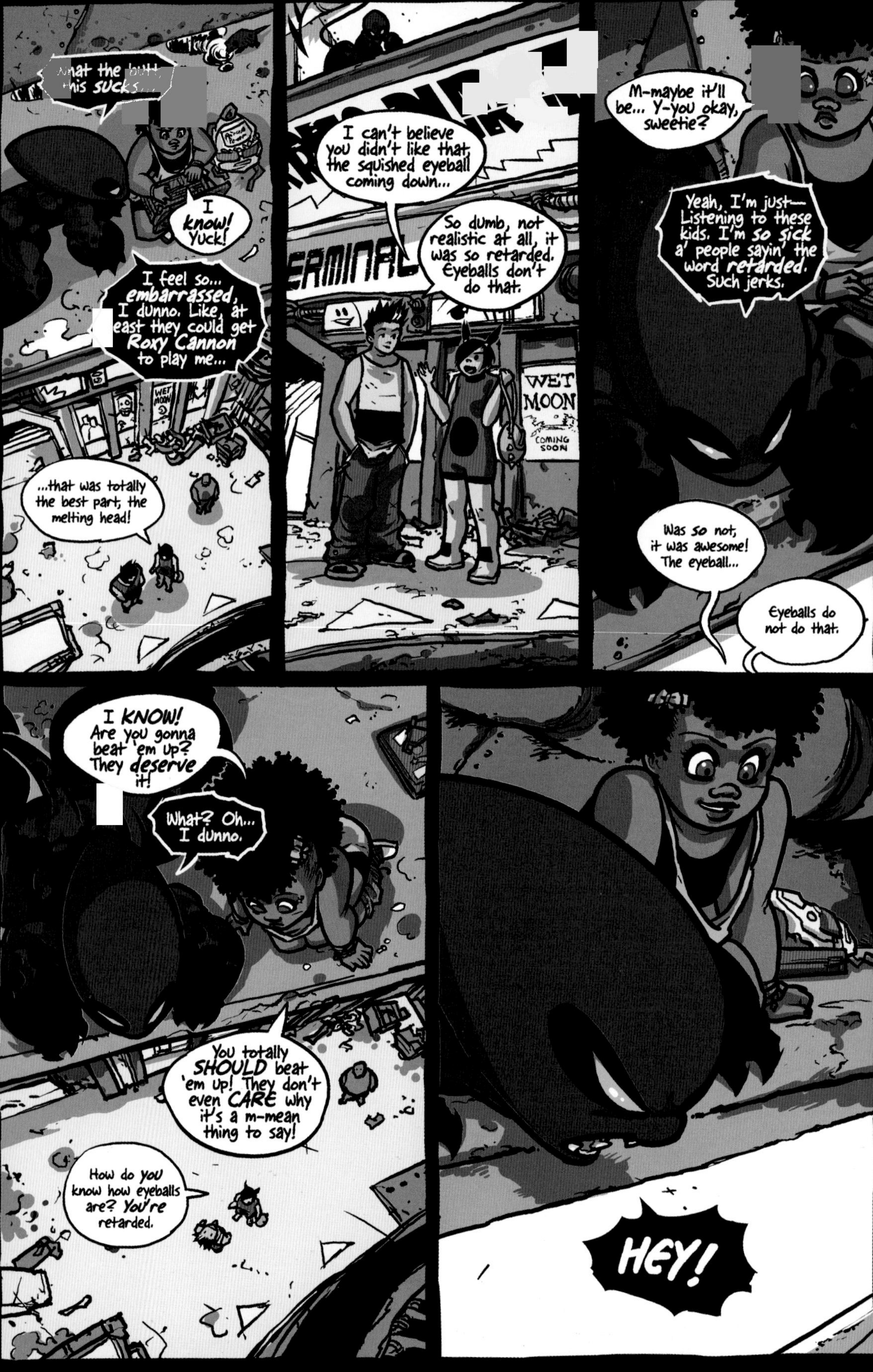
What the butt, this SUCKS...
I know! Yuck!
I feel so... embarrassed, I dunno. Like, at least they could get Roxy Cannon to play me...
...that was totally the best part, the melting head!
I can't believe you didn't like that, the squished eyeball coming down...
So dumb, not realistic at all, it was so retarded. Eyeballs don't do that.
ERMINAL
WET MOON
COMING SOON
M-maybe it'll be... Y-you okay, sweetie?
Yeah, I'm just— Listening to these kids. I'm so sick a' people sayin' the word retarded. Such jerks.
Was so not, it was awesome! The eyeball...
Eyeballs do not do that.
I KNOW! Are you gonna beat 'em up? They deserve it!
What? Oh... I dunno.
You totally SHOULD beat 'em up! They don't even CARE why it's a m-mean thing to say!
How do you know how eyeballs are? You're retarded.
HEY!

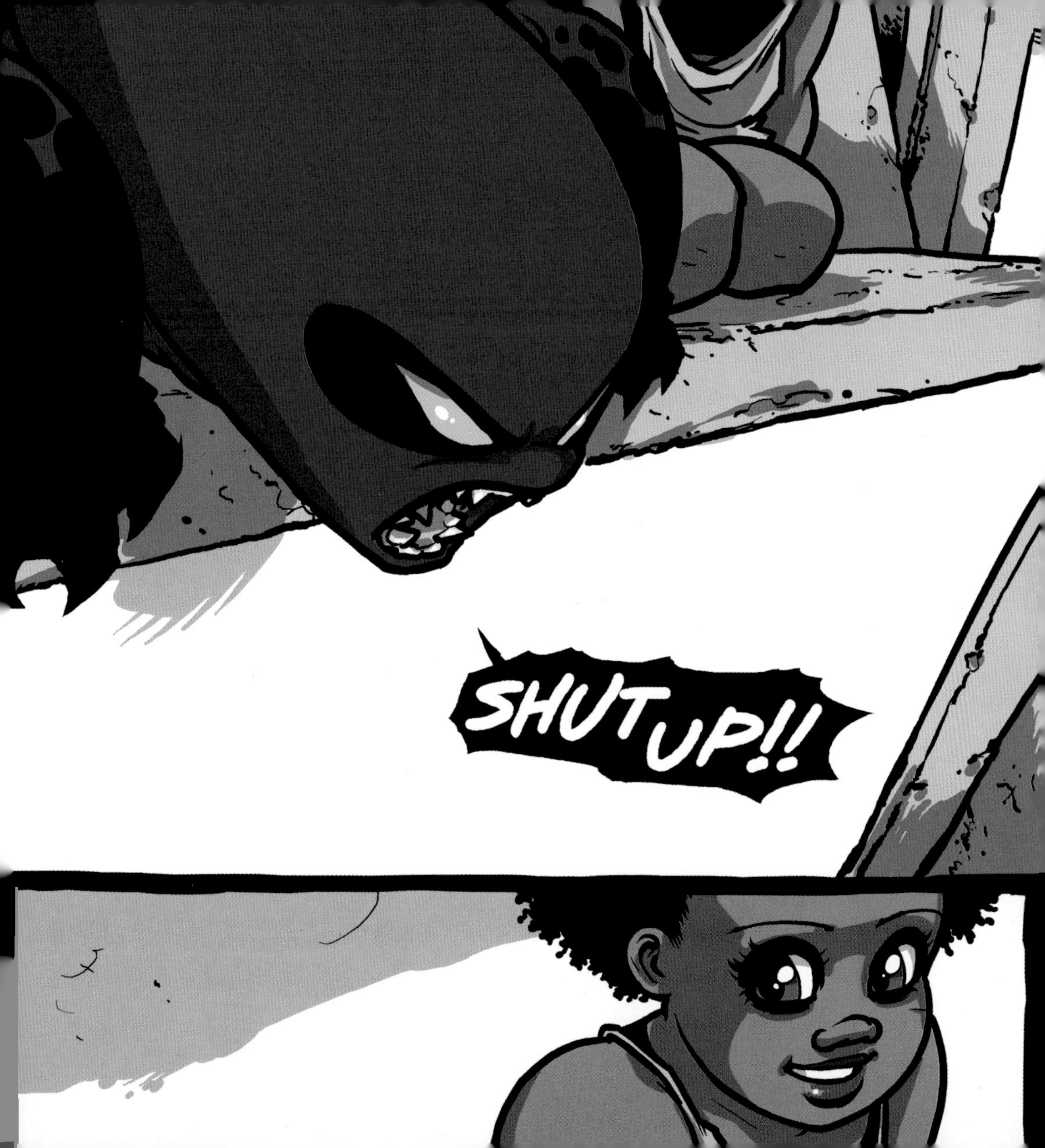
SHUT UP!!

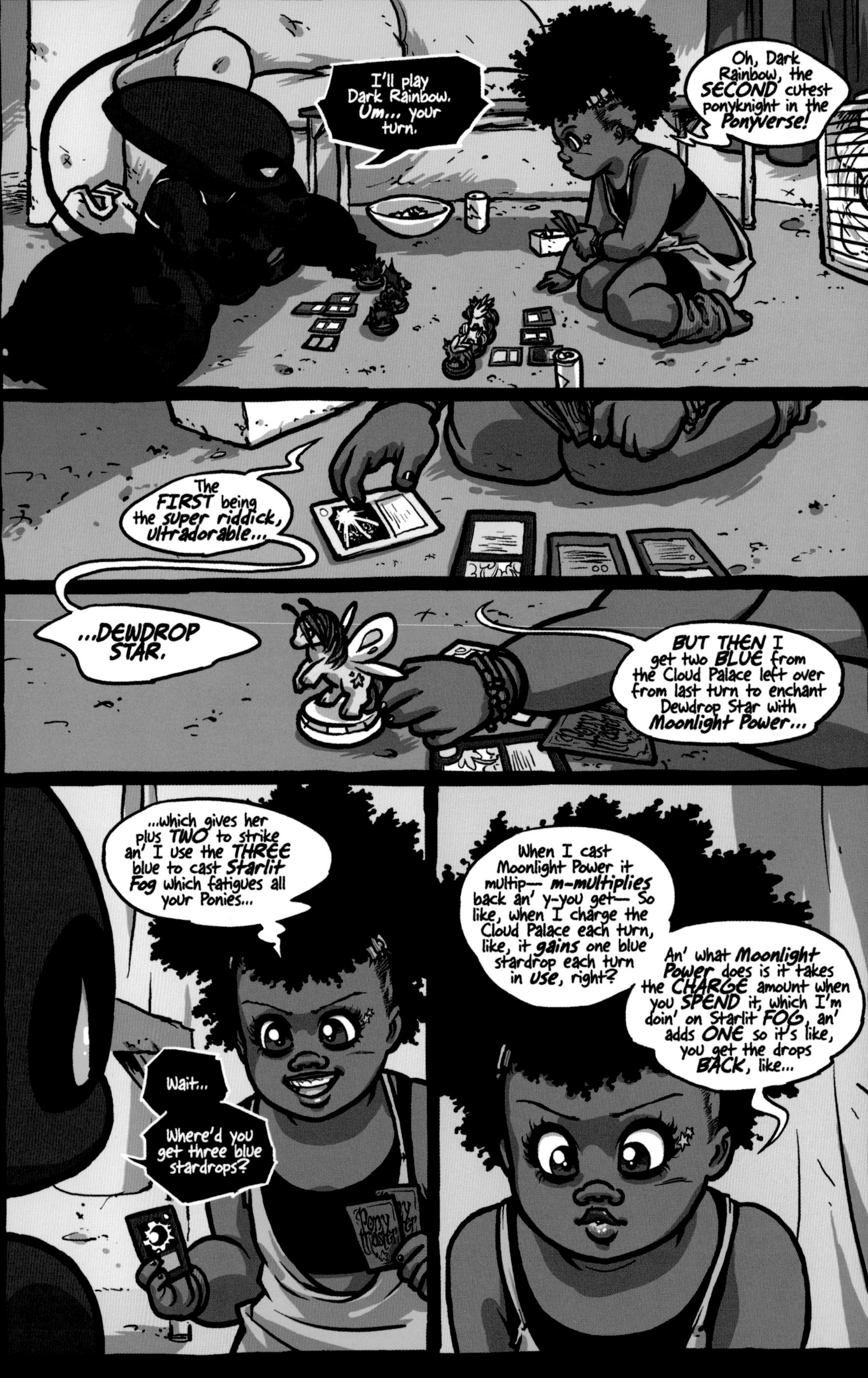

I'll play Dark Rainbow. Um... your turn.
Oh, Dark Rainbow, the SECOND cutest ponyknight in the Ponyverse!
The FIRST being the super riddick, ultradorable...
...DEWDROP STAR.
BUT THEN I get two BLUE from the Cloud Palace left over from last turn to enchant Dewdrop Star with Moonlight Power...
...which gives her plus TWO to strike an' I use the THREE blue to cast Starlit Fog which fatigues all your Ponies...
Wait...
Where'd you get three blue stardrops?
When I cast Moonlight Power it multip— m-multiplies back an' y-you get— So like, when I charge the Cloud Palace each turn, like, it gains one blue stardrop each turn in use, right?
An' what Moonlight Power does is it takes the CHARGE amount when you SPEND it, which I'm doin' on Starlit FOG, an' adds ONE so it's like, you get the drops BACK, like...

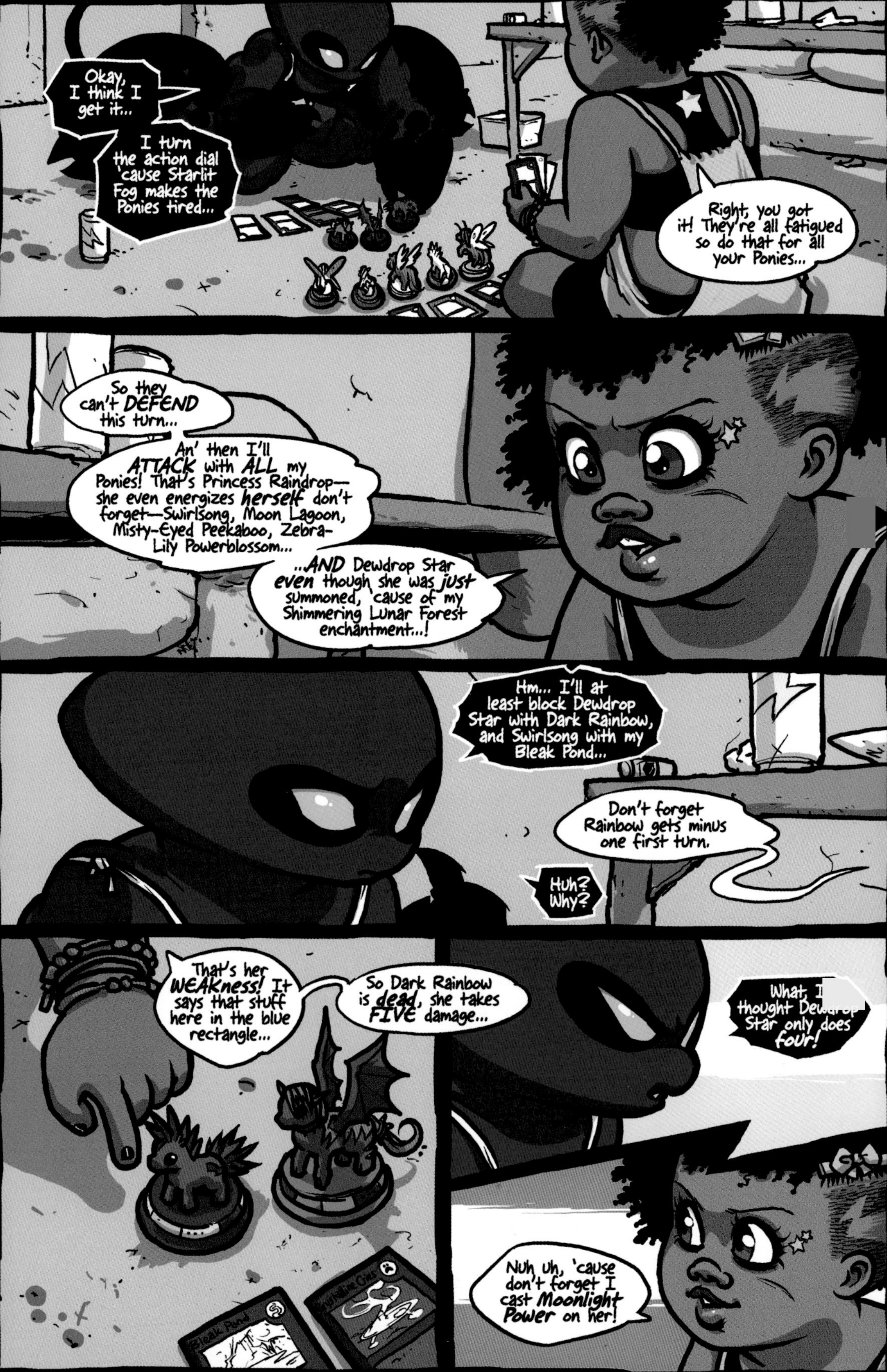
Okay, I think I get it...
I turn the action dial 'cause Starlit Fog makes the Ponies tired...
Right, you got it! They're all fatigued so do that for all your Ponies...
So they can't DEFEND this turn...
An' then I'll ATTACK with ALL my Ponies! That's Princess Raindrop— she even energizes herself don't forget—Swirlsong, Moon Lagoon, Misty-Eyed Peekaboo, Zebra-Lily Powerblossom...
..AND Dewdrop Star even though she was just summoned, 'cause of my Shimmering Lunar Forest enchantment...!
Hm... I'll at least block Dewdrop Star with Dark Rainbow, and Swirlsong with my Bleak Pond...
Don't forget Rainbow gets minus one first turn.
Huh? Why?
That's her WEAKness! It says that stuff here in the blue rectangle...
So Dark Rainbow is dead, she takes FIVE damage...
What, I thought Dewdrop Star only does four!
Nuh uh, 'cause don't forget I cast Moonlight Power on her!
Bleak Pond

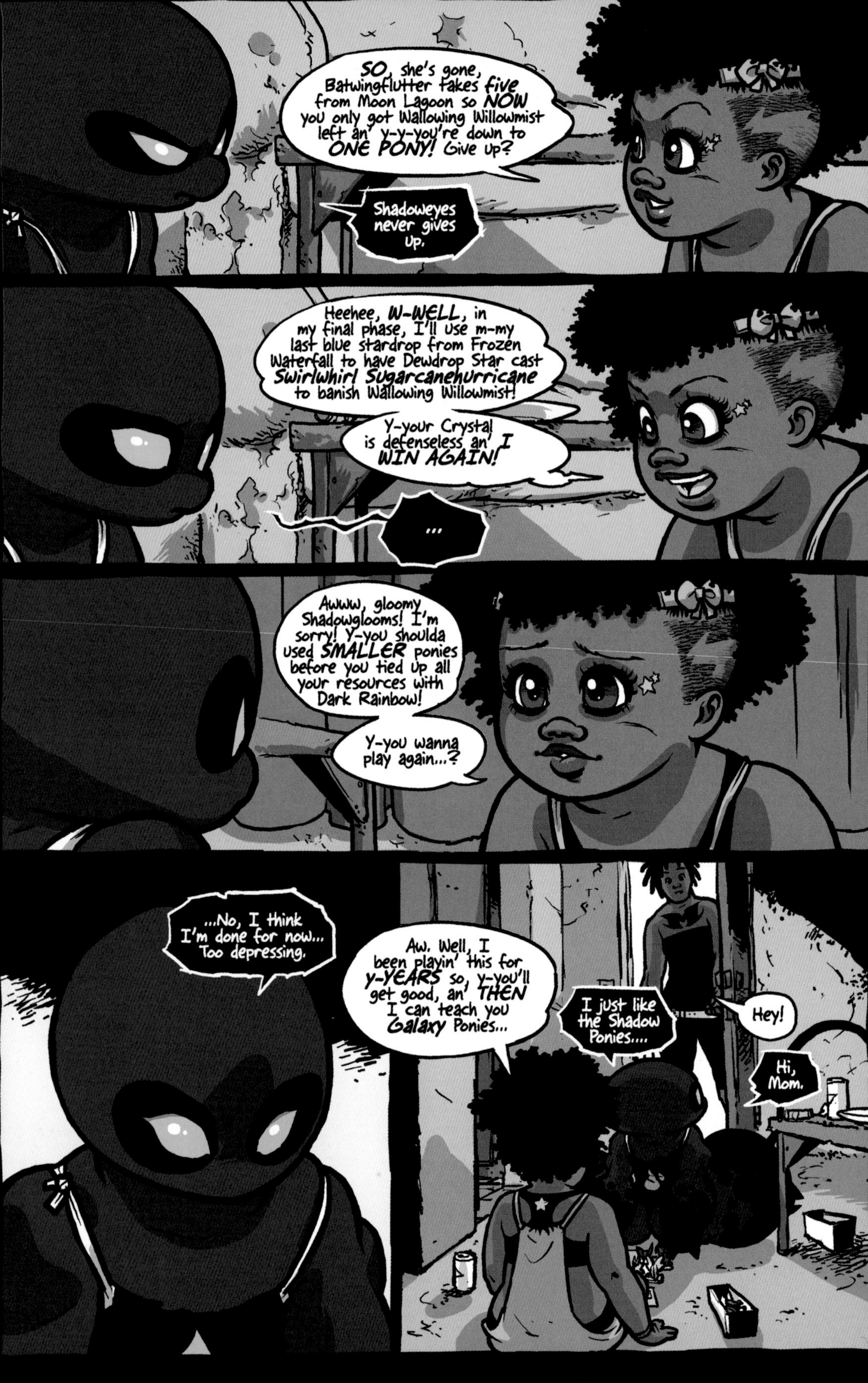
SO, she's gone, Batwingflutter takes five from Moon Lagoon so NOW you only got Wallowing Willowmist left an' y-y-you're down to ONE PONY! Give up?
Shadoweyes never gives up.
Heehee, W-WELL, in my final phase, I'll use m-my last blue stardrop from Frozen Waterfall to have Dewdrop Star cast Swirlwhirl Sugarcanehurricane to banish Wallowing Willowmist!
Y-your Crystal is defenseless an' I WIN AGAIN!
...
Awww, gloomy Shadowglooms! I'm sorry! Y-you shoulda used SMALLER ponies before you tied up all your resources with Dark Rainbow!
Y-you wanna play again...?
...No, I think I'm done for now... Too depressing.
Aw. Well, I been playin' this for y-YEARS so, y-you'll get good, an' THEN I can teach you Galaxy Ponies...
I just like the Shadow Ponies....
Hey!
Hi, Mom.

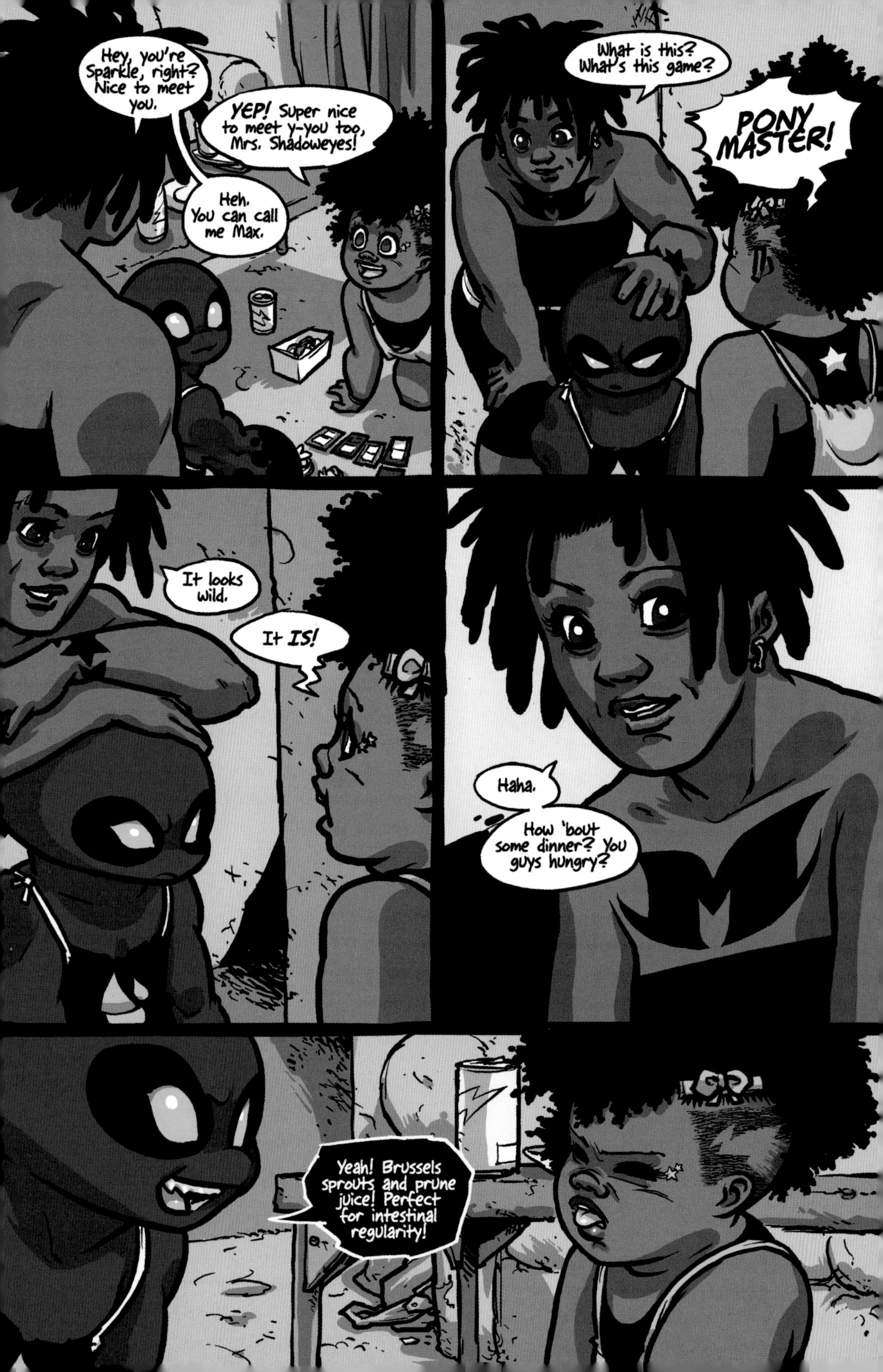
Hey, you're Sparkle, right? Nice to meet you.
YEP! Super nice to meet y-you too, Mrs. Shadoweyes!
Heh. You can call me Max.
What is this? What's this game?
PONY MASTER!
It looks wild.
It IS!
Haha.
How 'bout some dinner? You guys hungry?
Yeah! Brussels sprouts and prune juice! Perfect for intestinal regularity!

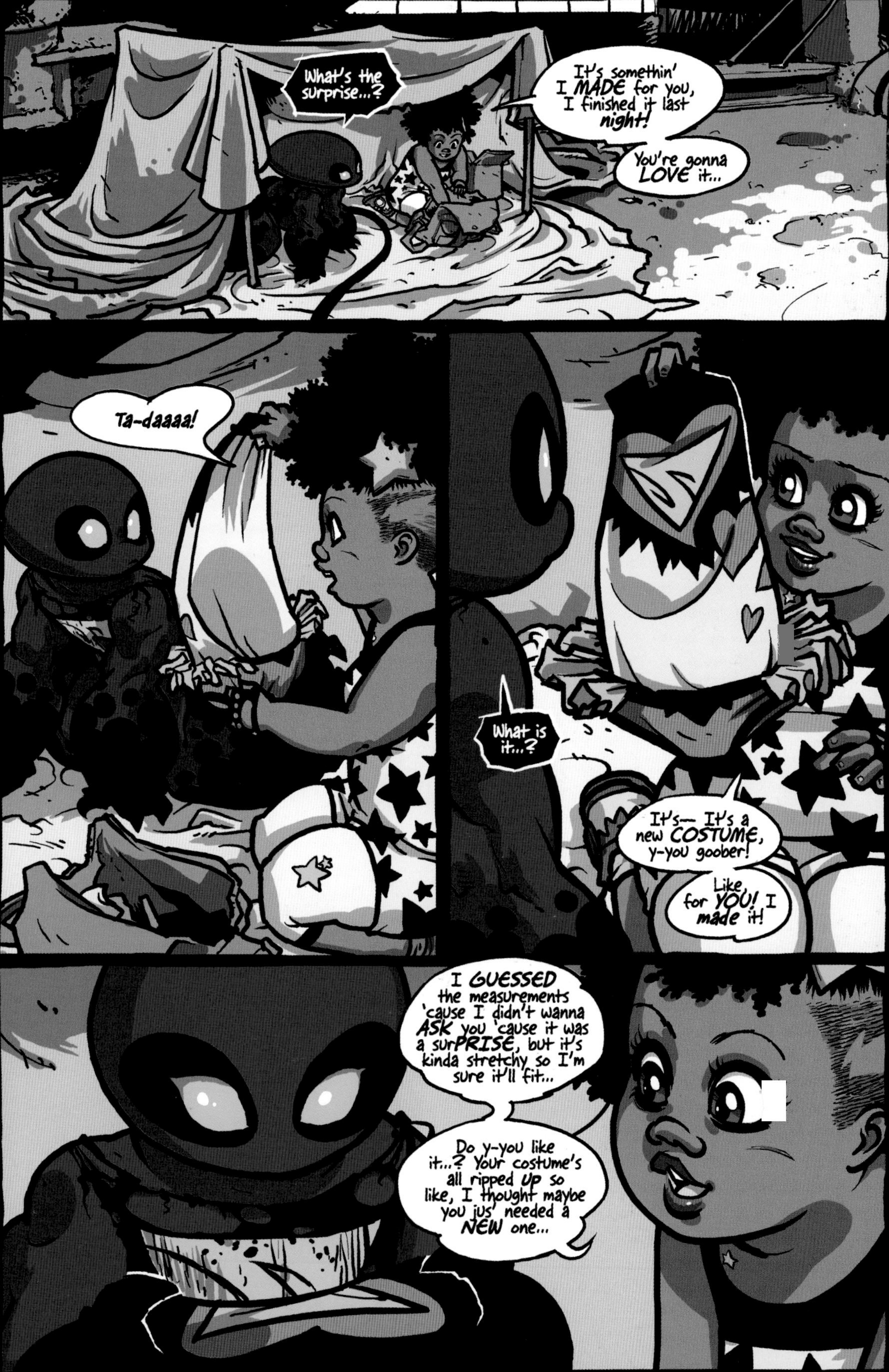
What's the surprise...?
It's somethin' I MADE for you, I finished it last night!
You're gonna LOVE it...
Ta-daaaa!
What is it...?
It's— It's a new COSTUME, y-you goober!
Like, for YOU! I made it!
I GUESSED the measurements 'cause I didn't wanna ASK you 'cause it was a surPRISE, but it's kinda stretchy so I'm sure it'll fit...
Do y-you like it...? Your costume's all ripped UP so like, I thought maybe you jus' needed a NEW one...

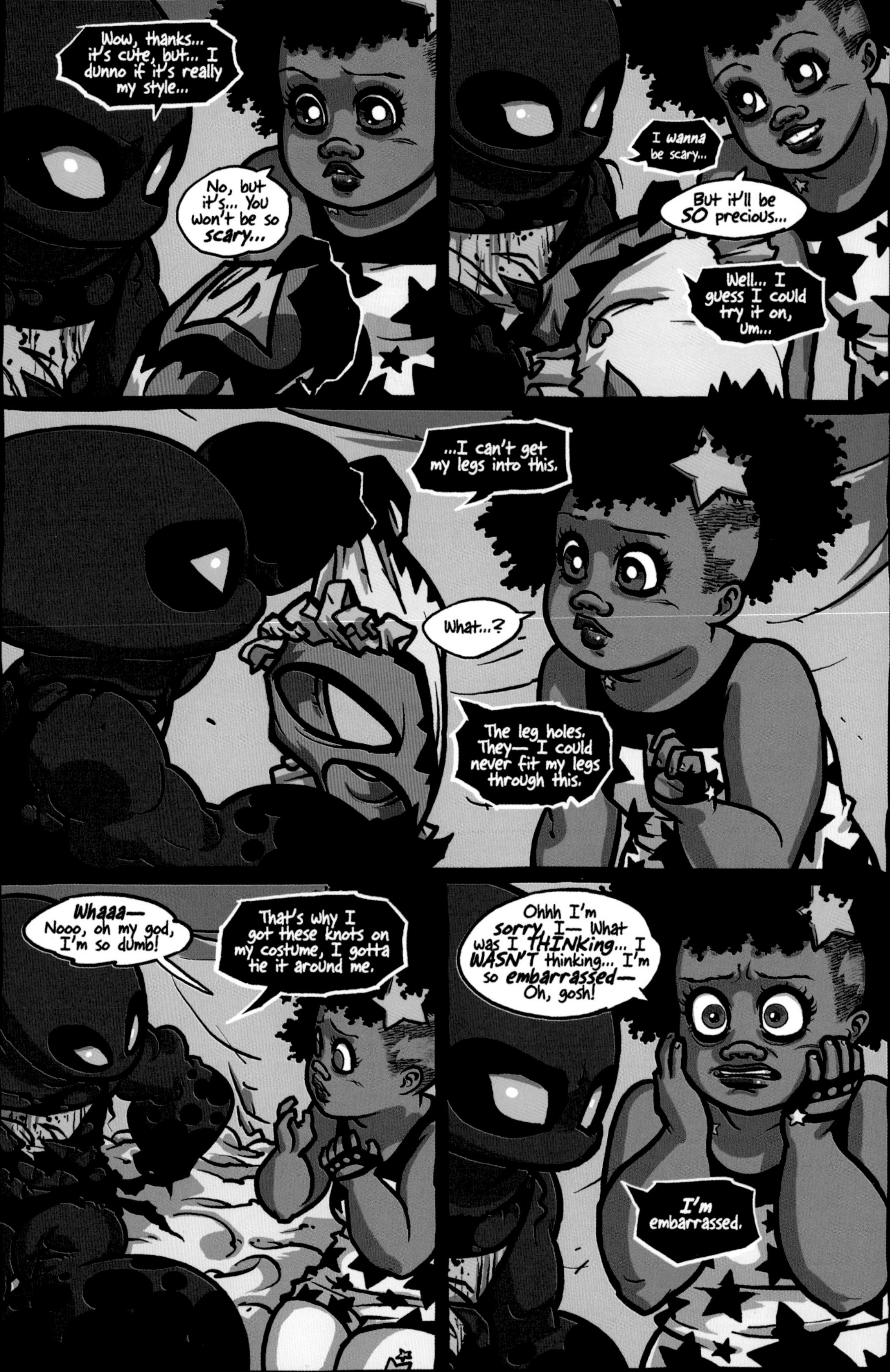

Wow, thanks... it's cute, but... I dunno if it's really my style...
No, but it's... You won't be so scary...
I wanna be scary...
But it'll be SO precious...
Well... I guess I could try it on, um...
...I can't get my legs into this.
What...?
The leg holes. They— I could never fit my legs through this.
Whaaa— Nooo, oh my god, I'm so dumb!
That's why I got these knots on my costume, I gotta tie it around me.
Ohhh I'm sorry, I— What was I THINKING... I WASN'T thinking... I'm so embarrassed— Oh, gosh!
I'm embarrassed.

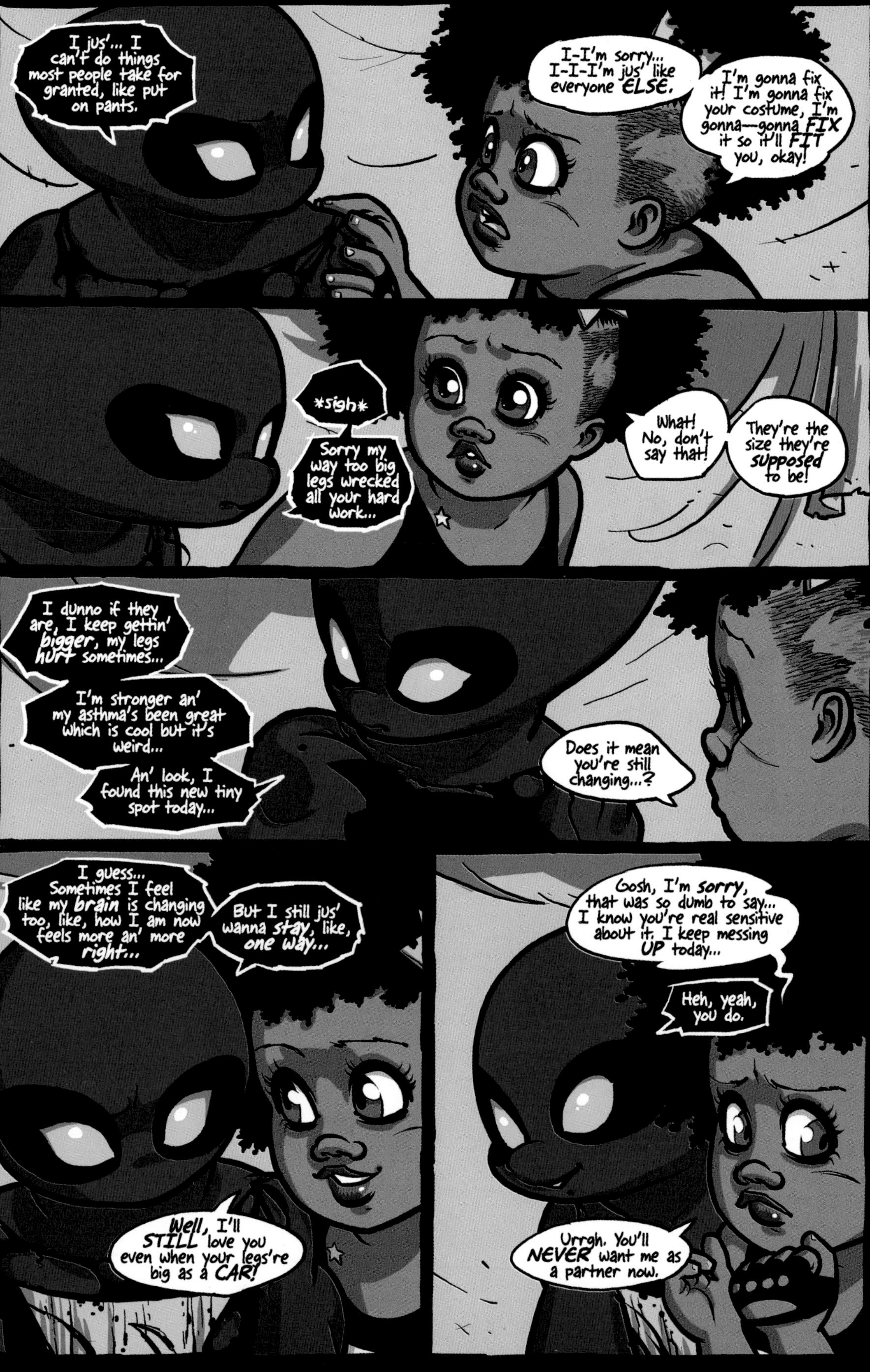
I jus'... I can't do things most people take for granted, like put on pants.
I-I'm sorry... I-I-I'm jus' like everyone ELSE.
I'm gonna fix it! I'm gonna fix your costume, I'm gonna—gonna FIX it so it'll FIT you, okay!
sigh
Sorry my way too big legs wrecked all your hard work...
What! No, don't say that!
They're the size they're supposed to be!
I dunno if they are, I keep gettin' bigger, my legs hurt sometimes...
I'm stronger an' my asthma's been great which is cool but it's weird...
An' look, I found this new tiny spot today...
Does it mean you're still changing...?
I guess... Sometimes I feel like my brain is changing too, like, how I am now feels more an' more right...
But I still jus' wanna stay, like, one way...
Well, I'll STILL love you even when your legs're big as a CAR!
Gosh, I'm sorry, that was so dumb to say... I know you're real sensitive about it. I keep messing UP today...
Heh, yeah, you do.
Urrgh. You'll NEVER want me as a partner now.

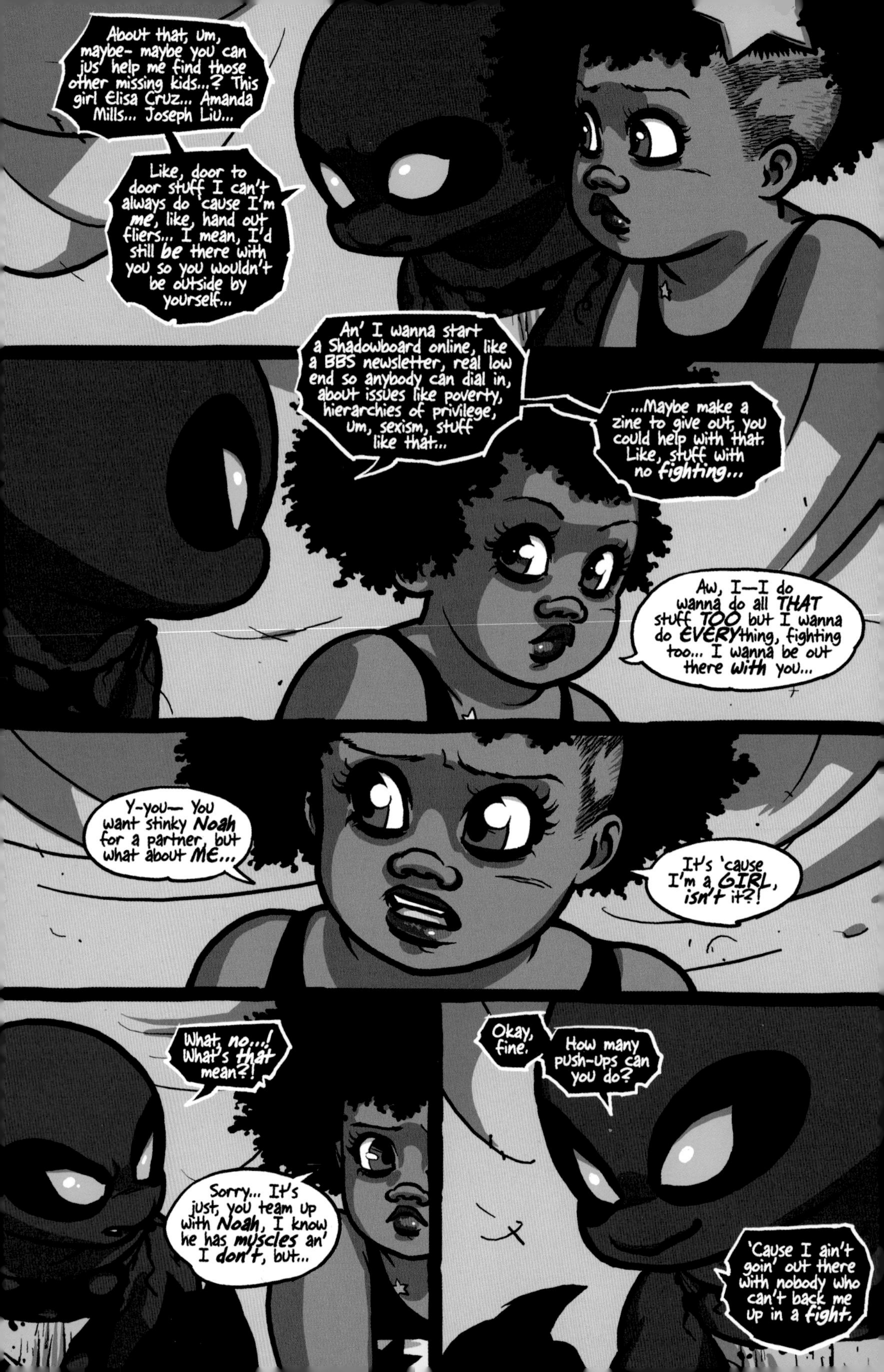
About that, um, maybe- maybe you can jus' help me find those other missing kids...? This girl Elisa Cruz... Amanda Mills... Joseph Liu...
Like, door to door stuff I can't always do 'cause I'm me, like, hand out fliers... I mean, I'd still be there with you so you wouldn't be outside by yourself...
An' I wanna start a Shadowboard online, like a BBS newsletter, real low end so anybody can dial in, about issues like poverty, hierarchies of privilege, um, sexism, stuff like that...
...Maybe make a zine to give out, you could help with that. Like, stuff with no fighting...
Aw, I—I do wanna do all THAT stuff TOO but I wanna do EVERYthing, fighting too... I wanna be out there with you...
Y-you— You want stinky Noah for a partner, but what about ME...
It's 'cause I'm a GIRL, isn't it?!
What, no...! What's that mean?!
Sorry... It's just, you team up with Noah, I know he has muscles an' I don't, but...
Okay, fine.
How many push-ups can you do?
'Cause I ain't goin' out there with nobody who can't back me up in a fight.

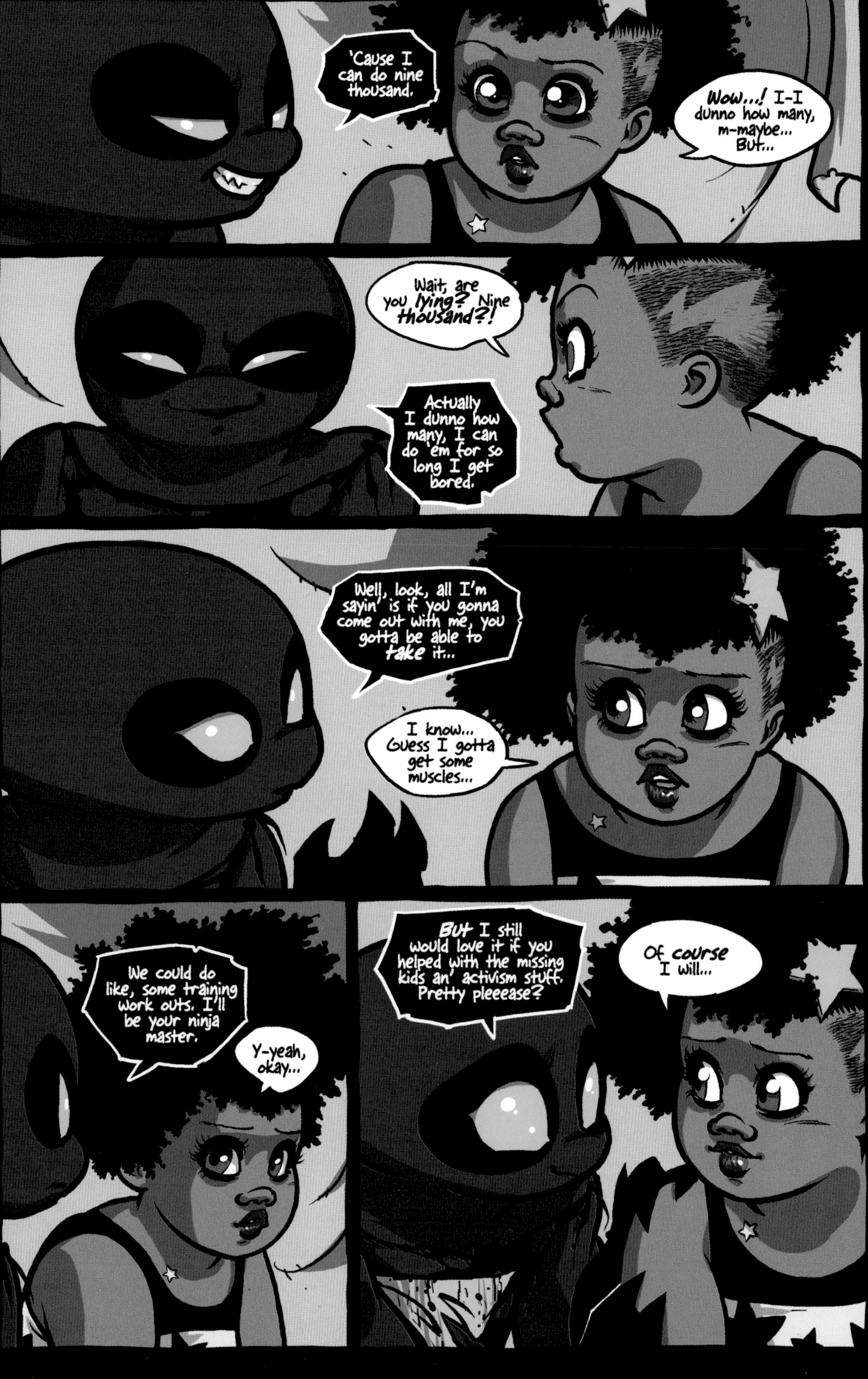
'Cause I can do nine thousand.
Wow...! I-I dunno how many, m-maybe... But...
Wait, are you lying? Nine thousand?!
Actually I dunno how many, I can do 'em for so long I get bored.
Well, look, all I'm sayin' is if you gonna come out with me, you gotta be able to take it...
I know... Guess I gotta get some muscles...
We could do like, some training work outs. I'll be your ninja master.
Y-yeah, okay...
But I still would love it if you helped with the missing kids an' activism stuff. Pretty pleeease?
Of course I will...

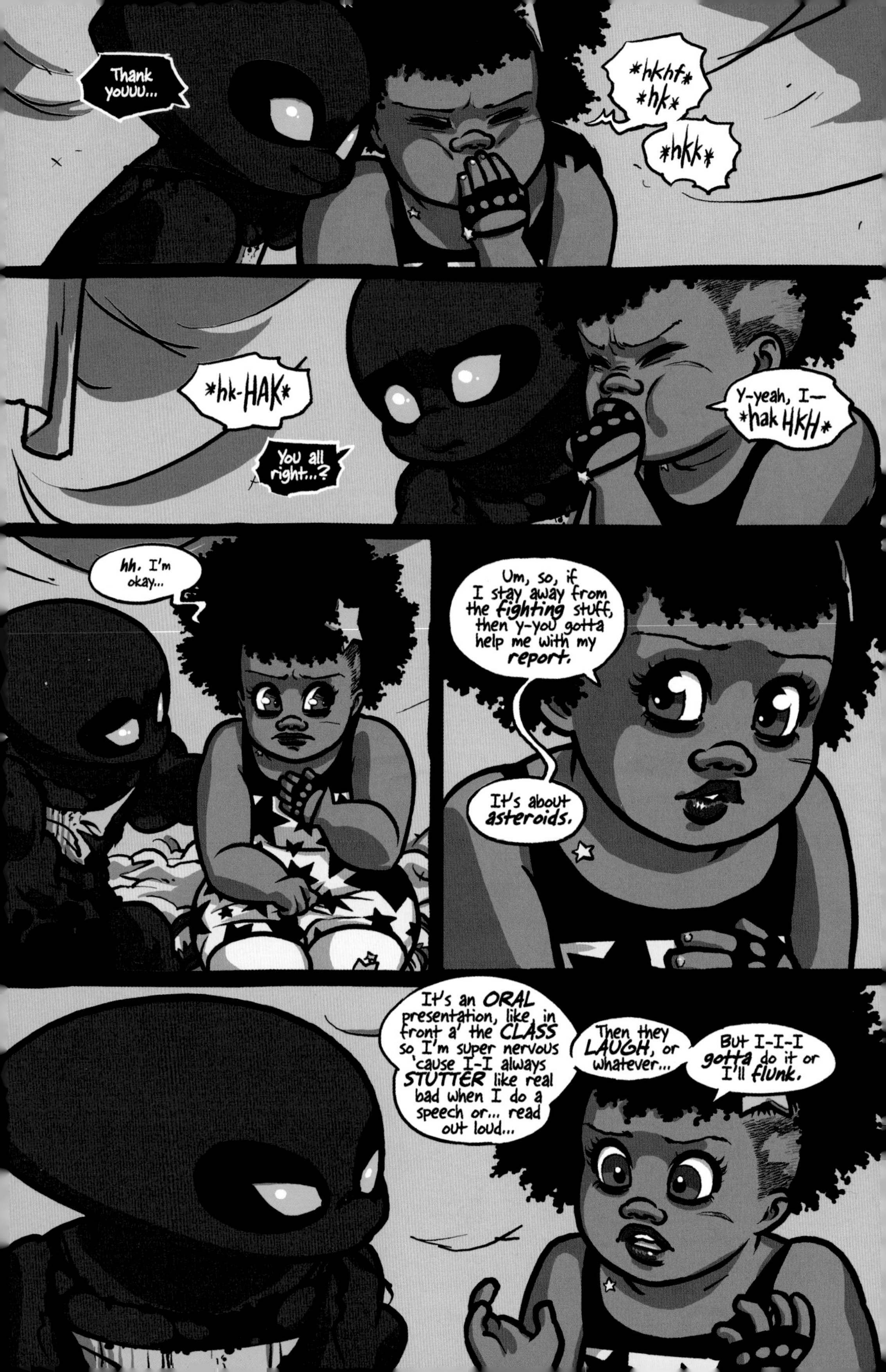

Thank youuu...
hkhf *hk*
hkk
hk-HAK
You all right...?
Y-yeah, I— *hak HKH*
hh. I'm okay...
Um, so, if I stay away from the fighting stuff, then y-you gotta help me with my report.
It's about asteroids.
It's an ORAL presentation, like, in front a' the CLASS so I'm super nervous 'cause I-I always STUTTER like real bad when I do a speech or... read out loud...
Then they LAUGH, or whatever...
But I-I-I gotta do it or I'll flunk.

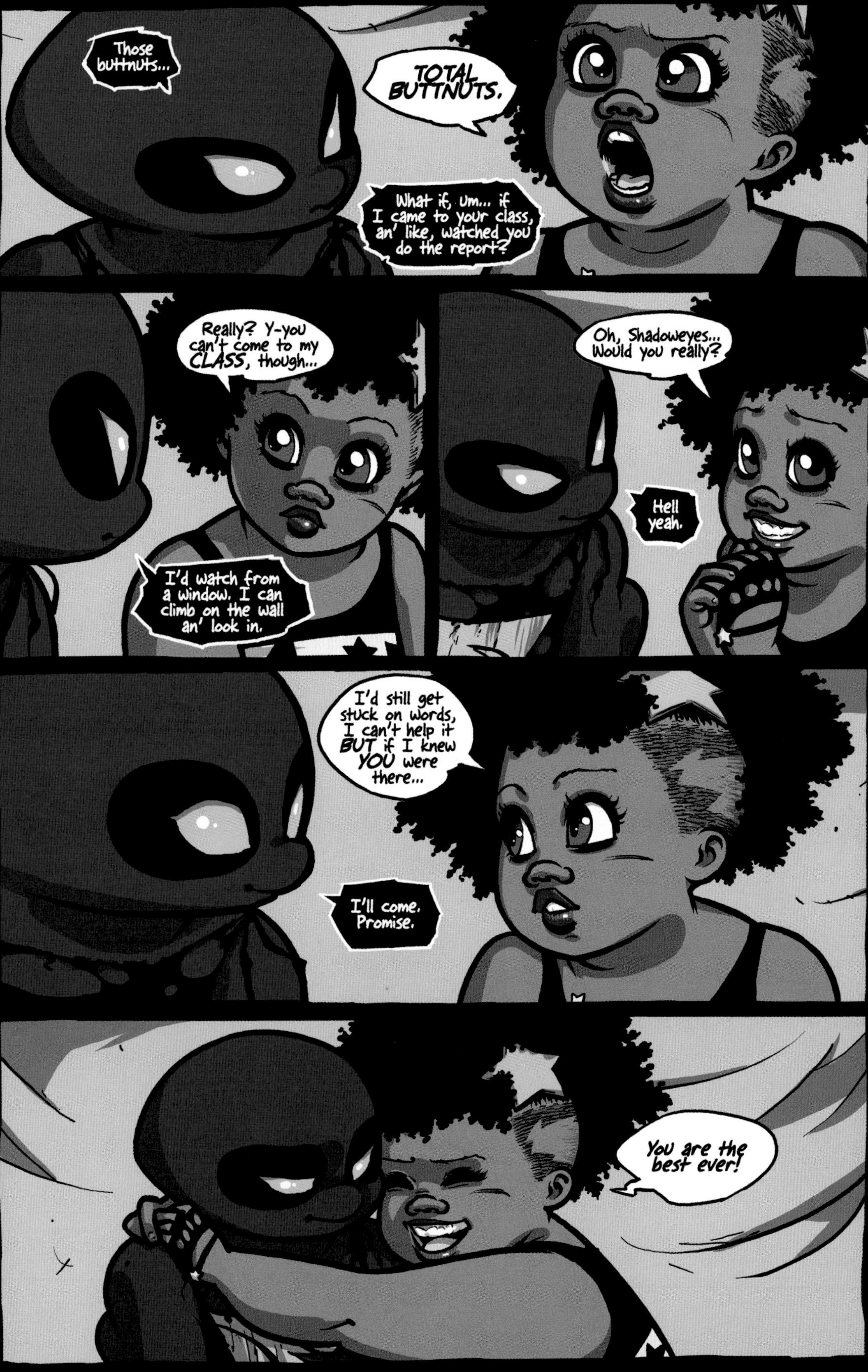
Those buttnuts...
TOTAL BUTTNUTS.
What if, um... if I came to your class, an' like, watched you do the report?
Really? Y-you can't come to my CLASS, though...
I'd watch from a window. I can climb on the wall an' look in.
Oh, Shadoweyes... Would you really?
Hell yeah.
I'd still get stuck on words, I can't help it BUT if I knew YOU were there...
I'll come. Promise.
You are the best ever!

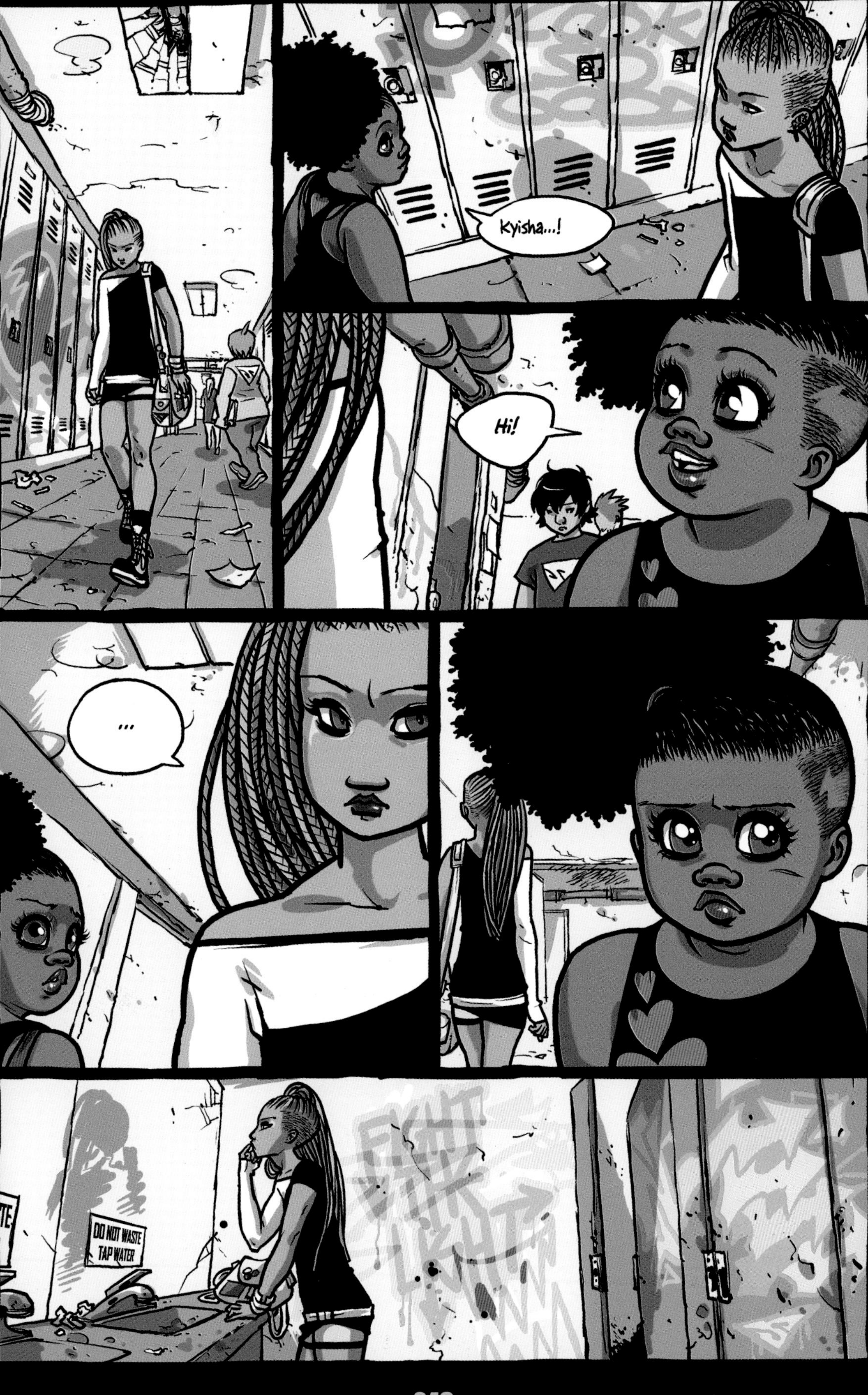
Kyisha...!
Hi!
...
DO NOT WASTE TAP WATER

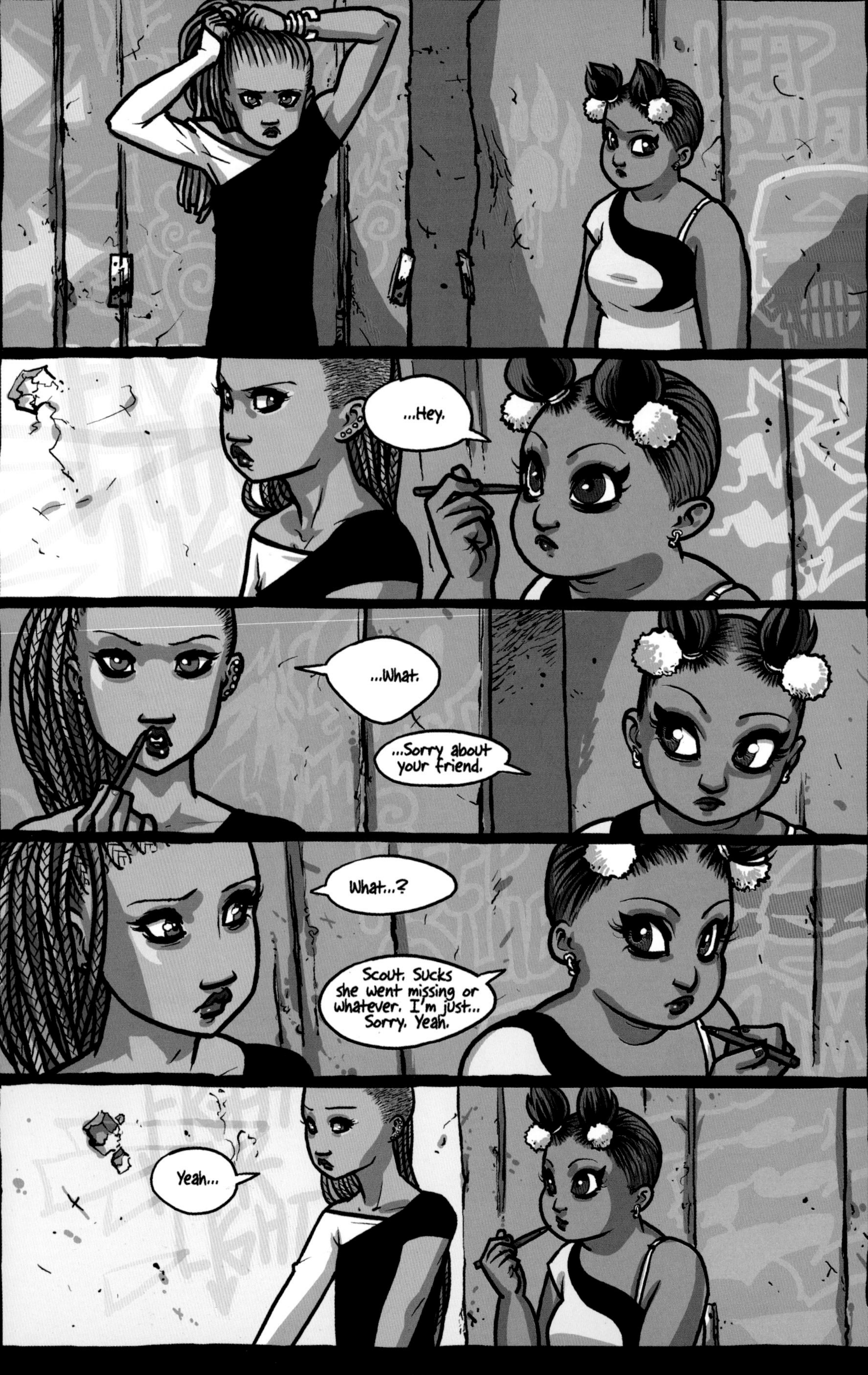
...Hey.
...What.
...Sorry about your friend.
What...?
Scout. Sucks she went missing or whatever. I'm just... Sorry. Yeah.
Yeah...

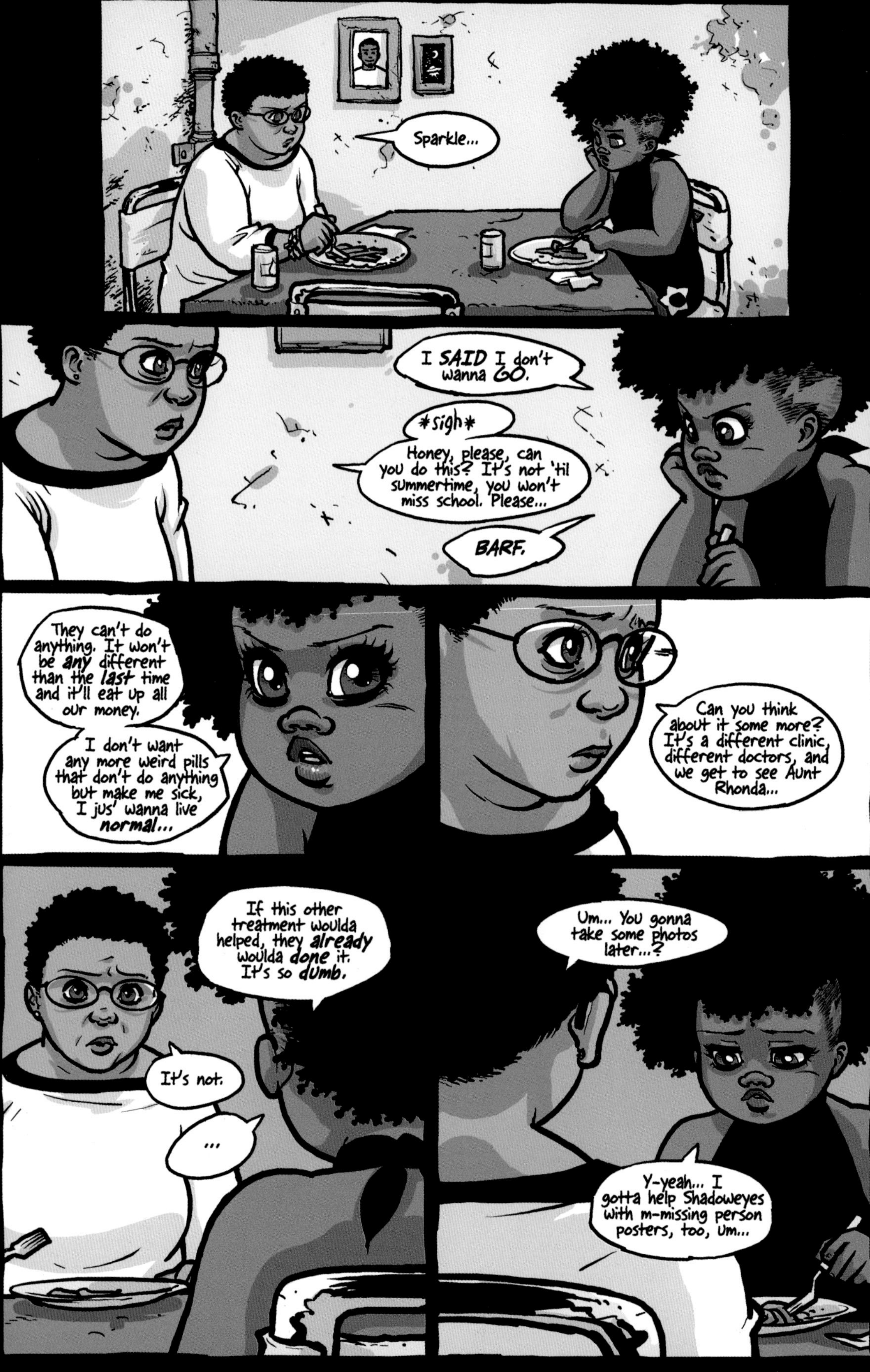
Sparkle...
I SAID I don't wanna GO.
sigh
Honey, please, can you do this? It's not 'til summertime, you won't miss school. Please...
BARF.
They can't do anything. It won't be any different than the last time and it'll eat up all our money.
I don't want any more weird pills that don't do anything but make me sick, I jus' wanna live normal...
Can you think about it some more? It's a different clinic, different doctors, and we get to see Aunt Rhonda...
If this other treatment woulda helped, they already woulda done it. It's so dumb.
It's not.
...
Um... You gonna take some photos later...?
Y-yeah... I gotta help Shadoweyes with m-missing person posters, too, um...

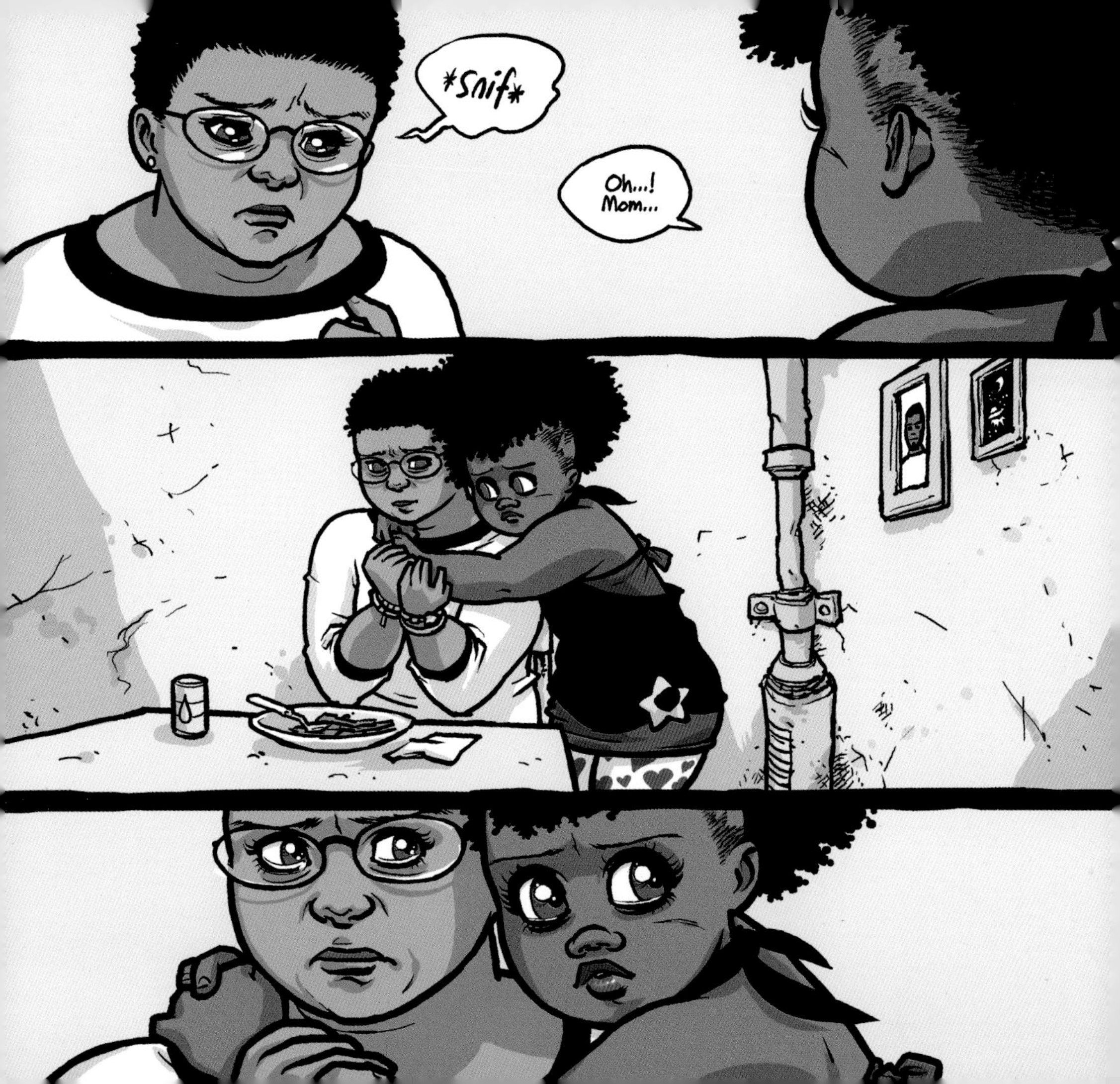
Snif
Oh...! Mom...

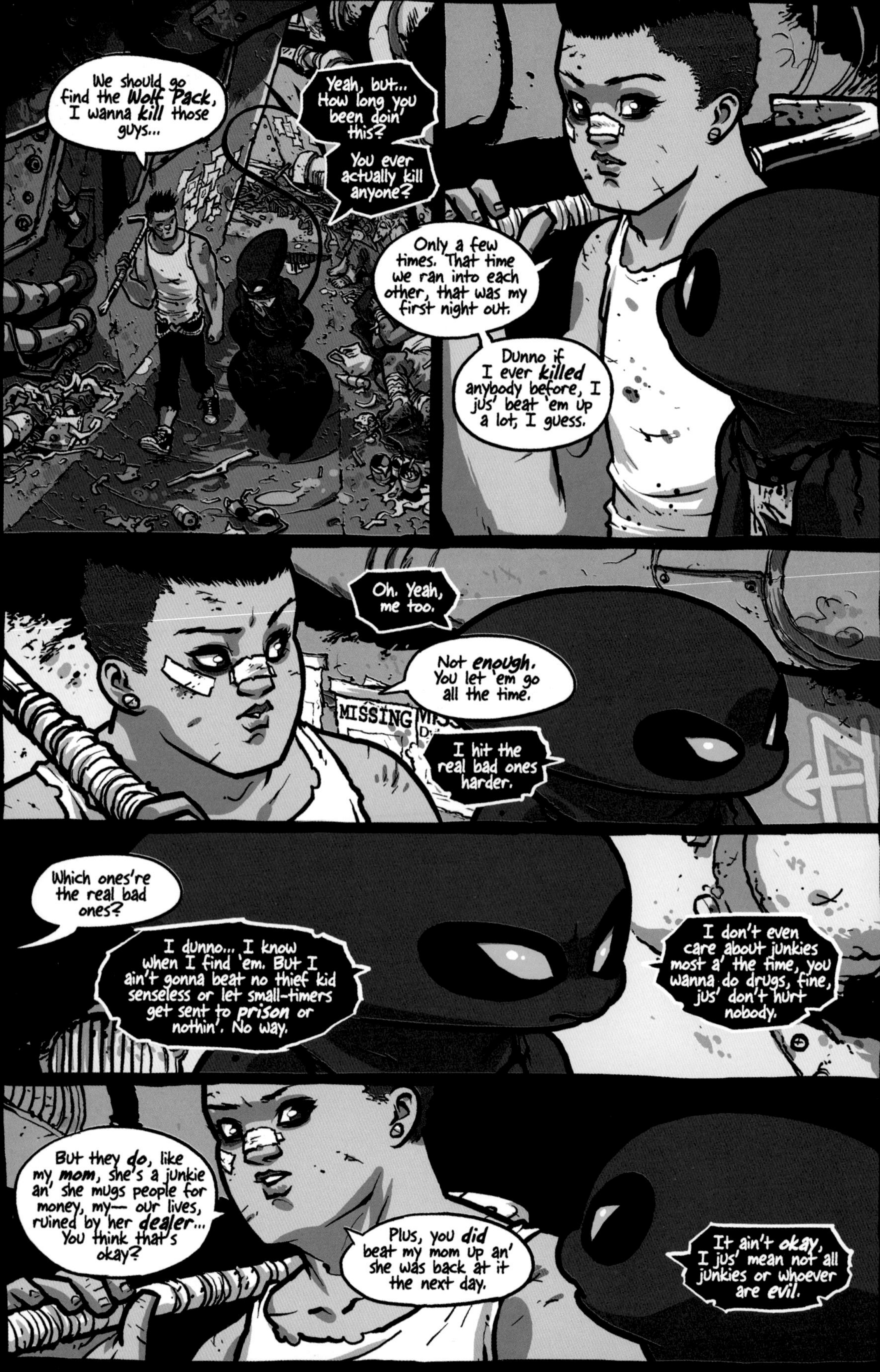
We should go find the Wolf Pack, I wanna kill those guys...
Yeah, but... How long you been doin' this?
You ever actually kill anyone?
Only a few times. That time we ran into each other, that was my first night out.
Dunno if I ever killed anybody before, I jus' beat 'em up a lot, I guess.
Oh. Yeah, me too.
Not enough. You let 'em go all the time.
MISSING
I hit the real bad ones harder.
Which ones're the real bad ones?
I dunno... I know when I find 'em. But I ain't gonna beat no thief kid senseless or let small-timers get sent to prison or nothin'. No way.
I don't even care about junkies most a' the time, you wanna do drugs, fine, jus' don't hurt nobody.
But they do, like my, mom, she's a junkie an' she mugs people for money, my— our lives, ruined by her dealer... You think that's okay?
Plus, you did beat my mom up an' she was back at it the next day.
It ain't okay, I jus' mean not all junkies or whoever are evil.

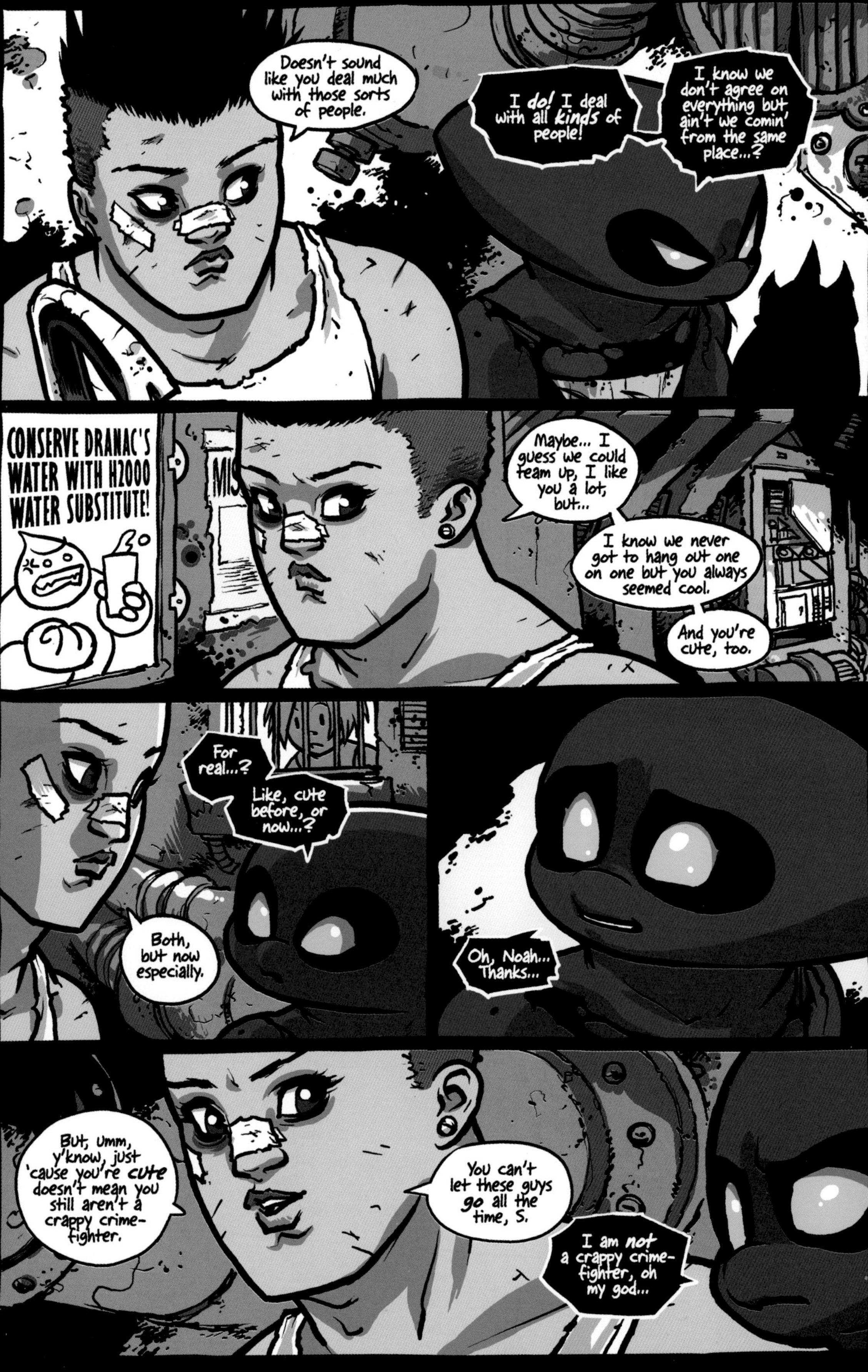
Doesn't sound like you deal much with those sorts of people.
I do! I deal with all kinds of people!
I know we don't agree on everything but ain't we comin' from the same place...?
CONSERVE DRANAC'S WATER WITH H2000 WATER SUBSTITUTE!
Maybe... I guess we could team up, I like you a lot, but...
I know we never got to hang out one on one but you always seemed cool.
And you're cute, too.
For real...?
Like, cute before, or now...?
Both, but now especially.
Oh, Noah... Thanks...
But, umm, y'know, just 'cause you're cute doesn't mean you still aren't a crappy crime-fighter.
You can't let these guys go all the time, S.
I am not a crappy crime-fighter, oh my god...

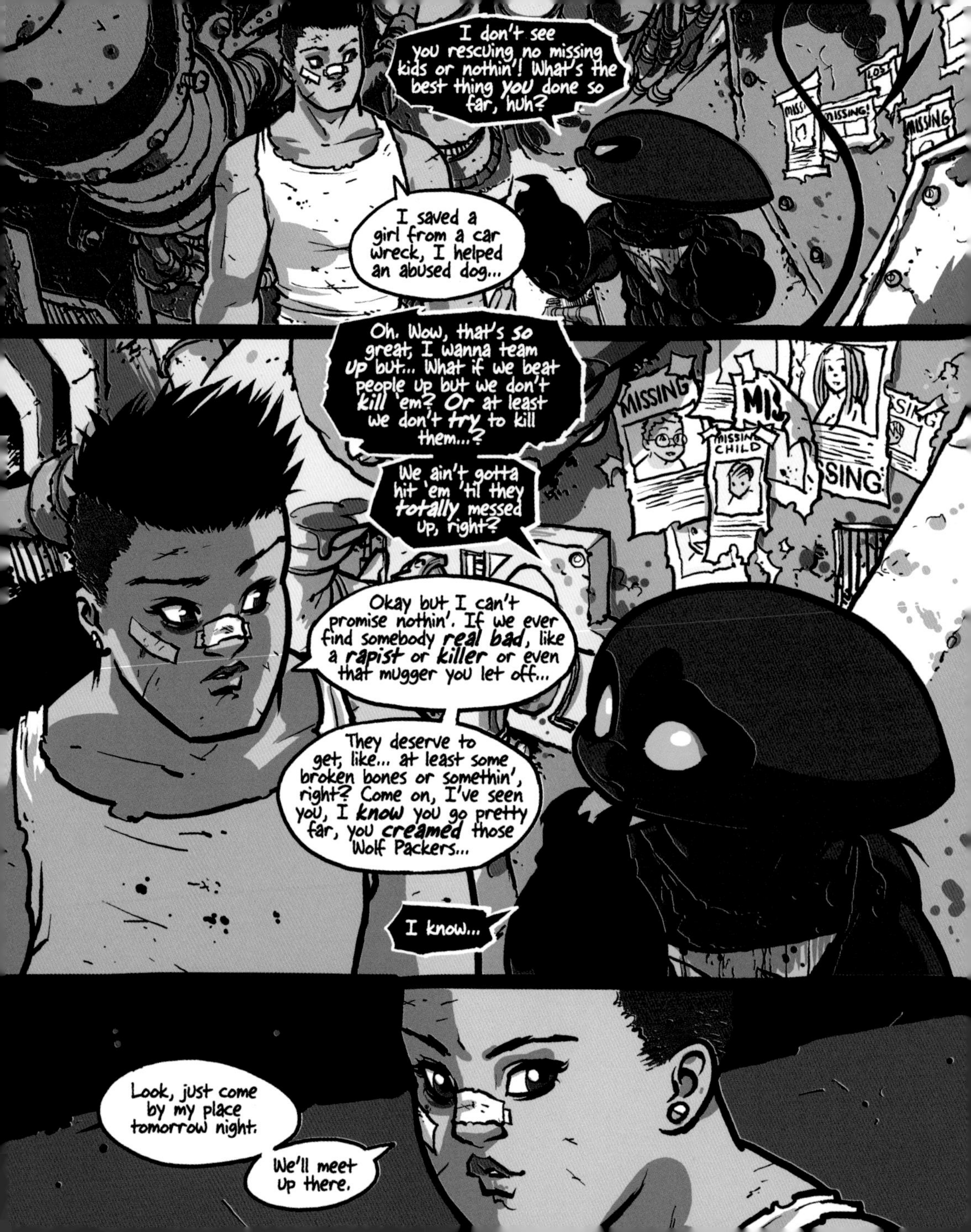

I don't see you rescuing no missing kids or nothin'! What's the best thing *you* done so far, huh?
MISSING
MISSING!
MISSING
LOST
I saved a girl from a car wreck, I helped an abused dog...
Oh. Wow, that's *so* great, I wanna team *up* but... What if we beat people up but we don't *kill* 'em? *Or* at least we don't *try* to kill them...?
MISSING
MISSING CHILD
SING
We ain't gotta hit 'em 'til they *totally* messed up, right?
Okay but I can't promise nothin'. If we ever find somebody *real bad*, like a *rapist* or *killer* or even that mugger you let off...
They deserve to get, like... at least some broken bones or somethin', right? Come on, I've seen you, I *know* you go pretty far, you *creamed* those Wolf Packers...
I know...
Look, just come by my place tomorrow night.
We'll meet up there.

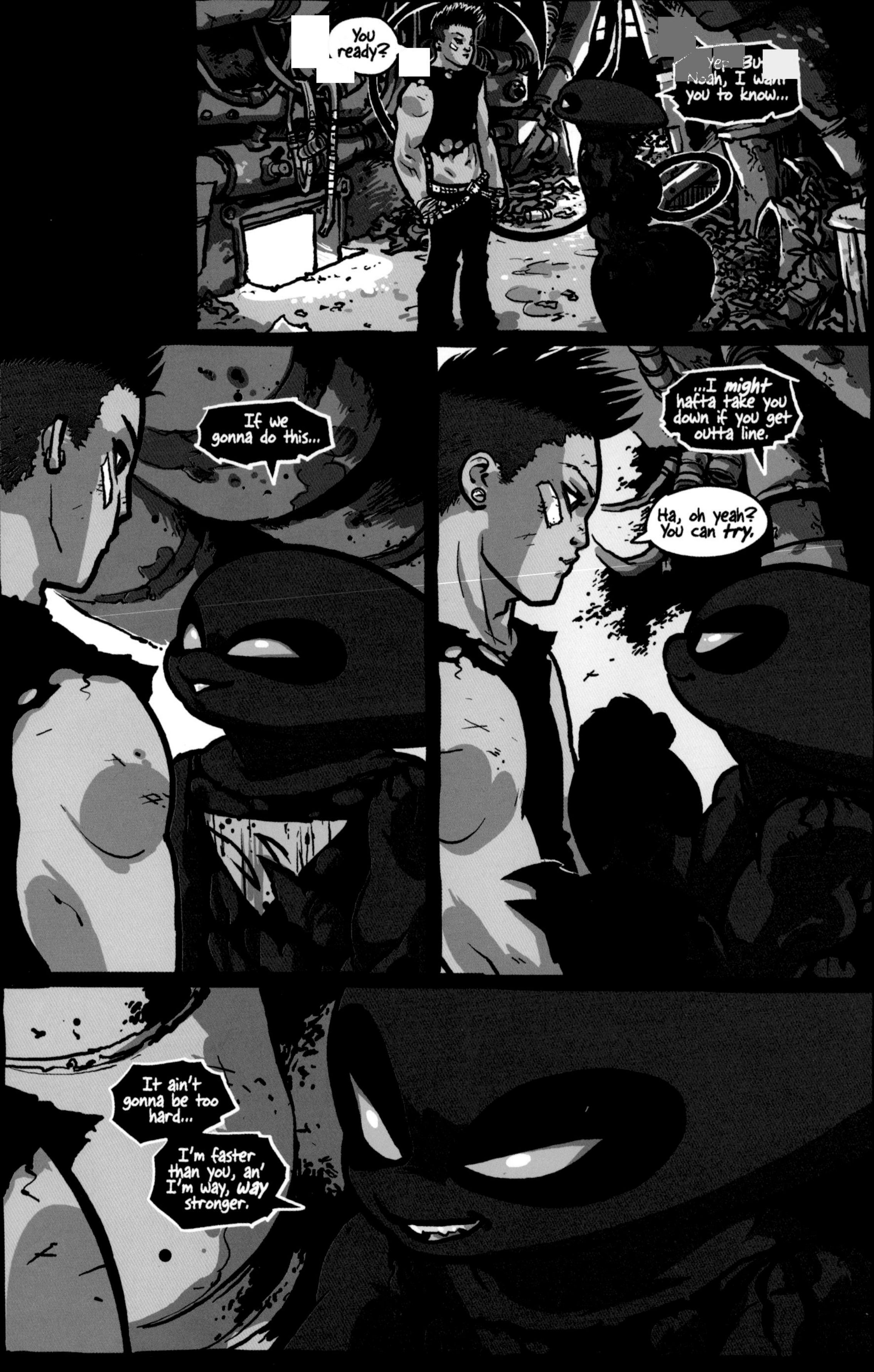
You ready?
Yep. Bu
Noah, I want you to know...
If we gonna do this...
...I might hafta take you down if you get outta line.
Ha, oh yeah? You can try.
It ain't gonna be too hard...
I'm faster than you, an' I'm way, way stronger.

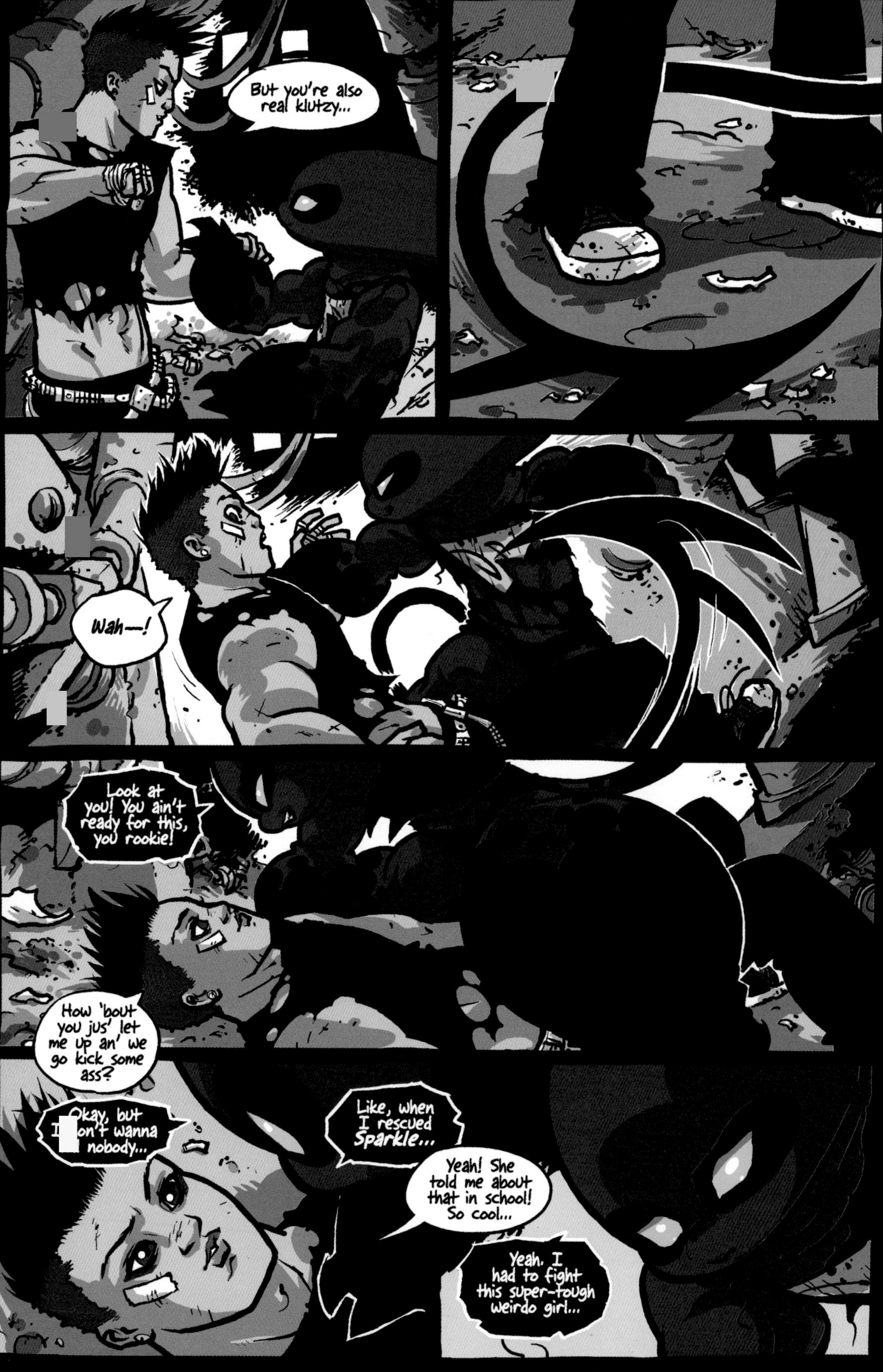

But you're also real klutzy...
Wah—!
Look at you! You ain't ready for this, you rookie!
How 'bout you jus' let me up an' we go kick some ass?
Okay, but I on't wanna nobody...
Like, when I rescued Sparkle...
Yeah! She told me about that in school! So cool...
Yeah. I had to fight this super-tough weirdo girl...

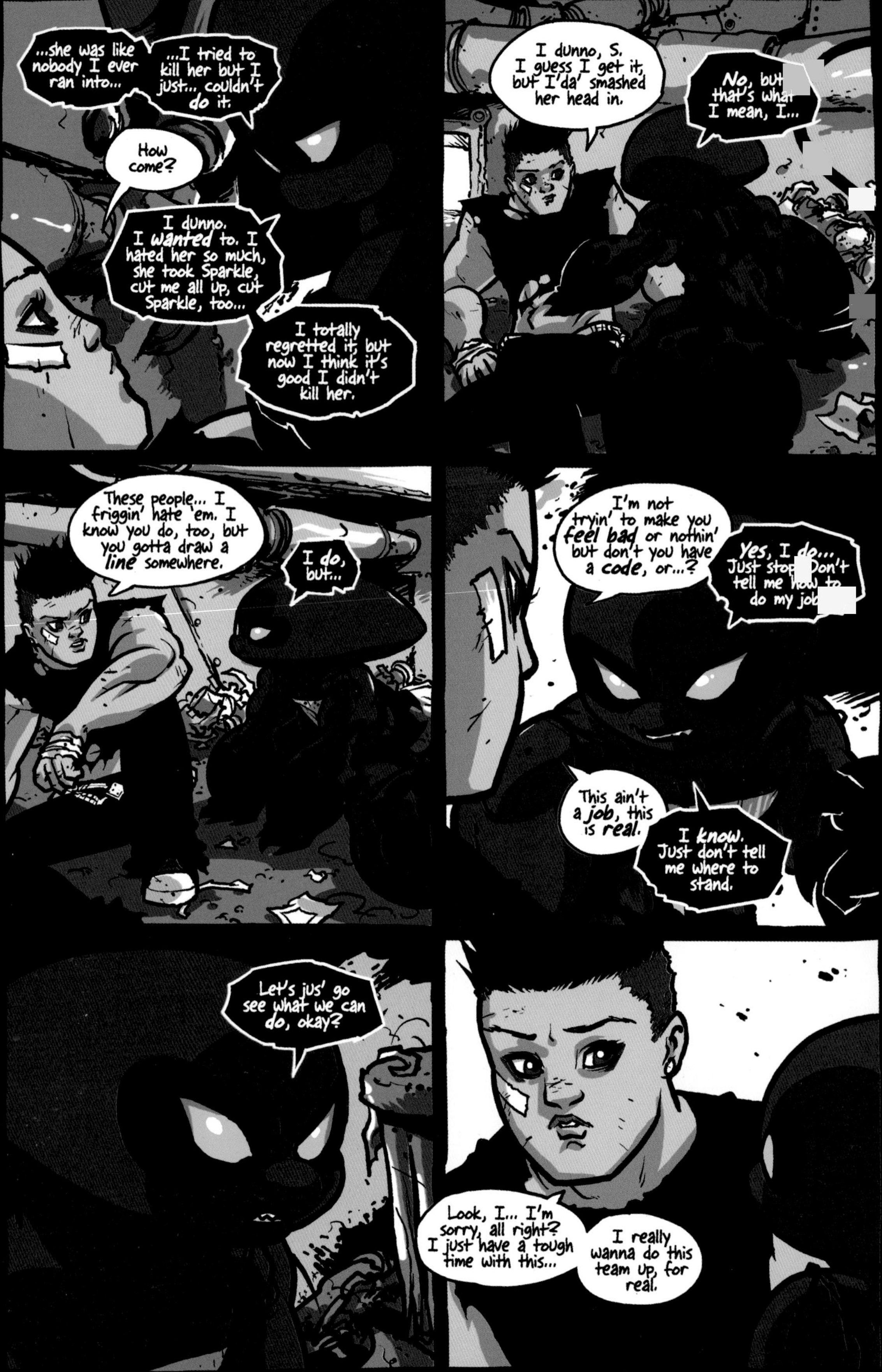

...she was like nobody I ever ran into...
...I tried to kill her but I just... couldn't do it.
How come?
I dunno. I wanted to. I hated her so much, she took Sparkle, cut me all up, cut Sparkle, too...
I totally regretted it, but now I think it's good I didn't kill her.
I dunno, S. I guess I get it, but I'da' smashed her head in.
No, but that's what I mean, I...
These people... I friggin' hate 'em. I know you do, too, but you gotta draw a line somewhere.
I do, but...
I'm not tryin' to make you feel bad or nothin' but don't you have a code, or...?
Yes, I do... Just stop. Don't tell me how to do my job.
This ain't a job, this is real.
I know. Just don't tell me where to stand.
Let's jus' go see what we can do, okay?
Look, I... I'm sorry, all right? I just have a tough time with this...
I really wanna do this team up, for real.

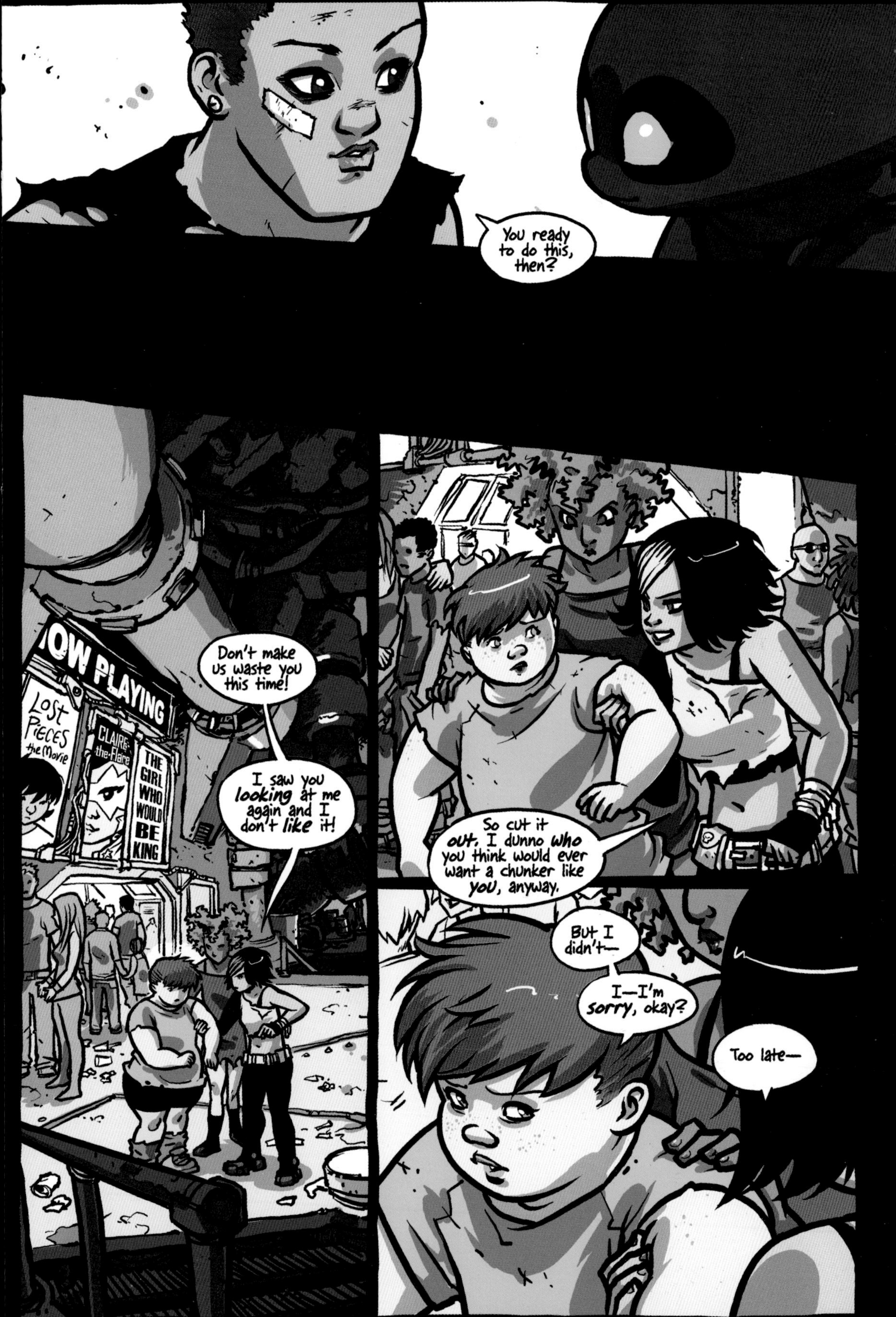
You ready to do this, then?
OW PLAYING
LOST PIECES the Movie
CLAIRE the Flare
THE GIRL WHO WOULD BE KING
Don't make us waste you this time!
I saw you looking at me again and I don't like it!
So cut it out. I dunno who you think would ever want a chunker like you, anyway.
But I didn't—
I—I'm sorry, okay?
Too late—

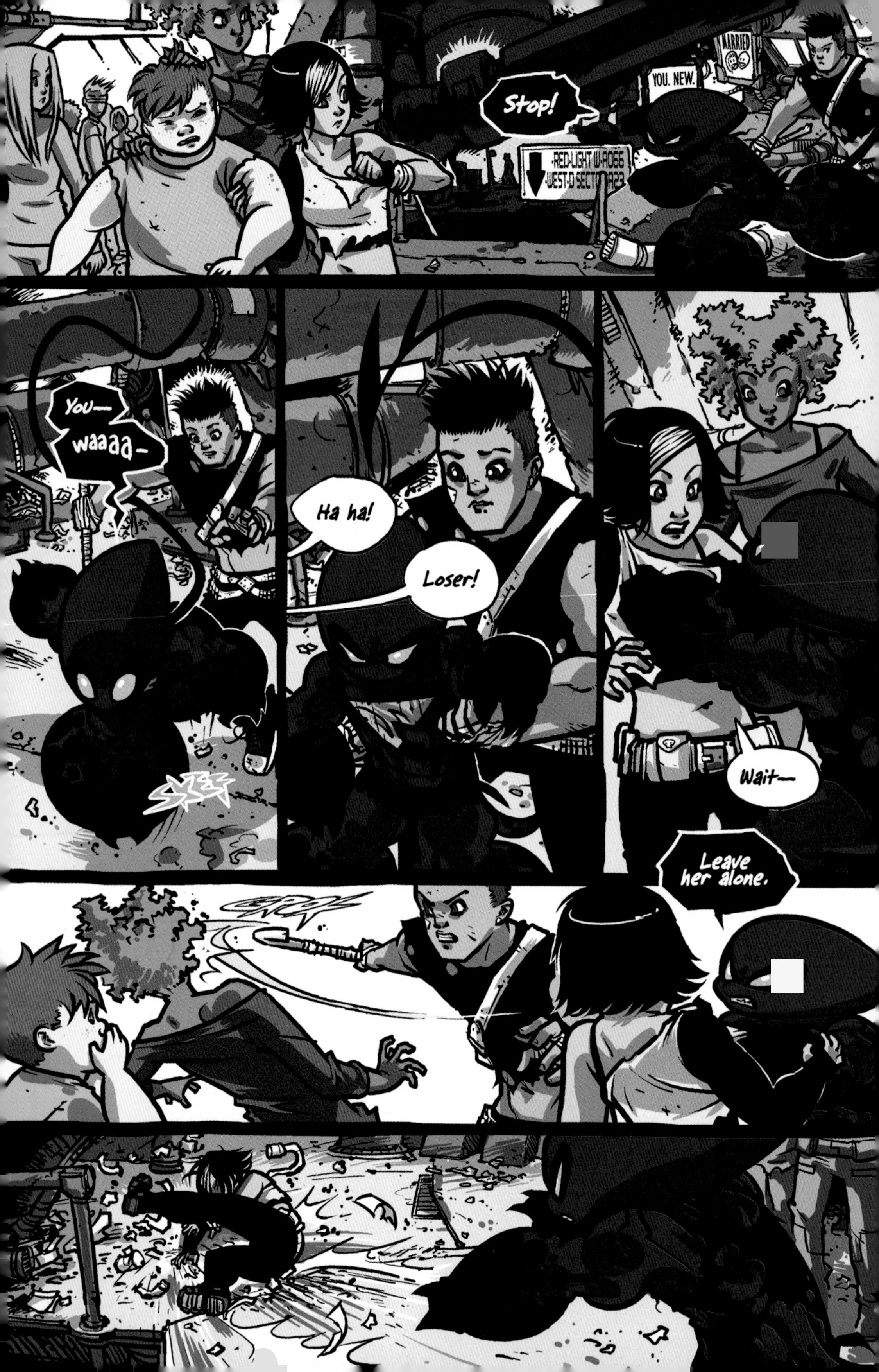
MARRIED
YOU. NEW.
Stop!
-RED-LIGHT W-RO66
-WEST-D SECT
You—
waaaa-
Ha ha!
Loser!
Wait—
Leave her alone.

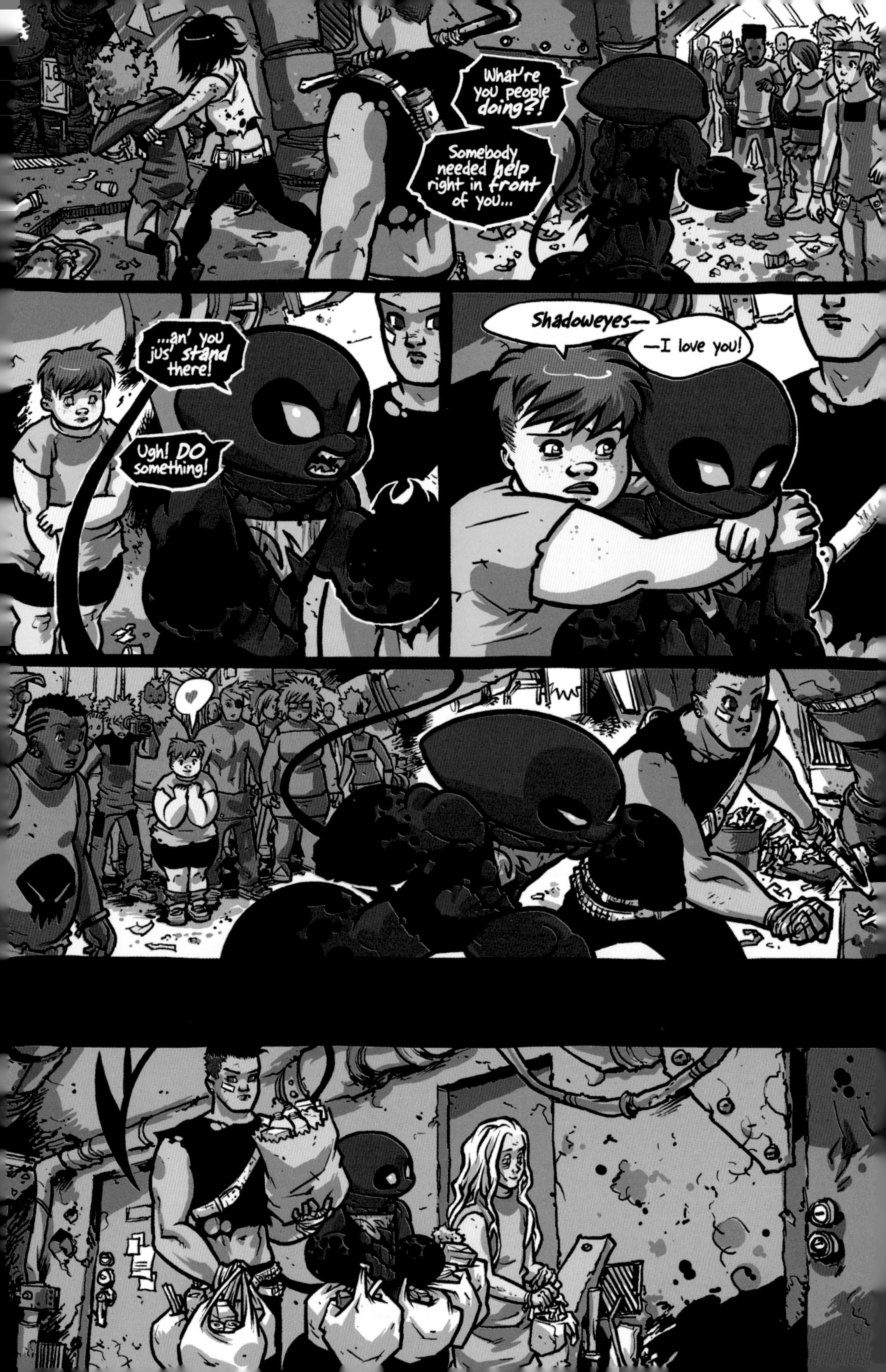
What're you people doing?!
Somebody needed help right in front of you...
...an' you jus' stand there!
Ugh! DO something!
Shadoweyes—
—I love you!

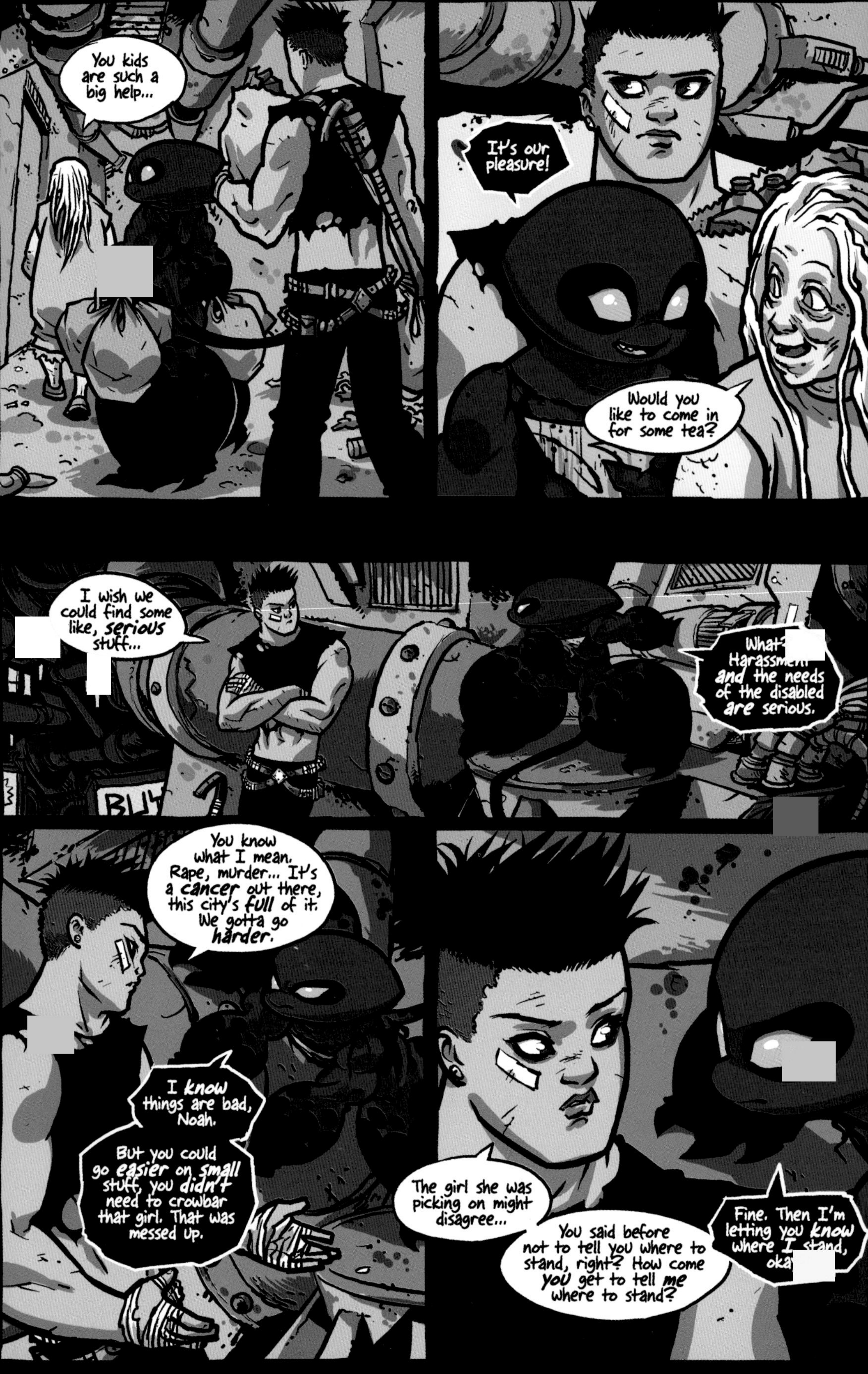
You kids are such a big help...
It's our pleasure!
Would you like to come in for some tea?
I wish we could find some like, *serious* stuff...
What? Harassment *and* the needs of the disabled *are* serious.
You know what I mean. Rape, murder... It's a *cancer* out there, this city's *full* of it. We gotta go *harder*.
I *know* things are bad, Noah.
But you could go *easier* on *small* stuff, you *didn't* need to crowbar that girl. That was messed up.
The girl she was picking on might disagree...
You said before not to tell you where to stand, right? How come *you* get to tell *me* where to stand?
Fine. Then I'm letting you *know* where *I* stand, oka

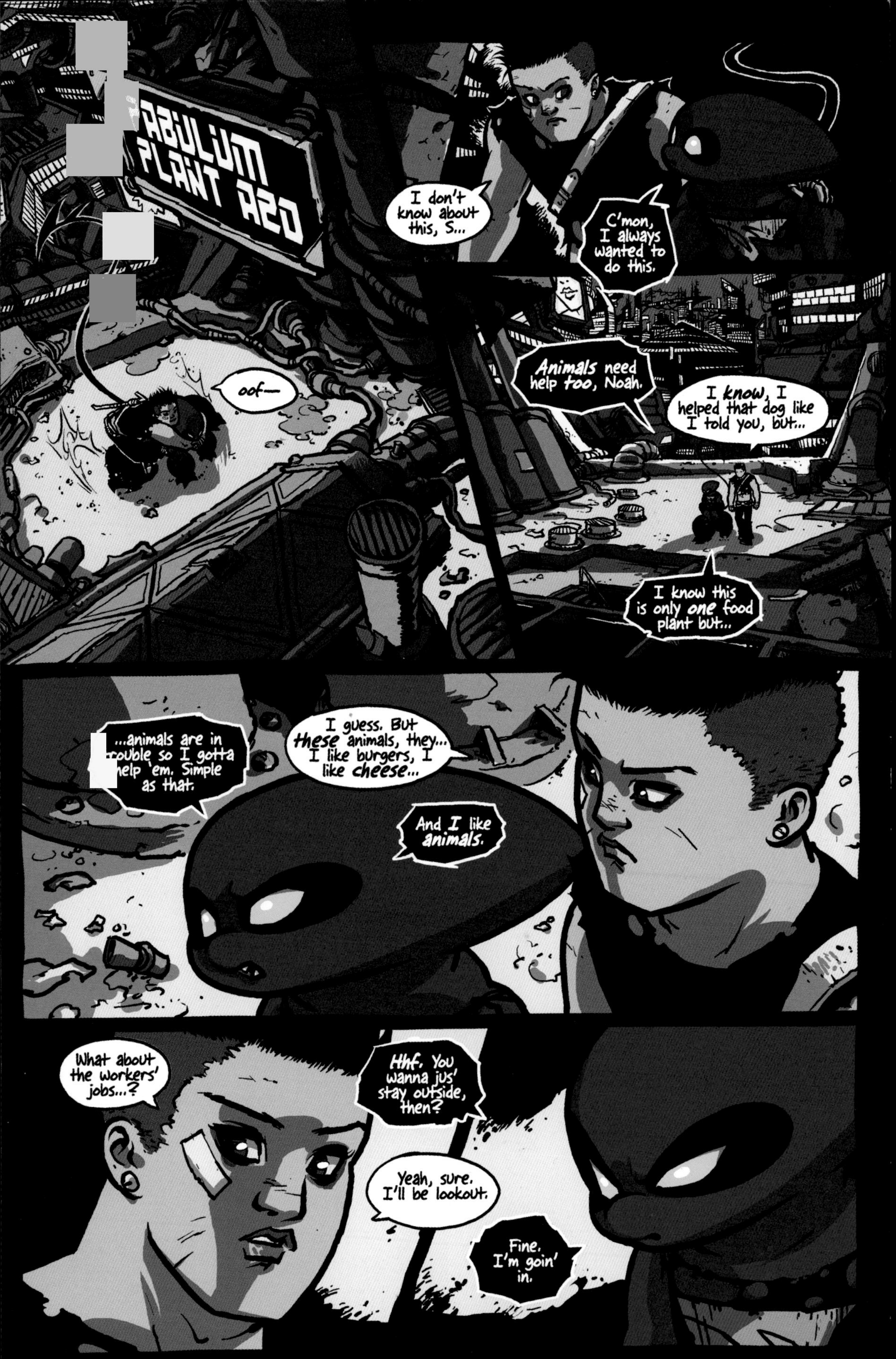
ABULUM
PLANT A20
I don't know about this, S...
C'mon, I always wanted to do this.
oof—
Animals need help *too*, Noah.
I *know*, I helped that dog like I told you, but...
I know this is only *one* food plant but...
...animals are in rouble so I gotta elp 'em. Simple as that.
I guess. But *these* animals, they... I like burgers, I like *cheese*...
And *I* like *animals.*
What about the workers' jobs...?
Hhf. You wanna jus' stay outside, then?
Yeah, sure. I'll be lookout.
Fine. I'm goin' in.

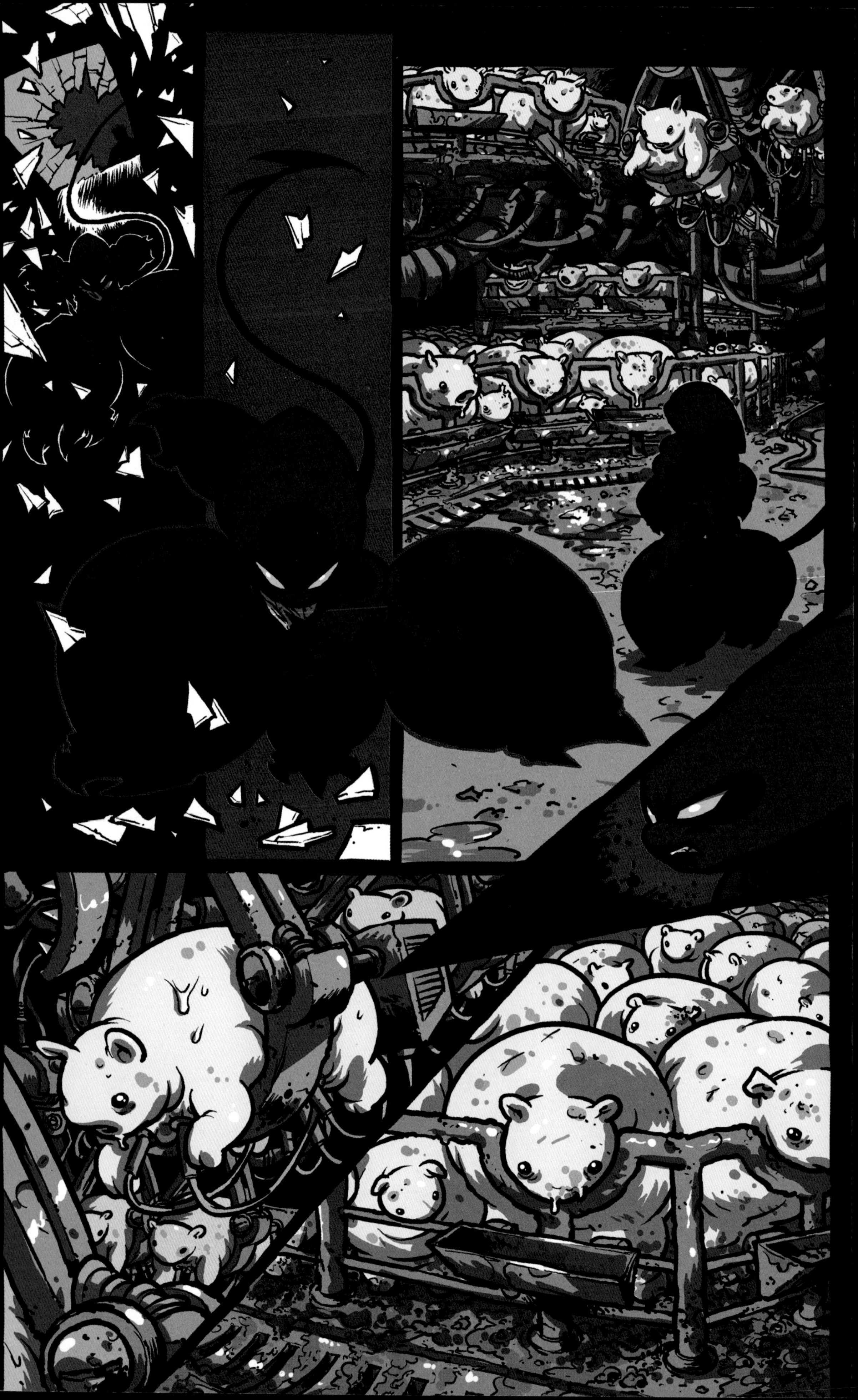

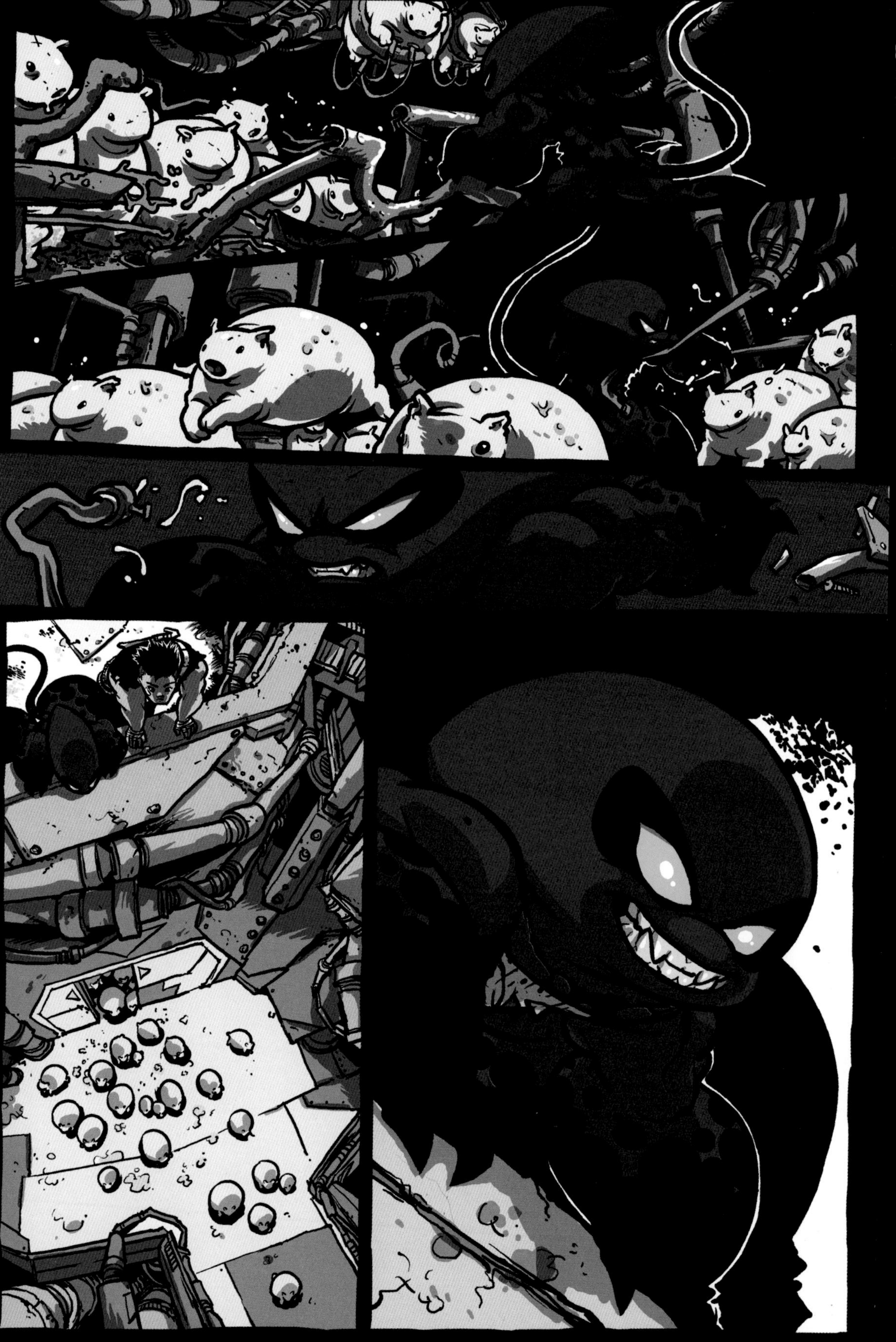

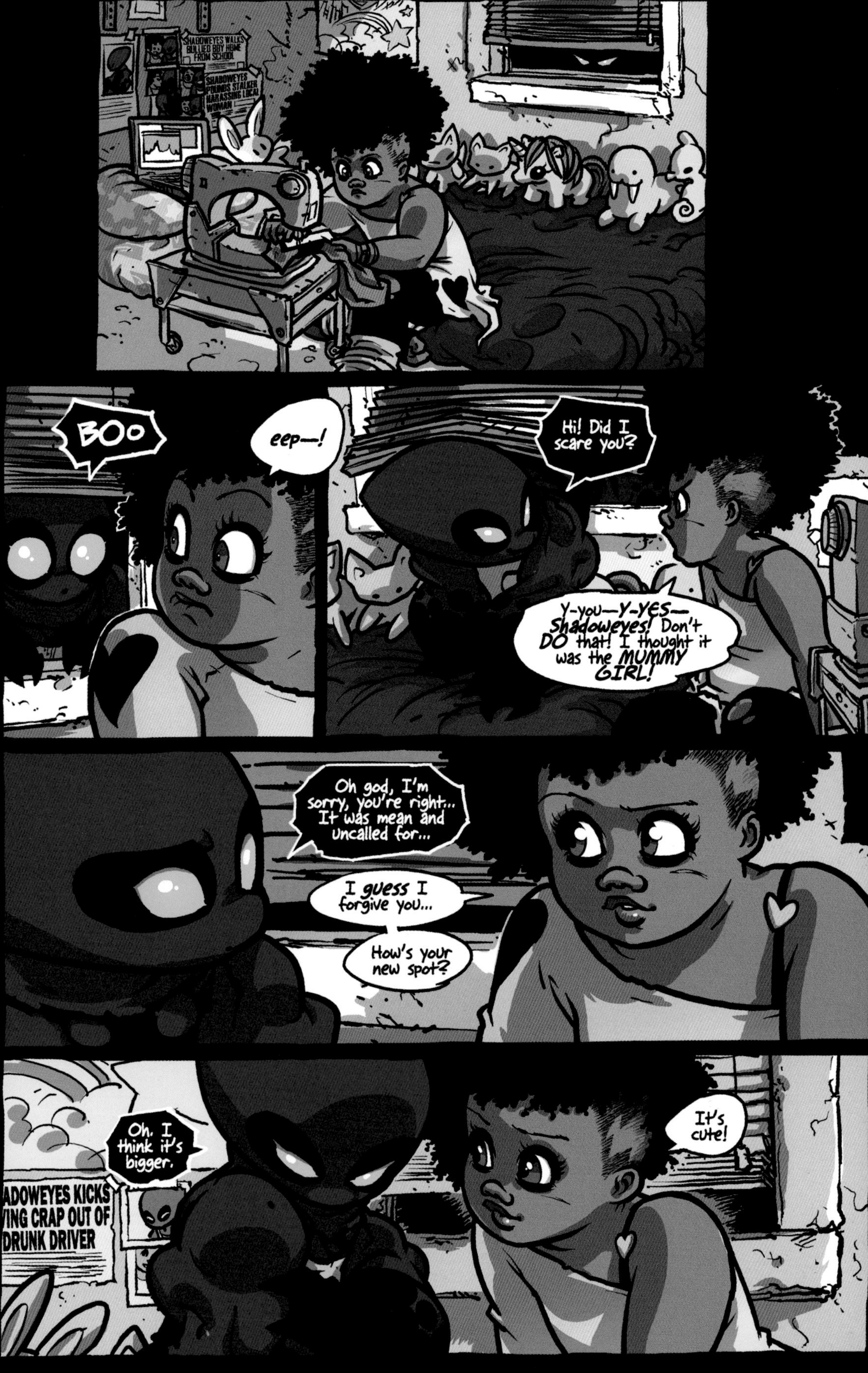
SHADOWEYES WALKS BULLIED BOY HOME FROM SCHOOL
SHADOWEYES POUNDS STALKER HARASSING LOCAL WOMAN
BOO
eep—!
Hi! Did I scare you?
Y-you—Y-YES— Shadoweyes! Don't DO that! I thought it was the MUMMY GIRL!
Oh god, I'm sorry, you're right... It was mean and uncalled for...
I guess I forgive you...
How's your new spot?
Oh. I think it's bigger.
It's cute!
ADOWEYES KICKS
VING CRAP OUT OF
DRUNK DRIVER

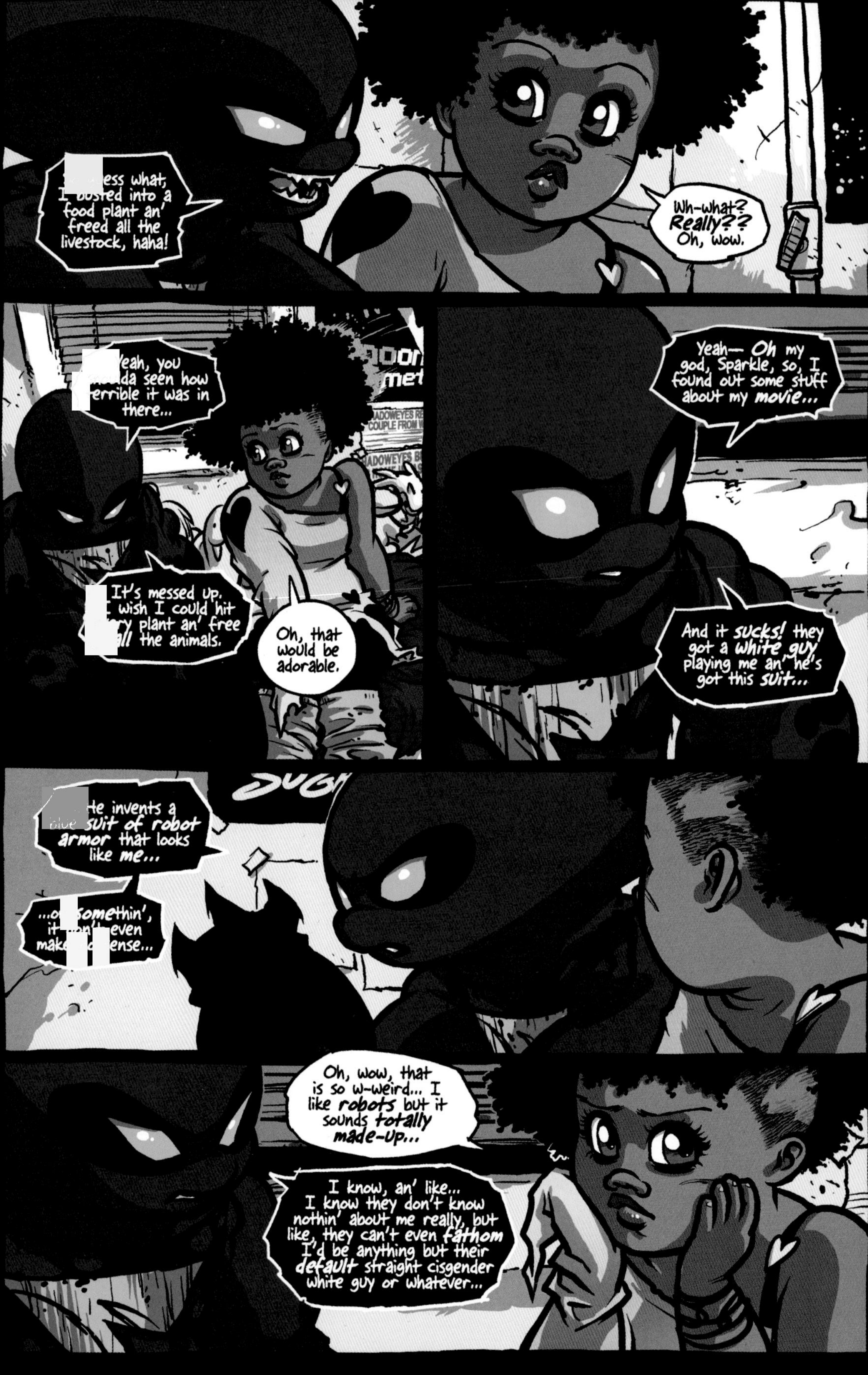
[redacted]ess what, I busted into a food plant an' freed all the livestock, haha!
Wh-what? Really?? Oh, wow.
[redacted]Yeah, you [redacted]oulda seen how [redacted]errible it was in there...
Yeah— Oh my god, Sparkle, so, I found out some stuff about my movie...
[redacted]It's messed up. [redacted] wish I could hit [redacted]ery plant an' free [redacted]all the animals.
Oh, that would be adorable.
And it sucks! they got a white guy playing me an' he's got this suit...
[redacted]He invents a [redacted]suit of robot armor that looks like me...
...o[redacted]somethin', it [redacted] even make[redacted]ense...
Oh, wow, that is so w-weird... I like robots but it sounds totally made-up...
I know, an' like... I know they don't know nothin' about me really, but like, they can't even fathom I'd be anything but their default straight cisgender white guy or whatever...

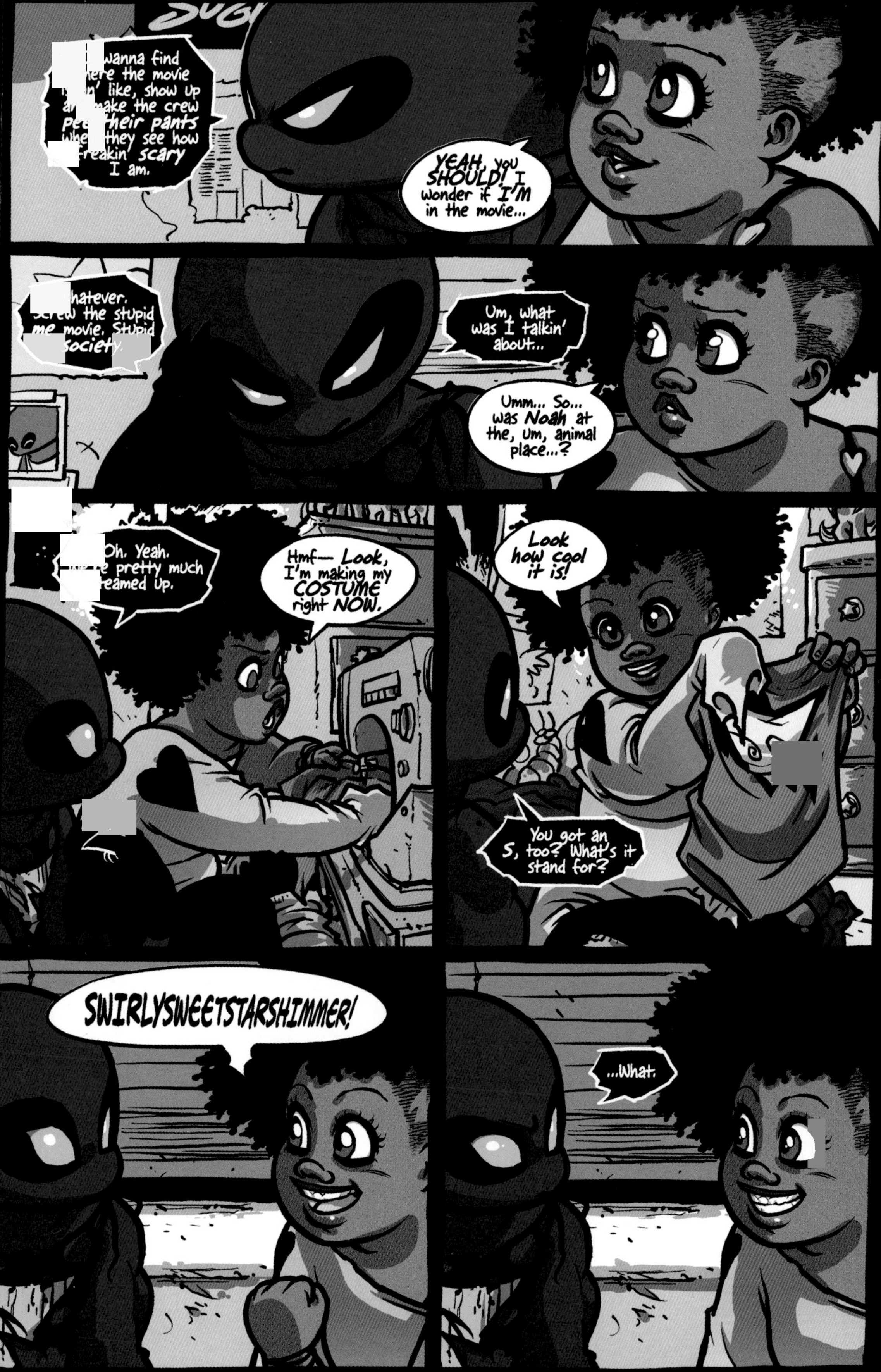
[redacted]wanna find [redacted]here the movie [redacted]n' like, show up a[redacted]make the crew pee[redacted]their pants whe[redacted] they see how [redacted]freakin' scary I am.
YEAH, you SHOULD! I wonder if I'M in the movie...
[redacted]hatever. Screw the stupid me movie. Stupid [redacted]society[redacted]
Um, what was I talkin' about...
Umm... So... was Noah at the, um, animal place...?
[redacted]Oh. Yeah. [redacted]re pretty much [redacted]eamed up.
Hmf— Look, I'm making my COSTUME right NOW.
Look how cool it is!
You got an S, too? What's it stand for?
SWIRLYSWEETSTARSHIMMER!
...What.

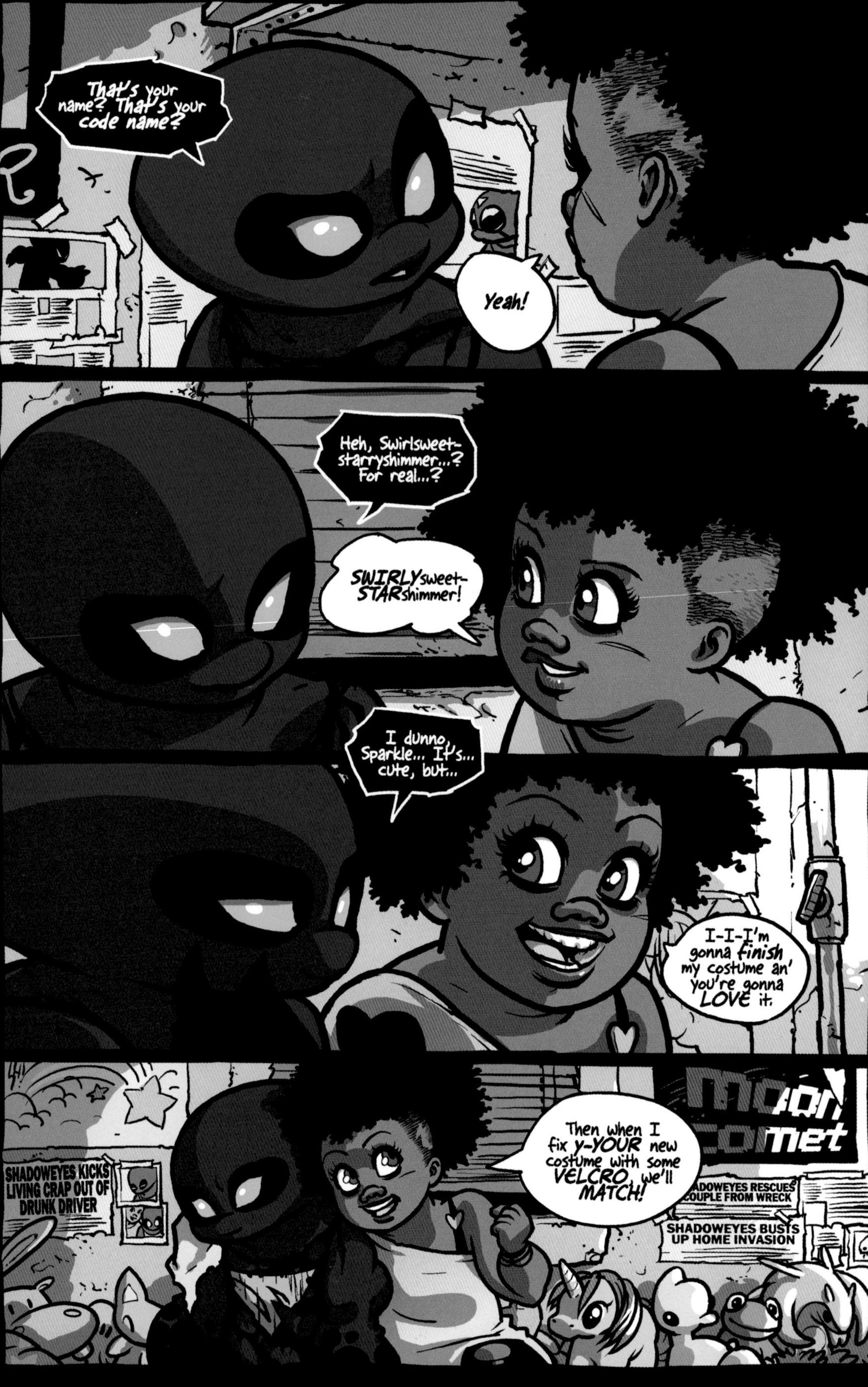
That's your name? That's your code name?
Yeah!
Heh, Swirlsweet-starryshimmer...? For real...?
SWIRLYsweet-STARshimmer!
I dunno, Sparkle... It's... cute, but...
I-I-I'm gonna finish my costume an' you're gonna LOVE it.
SHADOWEYES KICKS LIVING CRAP OUT OF DRUNK DRIVER
Then when I fix y-YOUR new costume with some VELCRO, we'll MATCH!
ADOWEYES RESCUES COUPLE FROM WRECK
SHADOWEYES BUSTS UP HOME INVASION

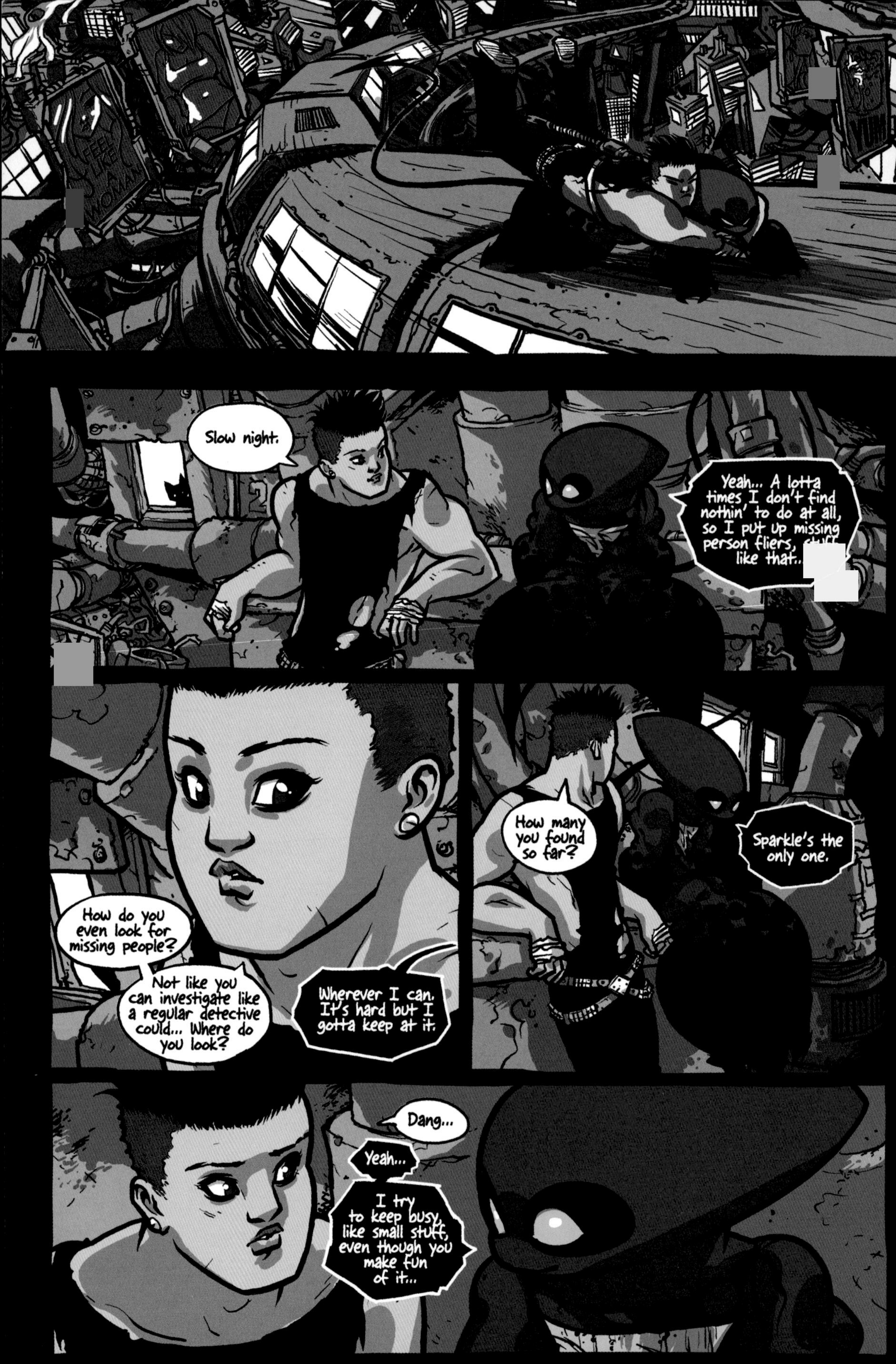
FEEL LIKE A WOMAN
YUM
Slow night.
Yeah... A lotta times I don't find nothin' to do at all, so I put up missing person fliers, stuff like that..
How do you even look for missing people?
Not like you can investigate like a regular detective could... Where do you look?
Wherever I can. It's hard but I gotta keep at it.
How many you found so far?
Sparkle's the only one.
Dang...
Yeah...
I try to keep busy, like small stuff, even though you make fun of it...

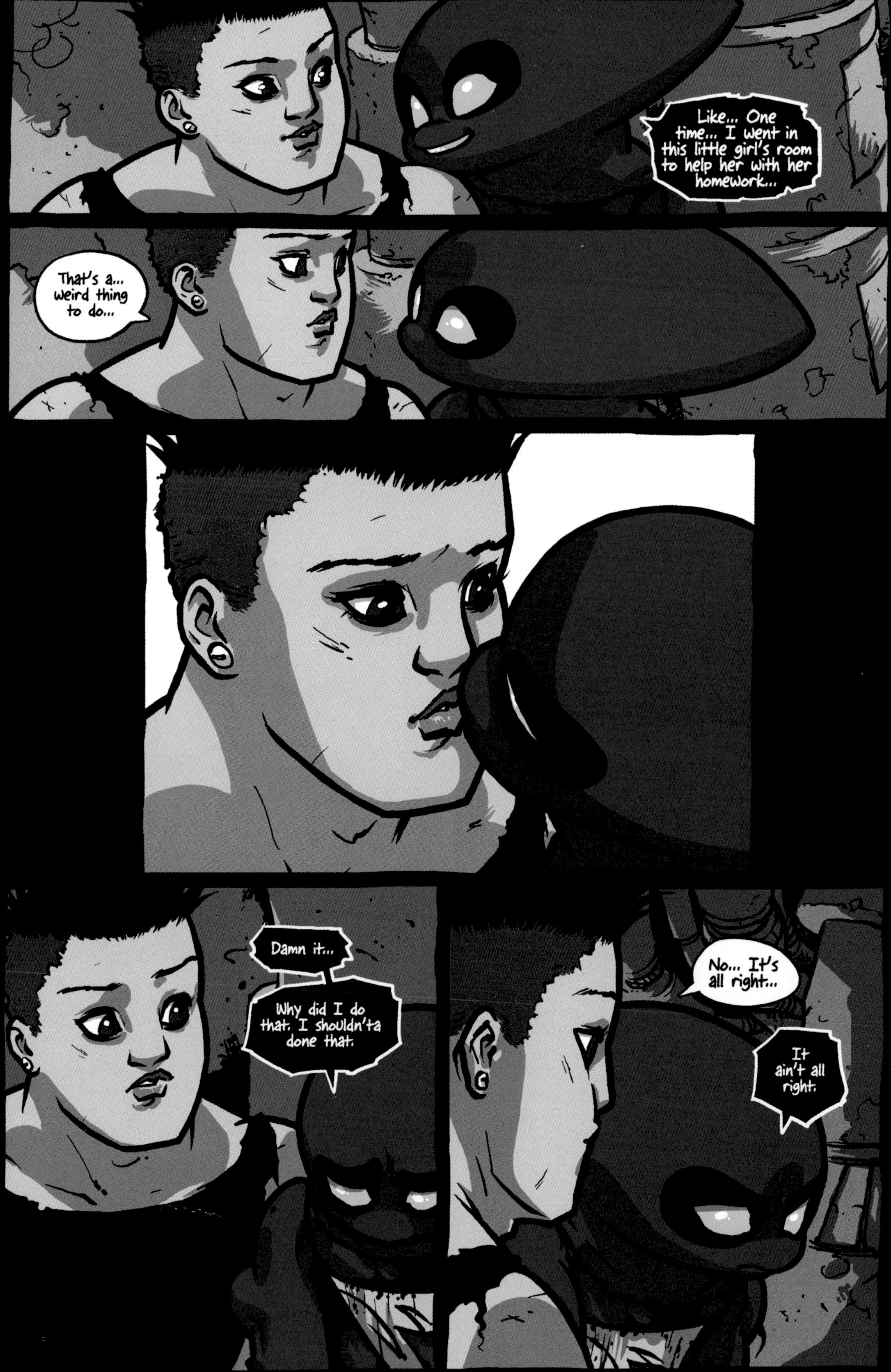
Like... One time... I went in this little girl's room to help her with her homework...
That's a... weird thing to do...
Damn it...
Why did I do that. I shouldn'ta done that.
No... It's all right...
It ain't all right.

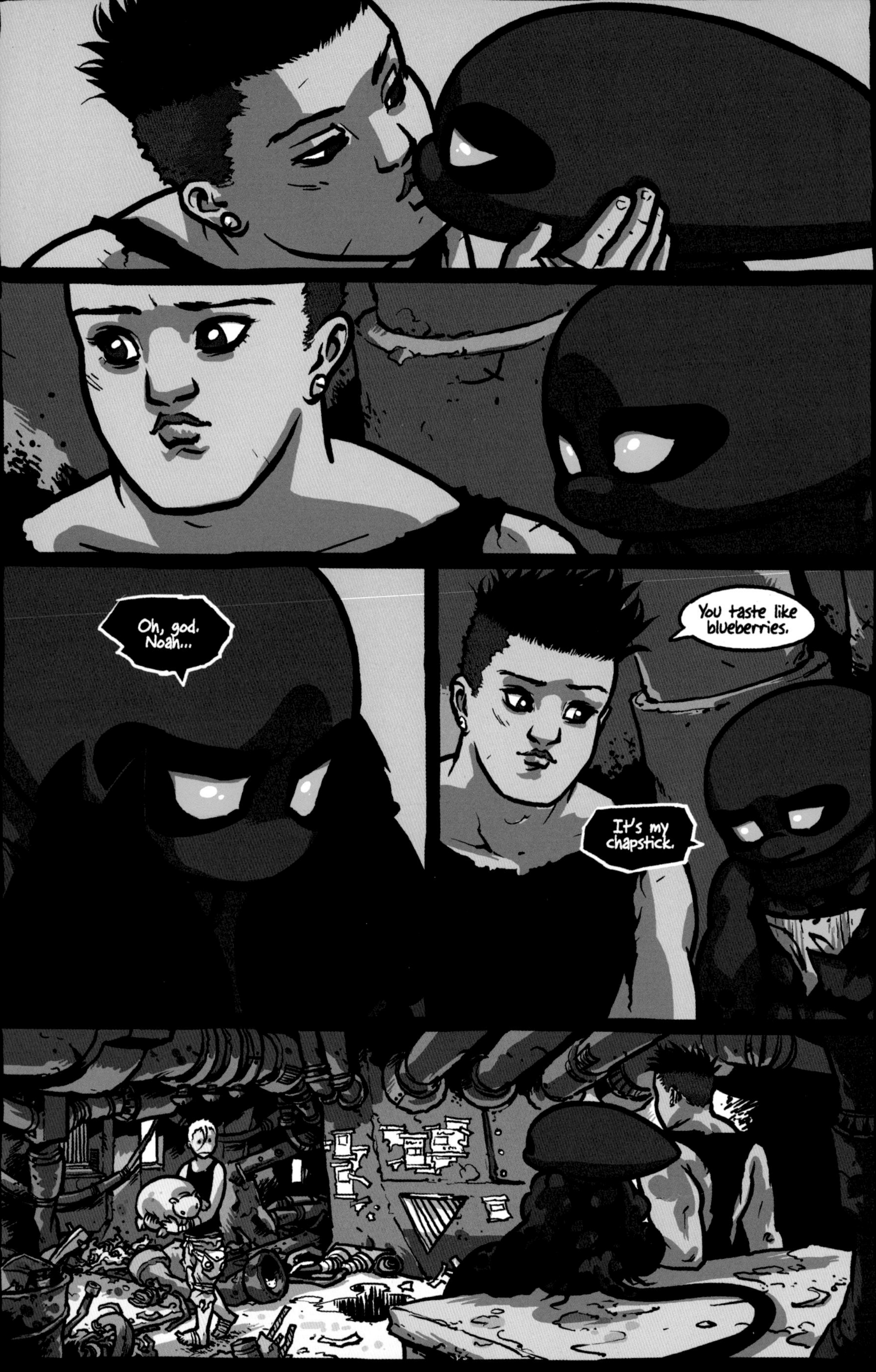
Oh, god.
Noah...
You taste like
blueberries.
It's my
chapstick.

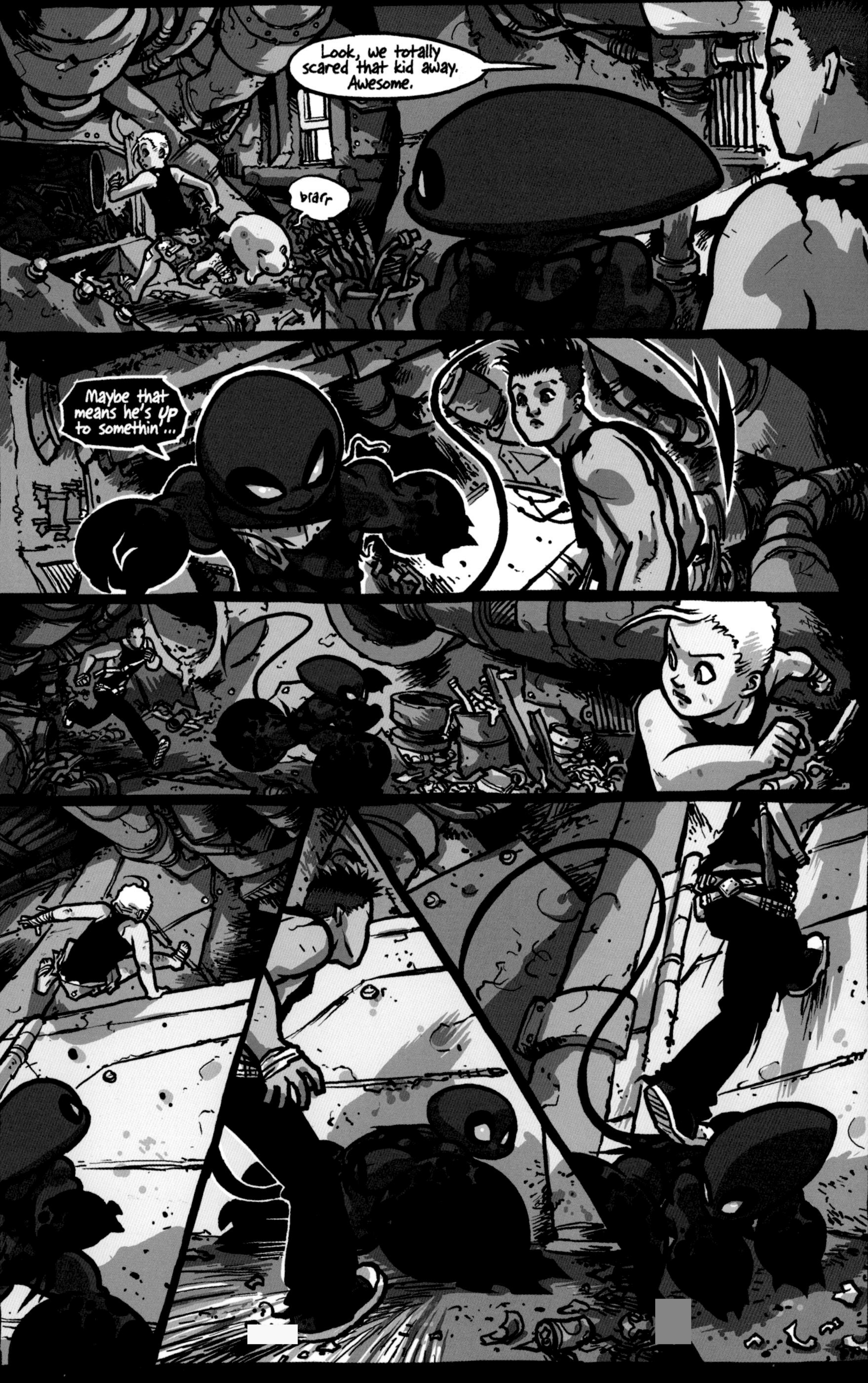
Look, we totally scared that kid away. Awesome.
brarr
Maybe that means he's up to somethin'...

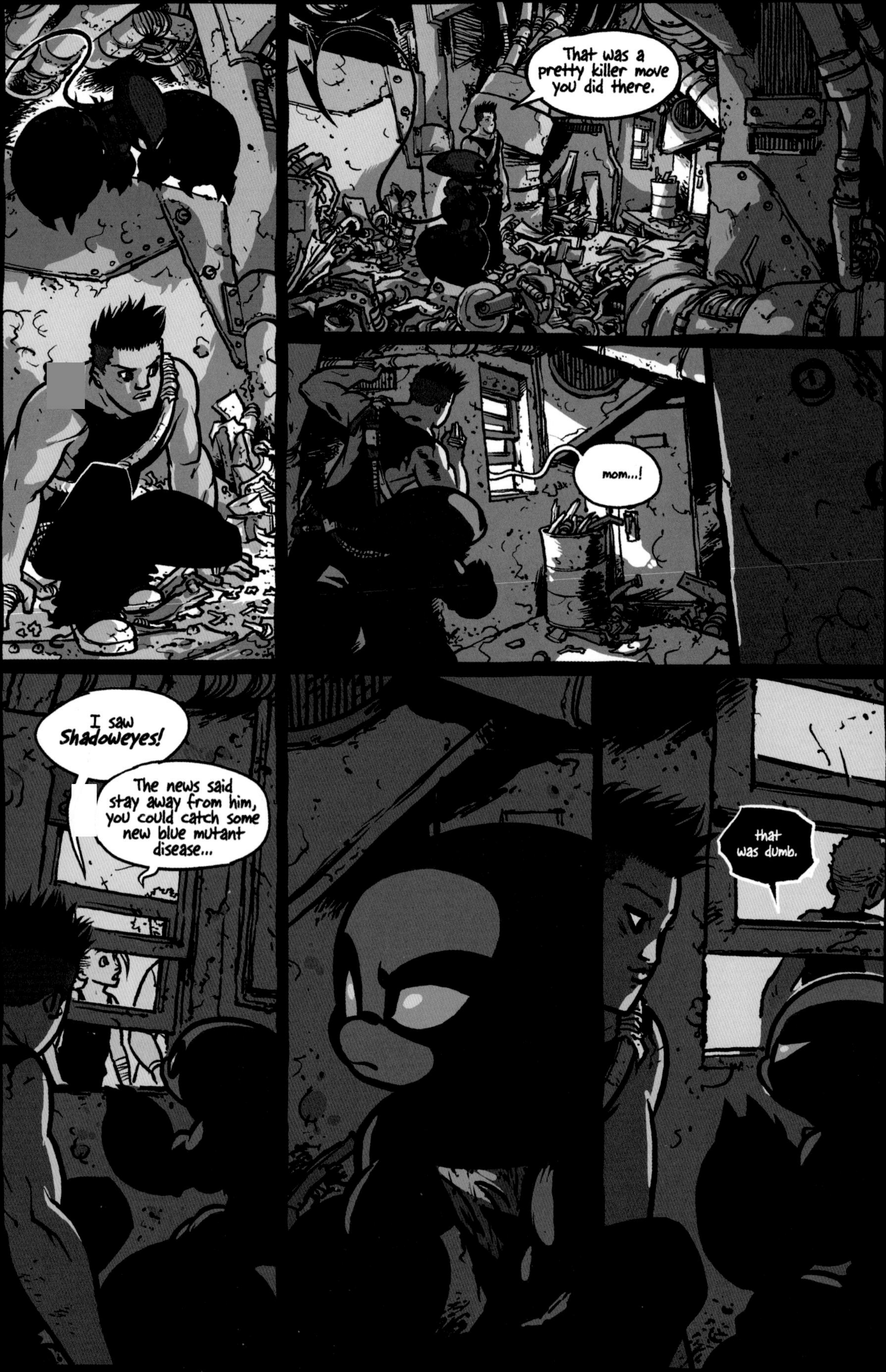
That was a pretty killer move you did there.
mom...!
I saw Shadoweyes!
The news said stay away from him, you could catch some new blue mutant disease...
that was dumb.

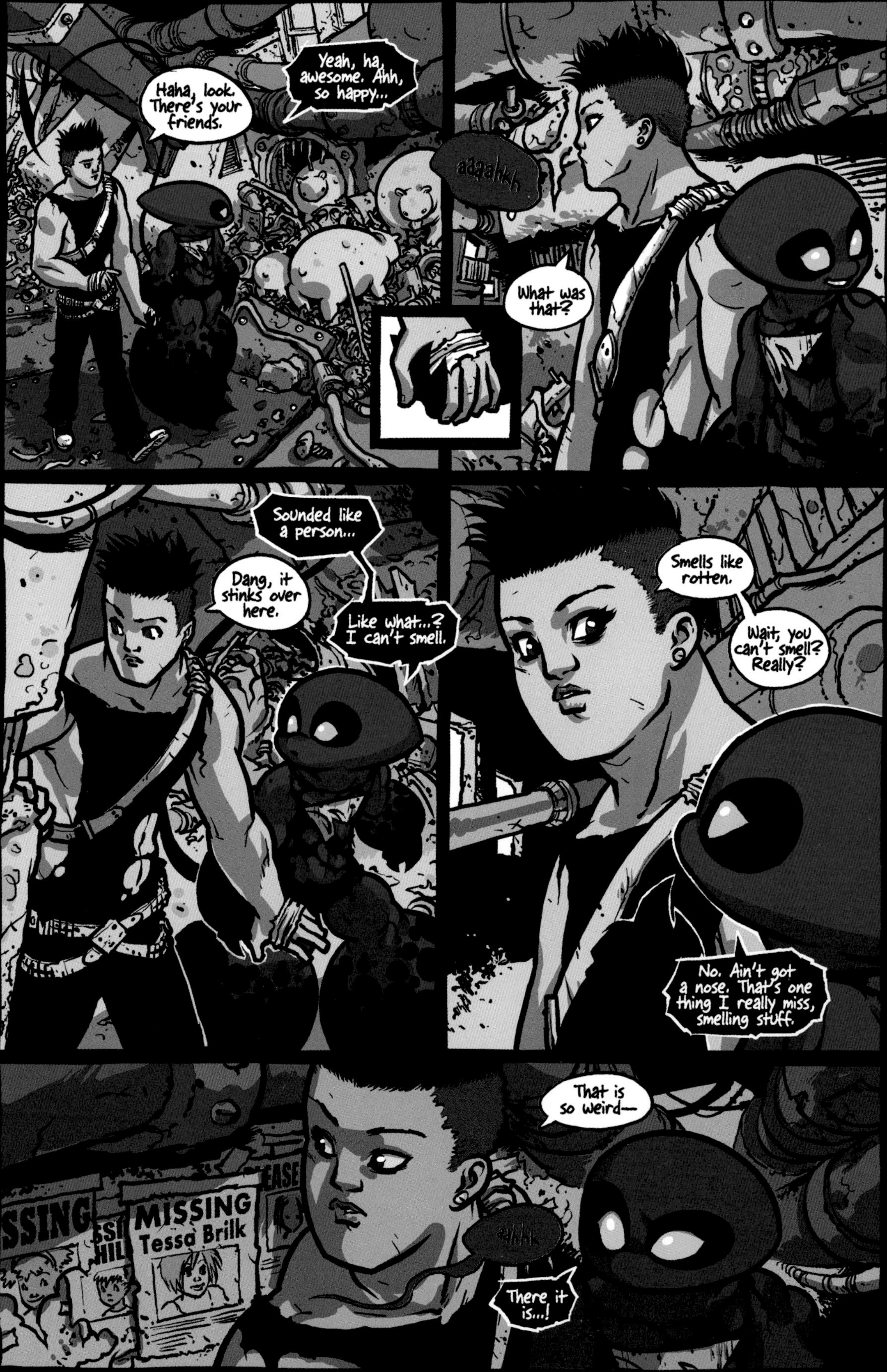
Haha, look. There's your friends.
Yeah, ha, awesome. Ahh, so happy...
aaaahhh
What was that?
Sounded like a person...
Dang, it stinks over here.
Like what...? I can't smell.
Smells like rotten.
Wait, you can't smell? Really?
No. Ain't got a nose. That's one thing I really miss, smelling stuff.
That is so weird—
MISSING
MISSING Tessa Brilk
There it is...!

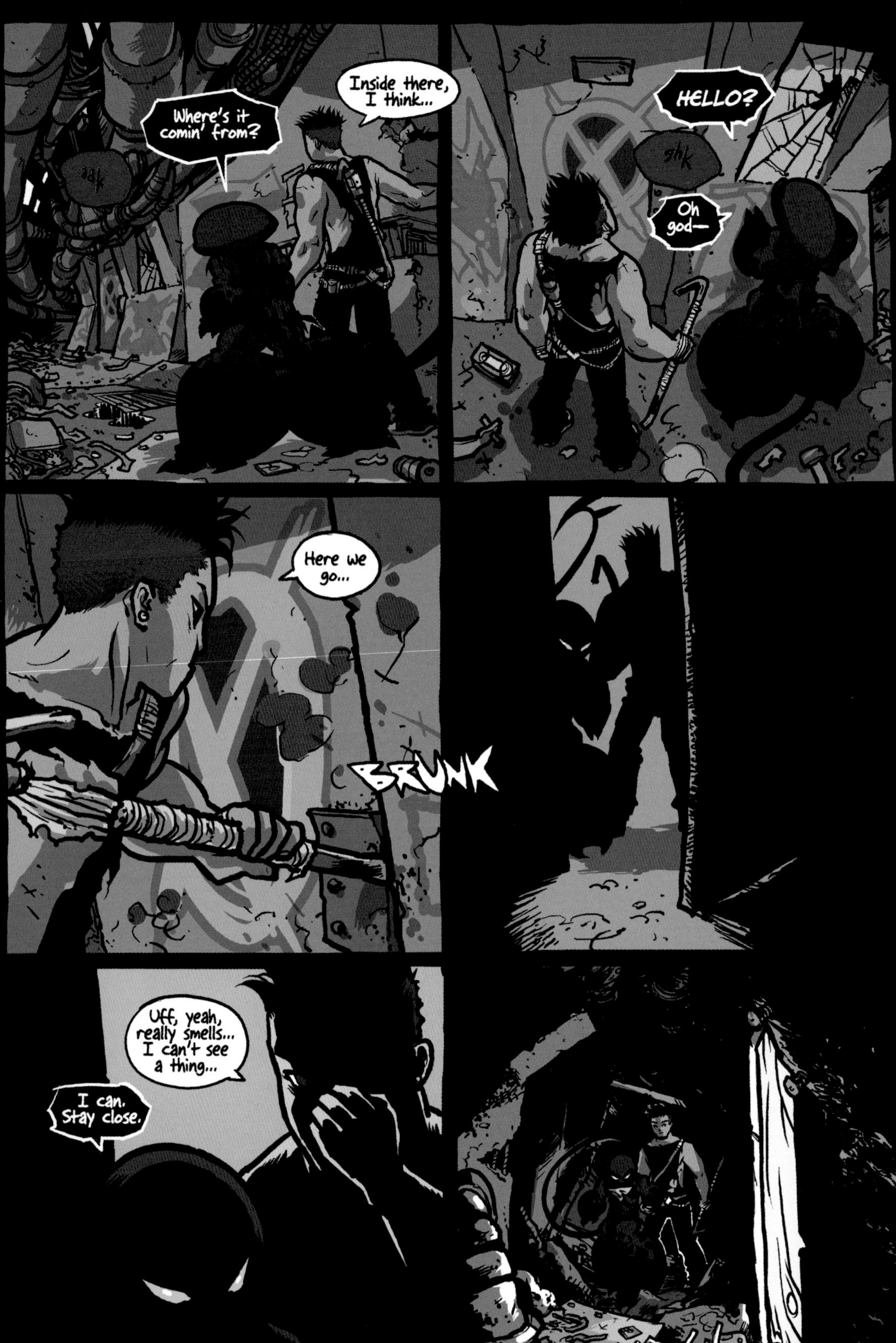
Where's it comin' from?
Inside there, I think...
HELLO?
ghk
Oh god—
Here we go...
BRUNK
Uff, yeah, really smells... I can't see a thing...
I can. Stay close.

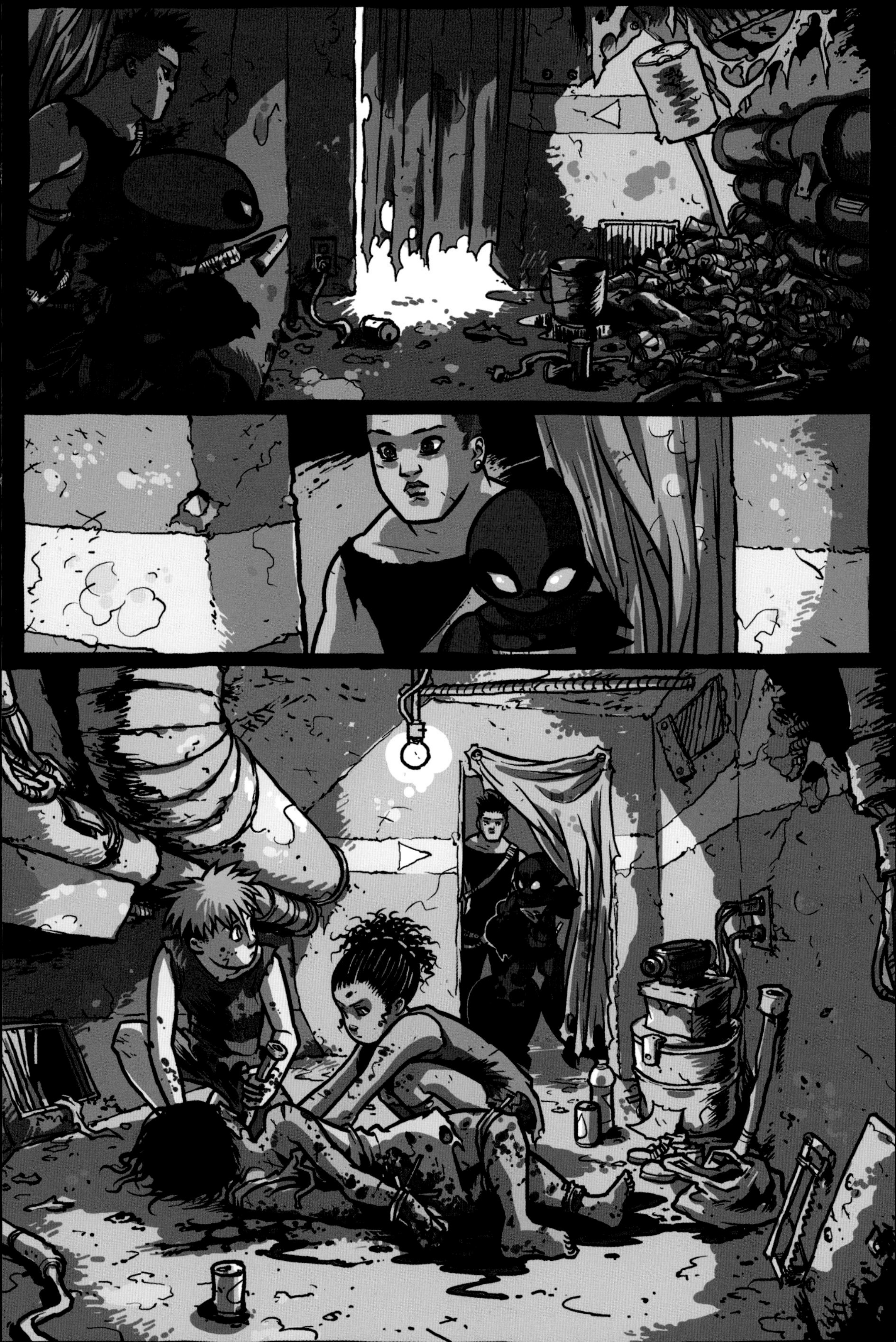

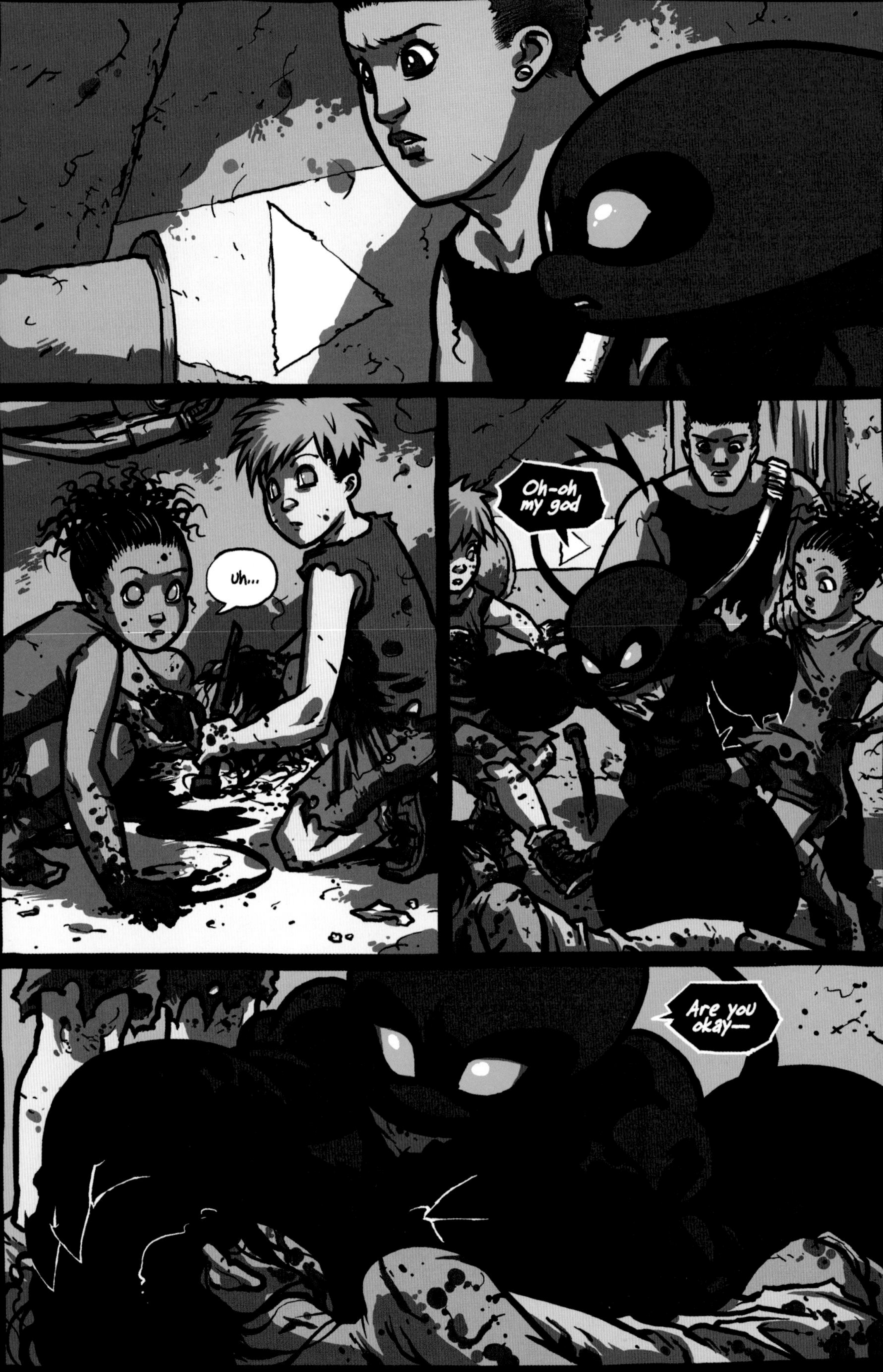
Uh...
Oh-oh my god
Are you okay—

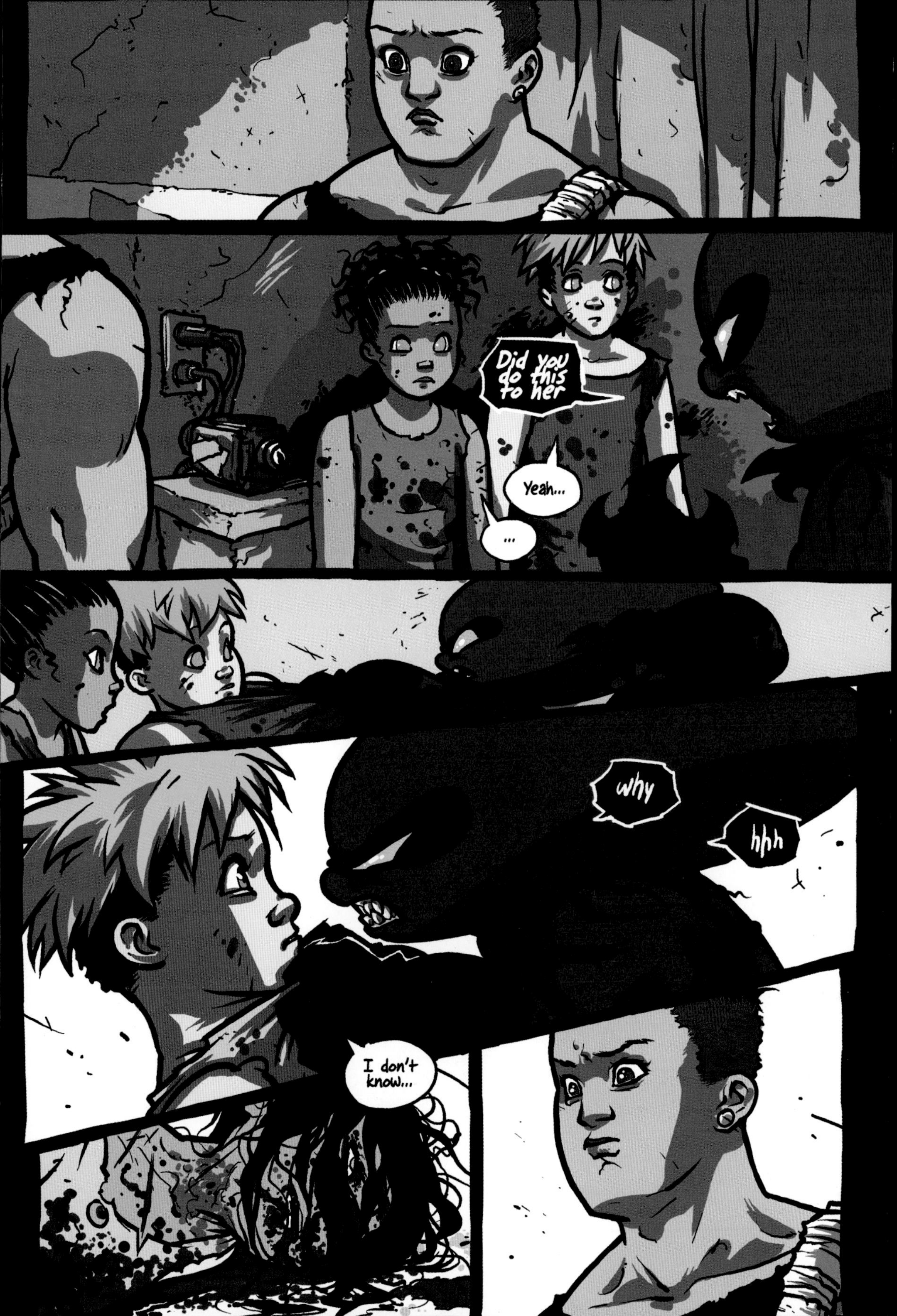
Did you do this to her
Yeah...
...
why
hhh
I don't know...

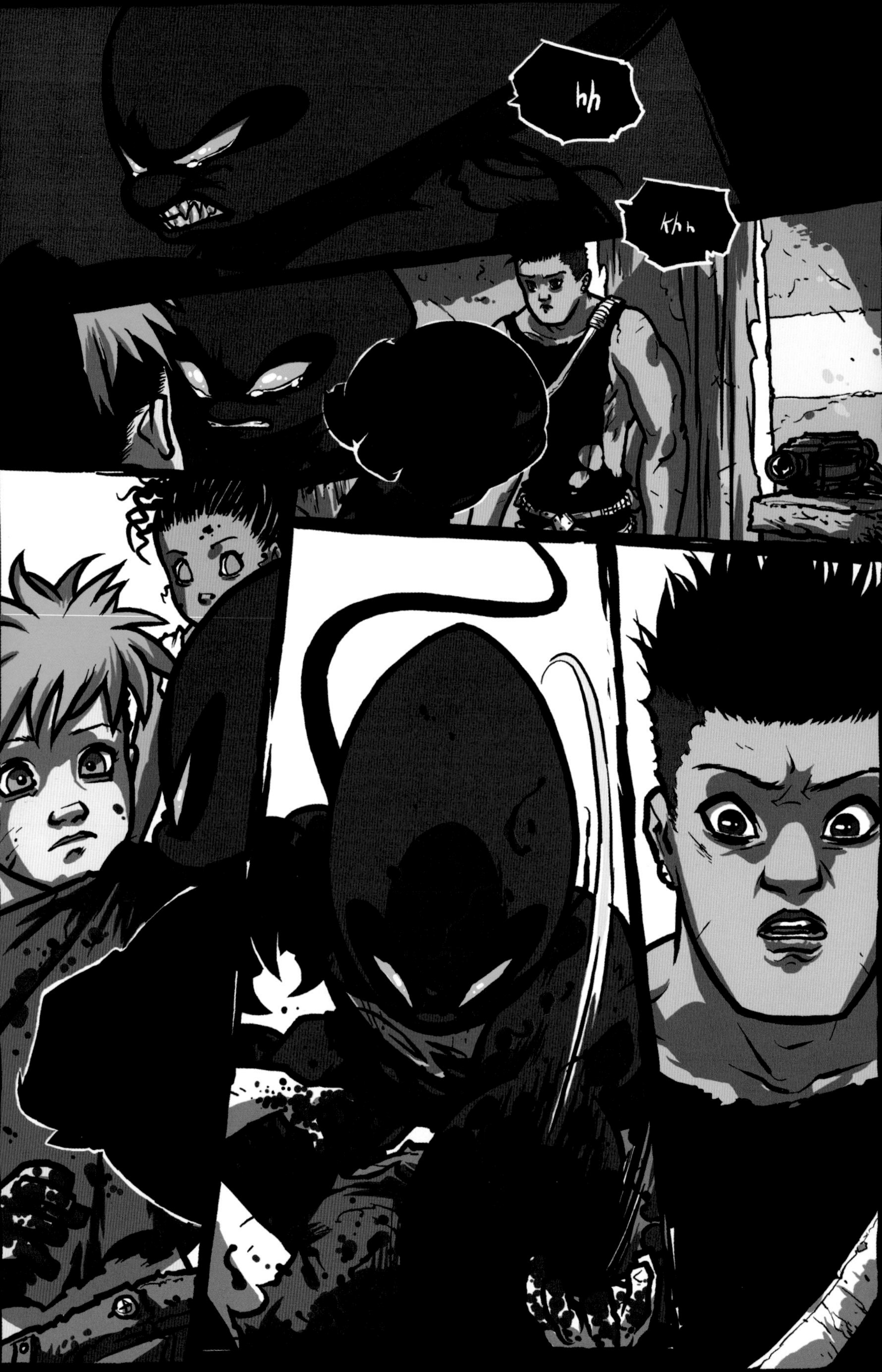
hh
khh

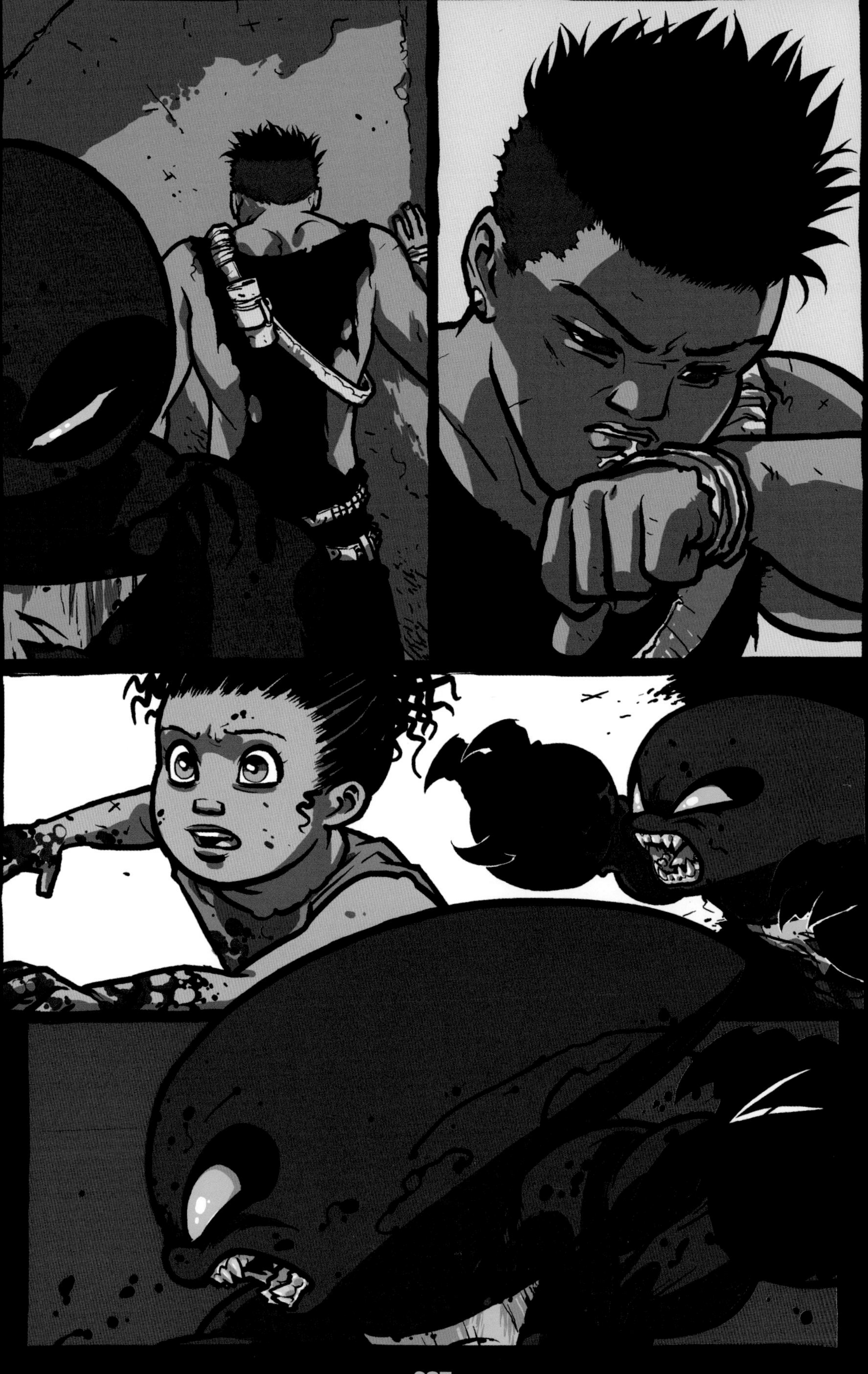

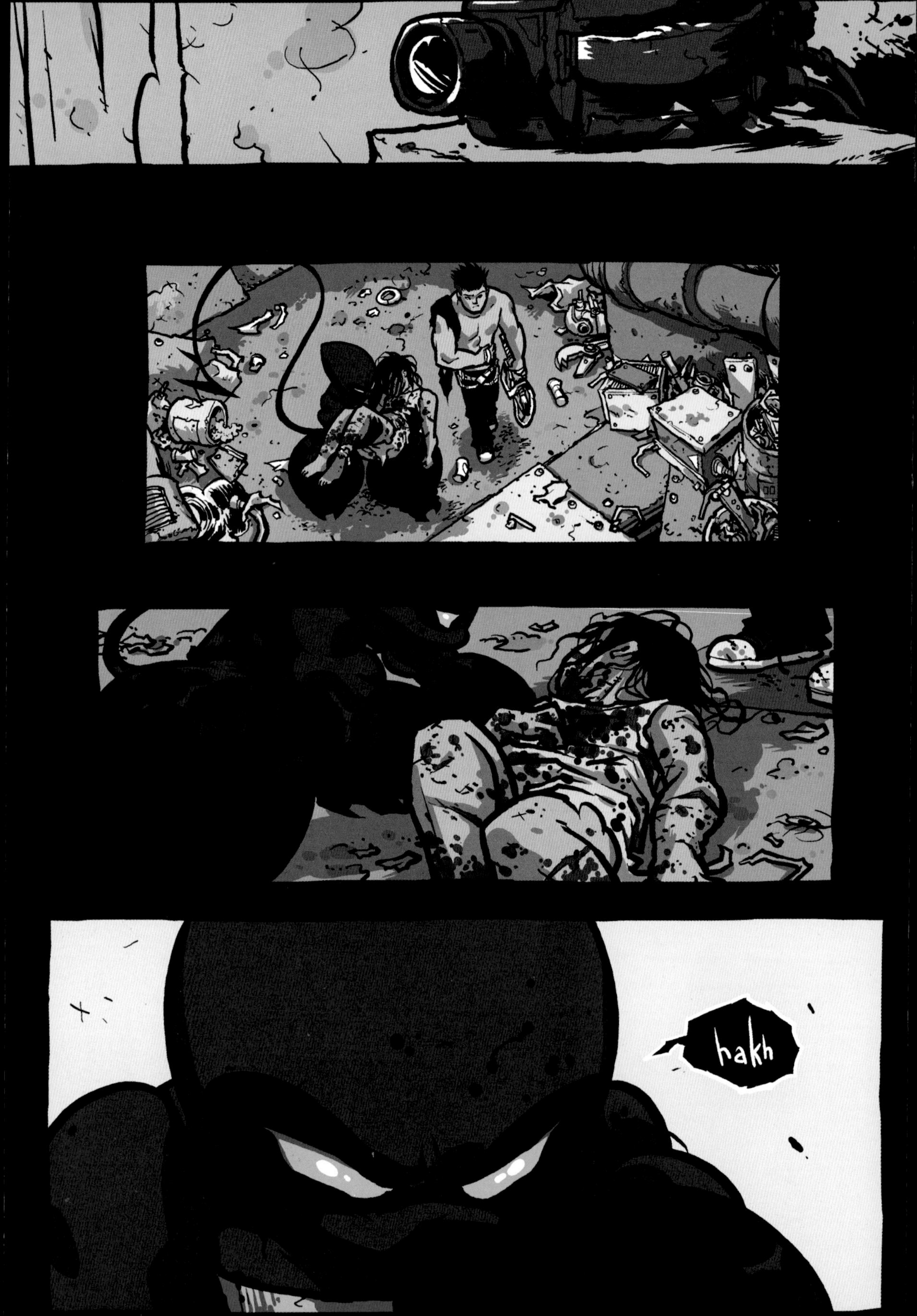
hakh

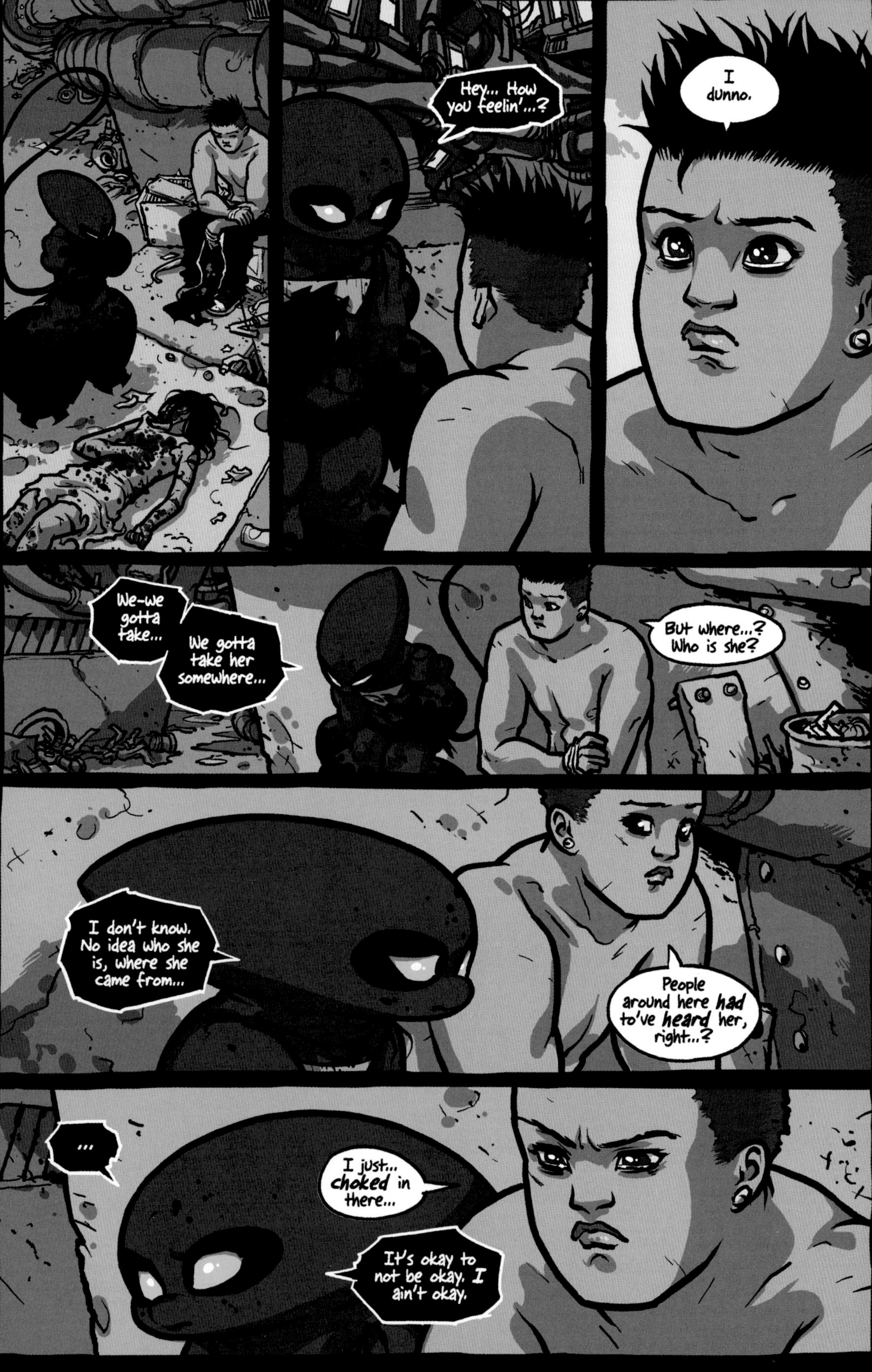
Hey... How you feelin'...?
I dunno.
We-we gotta take...
We gotta take her somewhere...
But where...? Who is she?
I don't know. No idea who she is, where she came from...
People around here had to've heard her, right...?
...
I just... choked in there...
It's okay to not be okay. I ain't okay.

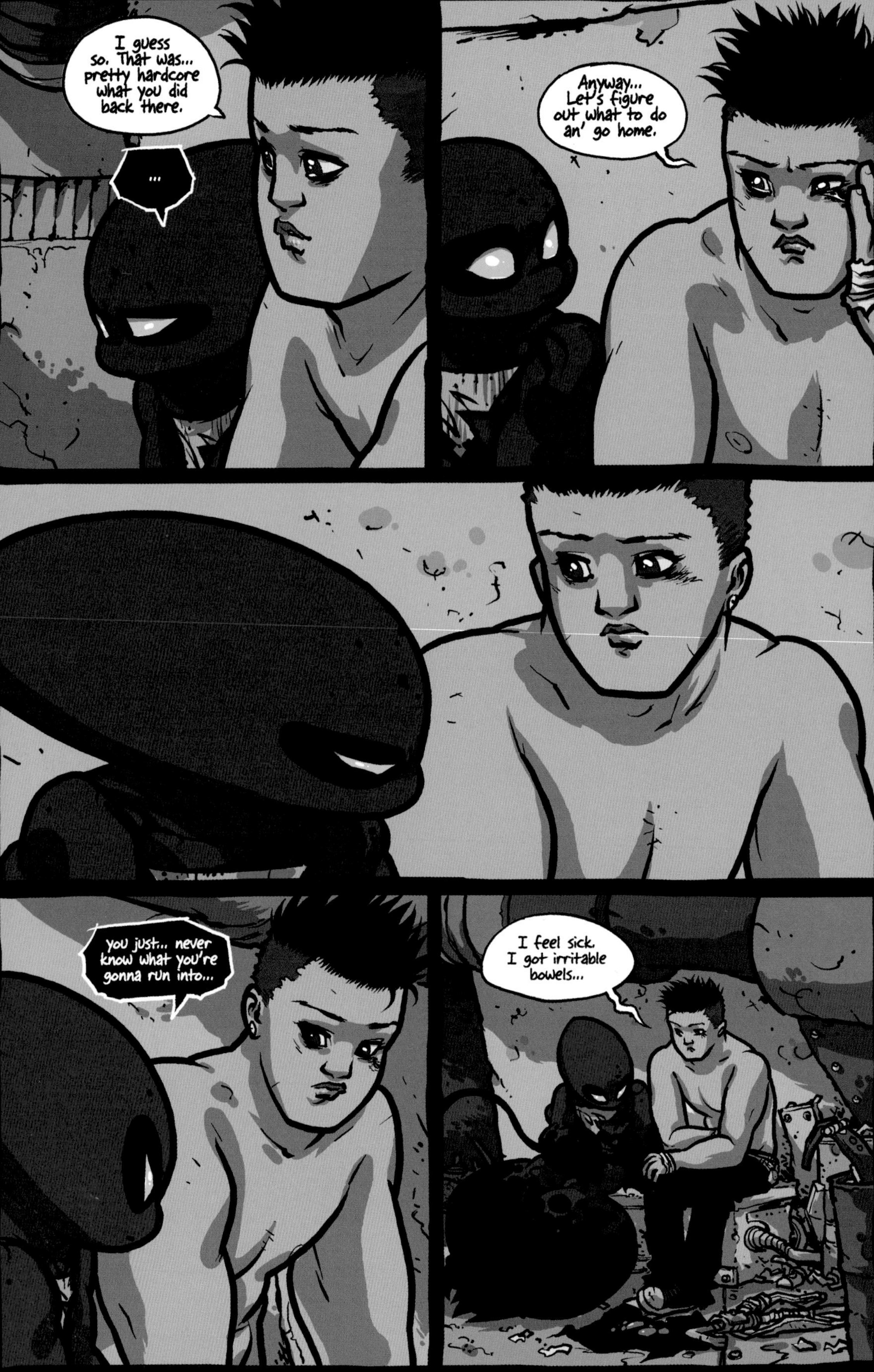
I guess so. That was... pretty hardcore what you did back there.
...
Anyway... Let's figure out what to do an' go home.
you just... never know what you're gonna run into...
I feel sick. I got irritable bowels...

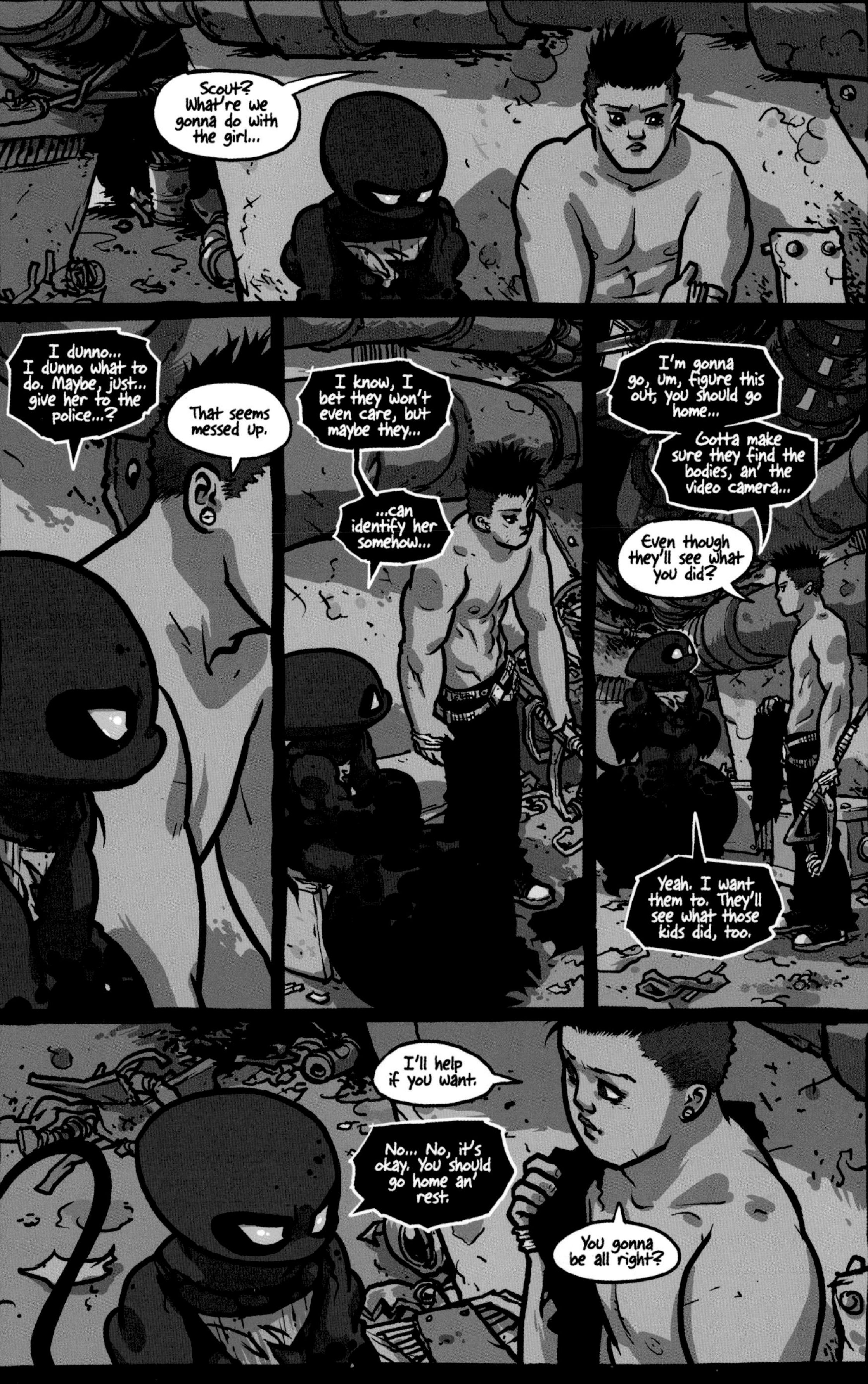
Scout? What're we gonna do with the girl...
I dunno... I dunno what to do. Maybe, just... give her to the police...?
That seems messed up.
I know, I bet they won't even care, but maybe they...
...can identify her somehow...
I'm gonna go, um, figure this out, you should go home...
Gotta make sure they find the bodies, an' the video camera...
Even though they'll see what you did?
Yeah. I want them to. They'll see what those kids did, too.
I'll help if you want.
No... No, it's okay. You should go home an' rest.
You gonna be all right?

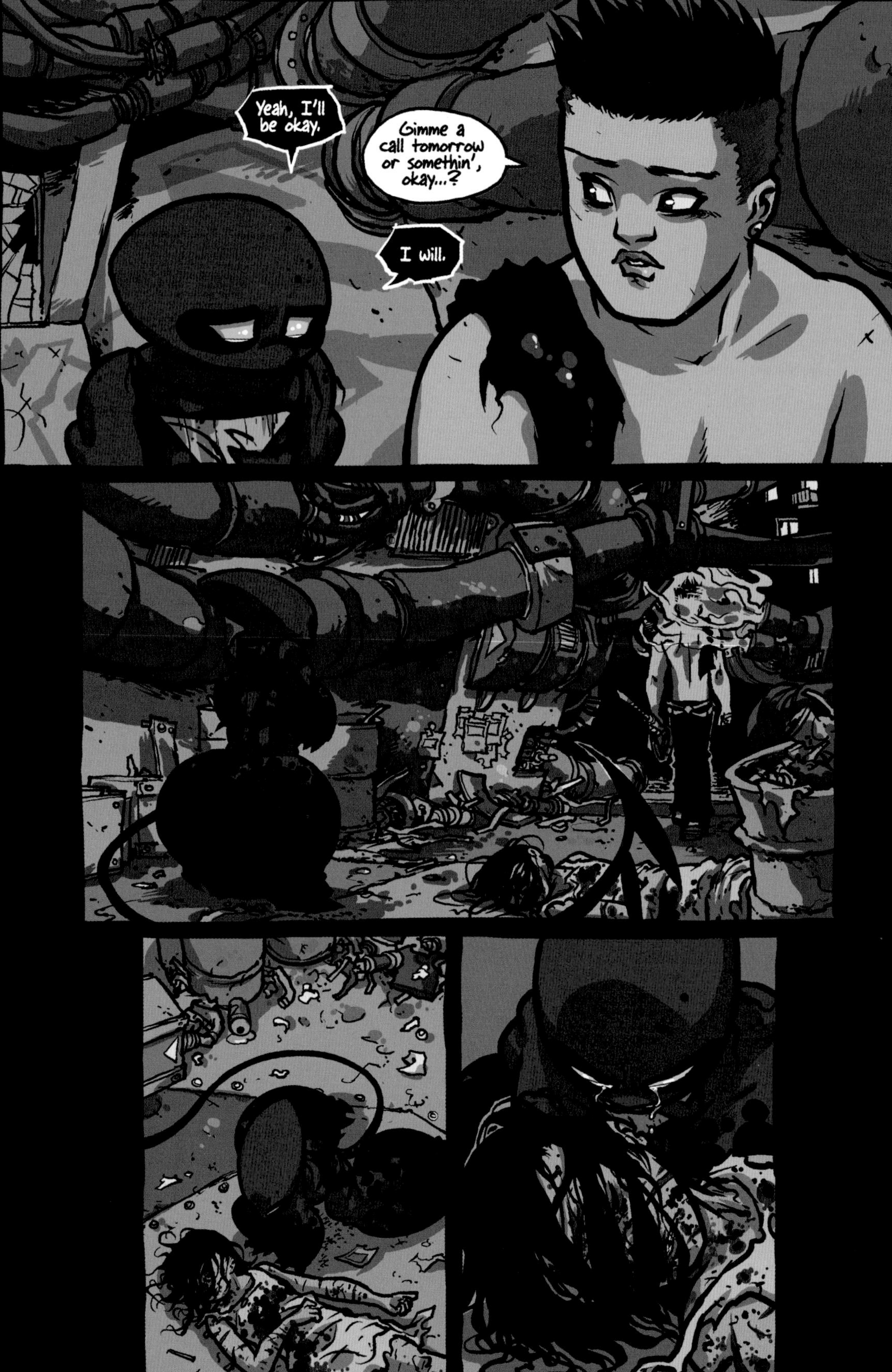
Yeah, I'll be okay.
Gimme a call tomorrow or somethin', okay...?
I will.

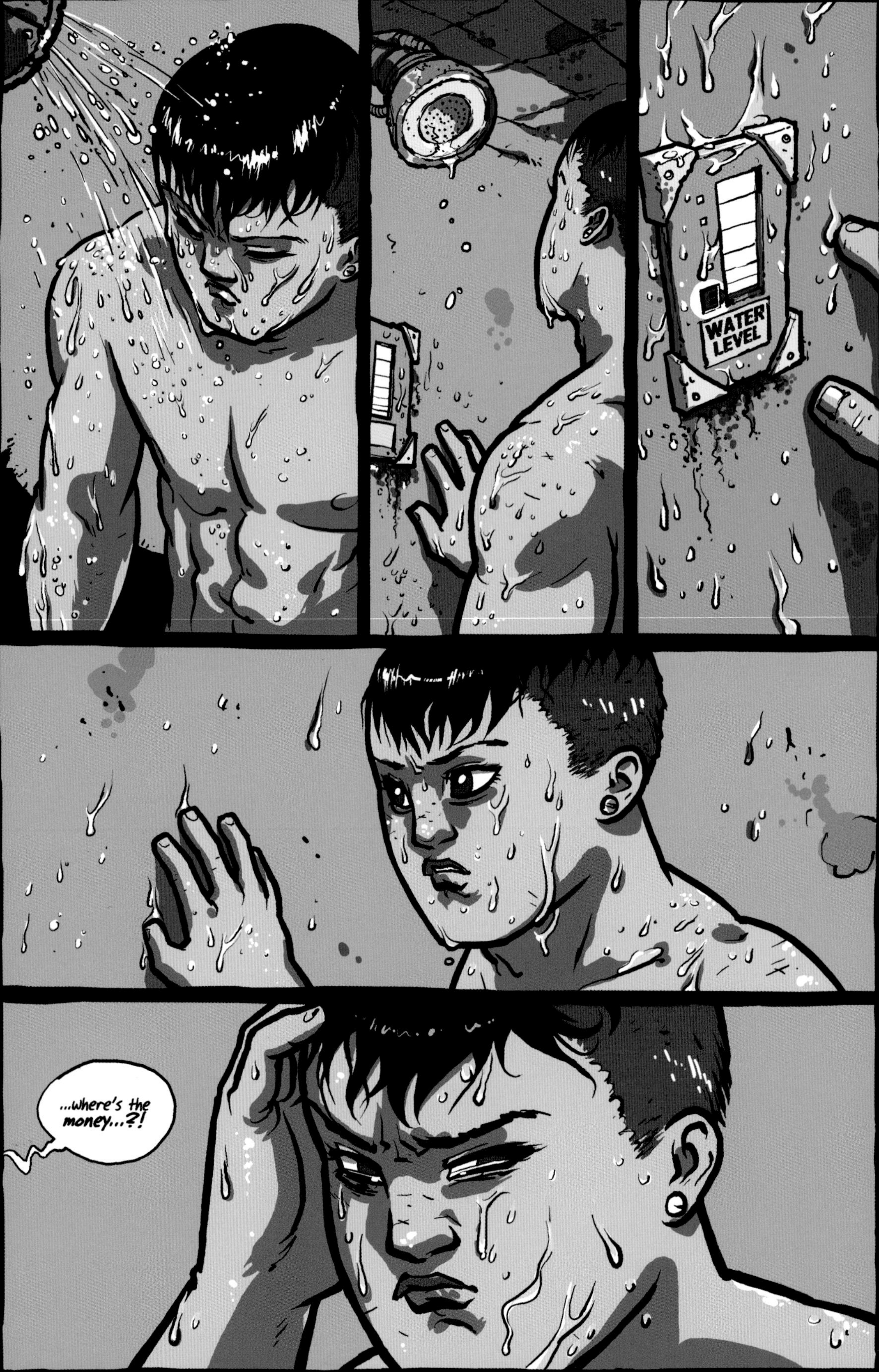
WATER LEVEL
...where's the money...?!

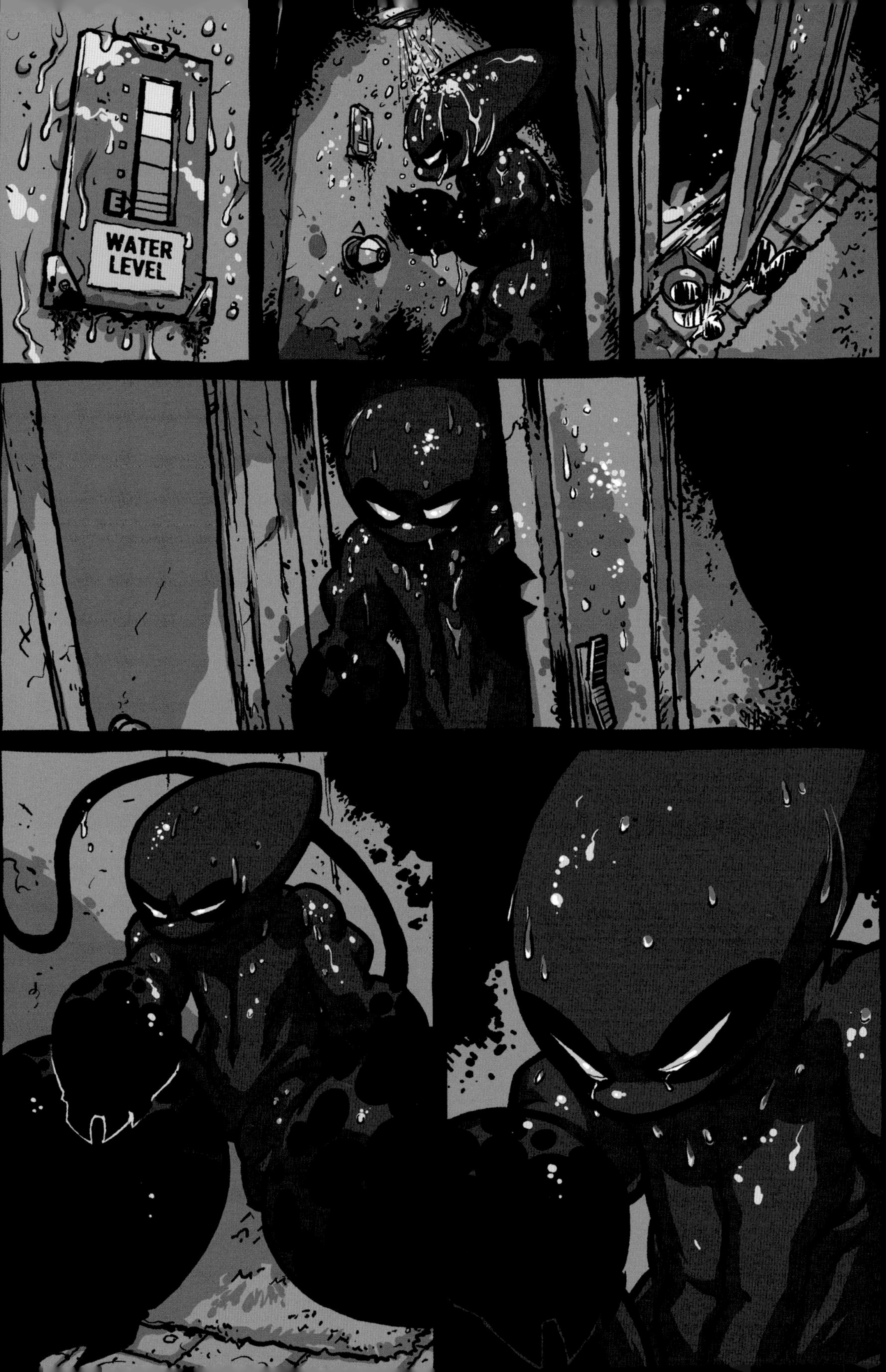
E
WATER
LEVEL

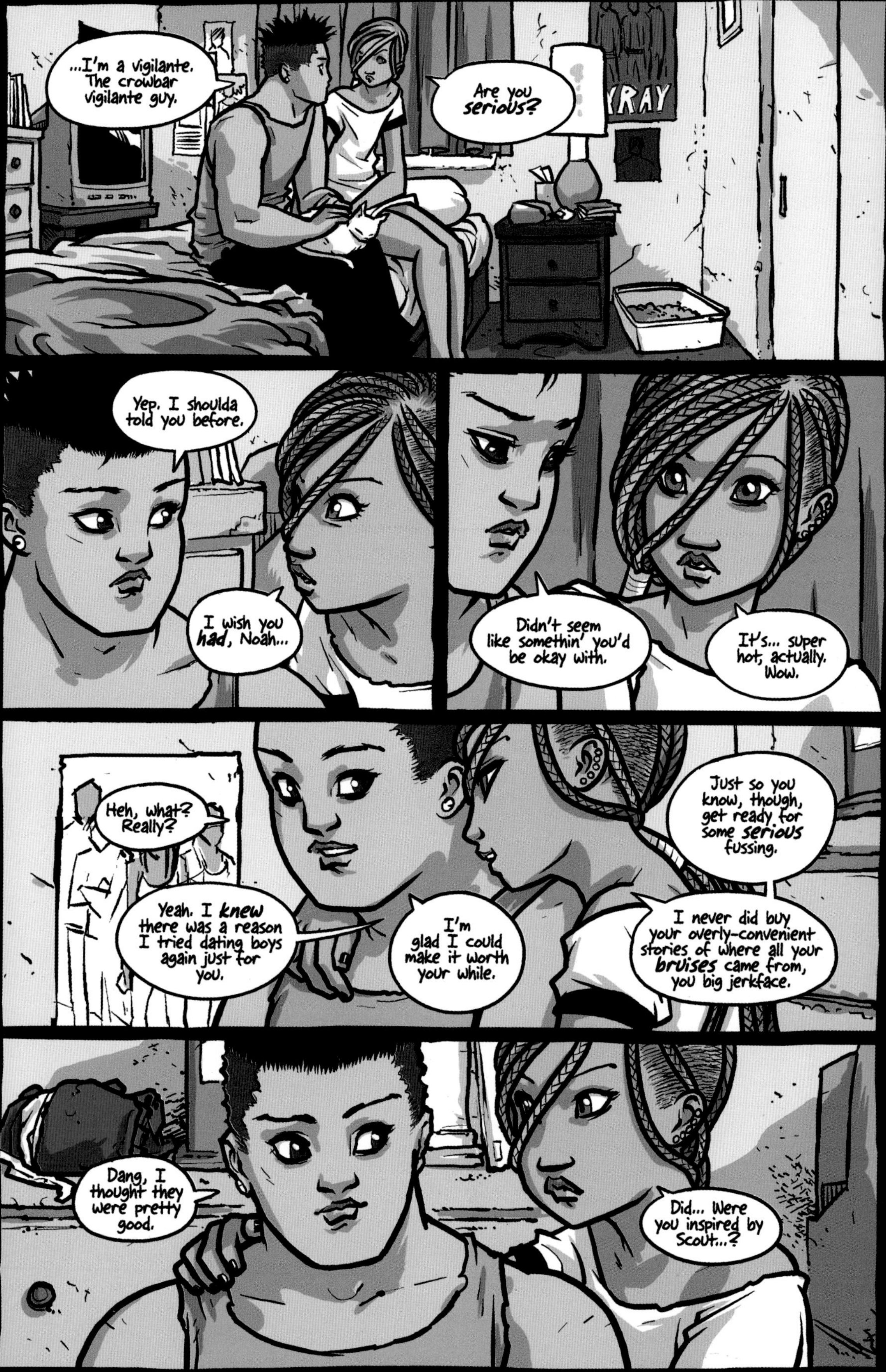
...I'm a vigilante. The crowbar vigilante guy.
Are you serious?
RAY
Yep. I shoulda told you before.
I wish you had, Noah...
Didn't seem like somethin' you'd be okay with.
It's... super hot, actually. Wow.
Heh, what? Really?
Yeah. I knew there was a reason I tried dating boys again just for you.
I'm glad I could make it worth your while.
Just so you know, though, get ready for some serious fussing.
I never did buy your overly-convenient stories of where all your bruises came from, you big jerkface.
Dang, I thought they were pretty good.
Did... Were you inspired by Scout...?

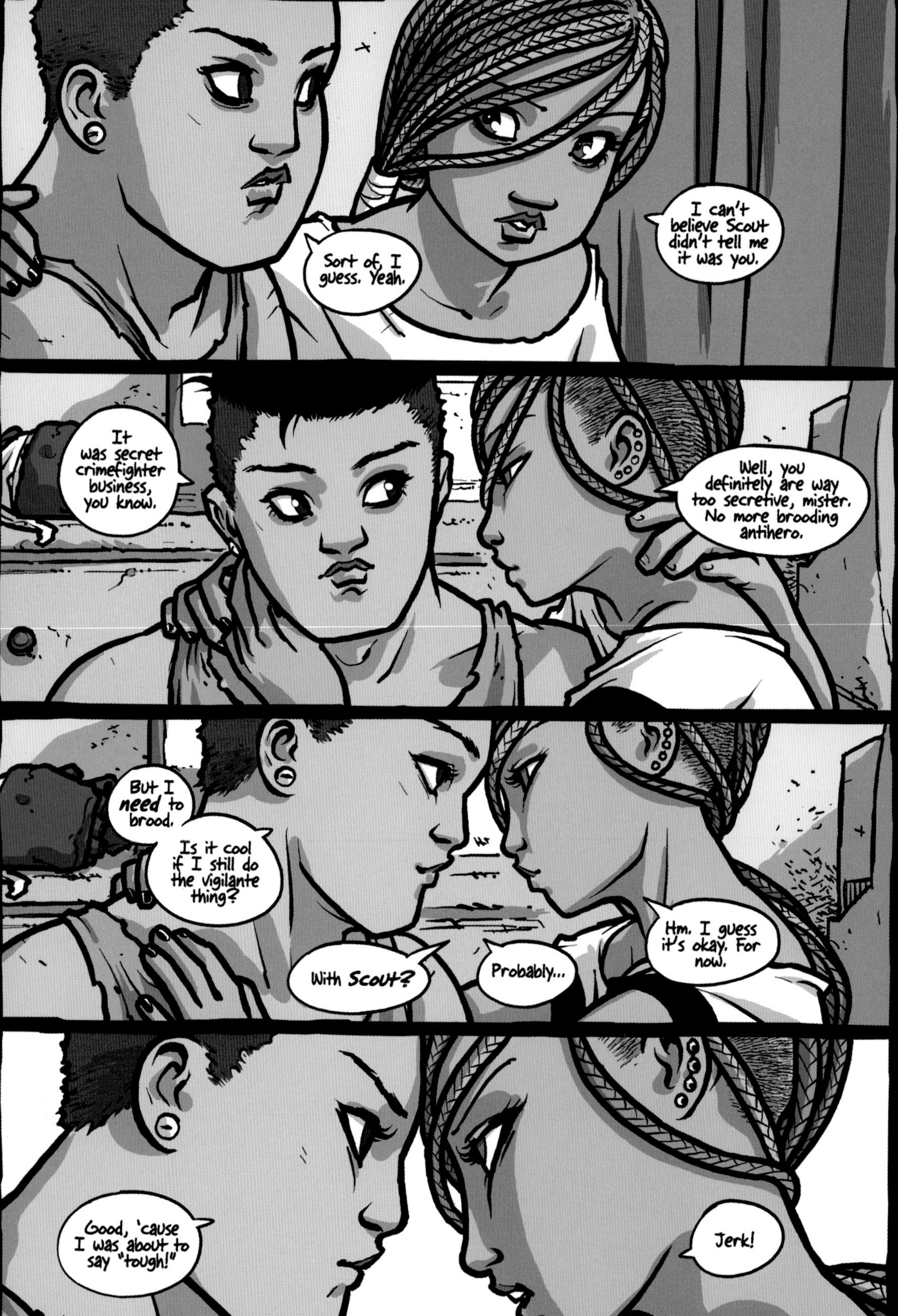
Sort of, I guess. Yeah.
I can't believe Scout didn't tell me it was you.
It was secret crimefighter business, you know.
Well, you definitely are way too secretive, mister. No more brooding antihero.
But I *need* to brood.
Is it cool if I still do the vigilante thing?
Hm. I guess it's okay. For now.
With *Scout?*
Probably...
Good, 'cause I was about to say "tough!"
Jerk!

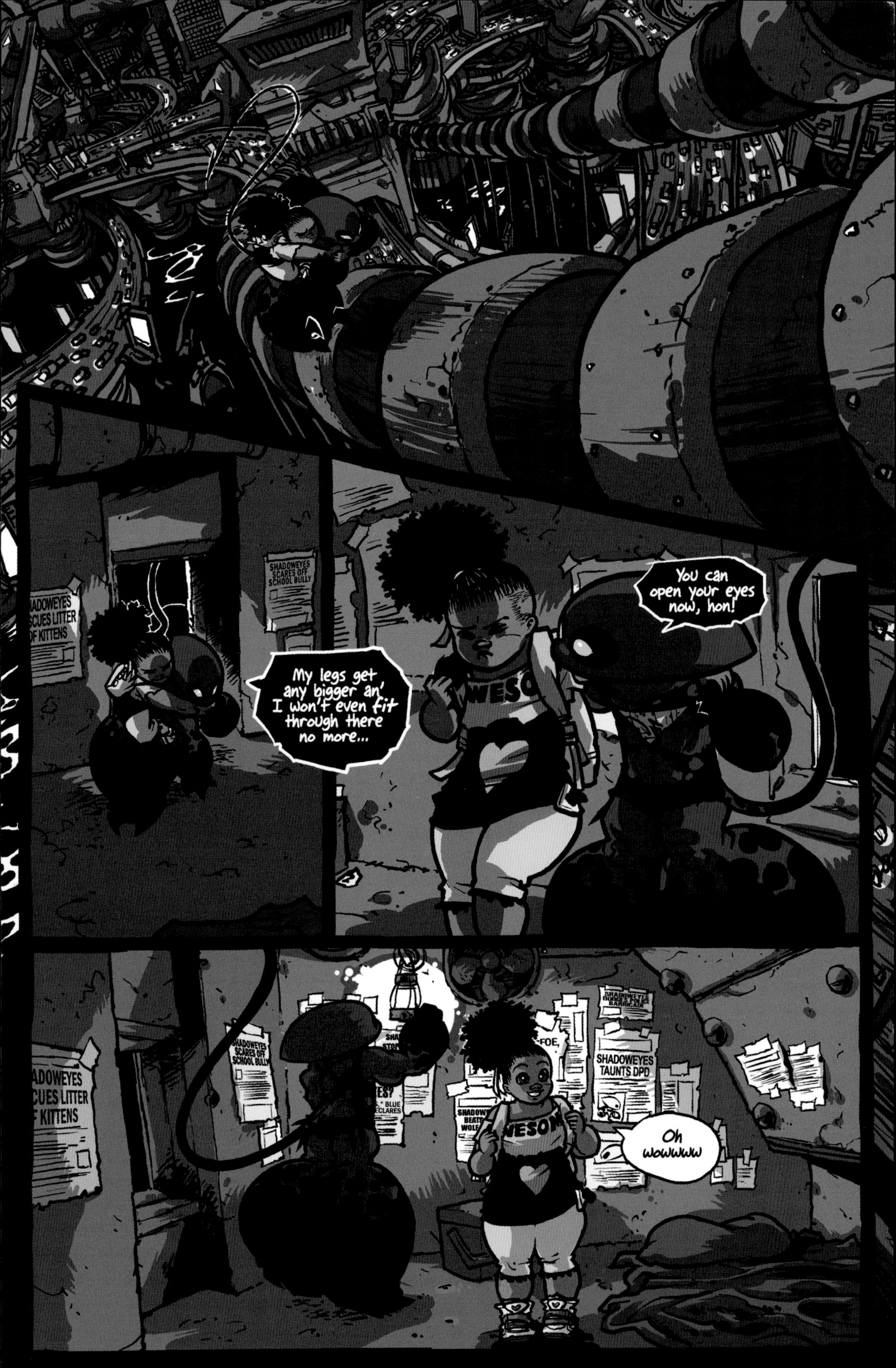
SHADOWEYES SCARES OFF SCHOOL BULLY
My legs get any bigger an' I won't even fit through there no more...
You can open your eyes now, hon!
SHADOWEYES TAUNTS DPD
Oh wowwww

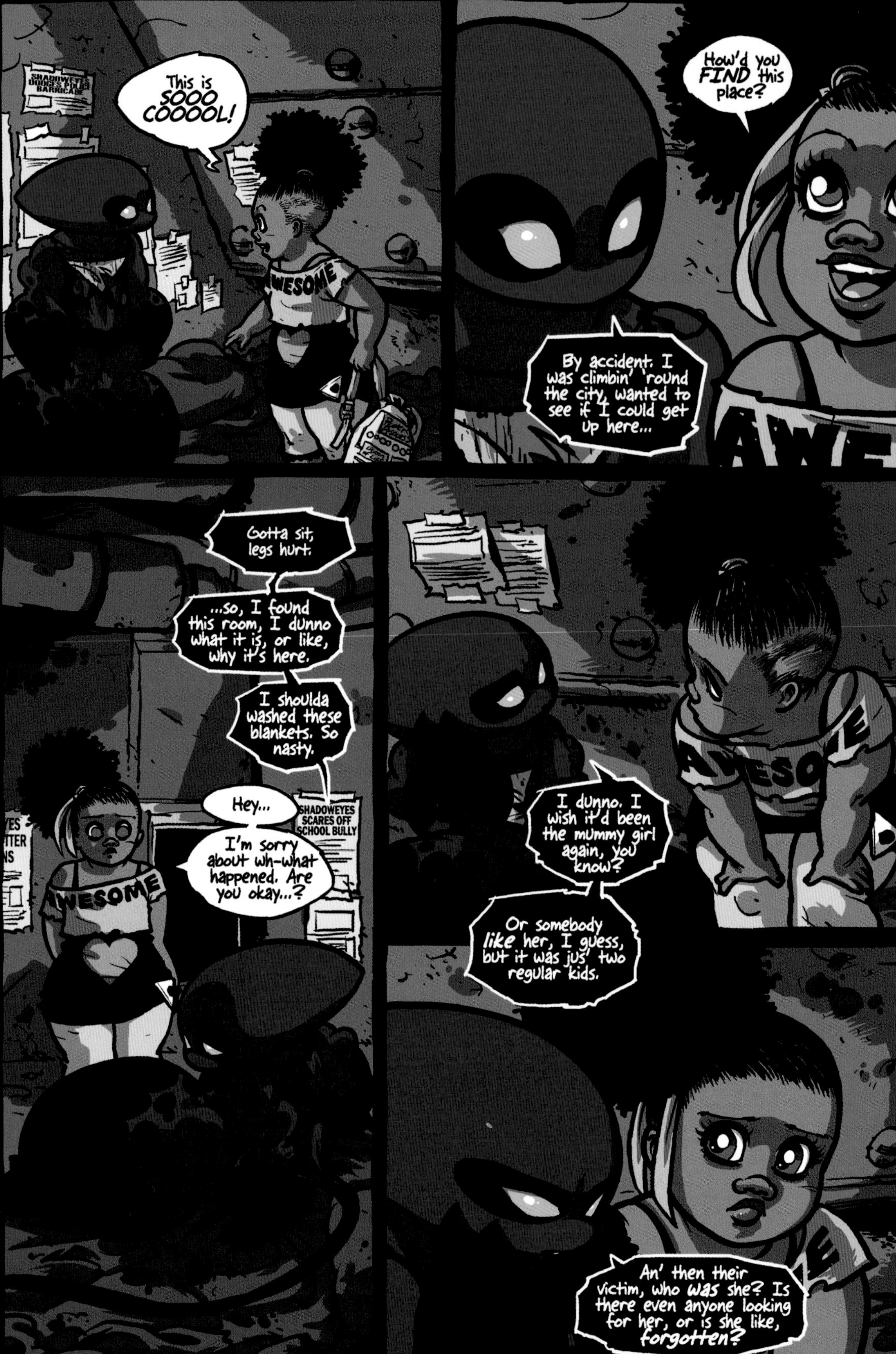
SHADOWEYES DODGES POLICE BARRICADE
This is SOOO COOOOL!
AWESOME
How'd you FIND this place?
By accident. I was climbin' 'round the city, wanted to see if I could get up here...
Gotta sit, legs hurt.
...so, I found this room, I dunno what it is, or like, why it's here.
I shoulda washed these blankets. So nasty.
SHADOWEYES SCARES OFF SCHOOL BULLY
Hey...
I'm sorry about wh-what happened. Are you okay...?
I dunno. I wish it'd been the mummy girl again, you know?
Or somebody like her, I guess, but it was jus' two regular kids.
An' then their victim, who was she? Is there even anyone looking for her, or is she like, forgotten?

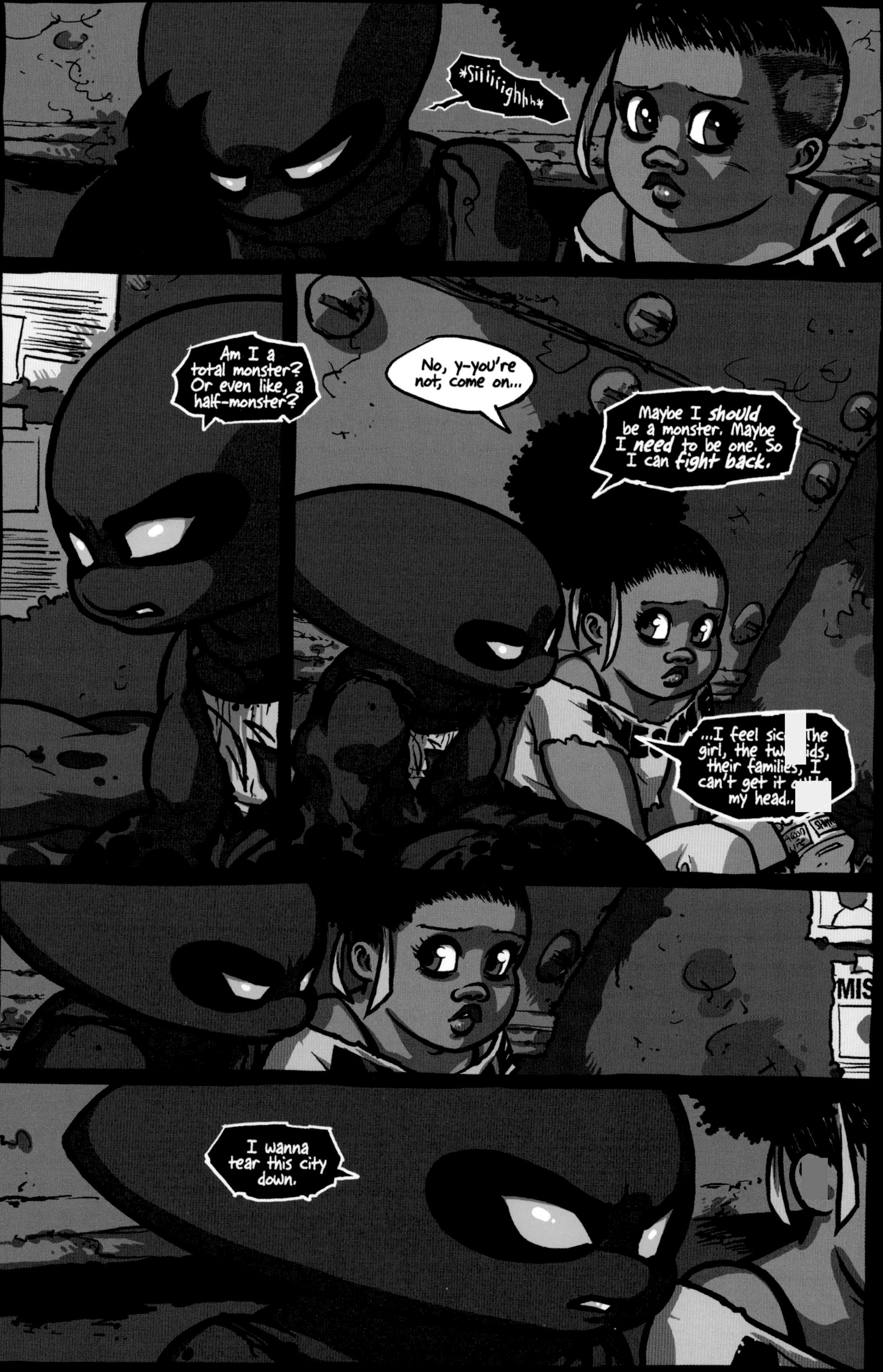
Siiiiighhh
Am I a total monster? Or even like, a half-monster?
No, y-you're not, come on...
Maybe I should be a monster. Maybe I need to be one. So I can fight back.
...I feel sic The girl, the tw ids, their families, I can't get it my head..
I wanna tear this city down.

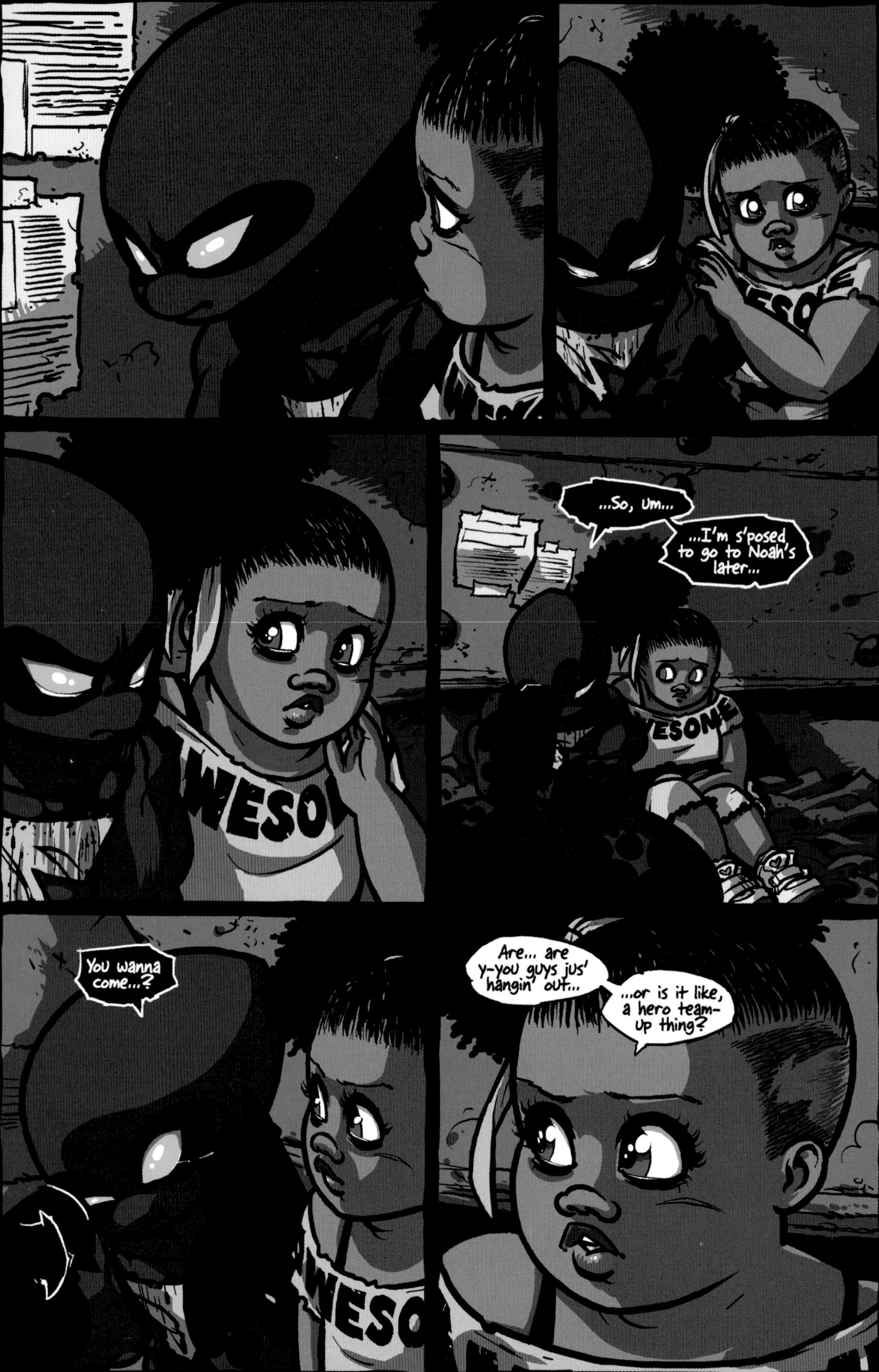
...So, um...
...I'm s'posed to go to Noah's later...
You wanna come...?
Are... are y-you guys jus' hangin' out...
...or is it like, a hero team-up thing?

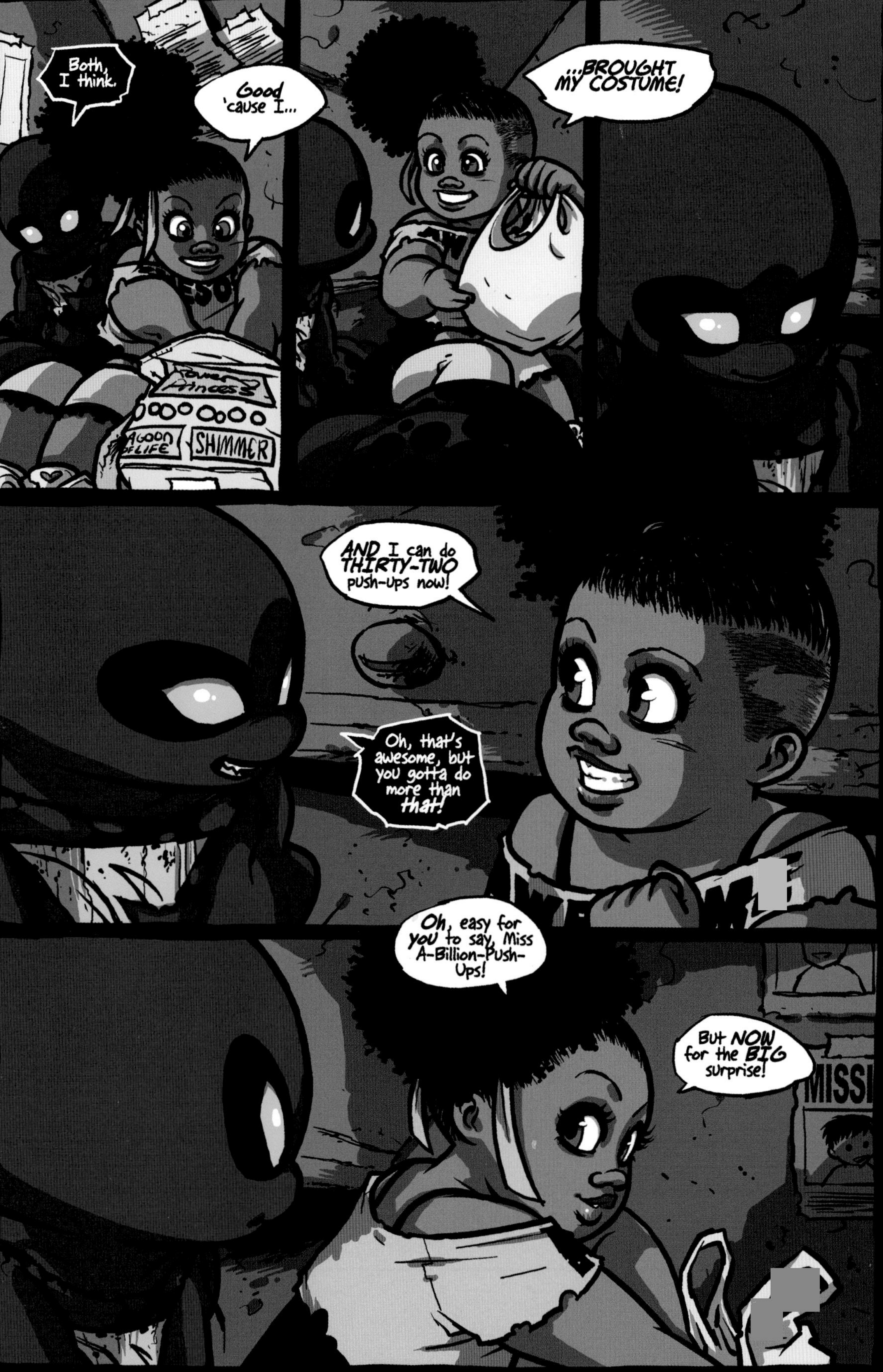

Both, I think.
Good 'cause I...
...BROUGHT MY COSTUME!
Power Princess
LAGOON OF LIFE
SHIMMER
AND I can do THIRTY-TWO push-ups now!
Oh, that's awesome, but you gotta do more than that!
Oh, easy for YOU to say, Miss A-Billion-Push-Ups!
But NOW for the BIG surprise!
MISSI

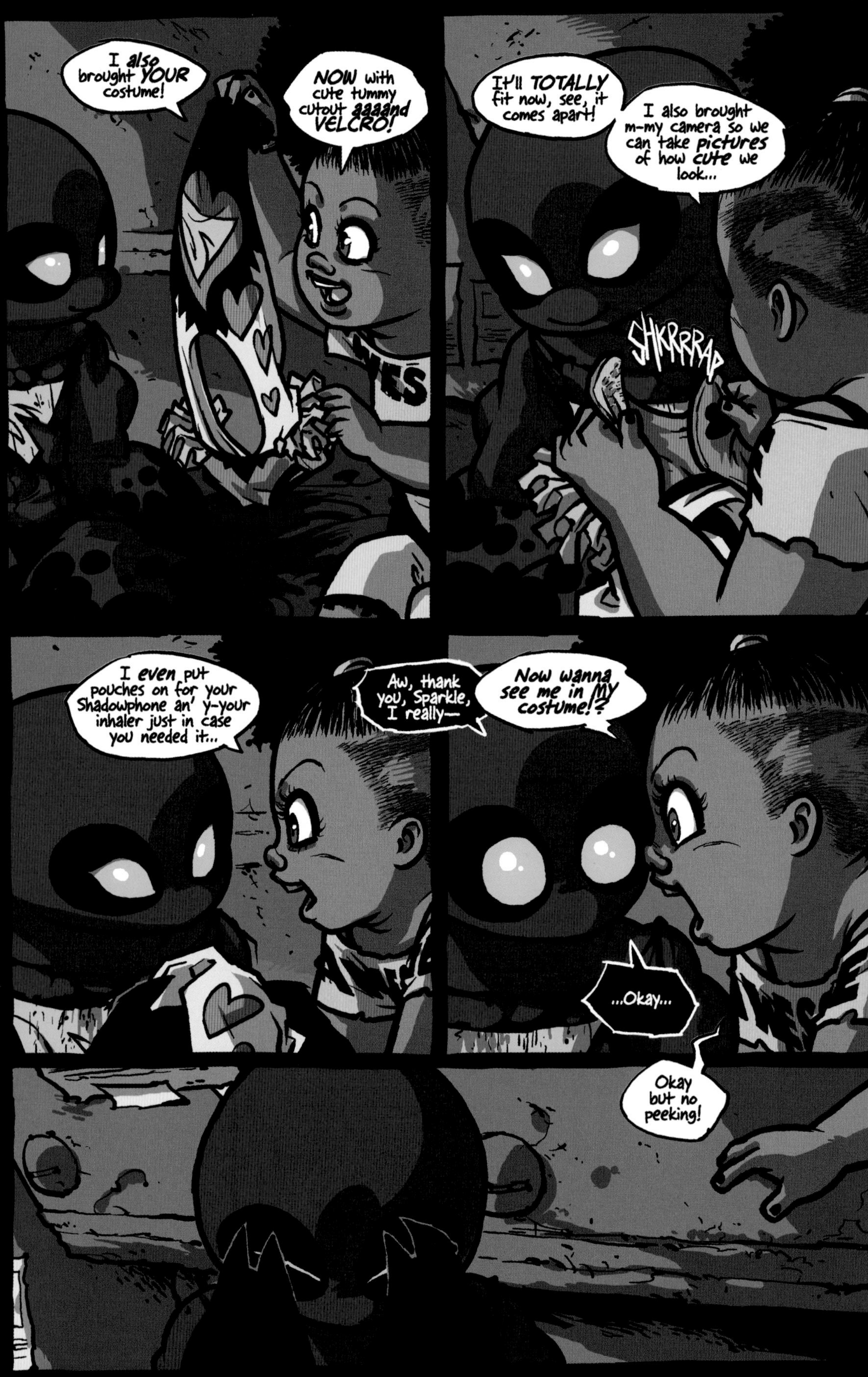

I also brought YOUR costume!
NOW with cute tummy cutout aaaand VELCRO!
It'll TOTALLY fit now, see, it comes apart!
I also brought m-my camera so we can take pictures of how cute we look...
SHKRRRAP
I even put pouches on for your Shadowphone an' y-your inhaler just in case you needed it...
Aw, thank you, Sparkle, I really—
Now wanna see me in MY costume!?
...Okay...
Okay but no peeking!

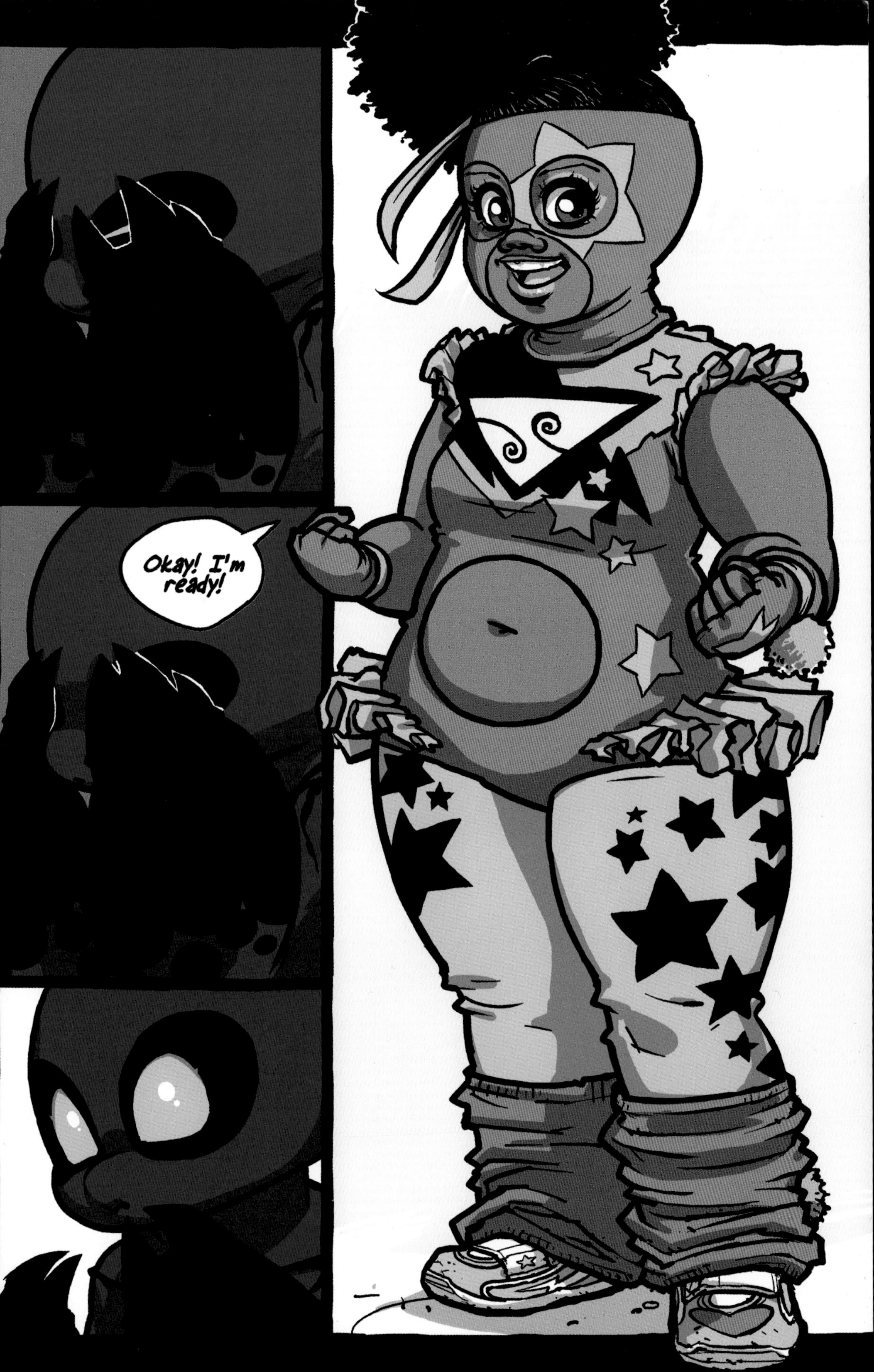
Okay! I'm ready!

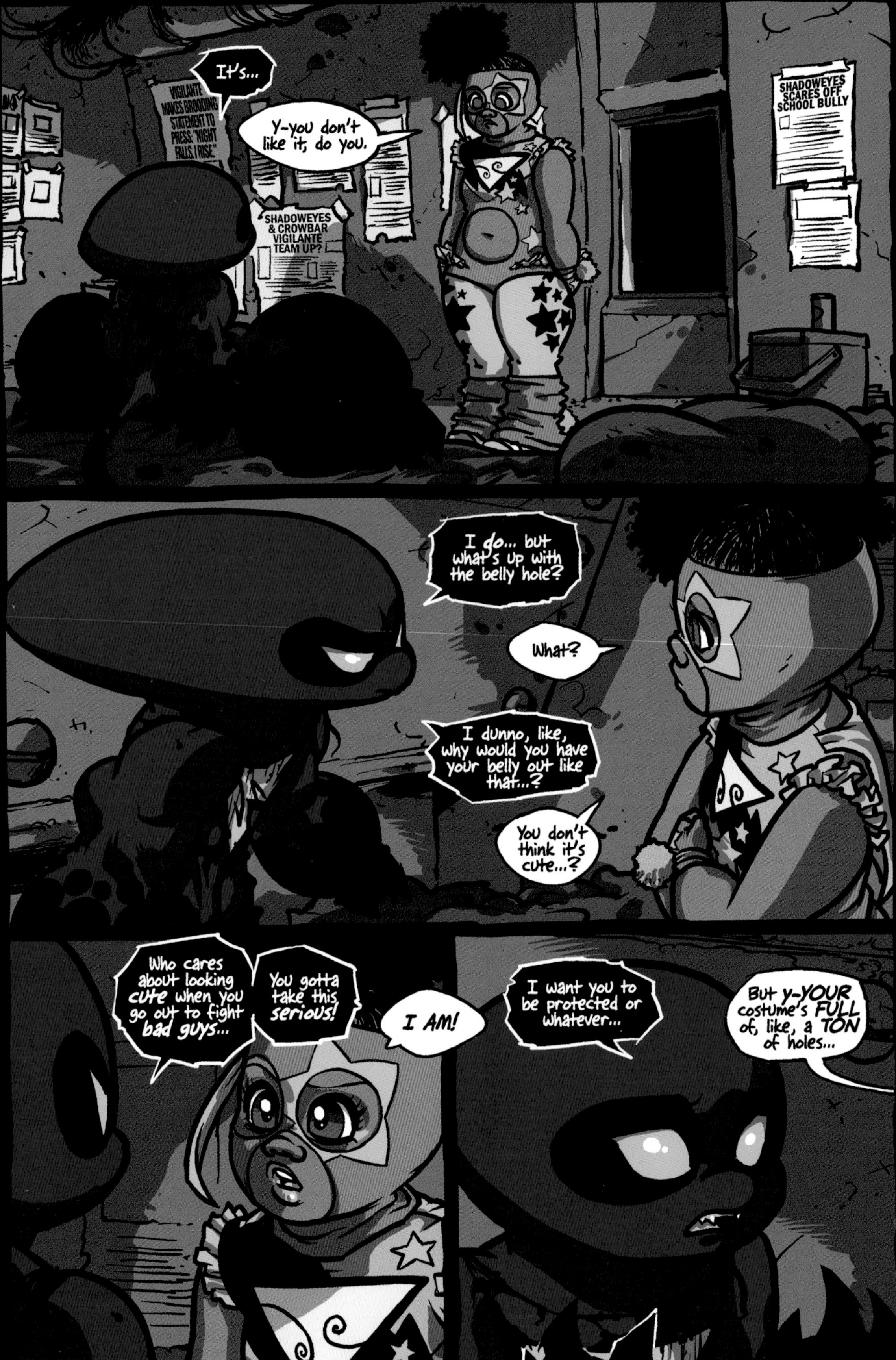

VIGILANTE MAKES BROODING STATEMENT TO PRESS: "NIGHT FALLS, I RISE."
SHADOWEYES & CROWBAR VIGILANTE TEAM UP?
SHADOWEYES SCARES OFF SCHOOL BULLY
It's...
Y-you don't like it, do you.
I do... but what's up with the belly hole?
What?
I dunno, like, why would you have your belly out like that...?
You don't think it's cute...?
Who cares about looking cute when you go out to fight bad guys...
You gotta take this serious!
I AM!
I want you to be protected or whatever...
But y-YOUR costume's FULL of, like, a TON of holes...

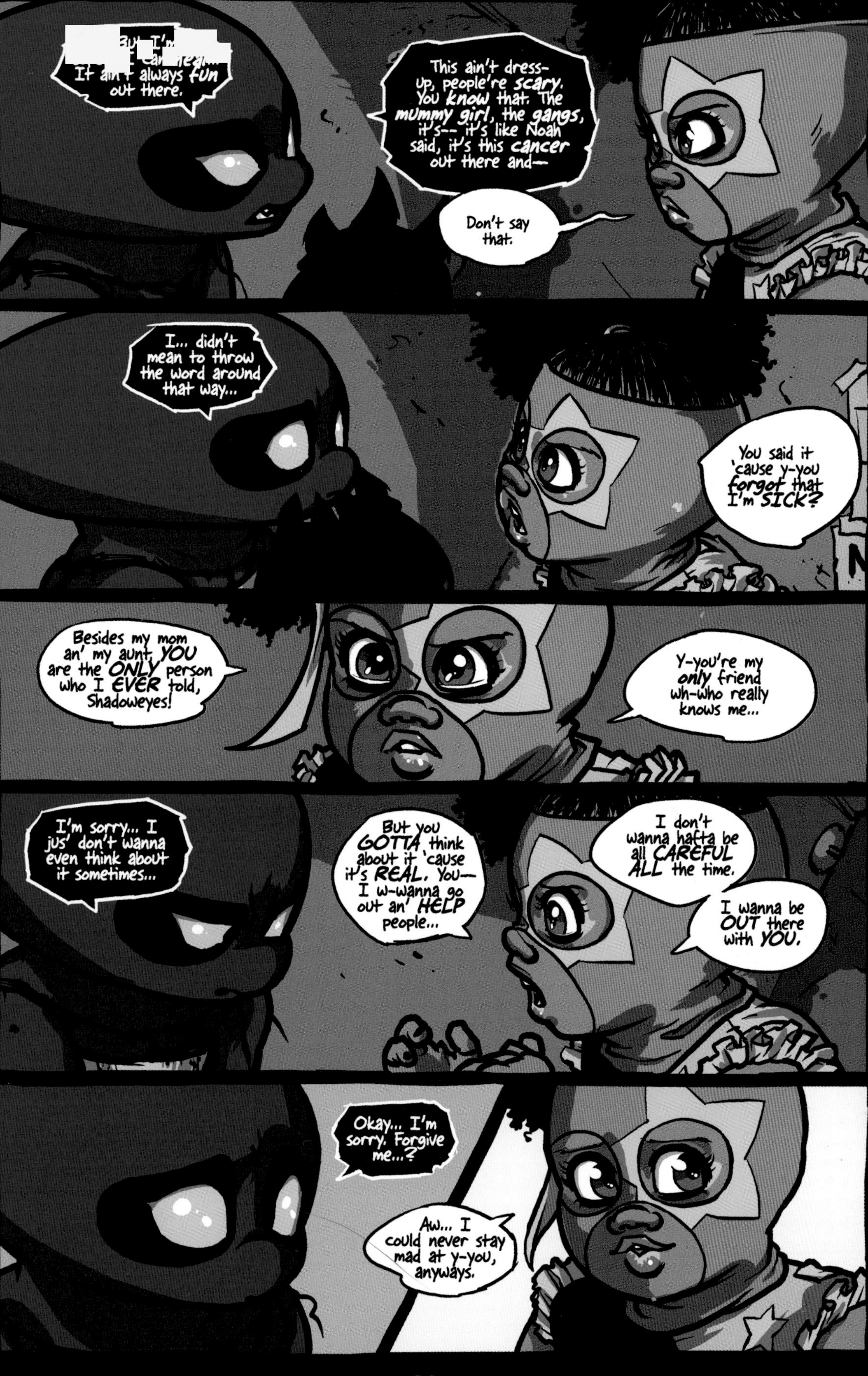
It ain't always fun out there.
This ain't dress-up, people're scary. You know that. The mummy girl, the gangs, it's-- it's like Noah said, it's this cancer out there and—
Don't say that.
I... didn't mean to throw the word around that way...
You said it 'cause y-you forgot that I'm SICK?
Besides my mom an' my aunt, YOU are the ONLY person who I EVER told, Shadoweyes!
Y-you're my only friend wh-who really knows me...
I'm sorry... I jus' don't wanna even think about it sometimes...
But you GOTTA think about it 'cause it's REAL. You— I w-wanna go out an' HELP people...
I don't wanna hafta be all CAREFUL ALL the time.
I wanna be OUT there with YOU.
Okay... I'm sorry. Forgive me...?
Aw... I could never stay mad at y-you, anyways.

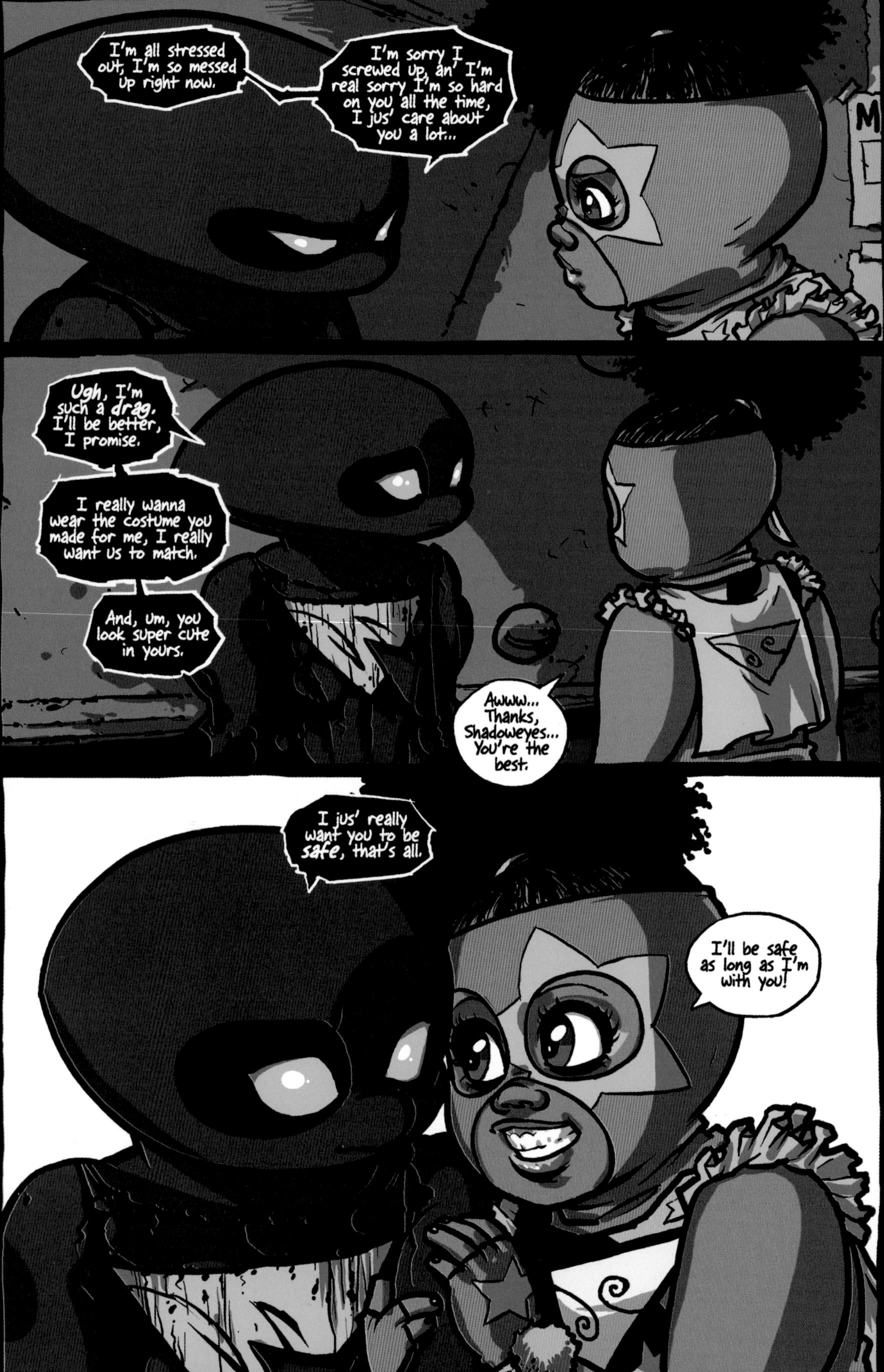

I'm all stressed out, I'm so messed up right now.
I'm sorry I screwed up, an' I'm real sorry I'm so hard on you all the time, I jus' care about you a lot...
Ugh, I'm such a *drag*. I'll be better, I promise.
I really wanna wear the costume you made for me, I really want us to match.
And, um, you look super cute in yours.
Awww... Thanks, Shadoweyes... You're the best.
I jus' really want you to be *safe*, that's all.
I'll be safe as long as I'm with you!

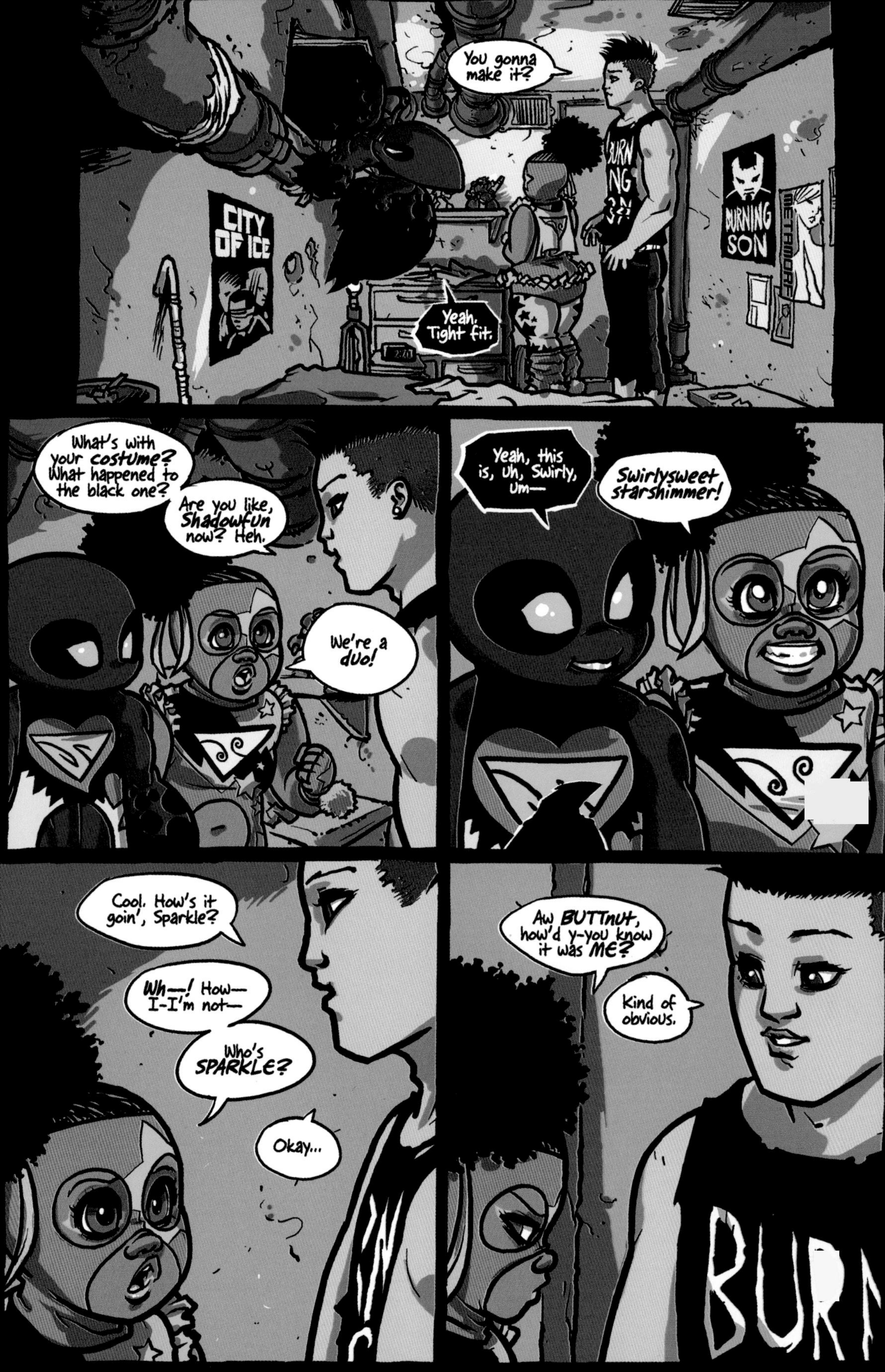

CITY OF ICE
BURNING SON
METAMORF
You gonna make it?
Yeah. Tight fit.
What's with your costume? What happened to the black one?
Are you like, Shadowfun now? Heh.
We're a duo!
Yeah, this is, uh, Swirly, Um—
Swirlysweet starshimmer!
Cool. How's it goin', Sparkle?
Wh—! How— I-I'm not—
Who's SPARKLE?
Okay...
Aw BUTTnut, how'd y-you know it was ME?
Kind of obvious.

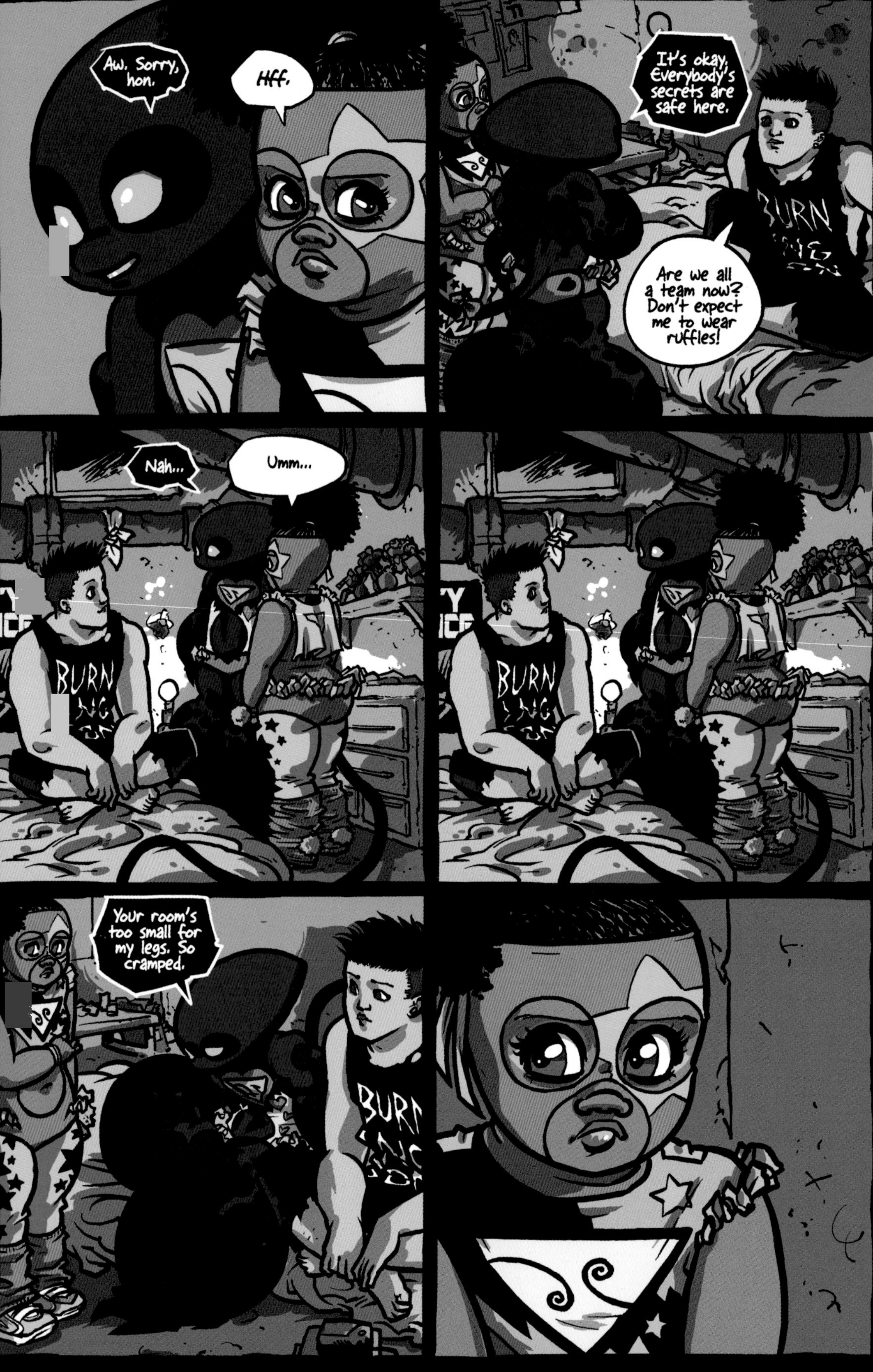
Aw. Sorry, hon.
Hff.
It's okay, Everybody's secrets are safe here.
Are we all a team now? Don't expect me to wear ruffles!
Nah...
Umm...
Your room's too small for my legs. So cramped.

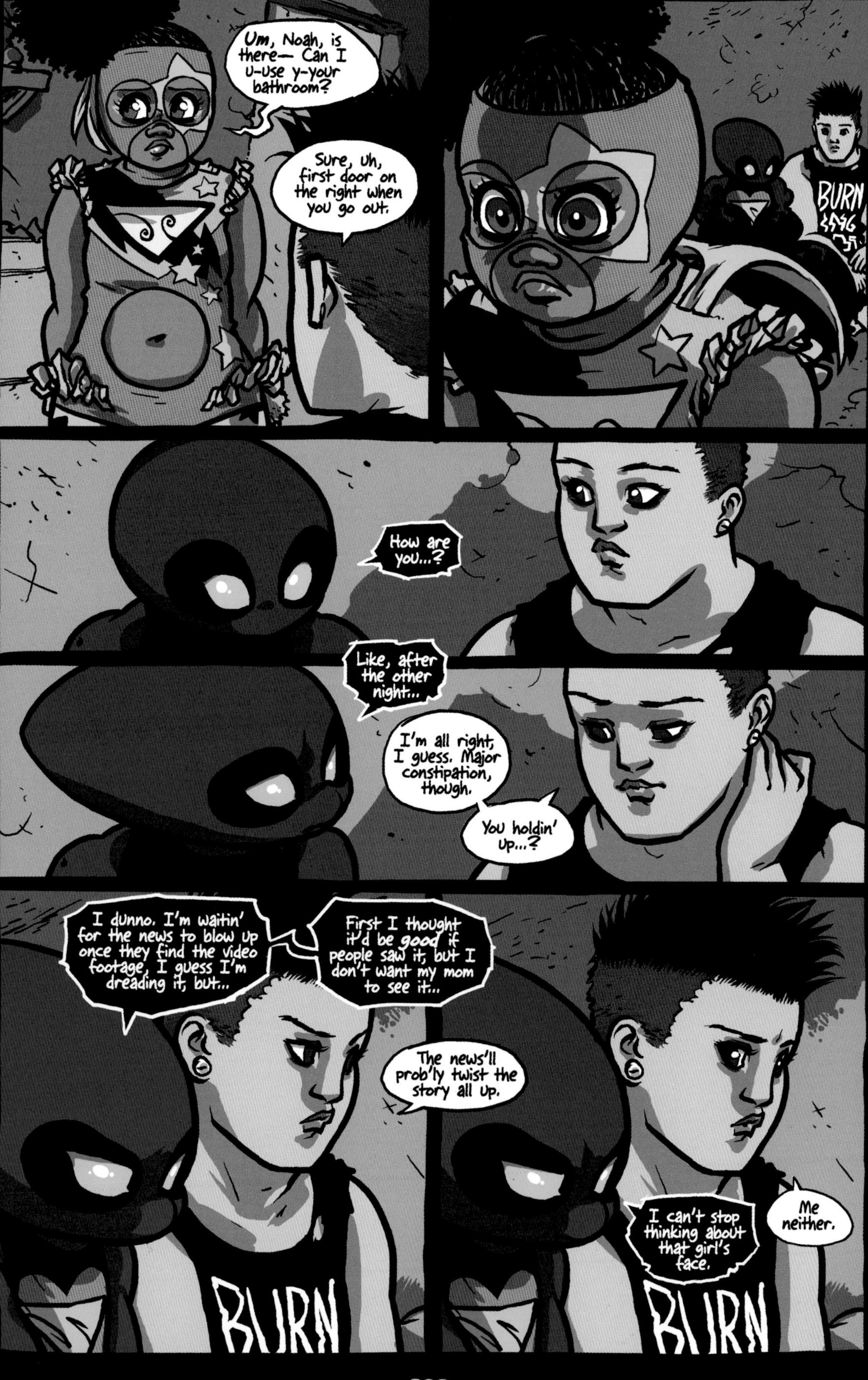

Um, Noah, is there— Can I u-use y-your bathroom?
Sure, uh, first door on the right when you go out.
BURN
How are you...?
Like, after the other night...
I'm all right, I guess. Major constipation, though.
You holdin' up...?
I dunno. I'm waitin' for the news to blow up once they find the video footage, I guess I'm dreading it, but...
First I thought it'd be *good* if people saw it, but I don't want my mom to see it...
The news'll prob'ly twist the story all up.
BURN
I can't stop thinking about that girl's face.
Me neither.
BURN

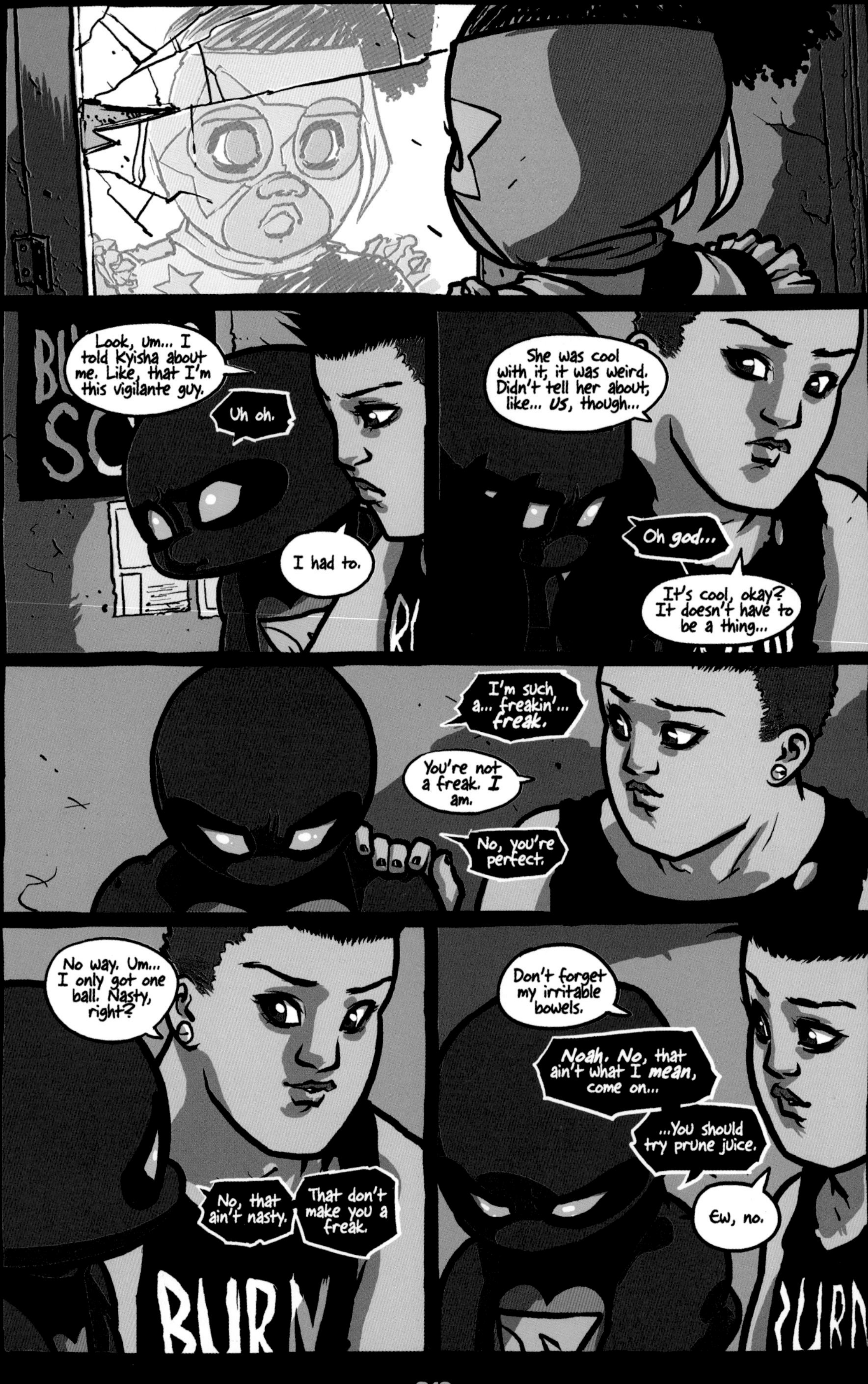
Look, um... I told Kyisha about me. Like, that I'm this vigilante guy.
Uh oh.
I had to.
She was cool with it, it was weird. Didn't tell her about, like... *US*, though...
Oh god...
It's cool, okay? It doesn't have to be a thing...
I'm such a... freakin'... *freak*.
You're not a freak. I am.
No, you're perfect.
No way. Um... I only got one ball. Nasty, right?
No, that ain't nasty.
That don't make you a freak.
Don't forget my irritable bowels.
Noah. No, that ain't what I *mean*, come on...
...You should try prune juice.
Ew, no.

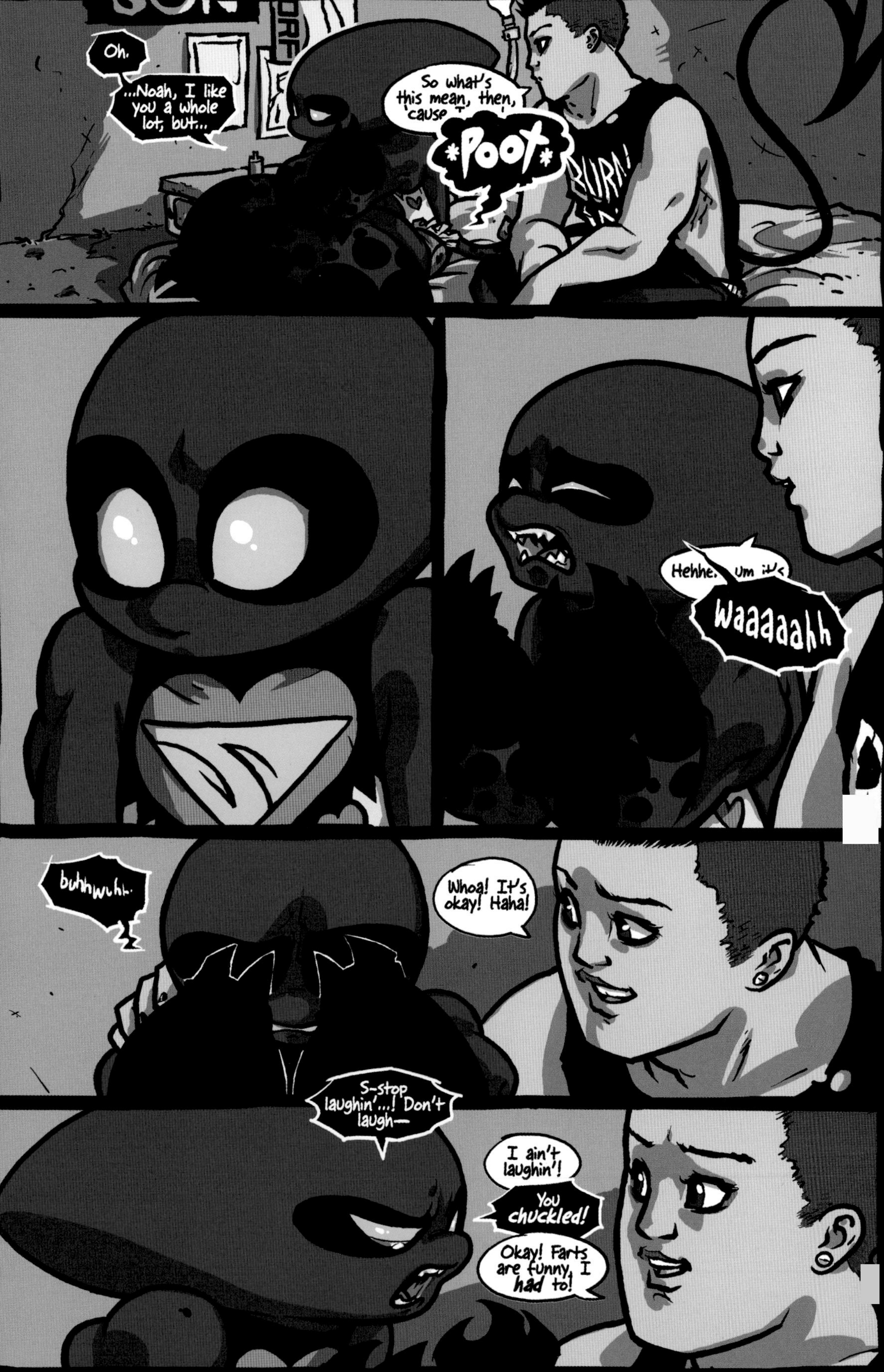
Oh.
...Noah, I like you a whole lot, but...
So what's this mean, then, cause
POOT
Hehhe. Um it's
waaaaahh
buhhwuh.
Whoa! It's okay! Haha!
S-stop laughin'...! Don't laugh—
I ain't laughin'!
You chuckled!
Okay! Farts are funny, I had to!

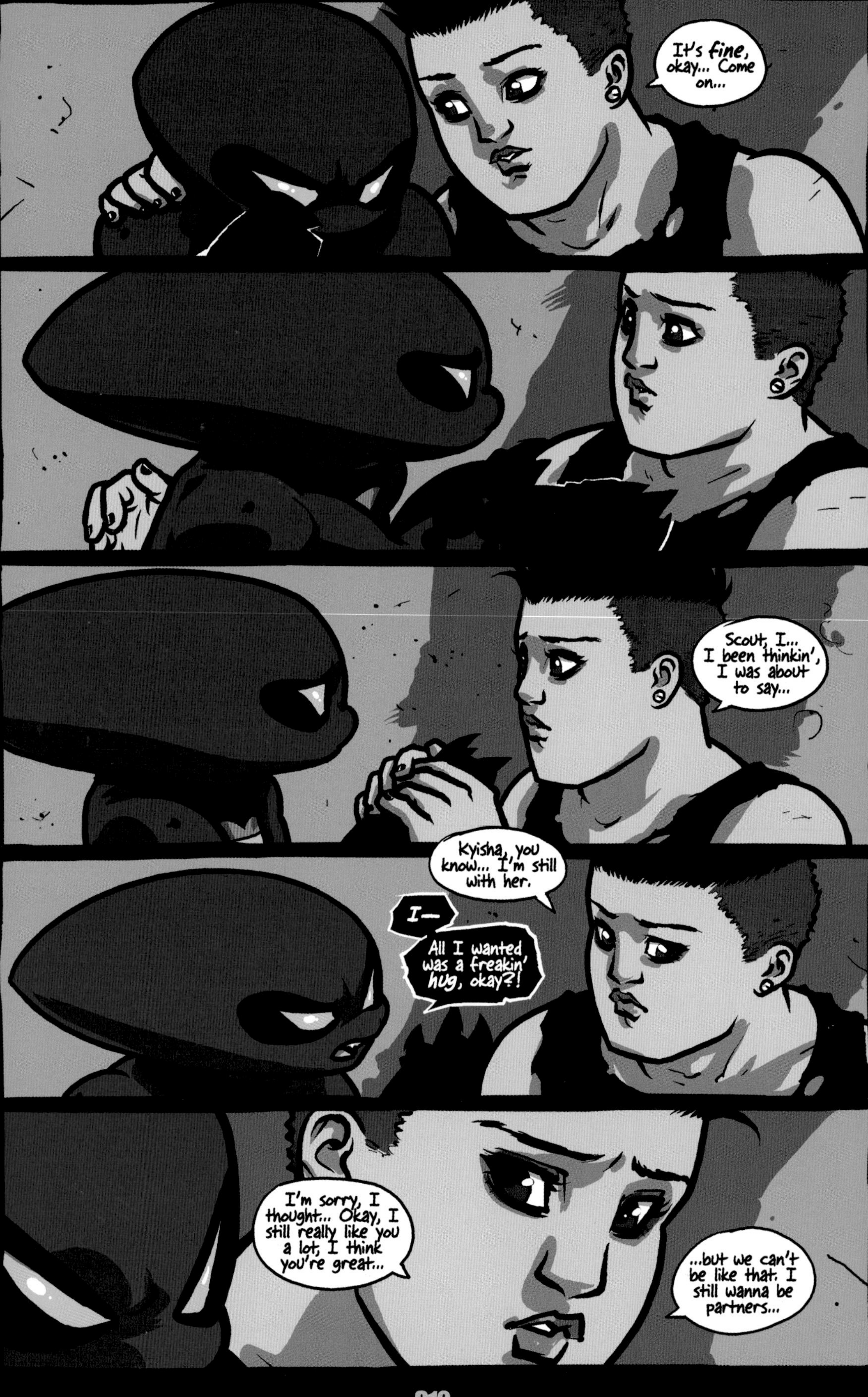
It's fine, okay... Come on...
Scout, I... I been thinkin', I was about to say...
Kyisha, you know... I'm still with her.
I—
All I wanted was a freakin' hug, okay?!
I'm sorry, I thought... Okay, I still really like you a lot, I think you're great...
...but we can't be like that. I still wanna be partners...

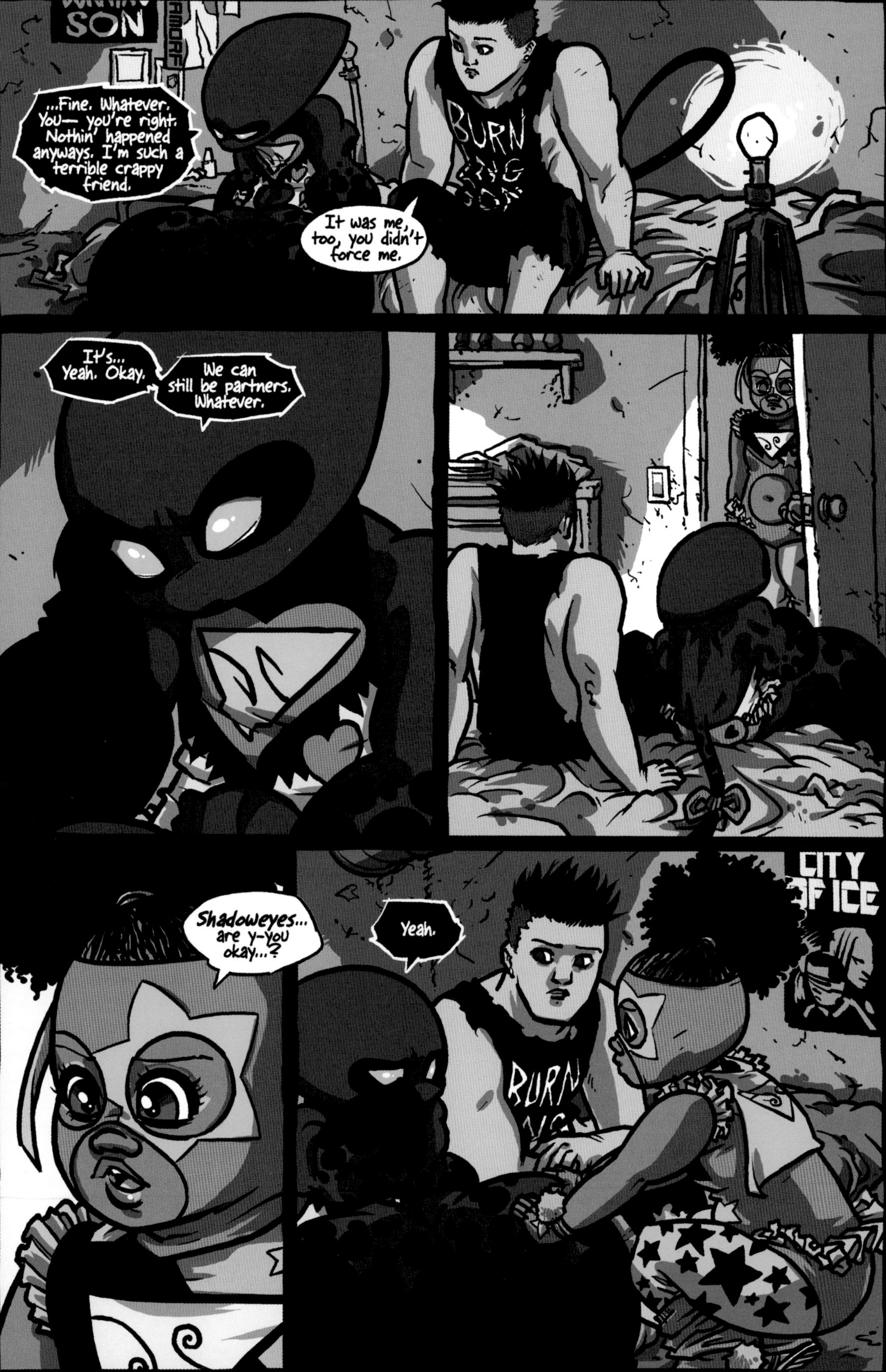
SON
...Fine. Whatever. You— you're right. Nothin' happened anyways. I'm such a terrible crappy friend.
BURN
It was me, too, you didn't force me.
It's... Yeah. Okay.
We can still be partners. Whatever.
CITY OF ICE
Shadoweyes... are y-you okay...?
Yeah.
BURN

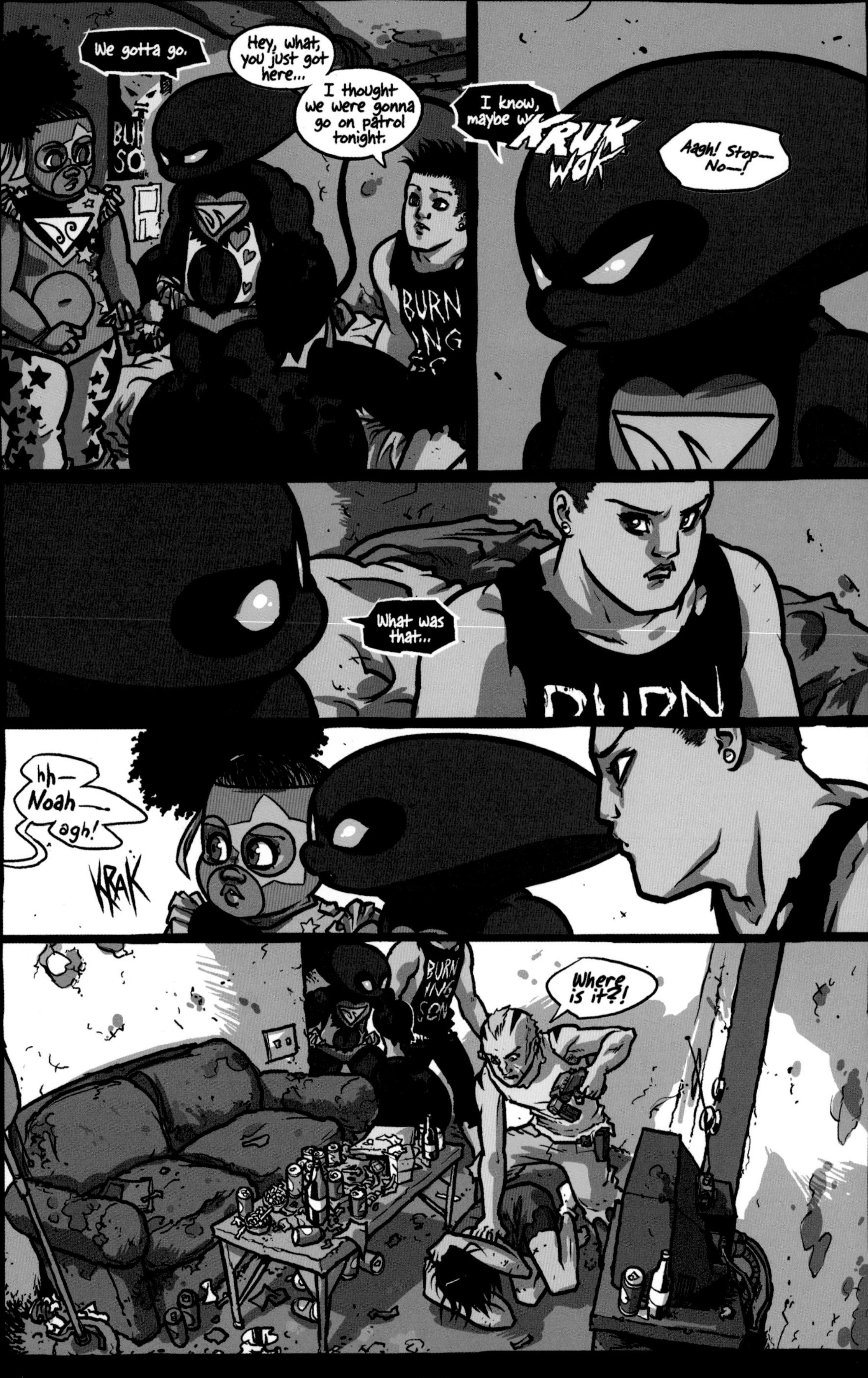
We gotta go.
Hey, what, you just got here...
I thought we were gonna go on patrol tonight.
I know, maybe w
KRUK
WOK
Aagh! Stop— No—!
What was that...
hh— Noah— agh!
KRAK
Where is it?!

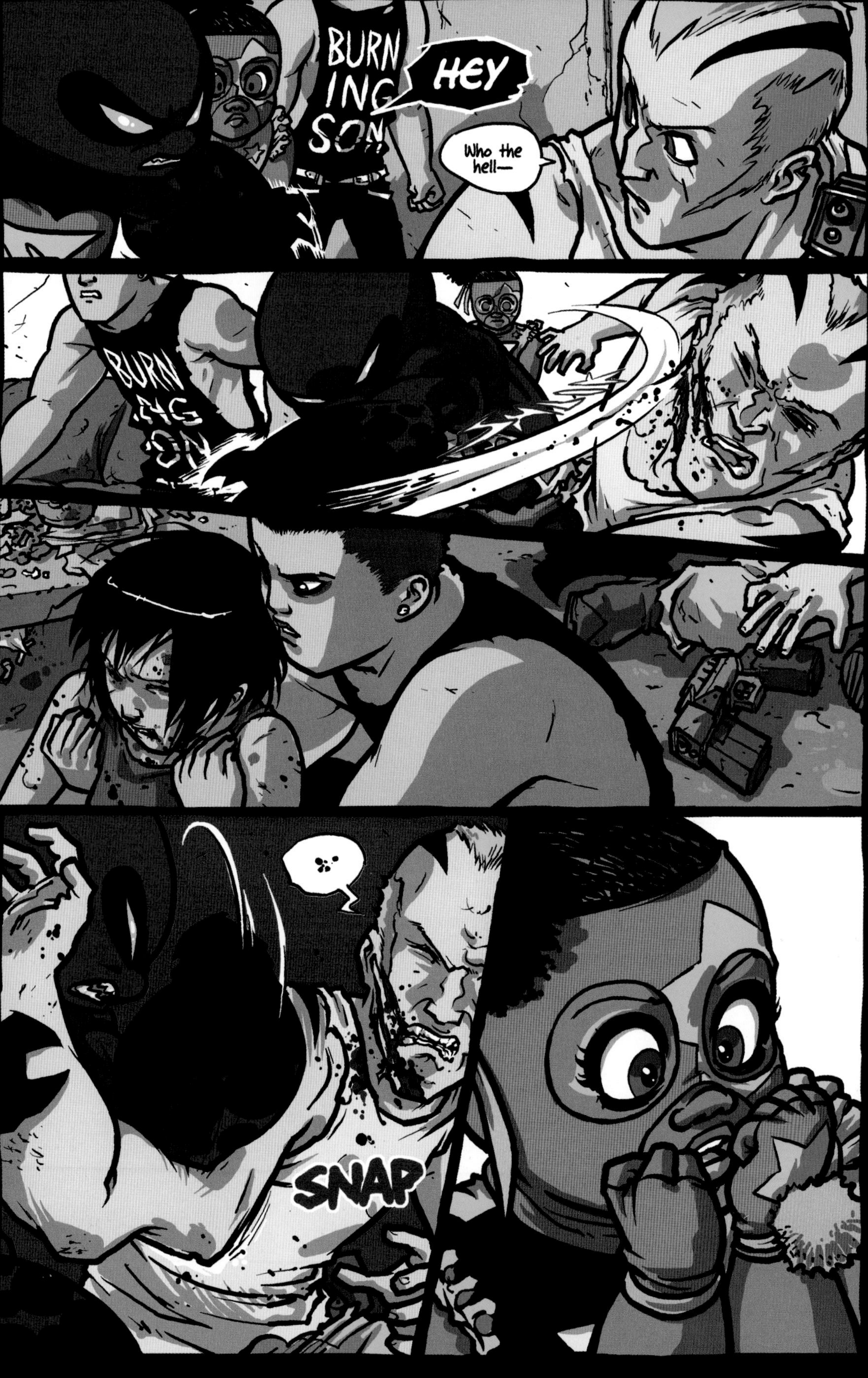
BURNING SON
HEY
Who the hell—
SNAP

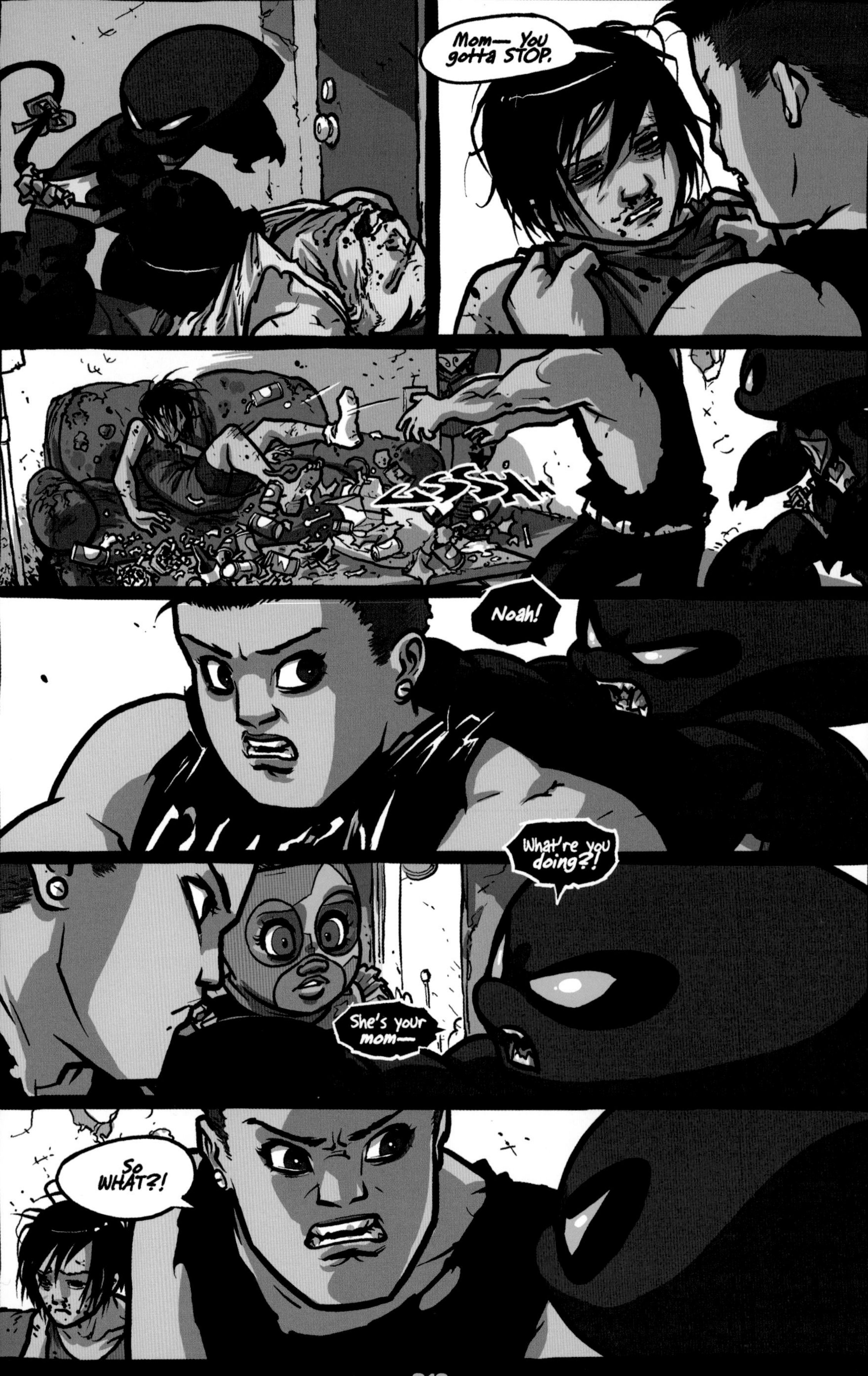
Mom— You gotta STOP.
Noah!
What're you doing?!
She's your mom—
So WHAT?!

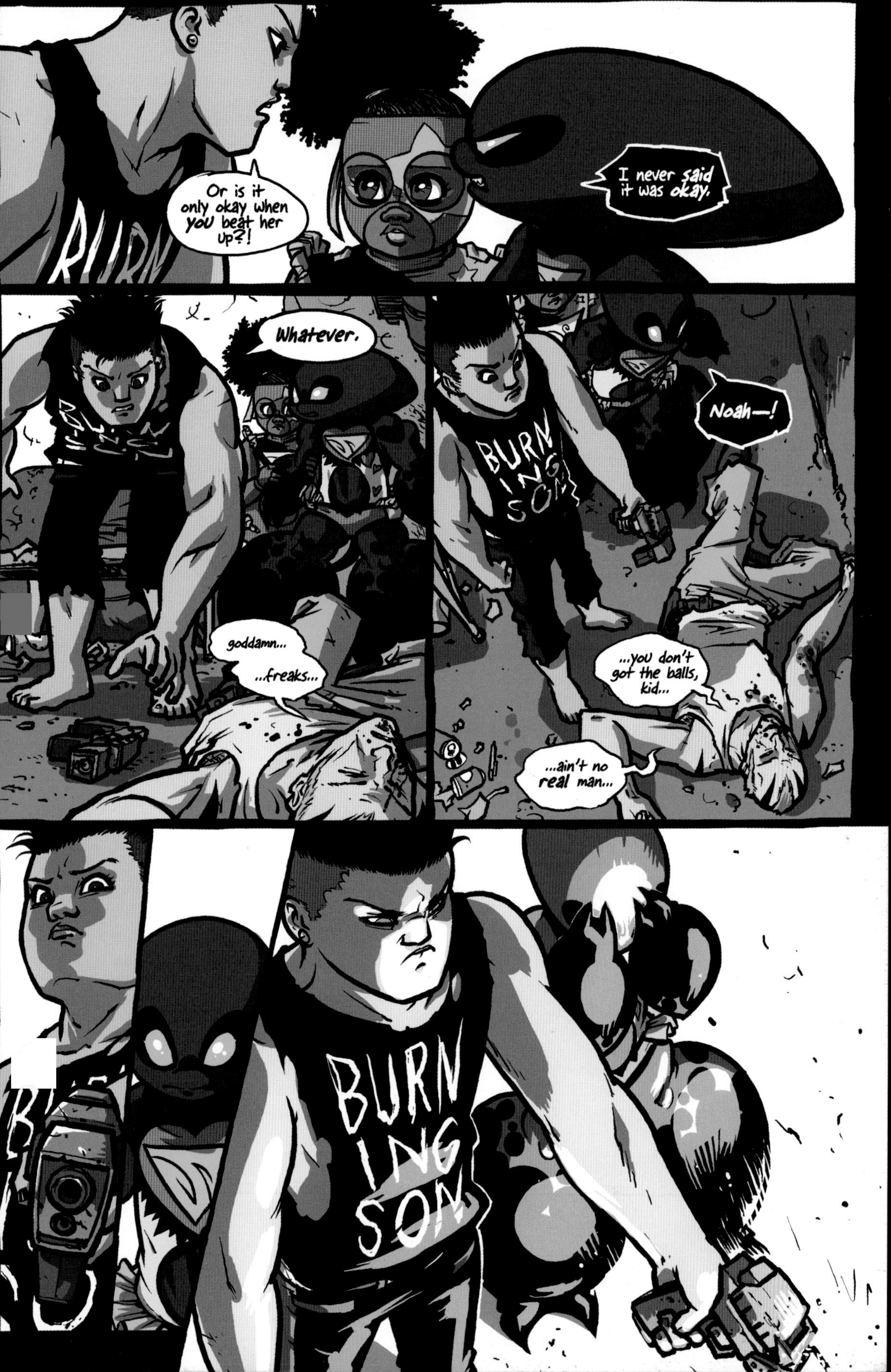
Or is it only okay when you beat her up?!
I never said it was okay.
Whatever.
goddamn...
...freaks...
Noah—!
...you don't got the balls, kid...
...ain't no real man...
BURN ING SON

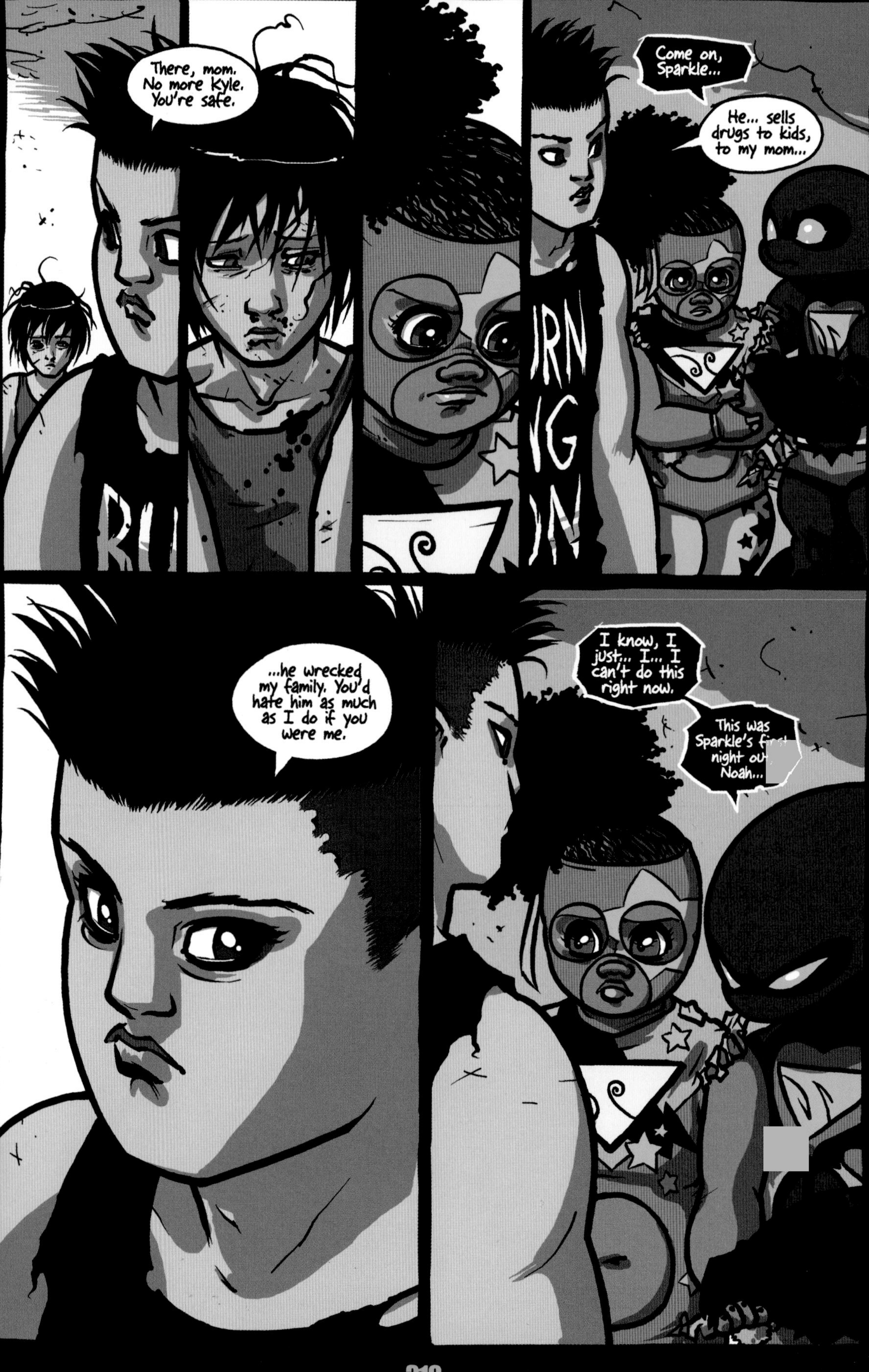
There, mom. No more Kyle. You're safe.
Come on, Sparkle...
He... sells drugs to kids, to my mom...
...he wrecked my family. You'd hate him as much as I do if you were me.
I know, I just... I... I can't do this right now.
This was Sparkle's first night out, Noah...

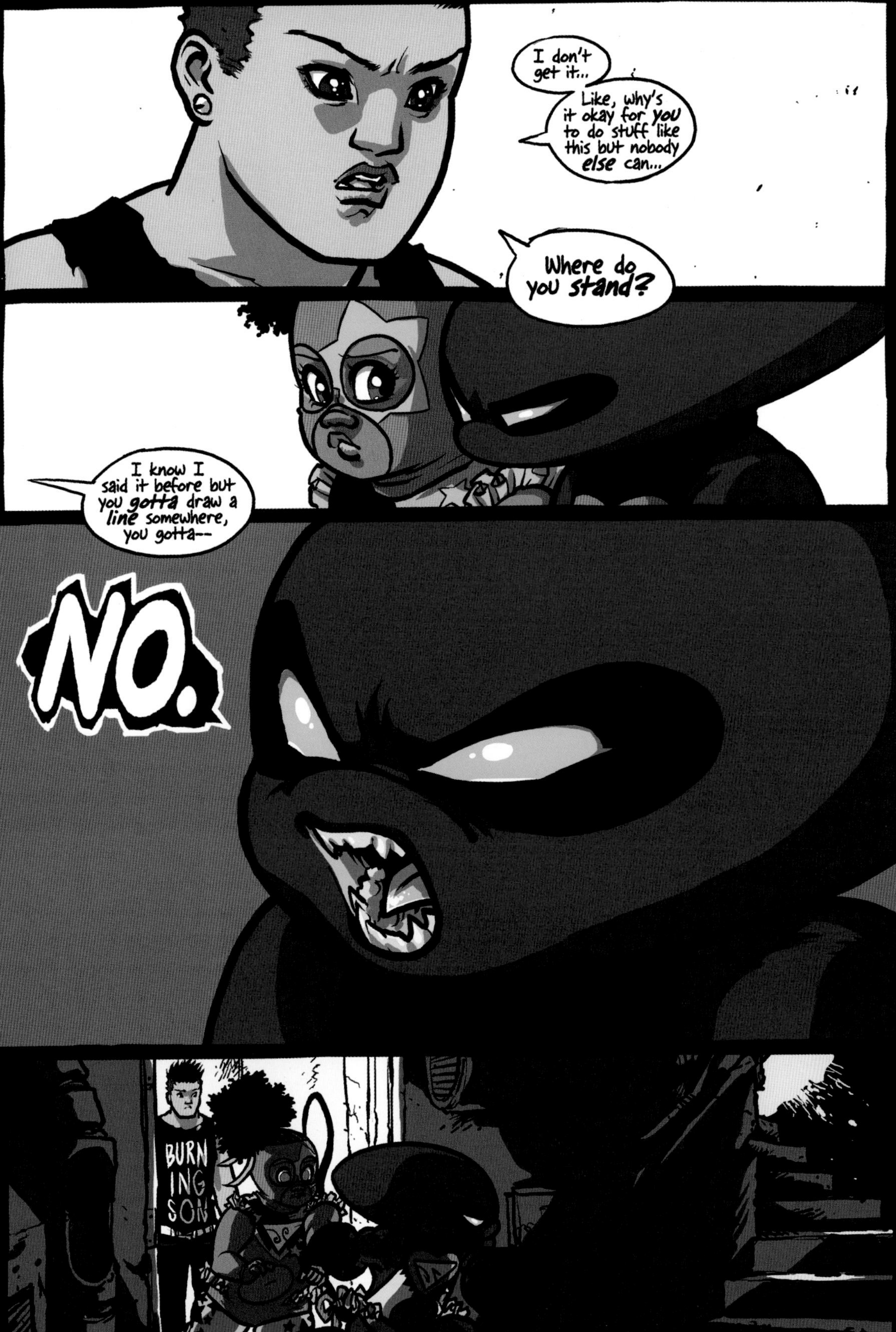
I don't get it...
Like, why's it okay for you to do stuff like this but nobody else can...
Where do you stand?
I know I said it before but you gotta draw a line somewhere, you gotta--
NO.
BURN ING SON

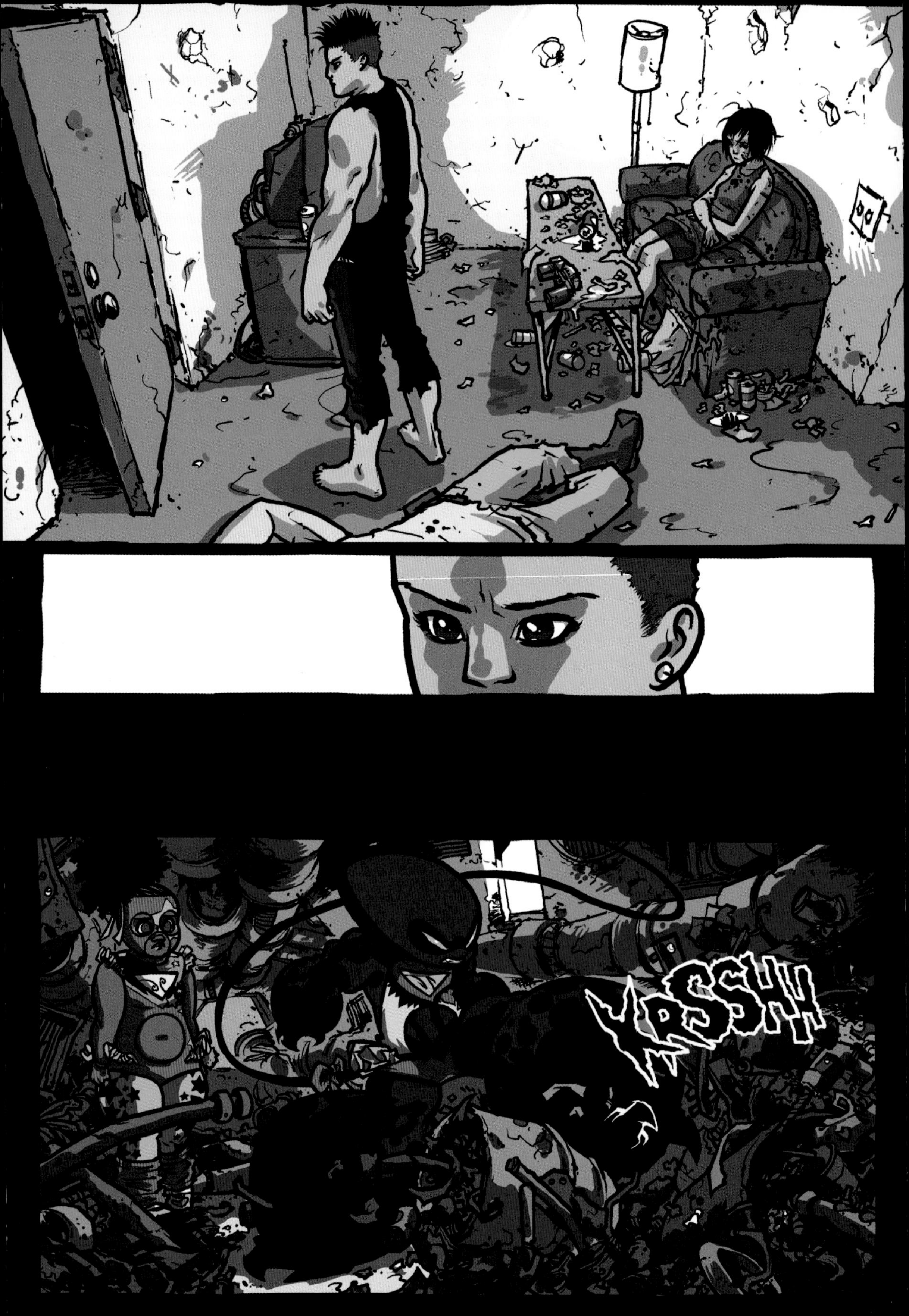
KRSSHH

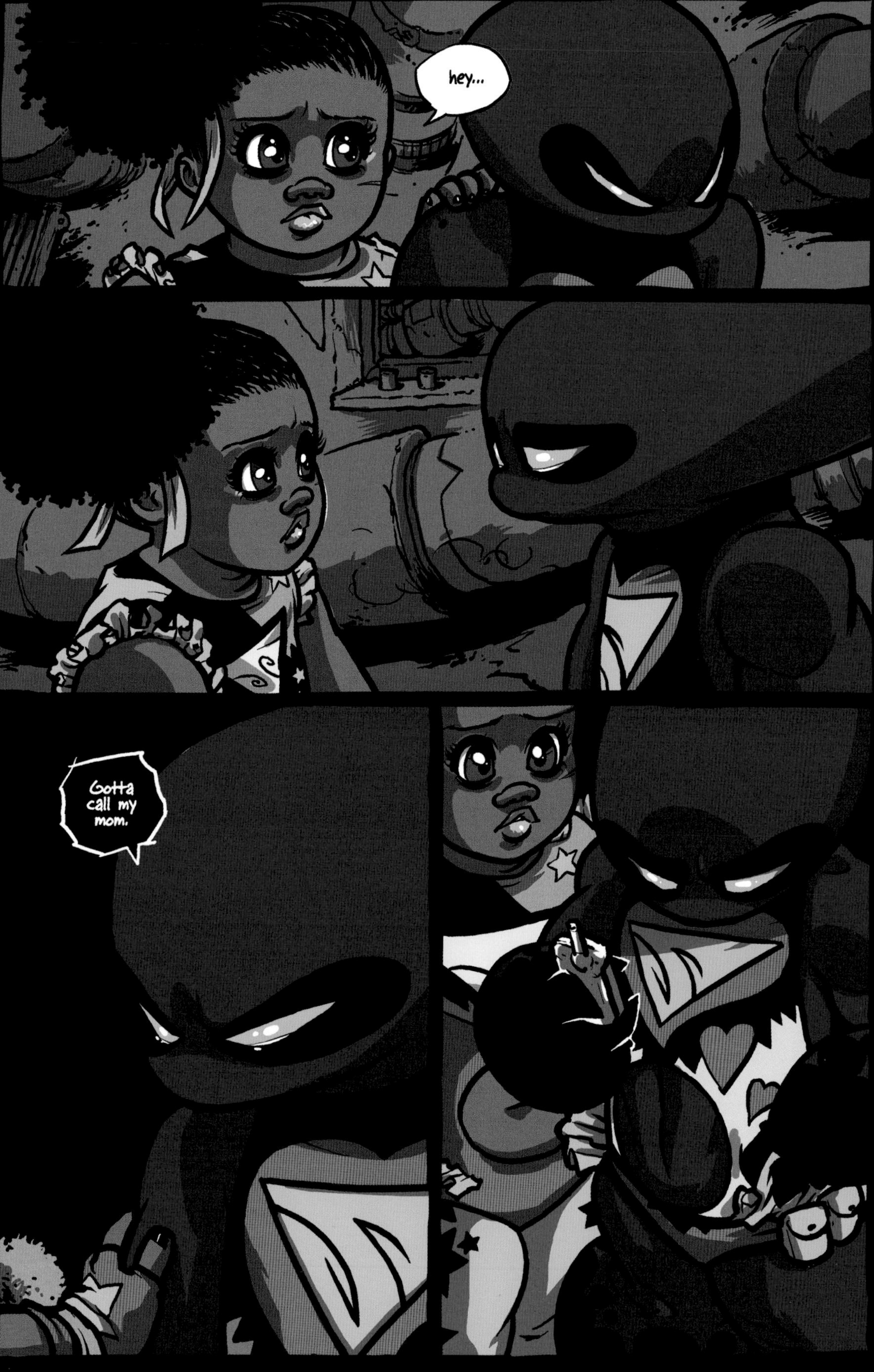
hey...
Gotta call my mom.

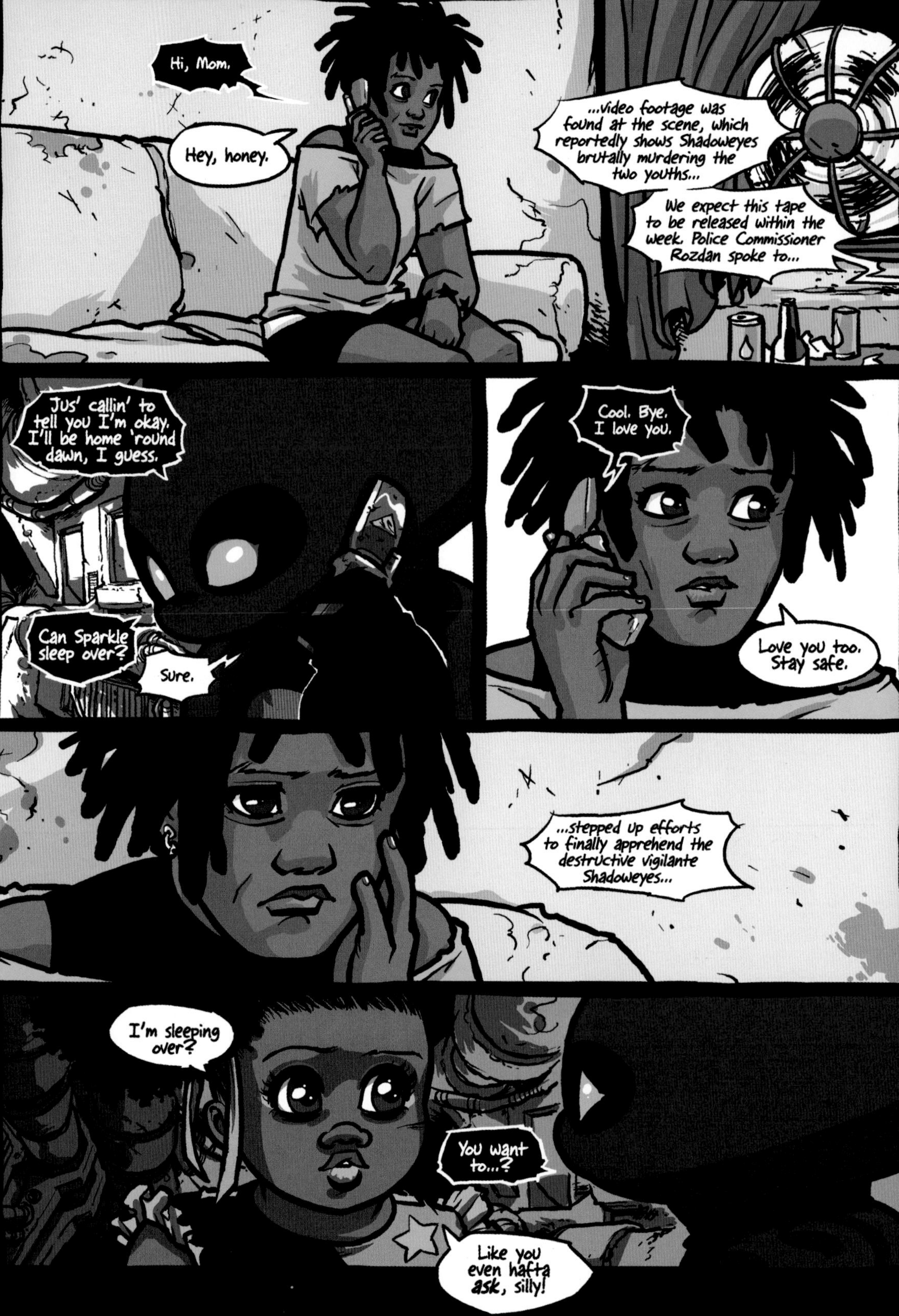
Hi, Mom.
Hey, honey.
...video footage was found at the scene, which reportedly shows Shadoweyes brutally murdering the two youths...
We expect this tape to be released within the week. Police Commissioner Rozdan spoke to...
Jus' callin' to tell you I'm okay. I'll be home 'round dawn, I guess.
Can Sparkle sleep over?
Sure.
Cool. Bye. I love you.
Love you too. Stay safe.
...stepped up efforts to finally apprehend the destructive vigilante Shadoweyes...
I'm sleeping over?
You want to...?
Like you even hafta ask, silly!

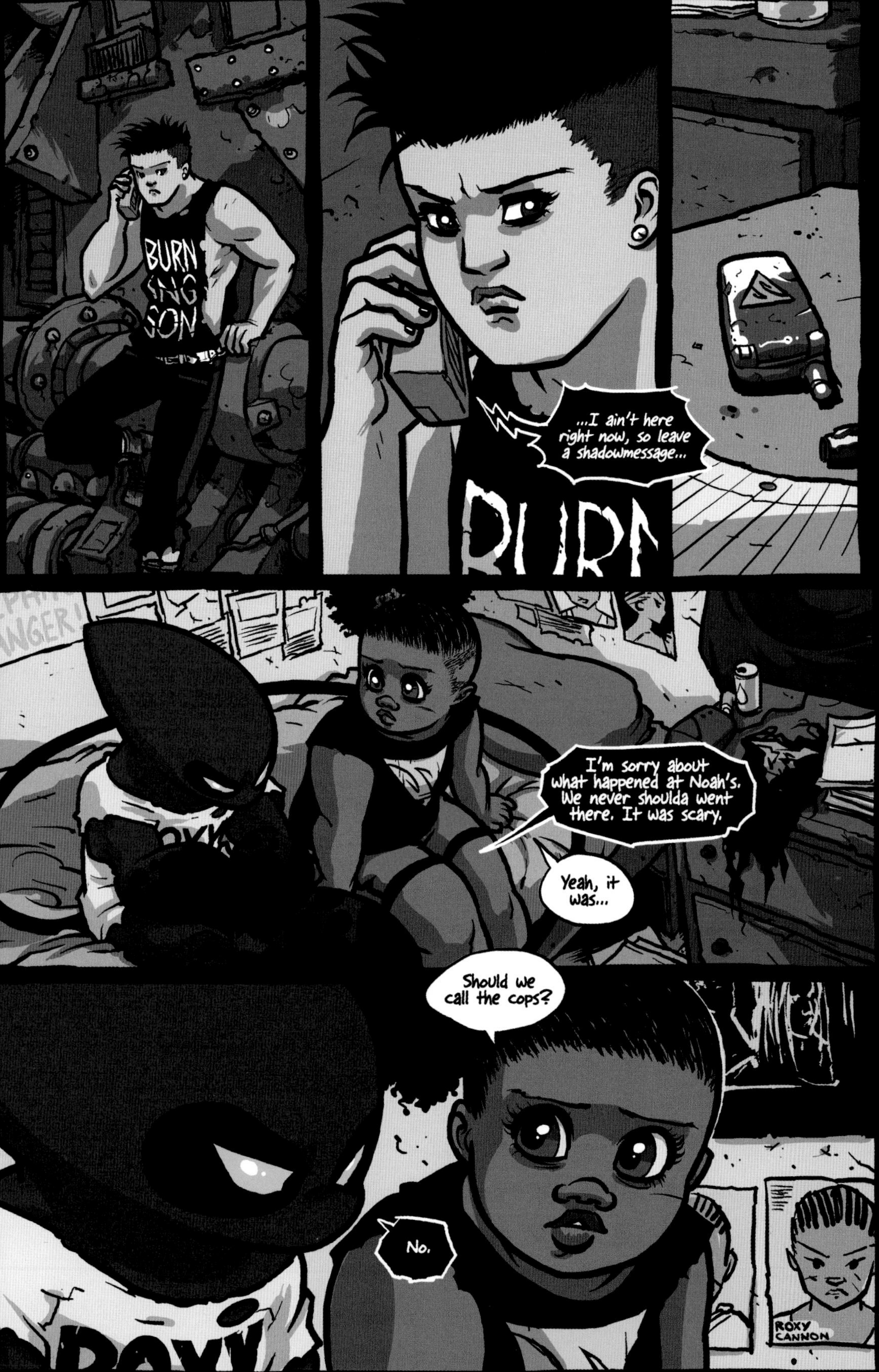
BURN SNGSON
...I ain't here right now, so leave a shadowmessage...
BURN
ANGER!
I'm sorry about what happened at Noah's. We never shoulda went there. It was scary.
Yeah, it was...
Should we call the cops?
No.
ROXY CANNON

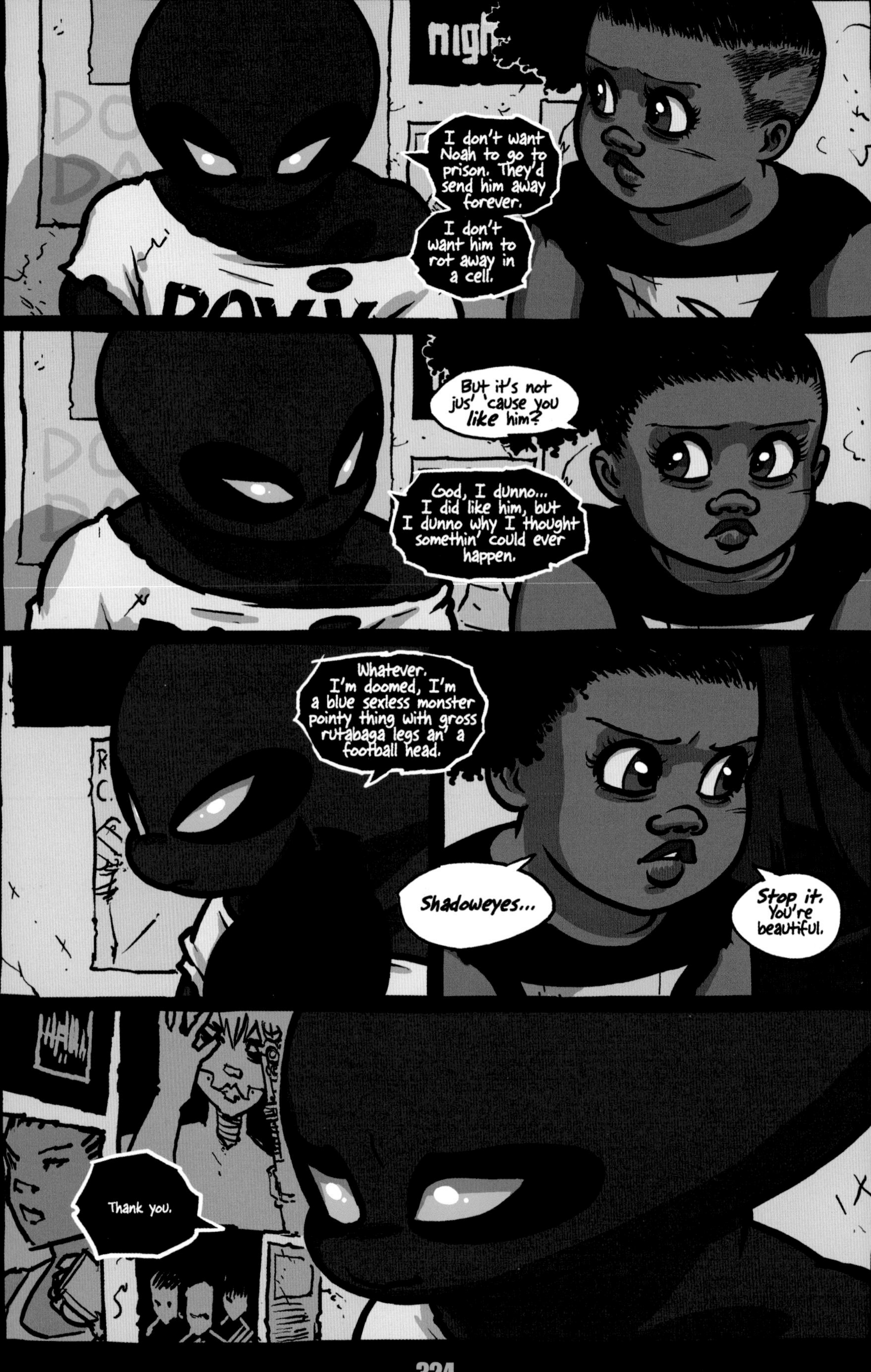
I don't want Noah to go to prison. They'd send him away forever.
I don't want him to rot away in a cell.
But it's not jus' 'cause you *like* him?
God, I dunno... I did like him, but I dunno why I thought somethin' could ever happen.
Whatever. I'm doomed, I'm a blue sexless monster pointy thing with gross rutabaga legs an' a football head.
Shadoweyes...
Stop it. You're beautiful.
Thank you.

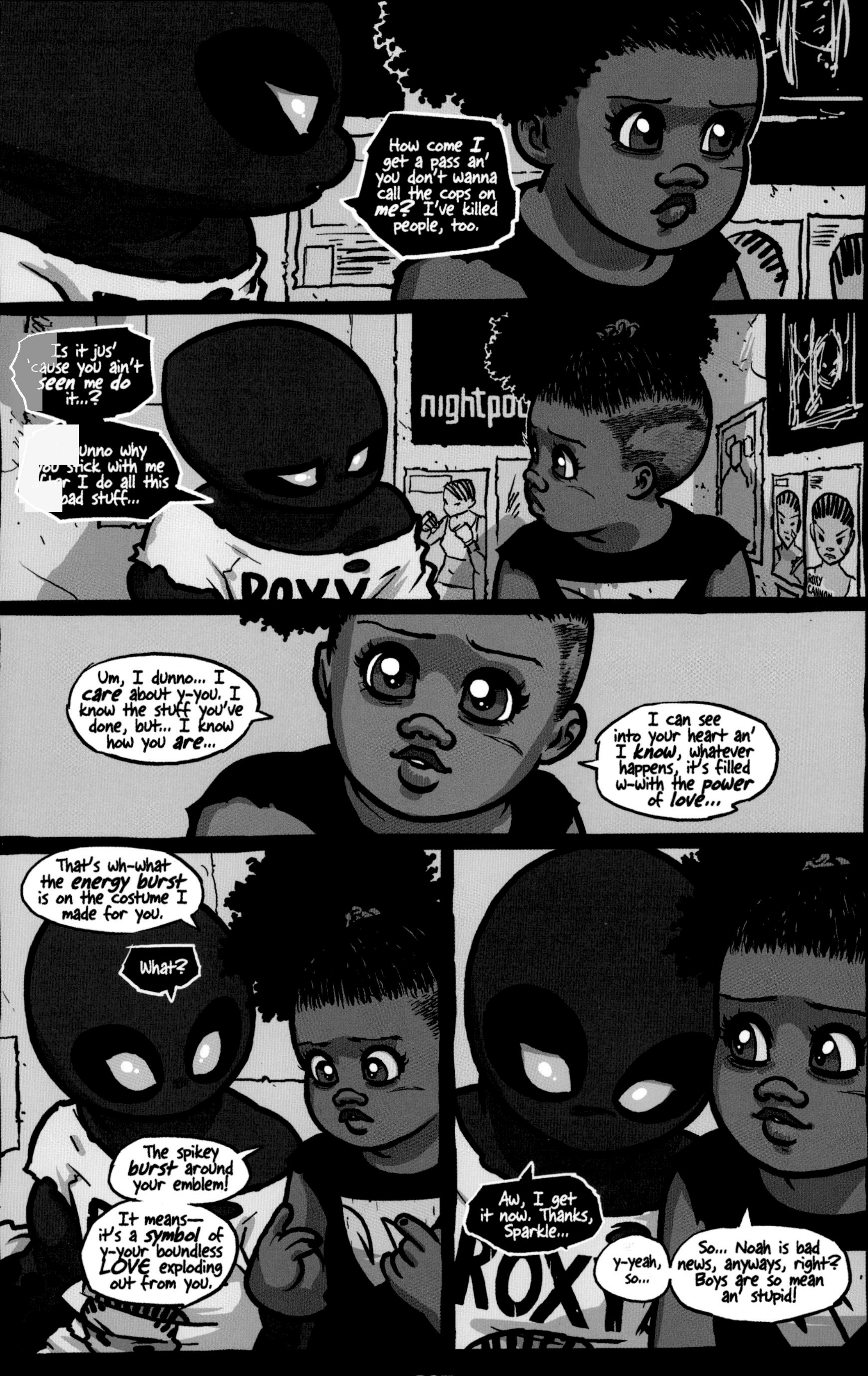
How come *I* get a pass an' you don't wanna call the cops on *me?* I've killed people, too.
Is it jus' 'cause you ain't *seen* me do it...?
unno why ou stick with me fter I do all this bad stuff...
nightpo
ROXY
ROXY CANNON
Um, I dunno... I *care* about y-you. I know the stuff you've done, but... I know how you *are*...
I can see into your heart an' I *know*, whatever happens, it's filled w-with the *power of love...*
That's wh-what the *energy burst* is on the costume I made for you.
What?
The spikey *burst* around your emblem!
It means— it's a *symbol* of y-your boundless *LOVE* exploding out from you.
Aw, I get it now. Thanks, Sparkle...
ROXY
Y-yeah, so...
So... Noah is bad news, anyways, right? Boys are so mean an' stupid!

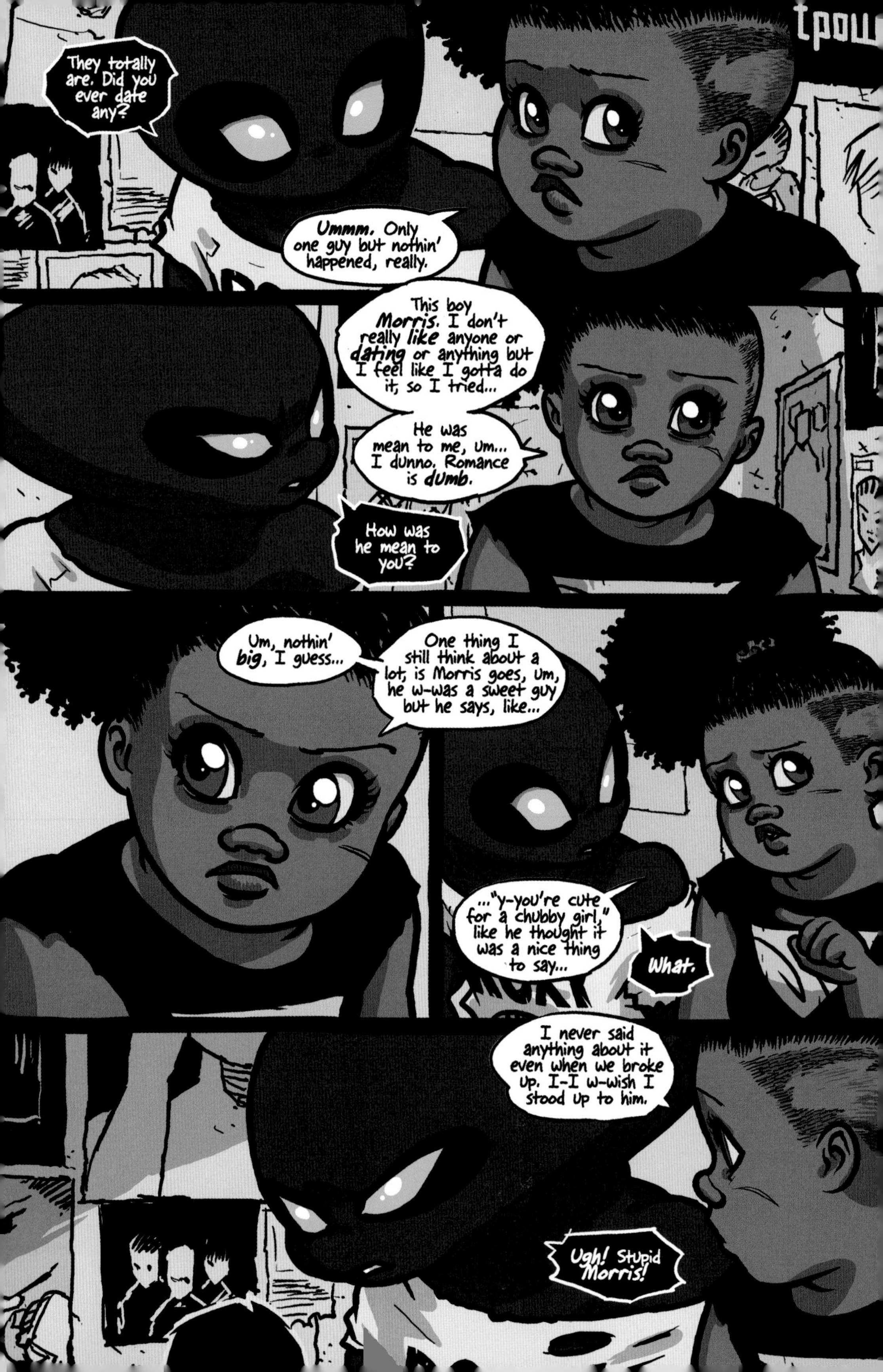

They totally are. Did you ever date any?
Ummm. Only one guy but nothin' happened, really.
This boy Morris. I don't really like anyone or dating or anything but I feel like I gotta do it, so I tried...
He was mean to me, um... I dunno. Romance is dumb.
How was he mean to you?
Um, nothin' big, I guess...
One thing I still think about a lot, is Morris goes, um, he w-was a sweet guy but he says, like...
..."y-you're cute for a chubby girl," like he thought it was a nice thing to say...
What.
I never said anything about it even when we broke up. I-I w-wish I stood up to him.
Ugh! Stupid Morris!

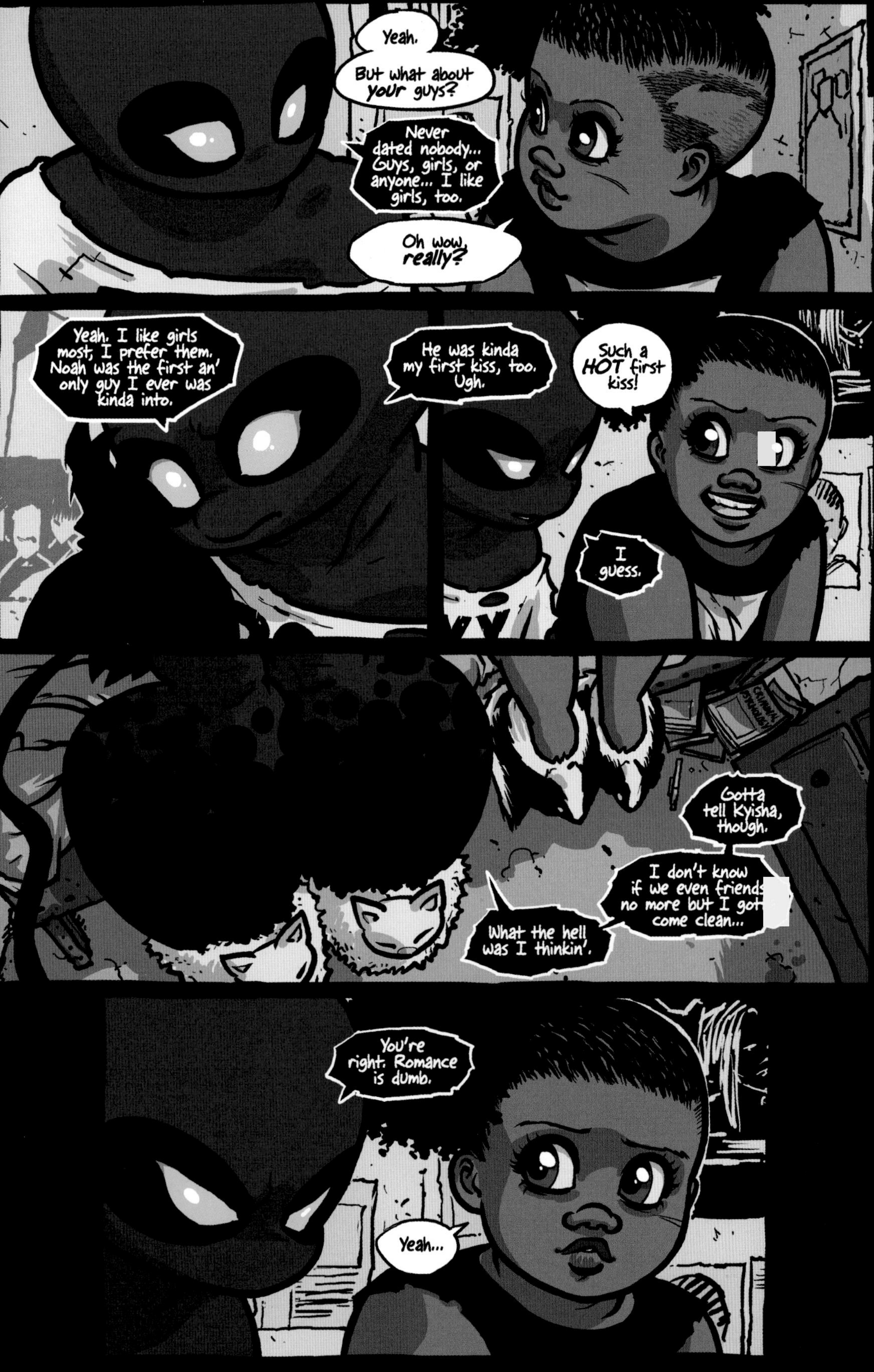
Yeah.
But what about your guys?
Never dated nobody... Guys, girls, or anyone... I like girls, too.
Oh wow, really?
Yeah. I like girls most, I prefer them. Noah was the first an' only guy I ever was kinda into.
He was kinda my first kiss, too. Ugh.
Such a HOT first kiss!
I guess.
Gotta tell Kyisha, though.
I don't know if we even friends no more but I got come clean...
What the hell was I thinkin'.
You're right. Romance is dumb.
Yeah...

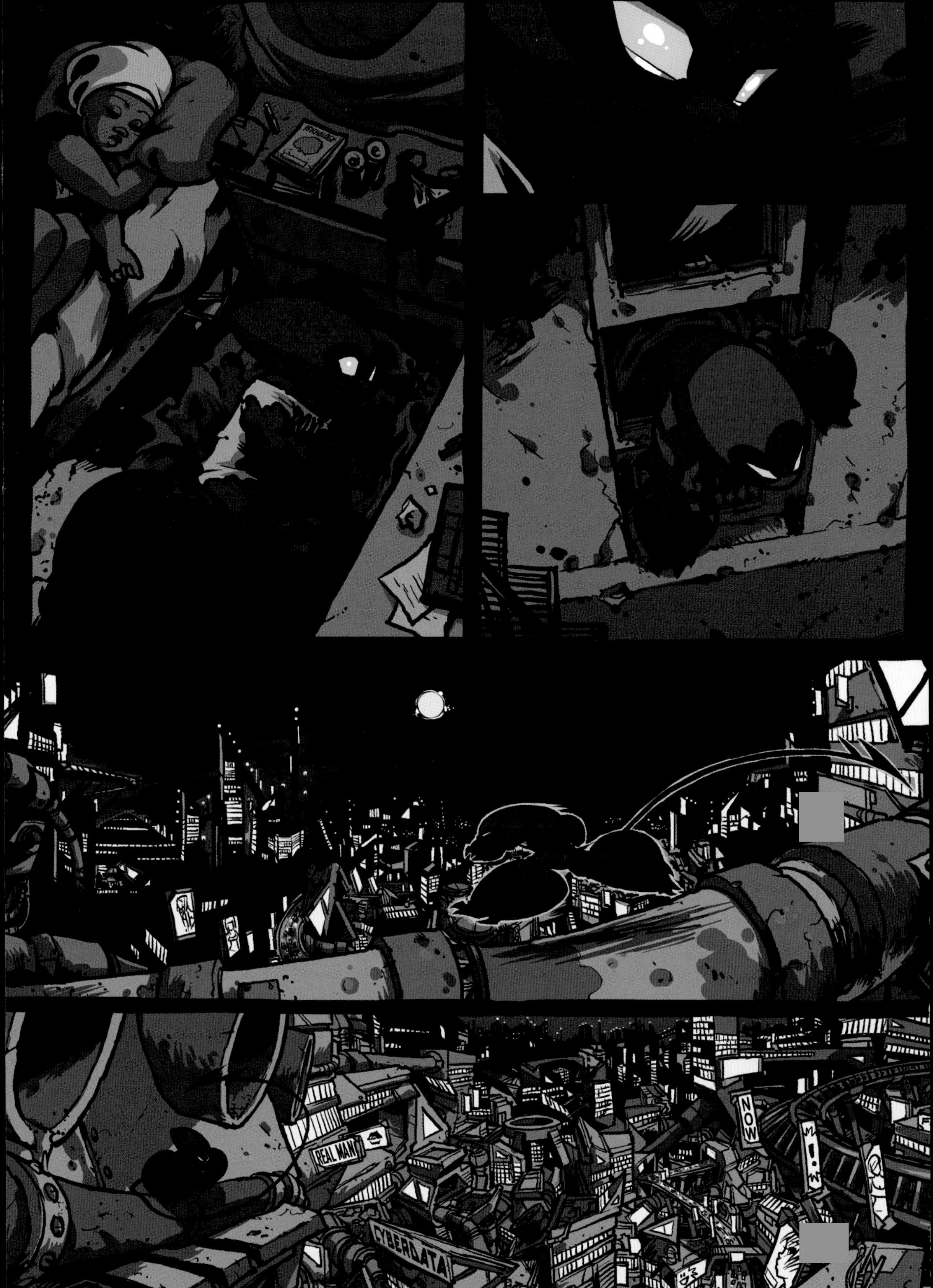
REAL MAN
CYBERDATA
NOW

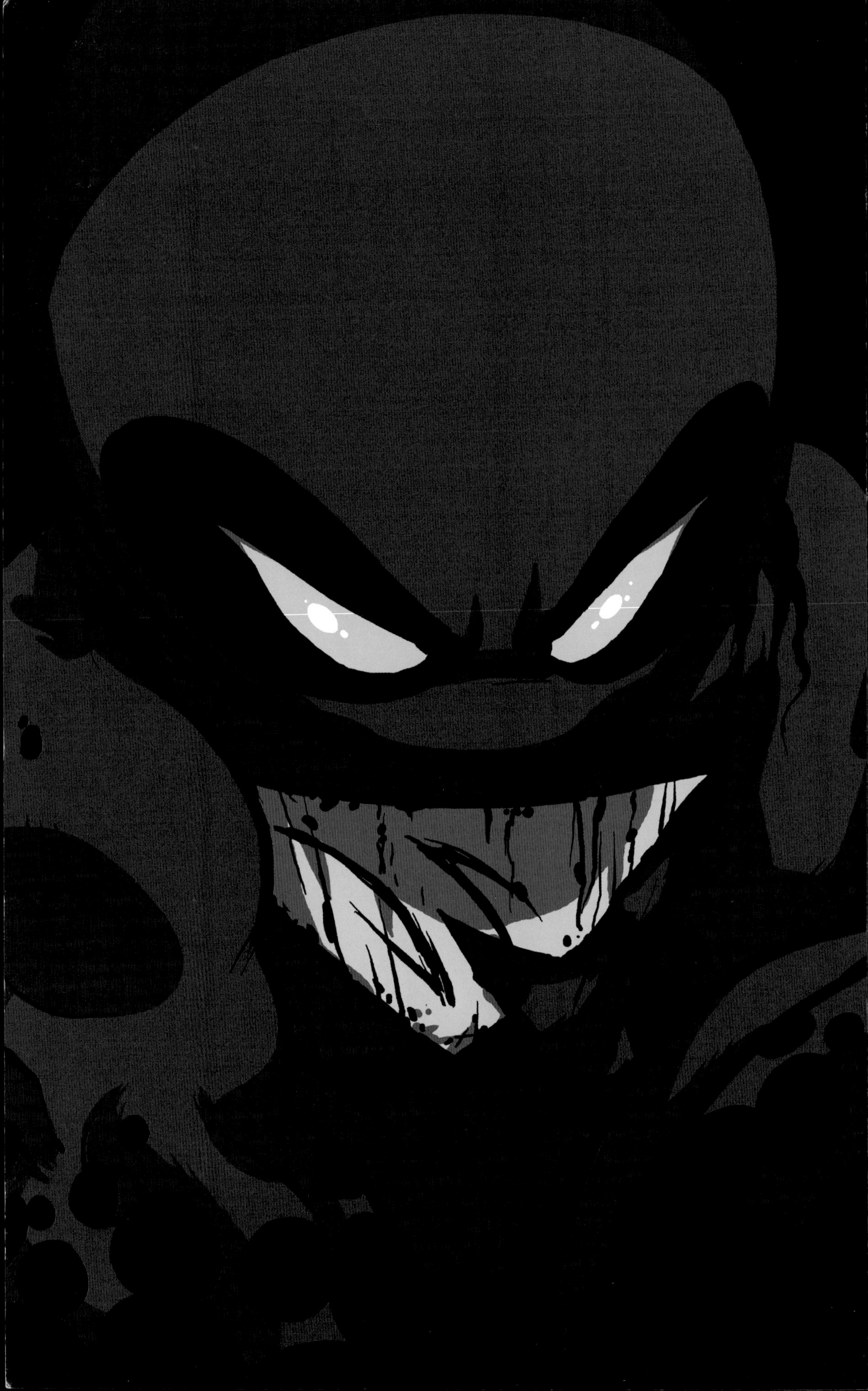

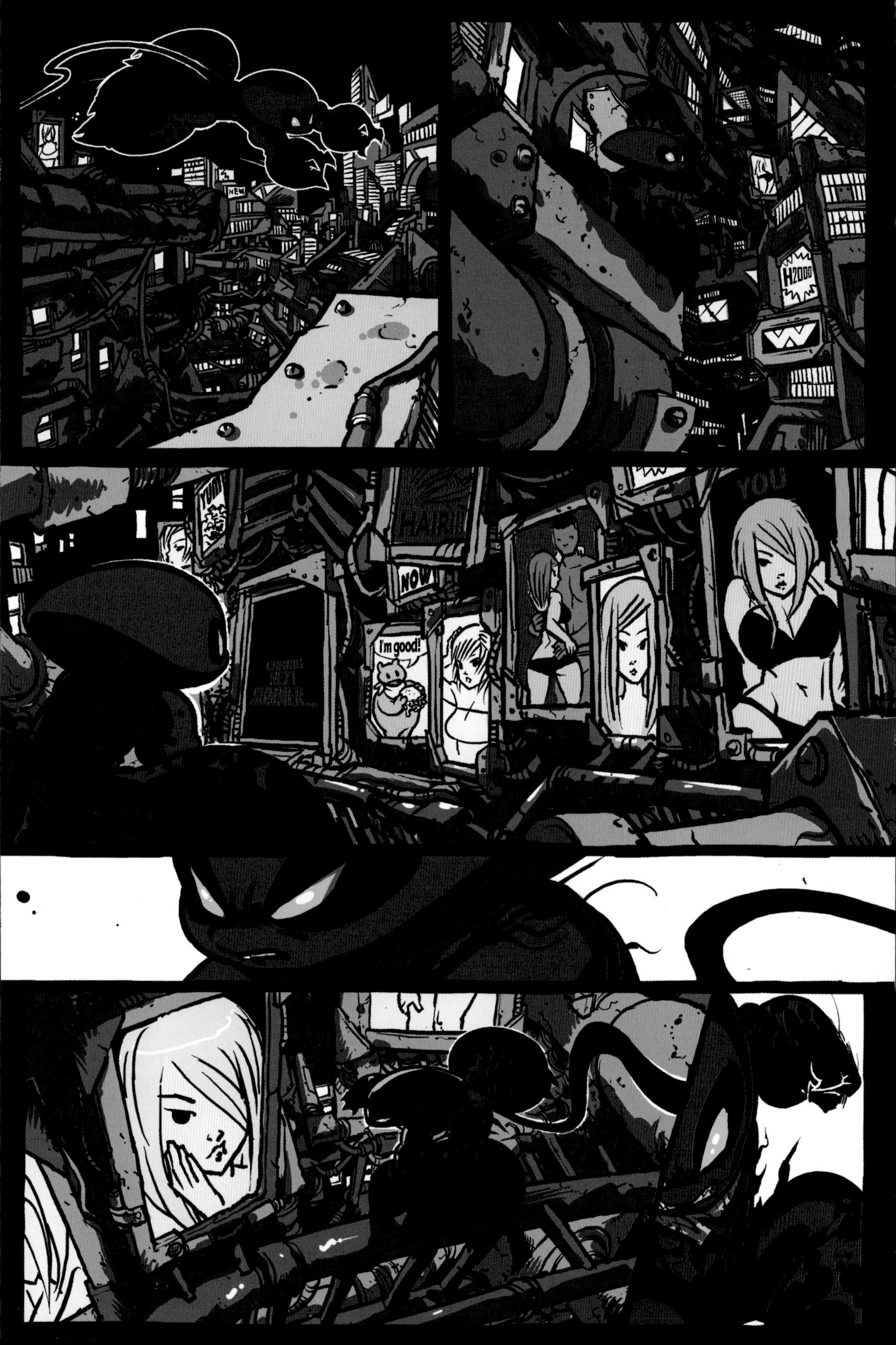
NEW
H2000
YUM
HAIR!!
NOW
YOU
NEXT
SUMMER...
I'm good!

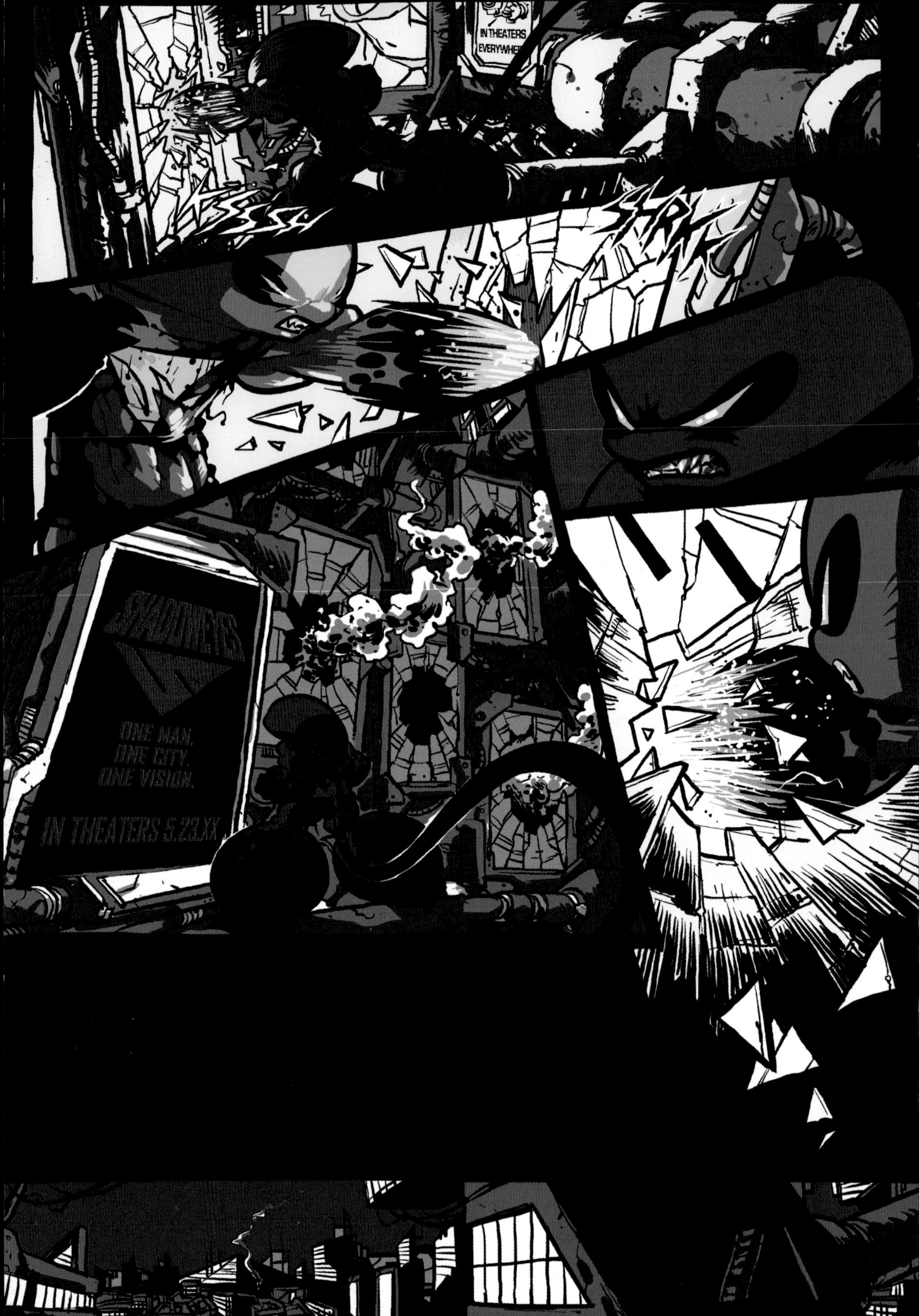
IN THEATERS
SHADOWEYES
ONE MAN.
ONE CITY.
ONE VISION.
IN THEATERS 5.23.XX

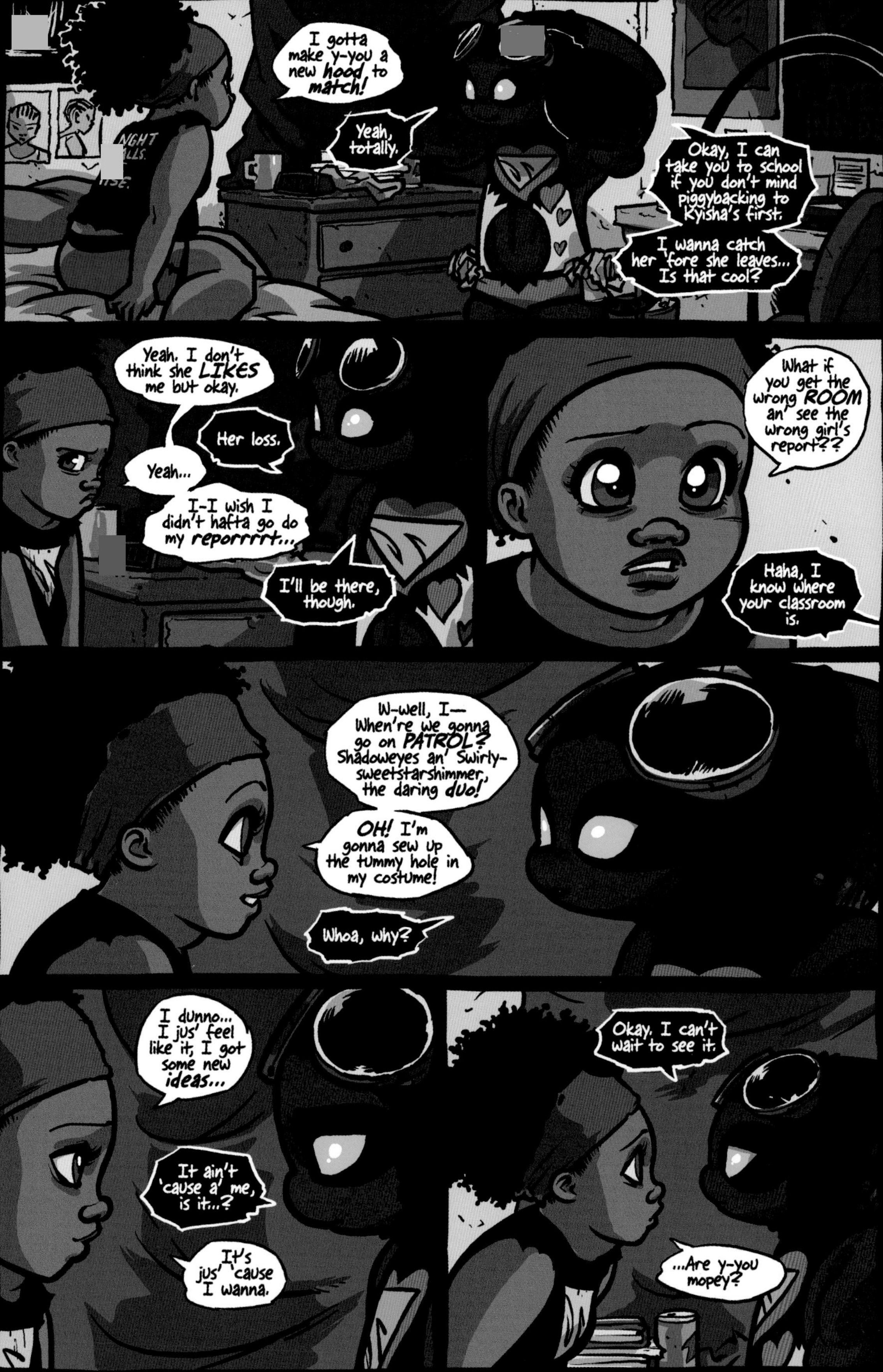

NGHT
ALLS.
TISE.
I gotta make y-you a new hood to match!
Yeah, totally.
Okay, I can take you to school if you don't mind piggybacking to Kyisha's first.
I wanna catch her 'fore she leaves... Is that cool?
Yeah. I don't think she LIKES me but okay.
Her loss.
Yeah...
I-I wish I didn't hafta go do my reporrrrt...
I'll be there, though.
What if you get the wrong ROOM an' see the wrong girl's report??
Haha, I know where your classroom is.
W-well, I— When're we gonna go on PATROL? Shadoweyes an' Swirly-sweetstarshimmer, the daring duo!
OH! I'm gonna sew up the tummy hole in my costume!
Whoa, why?
I dunno... I jus' feel like it, I got some new ideas...
It ain't 'cause a' me, is it...?
It's jus' 'cause I wanna.
Okay. I can't wait to see it.
...Are y-you mopey?

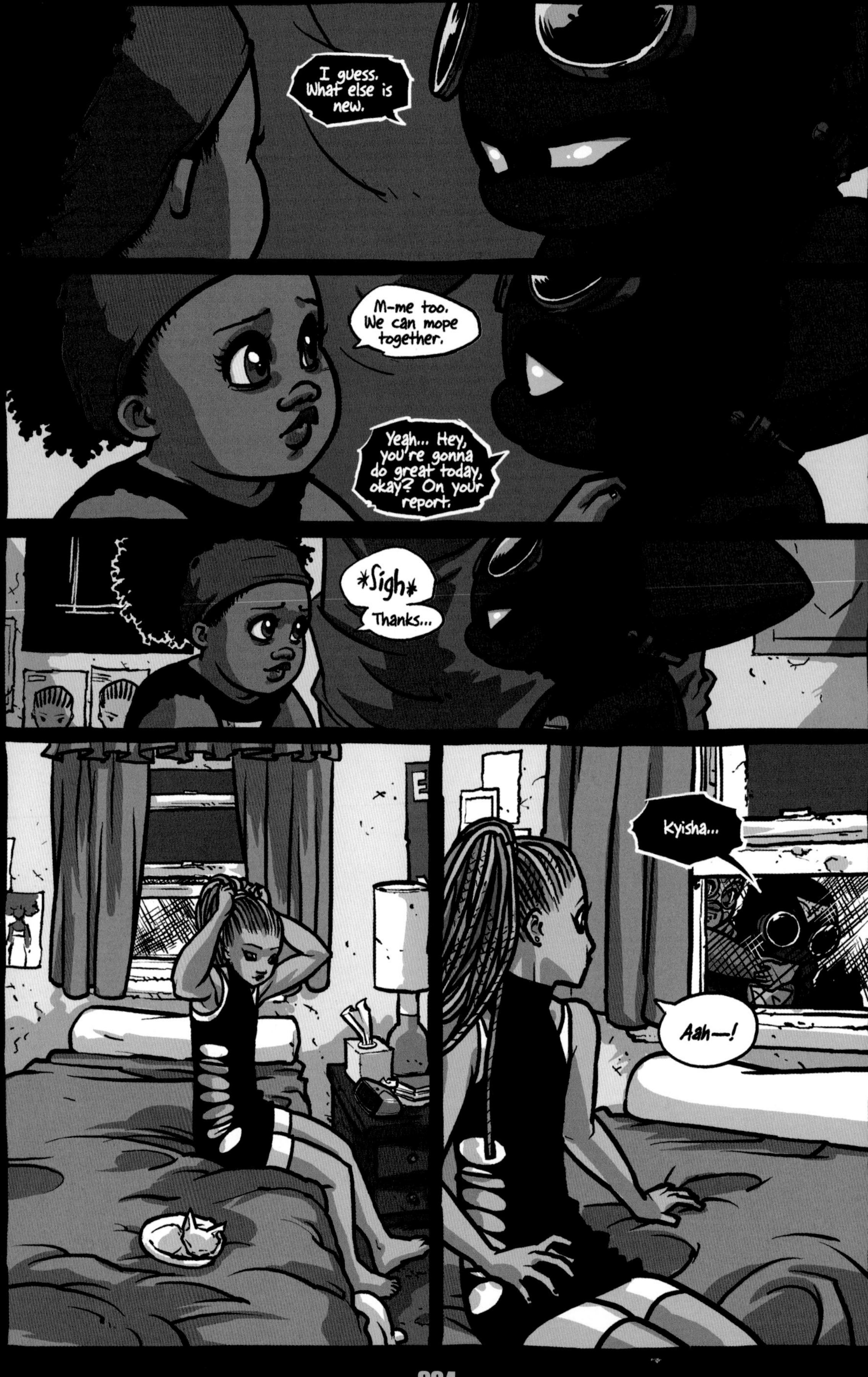
I guess. What else is new.
M-me too. We can mope together.
Yeah... Hey, you're gonna do great today, okay? On your report.
Sigh Thanks...
Kyisha...
Aah—!

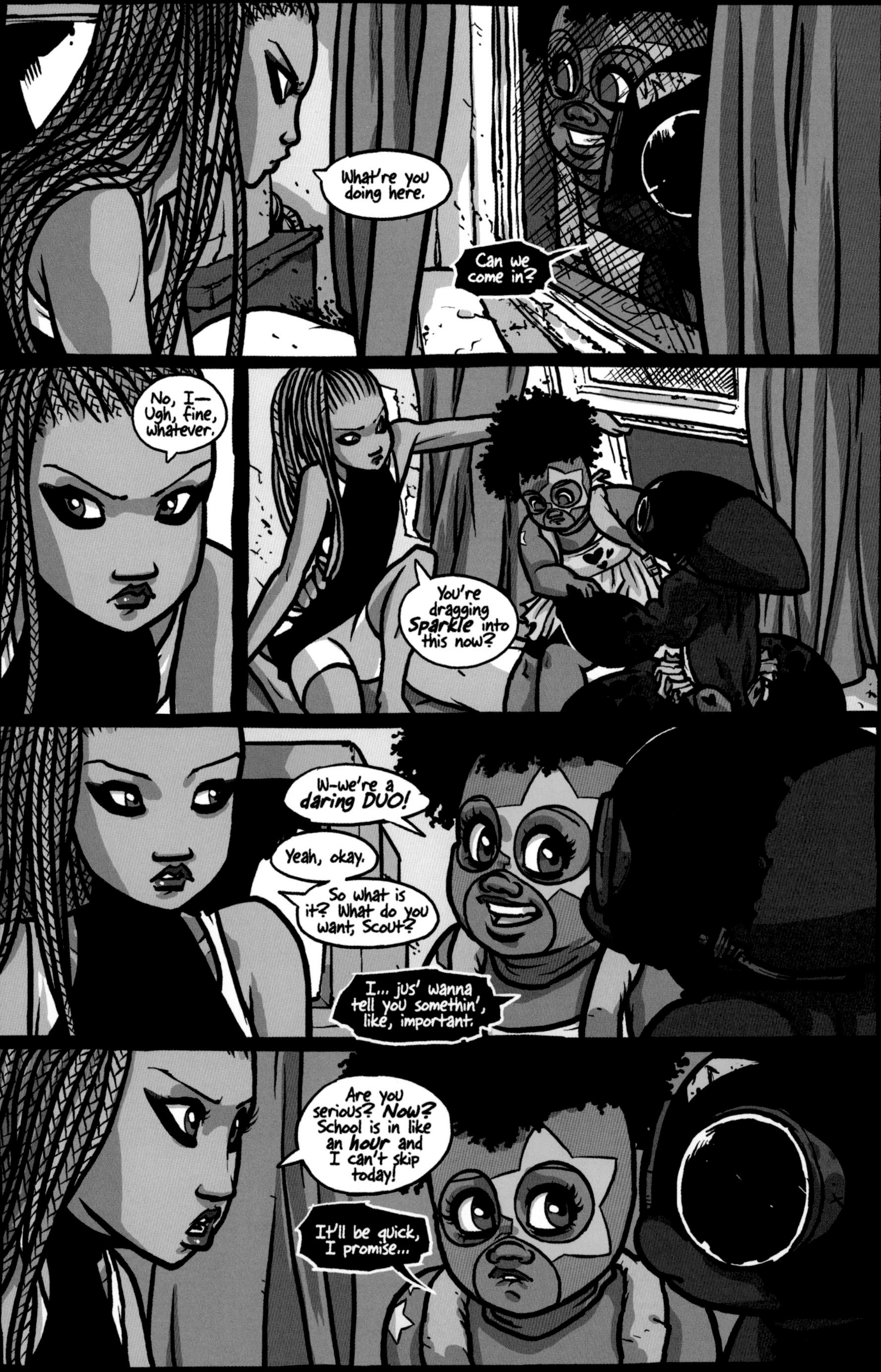
What're you doing here.
Can we come in?
No, I— Ugh, fine, whatever.
You're dragging Sparkle into this now?
W-we're a daring DUO!
Yeah, okay.
So what is it? What do you want, Scout?
I... jus' wanna tell you somethin', like, important.
Are you serious? Now? School is in like an hour and I can't skip today!
It'll be quick, I promise...

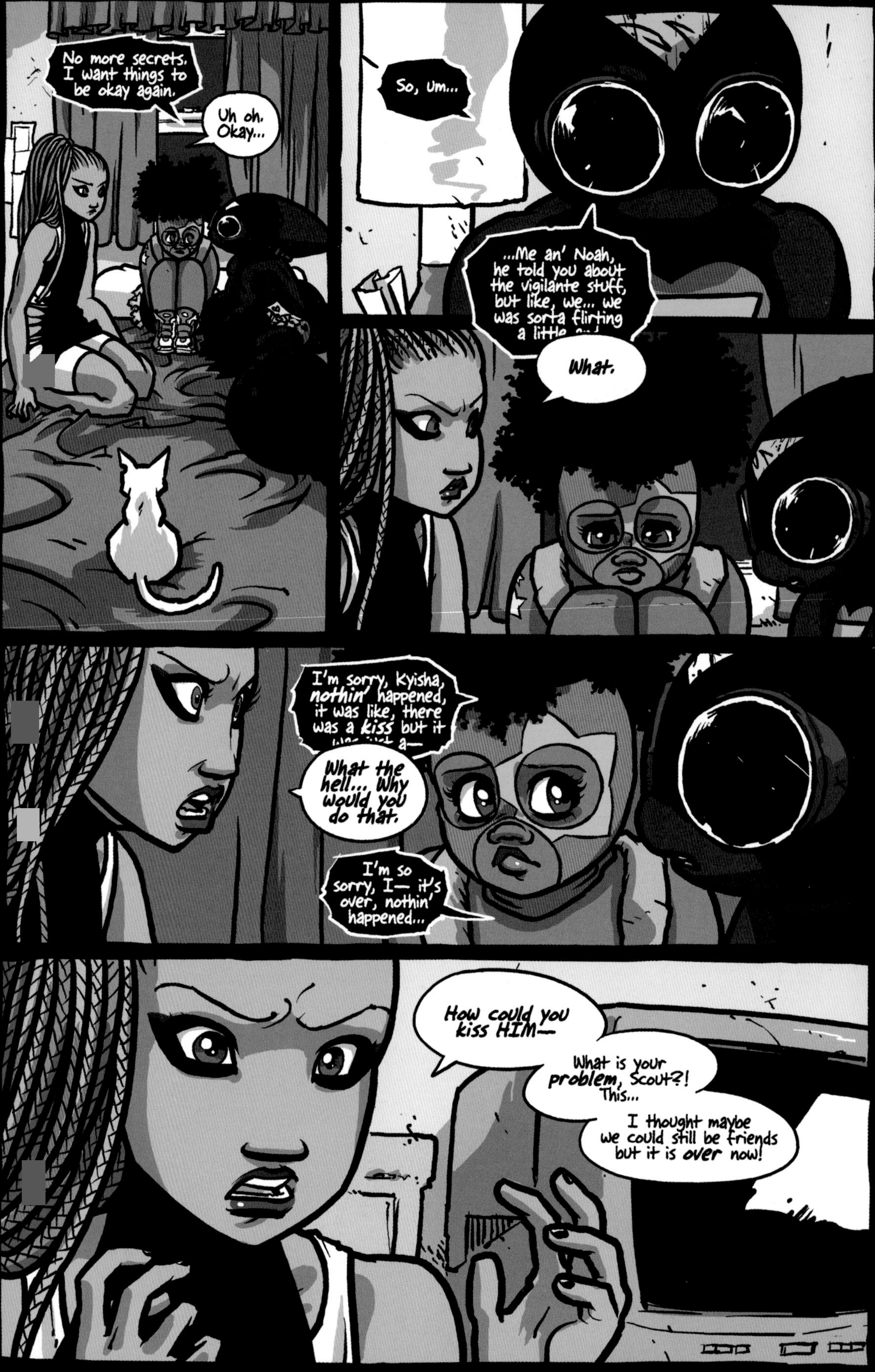
No more secrets. I want things to be okay again.
Uh oh. Okay...
So, um...
...Me an' Noah, he told you about the vigilante stuff, but like, we... we was sorta flirting a little
What.
I'm sorry, Kyisha, *nothin'* happened, it was like, there was a *kiss* but it
a—
What the hell... Why would you do that.
I'm so sorry, I— it's over, nothin' happened...
How could you kiss HIM—
What is your *problem*, Scout?! This...
I thought maybe we could still be friends but it is *over* now!

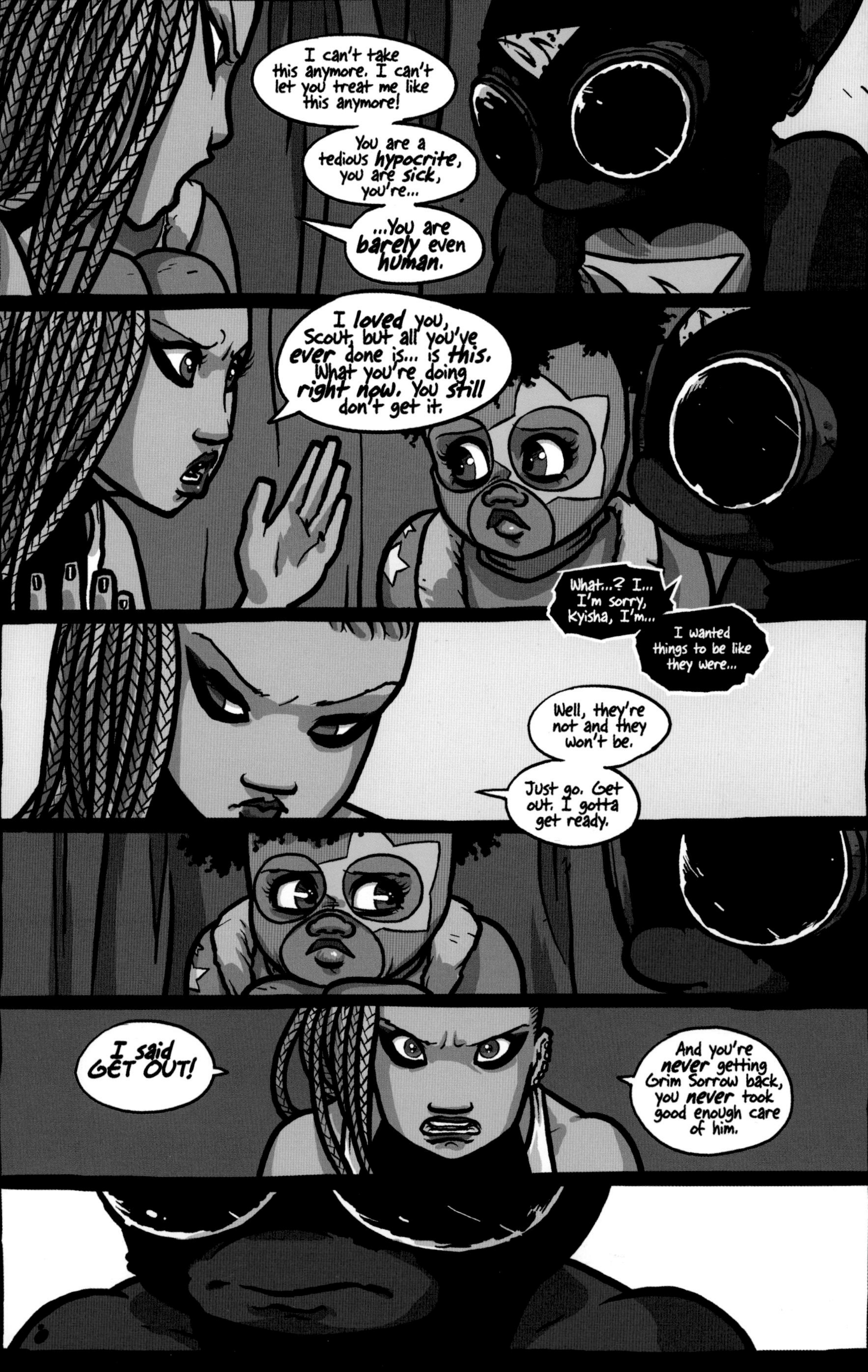

I can't take this anymore. I can't let you treat me like this anymore!
You are a tedious hypocrite, you are sick, you're...
...You are barely even human.
I loved you, Scout, but all you've ever done is... is this. What you're doing right now. You still don't get it.
What...? I... I'm sorry, Kyisha, I'm...
I wanted things to be like they were...
Well, they're not and they won't be.
Just go. Get out. I gotta get ready.
I said GET OUT!
And you're never getting Grim Sorrow back, you never took good enough care of him.

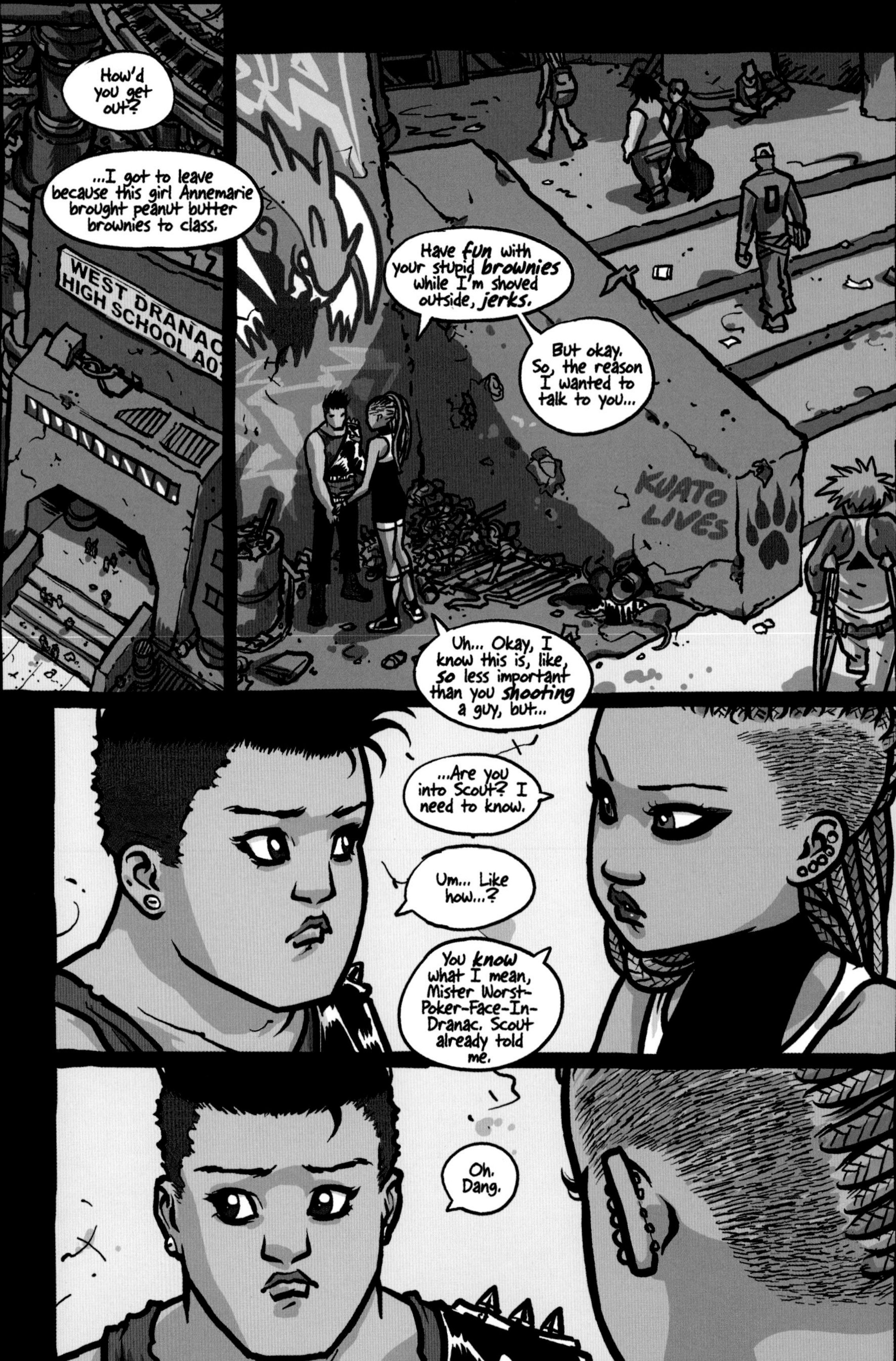
How'd you get out?
...I got to leave because this girl Annemarie brought peanut butter brownies to class.
WEST DRANAC HIGH SCHOOL A07
Have fun with your stupid brownies while I'm shoved outside, jerks.
But okay. So, the reason I wanted to talk to you...
KUATO LIVES
Uh... Okay, I know this is, like, so less important than you shooting a guy, but...
...Are you into Scout? I need to know.
Um... Like how...?
You know what I mean, Mister Worst-Poker-Face-In-Dranac. Scout already told me.
Oh. Dang.

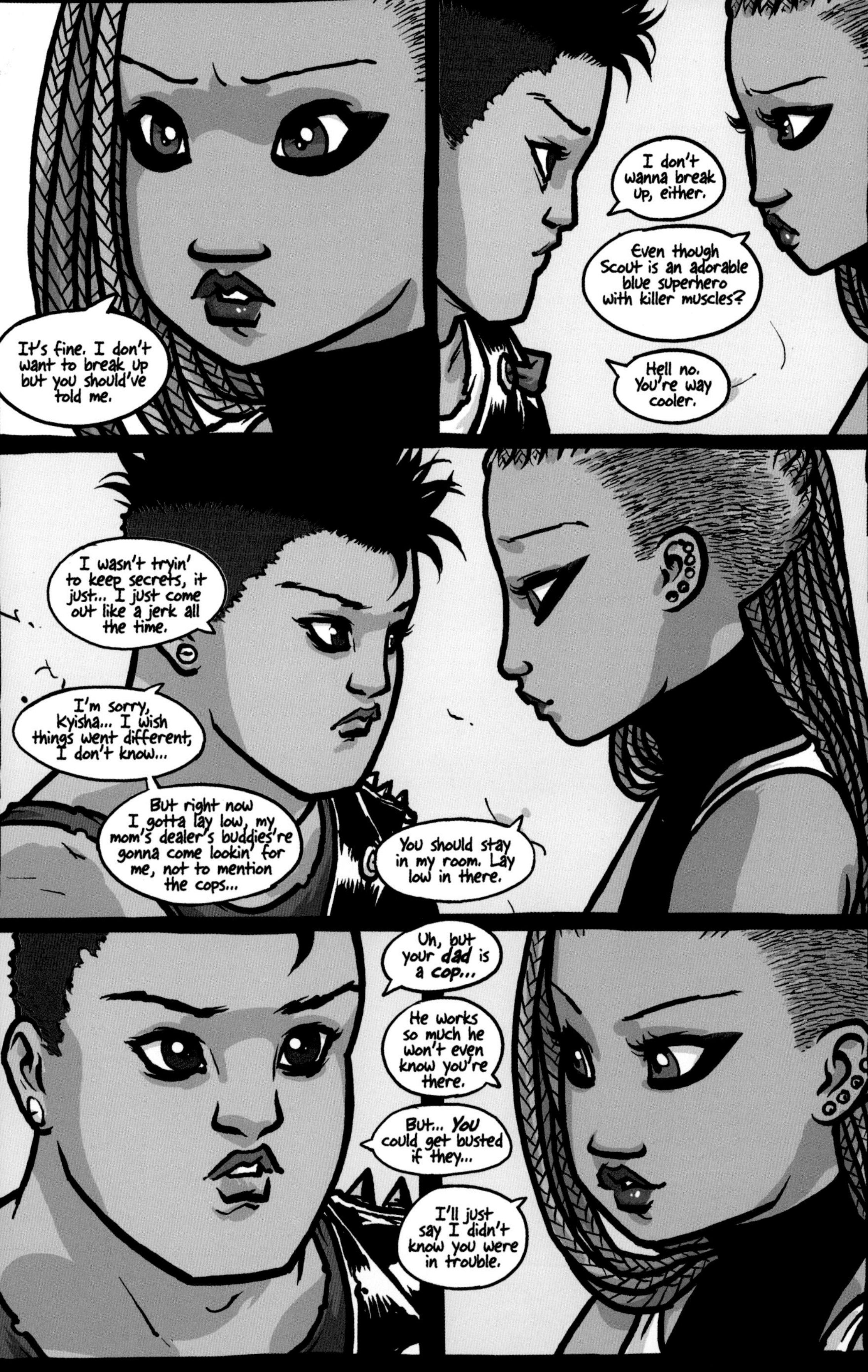
It's fine. I don't want to break up but you should've told me.
I don't wanna break up, either.
Even though Scout is an adorable blue superhero with killer muscles?
Hell no. You're way cooler.
I wasn't tryin' to keep secrets, it just... I just come out like a jerk all the time.
I'm sorry, Kyisha... I wish things went different, I don't know...
But right now I gotta lay low, my mom's dealer's buddies're gonna come lookin' for me, not to mention the cops...
You should stay in my room. Lay low in there.
Uh, but your dad is a cop...
He works so much he won't even know you're there.
But... You could get busted if they...
I'll just say I didn't know you were in trouble.

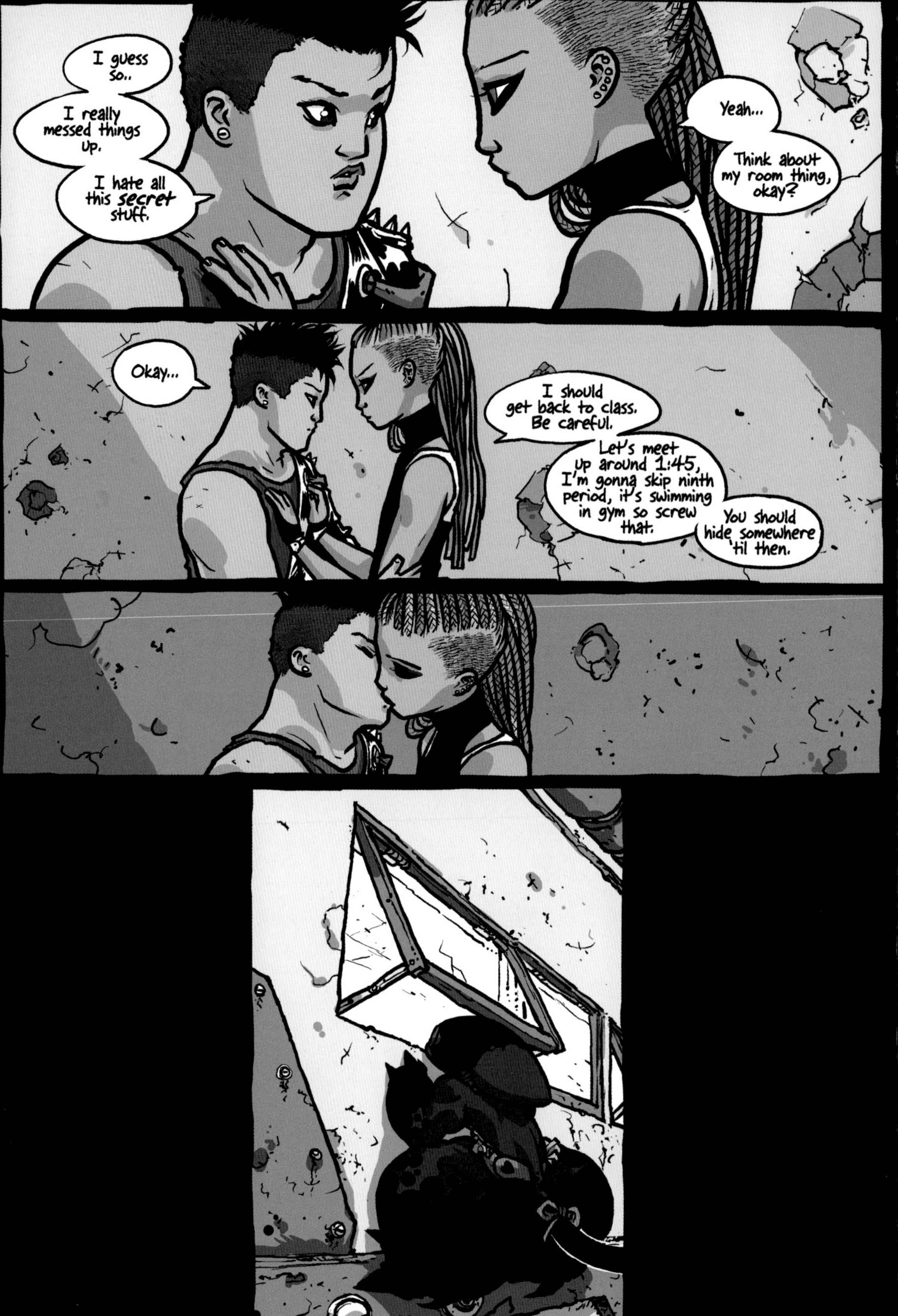
I guess so..
I really messed things up.
I hate all this secret stuff.
Yeah...
Think about my room thing, okay?
Okay...
I should get back to class. Be careful.
Let's meet up around 1:45, I'm gonna skip ninth period, it's swimming in gym so screw that.
You should hide somewhere 'til then.

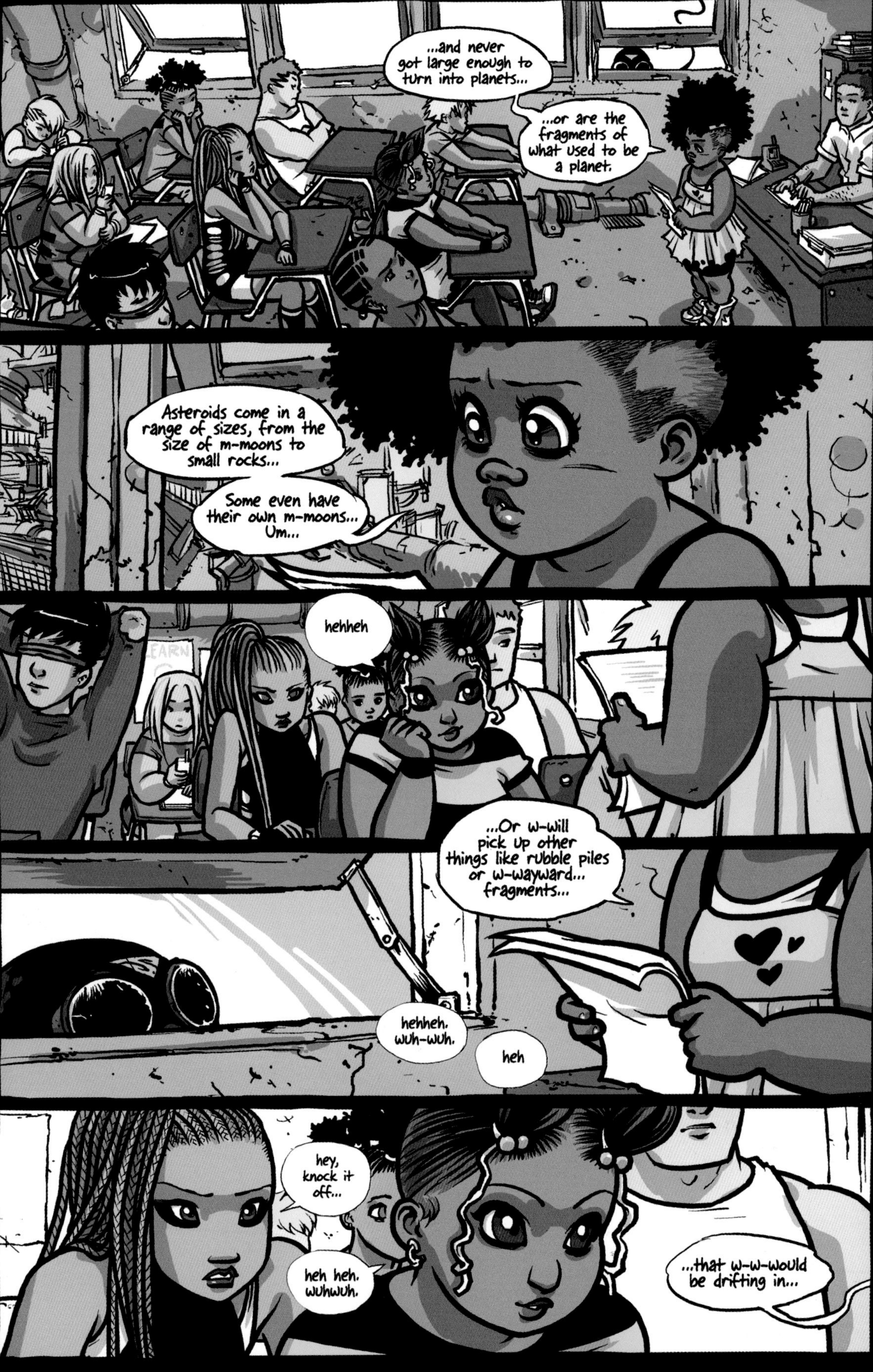
...and never got large enough to turn into planets...
...or are the fragments of what used to be a planet.
Asteroids come in a range of sizes, from the size of m-moons to small rocks...
Some even have their own m-moons... Um...
hehheh
...Or w-will pick up other things like rubble piles or w-wayward... fragments...
hehheh. wuh-wuh.
heh
hey, knock it off...
heh heh. wuhwuh.
...that w-w-would be drifting in...

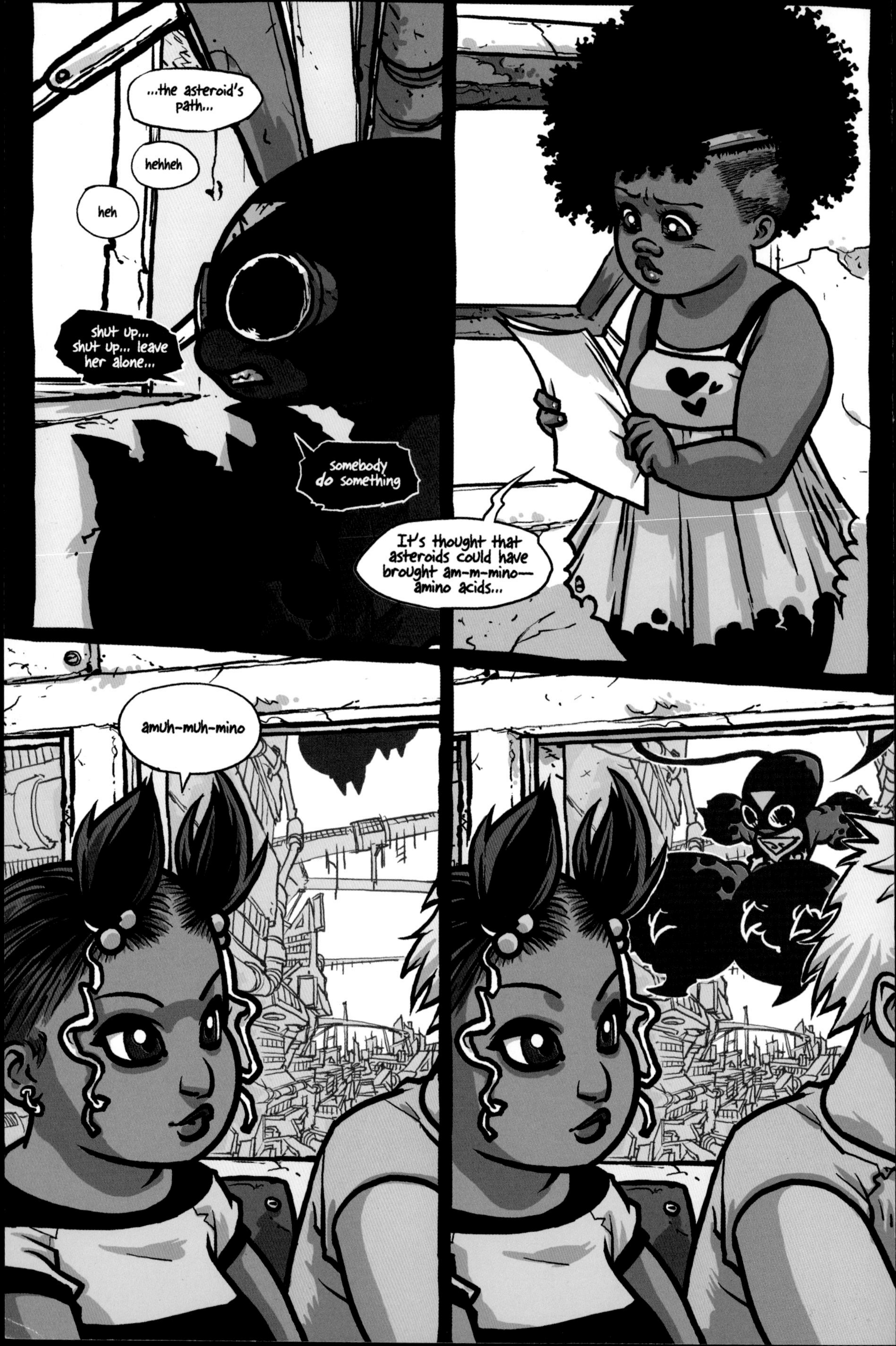
...the asteroid's path...
hehheh
heh
shut up... shut up... leave her alone...
somebody do something
It's thought that asteroids could have brought am-m-mino— amino acids...
amuh-muh-mino

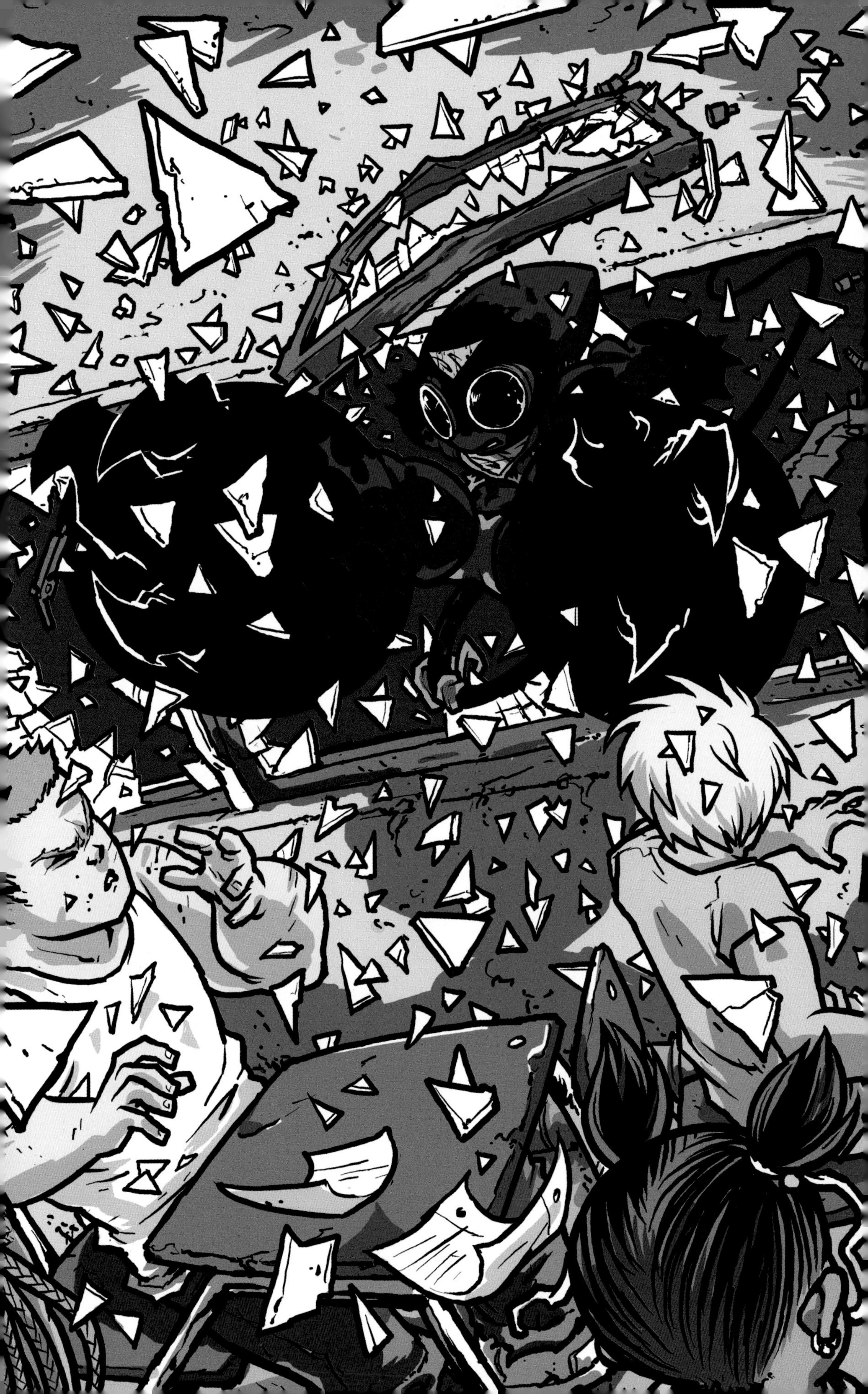

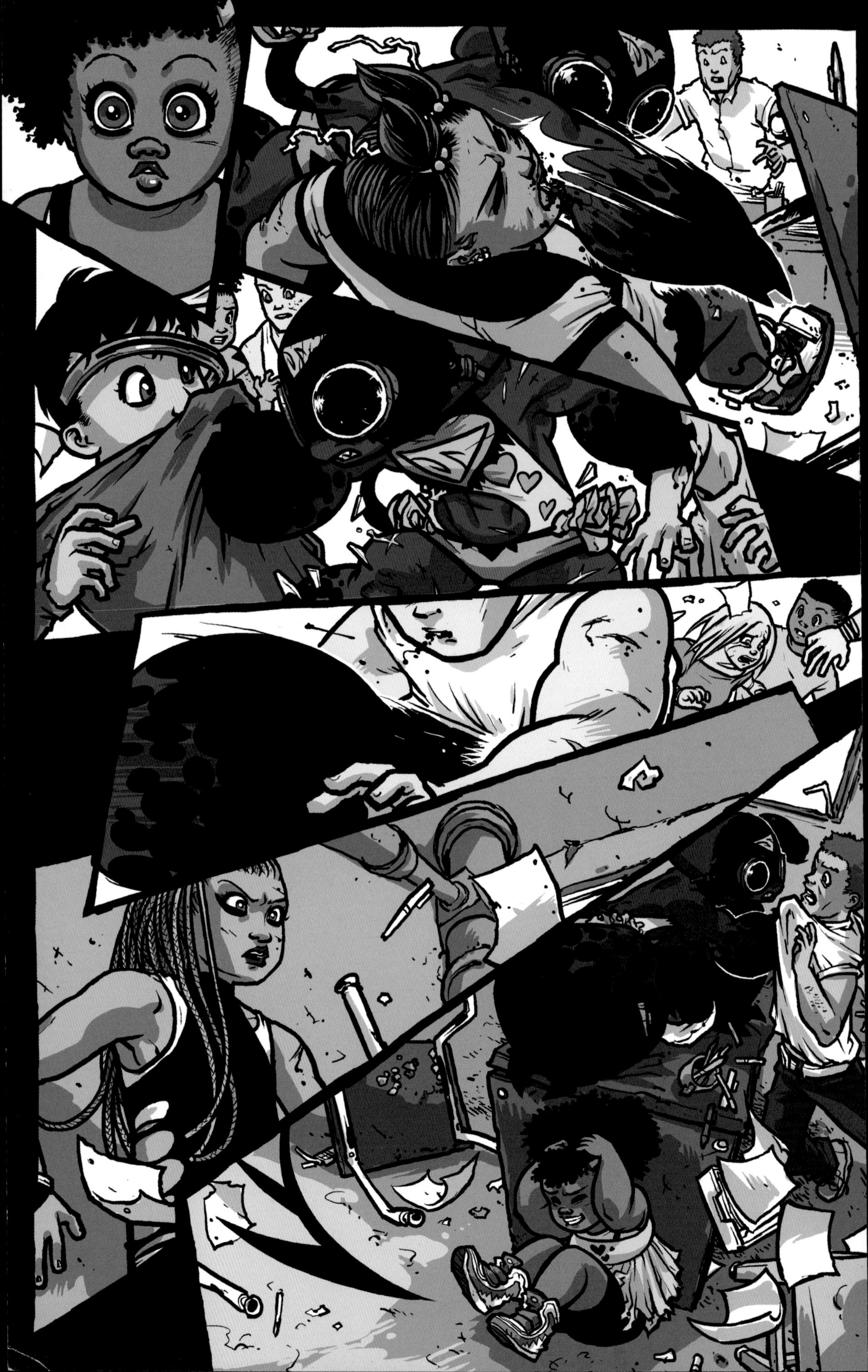

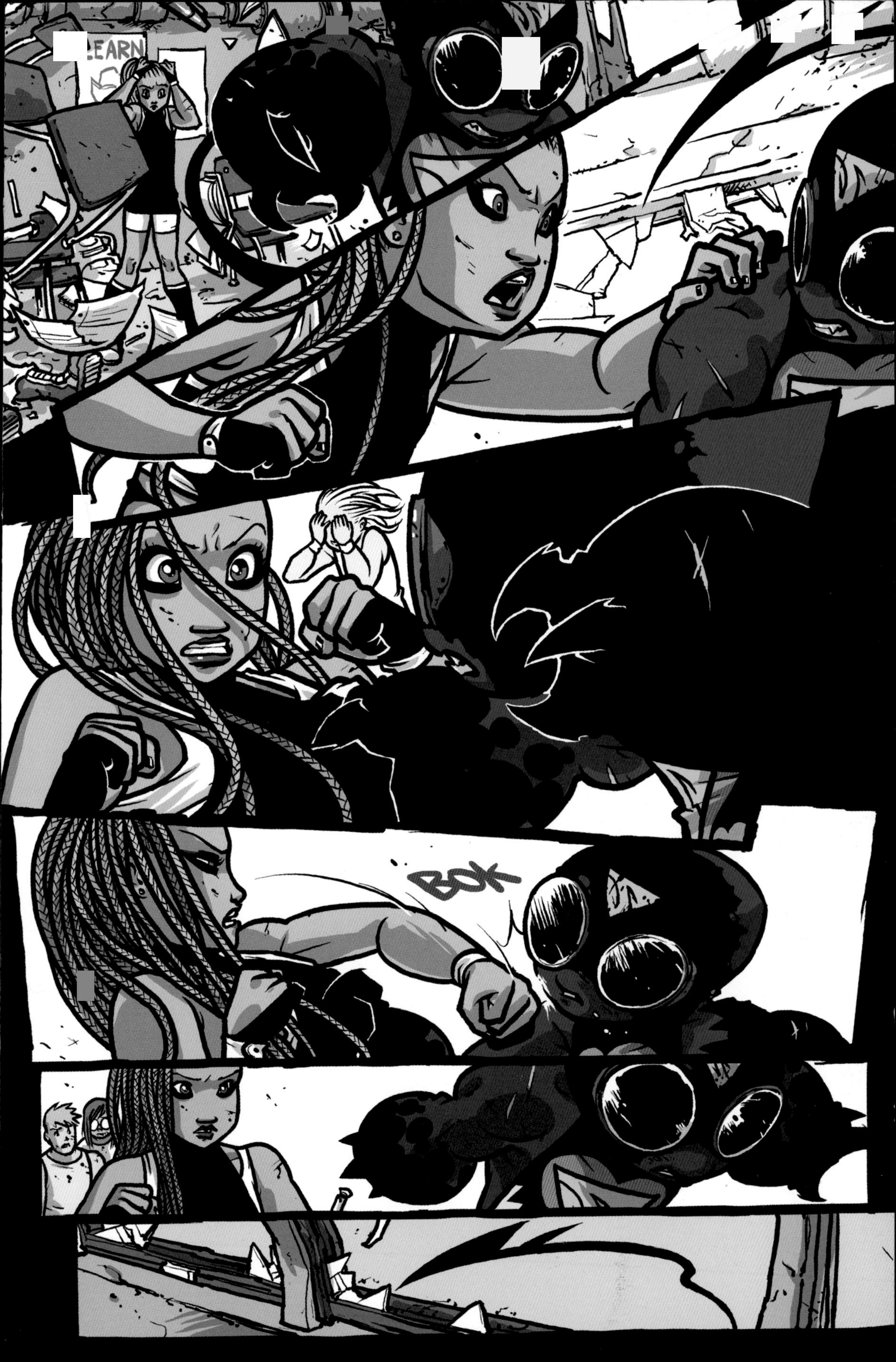
LEARN
BOK

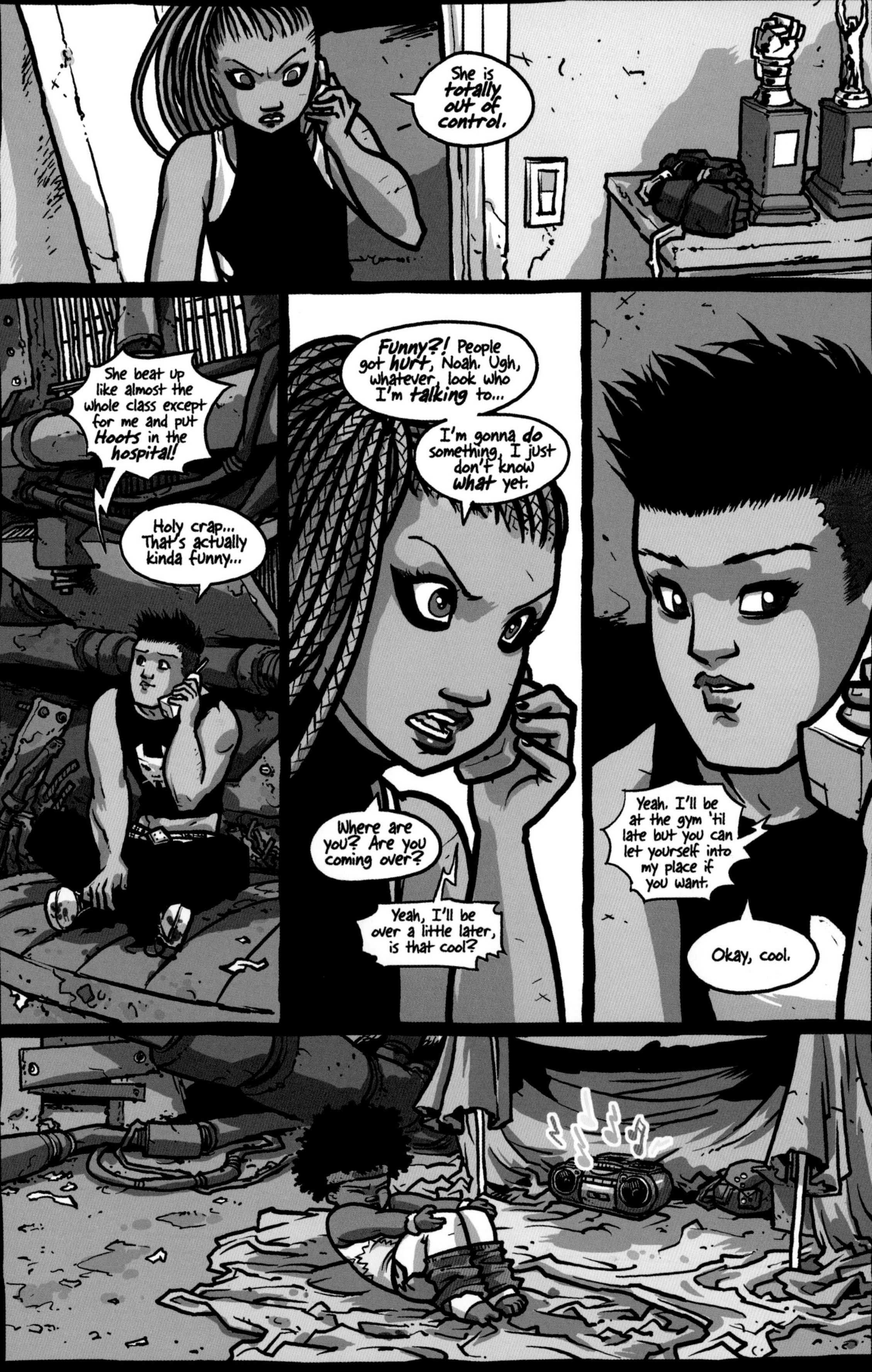
She is totally out of control.
She beat up like almost the whole class except for me and put Hoots in the hospital!
Holy crap... That's actually kinda funny...
Funny?! People got hurt, Noah. Ugh, whatever, look who I'm talking to...
I'm gonna do something, I just don't know what yet.
Where are you? Are you coming over?
Yeah, I'll be over a little later, is that cool?
Yeah. I'll be at the gym 'til late but you can let yourself into my place if you want.
Okay, cool.

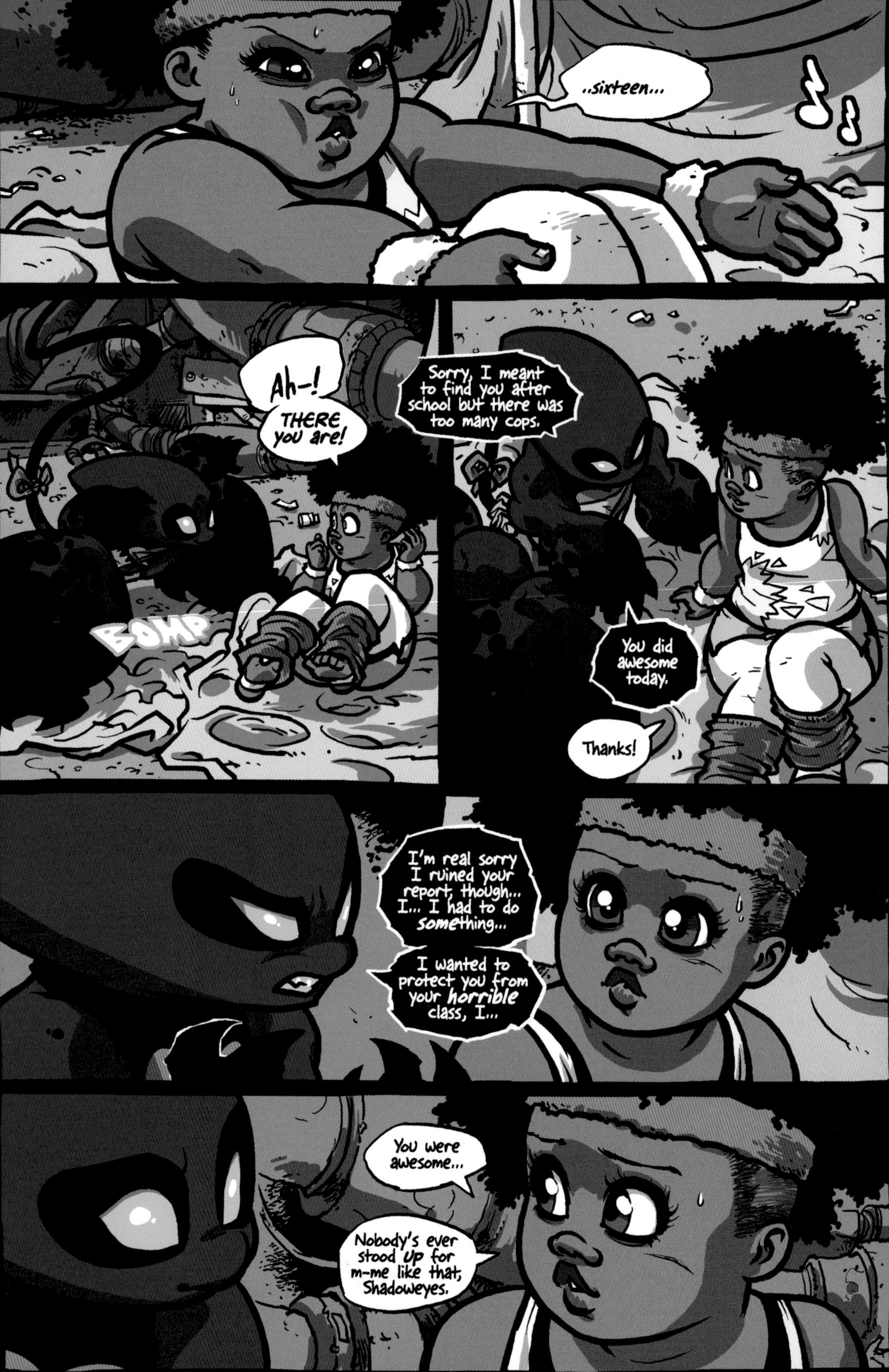
..sixteen...
Ah-!
THERE you are!
BOMP
Sorry, I meant to find you after school but there was too many cops.
You did awesome today.
Thanks!
I'm real sorry I ruined your report, though... I... I had to do *some*thing...
I wanted to protect you from your ***horrible*** class, I...
You were awesome...
Nobody's ever stood **UP** for m-me like that, Shadoweyes.

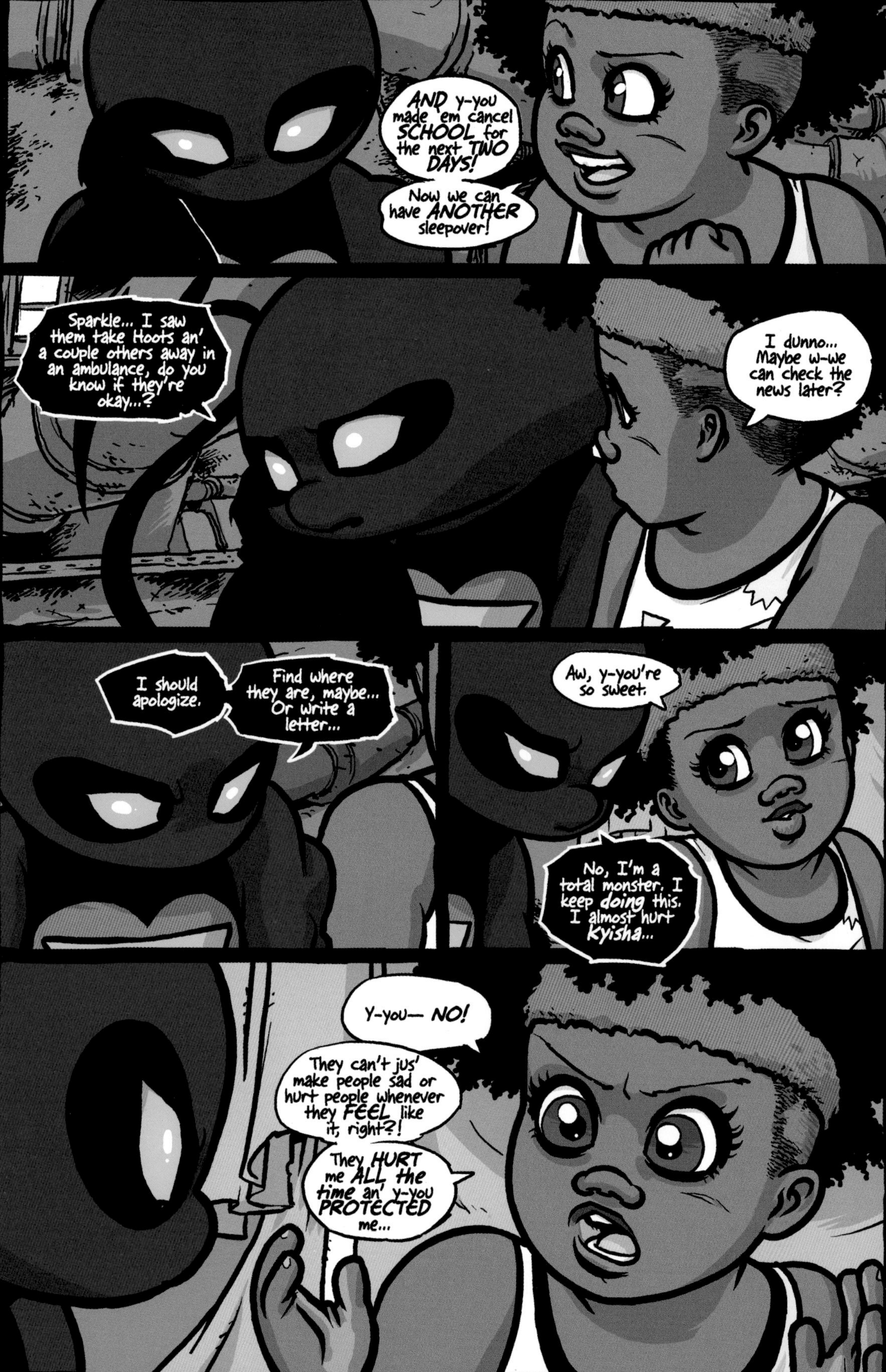
AND y-you made 'em cancel SCHOOL for the next TWO DAYS!
Now we can have ANOTHER sleepover!
Sparkle... I saw them take Hoots an' a couple others away in an ambulance, do you know if they're okay...?
I dunno... Maybe w-we can check the news later?
I should apologize.
Find where they are, maybe... Or write a letter...
Aw, y-you're so sweet.
No, I'm a total monster. I keep doing this. I almost hurt Kyisha...
Y-you— NO!
They can't jus' make people sad or hurt people whenever they FEEL like it, right?!
They HURT me ALL the time an' y-you PROTECTED me...

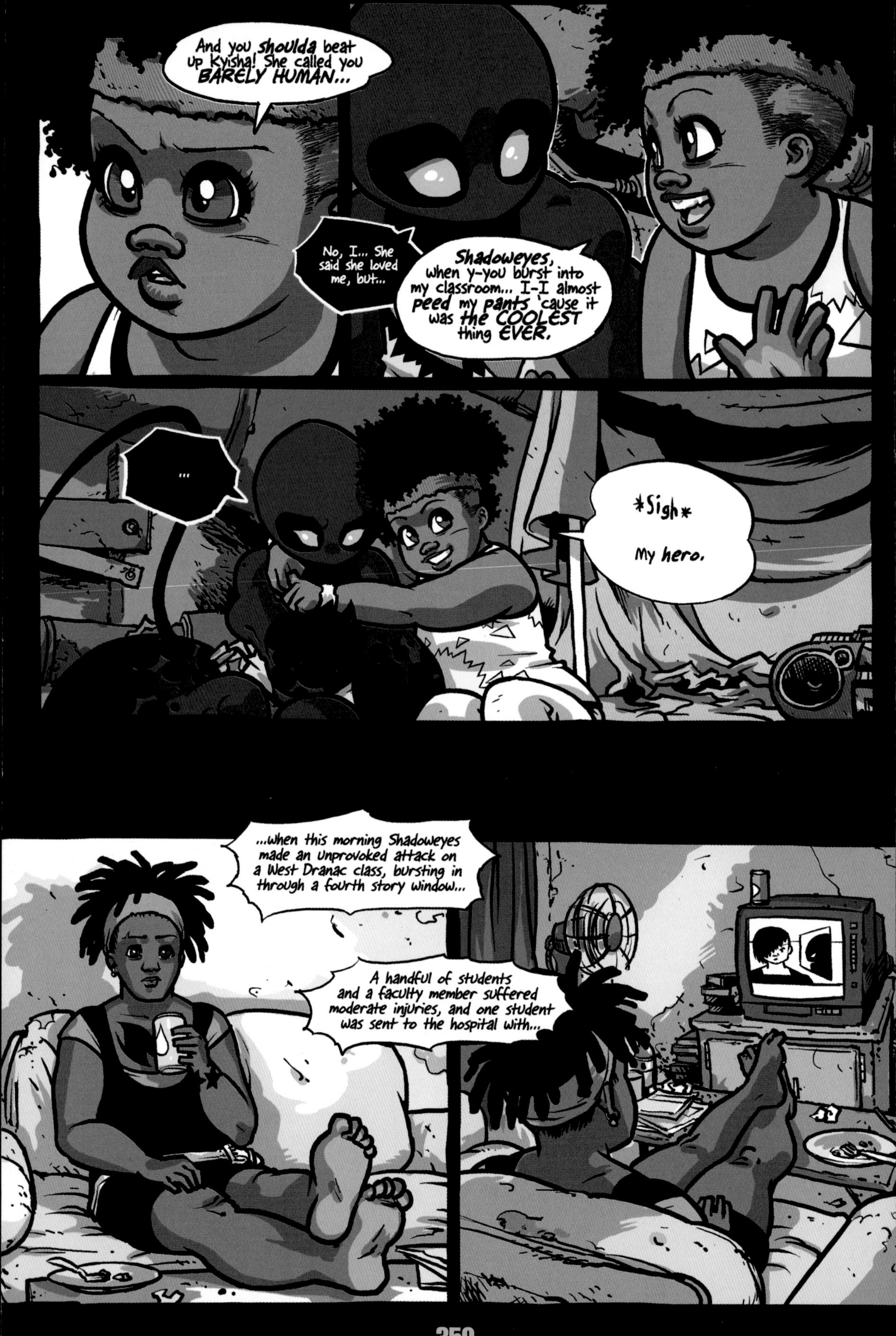
And you shoulda beat up Kyisha! She called you BARELY HUMAN...
No, I... She said she loved me, but...
Shadoweyes, when y-you burst into my classroom... I-I almost peed my pants 'cause it was the COOLEST thing EVER.
...
Sigh My hero.
...when this morning Shadoweyes made an unprovoked attack on a West Dranac class, bursting in through a fourth story window...
A handful of students and a faculty member suffered moderate injuries, and one student was sent to the hospital with...

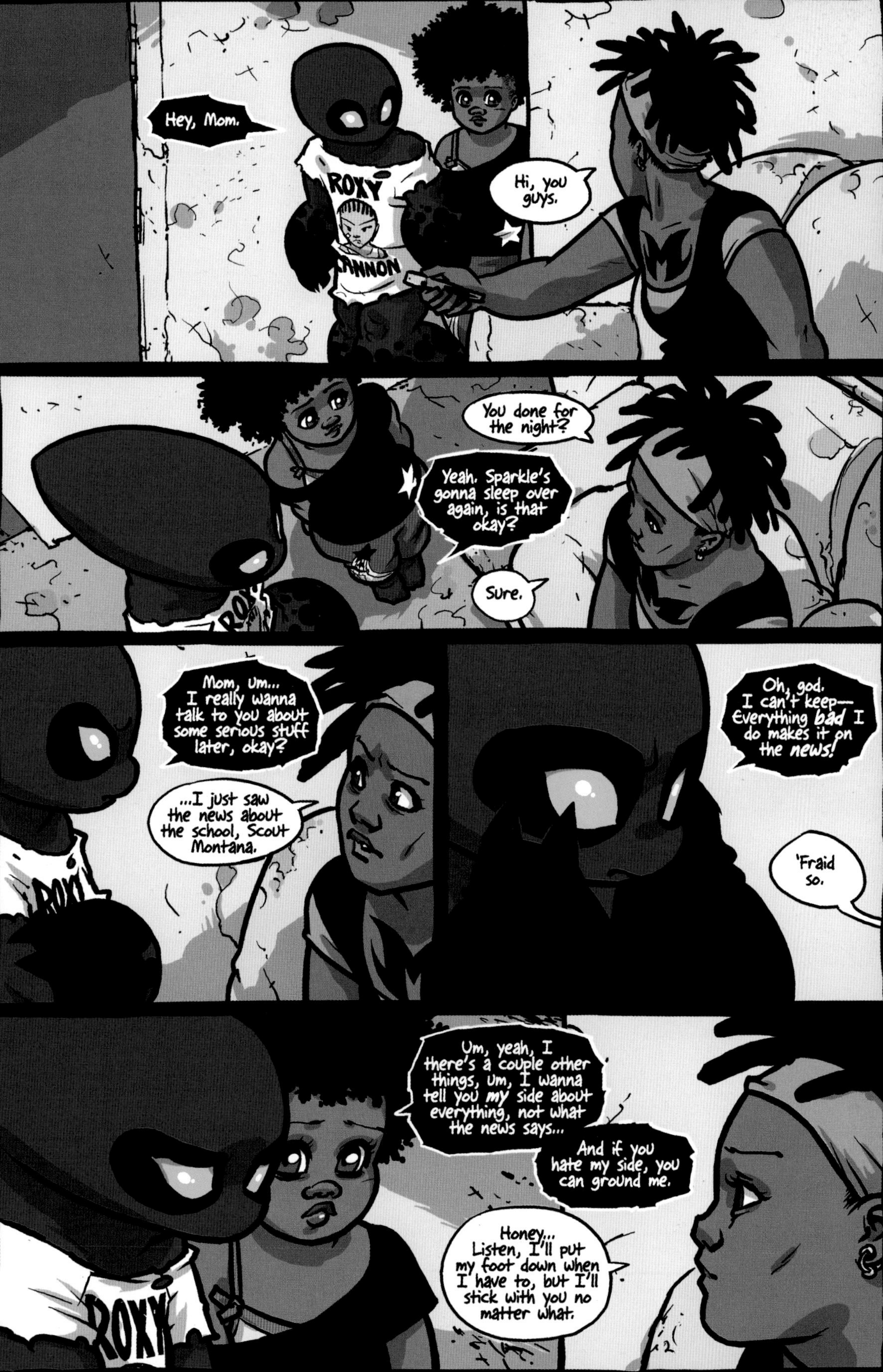
Hey, Mom.
ROXY CANNON
Hi, you guys.
You done for the night?
Yeah. Sparkle's gonna sleep over again, is that okay?
Sure.
Mom, um... I really wanna talk to you about some serious stuff later, okay?
...I just saw the news about the school, Scout Montana.
Oh, god. I can't keep— Everything *bad* I do makes it on the *news*!
'Fraid so.
Um, yeah, I there's a couple other things, um, I wanna tell you *my* side about everything, not what the news says...
And if you hate my side, you can ground me.
Honey... Listen, I'll put my foot down when I have to, but I'll stick with you no matter what.

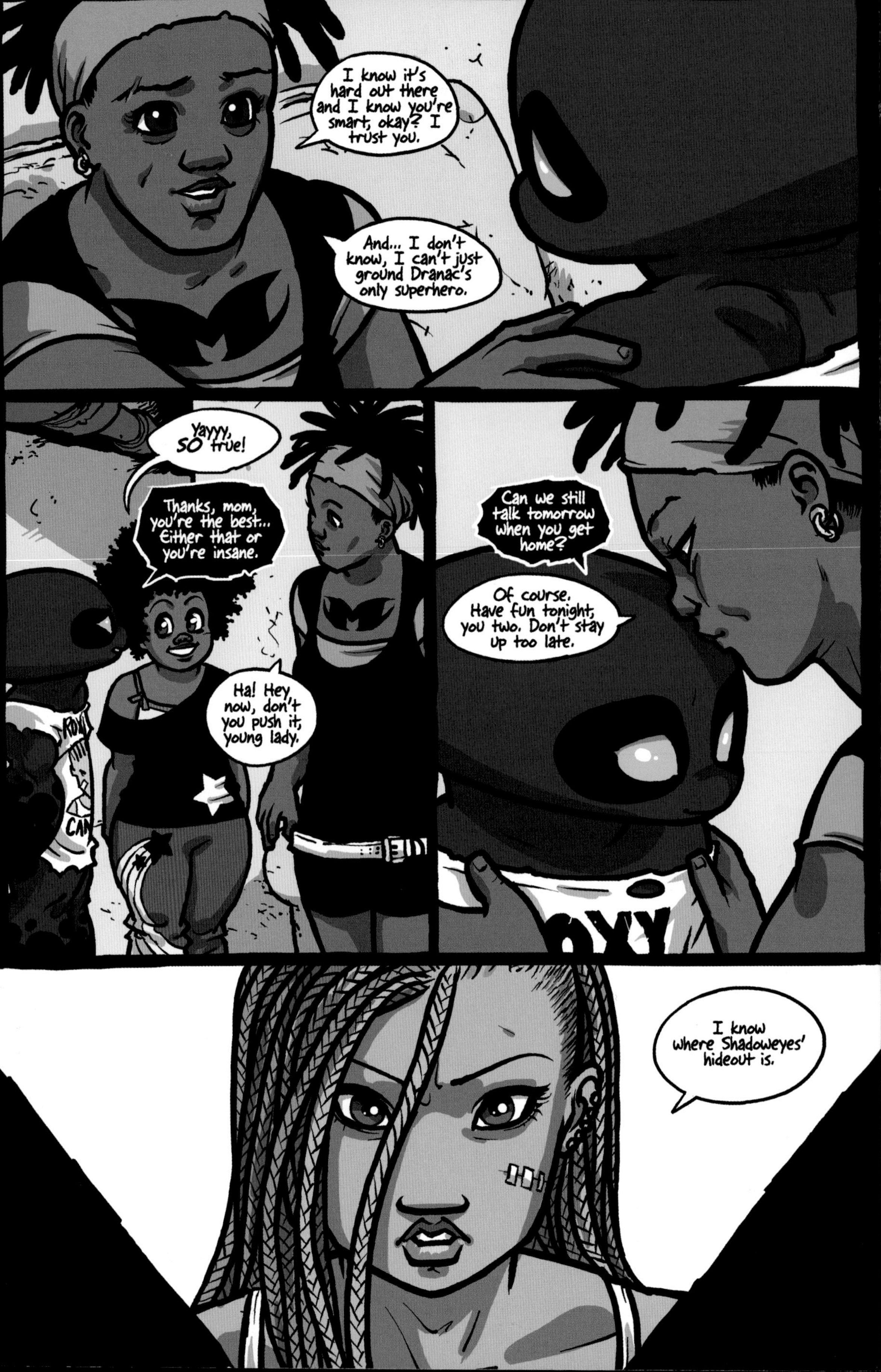
I know it's hard out there and I know you're smart, okay? I trust you.
And... I don't know, I can't just ground Dranac's only superhero.
Yayyy, SO true!
Thanks, mom, you're the best... Either that or you're insane.
Ha! Hey now, don't you push it, young lady.
Can we still talk tomorrow when you get home?
Of course. Have fun tonight, you two. Don't stay up too late.
I know where Shadoweyes' hideout is.

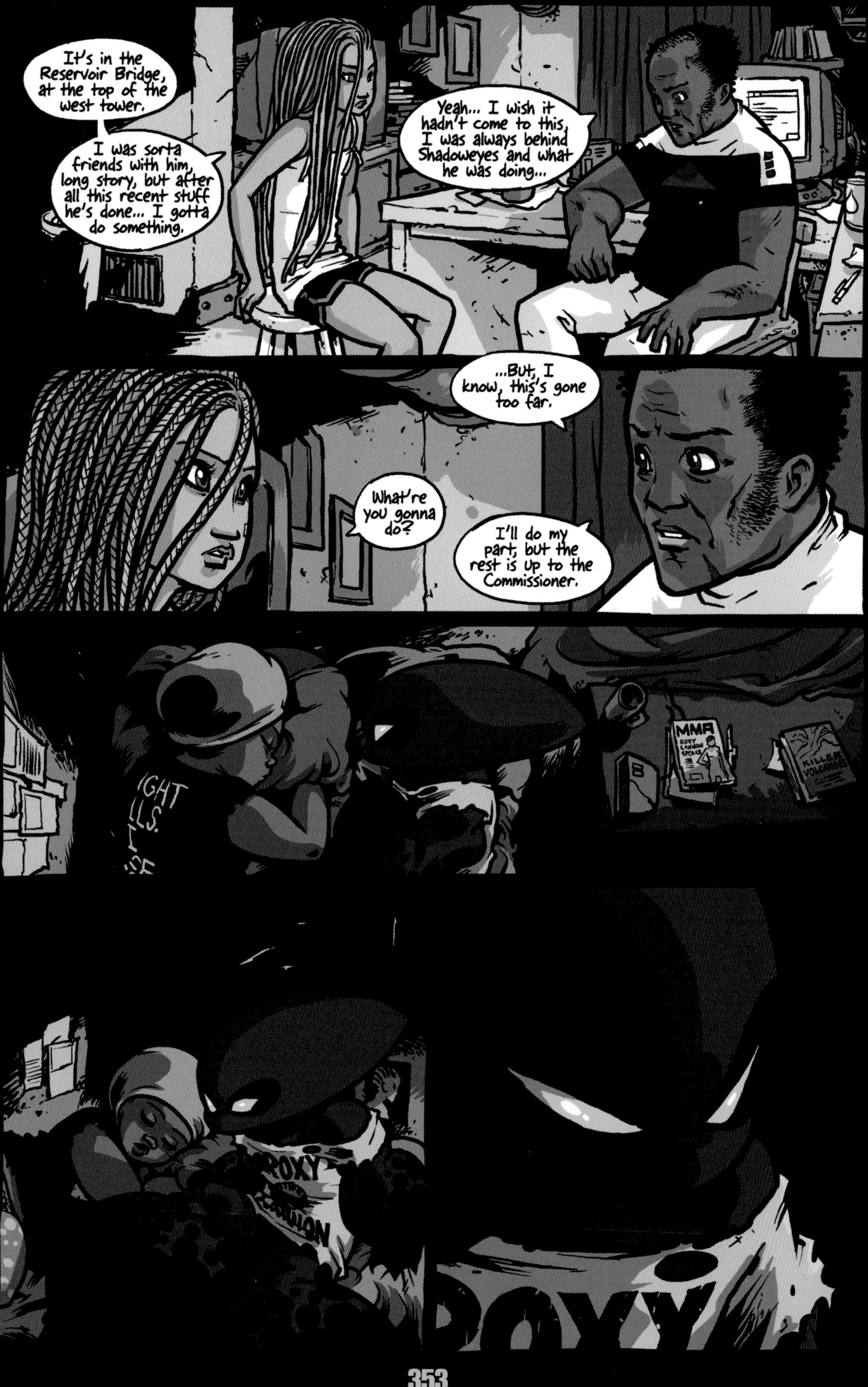
It's in the Reservoir Bridge, at the top of the west tower.
I was sorta friends with him, long story, but after all this recent stuff he's done... I gotta do something.
Yeah... I wish it hadn't come to this, I was always behind Shadoweyes and what he was doing...
...But, I know, this's gone too far.
What're you gonna do?
I'll do my part, but the rest is up to the Commissioner.
MMA
ROXY CANNON SPEAKS
KILLER VOLCANOES
ROXY
ROXY

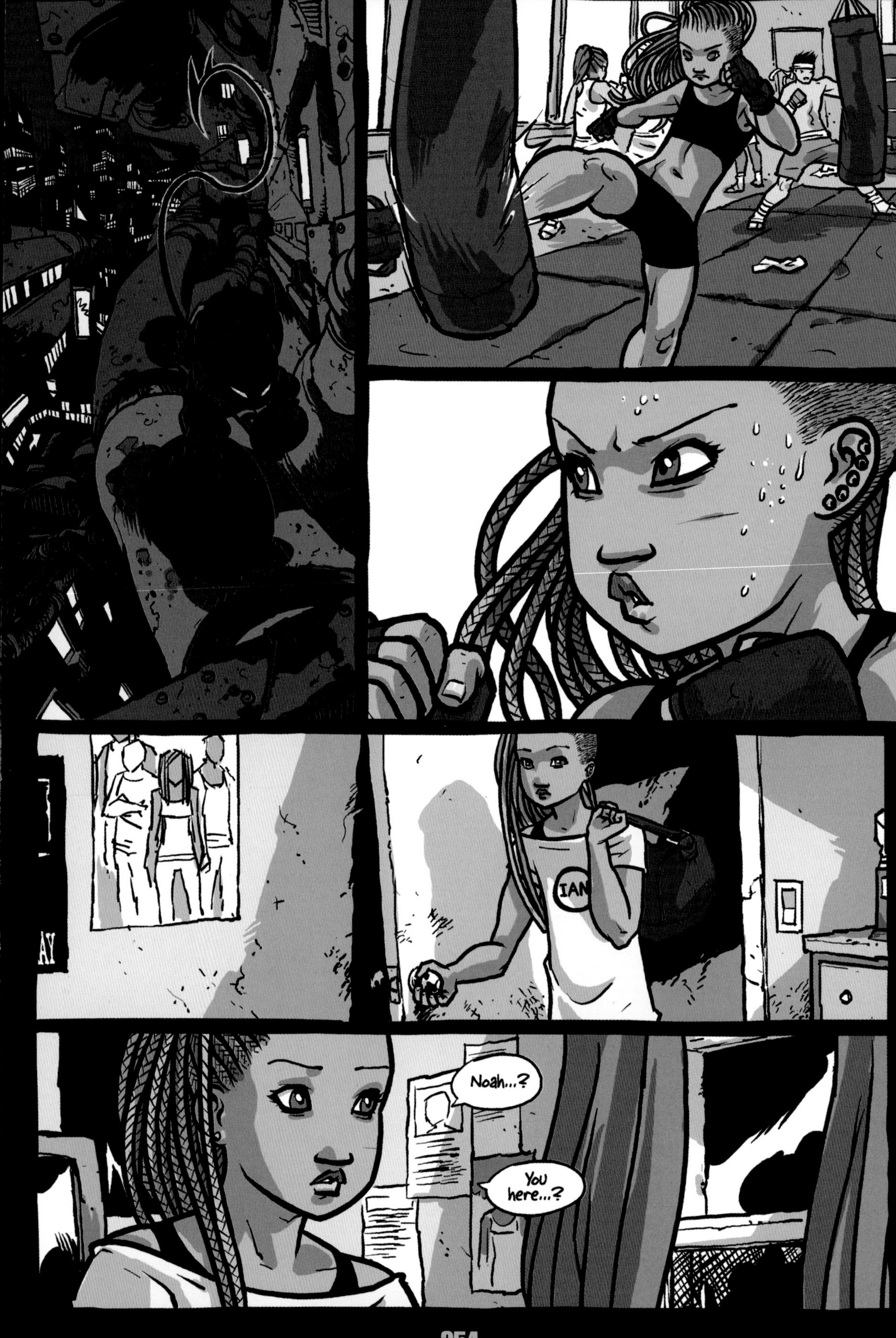
Noah...?
You here...?

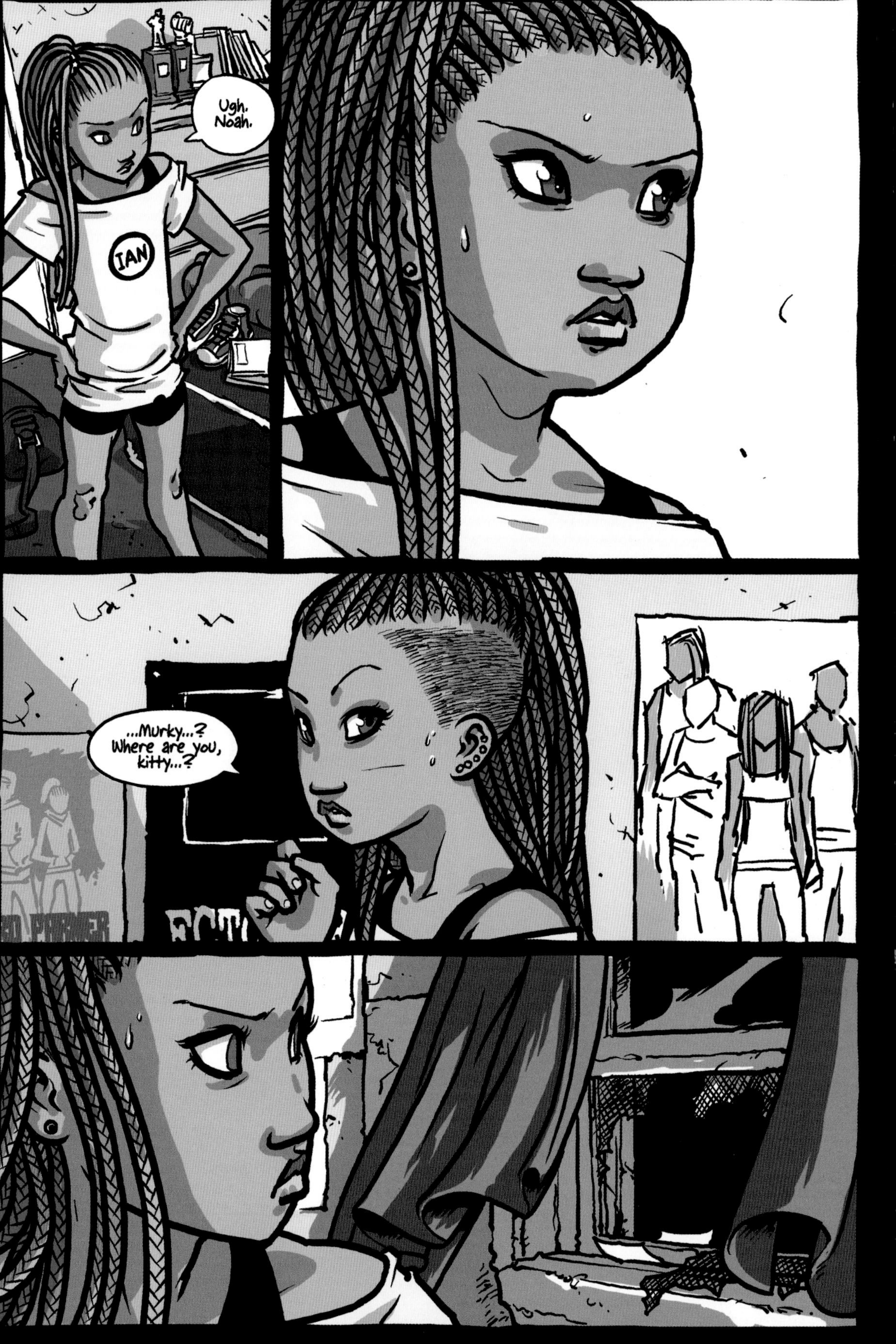
IAN
Ugh. Noah.
...Murky...? Where are you, kitty...?

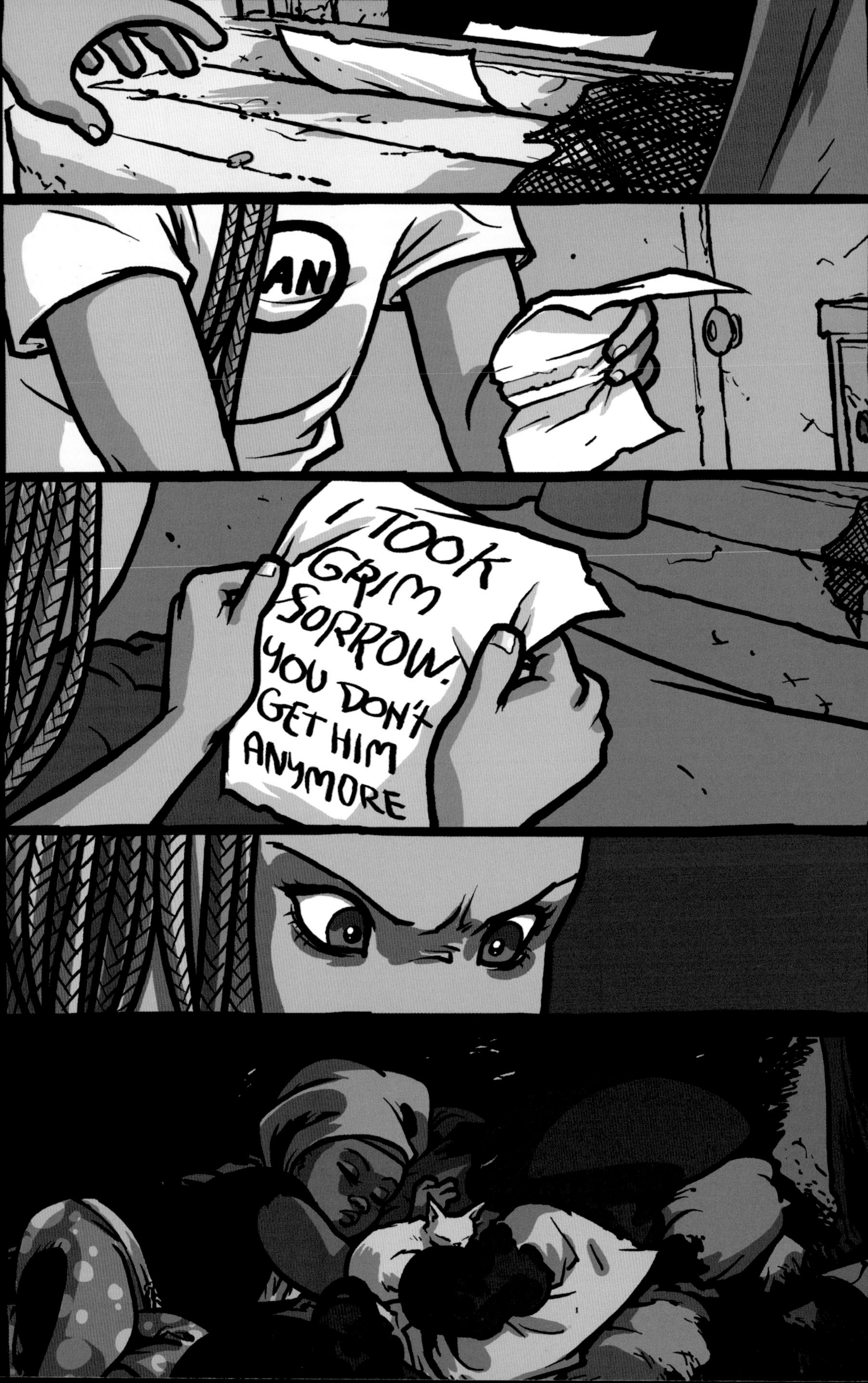
AN
I TOOK GRIM SORROW. YOU DON'T GET HIM ANYMORE

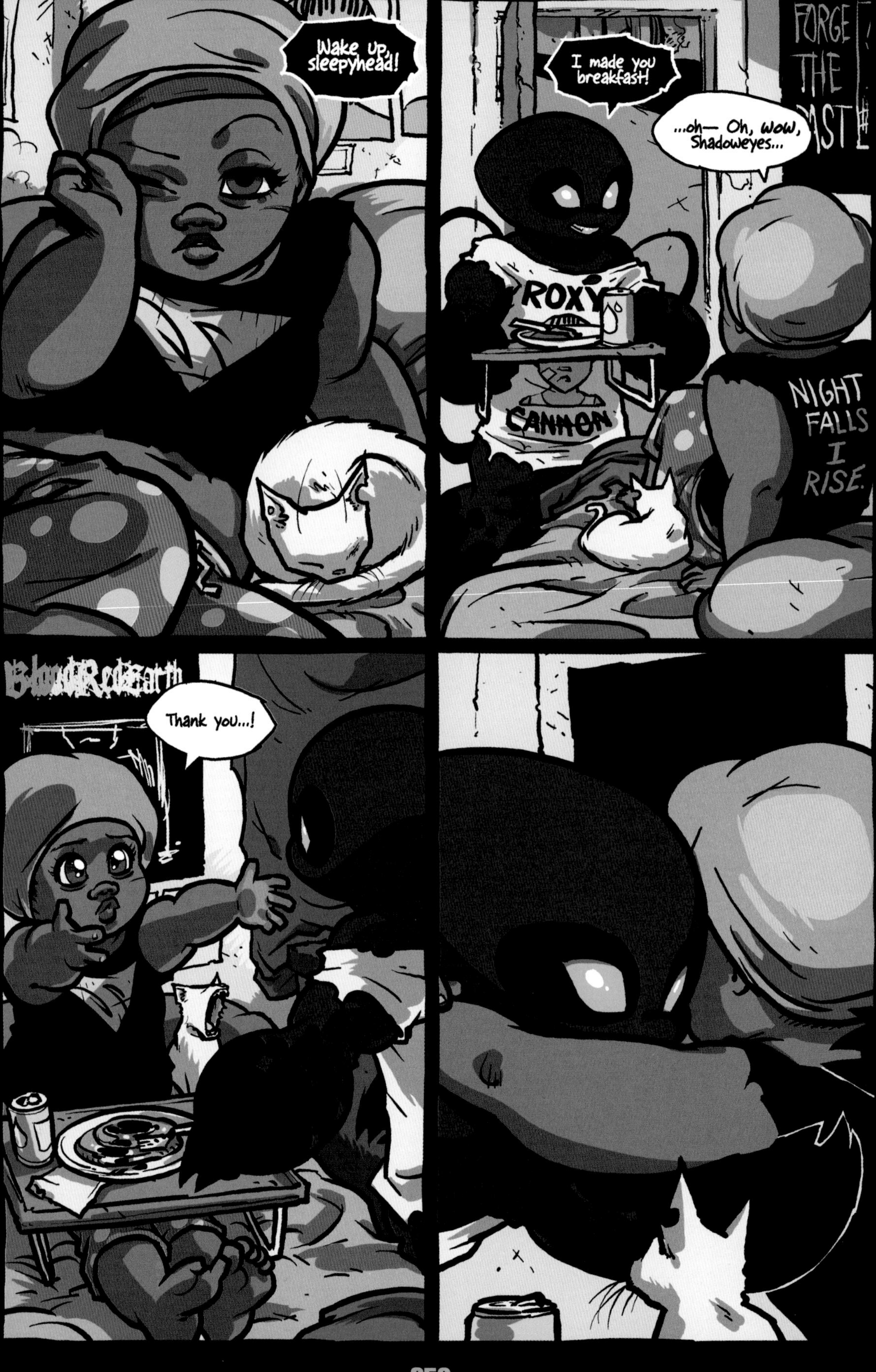
Wake up, sleepyhead!
I made you breakfast!
FORGE THE
...oh— Oh, wow, Shadoweyes...
ROXY CANNON
NIGHT FALLS I RISE.
Thank you...!

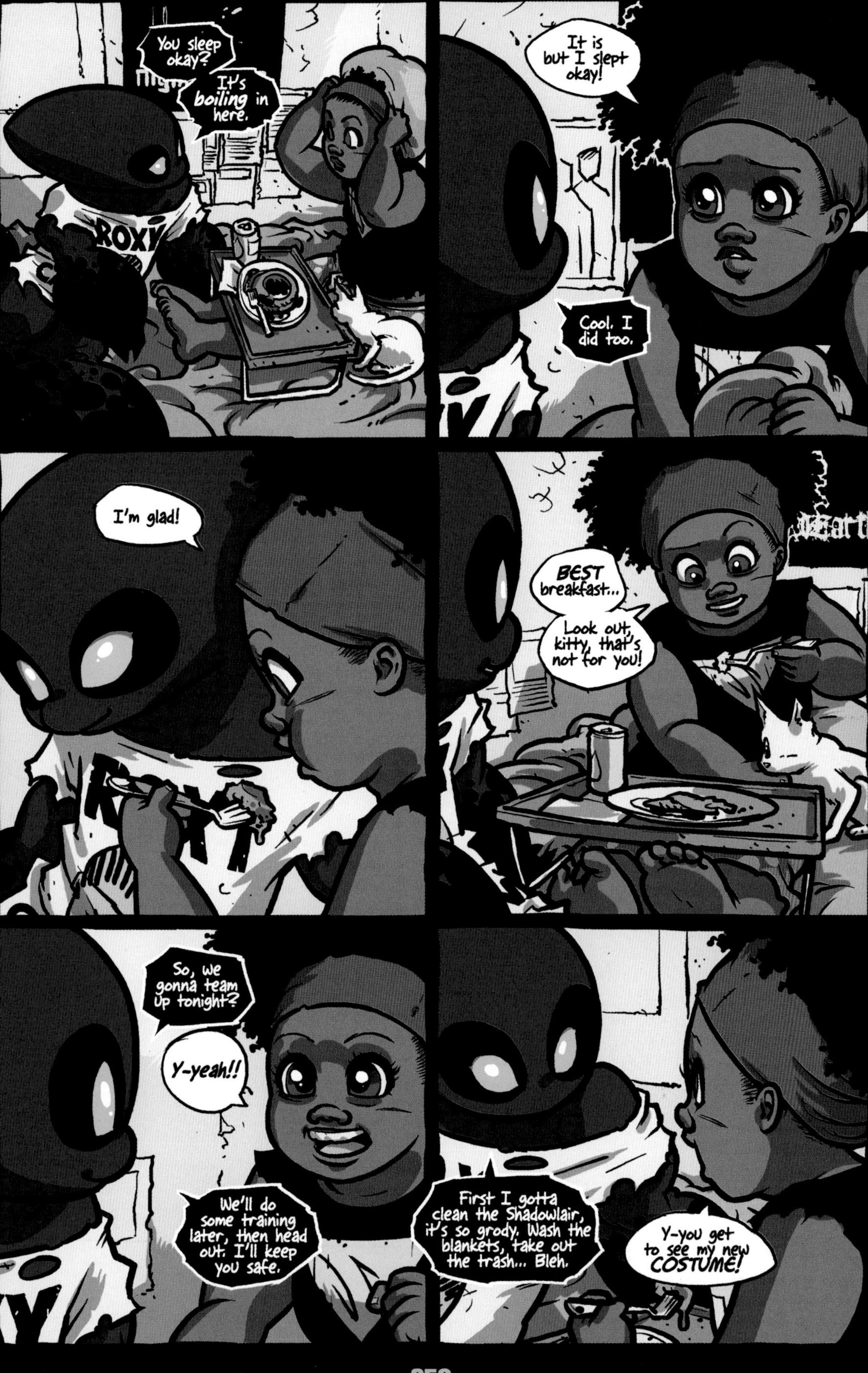
You sleep okay?
It's boiling in here.
ROXY
It is but I slept okay!
Cool. I did too.
I'm glad!
BEST breakfast...
Look out, kitty, that's not for you!
So, we gonna team up tonight?
Y-yeah!!
We'll do some training later, then head out. I'll keep you safe.
First I gotta clean the Shadowlair, it's so grody. Wash the blankets, take out the trash... Bleh.
Y-you get to see my new COSTUME!

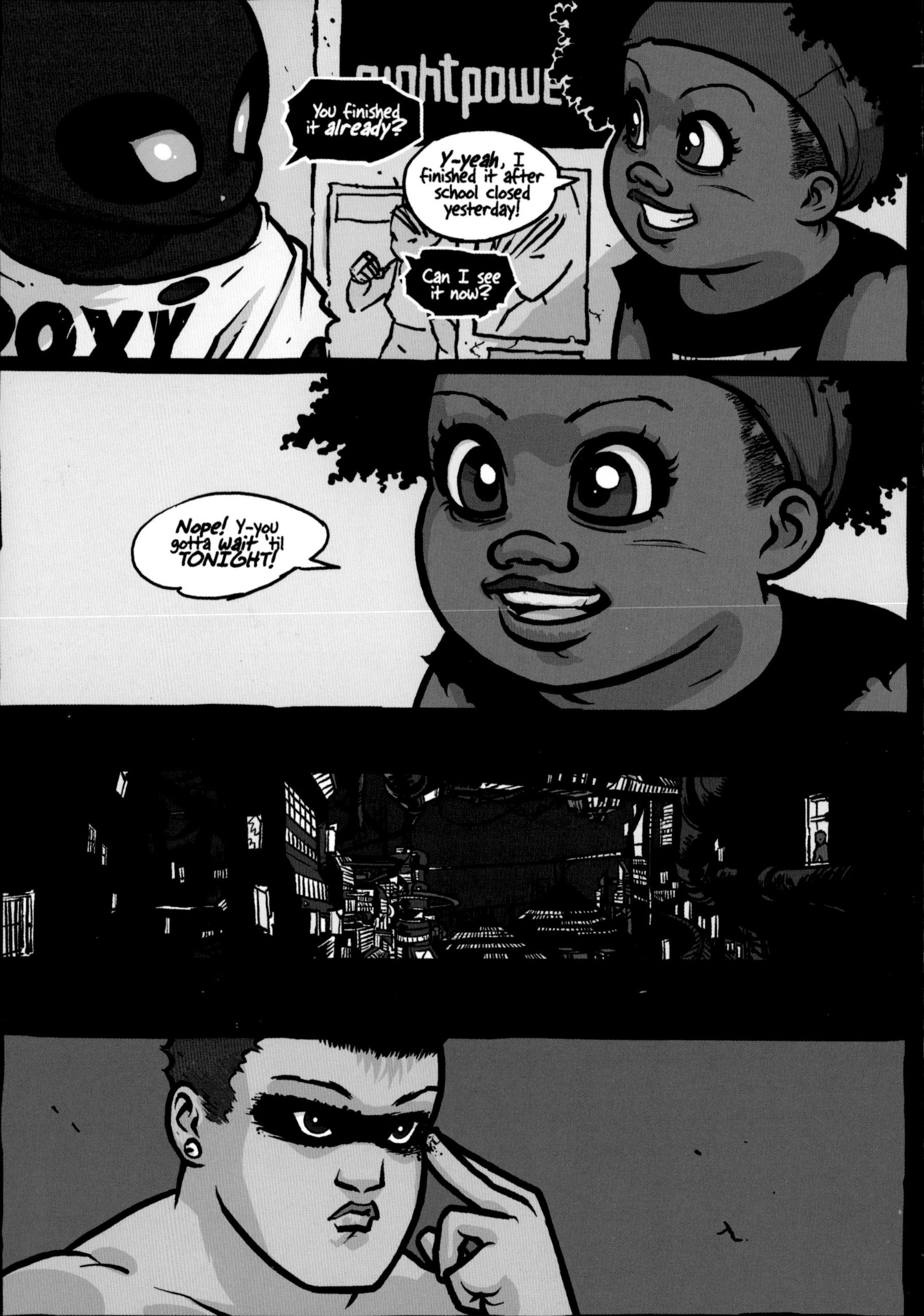

You finished it already?
Y-yeah, I finished it after school closed yesterday!
Can I see it now?
Nope! Y-you gotta wait 'til TONIGHT!

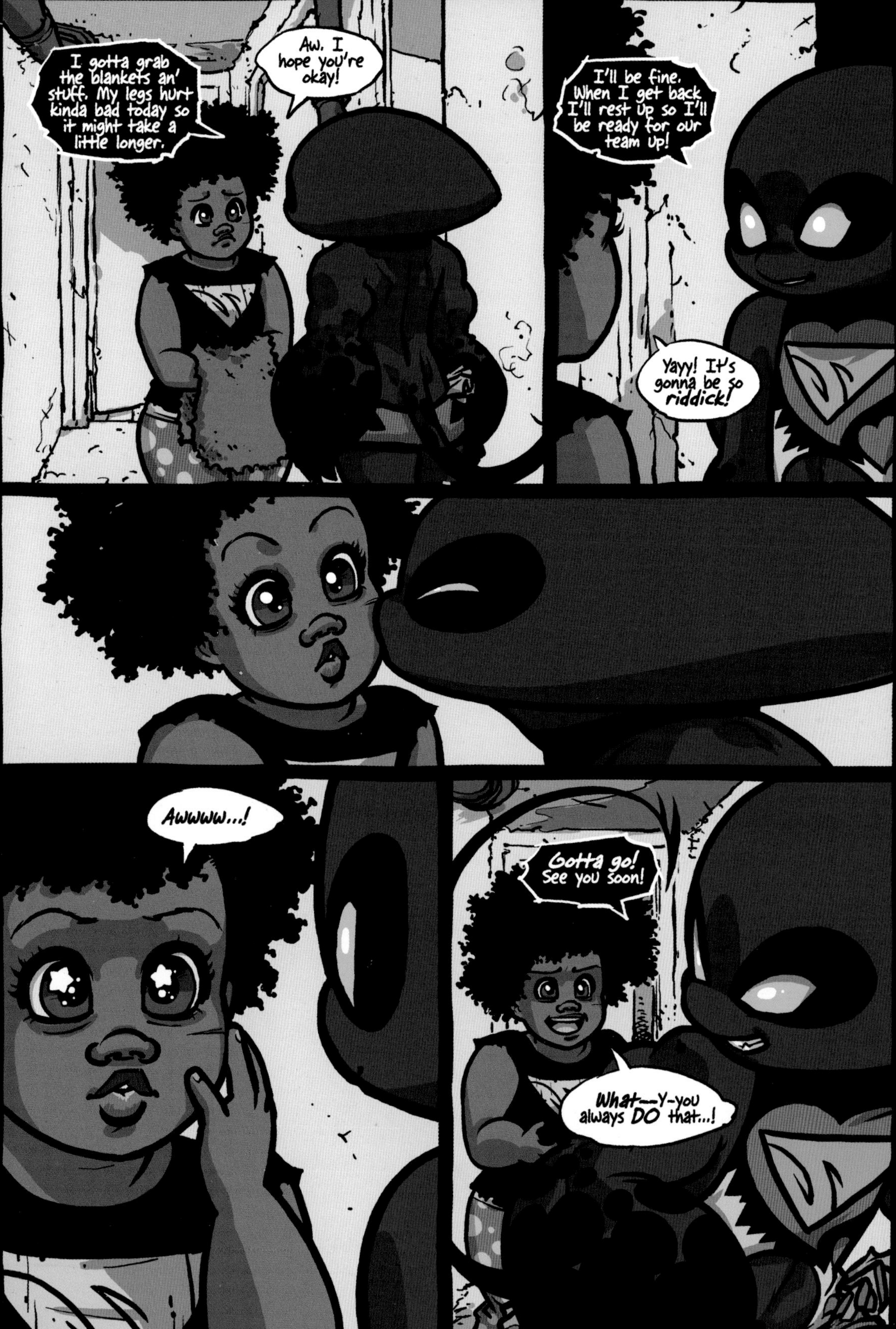
I gotta grab the blankets an' stuff. My legs hurt kinda bad today so it might take a little longer.
Aw. I hope you're okay!
I'll be fine. When I get back I'll rest up so I'll be ready for our team up!
Yayy! It's gonna be so riddick!
Awwww...!
Gotta go! See you soon!
What—Y-you always DO that...!

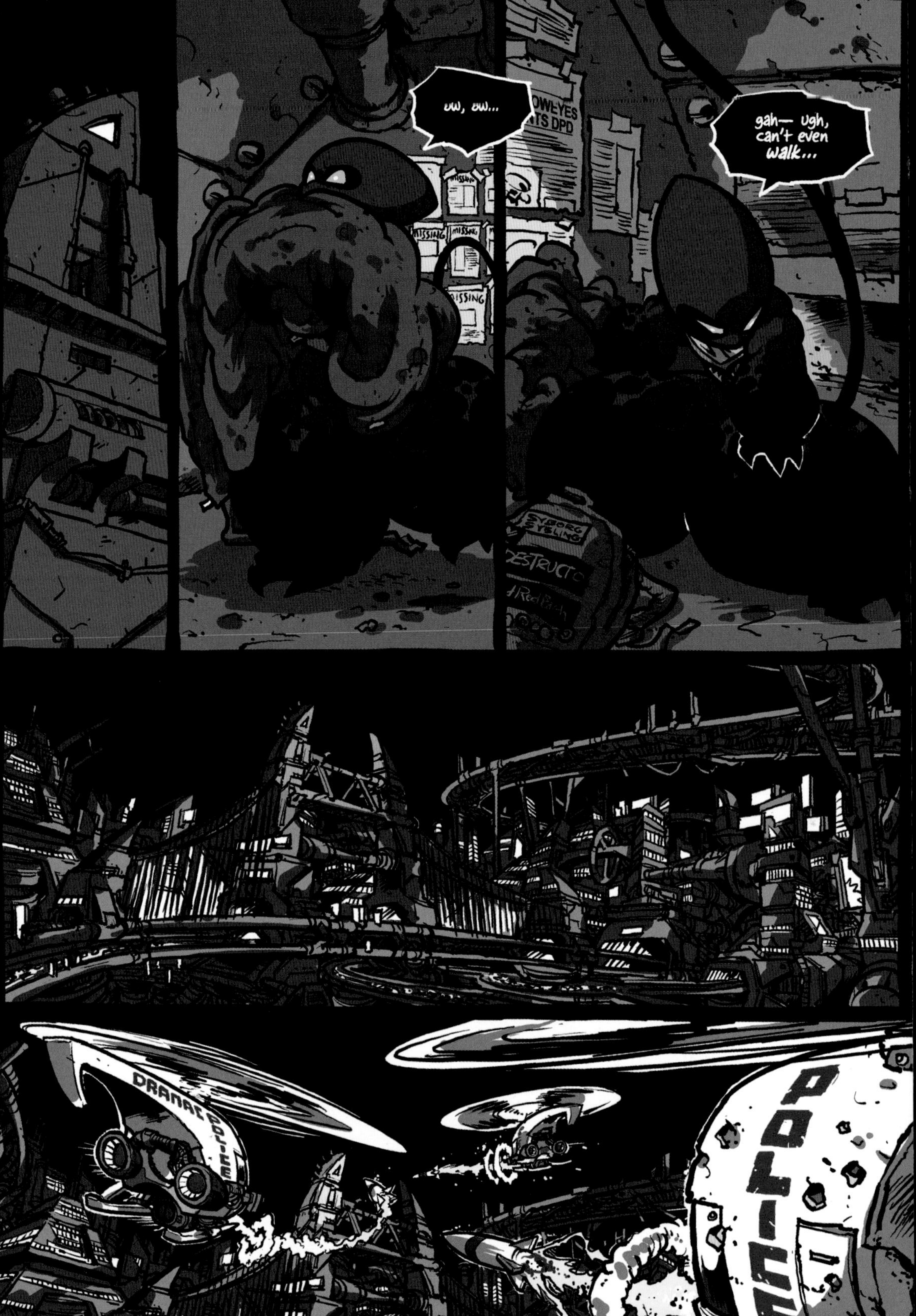
ow, ow...
MISSING
MISSING
MISSING
MISSING
gah— ugh, can't even walk...
SYBORG STYLING
DESTRUCTO
#RedPatch
DRANAT POLICE
POLICE

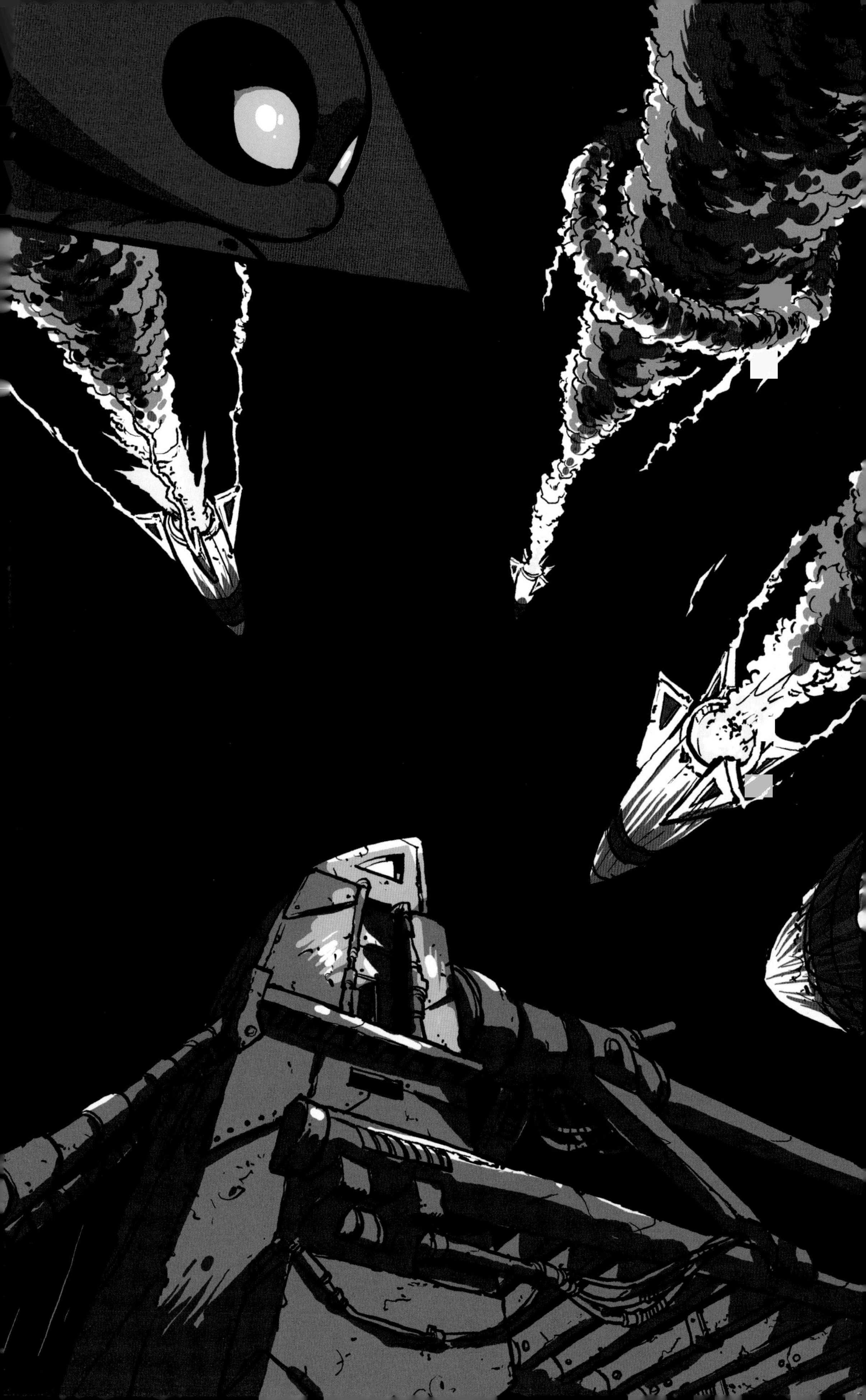

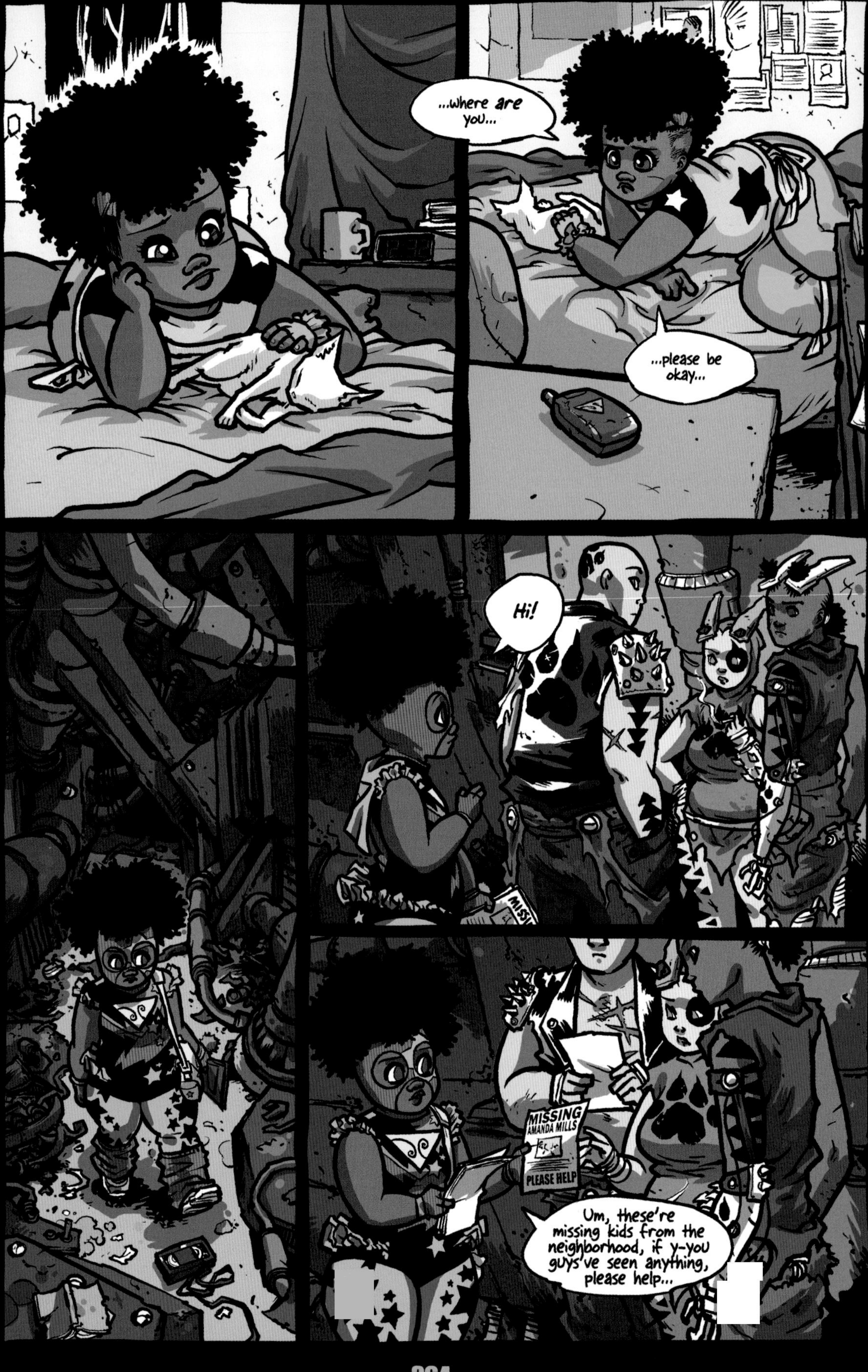
...where are you...
...please be okay...
Hi!
MISSING
AMANDA MILLS
PLEASE HELP
Um, these're missing kids from the neighborhood, if y-you guys've seen anything, please help...

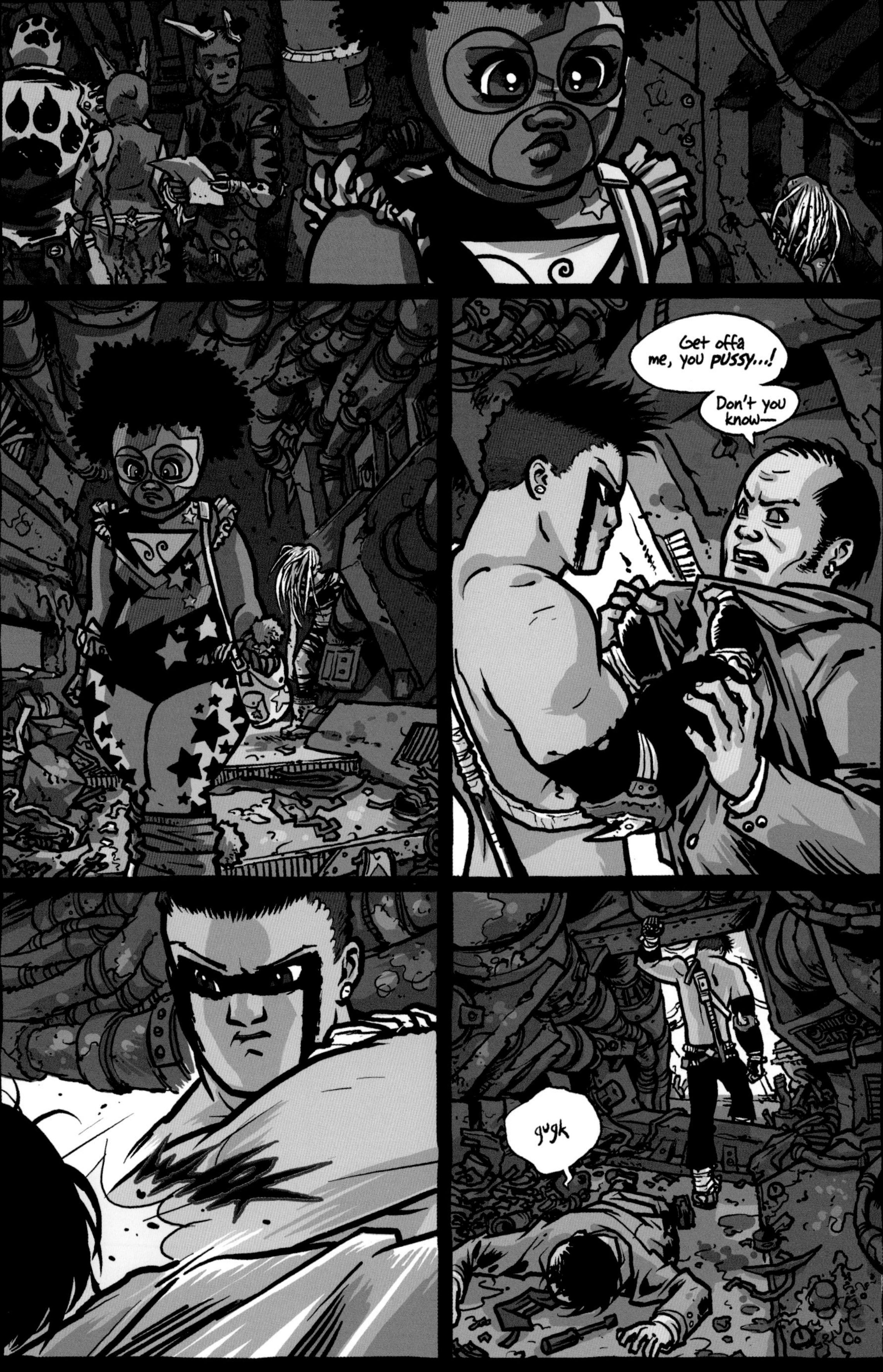
Get offa me, you PUSSY...!
Don't you know—
gugk

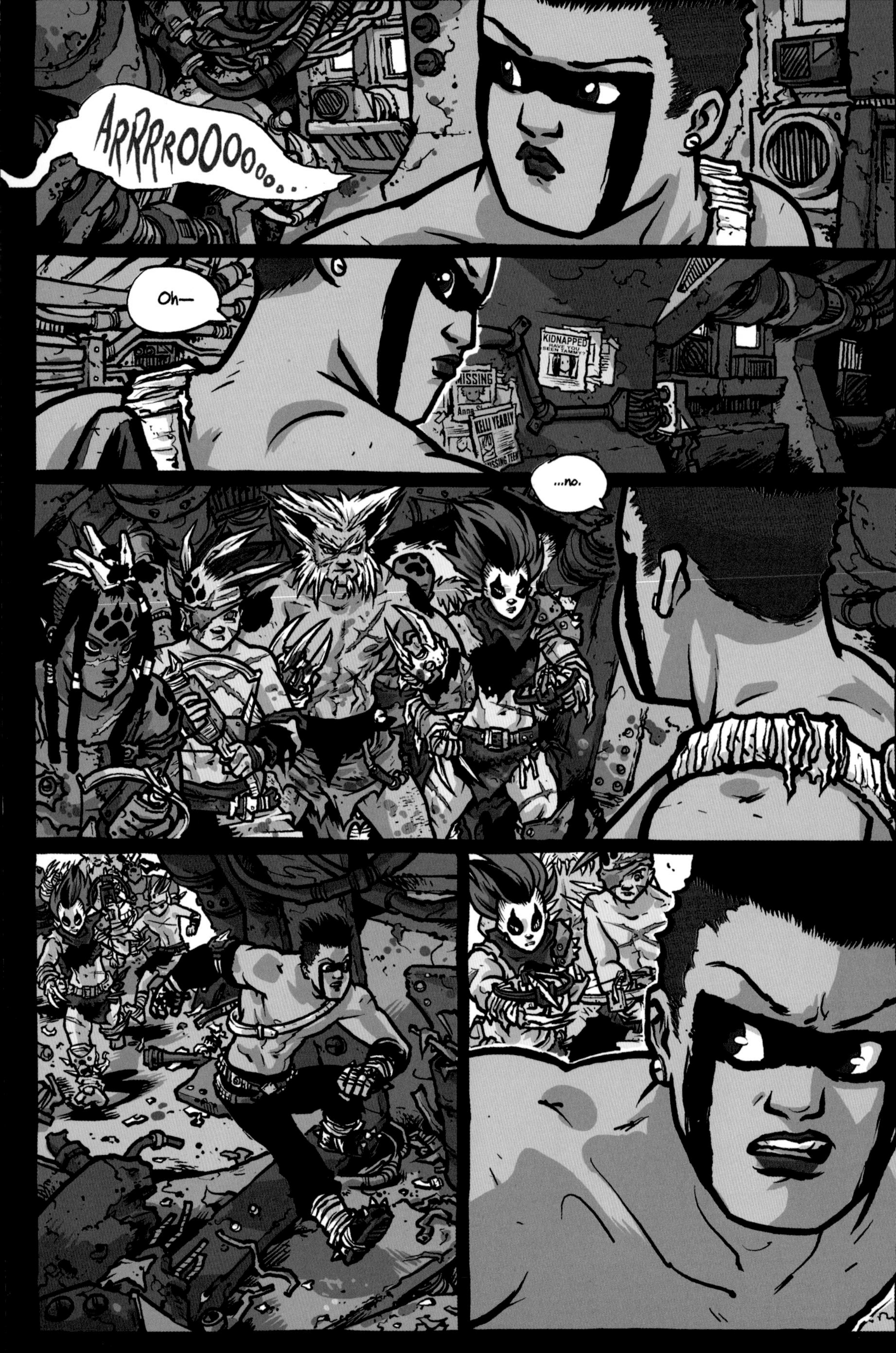
ARRRROOOOo...
Oh—
KIDNAPPED
HAVE YOU SEEN TAMMY?
KELLI YEARLY
...no.

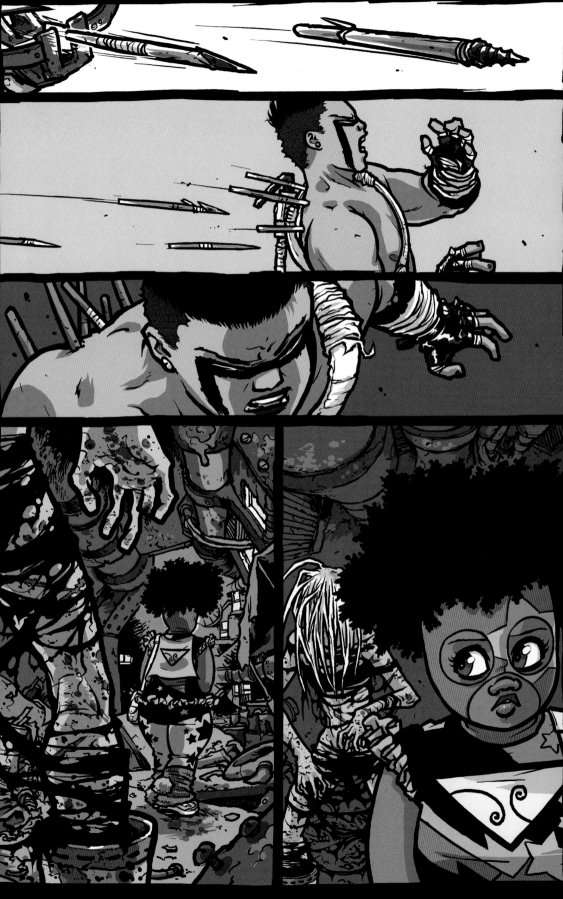

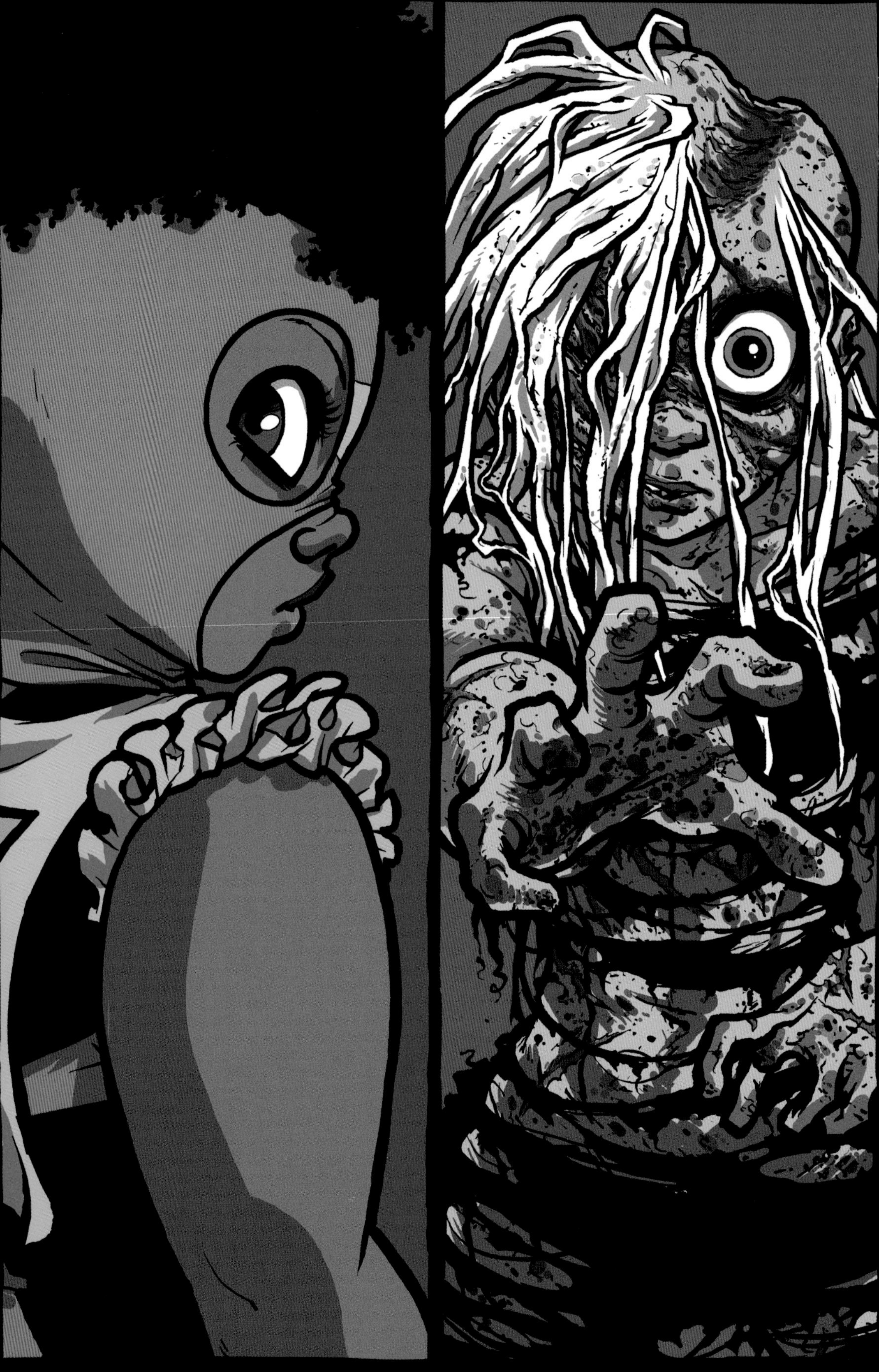

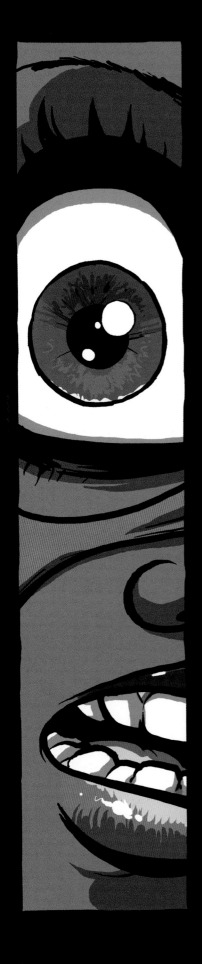

to be
continued

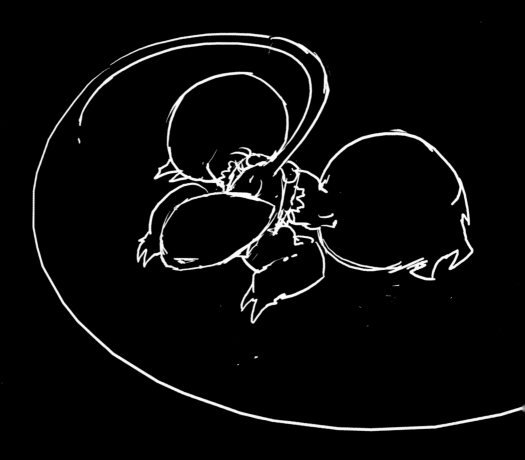

find Sophie at

mooncalfe.tumblr.com
mooncalfe-art.tumblr.com
shadoweyescomic.tumblr.com
cantlookbackcomic.tumblr.com
twitter.com/mooncalfe1
www.greenoblivion.com

find Erin at

missgreeney.tumblr.com
missgreeneyart.tumblr.com
lostpieces.smackjeeves.com
twitter.com/missgreeney

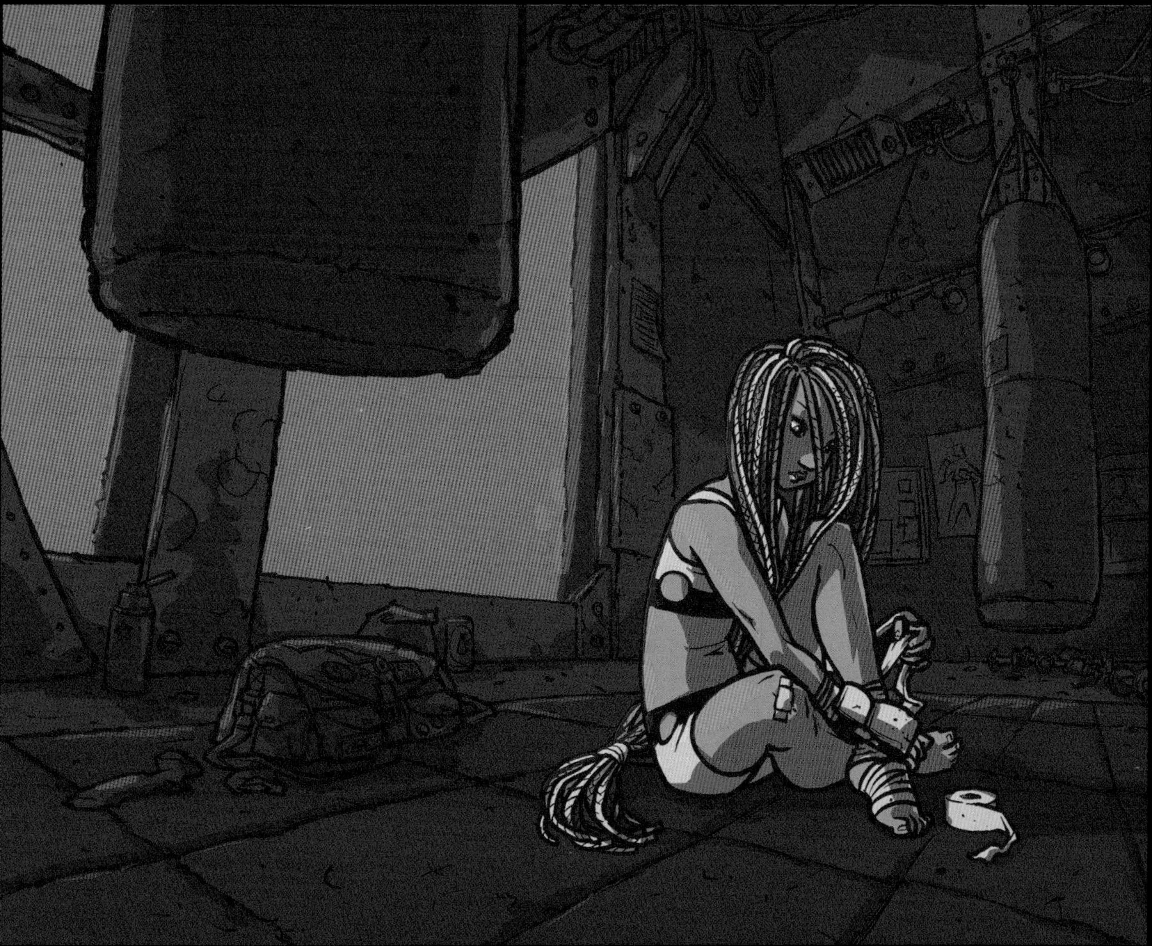

by Sophie Campbell

CRIMINAL PSYCHOLOGY

by Sophie Campbell

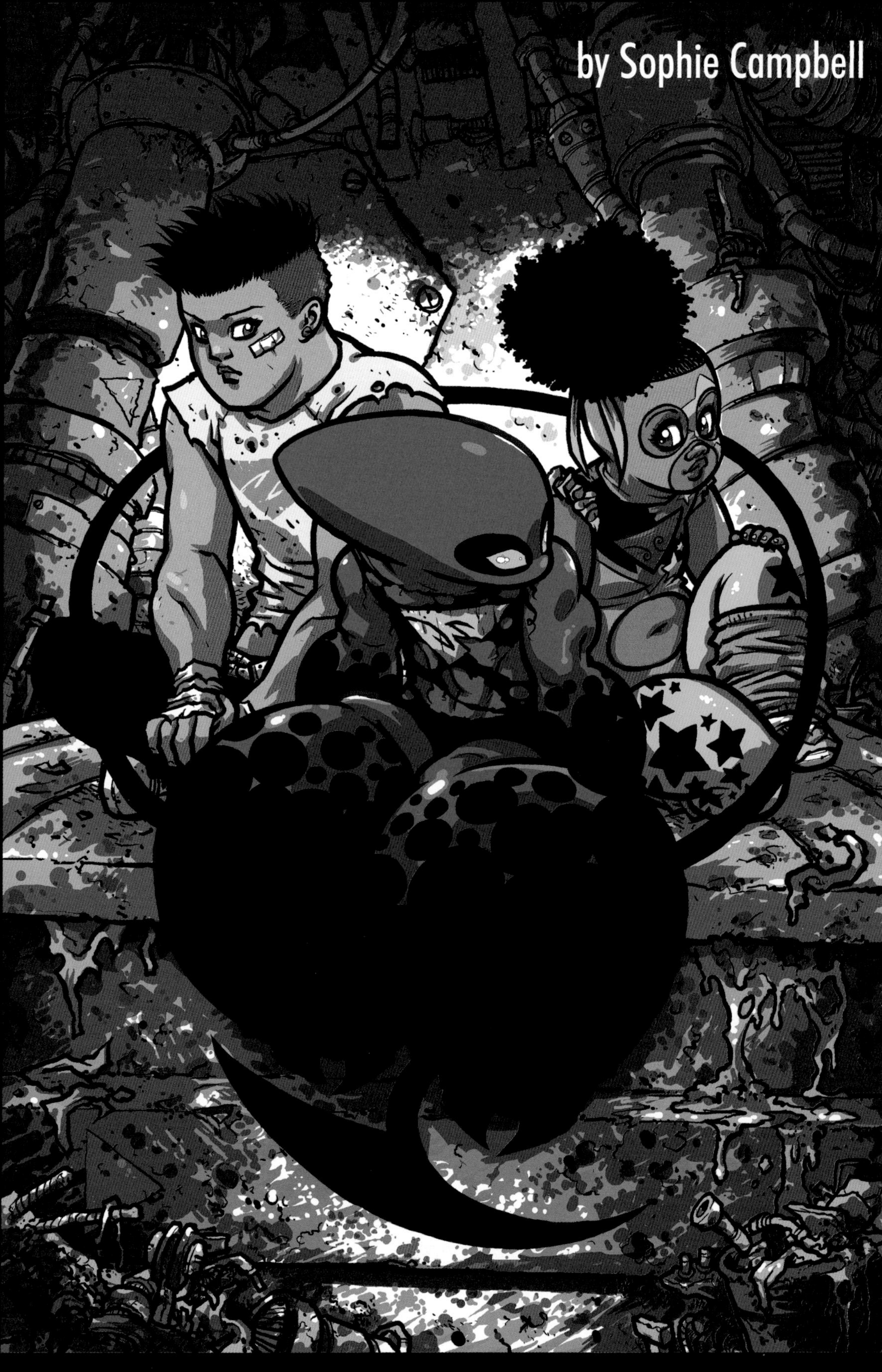
by Sophie Campbell

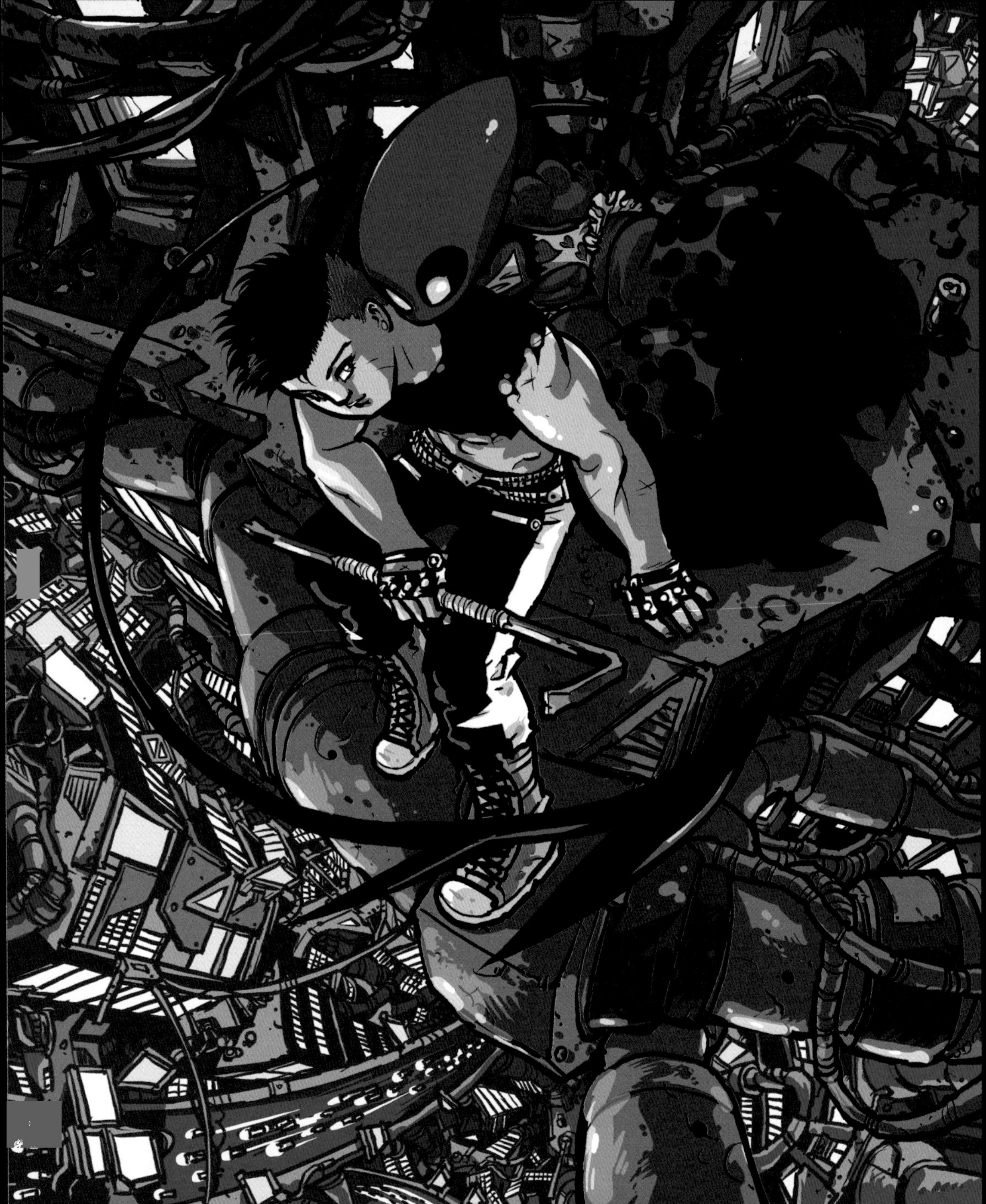

by Sophie Campbell

by Sophie Campbell

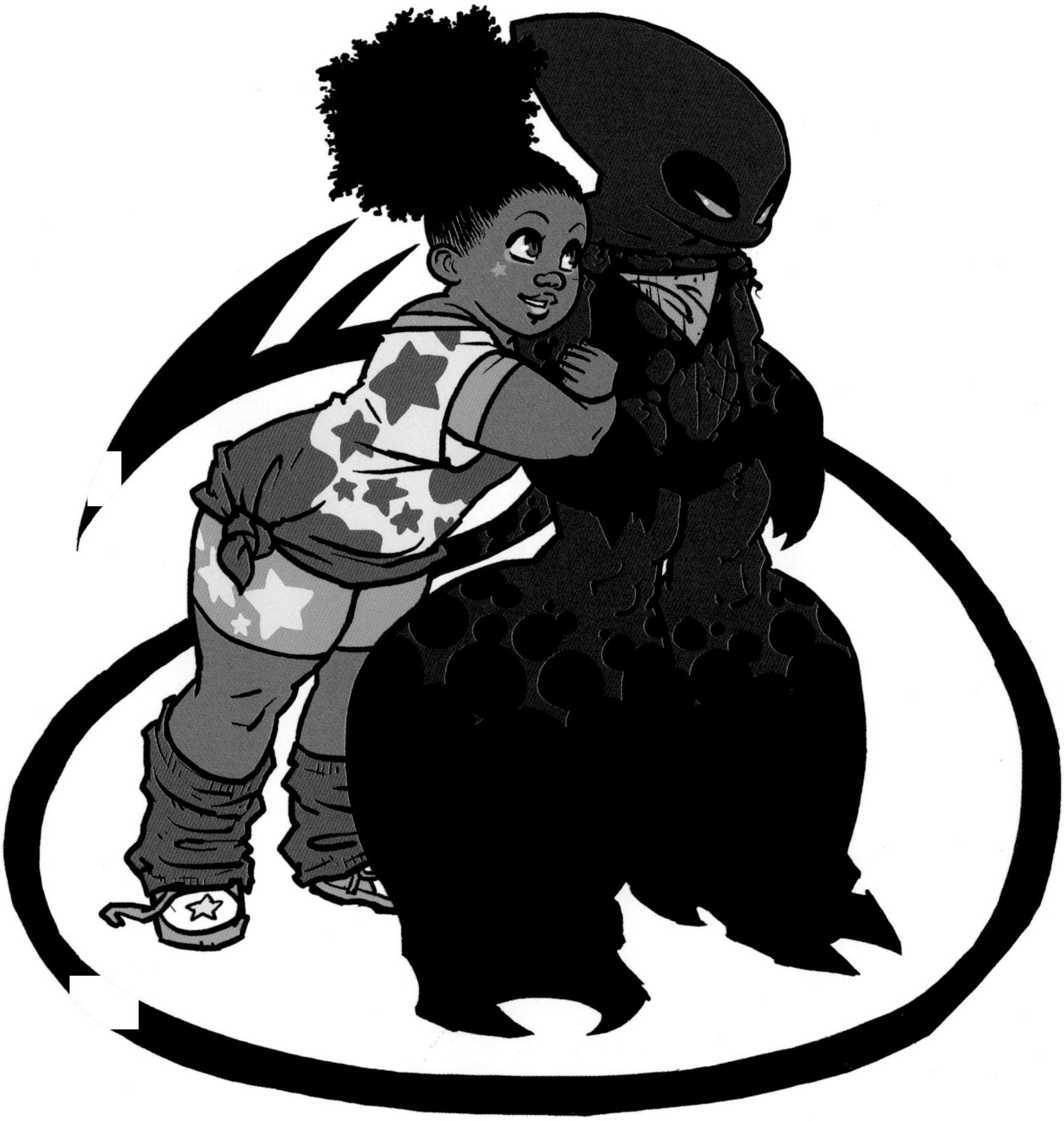

by Erin Watson

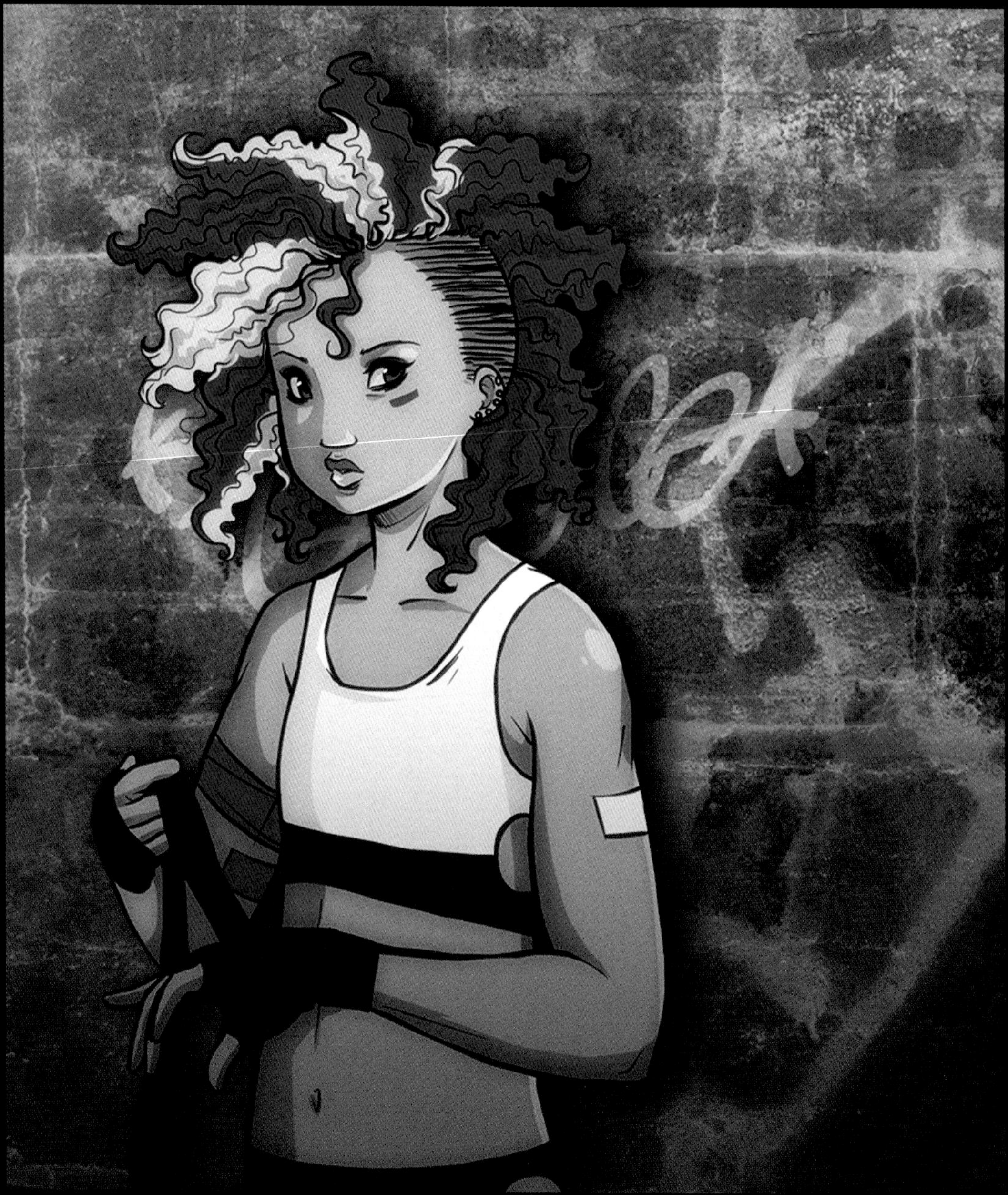

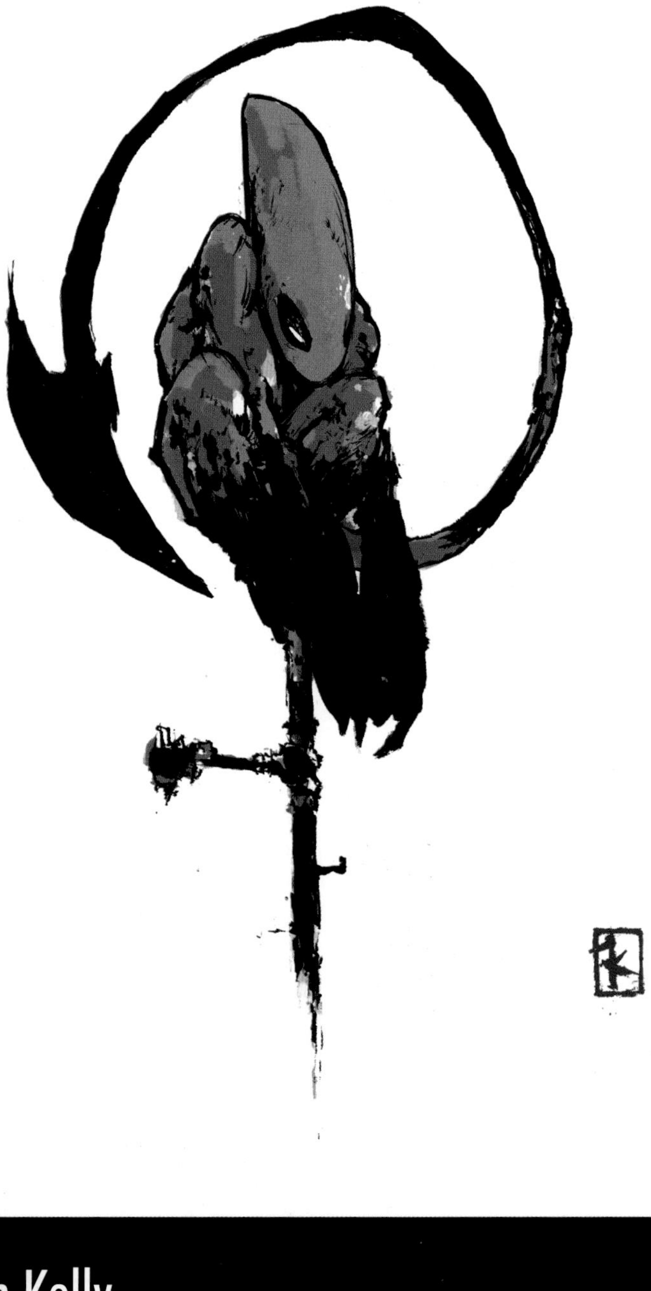

by Tim Kelly

by Jeffrey "Chamba" Cruz

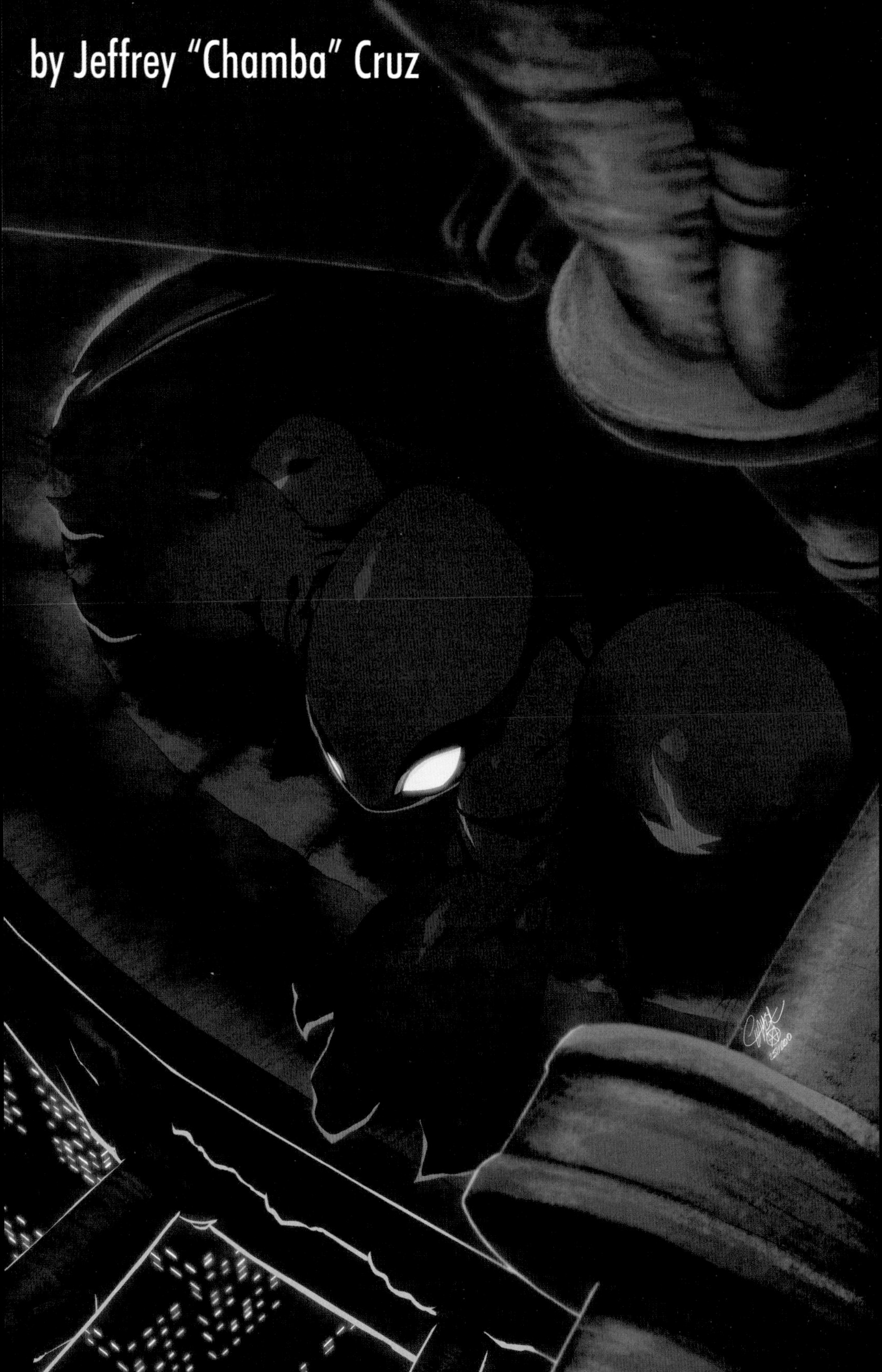

by Liz Suburbia

EL SUB ♡

by Bo Bradshaw

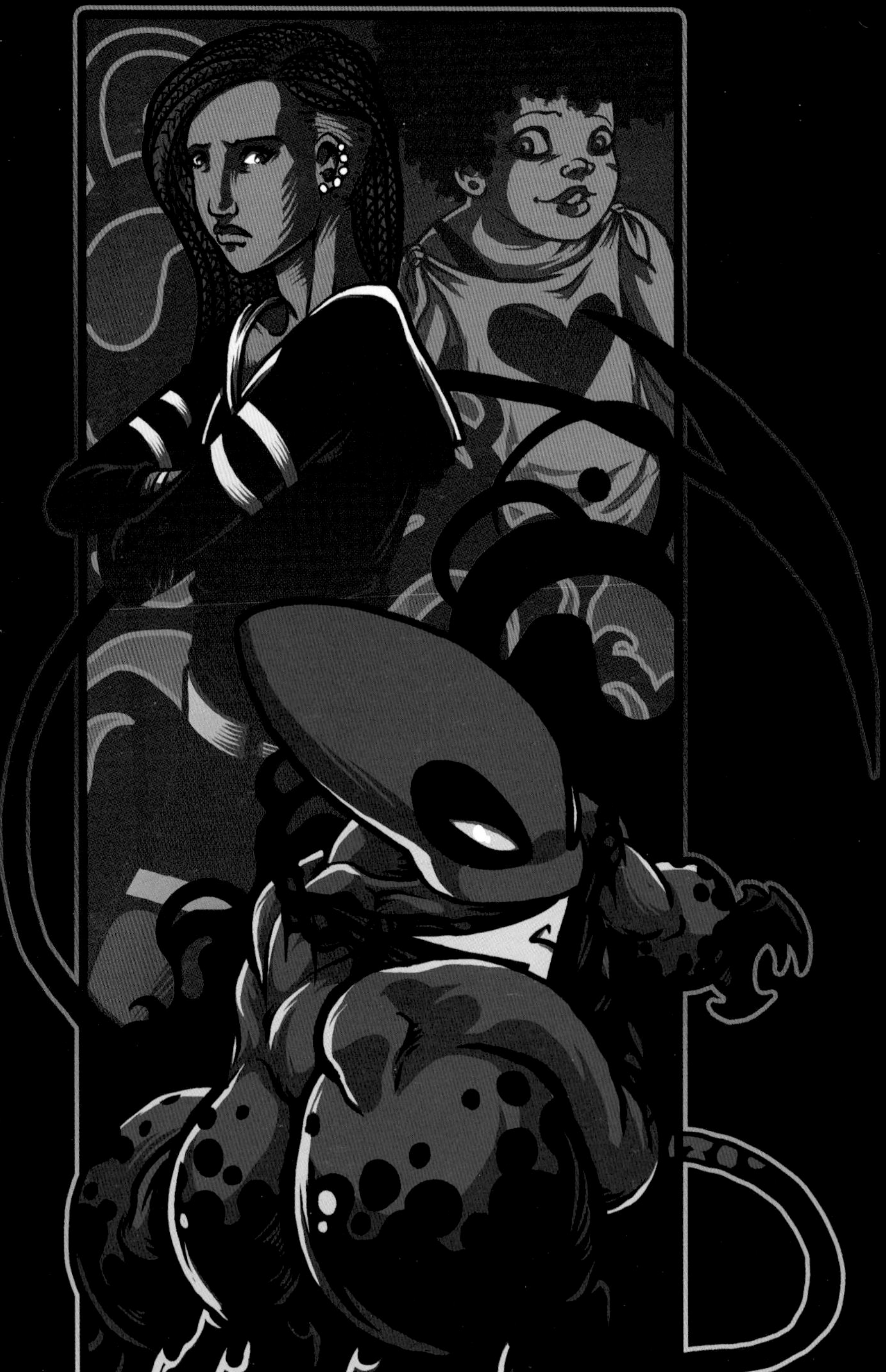